Lords of Misrule

Roundheads & Cavaliers - Book 4

Stella Riley

Copyright © 2016 Stella Riley
All rights reserved.
ISBN-13:978-1530592142
ISBN-10:1530592143

CONTENTS

	Page
PROLOGUE - London - December 16th, 1653	1
PLOTTERS ALL AWRY - London – January to May 1654	6
WINDS OF CHANGE - May to October, 1654	146
SHADOW DWELLERS - October 1654 to January 1655	285
THE GOLDEN KEY - London, February to April, 1655	430
EPILOGUE - Thorne Ash, Oxfordshire	592
Author's Note	603

Westminster Hall, December 11th 1653

On entering the House and finding a few Godly men still remaining, an Army officer asked, 'What do you do here?'
'We are seeking the Lord,' came the lofty reply.
The officer gave a sardonic smile.
'Then you may go elsewhere; for, to my certain knowledge, he has not been here these twelve years.'

PROLOGUE
London - December 16th, 1653

The procession was a long one and Eden Maxwell, marching alongside his fellow Colonels in the wake of the Captain-General's coach, was at the back of it. The entire route from Whitehall to Westminster was lined on both sides with infantry and, ahead of them rumbled carriages containing every important official in the City. Judges, Barons, the Lord Mayor and Aldermen, Lords Commissioners of the Great Seal, members of the Council ... not a man-jack of them had been left out. And yet the streets were no more crowded than usual and the faces of those who stopped to watch the mighty cavalcade wore expressions ranging from mild curiosity to total bafflement.

This wasn't surprising. As far as anyone knew, this was just an ordinary Friday afternoon. There had been no Proclamation announcing what was about to happen and wouldn't be until Monday – although doubtless the ceremony due to take place in Westminster Hall would find its way into one or more of the newspapers before then.

Really, thought Colonel Maxwell acidly, *the whole thing looks more than a little* furtive.

Although he was careful not to let it show, Eden was in an extremely sour mood. Truth to tell, he'd been in an increasingly sour mood for the best part of eight months – throughout which, despite repeated requests for leave of absence, he'd been kept chained to his desk in the

Intelligence Office due to the conviction of both Thomas Scot and Secretary Thurloe that he couldn't be spared.

First it had been the seemingly endless paperwork generated by the so-called Nominated Assembly which the Council, in its wisdom, had decreed was to replace the recently dissolved Rump. Since the entire country had been crying out for fresh elections and a new Parliament and clearly didn't want to be ruled by a clutch of fellows selected on the strength of their Godliness, Eden had wondered who'd come up with this asinine idea. Not that he'd cared very much because, once July came and the Assembly was in session, he would finally get his long-awaited leave.

And he might have done had not Thomas Scot suddenly quit his position.

Eden had known that Scot was highly critical of both the forcible expulsion of the Rump and of it being replaced with a non-elected body – now commonly known as the Barebones Parliament; what he *didn't* know was whether he'd resigned voluntarily or been pressured into doing so. But whatever the reasons behind it, the result had been the same. Thurloe had insisted that Colonel Maxwell remain to fill Scot's vacant shoes and deal with correspondence that would undoubtedly continue to arrive in his office.

After that, everything had gone rapidly downhill – and Eden's mood with it.

Reports came in of a gathering of Highland chiefs at Lochaber; of discontent in the fleet over arrears of pay; of Royalist plots to seize Poole, Portland and Portsmouth. And then, despite having been banished on pain of death by the Rump, John Lilburne returned from exile and was promptly imprisoned, pending trial – which just added fuel to the fire. Throughout August, the streets around Westminster brimmed with his supporters and pamphlets and petitions demanding his release arrived daily by the basket-load; and Eden had suffered the continual harassment of Sam Radford who appeared to think he had more influence than he actually did.

'They're trying John for his *life*,' Samuel had said furiously. 'You're on the inside. There must be *something* you can do.'

'There isn't. I'm just a cog in the bloody wheel – and a damned *busy* cog, at that,' Eden had snapped back. 'Use your head, Sam. No jury is going to be stupid enough to cause mass riots by sending Free-born John to the gallows. So get back to your own work and leave me to mine.'

More or less as Eden had predicted, the jury had eventually settled on a tactful verdict of *'not guilty of any crime worthy of death'* ... which, not being exactly an acquittal, had put Lilburne back in the Tower and caused another tidal wave of pamphlets.

For a brief time during September, despite the increasing unpopularity of the Barebones Parliament, peace had reigned ... and Eden began to entertain hopes of escape. But the following month hundreds of angry sailors had besieged Whitehall until the Army came along to disperse them. And in November, a fracas in the New Exchange had resulted in the death of an innocent bystander and the arrest of the Portuguese Ambassador's brother for murder. Eden, who already had more than enough to do, had sworn long and silently. Then, beginning with the intended victim – one Colonel John Gerard, in whom, for other reasons entirely, Eden had some interest – he'd started taking witness statements.

In Westminster, the Parliament had kept itself busy with a stream of largely non-essential legislation. Although none of its Members were lawyers, it voted to abolish the Court of Chancery without apparently sparing a thought for what might replace it; it prepared a new Marriage Act declaring that only ceremonies conducted by a Justice of the Peace would henceforth be legal; and it gradually slid into head-on conflict with Cromwell over the question of whether or not to abolish tithes.

Then, on December 11th, seemingly without any prior warning, the Assembly had handed its powers back to the Captain General ... and quietly abdicated. And the result was that, five days later, here they all were processing down to Westminster for the so-far unannounced purpose of inaugurating Oliver Cromwell as Lord Protector.

The ceremony was to take place inside the Court of Chancery, where the great and good were already taking their designated places around the Chair of State. To one side stood the Lord Mayor, scarlet-robed

Aldermen and black-clad judges ... and to the other, Lambert, Desborough and all the chief officers of the Army – with the notable exception of Harrison who heartily disapproved of the entire business. One of the last to enter, Eden removed his hat and occupied a discreet spot against the wall while, clothed in a plain black suit and cloak, Cromwell walked slowly through a silence broken only by shuffling feet and the occasional cough.

Like the rest of them, the Captain-General remained on his feet and stood, hat in hand, while one of the Council secretaries read out the lengthy, written constitution drafted by Lambert some eight months earlier which laid down the terms of the Protectorate. Lambert had called it *The Instrument of Government*. Eden mentally re-christened it *How to Make Military Rule look Respectable*.

During the seemingly endless time it took to read, he learned that the power of government would henceforth be held by the Lord Protector and a Council of State; that though Cromwell would remain Protector for life, the office was not an hereditary one; and that, every three years, the Protector was obliged to call a Parliament of no less than five months duration.

Announcement of the date set for the first Protectoral Parliament brought a sardonic curl to Colonel Maxwell's mouth. September 3rd; the anniversary of Cromwell's victories at both Dunbar and Worcester. It also, thought Eden cynically, granted Oliver a full nine months in which to order matters as he saw fit without parliamentary interference.

For the rest, control over the military was to be shared between Protector and Parliament – or the Council, when Parliament wasn't sitting. There were various changes to constituencies and the franchise, aimed at reducing the influence of the gentry; religious toleration was granted to everybody except the Papists; and, inevitably, both Catholics and known Royalists were denied the right to vote at all

It was all as eminently reasonable as one would expect of something issuing from Lambert's pen. It was also tedious. Eden smothered a yawn and had to remind himself not to lean against the wall. He prayed that the ceremony didn't require Oliver to make a speech. If it did, they'd all be here half the day.

When the *Instrument* had been read out cover to cover and Cromwell had sworn an oath of acceptance, he was invited, as Lord Protector of England, Scotland and Ireland, to occupy the Chair of State ... and, replacing his hat – significant, Eden thought, only because no one else replaced theirs – he did so. There followed a great deal of solemn passing to and fro of ceremonial items, most of which Eden was standing too far away to identify ... and finally it seemed that the thing was done. The Aldermen and Council led the newly-installed Lord Protector from the court and out to the waiting carriages for the journey back to Whitehall.

This time their progress was accompanied by a certain amount of cheering – though, as far as Eden could tell, the only ones doing it were the soldiers lining the route. Everyone else, of course, was as much in the dark as they'd been a couple of hours ago. And even if they'd known that they were witnessing the first moments of His Excellency's rule as Lord Protector, Eden had a sneaking suspicion that there would probably still have been a distinct dearth of *joie-de-vivre*.

Speaking for himself, he'd run out of that particular quality eight months ago.

PLOTTERS ALL AWRY
London – January to May 1654

A Protector! What's that? Tis a stately thing
That confesses itself the Ape of a King
The fantastic shadow of a Sovereign Head
The Arms-Royal reversed and disloyal instead.
In fine, he is one we may Protector call
From whom the King of Kings protect us all!

Major-General Overton

ONE

Her arms full of ledgers, Lydia Neville fumbled awkwardly with the latch of the front door. It would have been easier to pull the bell but, if she did that, they'd know she was home and someone would probably intercept her before she got more than three steps across the hall. It had been a long day. She was cold, tired and grubby. And the thought of having to endure the usual litany of criticism and complaint before she'd had time to wash her hands was more than she could tolerate.

The door opened unexpectedly, catapulting her inside and sending the ledgers flying across the floor along with a scattering of loose papers.

'Sorry, Miss Lydia,' whispered the maid, dropping to her knees and helping to gather up the books. 'I was looking out for you and thought to let you in quiet-like.'

'Pity it didn't work,' muttered Lydia, snatching up loose bills and invoices. Then, 'It's not your fault, Nancy. We'll just have to be quick.'

'Won't do no good. That's what I wanted to warn you about. They're all in the best parlour.'

Lydia's hands froze and she looked up.

'What do you mean – *all*?'

'Well, Mr Joseph and Mistress Margaret, of course ... and Mr Gideon and Mistress Elizabeth are up from the country visiting his sister in Lambeth. And the Reverend Geoffrey's here an 'all. They've been in there two hours and more, I reckon.'

'Oh God.' Lydia swept everything up willy-nilly and clutched the entire untidy heap against her chest. 'What *now*?'

'Lydia,' said the glacial voice of her step-daughter-in-law from the turn of the stairs. 'We thought it must be you.'

Brilliantly deduced, thought Lydia irritably. But she merely turned and said, 'Yes. I'm a little later than I'd hoped.'

'So we'd noticed.' Margaret remained where she was, her eyes taking in every detail of Lydia's appearance and her mouth tight with disapproval. 'I was about to suggest that you join us in the parlour ... but perhaps it might be best if you tidied yourself first.'

'In most particulars, that was precisely what I had in mind,' replied Lydia, dropping her cloak over a settle and heading for the stairs. 'Perhaps you can bring some hot water up, Nancy? And then I'd like to change my gown.'

'Right away, Mistress Neville.' With a brisk curtsy, the maid whisked herself away in the direction of the kitchen.

Lydia swallowed a grin. Nancy only ever addressed her formally when Margaret was around to be irritated by it. Margaret, of course, wanted to be the one and *only* Mistress Neville and particularly disliked sharing the name with her late father-in-law's second and, in Margaret's opinion, extremely unnecessary wife.

'That girl,' remarked Margaret, 'is impertinent.'

'Really? I don't find her so.'

'No. You wouldn't.' Her tone suggested that Lydia wouldn't recognise impertinence if it came up and smacked her in the face. 'I also take exception to having your – your charity cases employed in this house.'

'Yes. So you've said.' *Far, far too often.* 'But since Nancy is my personal maid and Tam never stirs above stairs, you need scarcely see either of them.'

Hoisting her skirts in one hand and holding tight to the ledgers with the other, Lydia tramped up the stairs only to halt a step below the half-landing because Margaret was still planted firmly in her way. She said, 'May I pass, do you think?' There was a moment of hesitation before the other woman stepped aside. 'Thank you.'

'Elizabeth and Gideon are here,' remarked Margaret from behind her. 'And Cousin Geoffrey.'

'Again?' Continuing on her way, Lydia neither paused nor turned her head. 'He's here so much these days that perhaps you should have a bed made up for him.'

And she set off up the second flight without waiting for an answer.

Once inside the safety of her room, Lydia dropped the ledgers on the bed and sank down beside them to draw a long, calming breath. The entire family seemed hell bent on driving her demented – though Margaret was by far the worst. That, reflected Lydia sardonically, was what came of having a step-daughter-in-law ten years older than she was herself. Their relationship had never been a comfortable one. But in the six months since Stephen's death, it had deteriorated into a nightmare.

Lydia sighed and started stripping off her dusty, ink-stained cuffs.

She didn't suppose anyone would believe that she missed Stephen. Margaret certainly wouldn't. She'd made it plain from the very first that she considered her father-in-law re-marrying at the age of sixty-two – and to a woman forty years his junior – a massive and frankly ludicrous mistake. The fact that Stephen Neville's reasons for doing so had nothing to do with acquiring a nubile young wife and everything to do with fulfilling what he saw as a duty to the second-cousin who'd been his closest friend, didn't weigh with Margaret at all. In her opinion, Stephen Neville could have put *any* roof over the heads of Sir Marchmont Durand's destitute children. It didn't have to be this one. And it *certainly* didn't have to involve marriage.

But Stephen had seen it differently. He'd insisted on giving Lydia the protection of a well-respected name; he'd provided her brother with both a home and employment in the family pewter-making business; and for five years he'd been a bulwark of kindness to both of them. And Lydia missed him.

A tap at the door heralded Nancy with the hot water. Lydia cleared her throat of the lump threatening to form there and stood up. There was no point in repining. Life was what it was. The only question was whether she could endure this house for the remaining six months of her mourning period.

'Is my brother at home?' she asked, as Nancy started unlacing her gown.

'No. He went out around noon and hasn't been back since that I know of.'

Lydia suppressed a groan. She knew what that meant. It meant Aubrey was in a tavern somewhere associating with God knew whom. The best she could hope for was that he'd come back sober and alone –

or whatever trouble was currently brewing downstairs in the parlour would only get worse.

Margaret liked Aubrey even less than she liked Lydia. It was tempting to wonder if the main reason for this was that Aubrey had inherited the baronetcy given to their father by the late King. It didn't seem a very *good* reason ... but the way Margaret always uttered his title in a tone dripping with sarcasm suggested that it wasn't far from the truth. Of course, another reason might be that, having decided becoming Lady Durand might be no bad thing, Margaret's elder daughter had recently started all-too-obviously setting her cap at him – and was getting precisely nowhere.

Having washed and changed into a fresh gown, Lydia sat before the mirror while Nancy attempted to restore her hair to some sort of order. It had to be admitted, she thought clinically, that black wasn't her colour. Some widows managed to look delicate and ethereal. She didn't. She merely looked pale, insipid and a bit crow-like. The last thought brought a slight curl to her mouth. It didn't matter if she looked like a crow. Black might not suit her but the reason she was wearing it was her protection from the plot that she suspected was being hatched on the floor below.

Finally, when she could delay no longer, she said, 'Oh well. Best get it over with, I suppose. There's only an hour before supper so I ought to be able to last that long without murdering one of them.'

'You keep your chin up, Miss Lydia. They can go on at you all they like but they can't *do* nothing. Mr Neville made sure of that.'

'He did,' agreed Lydia. 'And that, of course, is half the problem.'

* * *

By the time Lydia entered the room, the family gathering in the parlour and run out of a number of things. Patience was one of them and, having talked themselves to a standstill for nearly three hours, conversation was another. Ably assisted by both his cousin and his brother-in-law, Margaret's husband, Joseph, had virtually finished off the wine ... while his sister, Elizabeth, had demolished most of the fruit tartlets. As usual, Margaret looked ready to hit someone.

Lydia allowed herself to smile. She also allowed herself to stand perfectly still, just inside the door and wait, with slightly raised brows, for the three gentlemen to remember their manners. Belatedly and a little untidily, they hoisted themselves to their feet.

Lydia dropped the merest suggestion of a curtsy and sank into the nearest empty chair. Joseph and Gideon resumed their seats and Geoffrey hovered by the mantelpiece.

'You took your time,' snapped Margaret.

'Not especially. And I wasn't aware that there was any hurry.'

'There isn't, Cousin – no hurry at all.' The Reverend Geoffrey Neville crossed the room to possess himself of one of her hands and bow over it. 'As always, it's a great pleasure to see you – though, if you will forgive me saying so, you look rather more tired than when I saw you last.'

'Surely that was only two days ago?' Lydia freed her fingers with a deft tug and smiled sweetly up at him. 'I had no idea you studied me so closely, Cousin.'

For a moment, no one said anything and Lydia waited to see which of them would embark on the usual refrain; the collective chorus that had started within days of Stephen's funeral and been going on ever since. It also occurred to her with a faint quiver of amusement that she wasn't the only one who looked like a crow. Clad in the unrelieved black of full mourning, all six of them did.

Joseph Neville had none of his late father's spare, silver-haired elegance and also lacked his height. At the age of forty-three, his complexion was decidedly florid and he was already losing his hair. A few years younger and several inches taller, Margaret, his wife, might still have been considered a handsome woman but for the lines of discontent marking her face. His sister's passion for cakes and pastries was having the inevitable effect on her hips and his brother-in-law's weak chin was twinned with an even weaker character. As for Cousin Geoffrey, for whom Lydia suspected the family had plans ... he had a long nose, narrow shoulders and perpetually sweaty palms.

She wished he'd stop smiling at her. It was making her teeth hurt.

Plainly tired of waiting, Margaret shot her husband a look as sharp as a kick to the shin.

'Ah,' said Joseph. 'Yes. We wanted to speak to you, Lydia. As a family.'

'Did you? About what?' *As if I didn't know.*

'About your ... er ... outside activities.'

Lydia folded her hands in her lap and fixed him with a cool stare.

'You have something new to add?'

This seemed to throw Joseph off his stride. 'New?'

'Well, yes. I presume you're referring to the lorinery and the haberdashery – or more specifically, to the fact that both employ crippled ex-soldiers and war-widows. And if that's so, I can't imagine what more there can possibly be to say since you've spoken of little else for the last six months.' She paused and drew a bracing breath. 'To be honest, Joseph, I'm quite *tired* of discussing it. And I would have thought that, by now, you would be, too. Both you and Margaret must surely have realised that I have no intention of giving up either business – and that there's nothing you can do to make me.'

That did it. All five of them started to talk at once until, inevitably, Margaret emerged triumphant.

'Why must you be so stubborn?' she demanded angrily. 'These aren't suitable occupations for a respectable widow!'

'Nonsense. Lots of widows have their own businesses these days.'

'*Normal* ones, yes. Not the likes of yours! Associating with women who are little better than whores --'

'I really wish you'd stop calling them that, Margaret. They are *not* whores. Do you honestly think the Haberdasher's Guild would have admitted them if they were running a brothel out of the back room?'

'What makes you so sure they're not?' asked Elizabeth, dusting pastry from her fingers. 'How do you know *what* they get up to when your back is turned?'

'I *know* because I don't just take people off the street at random,' returned Lydia, striving for patience. 'The women I employ are the only bread-winners in their families. By providing them with a couple of rooms and a modicum of equipment, I make it possible for them to earn a basic living with their embroidery and lace-making and so on. How much more respectable do you think it can get?'

'No one is saying you're doing anything wrong, Cousin,' interposed Geoffrey earnestly. 'Indeed, your desire to help these poor unfortunates does you a great deal of credit. But you must see that things are different now. As a widow, you should give some serious thought to – to how it all looks.'

'But I don't care how it looks.'

'Then you should,' remarked Elizabeth. 'People talk, you know. Several of my friends have even commented to me directly about the way you spend your time – so I hate to think what's being said behind my back.'

'I'm surprised your friends are so interested. But the next time the subject comes up, you might tell them that, if they buy their lace from Bennett's in Paternoster Row or from Howell's in the New Exchange, it was probably made by my ladies in Strand Alley.'

'*Ladies?*' scoffed Elizabeth. 'They are hardly that. And as for yourself – what was just about acceptable in my father's wife is not at all appropriate in his widow. His rather *young* widow, I might add.'

'Your father made it possible for me to do more than offer a few coins or a basket of food,' said Lydia flatly. 'People don't want charity. They want self-respect and honest employment. The lorinery provides that. Every man who works there --'

'Rogues and vagabonds, the lot of them,' snapped Margaret. 'My God – some of them are even *Royalists!*'

'So they are. Odd as it may seem, men on both sides lost limbs and eyes – thus making them less desirable employees than the able-bodied. I take on men who need help – irrespective of their politics.'

'But you risk fights breaking out amongst them, do you not?' drawled Gideon Parker, speaking for the first time. 'Or are they all just one big happy family?'

'Yes. In essence, that's *exactly* what they are.'

'You'll forgive me if I find that rather hard to believe.'

'Then perhaps you should visit Duck Lane and see for yourself,' she suggested, knowing he wouldn't. Then, 'It's very simple, Gideon. We have one rule and one only. No one asks who fought for whom and when and where. And it works.'

'Until they get drunk,' spat Margaret. 'Don't try telling me half of them don't drink themselves silly on Neville money.'

Ah. Now we're getting down to it, thought Lydia cynically. *Money. None of this has anything to do with the lorinery or the haberdashery or what is or isn't a respectable occupation for a widow. It's to do with Stephen's will and the fact that they're all still smarting over him leaving me a good deal more than they expected.*

Keeping her voice as level as she could, she said, 'Anyone would suppose that whatever costs there may be are coming out of your own pocket – which we know isn't the case. Also, as I believe I've mentioned before, the lorinery is now breaking even and within a year is likely to be making a profit. Every bridle, bit, harness and spur we make is bought by either Mortimer's Saddlery or by Cotterell's and paid for at Guild rates. As for the men we employ – they all work hard and to the best of their ability, limited as that may be. There has never been a hint of trouble and not one of them has ever offered me the least disrespect – nor would they.'

'I'm sure we're all relieved to hear that,' began Joseph. 'But --'

'Good. Then let that be an end to it.'

'But caring for unemployed soldiers or their widows and orphans isn't your responsibility.'

'No. It isn't. Currently, it's the responsibility of His Highness, the Lord Protector,' retorted Lydia trenchantly. 'And I'd hope to see him getting on with it when he's got comfortable in his new chair and can spare a thought for the men who fought under him. Certainly, despite a lot of well-meaning talk, neither the Rump nor the Barebones Parliament ever made any proper provision either for crippled ex-soldiers or the fellows currently fighting the Dutch at sea. So while we wait for Cromwell to rectify that, I'll continue doing what I can – because, though Parish Relief may work well enough in the smaller towns, it's never going to be sufficient in London where the demand is so much greater.'

'What makes *you* such an expert?' asked Margaret sourly.

'Common sense. Something we haven't seen too much of recently in the powers-that-be.'

'Meaning what?'

'It's clear enough, isn't it? Cromwell threw out the Rump at sword-point, then replaced it with the Nominated Assembly – which was the last thing anybody wanted. Then, when Praise-God Barbone and the rest of the Saints didn't live up to his expectations, he pushed them out of the way so he could assume power himself.' Lydia paused and looked Joseph in the eye. 'You know what your father would have said about the current government. He'd have called it a dictatorship, veiled by a flimsy cloak of constitutionalism and he'd have disapproved of it heart and soul – in which he'd have been by no means alone.'

'I don't deny that,' said Joseph, knowing he couldn't do so. Stephen Neville had been a staunch Presbyterian, standing squarely behind men like Sir William Waller and Sir Arthur Haselrig. 'But the Lord Protector has promised elections and a new Parliament and --'

'He has indeed,' agreed Lydia. 'And we must hope that he likes it better than the previous effort – or it could be equally short-lived.' She rose from her seat and smiled at them all. 'Was there anything else?'

She knew there was. She just wondered, watching the glance that passed between Joseph, Margaret and Geoffrey, if any of them would be crass enough to actually say it.

'I'm sure I speak for us all,' said Geoffrey smoothly, 'when I ask you to at least *consider* what we have said. It is well-meant. And I'm sure that if Stephen were here --'

'If Stephen were here,' said Lydia, moving towards the door, 'there would be no need to have this conversation at all.' She turned, her hand on the latch and added, 'I know it doesn't suit you to admit it ... but Stephen would tell me to carry on the work he and I started. And he'd tell all of *you* to let me alone to get on with it.'

* * *

Not surprisingly, supper was an uncomfortable affair and not much improved by the departure of Elizabeth and Gideon, Cousin Geoffrey's unsuccessful attempts to be charming or the presence of Joseph and Margaret's daughters. Janet and Kitty spent the entire meal bickering about which of them owned a silk shawl until Lydia felt like banging their heads together. Then, just when she was wondering how soon she could escape to her bedchamber, rescue arrived in a form she could have done without.

Voices in the hall told her that her brother was home … and that he'd brought company.

'Sir high-and-mighty Aubrey, of course,' said Margaret. 'And who do you suppose he has with him *this* time?'

'I have no idea,' sighed Lydia rising. 'But there's no need for you to be troubled by them.'

'We'd be even less troubled if he stopped treating this house like his own private tavern.'

'I know – and I'll speak to him.' *Again.* 'Meanwhile, I'll put them in the back parlour. There's no fire lit in there so they won't get too comfortable.'

'Why can't they sit with us?' demanded Kitty, also quitting her chair. 'I like Aubrey's friends. They're the only interesting men I ever meet.'

'You're only saying that because the last fellow he brought home was drunk and leered at you,' said Janet. 'It was disgusting.'

'I bet you wouldn't say that if he'd been leering at you.'

Lydia looked from one to the other of them and despaired.

'Excuse me,' she muttered. And fled.

* * *

Sir Aubrey Durand ushered his guests into the back parlour saying, 'I apologise for the chill in here – but it's better than trying to be civil to my sister's relatives by marriage.'

'That bad, are they?' asked the younger of his two friends with a grin.

'Worse.' He moved around the room, lighting candles. 'Stephen was a decent fellow and a good husband to Lydia, despite being so much older. But the son is an ass and the daughter-in-law, a bloody nightmare.' He stopped as the door opened and his sister walked in. 'Hello, Lyd. Please tell me the others aren't hard on your heels.'

'They're not.'

'Not even the dreadful girls?'

'Not even them – though Kitty made an attempt.'

Aubrey shuddered, then gestured to his companions.

'I'm forgetting my manners. Gentlemen, this is my sister, Mistress Neville. Lyd ... allow me to present Colonel John Gerard and Sir Ellis Brandon.'

The young, slightly-built Colonel smiled and bowed. Lydia dipped a curtsy and wondered why his name rang a distant bell.

Sir Ellis meanwhile, older and elegant in tawny velvet, sauntered across to take her hand and, with an extravagant bow, murmured, 'Mistress Neville ... a pleasure. But I fear that we should apologise for our intrusion.'

Lydia withdrew her hand and said prosaically, 'Thank you – but I'm used to it.' And, to her brother, 'I'll send Nancy in with wine – though, if you want to avoid the usual lecture, I'd advise you against making a night of it.'

'We won't. But perhaps you could bring the wine yourself? We have matters to discuss and would rather not have servants tripping about while we do so.'

Lydia shot him an acute glance, wondering what these three had in common that created a need for secrecy. Then, having no objection to listening outside the door if needs be, she nodded and left the room.

When she returned with a bottle and glasses, the gentlemen had their heads together around the table. She caught the words, *'That business with Pantaleon --'* before Sir Ellis stopped speaking. And that was when she realised why Colonel Gerard's name had seemed familiar.

Setting down the tray and taking her time about filling the glasses, Lydia said, 'Perhaps I'm mistaken, Colonel ... but aren't you the gentleman the Portuguese Ambassador's brother tried to murder a few weeks ago?'

A warning glance passed between the three of them. Then, sighing slightly, John Gerard said, 'You're not mistaken, Madam. The whole affair was extremely unfortunate.'

'So I understand.' Like half of London, she'd read about it in the newspaper. 'The *Intelligencer* said it began as an 'affair of honour' – though it didn't much sound like one to me.'

'It wasn't. Dom Pantaleon and his friends were in their cups and full of arrogant bravado. It began with a lot of unmannerly jostling and progressed to loud and extremely offensive insults which, foolishly perhaps, I didn't choose to ignore.'

'In English?' asked Lydia. And when he looked at her, 'I thought it was odd that they were apparently insulting one and all in English rather than Portuguese.'

He shrugged. 'They were spoiling for a fight. I tried to remonstrate with them and got a blade in my shoulder for my pains – which is where my part in the incident ended. But the next night, Pantaleon took an armed escort and went back to the New Exchange hunting for me. I wasn't there, of course … but a young man of approximately my height and build was buying ribbons for his bride-to-be.' He paused and then added tightly, 'Dom Pantaleon killed him.'

'And has been tried and found guilty of murder,' remarked Aubrey. 'Somewhat awkward since Cromwell's been negotiating a treaty of sorts with the Portuguese.'

'It will be even more awkward if they hang him,' drawled Sir Ellis.

'Do you think they will?' Lydia asked. 'An Ambassador's brother?'

'Guilty of murder in a public place and in front of a dozen witnesses? They can't afford *not* to – though I imagine they'll take their time about it.'

'Probably.' The Colonel frowned into his wine. 'With hindsight, I wish I'd stayed out of it. If I'd kept my mouth shut and just let them roister their way through the Exchange that night, none of the rest of it would have happened. The murdered man's family wouldn't be mourning his loss. That idiot, Pantaleon, wouldn't be awaiting execution. Cromwell would be getting his treaty. And I'd have been spared both a painful wound and several uncomfortable hours in the Secretary of State's office, answering questions and making a formal deposition.' He looked up, his eyes locking with those of Sir Ellis Brandon. 'Whichever way you look at it, the ramifications are both numerous and undesirable.'

'That,' agreed Sir Ellis, in what Lydia thought was a rather odd tone, 'is indisputably true.'

TWO

On the following morning, Colonel Maxwell had been at his desk for no more than ten minutes before he was peremptorily summoned to the Secretary's office.

Taciturn as ever, Thurloe glanced up briefly and pushed a few sheets of paper across the desk, saying, 'Take a look through those, Colonel. It's probably nothing that need concern us but there might be a few new names worth noting for future reference.'

Eden thought of the dozen or so reports and letters lying on his own desk from agents in Paris, Madrid, Lisbon and Stockholm, some of them coded and some not even in English.

The familiar feeling of angry frustration boiled up inside him and he very nearly said, *'Certainly. I'll be happy to waste my morning on the latest trivia dug up by your creatures.'* Then, because he actually couldn't trust himself to say anything at all, he simply nodded, swept up the papers and strode out.

Back in his own room with the door firmly shut, he communed silently with the ceiling while he tried to master his temper. This couldn't go on. Thurloe – this room – the endless, daily tedium of the work he was required to do … all of it was stifling him. If he couldn't obtain leave of absence soon or better still, be re-assigned to more active work, he was either going to explode or bounce some unfortunate person off a few hard surfaces. Only that morning, he'd bitten Deborah's head off for no reason at all and managed to start an argument with Tobias – something that was normally impossible.

He could resign, of course. But, if he did that, he wasn't sure what he'd do with his time and the idea of days filled with nothing either constructive or purposeful wasn't inviting. He could apply, yet again, to Lambert for a change of direction – something which he'd tried twice already with a singular lack of success. Or he could apply to Lambert, *threaten* to resign and hope his bluff wasn't called.

And in the meantime, he could leaf through Thurloe's bloody papers and hope there was something interesting in them.

On first sight, the scribblings of one Roger Cotes didn't look promising. He had managed to fill half a dozen sheets with laborious accounts of a handful of men holding what, in Eden's view, might or might not have been meetings of a political nature in various taverns. Their favourite haunt, though by no means the only one, appeared to be the Ship on the corner of Newgate Street and Old Bailey and Mr Cotes' jottings suggested that the fellows in question did more drinking and flirting with the tavern wenches than anything else. Then, just when Eden was about to lose interest and toss the whole lot aside, a particular name caught his eye and succeeded in capturing his wandering attention.

John Gerard.

Well, now ... this might be interesting, after all.

The name Gerard was one Eden was accustomed to seeing in reports from Paris. Lord Charles Gerard was an active Royalist, a friend of Prince Rupert and an open opponent of Edward Hyde. So when the Dom Pantaleon debacle had brought Colonel John Gerard to Eden's attention, he had wondered if the two men were related – and quickly established that they were cousins. Consequently, the natural inference was that Lord Charles and Colonel John might share allegiances as well as blood.

Eden read on. Two other names were regularly mentioned; Captain Dutton and Colonel Whitley – the latter also being related to Lord Gerard by marriage. Cotes maintained that the group planned to incite apprentice riots and seize the City – an idea that made Eden groan at the sheer, mind-blowing idiocy of it.

God. How stupid are these people? Can't they see it will never come to anything?

Then another well-known name caught his eye.

Sir Ellis Brandon.

This time, despite himself, Eden laughed. Ellis Brandon; Gabriel Brandon's half-brother, last heard of dabbling in counterfeiting ... and, not just the least successful but also probably the least *reliable* conspirator in the entire history of plotting. If the plan had looked ridiculous before, Brandon's involvement doomed it to disaster.

The semi-literate ramblings ended on the previous evening when, on leaving the tavern, Gerard and Brandon had accompanied another gentleman – one Sir Aubrey Durand – to a large house just off John Street in Clerkenwell. Mr Cotes had not been invited to join them but had followed at a discreet distance, then been prevented by the icy weather from lingering outside until they left.

Eden dropped the pages in a drawer. The chances of it amounting to more than a few hot words over numerous tankards of ale were miniscule but it would do no harm to keep half an eye on the situation.

* * *

He spent the afternoon dutifully decoding reports, sending others for translation and making notes in the appropriate files. Then, when his neck had grown stiff and his fingers cramped, he reached for his hat and cloak and set off home to mend a few of the morning's fences.

Tobias was in the room that had once more been transformed into a goldsmith's shop and was surrounded by three pretty women. This was becoming such a normal occurrence that Eden wondered how his brother ever managed to get any work done. The assistant employed to deal with customers lounged in a corner, grinning, while the ladies vied for Mr Maxwell's attention under the pretence of choosing which earrings one of them would buy. The apparent problem was choosing between rubies and amethysts. The *real* problem was that Mr Maxwell attracted women like flies and never seemed inclined to brush them off.

Glancing up, Tobias met Eden's eyes briefly and then returned his attention to the ladies. With a ridiculously charming smile, he said, 'I believe that the amethysts will complement your complexion best, Mistress Crowley – but the choice must be yours. And now, I'm afraid that my brother requires a little of my time so I must leave you to be attended by Mr Turner. Forgive me.'

Knowing Toby wouldn't get away so easily because he never did, Eden smiled to himself and went upstairs. Ten minutes later and having poured ale for them both, he looked up when his brother came in and said, 'What was it this time? An invitation to supper or an evening stroll around the Exchange?'

'Supper,' replied Tobias, dropping into a chair by the fire and taking the mug Eden offered him. 'I might have accepted, there being safety in numbers ... but all three of them talking at once is a bit too much.'

'Yes. I would imagine it might be. Perhaps you should occasionally let Turner do what you pay him for. Unless you enjoy the attention?'

'Of course I enjoy it. Wouldn't you?'

'Never having had the experience, I wouldn't know,' said Eden dryly. Then, curiously, 'Will they buy anything?'

'Probably.' Tobias took a deep draft of ale. 'It's their second visit.'

'You mean you've been through the same rigmarole with them before?'

'More or less. But two is all any of them get.'

Eden blinked. 'I don't follow.'

'It's easy enough. The Crowley girls are the sort of customers who are more likely to buy if I attend them personally – so Matt and I have a system. If they ask for me and I can leave what I'm doing, I'll put in an appearance – but only twice. If they come back a third time, I'm never available.' He grinned suddenly. 'Word gets around. You know how it is.'

'I don't, actually. I'm still reeling from the realisation that my little brother is positively Machiavellian.'

'It's not Machiavellian – it's just good business. But if it was ... what can you expect? I spent years with the most unscrupulous manipulator of them all.' Tobias downed the remainder of his ale and, in a slightly different tone, said, 'I take it that your mood has improved somewhat since we last spoke?'

'Not very much,' admitted Eden, frowning down into his mug. 'But I apologise for this morning. I had no business speaking to you that way.'

'No. You didn't,' came the blunt reply. 'And no business snarling at Deborah either.'

'I'm aware of that and will do my best to mend matters.'

'Do. When she's upset, the pastry suffers.'

Eden gave a brief crack of laughter and then stopped, looking concerned.

'*Is* she upset?'

'What do you think?'

'Where is she?'

'Somewhere about. Staying out of your way until she knows whether you're likely to be civil or not, I should imagine.' The normally smiling grey eyes became unexpectedly serious. 'It's no business of mine but I'm going to say it anyway. Your relationship with Deborah has been going on for two years ... but you're not going to marry her, are you?'

'No.'

'Why not? Because of her birth and background?'

'No! I just don't want to marry at all.'

'Then you ought to think about what you're doing.' Tobias got up and stretched. 'Unless I'm mistaken, both the vintner and the fellow who delivers the vegetables wouldn't mind courting her. But she won't look at anyone else while you're in her life ... and you can't offer her a future that's either respectable or permanent. Perhaps you should ask yourself if that is fair.' He paused. Then, 'And now – before this conversation descends into another argument – I'm going back downstairs to see what my apprentices are up to. I'll swear I was never as much trouble to Luciano as those two are to me. I'm just grateful their families are nearby so I don't actually have to have them living in the house.'

* * *

On his way upstairs in search of Deborah, Eden ran into his resident house-guest.

Sir Nicholas Austin, the one-armed Catholic Royalist that he'd rescued at Worcester immediately said, 'Eden – I've been trying to talk Sam into mentioning Neville's in the piece he's writing about the government's lack of support for war veterans but he's not convinced. There wouldn't be any harm in it, would there?'

'Since I haven't the remotest idea what you're talking about --'

'Neville's!' said Nicholas impatiently. 'The lorinery in Duck Lane and the sewing widows in Strand Alley. Surely you know about them?'

'Clearly I don't – and neither, just now, do I want to. Have you seen Deborah?'

'She's upstairs. But --'

'Thank you,' replied Eden, continuing on his way.

He found Deborah in the top floor room she used for storing and mending the household linen. When he appeared in the doorway, she looked up with a sort of questioning wariness, causing him to say quickly, 'I'm sorry – I'm sorry. I behaved atrociously and deserved to have something thrown at my head.'

'Yes. You did.'

'You could do it now, if you like.'

'Would it make you feel better?'

'Probably.'

'Ah. In that case, I shan't bother.' She smiled a little. 'As for why you behaved as you did ... I *do* understand, you know. You need time away. You've needed it for months now – but they won't let you go.'

'That's an explanation – not an excuse.' He paused, not wanting to ask but knowing that he had to. 'Do you think I need time away from you?'

'Don't you?' she asked gently. And then, when he said nothing, 'This arrangement of ours was never going to be permanent, Eden. We've both always known that. And – in case you were wondering – I've neither hoped nor expected that it would change.'

Eden shook his head slightly. He wondered how to say what was in his mind – and indeed, whether it would be a mistake to say it at all.

'If someone ... if some other man were to ask ... you could marry.'

There was a long silence. Finally, she said calmly, 'Toby's told you about the vintner.'

'Also, the fellow who brings the vegetables, apparently.'

'Really? Your brother seems to know more than I do.'

'He thinks I'm being unfair to you. And he's worried about the pies.'

Unexpectedly and despite the growing pain in her chest, Deborah laughed.

'Of course he is. Between his work and his women, he has a constant need to keep his strength up.' She hesitated, and then said, 'You know he's getting something of a reputation, don't you?'

'I've suspected as much. But no doubt he'll settle down in time.'

'He might ... but only if he falls in love with a woman who can cook.'

'That is probably all too true. But we're digressing. I didn't come up here to talk about Toby. I came to apologise.'

'And you've done so. But that's not all, is it?'

He frowned down at his hands.

'No. What Toby said has made me recognise that there are fellows who could give you what I can't. Men who could offer you a home of your own and children; men who'd respect and value you and consider themselves lucky to have you.' He paused, looking up at her. 'You're still young, Deborah and you deserve a real life – not this half-and-half existence you have with me. I don't ... it's just that, if a chance like that came your way, I wouldn't want to be the cause of you throwing it away.'

'I see.' With an effort of will, she kept her voice perfectly even. 'If you feel our time together has run its course --'

'It's not that.' An uneasy voice in his head said, *At least, I don't think it is.* 'I could quite happily go on as we are. But at some point, a change is inevitable. And when it comes – selfishly, perhaps – I want to know that you will be secure and happy.' He paused and then added gently, 'There's no hurry. I'm not asking you to decide now – indeed, I'd rather that you didn't. Also, if it's not what you want, then there's no more to be said. But I would ask you to at least consider it. Will you?'

'Yes.' *Even though it's slicing my heart into small pieces.* 'Yes. I'll consider it.'

* * *

A week went by during which Eden received no further tavern gossip from Mr Cotes but had more than enough other work to keep him occupied.

In the world outside his office, an envoy from Cardinal Mazarin arrived to open negotiations with the Lord Protector; while, at much the same time, thanks to the rantings of Major-General Harrison and his

Fifth Monarchist preacher friends, the Council of State issued an ordinance declaring that criticism of the Protectorate was now treason. Harrison himself, having already been deprived of his commission for refusing to serve under the new regime, was ordered to take himself back to Staffordshire.

Eden wondered if this was a sign of things to come. He didn't like Harrison and never had but the fellow had always been one of Cromwell's favourites. And if a mere opinion ... not a threat, just an *opinion,* however critical ... could be called treason, it didn't bode well for a good many things; things, for example, such as Samuel Radford's Leveller newspaper. It also didn't say much for the Lord Protector's confidence.

During the first week in February, Mr Cotes surfaced again, adding a couple more names to his existing list. He also reported that none of the would-be plotters were prepared to put their hands in their pockets and contribute hard cash to their common cause. Neither, as far as he was aware, had they received any commission from Charles Stuart to attempt anything on his behalf. Eden added the names Bunce, Ross and Henshaw to his notes, then put them back in the drawer.

In between the various other matters consuming his time, Eden thought long and hard about the conversation he'd had with Deborah, hoping that he'd done the right thing in suggesting she consider a future without him. It was possible, he supposed, that he'd let their relationship go on longer than he should. It was easy and comfortable and he was genuinely fond of her. But fondness wasn't love; and, even if it had been, he had no intention of re-marrying. Neither could he see himself spending the rest of his days living in his brother's business premises. He was thirty-four years old, for God's sake and ought to take control of his life instead of letting it drift by in this smooth, well-established channel. So perhaps Toby was right. Perhaps he really *was* being unfair to Deborah ... selfish, even.

He'd neither expected nor wanted her to fall in love with him but had done nothing about it when he realised that she had because what she offered was so exactly what he'd needed at the time. In some ways, it still was. But, though he couldn't bear to hurt her by admitting it, he was aware that, deep down, he did want time to himself; time away from London, from the Intelligence Office, from the eternal politics ... and even from Deborah.

Leave of absence and the opportunity to visit Gabriel in Yorkshire was the obvious answer to all of this but that continued to be denied him. And the only other solution that he could see – since the Cheapside house was as much Deborah's home as it was his – was for him to move out and lodge elsewhere. It would be awkward and raise questions. But it would create a natural break and allow Deborah time to determine her future. And as long as his favourite pies and pickles continued to arrive on the table, Toby would be happy.

Before he could reach any firm decision on this, what ought to have been no more than a trivial incident, suddenly leapt into prominence. On February 8th, the Lord Mayor and Aldermen invited the Lord Protector and his Council to a banquet in the Grocer's Hall. Despite being received with all the ceremony usually accorded to royalty, Cromwell's day didn't start well. The whole route from Temple to Old Jewry was lined with members of the City Companies but though he repeatedly doffed his cap, neither they nor the watching crowds raised a single cheer. They merely looked on in silence.

The banquet itself, so far as Eden could tell, had gone rather better. Sumptuous food, specially composed music and verses, and a gift of gold plate worth roughly £2000; all these must have gone some way towards lifting Cromwell's spirits. At all events, he didn't leave the Grocer's Hall until well after dark and rode back to Whitehall lit by three hundred torches. But, as they had done that morning, the crowds thronging the streets maintained a sullen silence; and a large stone was hurled from an upper window at the Lord Protector's carriage – missing its target by no more than a foot.

Summoned once more into Thurloe's office on the following morning, Colonel Maxwell said, 'I suppose throwing a rock at the Protector must be treason, must it not? Did they find the person responsible?'

'No. And your flippancy is not appreciated, Colonel.'

No. Of course it isn't.

'My apologies, sir.'

'That rock is but one symptom of public discontent – which is something I take seriously. I'm told people are muttering about dire omens, prophesying the end of the Protectorate.'

'Yes. I've heard them. The Thames ebbing and flowing a couple of hours earlier than it should ... part of Paul's Cathedral crumbling ... a comet in the heavens and the ghost of the late King gliding through Whitehall.' Eden shrugged slightly. 'You can't fight superstition.'

'I'm aware of that,' returned the Secretary testily. 'We can, however, ensure that it doesn't translate into anything more. These tavern meetings Roger Cotes has been privy to ... what do you make of them?'

'Nothing. Apparently they talk of inciting apprentice riots and taking the City – but they've no money, no authority from Paris and no backing from men of substance. It's all talk and no possibility of action, that I can see.'

'You have the names of everyone involved?'

'Most of them, I believe.'

'Good. Bring me your list.' Thurloe paused briefly and then said slowly, 'It's time we made a few arrests. Not all of them, perhaps ... but enough to give the rest pause.'

Eden looked at him. 'Whilst leaving them free to get into more trouble?'

'Yes. That, too.'

THREE

At around the time Colonel Maxwell was receiving his orders from the Secretary of State, Lydia Neville was paying her annual dues at both the Loriners and Haberdashers Guilds. It was the first time she'd had to go to either of them without Stephen's support and she had half-expected to be treated with less than the usual courtesy. But her worries proved groundless and the transactions in both places was conducted without the merest hint of a sneer.

From the Haberdashers Hall on Wood Street, she picked her way through the labyrinthine ways of Aldersgate to the lorinery in Duck Lane. As always, the place was a hive of industry but every man there looked up from his work and called out a greeting as she walked through to the foreman's tiny office. To most, Lydia responded with a smile and a lifted hand; with others, she paused to enquire after either their own health or that of a member of their family. Consequently, it took some time to reach Mr Potter – thus allowing him to tuck his empty left sleeve into the breast of his coat, dust off the room's only chair and shuffle his desk into some semblance of order.

'Mistress Neville,' he grinned, obviously pleased to see her. 'We was hoping you'd come along today. I didn't want to send a lad round to the house 'cos we all know how that goes down. But we got a bit of good news for you.'

'What is it?' She sat, eyeing him expectantly. 'A new order?'

'Better'n that, Miss. A new *customer*.'

Lydia's eyes widened.

'Really? Who?'

'Rayners. They ain't ordering bits and bridles and such – not yet, anyway. But they're asking us to supply saddle-trees – starting with an order of two dozen by next week.'

'That's wonderful! But can we do it? I mean – the order book is full and you're working to capacity already. Do you have enough men?'

'We'll manage – though a couple more, 'specially ones with a bit of carpentry training wouldn't go amiss. Meantime, we ain't going to risk losing a new customer – not if we can help it. It'll just mean working a few extra hours. And none of us'll mind that.'

'Note it all down, then. Extra hours mean extra pay.'

He shook his head. 'Maybe one day – but not yet.'

'But --'

'Beg pardon for arguing, Miss Lydia but we've all decided. After you and Mr Stephen setting this place up and using your own money to give us all a chance – why, there's not a man here who wouldn't be begging on the streets, but for you. And now, with us just about breaking even, this order from Rayners could see us turning a profit sooner'n we thought. So there's no question of extra wages 'cos we won't take 'em.'

Lydia felt tears pricking her eyes. She said, 'That ... that's exceptionally good of you.'

'No, Miss. It's only doing what's right.'

She left soon after and walked on towards Smithfield and Strand Alley where two clean, well-lit rooms were occupied by nine women and half a dozen young girls, all busy with various tasks. Exactly as at the lorinery, she was welcomed with smiles and murmured greetings but the only one who stopped work was the chief seamstress.

Dipping a curtsy, she said, 'Good morning, Mistress Neville.'

'And to you, Lily.' She glanced round and then said, 'Everyone seems very busy today. Are there any problems?'

'Not as such. The weekly order for Bennett's is ready for delivery but they sent a boy round asking for another dozen yards of the new cream lace as well. Bel and Marjorie are working on it now but it'll be a while before it's finished. So I was wondering whether to hold the order back till it's done or send it along anyway and tell them they'll get the lace by the end of tomorrow. What do you reckon?'

'Delivering the main order and sending the lace on later would probably be best,' replied Lydia. Then, 'How is your husband today?'

'He's as well as can be expected, thank you for asking.'

Lydia nodded, aware that the unfortunate man was blind in one eye, had severely restricted vision in the other and was prone to occasional violent headaches. She said, 'You'll tell me if there's anything I can do to help?'

Lily curtsied again. 'That's good of you, Mistress. But we manage well enough.'

Lydia recognised that was less an affirmative than a side-step but had learned long since that, like the men in the lorinery, these women had their pride. In most cases, it was *all* they had. Fortunately, while she was still wondering how best to respond, a voice from the other side of the room called out, 'How's our Nancy doing, Mistress? We ain't seen hide nor hair of her at home for a month or more.'

Smiling, Lydia turned to her maid's younger sister.

'She's fine, Mary. Truthfully, I don't know how I'd manage without her. But I'll make sure she visits you all as soon as possible.'

'Thank you, Miss Lydia – that'd be kind. Meantime, I'll tell Mam what you've said.' And then, hesitantly, 'I wouldn't want you to think our Nancy gossips about you, because she don't … but are Mr and Mistress Neville still nagging you to shut this place down?'

'Mary!' snapped Lily quickly. 'You're over-stepping yourself.'

'No,' said Lydia. 'It's all right. I don't mind her asking. In fact, I'd rather tell you the situation myself than leave you to speculate on what might or might not happen.' She looked around and raised her voice slightly, 'Mary is right. My husband's family don't like my involvement either here or at the lorinery and want me to stop. I have refused … and I shall continue to refuse. So none of you need worry.'

'Can they *make* you do what they want?' asked another voice anxiously.

'No.' Lydia managed a grim smile. 'All they can do is annoy me – and I won't deny that they do. But I'm not about to give way just for the sake of a little peace and quiet. I'm proud of everything you've achieved – and I want to see you flourish further.' She paused and then added, 'This morning, the men at the lorinery volunteered to work extra hours for nothing to complete a new order. Actually, they *insisted*. So - -'

'And they was right, Miss Lydia,' said Mary firmly. 'It's different for us 'cos we get paid for what we make, not the hours we work – but I reckon I can speak for us all when I say we'd do the same, if there was ever a need for it.'

A chorus of agreement followed her words.

Lydia spread her hands in a gesture that was half helpless, half embarrassed.

'I don't know what to say to you.'

'You don't need to say anything, Mistress Neville,' remarked Lily. 'But you should know that we talk to the men from time to time and we're all in agreement about one thing. If you ever need a rag-tag army to stand at your back, you can count on us. *All* of us.'

* * *

Later in the day, while his sister was hiding at the top of the house with her ledgers in order to avoid yet another visit from Cousin Geoffrey, Sir Aubrey Durand took leave of absence from his own work at Neville's Pewterers and joined his friends at the Ship Tavern.

'Cromwell must still be smarting over yesterday's lack of enthusiasm,' remarked Captain Dutton with a grin. 'Not a single cheer, I believe.'

'Did he expect them to throw their hats in the air?' asked Aubrey. 'He's never been less popular than he is right now.'

'Who threw the rock?' Roger Cotes' voice was casual. 'Does anyone know?'

'No – though I expect the spymaster is doing his damnedest to find out.' Ellis Brandon, reached for his tankard of ale. 'My own guess, for what it's worth is that – since whoever it was missed their target – it was probably a woman.'

There was a scattering of laughter into which John Gerard eventually said flatly, 'It's all very well to laugh – but that kind of thing does more harm than good. Even if the rock had actually *hit* Cromwell's carriage, what would it have achieved?'

'A round of applause?' suggested Dutton flippantly.

'Oh for God's sake!' snapped Gerard. 'Can we please take this seriously? Because, as Ellis has already said, Thurloe certainly will. He'll look for the guilty party but if he doesn't find them, he'll arrest anybody who comes to his attention. Do you think he doesn't have a list of virtually every Royalist in London? And any one of us could be on it.' He glanced round and added, 'Speaking for myself, I'd as soon not see the inside of a cell because some damned idiot threw a brick at the Protector.'

'I take your point,' said Dutton, 'but at least this person *did* something – which is more, despite three months' worth of talk, than can be said of ourselves.'

'Very true,' drawled Ellis. 'So perhaps it's time we changed that.'

'You have a suggestion as to exactly *how*?' asked Gerard.

'What's wrong with the original idea of inciting the apprentices to riot?'

'Quite a lot. It's just not enough and likely to about as effective as yesterday's rock – on top of which it would also earn us the enmity of every merchant and Guild in the City. People may be disenchanted with Cromwell – but they'll back him to the hilt if they think we're disrupting trade.'

'So what are you saying?' asked Aubrey. 'That we can't do *anything*?'

'At present, I don't believe we can.' Gerard pushed his ale aside and stood up. 'Think about it, gentlemen. In particular, think about the things – aside from a coherent plan – that we *don't* have. At the top of that list comes money – of which we have none at all and therefore can't afford to do any serious recruiting. Next comes support from men like Belasyse and Loughborough; Royalists with family connections and substantial influence. And finally there's the not-unimportant fact that we don't have the King's commission to act on his behalf.'

'I doubt His Majesty would let that worry him if we achieved something,' said Cotes.

'Perhaps not – *if* we did. But if we don't? If we go off half-cocked and plunge into yet another fiasco, there'll be a fresh round of arrests and even more of our friends choosing to stay at home in future.' Gerard paused again to glance round. 'I probably have a clearer picture of the situation in Paris than most of you. My cousin and his friends are anxious for some action and have been attempting to persuade His Majesty to sanction it. But Ned Hyde is urging caution and the King trusts him so it's Hyde's advice that is dictating policy at present – and it's his belief that nothing at all should be attempted until the time is right. In fact, he's rumoured to be forming an official unit to control all

Royalist conspiracies. I don't know how true that is but it sounds very likely. At any rate, the two opposing views are causing a lot of friction. And though I like it no better than you, our hands are tied until we can come up with a scheme promising enough to win the King's approval.'

'If that's so, we're wasting our time here,' said Dutton. 'Unless anyone has got a brilliant suggestion they've been keeping to themselves?'

'I know a man who *does* have an idea,' replied Gerard guardedly, 'though whether or not it's brilliant is debatable. Obviously, I'm not at liberty to reveal it without his permission. I also want to go to Paris to speak with my cousin and a few others … and get an audience with the King, if I can.'

'To get his commission?' asked Cotes negligently.

'To ask for it, at least. But it will be some ten days before I can get away – so I suggest we meet here again next week to consider Colonel Whitley's report on the likely level of support in Kent and Essex.' He stood up. 'And that, gentlemen, would seem to be as good a place as any to end this meeting.'

* * *

Ellis Brandon strolled out of the tavern beside Aubrey, saying, 'Gerard is very young – which makes his caution surprising. I'd expected a more positive approach. I imagine his cousin feels much the same.'

'Are you acquainted with Lord Gerard?'

'Oh yes. Truth to tell, there are precious few active Royalists I haven't come across over the years. At the moment, many are still keeping their heads down. But as it becomes plain just how unpopular the government really is, doubtless that will change. And when it does we'll need to be ready.'

'Indeed,' nodded Aubrey. Then, 'I know you fought in the first war and again at Preston. But am I right in guessing that this kind of thing isn't new to you? Plotting, I mean.'

'Good Lord, no. I've been working undercover for years now. I devised the scheme that enabled the Duke of York to escape and worked alongside others – rather less successfully as it turned out – to get the late King out of Carisbrooke.'

Aubrey eyed him with increased respect.

'In that case, you must find the current stagnation extremely frustrating.'

'I do. But I'm wise enough to know that forcing others into unwilling action isn't helpful.'

'No. I suppose not.' Aubrey thought for a moment and then, because he didn't want his new friend to think him totally inexperienced, said, 'I've fought, of course – in the Kent rising in '48 under Lord Norwich. But I was wounded at Chelmsford and my father died there, so I didn't get as far as Colchester.'

'For which I'm sure you are duly grateful.'

'Yes, well ... that was the only thing in that whole hellish year that I *could* be grateful for. My father had taken the oath not to fight again – so his part in the Kent rising cost us everything. And the loss of our home and land on top of Father's death was too much for Mother. She didn't see out the year.'

'Supporting the King comes at a high price, does it not? My own birthright is now in the hands of one of Cromwell's Colonels.' As with a number of other things, Ellis chose not to mention that the Colonel in question was his illegitimate half-brother. 'So you and your sister were left with nothing, I take it?'

'Scarcely a groat. If it hadn't been for Stephen, I don't know what we'd have done.'

'Ah. I was wondering how your sister came to be married to a man so much older than herself.'

Aubrey shrugged. 'There's a very distant kinship between our family and the Nevilles but Stephen was also Father's oldest and closest friend. He needn't have married Lydia. He could just have provided for us in some other way. But he said marriage and his name made us both safer – and Lydia didn't mind. She was fond of him. We both were.'

'You were very fortunate in having his support,' remarked Ellis thoughtfully. Then, 'Did he leave your sister adequately provided for?'

'More than adequately. That's why the rest of the family are so bloody awful to her – or part of the reason, anyway. They absolutely *hate* her continuing to run the lorinery.' Aubrey paused, smiling wryly.

'They want her to give it all up but she won't. And she spends half her time either at the work-places or keeping the ledgers up to date.'

'As a widow, she doubtless finds it helpful to keep busy – though one would imagine that in time she will re-marry. How long ago did Mr Neville die?'

'Six months. So poor Lyd's in black until August at the earliest.' Realising that they were only two streets away from his home, Aubrey said, 'I can't promise that we'll escape the rest of the family ... but I'd be happy to offer you some refreshment if you'd care for it?'

'I'd be delighted,' replied Ellis. And then, as if it was merely an afterthought, 'Perhaps your sister might do us the honour of joining us?'

* * *

'Why?' asked Lydia when, having tracked her down, her brother invited her to join himself and Sir Ellis in the parlour.

'Why not?' And then, coaxingly, 'Come on, Lyd. It won't hurt you to be sociable for a little while – and your books will wait. Also, Margaret and the girls are out so you might actually *enjoy* yourself for once.'

Part of her wanted to refuse. The other part suggested that it might be a good idea to find out precisely what kind of men Aubrey was associating with at present – since thus far he had managed to evade all her questions. So she tucked a stray lock of hair back into her cap and prepared, as subtly as possible, to interrogate Sir Ellis Brandon.

He bowed over her hand and said how pleased he was to have an opportunity to further their acquaintance. Lydia caught a calculating glint behind his easy smile and decided it suggested an ulterior motive.

For his part, Ellis saw a slender woman in unflattering black whose dark-brown hair was virtually hidden by an even more unflattering widow's cap. Her light blue eyes were fringed with long, silky lashes but their expression was a little too acute for his taste and the tilt of her chin suggested obstinacy. All in all, he found her ordinary.

Settling herself by the fire and accepting a small glass of wine, Lydia said, 'Do you live in London, Sir Ellis ... or do you merely have business here at present?'

'The latter – and very tedious it is, too. On the other hand, it's given me the opportunity to make new friends as well as seeing old ones.'

'Yes.' She smiled invitingly. 'Just how long *have* you and Aubrey been acquainted?'

If she hadn't been watching carefully she would have missed their brief exchange of glances. Then Aubrey said tersely, 'A few weeks.'

'Not very long, perhaps,' interposed Ellis smoothly, 'but long enough to discover how many things we have in common.'

Such as what? she thought acidly. *Which are the best taverns and whether cards are more fun than dice?* But said instead, 'A meeting of minds? How nice.'

In an attempt to take control of the conversation, Aubrey said, 'I was telling Ellis a little about your business projects.'

'A very little,' said Ellis, bathing her in an appreciative brown gaze. 'I'd love to hear more.'

I doubt that. You just want to stop me asking questions.

'It's very simple really.' And she calmly disposed of the doings in Duck Lane and Strand Alley in four brief sentences.

'Remarkable. And the gratitude of those you help must be enormously rewarding.'

'It is. But I don't do it for that. I do it to see them regain some self-respect.' Lydia decided to find out if, as she suspected, the fellow was trying to charm her. 'Do you know, sir … aside from my late husband and my brother, I believe you are the first person who has been able to appreciate the point of my endeavours.'

'You surprise me. Surely anyone can see that you're doing something both necessary and worthwhile.'

'Margaret and Joseph can't,' remarked Aubrey.

'No – that is perfectly true.' Lydia took a sip of wine and surveyed Sir Ellis over the rim of her glass. 'I promised myself I'd remain with Stephen's family throughout my year of full mourning but it isn't always … comfortable.'

'God, Lyd – it hasn't been remotely comfortable since Stephen died. Nowadays, if it isn't Margaret nagging and complaining, it's those wretched girls of hers. The only time they're not arguing is when one or the other of them is trailing round after me.'

Lydia frowned slightly.

'You're saying Kitty has started trying to engage your attention?'

'From time to time. But she only does it to annoy Janet.'

Ellis laughed.

'Are you sure about that? Two young girls living in the same house as a good-looking man who is only a very distant relation ... well, it must be something of a temptation.'

Aubrey coloured slightly. 'It's not. The older one fancies being Lady Durand and the younger just enjoys annoying her sister. It's nothing to do with me personally.'

Privately, Lydia thought that he might be mistaken about that. Tall and loose-limbed, Aubrey was twenty-five years old and had eyes as blue as a summer sky. Janet and Kitty might be stupid – but they weren't blind. However, because they had strayed from the point, she said, 'And you, Sir Ellis? Are you married?'

'No. I am not.' He leaned back in his chair, the perfect picture of effortless grace and looking deep into her eyes. 'I was once betrothed ... but the war made marriage impossible. And since then I suppose I haven't met the right lady.'

Lydia had the uncomfortable feeling that the words *'Until now'* were lingering in the air – for which she could think of only one explanation. In the hope of finally discovering something useful, she said, 'That is a pity. I imagine you would like a son to continue your name and inherit your family home.'

'Unfortunately, my family home went the same way as my erstwhile bride,' he replied carelessly. And then, as if regretting the remark, added, 'But many men are in far worse case than I. At least I have all my limbs and sufficient funds to live in reasonable comfort.'

Oh my God, thought Lydia, aghast. *So that's it. Why on earth didn't I guess?*

* * *

The moment Sir Ellis sauntered out of the house, Lydia rounded on her brother and said, 'He's a Royalist, isn't he? *Isn't he?*'

'Yes,' agreed Aubrey sulkily. 'But --'

'And Colonel Gerard ... he's one, too?'

'Yes.'

'And how many others? How many other Cavaliers are you associating with?'

'A few. Not that many.'

Lydia raised a hand to her head and stared at him in mingled anger and disbelief.

'Are you *completely* insane? After what happened to us because you and Father fought in the second war and knowing that Royalists are arrested all the time on the slimmest of pretexts ... don't you know the risk you're running?'

'You make too much of it. It's just a handful of fellows, sharing the same views. We *talk* – that's all. We haven't *done* anything.'

'You're not listening,' she snapped. 'You don't *need* to do anything. If any of these new friends of yours are known to the authorities, it's possible that they are being watched. And if they're seen meeting on a regular basis, it could be assumed they're plotting.'

'They're not,' he said hurriedly. And thought, Not really.

'That's not the point. The *assumption* is enough. And if you're seen with them, you'll be tarred with the same brush. For God's sake, Aubrey – you know how things are. At the first sign of any trouble, Thurloe's men start rounding up all and sundry.'

'You're exaggerating. And don't try telling me *you* wouldn't like to see the King back on his throne – because I know you damned well would!'

'All right. Yes. I would. But it's not going to happen. Worcester proved that.' She drew an exasperated breath. 'It's time to face reality, Aubrey. If His Majesty at the head of an army couldn't succeed – what chance do you think wishful thinking in the tavern has got?'

'Gerard and the rest aren't stupid, Lyd. And Ellis says --'

'I don't much care what Ellis says. In fact, I don't much care for Ellis at all. He's got a very high opinion of himself and is too smooth by half.'

'You're being unfair.' Aubrey's mouth curled slightly. 'He seemed very taken with you.'

'Yes. And that's another thing. What have you been telling him?'

'Telling him? About you? Nothing, really.'

'No? You didn't happen to mention anything about Stephen having left me a relatively rich woman?'

He opened his mouth, closed it again and stared at his feet.

Lydia looked back at him in total despair.

'You *idiot!*' she said.

FOUR

Having considered Colonel Maxwell's list of names for three days, Secretary Thurloe said curtly, 'Round them up next time they meet. Has Cotes supplied the date and place?'

Eden nodded reluctantly.

'The 16th at the Ship. Am I to arrest them all?'

'I have decided that would be best. There's no point in half-measures – though you'll be able to release most within a few hours.' The Secretary looked up for a moment. 'You have reservations?'

'Yes. Since they drink more than they talk, I think the whole exercise will be a waste of time.'

'Perhaps – perhaps not. I will be the judge of that.'

'Naturally. You wish to interrogate them yourself, sir?'

'I'll see Cotes. I want to know exactly what he's heard about this new network Edward Hyde is reputedly forming. But you can take care of the rest. See what you can get and furnish me with detailed reports.' He turned back to his work. 'Thank you, Colonel. That will be all.'

'Sir.'

Spinning on his heel, Eden left the room in the same irritable frame of mind he had entered it. He'd considered pointing out the advantages of picking up the so-called plotters separately from their various homes or lodgings so that none of them would be sure who else had been brought in. And if he'd ever known Thurloe take notice of anything he said, he might have done so … but, since he hadn't, it hardly seemed worth the effort.

He did, however, make one very firm decision. Tomorrow, at the first opportunity, he was going to seek an interview with Major-General Lambert.

Back in his office, he sent for his Major and issued the necessary orders.

Ned Moulton had known Colonel Maxwell for a long time and had fought under him until a severe wound had forced him to be shipped out just prior to the battle of Dunbar. Now, easing his stiff leg into a marginally more comfortable position, he said, 'Are any of them of particular interest?'

'I doubt it. The ones most likely to be are John Gerard and Roger Whitley – both of whom are related to Lord Gerard, currently in Paris with the court-in-exile. Another is Gabriel Brandon's half-brother who, to the best of my knowledge, is a buffoon. As to the rest – aside from Roger Cotes who, being Thurloe's man, will get a private interview upstairs – they're a collection of nobodies. But the Secretary wants them all questioned – so we'll question them. Then I can spend many happy hours writing yet more tedious reports which will, in all likelihood, tell us nothing we don't know already.'

Major Moulton grinned.

'I can see,' he said, 'that you're overjoyed at the prospect.'

'I'd rather have my fingernails torn out,' replied Eden. 'Unfortunately, I don't have that choice.'

* * *

On the evening the arrests were to be made, Eden sat in his office staring at the wall and trying to reach some decision about his personal life. It was becoming clear that he had to do something because, though on the surface nothing had changed, beneath it, everything had. For the last week, Deborah had not come to his room and neither had he asked her to. He couldn't. Until he'd worked out what he was going to do, it felt awkward and wrong. And Deborah, of course, would know that – just as she always did.

From two corridors away, he heard voices and the tramp of feet.

Here we go, he thought wearily. And then, with a flicker of dark humour, *But how remiss of me. I forgot to order the red-hot pincers.*

Major Moulton appeared in the doorway.

Eden stood up and said, 'Who have we got?'

'The men you mentioned and eight others.'

'There are *eleven* of them?'

'I'm afraid so.' He handed over a scrap of paper on which he'd scribbled the names of those he'd arrested. 'A couple of your fellows below stairs are writing this out properly and taking details of where they all lodge and I've left four troopers keeping order. So ... where do you want to start?'

'With the minnows. We'll save the bigger fish until last.' Eden scanned the paper. 'Have them send up Bunce, Ross, Horton, Mynott and Durand, in that order. And you can sit in with me yourself.' He grinned wryly. 'It's going to be a long night and I don't see why I should be the only one to suffer.'

The next hour went by precisely as Colonel Maxwell had expected and produced no surprises. Dr Ross, along with Messrs Bunce, Mynott and Horton all protested their complete ignorance of treasonable doings. They had merely spent a few sociable evenings in various taverns where they had occasionally and purely by chance bumped into other gentlemen with whom they had only the most superficial acquaintance. Eden knew it wasn't quite as innocent as they tried to make it sound – but, equally, he was prepared to accept that they didn't know anything because he didn't believe there was anything *to* know.

He ordered the four gentlemen to be detained over-night and released in the morning. Then he took a long, searching look at Sir Aubrey Durand.

Young, he thought. *Too young to have fought in the first war ... but old enough for the second? And right now, he's nervous. Good. He should be.*

Aubrey met the impersonal, hazel regard calmly enough but he could feel his palms starting to sweat. He wished the fellow would say something before he broke the silence himself and said something stupid.

Finally, Colonel Maxwell said, 'Sir Aubrey ... how well-acquainted are you with Colonel Gerard and Sir Ellis Brandon?'

It wasn't the question Aubrey had been expecting. As casually as he could, he said, 'Barely at all. I don't think I've met them more than twice.'

Another long, unnerving silence. Then, gently, 'That's not quite true, is it?'

'No. I mean yes. I think it is.'

'Then I suggest you reconsider.' Eden toyed idly with a quill. 'I doubt you are enjoying this ... and it will be over faster if you tell me the truth. Now. How well do you know Gerard and Brandon?'

He can't know anything, thought Aubrey. *It isn't possible. Is it?*

Shrugging, he said, 'As I said – not well at all. Though it's possible I've run across them more often than I thought. I really don't recall.'

'Indeed. And do you also not recall the Colonel and Sir Ellis spending an evening in your home?' He consulted one of the papers in front of him. 'Clerkenwell, isn't it? Just off John Street? And ... ah yes. On Friday, the third of this month, I believe?'

Something unpleasant lurched inside Aubrey's chest and he remembered what Lydia had said about the authorities watching known Royalists. If, as it now seemed, they'd been watching Gerard and Brandon, further denial was only going to make his current situation worse.

Clearing his throat, he said, 'I do recall it, yes. But it was just that one occasion and there was no particular significance to it. They took a glass of wine with my sister and me.'

'And talked about what?'

'That murder in the New Exchange. My sister was interested and she asked the Colonel about what happened.'

'I see. And doubtless your sister ... what is her name, by the way?'

Aubrey's mouth went dry. 'Lydia N-Neville.'

Colonel Maxwell wrote it down.

'And she could confirm this conversation?'

'Yes.' Aubrey swallowed hard, trying not to panic at the thought of Lydia being brought before this intimidating man. 'But there's no need to involve her in this. It's as I said. Sir Ellis and Colonel Gerard drank wine and talked about the murder. That's all.'

'If it really *is* all,' said Eden, his tone still completely bereft of expression, 'why did you try to conceal it?'

'Because I don't know why I'm here! Under those circumstances, what would *you* do?'

'I think I would probably work on the assumption that the arrest of myself and my friends is not a random act,' remarked Eden aridly. He left the words to hang in the air for a moment and then said, 'As for not knowing why you are here ... why don't you take a guess?'

'I can't.'

'That's disappointing. But perhaps you're just averse to stating the obvious.'

Aubrey was beginning to find Colonel Maxwell's urbane manner even more alarming than his questions. He searched his mind for something – anything – he could say that would get him out of this room and home before daylight. Then, failing, he said, 'All right. Clearly, Sir Ellis and the Colonel are of some interest to you – so I suppose it's because they are Royalists.'

You suppose? thought Eden. But he merely smiled faintly and said, 'Congratulations, Sir Aubrey. I felt sure you'd get it right eventually.' He paused. 'What are your own political allegiances?'

'I've never been part of a Royalist plot, if that's what you were asking.'

'It wasn't.'

Yet another silence developed while Colonel Maxwell waited. And finally Aubrey said tightly, 'My late father fought for the late King. I myself fought briefly in the Kent rising. That's it.'

'You weren't at Worcester?'

'No. For the last five years I've lived with my sister in her husband's house. He's dead now but, aside from owning the largest pewter manufactory in London, Stephen Neville was also a well-known Presbyterian and friendly with men like Sir William Waller. If you think he'd have allowed me to go marching off to a third war --'

'Thank you. The point is duly noted.' Eden scribbled something else on the sheet containing nothing but Lydia's name and then said, 'Major Moulton ... have the sergeant escort Sir Aubrey back downstairs and placed in custody.'

Appalled, Aubrey said, 'But I haven't *done* anything!'

'If that's so, we won't need to keep you long – possibly no longer than tomorrow. It will depend on Secretary Thurloe.' Rising, Colonel Maxwell said dispassionately, 'If you really are innocent of any wrongdoing, I have a piece of advice for you.'

'What?'

'Distance yourself from Sir Ellis Brandon. He has been involved in numerous plots over the years, none of which have gone well. In short, he's a liability of the sort that will put you behind bars.' And, with the merest hint of a shrug, 'But, of course, the choice is yours.'

Ned Moulton left the room to instruct his sergeant and re-entered it, saying, 'That was a low trick.'

'Which?'

'Letting him think you'd haul his sister in here.' And when he didn't get a reply, 'You wouldn't, would you?'

'No.' Eden rolled his shoulders and let his head drop back to ease the tension in his neck. 'But I think you misunderstand his reaction. He's less worried about his sister being questioned than about her finding out in which puddles he's been playing.'

'You think?'

'It's usually the case. They never want their womenfolk to know what they're doing. That might be because they don't trust their discretion or – as I think more likely – because they know how much trouble they'll be in at home if their antics come to light. And Sir Aubrey is new to the game. As you'll see later, the experienced players know better than to simply deny everything. They understand that, if they've been brought here, it's because we already have certain information. So they admit to anything that's of no consequence and they launch into long, inconsequential rigmaroles designed to confuse the issue. Sir Aubrey,' he concluded simply, 'has a great deal to learn if he plans to pursue the path he's just stepped on.'

The Major eyed him thoughtfully.

'You know who his sister is, don't you?'

'No. Should I?'

'I'd have thought so. She owns the lorinery in Duck Lane that employs crippled soldiers from either side – and *only* them. At least two men you'd remember work there. And if this,' he tapped his injured leg, 'had been any worse than it was, it's the kind of place I might have ended up myself.'

The hazel eyes narrowed as Eden tried to recall something Nicholas had said to him. Then, failing, he shrugged and said, 'If that's so, I'm surprised her brother didn't mention it.'

'If he wasn't intent on keeping his sister out of all this, he might have,' replied Ned. Then, 'The advice you gave him about Ellis Brandon ...?'

'Was well-meant,' came the terse reply. 'Let's get on, shall we? In fact, let's have Sir Ellis up next.'

Although, thanks to Gabriel, Eden knew quite a lot about Ellis Brandon, this was the first time he'd actually met the man. Now, watching him saunter into the room amidst a positive fog of careless bravado, he absorbed the glories of the single ear-ring, the artfully curled lovelocks and the tawny velvet coat ... and had to smother a smile. Gabriel had once remarked that amongst his half-brother's numerous character flaws was an ego the size of Yorkshire. Eden decided it might be fun to exploit that.

He said, 'Sit down, Sir Ellis. Perhaps you might begin by telling me why you are in London at this time – aside from the obvious, of course.'

'And perhaps *you* might begin by having the courtesy to introduce yourself.' Ellis lounged in his chair, crossing one leg over the other. 'I would also like an explanation of this ridiculous and extremely annoying inconvenience. Well?'

Eden subjected him to a long, cool stare. Really, the man was just asking for trouble.

'I am Colonel Maxwell, currently serving as one of Secretary Thurloe's senior aides. And you, sir, are under arrest for possible complicity in a Royalist plot. How long we will find it necessary to detain you will depend, to a large degree, on how cooperative I find you.' He waited to let this sink in and to see if Brandon had recognised his name. When it was clear that he hadn't, Eden returned to his original question. 'I asked why you are in London. It would be sensible to answer.'

'My business here is no concern of yours.'

'I fear we may disagree on that point. For example ... not so very long ago, you were involved in the making of false coin, were you not?'

Shock rippled across Ellis's face and for a moment he suddenly looked a great deal less composed. Then, summoning anger as a shield, he said, 'That is completely untrue!'

'Really?'

'Without doubt! Where did you get such a preposterous notion?'

Eden took his time about replying. Then he said gently, 'As it happens, I got it from your half-brother.'

'*What?*'

'Quite.' Another pause. 'Perhaps I should have mentioned that I had the privilege of serving under Colonel Brandon and am therefore aware that I may place absolute faith in his word.'

Some of the colour drained from Ellis's skin and one hand closed convulsively on the arm of his chair. He said, 'The bastard can't prove it – and neither can you.'

'You know, you really aren't helping yourself,' sighed Eden. 'Firstly, while in my presence, you will speak of the Colonel with more respect. Secondly, I'm sure he would be willing to testify that you repaid a debt to his lady wife with counterfeit coins. And thirdly, I saw those coins myself. Well?'

Ellis raised a hand as if to tug at his collar and then thought better of it.

'I didn't … that is, the coins you speak of were passed to me by – by a third party. I wasn't aware that they weren't genuine.' He swallowed and then said rapidly, 'You didn't have me brought here for this. So why don't you get on with your real reason?'

'Oh I will. Have no doubts on that score. But I think you will be more disposed to be helpful when you've had a little more time to consider. Major Moulton … have Sir Ellis taken back below and ask them to send Captain Dutton up.'

Ellis remained in his seat, eyes narrowed in fury.

'You can't keep me here indefinitely.'

'Actually, I can,' replied Eden pleasantly. 'Fortunately however, I don't have to endure your company while I do so. Major?'

* * *

They worked steadily on through the night and into the early hours of the morning. By the time it was finally the turn of Colonel Gerard, Eden's eyes felt full of grit and Ned was struggling with cramp. Neither of them let it show.

'Colonel Maxwell!' said Gerard with a surprised smile. 'I had no idea it was you I was to have the pleasure of seeing. How are you?'

'After hours of listening to drivel? Pretty much as you might expect,' returned Eden. 'Please sit down, Colonel ... and do us both the favour of keeping this brief and to the point.'

'Certainly. You want to know why I and the others you arrested have been meeting and whether we've hatched some sinister plot. Yes?'

'Yes. And?'

'We are – as you're perfectly well-aware – all Royalist sympathisers of the minor variety. We have no influence, no authority, no money and no little army hiding in the shadows. So we gather together in the tavern from time to time and enjoy wallowing in nostalgia. You know the kind of thing. Numerous toasts to the King and recollections of better days; much airing of grievances and a great deal of wishful thinking.' Pausing, he leaned forward and lowered his voice. 'From time to time, we even say rude things about the Protector. *Very* rude things, if I'm to be completely honest.' He sat back again and added cheerfully, 'But, since you didn't hear us saying them, you can't arrest us for that, can you?'

Eden suppressed a twinge of amusement – the first he'd felt throughout this very long night.

He said, 'So, Colonel. You haven't been plotting disturbances? No apprentice riots, for example – or other ways of seizing the City?'

'Oh – that.' Gerard's expression gathered a hint of mild despair. 'Someone – I don't recall who – came up with that sorry idea and, once they got sufficiently drink-sodden, a few of the fellows discussed it as if it was a viable possibility.' He shook his head. 'Fortunately, sense prevailed when they sobered up.'

You're very good at this, aren't you? thought Eden dryly. *Candid, plausible, relaxed ... your whole demeanour so exactly right. You, my friend, are the only man I've met tonight who is actually worth watching.*

'When did you last see Lord Gerard?' he asked, knowing the answer and wanting to see if the Colonel would tell the truth.

'Last autumn. October, I think it was – some weeks before the debacle at the Exchange.'

The right answer. Are you being sensible ... or have you guessed there's a spy in your camp?

'Do the two of you communicate?'

'No. Cousin Charles is too busy with his own affairs to have much interest in a very junior member of the family.'

That might be true or it might not. We haven't intercepted anything – but things slip the net from time to time.

Eden stood up, fully aware that he could try half a dozen different tacks and get precisely nowhere. He said, 'I think that's all for now, Colonel – though I'm afraid you'll be our guest for some little while.'

'Of course.' Gerard also rose, smiling a little. 'May I thank you for your courtesy, sir?'

'By all means. Just don't count on it lasting if you're brought before me again.'

'I'll remember that ... *if* I am.'

After the prisoner had been sent back downstairs, Major Moulton lifted an enquiring brow and said, 'I noticed you didn't warn *him* about Ellis Brandon.'

'No. He's a clever fellow and, despite his youth, remarkably astute – so I'm sure he'll work it out for himself eventually. And, should he ever actually put a plot in motion, Brandon's presence in it can only be to our advantage.'

* * *

Downstairs in a cold and rather dank part of the building, Aubrey Durand shared his accommodation with Roger Cotes, Mr Bunce and Dr Ross. By common consent, since there was no saying who might be listening, none of them spoke. So Aubrey hugged his cloak around himself and tried not to let his various worries escalate into full-blown panic.

He wondered how long they'd keep him there and whether he'd end up in the Tower. He hoped against hope that the fellow upstairs wouldn't decide he wanted to speak to Lydia. And he tried to figure out how – if and when he was finally released – he was going to explain all of this at home.

None of these thoughts were pleasant company but, like unwanted guests, they refused to leave. Across the room, Aubrey could hear somebody snoring. Given their current situation, he couldn't imagine how anybody could possibly sleep. He certainly couldn't. He just wanted to be sick.

FIVE

At home in Clerkenwell, Lydia didn't realise that Aubrey hadn't been seen since the previous day until she returned from Strand Alley in the early part of the afternoon and Nancy informed her that his bed hadn't been slept in.

'And he hasn't been home this morning?'

Nancy shook her head.

'No, Miss Lydia. I thought maybe he might have spent the night with a friend, then gone straight off to his work – so I sent Tam over to the pewter manufactory but he says they haven't seen him neither.'

Certain unpleasant possibilities crowded Lydia's mind. She told herself that there could be many reasons why Aubrey hadn't come home. He might have spent the night with a woman. Although it was never mentioned, she was aware that he did that sometimes. Or he could have drunk too much and ended up sleeping it off on someone's floor. Those were her preferred options. Other less acceptable ones included the possibility that he'd been attacked and left for dead in some alleyway ... or arrested along with his Royalist friends. Lydia discovered that she felt slightly unsteady.

She said, 'For now, we can't do anything except wait. But if he's not back by supper ... well, let's hope it doesn't come to that. In the meantime, don't mention his absence to anyone and let me know immediately if he turns up. I shan't leave the house until we know.'

'Right you are, Miss Lydia,' said Nancy comfortingly. 'It'll be all right, I'm sure.'

I wish I was, thought Lydia.

Three hours later, still without any sign of Aubrey, she had given up trying to add columns of figures and was reduced to lurking in the small parlour because it offered a view of the hall. And that was how, at a little past five o'clock, she saw her errant brother sidle through from the door to the kitchens, plainly hoping to avoid being seen.

Lydia shot into the hall to cut off his escape and, in a furious undertone, said, 'Where have you *been*? Did it never occur to you that I might be worried?'

'Sorry,' muttered Aubrey. 'I'd have sent you a message but --'

'Stop. Not one more word. We'll speak of this where we can't be overheard, if you don't mind.'

Aubrey did mind. He was hungry, tired and dirty. He was also aware that, if he could have reached his chamber undetected, he might have had some chance of talking his way out of this. He said, 'I'll be with you in half an hour or so, Lyd. I just want to clean myself up a bit first.'

'That can wait. I can't.'

And she set off up the stairs, leaving him with little option but to trail behind her.

Once inside her room with the door securely bolted, she said, 'What happened? And don't even *think* of lying to me because you know I can always tell.'

He sighed, tossed his cloak over a chair and sat down on the window-seat.

'I imagine – since you predicted it – that you can guess what happened.'

Lydia dropped on the edge of her bed.

'You were arrested?'

'Yes.'

'*Just* you?'

'No. Nearly a dozen of us.'

She wrapped one hand hard around the other.

'Did – did they hurt you?'

'No. It was fairly civil, actually.' *Except that it hadn't felt that way at the time.* 'We were all questioned individually and then held overnight. A couple of fellows were released earlier this morning; I got out about an hour ago; and some of the others are still there.'

'Who did the questioning? Secretary Thurloe?'

'No. An Army officer. A Colonel, I think – though he didn't trouble to introduce himself.' This had the advantage of being true and made it unnecessary to admit that, thanks to the troopers guarding his cell, he knew the Colonel's name well enough. 'I can't say I liked him much – but at least *he* kept it short.'

'And you'd like me to do the same? Yes. I've gathered that.'

'I'd like you to recognise that I've had a hell of a night and just want to wash, change my clothes and eat,' he replied, coming to his feet. 'If you *must* have a word-for-word account, I'll recite it for you later. Meanwhile --'

'Aubrey – no!' Lydia also stood up and planted herself in front of him. 'Can't you see that this is too important to just brush aside? You're the only family I've got – and I'm *frightened* for you. I'm frightened they'll send for you again.'

And I'm worried they'll send for you – but I can't tell you that any more than I can tell you someone followed me here the night I brought John and Ellis home with me.

'There's no reason why they should.'

'But they might. What did this Colonel ask about?'

'This and that.' During the course of a sleepless night, it had occurred to Aubrey that the things he *hadn't* been asked about were actually more worrying than those he *had*. Reluctantly, because she wouldn't let him alone until he answered, he said, 'He seemed especially interested in how well I know Ellis and John. And he asked me where my own political loyalties lie ... so, since there was no point in lying about it, I told him.' He ran a decidedly irritable hand through his hair. 'That's it, really. I got the impression that I, along with a few of the others, weren't of much interest and he wanted to get us out of the way in order to concentrate on those he considered more important.'

Lydia nodded slowly, hoping this might be true. She said, 'Promise me something. Promise you'll stay away from them in future.'

Even after last night's experience, Aubrey realised that he wasn't quite ready to promise that. Associating with Gerard and the others made his life less humdrum and gave him a sense of importance. So rather than lie outright, he said wryly, 'Given the current situation, I imagine everybody will be staying away from everybody else for the foreseeable future. As for myself – I promise I'll be careful.' He paused briefly and then pulled her into a hug. 'I'm sorry you were worried, Lyd. Really sorry.'

'Good.' She hugged him back. 'If you mean it, you won't let it happen again.'

* * *

During the course of the next week, life in the Neville household returned to its usual state of armed neutrality. Margaret carped and complained; Janet and Kitty bickered over everything from hair ribbons to which of them had the bigger slice of cherry pie; and Aubrey spent the whole of each day at his work and the whole of each evening at home. Then Lydia received a letter.

It came from Stephen's man-of-law who she hadn't seen since the reading of the will when the ensuing uproar had resulted in Joseph shouting that Mr Hetherington's services were no longer required and that all Neville's future business would be taken elsewhere. As soon as it was possible to make herself heard, Lydia had quietly informed the lawyer that Mr Joseph did not speak for her and that, should the need arise, she hoped Mr Hetherington would continue to act on her behalf. And that had been that ... until today.

The letter was brief and written in the little man's formal style. What struck her as odd about it was that, though Mr Hetherington was usually direct and to the point, his letter invited her to visit his office at her earliest convenience in order to discuss *"an advantageous opportunity that has arisen"* but didn't specify – or even hint – what it might be.

Consequently, the following morning found her smiling at Mr Hetherington across his desk and saying, 'I am mystified, sir – and somewhat intrigued. What is all this about?'

The lawyer laid a paper in front of him and then folded his hands upon it.

'It *is* a trifle unorthodox,' he admitted. 'I have received a communication from a fellow lawyer – Mr Philpott of Lincoln's Inn. He has approached me on behalf of his client, asking that I communicate this client's wishes to yourself.'

'That doesn't sound very unusual,' remarked Lydia. 'Isn't that how these things are often done?'

'Yes. But one is usually made aware of the client's identity. In this case, however, the gentleman ... at least, I am *assuming* it is a gentleman ... wishes to remain anonymous.'

'Oh.' She frowned a little. 'And what does this shy gentleman want with me?'

'He wants to buy your lorinery.'

It was unexpected but surprise didn't stop her knowing the answer.

'It's not for sale.'

Mr Hetherington tutted reprovingly.

'Let us not be hasty, Mistress Neville. When you hear the details you may feel differently.'

Lydia shook her head.

'I won't. The answer will still be no.'

Mr Hetherington looked down at the paper in front of him and sighed.

'The gentleman is offering a very generous price. If I might just --'

'Money is neither the issue nor a consideration. I own the Duck Lane premises outright and have a favourable lease on those in Strand Alley. Stephen also left me a thousand pounds a year and a twenty percent share in the pewter business – regardless of whether or not I remarry.' She paused. 'I don't need money ... and the lorinery isn't for sale.'

'I take your point,' said Mr Hetherington unhappily. 'But this really is an exceptionally good offer. I would be failing in my duty if I did not urge you to at least think about it. And your own situation should not be discounted. Since Mr Neville's death, there must have been occasions when you have missed his support.'

'I miss his support every day, sir – but that doesn't change anything. I'm afraid you will have to tell Mr Philpott that I won't sell.'

'And that is your final word?'

'Yes. In truth, I wouldn't sell the lorinery to anyone. But I *particularly* won't sell it to some nameless person who, for all I know to the contrary, may decide to put my people out of work.' She stood up, her expression pleasant but firm. 'I know you mean well, Mr Hetherington. But my mind is made up.'

* * *

On the walk home, Lydia thought long and hard about the mysterious offer.

It could be from a competitor – though, if that was so, she didn't see any reason why the would-be buyer should wish to remain anonymous. It might have come from one of the saddleries she currently had dealings with but that didn't seem very likely either because both the Saddlers and the Loriners Guild actively discouraged a combination of their respective trades. And that left just one other possibility that she could think of.

Despite all their nagging over the last six months, Joseph and Margaret had failed to persuade her to dispose of the lorinery. Lydia supposed they might have decided to try a different tack. Indeed, if Mr Hetherington hadn't been so impressed by the offer-price, she would have been certain of it. But since most of their ill-feeling derived from – in their opinion – the overly-generous provisions Stephen had made for her in his will, Lydia couldn't quite see them pouring more money into her pocket just to be rid of the lorinery. She rather wished now that she'd let the lawyer name the figure. Knowing just how much money was at stake might have answered her doubts one way or another. But for now, she decided to say nothing to either Joseph or Margaret. She would bide her time and see what, if anything, happened next.

* * *

For the next week as March roared in like a lion, nothing especially unusual happened.

In Duck Lane, a couple of burly and perfectly able-bodied individuals turned up seeking work. Mr Potter informed them that he didn't need extra hands at present but, being reluctant to take no for an answer, the men argued a great deal before being persuaded to leave. Two days later, the foreman unhesitatingly took on a sailor who'd lost half of his left leg ... and, within hours, the belligerent pair re-appeared with loud and resentful demands. At this point, realising that they must have been watching the premises, Mr Potter was finally forced to point out that Mistress Neville only employed men whose disabilities made them unable to get work elsewhere. This, inevitably, did not go down well; and, faced with behaviour that was becoming decidedly threatening, the foreman summoned reinforcements from the workshop to eject his unwelcome visitors from the premises.

In Strand Alley, Lily Carter asked Mistress Neville to join her in interviewing two new applicants. Agreeing that both women seemed respectable and the samples of work they had brought with them were of an acceptable standard, Lydia offered the pair the usual month's trial period and thought no more about it.

Then, a few days after the scuffle at the lorinery, Lydia arrived there to find visitors of a different kind.

A well-dressed and pleasant-looking young man lacking his left arm was being instructed in the finer points of harness-making by Tom and Nathan while, further down the main room, another man, one hip perched on the work-bench, was provoking three of her most long-standing employees into gales of laughter.

As soon as he saw her, the young man stood up and bowed.

'Please forgive us for intruding unannounced, Mistress Neville. Your foreman said we ought really to have asked permission but ... well, here we are.'

'So I see,' replied Lydia dryly. 'And, *since* you are, I've no choice but to forgive you, have I? However ... you seem to have the advantage of me, sir.'

He grinned and bowed again.

'Nicholas Austin – very much at your service.'

Lydia curtsied slightly and said, 'May I ask *why* you are here?'

'Actually, I've wanted to visit your workshop for quite a long time – ever since I first learned of it, in fact. I think what you are doing is remarkable. And, as you can see,' he gestured lightly to his empty sleeve, 'had my circumstances turned out differently, it's a place I might have been glad of myself.'

Lydia found that strange. Appearances could be deceptive, of course. But he neither looked nor sounded as if he came from the kind of family which would leave him on the street.

She said, 'So what has prompted your visit today?'

'My friend over there. He learned that some of his former troopers worked here and wanted to see how they were getting on – so I took the opportunity to join him.'

She looked across at the other man of whom, since he had his back towards her, she could see nothing but a pair of well-formed shoulders and long, mahogany hair.

'The gentleman is a soldier?'

Nicholas nodded. 'A colonel – though currently tied to a desk. May I introduce him?'

'That,' agreed Lydia, 'would be a very good idea.'

Abandoning his casual pose as soon as he became aware of their approach, Eden appraised Sir Aubrey Durand's sister without seeming to do so. She didn't bear any great resemblance to her brother and was also, since Stephen Neville had apparently died recently at the age of sixty-seven, much younger than he had expected. She was small and slender with delicate features and silvery-blue eyes, fringed by extravagant lashes. But her expression was shrewd, her chin set at a determined angle and her spine, ramrod straight.

Nobody's fool, he decided. *And, at present, mildly annoyed and just a touch suspicious.*

'Mistress Neville – my friend, Colonel Maxwell,' said Nicholas. And then, in a mock-conspiratorial whisper, 'I suspect the lady is not pleased with us, Eden, so best mind how you tread.'

'I always do,' came the negligent reply as he bowed formally over Lydia's hand. 'It is a pleasure to meet you, Mistress. Troopers Collis, Buxton and Hayes have been singing your praises in solo and chorus ever since I arrived.'

Lydia met a quizzical hazel gaze and, whether due to that half-smile or the thin white scar marring his left cheek, heard warning bells.

'Really? And the laughter I heard as I came in?'

'That was my fault, I'm afraid. Trooper Hayes and I were describing our undignified progress across the bridge at Upton a couple of years ago.'

"Twere right funny,' said Dan Hayes, still wiping his only eye. 'It ain't every day you see an officer hopping across a plank on his arse – begging your pardon, Miss Lydia.'

She smiled to show she wasn't offended but before she could speak, the Colonel murmured, 'It wasn't funny at the time. I recall having nightmares about it.'

'Reckon we all did, Colonel. But you got us to the other side, all right – *and* out of that burning church after.'

Lydia decided it was time to put an end to this before her only hard and fast rule was breached any further. She said, 'Colonel Maxwell ... might I have a few words in private?'

'Of course.'

'Thank you. We'll borrow Mr Potter's office for a minute or two.'

Eden followed her, wondering whether she knew about her brother's activities or whether she had something entirely different she wanted to say. Then, when the door was closed behind them, Lydia turned to him saying pleasantly, 'You wouldn't be aware of it, Colonel – but we have one very important rule here. It's necessary because we make no distinction between those who fought for the Parliament and those who fought against it.'

'And your rule?'

'The men here are asked never to talk about the wars in specific detail. Not the side they fought for or in which battles or under which commanders. It is instrumental in keeping the peace. And though I appreciate you showing those men they haven't been forgotten --'

'*None* of the men who fought under me are forgotten,' interposed Eden blandly. 'But, of course, I take your point and beg your pardon.'

'There's no need for that. As I said, you weren't to know. It's just that the conversation seemed to be ...' She stopped and spread expressive hands.

'Heading in an inappropriate direction?' suggested Eden, helpfully.

A hint of colour warmed her skin but she continued to look him in the eye.

'Yes. I know how such a rule must look to you but --'

'The word that springs to mind is 'sensible',' he said. Then, 'How many men do you have working here?'

'Nineteen, at present. Of course, it's not possible to employ every crippled soldier or sailor reduced to begging on the street – though we *do* take in any particularly needy cases that come to our attention, even if we don't always have work for them. But as our order books grow fuller, we increase the work-force accordingly – which is fortunate as the war with the Dutch was sending fresh casualties our way.'

He nodded and then asked curiously, 'What made you start this?'

The expression that crossed her face told him that this was a stupid question and her next words confirmed it.

'Have you spent much time in London over the past few years, Colonel?'

'A fair amount, yes.'

'Then you must know the answer to that. My *reasons* are on every corner and have been for years.'

'Reasons most people seem to have no difficulty in ignoring,' replied Eden provocatively.

'Yes,' she said bitterly. 'And there's my whole point. If the various governments we've been subjected to recently had ever dealt with the problem effectively, our little enterprise here wouldn't be necessary.'

He noticed with interest how she always said 'we' and 'our' but, instead of commenting upon it, chose to ask whether her 'enterprise' was financially viable.

'It wasn't back in '48 when we started – but fortunately my late husband agreed with me that something must be done and didn't mind absorbing the cost.' A tiny glow of pride touched her face. '*Now*, however, we're breaking even and have hopes of going into profit within the next few months.'

Eden saw with sudden clarity how honestly passionate she was about what he recognised was a very real achievement. The men he'd spoken to in the work-shop were cheerful and relaxed and, above all, confident. He'd seen too many others who were none of those things, thanks to shattered limbs, sightless eyes and – worse than either – a future of being regarded as useless. He also remembered how long it had taken

Nicholas to become accustomed to managing with only one hand ... and wondered how much will-power had been needed to enable Tom Grey to sit at a bench, similarly handicapped and link bridles to bits.

'I congratulate you, Mistress Neville – and wish you every success. But now, since I'm sure you have a great deal to do, I should leave so that you can get on with it.' He opened the door and followed her through it. 'Perhaps – if I promise to remember your rules – I might be allowed a parting word with my old comrades-in-arms?'

'By all means.' Then, a shade crossly, 'And there's only *one* rule. You needn't make it sound as if we have more regulations than a cheap lodging house.'

Eden looked down at her, a very slow smile curling his mouth.

'I beg your pardon. One rule. Of course.'

Lydia had the feeling he wasn't apologising at all and that, not for the first time, he was deliberately provoking her. She also mistrusted that smile which was a lot more charming than any smile had a right to be and was making it very difficult not to respond.

Keeping her own expression as severe as she could, she said stiffly, 'And don't pretend I'm chasing you away. If you wish to spend a little more time with --'

Her words ended in a yelp as a large brick came flying through one of the windows.

Mercifully, it didn't hit anybody but shards of glass flew in all directions.

In the space of a heartbeat, Colonel Maxwell had seized Lydia's arm and flung her down behind a work-bench, before taking off at a run, closely followed by Nicholas Austin and the only four of her employees who had two good legs.

Lydia sat on the floor for a moment, breathing rather hard and looked up at a circle of anxious faces.

'Are you hurt, Miss Lydia?' asked one.

'No.' There was a cut on her hand and bits of glass were dropping from her hair. 'Is anyone else?'

'A few scratches, Miss. Nothing to worry about.'

Mr Potter appeared, holding the missile. He said, 'There's something wrapped round it.'

She scrambled to her feet and reached for the paper.

'Let me see.'

The message was dirty, ill-written and brief.

Cripple-loving bitch. We'll get you.

Despite the shiver than ran down her back, Lydia crumpled the note in her hand and managed a careless shrug.

'It's nothing. Some foolish apprentice boy, I should imagine – or perhaps a drunk. Whoever it was, they'll be sorry if our visitors catch up with them.'

'They will that,' agreed Dan Hayes. 'The Colonel will knock seven bells out of 'em.'

At that moment, the Colonel and all those who had followed him with the exception of Nicholas reappeared in the doorway.

'No sign,' said Eden tersely. 'I imagine he, or they, will be well-away by now – though Nick is still looking.' His gaze skimmed over Lydia. 'Your hand is bleeding. I hope my rough treatment wasn't responsible?'

She shook her head. A moment ago, keeping her voice steady hadn't been too difficult. Now, as shock and a tiny tremor of fear took root, she didn't dare trust it.

The Colonel's eyes narrowed and he advanced on her.

'What do you have there?'

She tried, belatedly, to hide the paper in her skirts and said, 'It's nothing.'

Behind her, the men exchanged glances before staring meaningfully at the foreman.

'It's a note, Colonel,' said Mr Potter firmly. 'It was tied round --'

'Stop this instant!' Lydia spun round, her face furious. 'It's neither your business nor his!'

'Begging your pardon, Miss Lydia,' remarked Will Collis, 'but we reckon it is. Only you wasn't going to let us see it, was you? And somebody ought to.'

'Quite right.' Eden advanced on her and held out his hand. 'If you please, Mistress Neville?'

'No.' She backed away, shaking her head. 'It's a stupid note, meant for me and nothing to do with anyone else – particularly not you. You – you are exceeding your authority here.'

'And you are exceeding my patience,' he replied, stepping forward to take her wrist in a firm clasp and calmly twitching the paper from her.

Lydia watched him smooth it out and read it. She didn't know whether to scream or hit him. Then he looked up, frowning, and said, 'Has there been anything like this before?'

'No.'

'Never?'

'*No*. For God's sake – it's just a bit of spite, not worth the paper it's written on.'

'Perhaps.' He paused as Nicholas returned, dishevelled and sweating. 'Anything?'

'No. Too many places to lose yourself around here. Sorry.'

The Colonel's attention returned to Lydia.

'I gather you visit the workshop most days, Mistress Neville. How do you get here?'

'How do you think?' she snapped. 'I walk.'

'Alone?'

'No. I bring a maid, three footmen and a very large dog.'

Though Eden's mouth quivered with something that might possibly have been amusement, his voice remained coolly impassive. He said, 'You've been threatened, Mistress Neville. Sarcasm is both misplaced and unhelpful – as is pretending it didn't happen. I suggest that, in future, you ask your brother to escort you.'

Lydia scowled, instantly suspicious. 'How do you know I *have* a brother?'

He shrugged, annoyed at the slip and prompt to hide it.

'I thought someone mentioned him – but perhaps I misunderstood. Did I?'

She stared mutinously back at him and took her time about answering. Had it not been for the clutch of over-protective nursemaids behind her, she'd have lied. As it was, there was no alternative but to simply say, 'No.'

'Good. Then you'll be sensible and enlist his assistance for a time.'

'And if Sir Aubrey'd walk you here of a morning,' volunteered Jem Buxton helpfully, 'one or more of us'd be happy to see you home again after. Just following along behind, like. No need for you to be seen with us.'

'I'm perfectly happy to be seen with you,' she shot back. And then, recognising her mistake, added, 'But you're all talking as if someone's out to murder me. It was a brick through the window and a nasty note. That's all. And I will *not* have my life ruled by it.'

Eden looked round the faces behind her and suddenly grinned.

'Actually,' he said, 'I rather suspect that you will.'

* * *

Lydia wasn't happy when Dan Hayes insisted on following her home. She was even less happy when, an hour or so later, her brother stormed into her little office saying, 'You weren't going to tell me, were you? And don't pretend you don't know what I'm talking about. One of your workers was waiting for me.'

'Not you as well,' muttered Lydia. 'Why is everybody making so much of this? It was just a moment of spite – probably from a couple of men we refused to employ. It doesn't mean they're actually going to *do* anything.'

'We'll damned well make sure they won't get a chance. From now on, I'll be walking to Duck Lane with you.'

'You certainly will not!' she said, completely aghast. 'If you do that, Margaret will want to know why – and I'm having enough trouble with the family as it is.'

'Would you rather find yourself being dragged into some alley with a knife at your throat?'

'I'd *rather* you stopped being hysterical. Nothing is going to happen – and I don't need an armed guard.'

'According to my one-eyed friend, that's not what this Colonel of his thinks.'

'Oh – him.' Lydia sniffed disparagingly. 'He shouldn't even have *been* there – never mind giving out orders as if I was one of his blasted troopers.'

'Why *was* he there?'

'He found out that some of his old comrades worked at the lorinery and decided to pay them a visit. When I walked in they were all merrily reminiscing about the good old days at some battle or other. I put a stop to it, of course – but I don't suppose Colonel Maxwell is accustomed to having women lay down the law to him.'

'*Who?*' Aubrey's nerves snarled into a painful tangle. 'Colonel *who?*'

'Maxwell. Why --?' She stopped abruptly as his expression of utter horror made the question unnecessary. 'Oh. Is he the one ... was it him who had you arrested?'

He felt sick but knew that denial was pointless now.

'Yes. Did he say anything about that?'

'Not a word.' Her eyes darkened with sudden anger. 'But it's why he came, isn't it? Dropping in for a chat with his men was just an excuse. He knows I'm your sister and decided to find out if the lorinery is just a smokescreen for – well, for God knows what.' She paused and drew an uneven breath. 'The devious *bastard!*'

Aubrey managed a feeble smile, trying to take comfort from the fact that Maxwell had neither questioned Lydia about her conversation with Gerard and Brandon nor revealed that the three of them had been followed that night.

'Steady on, Lyd. It might not have been that at all. I mean ... if he didn't say anything about me or ask you any questions, it might have been a coincidence.'

'Rubbish! He came to poke and pry but he wanted to be discreet about it. And when I think about how concerned he was regarding my safety, I could spit. As for you ...' Lydia paused again, impaling her brother on a fulminating stare, 'As for *you*, it's your fault he decided it might be worth taking an interest in me. If you'd never brought yourself to his attention, he wouldn't have known I *exist.*'

'No. And I've said I'm sorry. But it doesn't seem that there's any harm done. After all, he's hardly likely to make visiting the lorinery a habit.'

'He'd better not – though I can think of a few things I'd like to say to him.'

'I daresay. But hopefully you wouldn't be stupid enough to actually *say* them,' said Aubrey, realising that, if she subjected the Colonel to a verbal attack, all manner of things might come out. 'And right now, this is beside the point. The important thing is that you've been threatened with violence and will need to be more careful – at least for a while. So as I said, I'll be escorting you to --'

'And as *I* said – you won't.' She met his eyes with a look as stubborn as his own. Then, realising that he'd argue until Doomsday if necessary, she said crossly, 'All right. I'll take Tam with me for the next couple of days.'

'Tam? What good do you think he'll be? Oh – he'd do his best, I grant you. But he's sixty years old and half crippled with rheumatism.'

Lydia tilted her head. 'Fine. Then I'll take Nancy.'

'Now you're being ridiculous.'

'Not at all. Nancy never leaves the house without a weapon.'

Aubrey folded his arms, clearly unimpressed. 'What sort of weapon?'

'It varies,' said Lydia firmly, preferring not to admit that it was either a meat mallet or a pair of scissors. Then, 'Be honest. Would *you* want to get on the wrong side of Nancy?'

He thought about it and then gave a reluctant laugh.

'Not if I could avoid it. I've seen her when her blood is up.'

SIX

'You mean,' said Nicholas slowly, 'that you recently had her brother arrested and brought in for questioning – and you didn't think it worth mentioning?'

It was later that evening and he, Eden and Tobias were relaxing over a glass or two and a deck of cards

'Mention it to whom? Mistress Neville? Absolutely not.'

'But --'

'Damn, Nick – he oughtn't to be mentioning it to *us*, never mind the fellow's sister,' objected Tobias. 'He doesn't normally tell us anything at all.'

'And normally there's a very good reason for that,' Eden said. 'In this case, however – aside from trusting your discretion – there was nothing to the entire affair. Just empty talk over a few tankards of ale.'

'And Mistress Neville?' asked Nicholas, a shade disapprovingly.

'Is unlikely to know anything of the matter at all – which is how her brother would doubtless prefer it to stay.' Eden turned an oblique and faintly mischievous look on the younger man and said, 'I'm aware that you're very taken with her, Nick, but --'

'It's nothing of the sort! It's just that, when you consider what she's trying to do in that place, it seemed wrong to deliberately deceive her. But ... well, I suppose you may have a point.'

'Thank you.'

'My trick,' observed Tobias, laying down his cards and reaching for the stack. Then, 'This note said they'd 'get' her. Clearly it's a threat ... but a serious one?'

'I doubt it. I suspect the lady was right to dismiss it as a random act of spite. Her foreman told me there had been a couple of fellows in demanding work and refusing to accept that they weren't going to get it. What happened today was probably them registering their disapproval. But it doesn't hurt to take the odd precaution.' He looked at his cards and then across at his brother. 'Is dealing me the worst possible hand just my bad luck – or has somebody taught you to fuzz the deck?'

Tobias grinned. 'Look on the bright side. Don't they say 'Lucky at cards, unlucky in love'? So presumably it works the other way as well.'

'Not that I've noticed.' Eden played his only decent card. Then, because he had no intention of being drawn into a discussion about Deborah, he said, 'I spoke to Lambert again yesterday.'

'And?' asked Nicholas, most of his mind on the game.

'And he said this business in Scotland might be a chance to prise me out of Thurloe's clutches.'

'*Scotland?*' echoed Nicholas. 'My God. If you think that will be an improvement on your current situation, you *must* be desperate.'

'I am.'

'I had the impression,' remarked Tobias, 'that the Scottish rising was about as serious as the brick through the lorinery window – that is to say, not very.'

'That was true last summer when it first began but is less so now. The Earl of Glencairn has drawn a surprising number of powerful lairds to his side; Huntly, MacDonald of Glengarry, Seaforth – even Argyll's heir. And for months now, Rob Lilburne has been trying to make Cromwell understand that, without reinforcements and essential supplies, he can't keep the lowlands garrisoned and also go chasing Glencairn through the mountains.' Eden paused and reached for his wine. 'By the turn of the year, it had got so bad he wrote asking the Council to send General Monck to replace him.'

'And will they?'

'Lambert thinks it likely. Certainly, he's personally in favour of it. With the Dutch War finally over – not that they've agreed the terms of the peace yet – Monck is no longer needed at sea and he's a damned fine field commander. And recently we had a report that Major-General Middleton has arrived to take over charge of the Royalist forces from Glencairn.' He glanced at Nicholas. 'I never came up against Middleton – but the general opinion seems to be that, like Monck, he knows what he's doing.'

'He does,' said Nicholas shortly.

'In that case, it's a pity he doesn't have a modicum of tact. He's apparently made Sir George Munro his second-in-command rather than Glencairn – which resulted in the two of them fighting a duel. Monro was wounded and Glencairn's gone off in a huff.'

Nicholas was tempted to ask if Eden also knew what any of the men he'd mentioned ate for breakfast ... but settled for saying, 'A pity for the Scots Royalists – but nice for you.'

There was silence for a few moments, then Eden said mildly, 'I appreciate that this isn't easy for you, Nick. But a rising in the highlands isn't going to put the Charles Stuart back on the throne. It's not even going to conquer the whole of Scotland.'

'I know.'

'You know ... but you still hope.'

'You're saying I shouldn't?' Nicholas reached for his glass and drained it. 'Don't think I don't appreciate what you did for the King last year. Nobody knows better than I do that you bear him no animosity. But there are others who do.'

'I'm aware. What are you trying to say?'

'That he's not his father. And that there are a lot of people these days – and I don't mean only the Royalists – who'd prefer him to Oliver Cromwell.'

'Are we going to finish this game?' asked Tobias. He had never heard Eden and Nicholas argue about their diverse allegiances before but recognised that there was a first time for everything.

'Presently,' said Eden. 'I'm aware of that too, Nick. Sam Radford and his Leveller friends to name but a few. But without a national upheaval in the King's favour, it's never going to be enough. And there's been too much blood shed over this already.'

'Yet you'll still go to Scotland and help shed some more?'

'If I'm asked. To be honest, I'll go anywhere that gets me out of Thurloe's office. But that's not what this is about, is it? You're finding it hard to hear of others doing what they can for the Cause but not being part of it yourself – and you're starting to feel that your days are empty of purpose. I understand that. But what you need to remember is that, during the two years you've been living in this house, no one outside it has been made aware of either your religion or your loyalties.' Eden paused and then said, 'If that should change, your presence here could become ... problematic.'

'I know that. And do you honestly think I'd do anything that might compromise either you or Toby?'

'No. What I think is that, if you got wind of some conspiracy that sounded likely to succeed, you might decide to vanish in order to join it.'

Nicholas coloured slightly but said nothing.

Silence stretched out for several moments until Tobias said bluntly, 'Is he right, Nick? *Might* you do that?'

'Perhaps. I won't deny that the idea has occurred to me.'

'Then you're a bloody idiot!'

'I knew you'd say that,' sighed Nicholas. And to Eden, 'I suppose you think the same?'

'Not exactly,' came the flat reply. 'But you'll be a bloody idiot if you let yourself get tangled up with John Gerard and Ellis Brandon. Everything I hear from Paris says that the whole Gerard faction are apt to throw themselves into any scheme, no matter how stupid or reckless. And Brandon's a braggart whose only talent is disappearing – while his loose mouth and general carelessness gets the rest of his friends arrested.' He paused. 'I should add that Thurloe is releasing him for just that reason.'

* * *

Down in the kitchen, Deborah was engaged in transferring a new batch of sweet chutney from the pan to numerous small earthenware pots when she heard Eden's footsteps on the stairs. In the space of a heartbeat, the gnawing ache which had been simmering inside her for days became a piercing pain. It was time to keep her promise and do what she had always known would one day become necessary. It was time to make it easy for him.

Just for a second, her own sense of desolation threatened to choke her. Then, summoning sufficient power to master it, she sent him a fleeting smile and, restoring her attention to the task in hand, said lightly, 'Has Toby emptied your pockets?'

'Almost.' Eden sat down on the far side of the table and watched her methodically spooning chutney into pots. 'That smells good.'

She glanced at him again, seeing doubts and confusion hovering about him like a muddy cloud. And something else; something new. She said, 'What has happened?'

As always, a small tremor of shock rippled through him. And, as always, he refrained from asking how she knew.

'There is a possibility ... and at present it's *only* that ... of my being sent to Scotland.'

'Ah.' Having filled the pots, she reached for the neat squares of linen with which to cover them. 'Soldiering?'

'Yes.'

'Good. It's what you've wanted, isn't it?' She tied string round the first pot. 'How soon would you have to leave?'

'Not for a while yet. A couple of months, probably.'

So soon? Only a few short weeks ... a mere handful of precious days before I have to let you go and the world becomes a desert.

Somehow she managed to smile at him and, as if it was the easiest thing in the world, say, 'I'm pleased for you.'

'You are?' he asked, surprised and a little cautious.

'Oh – for heaven's sake, Eden! Of course I am. You haven't been happy for a long time and this is just what you need. Also, I've some news of my own ... or I think I may have soon.' She continued covering her pots so that she wouldn't have to look at him. 'I heeded your suggestion and furthered my acquaintance with Mr Fisher and Mr Brent.'

Without warning, something cold and hard twisted in his chest.

'The vintner and the vegetable man?'

'Yes. It turns out that they are both ... interested.'

'That doesn't surprise me. You are a remarkable woman.'

'No. But thank you for saying it.' She tied off another pot. 'I suspect that Mr Brent – the vegetable man – is looking for something rather less permanent than marriage. But --'

Instantly, the odd sensation turned into a flare of anger.

'Has he importuned you in any way?'

Deborah heard the protectiveness behind the anger and wanted to cry.

'No.'

'Are you sure? If he has --'

'He hasn't. And you know I can take care of myself in that way.'

Yes. But you shouldn't have to.

Eden forced himself to let it go. 'What of the other fellow?'

'Mr Fisher? He's another matter. He's a widower with two young children and has made it clear that he's looking for a wife.' She managed to inject a note of satisfaction into her tone as she added, 'He's also made it clear that he finds me … appealing. He hasn't asked yet but I believe he will do so if he has hopes of a favourable reply.'

His throat felt tight. 'And has he?'

'Yes. I'd be foolish to turn him down, wouldn't I?'

'I don't know. Do you like him?'

'Yes. He's a little younger than you and by no means ill-looking. He's kind and well-mannered. He has a pleasant house across the river in Southwark and owns a thriving business. What more could I hope for?'

'I don't know.' *I shouldn't mind. I've no right to mind. It's for the best. I know that. I just never expected to feel like this when it happened.* 'Can I meet him?'

Deborah's hands stilled and she looked up.

'He knows a lot less about me than he thinks he does. He thinks I'm a respectable widow and that you employ me as your housekeeper. Nothing more.'

'And he'll hear nothing more from me,' said Eden, more sharply than he'd intended. 'I won't spoil anything. I just … I'd just like to be satisfied that he's what he seems.' He hesitated and then said, 'I know it's your decision – that you must do what you see fit. But I find I can't let you go without being sure you'll be all right. So may I meet him? Please?'

Everything inside her was crumbling but somehow she found the strength to smile and say, 'I can hardly refuse, can I? But you must promise not to intimidate the poor man.'

'I would hope he won't let me. And he's likely to have more trouble with Toby.'

'No.' She shook her head and her voice was suddenly very firm. 'You are *not* going to involve Toby.'

'Yes, I am. And Nick – who hasn't forgotten that you saved his life. My dear, your Mr Fisher is going to understand that there are three men who will defend you to the hilt, should the need ever arise.' He took her hand and kissed it. 'I'm sorry it couldn't be me, Deborah. But I can't contemplate marriage ... and you deserve more than I have to give.'

I never wanted more. I only ever wanted you. I still do. But I've always known it couldn't happen. I wish I didn't. If I didn't know what lies ahead for you, do you think I'd give you up?

Her eyes darkened, as she saw again that hazy vision of an inevitable future.

'I know you still choose not to believe it ... but you *will* marry again.'

'So you've always maintained.'

'You think it merely a feeling I have? It isn't.'

'I prefer not to know *what* it is,' he replied truthfully. *The idea that you can predict the future or that you really are what they said you were in that Worcester courtroom has never ceased making me nervous.* Then, putting the thought aside and, trying for a note of humour, he said, 'But I don't see how I'm ever to meet this mythical bride you say is out there waiting for me. The only women I ever meet are the ones I trip over downstairs, drooling over Toby. And God forbid I should ever think of marrying one of those – even supposing she should tear her eyes away from my brother long enough to notice me. If there really *is* a fate worse than death, I think that would be it.'

* * *

In the offices around Westminster, bets were being taken on which of the two foreign Ambassadors currently courting the Lord Protector would finally win his hand. Most of Europe had been at peace since 1648 but Spain and France obstinately refused to let go of their grievances and were still fighting over pretty much the same ground they'd been squabbling over for the last five years. So now that England's war with the Dutch was over, both countries were vying with each other to gain English support ... and the ensuing bidding war was providing a good deal of amusement to those in the know.

On behalf of Philip of Spain, Ambassador Cardĕnas had promised £120,000 a year. Not to be outdone, Cardinal Mazarin immediately instructed Ambassador Baas to match this figure and also put a promise of giving no further help to the House of Stuart on the table. Those with substantial wagers waited with bated breath.

For a few days nothing happened. Then rumour said that Cromwell was making the most of his sudden popularity and playing the coy virgin to see what further inducements might be forthcoming. Cardĕnas was asked if King Philip would consider adding Calais to the mix ... and Baas told the Cardinal that the Protector wouldn't consider an alliance that didn't include better treatment for French Protestants. Once again, everything ground to a halt.

Meanwhile, the non-event that, for want of a better name, Colonel Maxwell's clerks referred to as the Ship Tavern Plot had only one significant repercussion. Although Captain Dutton and a couple of others remained in prison, Colonels Gerard and Whitley were eventually released without charge ... as, after as long a delay as Eden could manage, was Sir Ellis Brandon. But Secretary Thurloe's interest in all these men was now minimal. He was intent on tracing a single shred of rumour and discovering what, if anything, lay behind it.

In pursuit of this, he sent for Colonel Maxwell.

'Who is currently our best agent in Paris?'

'Best in what sense, sir?' asked Eden, sighing inwardly. 'Regularity? Accuracy? A nose for what will be useful? And are you seeking intelligence about French policy or --'

'Don't be obtuse, Colonel. I want to know what plans Sir Edward Hyde may be hatching with regard to the management of future conspiracies.'

'We're talking about the rumour Cotes got wind of regarding the establishment of some kind of controlling executive body?'

'I believe it's more than a rumour. Recently, I've seen two intercepted letters referring to something called the 'sealed knot' and I want to know precisely what that is. Which of our people is best-placed to find out?'

'At present? None of them.'

The Secretary looked up, scowling. 'None?'

'No, sir. I have three fairly useful agents operating around the fringes of the court-in-exile – but none has access to the internal workings of Charles Stuart's council. They'll pick up gossip, of course – should there be any. But in a case such as this, I doubt --'

'What about Bampfield?'

'He still sends reports … but since the Royalists have known about him for quite some time his information isn't to be relied upon.'

Thurloe stared back with acute displeasure.

'So what *can* you give me, Colonel?'

'I can instruct our people to keep a close eye on everyone entering Hyde's office and to find out exactly who Charles Stuart is receiving these days. Those names may be sufficient to confirm or deny the existence of this 'sealed knot' and may even give an indication of which men are part of it. My guess is that there won't be many because the more people who are involved, the less secret it becomes.'

'I hardly need you to tell me that,' said the Secretary testily. Then, restoring his attention to the sea of papers in front of him, 'Very well, Colonel. If that's the best you can do – get on with it.'

* * *

March became April. On the 5th, the long-awaited Treaty finally concluded the Dutch War; on the 8th, General Monck was appointed Commander-in-Chief of the Army in Scotland; and from his office in Westminster, Eden sent out orders to his agents in Paris and then continued to deal with the usual day-to-day business while he waited for their replies. Meanwhile, at home in Cheapside, Deborah Hart slowly let Jeremiah Fisher know that she might not be averse to hearing his addresses.

A shy and rather gentle man, Mr Fisher finally stammered out a proposal and then beamed with unadulterated pleasure when Mistress Hart accepted. He said, 'My dear … thank you. I was afraid that I stood little chance of winning you and, even now, can hardly believe my good fortune.'

Deborah's heart lay like lead in her chest. He was a good, kind man who deserved a better bargain than the one he was getting. Keeping a tranquil smile in place, she said, 'You are too modest. I have no doubts that we will deal admirably together ... and I look forward to caring for your children – though it might be best to make it clear that I'm not trying to replace their mother.'

He shook his head.

'They already like you, Deborah and will become fond when they know you better.' He paused. 'I have not asked ... but what are the terms of your employment with Colonel Maxwell? Are you obliged to give notice?'

'No – though I can't possibly leave until I've found a suitable replacement.' She spread her hands. 'I've worked here for over two years and the household has come to rely on me.'

He nodded. 'I imagine the gentlemen will be very sorry to see you go.'

'It's a bit more than that.' Deborah managed a tiny laugh. 'Mr Tobias has a prodigious appetite and is particularly addicted to anything involving pastry. Sir Nicholas is easy to please but has the unshakeable conviction that I saved his life after he lost his arm. And, probably as a result of years spent caring for his regiment, the Colonel feels responsible for me.' She kept her eyes on his face to see how he would take her next words. 'They'd all like to meet you.'

'Ah.' Mr Fisher swallowed hard. 'That sounds ... rather alarming.'

'I know. But you need not worry. I have no doubts at all that the gentlemen will like you.' She paused and added resolutely, 'Also, I have promised to marry you – and I will.'

* * *

Telling Eden that her future was now settled was no easier than she had expected it to be and was made all the more difficult by what she saw in his eyes.

Somehow, past the hiatus in his chest, he said, 'Are you sure about this?'

'Yes.' *Sure, at any rate, that – for your sake – it's the right thing to do.*

'It … it seems rather soon.' *Too soon. I never thought it could happen so quickly.* 'There's time, you know. You don't need to rush into anything.'

'I know. But --'

'Tell him you want a long betrothal,' he said, half way between entreaty and command. 'At least two or three months.'

Deborah looked at him in silence for a moment.

'And what would be the point of that?'

'You'd allow yourself time to know him better. Time to be absolutely sure.'

'As I just said, I'm sure now. He'll suit me well enough and better than most,' came the flat reply. 'And I'm hardly likely to rush out and get married tomorrow, am I? You know I won't leave until I've found someone to take my place. So --'

'Deborah, no one can ever do that.'

'Don't!' The word was out before she could stop it and she had to shut her eyes for a moment so that he wouldn't see what this was costing her. 'I know you mean it kindly – but it isn't helpful.'

'No.' He stared down at his hands. 'No. I suppose not. I'm sorry.'

She nodded. 'I've started looking about for someone suitable to look after the three of you. Meanwhile, I've told Jeremiah that you wish to meet him. If you still want that, tell me when and I'll arrange it.'

Eden tried to think of a way – any way – to make this better. She was using every means she had to make it easy for him but he knew that, behind that cool facade, was a vortex of pain that far exceeded his own. He wished she'd pile it on his shoulders where it belonged. He might feel less of a bastard if he could just put his arms around her and absorb some of her hurt into himself. But since he couldn't, he forced himself to say evenly, 'I'll do whatever will suit you best. That is the very least I owe you.'

SEVEN

For Lydia, the first week of April brought no further hints of danger, thus enabling her to dispense with the escort of both Nancy and her workmen on her journeys to and from Duck Lane. What it *did* bring, however, was Cousin Geoffrey who took to visiting on a daily basis until Lydia started to feel hunted and wanted to strangle Margaret for the regularity with which she managed to find a reason to leave them alone.

'What was that fellow doing here again?' asked Aubrey one day, as soon as Lydia had managed to send the Reverend Neville on his way. 'Hasn't he got anything better to do?'

'Apparently not. As for why he visits so often, I'm surprised you haven't guessed. He's not exactly being subtle – and neither is Margaret.'

'What are you talking about?'

Lydia managed a sardonic smile.

'They want me to marry him. To keep my inheritance from Stephen in the family, as it were – and to curtail what they persist in calling my "outside activities".'

Aubrey opened his mouth, then closed it again. Finally, he said, 'Are they completely insane? Aside from the fact that the man's a weasel, you're still in mourning.'

'Yes – which is the only reason nothing has been said yet. But as soon as I put off my blacks, I'll wager that I'll have Geoffrey going down on one knee.'

'God forbid!' he muttered. And then, 'I trust you'll send him off with a flea in his ear?'

'If it comes to it, yes. But the best plan might be for us to look around for a house of our own a bit sooner than we'd planned,' she said calmly. 'Otherwise, I'm likely to end up in the madhouse.'

* * *

Four days later, Lydia received a renewed offer for the Lorinery.

This time, Mr Hetherington was able to reveal that the potential purchaser was a gentleman who wished to buy the business as a wedding gift for his son. There would be no question of dismissing her current employees and the offer price was increased to the sum of fifteen hundred pounds. Lydia knew the Lorinery was worth little more than half that – even including the premises. She was also sceptical of this shy gentleman's real intentions. So she sent a polite refusal to Mr Hetherington and promptly forgot about the matter when she arrived in Strand Alley on the following morning to learn that Lily had curtailed the newcomers' trial period and dismissed them out of hand.

'I know I should've spoken to you first, Mistress Neville – but I didn't dare keep them a day longer,' said Lily briskly. 'That work they showed us had been done by somebody else because neither one of them could even knot a fringe. But that wasn't the worst of it.'

'It wasn't?'

'No. Underneath their cloaks and shawls they weren't dressed like decent women. And then I caught them loitering in the alley,' she said darkly. 'Laughing and flirting and kicking up their skirts with *men*.'

'Oh.' Lydia's heart sank. 'You think they were --?'

'Trollops? Yes. Standing outside our door, plying their trade bold as brass. But what bothers me is *why* they came – when they must have known we wouldn't keep them on once we realised they didn't know which end of a needle to thread. It doesn't make any sense.'

Lydia had a sudden very unpleasant thought. She said slowly, 'It doesn't ... unless someone put them up to it.'

'What?' Lily stared at her, baffled. 'But who'd do that? And why?'

'To give the impression that none of you are quite as respectable as you seem.'

'But – but that's just *spiteful*!'

'Yes. It is, isn't it?' said Lydia grimly. 'As for the who ... I can't prove it, of course – but I could take a reasonable guess.'

Lily's gaze sharpened.

'Mr Stephen's family? No. Surely they wouldn't do something like that?'

'I've given up guessing what they might or might not do. But I'll do my damnedest to make sure they don't try anything else.'

* * *

She was half-way to Duck Lane before she realised quite how angry she was; not only because of what she believed Margaret and Joseph had done but because, without proof, she knew she couldn't accuse them openly.

The morning wasn't destined to get any better.

At the lorinery, she walked in to the all-pervading odour of something very like rotting fish and a feeling that everyone was avoiding her eyes. Mr Potter apologised, said that the smell had been caused by a batch of incorrectly mixed glue and went on to tell her more about that process than she'd ever wanted to know.

Lydia nodded and tried to breathe through her mouth. Then, muttering something about an urgent errand, she collected the ledgers for the previous quarter and headed for the fresh air beyond the door. On the threshold, she collided with Will Collis, almost knocking his wooden leg from under him and immediately noticing that his right hand and forearm were heavily bandaged up to the elbow. When asked what had happened, he turned rather red and said, 'Had a bit of an argument with my neighbour's dog. But it's nothing to worry about, Miss Lydia. Healing up nicely now it is and it'll soon be good as new.'

Lydia shook her head at him and promised to send Nancy round with a pot of salve. Then she set off home, moodily wondering what else the day would bring.

* * *

For the first time since the night he'd been arrested, Aubrey failed to join them for supper.

Typical, thought Lydia. *Just when it might have been helpful to have some support.*

Swallowing her annoyance, she waited until supper was nearly over before saying mildly, 'I discovered something extremely vexing today.'

Joseph said nothing, Margaret kept her eyes on her plate and Kitty continued bickering with Janet. It was therefore left to Geoffrey to say winsomely, 'Dear me. And what might that have been?'

'I found out that our two newest employees in Strand Alley were … women of dubious morality.' Lydia sent a bright smile around the table. 'Needless to say, Mistress Carter dismissed them forthwith. But what interests me is why – since neither had any skill with a needle – they applied for work with us.' She paused, letting the words linger in the air for a moment. 'It seemed quite a mystery ... until I was able to give it a little thought. And then the answer seemed fairly clear.'

'Really?' Margaret continued busily sawing up a piece of mutton.

'Really,' agreed Lydia. 'The only possible explanation is that someone paid them to do it for the purpose of damaging the good name of the other women.'

'Not the *only* one, surely?' Joseph laid down his knife in order to run a finger round his collar, as if it suddenly felt too tight. 'Perhaps they were acquainted with some of the others and thought --'

'No, Joseph. They were strangers. They claimed to be supporting their husbands and children and they brought samples of work which they most assuredly did not make themselves.' She smiled again, toying with her wine-glass. 'They didn't go to all that trouble for the sake of a few days' work, knowing how quickly they'd be found out. So the idea must have originated elsewhere for the reason I said.'

'My goodness,' jeered Margaret. 'What an imagination you have!'

'You think so? Then how would you explain it?'

'I haven't the remotest *interest* in explaining it.'

'Oh. That's disappointing. I was quite sure you would have a theory.'

Margaret's knife hit the plate with a clatter.

'What *is* this? Are you accusing me?'

Lydia's eyes widened mockingly.

'Heavens, Margaret – perish the thought! Why on earth do you suppose I might do that? After all, whoever was responsible for what, if I wished to be charitable, I might consider no more than a tasteless joke, must be acquainted with harlots – or at least know where to find them. That couldn't apply to you, could it?' She rose gracefully from her seat and added, 'They're also fairly stupid, of course – sending women who can't sew to save their lives. And I'm entirely sure you'd *never* have made a mistake like that.'

Upon which note she walked out of the room and left them to digest what she'd said.

* * *

Lydia would have been even more annoyed with her brother had she known where he was.

When the note from Colonel Gerard had first arrived, Aubrey had known that the sensible course was either to ignore it or to send back a polite excuse. In the end, however, he'd done neither – which was how he came to be passing the evening in the back room of the Belsavage on Ludgate Hill with Gerard, Colonel Whitley and five men he'd never met before.

Offering his hand, Gerard said, 'Welcome, Aubrey. I'm glad you were able to join us. Allow me to introduce Colonels Deane and Aldridge. Also, Majors Henshaw and Halsall and Captain Griffiths. Gentlemen – Sir Aubrey Durand.'

Aubrey acknowledged the other men with a brief nod and took a seat at the table.

Major Henshaw subjected him to a gimlet stare and then, turning to Gerard, said tersely, 'I take it you can vouch for him?'

'He wouldn't be here if I couldn't,' replied Gerard, sliding on to a bench and sending a cool smile around the table. 'Like Major Henshaw, some of us here are recently returned from Paris so, if those gentlemen will bear with me for a few minutes, perhaps I should begin by giving the rest of you an outline of the current situation.'

'Make it brief,' grunted Henshaw. 'I've a meeting across the river with Colonel Haines in an hour.'

'Then we'll try not to keep you,' came the smooth reply. 'The King and Prince Rupert are currently at odds over possession of the prize-money from the Prince's recent activities in the Caribbean. I only mention this because it has inevitably brought Hyde and Rupert into conflict with each other – and since Hyde is all for caution, Rupert is naturally the exact opposite and therefore willing to support a scheme proposed by Major Henshaw.' He paused, shrugging slightly. 'Despite his best efforts, Rupert couldn't persuade Charles to receive the Major when he was in Paris last month. However, His Majesty *did* send for Colonel Fitzjames ... and it was through him that some of us gained an audience.'

'Who?' asked Colonel Deane. 'Which of you met with Charles?'

'Myself and my cousin, Lord Gerard. Also Colonel Whitley, Captain Griffiths and Fitzjames himself, of course.' An expression of sorrow darkened Gerard's eyes. 'I know that not everyone here was acquainted with Fitz ... but I hope we can all mourn his loss.'

'He's *dead*? How?'

'Drowned on the return crossing from France,' supplied Roger Whitley. 'A stupid, tragic accident.'

'Bugger,' said Deane. He took a hefty swallow of ale. 'Right. Let's hear the rest of it.'

'At the urging of my cousin, we laid certain proposals before the King. In essence, they were the same ones Major Henshaw had already discussed with Prince Rupert – so I'll leave him to give you the details in a moment. Suffice it to say that His Majesty is still in agreement with Hyde and not inclined to sanction anything risky. And so, although he didn't *entirely* dismiss Henshaw's plan, he refused to approve it for implementation right now.' Gerard glanced around the assembled faces. 'There are still whispers of an official body to control all loyal conspiracies – but no one we spoke to seems to know who is involved. One might guess, of course. Men like Ned Villiers and Nicholas Armourer. But the upshot is that we have neither the King's blessing nor that of this secret organisation and so --'

'What we *do* have is the backing of Lord Gerard and Lord Keeper Herbert,' interrupted Henshaw belligerently. 'These – and to a degree, Prince Rupert – are keen to see some action in the near future. Damn it – am I the *only* one who's bloody tired of sitting on my hands?'

'No. Everyone in this room feels the same. But it's possible there are some here who won't want to act without the King's authority,' returned Gerard flatly. 'In truth, I'm not entirely comfortable with it myself even though I've allowed my cousin to persuade me to his way of thinking. Consequently, I've called this meeting so you can outline your plan and we can discuss both the idea and its ramifications in detail.'

'Tell them about the Proclamation first,' suggested Colonel Whitley before Henshaw could continue arguing.

'Oh – that.' Gerard reached into his pocket and drew out a much-creased piece of paper. 'Anyone who wishes to read the whole may do so later. Basically, it offers five hundred pounds a year and a knighthood or the rank of colonel to any man who *"by pistol, sword, poison or by any other means whatsoever"* succeeds in murdering Oliver Cromwell.'

Major Halsall shifted uneasily. 'Who offers this? The King?'

'I doubt it. Granted, it's been issued in his name. But I'd put money, supposing I had any, on it actually being the handiwork of Sir Edward Herbert.'

Aubrey unlocked his jaws and spoke for the first time.

'But the King will be held responsible for it – which won't do his reputation any good whatsoever. Unless I'm missing something?'

'If you are, then so am I,' remarked Halsall. 'His Majesty should issue a retraction, disclaiming all knowledge. Or someone should do it for him.'

'That's a completely separate issue and nothing to do with us,' said Henshaw irritably. 'Can we please get on with the business in hand?'

'By all means,' agreed Gerard. And with an elegant shrug, 'The floor is yours, Major.'

'About time, too.' The Major pushed back his stool and got to his feet. 'We need to begin by recruiting as many of His Majesty's old soldiers as we can reach and who can be persuaded to join us. It's a pity Dutton is still in the Tower because he's good at that. However, my brother-in-law, John Wiseman, and I have already embarked on the task and can count on some six or seven hundred stout fellows between us. Colonel Finch has taken on the task of raising the young bloods in the City and Somerset Fox will stir up the apprentices. A schoolmaster in Islington – one Peter Vowell – believes it may be possible to round up Army horses which are left to graze on the fields near his home ... and everyone involved will need to acquire as many pistols as they can – along with powder and shot. Then, when our numbers are great enough and we've amassed sufficient horses and arms, we will strike.'

'Strike?' asked Colonel Deane tersely. 'How?'

'Our first move is the most difficult and also the most crucial,' replied Henshaw, 'and will doubtless lead to a great deal of discussion. That being so, I'll leave explaining that part of the plan until later. Once this critical stage has been successfully accomplished, we will move on to the more widespread part of my plan. I propose to begin with a diversionary assault on Colonel Ingoldsby's regiment in Southwark – the aim being to draw a proportion of Cromwell's troopers away from their normal positions. This done, our main forces will launch simultaneous attacks on Whitehall, Horseguards, St James's and the Mews.'

Bloody hell, thought Aubrey. But merely said, 'That sounds rather ... ambitious.'

'Caution and half-measures won't serve,' snapped Henshaw. 'This has to be all or nothing. And if everyone fulfils their part and no word of our intentions is allowed to reach Thurloe, we have a good chance of success.'

'Do we know exactly how many troopers are stationed at the various locations?'

'Not as yet – but I'll find out. In general terms, we know that the Mews is not heavily guarded and that the various regiments of Foot withdraw from their posts to muster on Tothill Fields three times a week.' He paused for a swallow of ale. 'And now to each man's specific duties on the day. As I said, Mr Fox will be responsible for rousing the City apprentices and Mr Vowell has undertaken to provide us with some horses. Colonel Daniel, Captain Griffiths and myself will continue recruiting outside London – in which,' he added, staring across the table, 'I would hope Colonels Whitley and Deane will agree to lend their assistance.'

Deane immediately nodded. Whitley's expression remained somewhat doubtful but, after a moment's hesitation, he signified also his assent.

'Good,' said Henshaw. 'Colonel Aldridge ... I'd ask you to help Colonel Finch create divisions within the soldiery. You know the kind of thing – just sow as much discontent as you can. And Halsall ... you and Sir Aubrey will occupy yourselves with seeking out every loyal man in the City and drawing them to our cause. But for God's sake don't reveal our specific goals. Needless to say, that rule applies to everyone.' He glared around him as if daring anyone to argue. 'Then, on the day appointed, Colonel Haines will surprise Southwark and I'll engage to secure Horseguards and the Mews; Colonel Gerard will take Whitehall and Colonel Deane, St James's. Clear so far?'

Aubrey said nothing while, around him, there was a muted rumble of assent. Then Major Halsall said tentatively, 'Should we be attempting something of this magnitude? Indeed, without His Majesty's commission, should we be doing anything at all?'

'Possibly not,' said Gerard. 'But Major Henshaw is right. With sufficient effort and organisation, the plan will work. And the King won't disown us if we succeed.'

For almost a full minute there was silence. Then, turning to Henshaw, Deane said, 'You spoke of a critical opening move that will precede everything you've just described. What is it? And who is to undertake it?'

'Gerard and myself – at the head of thirty men, all armed and mounted.' Henshaw paused briefly, as if choosing his words. 'As to what it entails ... it's something that will put an end to this sorry government for once and all.'

'Excellent.' Deane stretched out his legs and crossed one ankle over the other. 'How?'

Across the table, Major Henshaw's eyes met those of Colonel Gerard and he took his time about replying. Then almost carelessly and as if it were the simplest thing in the world, he said, 'We're going to kill Cromwell.'

The ensuing silence was so acute that Aubrey could have sworn he heard his own heart beating.

Then everyone started talking at once.

EIGHT

Aubrey's nerves kept him awake for the whole of the night.

Although the notion of cold-blooded murder didn't sit well with him, he could see both logic and a certain justice in somebody shooting the Protector. After all, the fellow had killed the late King and was preventing the return of the rightful heir by occupying the throne himself. On the other hand, Aubrey wasn't at all sure how involved he wanted to be in an assassination plot. If it failed – and even if it didn't … if it went awry in any particular … everyone who'd had a hand in it was likely to find themselves decorating the end of a rope. He also, somewhat uneasily, recalled what Colonel Maxwell had said about Ellis Brandon and wondered if he shouldn't pass the warning on to John Gerard – just in case.

He got up the following morning still with no clear idea of what he intended to do. Perhaps, he thought, he could start by sounding out the views of the man he was supposed to be working with. From what he'd seen so far, Major Halsall was no more eager to stick his head in a noose than Aubrey was himself.

Yes. A few words between the two of them might clarify matters.

If he'd known what was happening across the City in Westminster, he might have considered jumping on the first ship ready to sail.

* * *

On the same morning, Eden left early for his office because he wanted to get out of the house. Today was the one on which he was to have the dubious pleasure of meeting Deborah's future husband. And on the previous evening, he had finally brought himself to tell Tobias and Nicholas what was happening.

It had not gone well.

'She's what?' demanded Tobias sharply.

'Marrying the vintner. His name's Fisher, apparently.'

'Why?' asked Nicholas, baffled. 'I mean … it's a bit sudden, isn't it?'

'Not especially. He proposed to her a few weeks ago.'

'But you didn't think to mention it.' Tobias again, arms folded across his chest and a dark look in his eyes. 'Nick's right. It's *damned* sudden. What did you say to her?'

'Nothing you didn't put in my head.' Eden faced his brother squarely and with more than a little annoyance. 'Hell, Toby – this was your idea.'

'It wasn't an idea so much as something I thought you should consider. I didn't expect you to go rampaging off and give her her marching orders.'

'And I didn't. I told her not to rush into anything. I even tried to talk her out of it. But it's her choice. Ask her yourself, why don't you?'

'I will,' vowed Tobias, turning towards the door.

'Wait,' snapped Eden. He knew his brother. Easy-going as Tobias usually was, he could also be the most stubborn man God ever made. 'Talk to Deborah, by all means – but remember one thing. You will be civil to Fisher until there's a reason not to be. And you will do it for her sake, not his.'

Tobias made a sound not unlike a grunt and stalked out, shutting the door behind him with a snap.

Nicholas looked at Eden in silence for a moment and then said, 'I don't understand. I thought she ... that you and she were happy together.'

'We were.' Eden dropped wearily into a chair and ran his hands over his face. 'But my one taste of matrimony was enough for me – so our relationship was always destined to end at some point.' He looked up. 'Deborah deserves a wedding ring and a home of her own, don't you think?'

'Yes. Yes, I suppose so.' Trouble still lurked in the younger man's eyes. 'But how is this supposed to work when it's as clear as day that she loves you?'

'Oh God, Nick. I don't know. I'm just hoping for the best and that she knows what she's doing. And, unless I'm mistaken and you ride to Shoreditch much less often these days for some other reason than the one I've assumed, you ought to have some inkling of how I feel. After all, you don't want to marry Verity Marriot, do you?'

This time the silence was a long one. Then Nicholas said slowly, 'No. I don't feel that way about her. In the beginning, I thought perhaps ... but it didn't happen. Truthfully, she's like my sister.'

'But she doesn't see you as a brother.'

'No.'

'Well, then,' said Eden, hauling himself to his feet. 'There you have it. My situation, more or less exactly.'

After this conversation and a further, unusually terse one with Tobias, Eden had got out of bed determined to avoid any repetition. His office, he decided, was preferable.

The first letter he picked up went some way to improving his mood. Major-General Lambert was summoning him to Whitehall that afternoon to discuss requests recently arrived from General Monck in Scotland. This sounded promising. Eden prayed that it was but permitted himself only the smallest fragment of hope. Then he reached for the three new reports which his clerk had placed in the box labelled 'Paris'.

Ten minutes later, wheeling away from his desk to slam his fist into the wall, he had only one lucid thought.

Bloody buggering hell. I'll never get away now.

* * *

Secretary Thurloe deigned to pause in his labours and said, 'You wished to see me, Colonel?'

No. I'd be ecstatic if I never had to see you again.

'Yes, sir. I've had word from two of our agents in Paris – some of which I felt you should be made aware of immediately.'

'Ah.' Thurloe gestured to a chair. 'Well? You have something about this sealed knot?'

'Not specifically – though I'm told that Hyde has recently met with Colonel John Russell on more than one occasion. Edward Villiers and Nicholas Armourer are also regular visitors. I can only speculate ... but if this secret group exists, it's likely that those three either know of it or are members. I don't know about Armourer but I'm informed that Russell and Villiers are now in England – so you may wish to have them found and followed.'

'Arrange it,' said Thurloe, glancing back down at his desk. 'Anything else?'

'Yes. Something rather more serious.' Colonel Maxwell waited until the Secretary graced him with his full attention. 'I have a letter here addressed to Thomas Scot – presumably from someone who doesn't know he's left the service. It offers no details but it refers to a possible plot to assassinate the Protector.'

Thurloe tossed down his quill.

'Heaven help us. *Another* one?'

'Yes. I realise that these rumours arise from time to time and that, so far, they have amounted to little or nothing. But, in this particular instance, there may be something more.'

'Go on.'

'A proclamation has been issued in Paris offering a substantial reward for any man who contrives Cromwell's death. It purports to come from Charles Stuart - though the agent who brought it to my attention believes it to be the work of someone in the Queen's party, most likely Edward Herbert.' Eden held up his hand as Thurloe would have spoken. 'There's more. Charles recently granted Lord Gerard, his cousin Colonel John Gerard and his brother-in-law, Colonel Whitley a private audience. Also present, apparently, were Colonel Fitzjames and one Captain Griffiths – the latter being the only one whose name is unfamiliar to me.' He paused briefly. 'The same agent informed me that, with the sole exception of his lordship, all of them set off back to the coast over a week ago – which I assume means they're now in England. But a separate report from Dover indicates that Fitzjames was somehow lost at sea en route. That may merely have been bad luck on his part – or it might not. He was one of our sporadic informers. Not an enormously useful one, it's true – but an informer nonetheless.'

'You're suggesting one of his colleagues discovered that and took the opportunity to toss him overboard?'

Eden shrugged. 'It can't be discounted. And neither can the fact that the Gerard faction aligns itself with the Queen's party and is rash to the point of lunacy. Taken all in all, I think an attempt on the Protector's life might be a real possibility.'

The Secretary nodded. 'You may be right. Precautions should certainly be taken.'

Rising from his seat, Colonel Maxwell said, 'I'll be speaking to Major-General Lambert later today. Do you wish me to brief him about this?'

'By all means. And keep me informed of any further developments.'

'Of course, sir.'

Eden walked slowly back through the corridors, acutely aware that it was not yet nine o'clock in the morning and he yearned to sit down with a bottle of brandy. He even contemplated doing it ... and was *still* contemplating it when he walked into his room to find Major Moulton entertaining Will Collis.

Before he could say anything, the old soldier burst into speech.

'Colonel – I'm sorry to come troubling you but things is going from bad to worse and we didn't know what else to do so I said as I'd come and ask you.'

Battening down his own feelings and dismissing the Major with an almost imperceptible gesture, Eden said, 'Ask me what? Or no. Never mind. Just sit down and start at the beginning.'

'Thank you, sir.' He sat on the edge of a chair and tortured the brim of his hat. 'It's the lorinery. You remember that business with the brick?'

'Vividly.'

'Well, nothing happened for a bit after that – though we made sure Mistress Neville wasn't going to and fro on her own till we was sure she'd be safe. Then last week, I was first in and somebody'd shut a pair of great vicious dogs in the yard.' Will held out his arm. 'Nearly had me hand off they did afore I got rid of 'em.'

Eden frowned. 'Dogs? They couldn't have got in there on their own?'

'Not a chance, Colonel. Somebody had to've unbarred the gate, then shut it behind 'em. Made us all sweat, I can tell you – thinking it might've been Miss Lydia who opened that gate instead of one of us.' He drew a long breath. 'Then yesterday it was rotten fish. Half a barrel of it, shoved through the only window that's got a weak catch. The smell was bloody evil, even after we'd cleared it all away – still is, come to that. But the worst thing happened this morning.'

'And that was?'

'It was poor old Dan – Trooper Hayes, I should say. You'll remember him an all.'

'Of course. What's happened to him?'

'He's broke his arm, sir. He was going up the ladder to check the stock in the loft same as he does every week – him being the only one of us with four good limbs – and he was nearly at the top when a rung snapped and Dan come down like a ton of bricks with his arm all busted up. Only when we had a look at the ladder, it hadn't snapped at all, Colonel. It'd been sawn through deliberate.'

'You're sure about that?'

'Bloody certain, sir.'

Eden's frown intensified.

'Does Mistress Neville know about all this?'

'She will do now,' replied Trooper Collis unhappily. 'We kept it from her about the dogs and the fish. But Mr Potter had to send for the sawbones to see to Dan's arm and he said it weren't right to do that without telling Miss Lydia – so he sent round a note. I reckon she'll be at the yard by now. And hopping mad, most like.'

'No doubt.' As he reached for his hat, Eden glanced briefly at the man's wooden leg and said, 'How did you get here?'

'A log-seller gave me a ride on his barrow.' Will rose from the chair, his expression both eager and hopeful. 'Are you coming to take a look, Colonel?'

'Yes. I keep a horse here but I draw the line at taking you up behind me, so --'

'I can walk well enough.'

'From here to Aldersgate? Don't be an idiot. I'll have Major Moulton find a cart or some such. In fact, he may as well come, too. There's no saying that we might not find a use for him.'

* * *

By the time Colonel Maxwell rode into the yard in Duck Lane, a hefty measure of spirits had been poured down Trooper Hayes throat and the surgeon had set his arm. Then, accompanied by Nancy with orders to stay until his daughter came back from her work at the laundry, Lydia had paid two brawny fellows to carry him home on a hurdle.

Consequently, Eden arrived at the doorway to the workshop just in time to hear Mistress Neville say crisply, 'And now, gentlemen, you will all sit down and, without further omissions or prevarications, tell me *exactly* what has been going on here.'

Seventeen pairs of eyes stared miserably down at the floor and no one spoke.

'Well?' she said. 'I'm waiting.'

Eden stepped back outside before anyone should notice him, a faint smile curling his mouth. He'd been right about Lydia Neville. She might *look* like a slip of a thing but her backbone was pure steel.

Assuming the workers couldn't add anything to what Collis had already told him, Eden decided to take a look around the yard. The first thing he noticed was that gate had no lock and was merely fastened by a bar.

This is ridiculous. What are they thinking? It's an open bloody invitation.

The broken ladder lay on its side against a wall. Eden dropped to one knee and examined it. The rung that had given way had been sawn almost clean through and the ones above and below also showed signs of tampering. Someone had been very thorough. He stood up and considered what he knew. The rotting fish was the sort of practical joke played by youthful apprentices. But the dogs had been a vicious trick which might, as Collis had said, have had very nasty consequences. As for the business with the ladder ... if Hayes had fallen differently and his head had hit either the cobbles or the corner of any of those iron-bound boxes, he'd be dead.

This was no game. Somebody was apparently set on damaging – or even destroying – a business that was too small to be a threat to anyone ... which suggested a grudge either against Lydia Neville personally or her work-force of semi-crippled war veterans. The question, thought Eden grimly, was *why*. If he knew that, he might be able to figure out the *who*.

A cart rumbled to a halt beyond the gate and, more nimbly than might be expected of a man with a false leg, Trooper Collis made it to the ground. Colonel Maxwell watched Major Moulton tethering the horse and said, 'We need a padlock, Ned. A good, stout one and the fittings for it – and at least two keys. Buy one and I'll help you attach it. I'll be inside having a word with Mistress Neville.'

Major Moulton nodded and limped away towards St Martin's Lane and the shops of Cheapside. Trooper Collis looked warily at the Colonel and said, 'Miss Lydia's here, then?'

'She is indeed – and, when last I looked, was giving your friends a rare grilling.'

'Gawd,' breathed Will. 'Reckon I might just stop out here for a bit.'

The hazel eyes gleamed.

'Craven, Will?'

'No. I just knows when to keep me head down.' The seamed face cracked into a grin. 'Learned that from you, Colonel.'

Eden gave a snort of laughter and turned away, saying, 'She'll catch up with you – see if she doesn't. You can't hide forever.'

Inside the workshop, men were now returning to their benches and Mistress Neville had disappeared – presumably to confer with the foreman in his office. A few heads were nodded and hands raised in greeting as he strolled through but no one said anything. Clearly, thought Eden sardonically, they were going to leave him to announce himself.

The door to the office stood slightly ajar and the lady had her back to it. Consequently, it was left to Mr Potter to say weakly, 'Ah. Miss Lydia? The Colonel's here.'

She wheeled round, her face a picture of shock, swiftly merging into frigid dislike. Then she said furiously, 'You again. What the *hell* do you want this time?'

Her anger seemed greater than the situation warranted. His eyes narrowing slightly, Eden said mildly, 'I was sent for. Did no one mention it?'

'No.' She swung back to Mr Potter. 'You knew about this?'

He nodded. 'We sent Will Collis. It was for the best, Mistress.'

'That's a matter of opinion. And I suppose it had to be *him*?' Then, when the beleaguered foreman frowned in palpable confusion, 'Oh – never mind. You weren't to know, I suppose. Just go away and see that everyone has got over the upset. I need a private word with the Colonel.'

Mr Potter edged between his desk and the lady, glad of the chance to escape.

Lydia held her ground and waited while Colonel Maxwell came in, closed the door and, in deference to the lack of space, leaned negligently against it with his arms folded. Then she said coldly, 'Well, Colonel? If you investigate *every* instance of a man falling from a ladder, you must be kept extraordinarily busy. Or was your previous visit not enough to convince you that my business is *not* a hot-bed of conspiracy?'

Ah. So that's it. Sir Aubrey must have let himself be caught out. I suppose I ought to have guessed he might not be clever enough to keep quiet. And now I'm the villain of the piece.

He said, 'I *am* extraordinarily busy, Mistress – as doubtless your brother can testify. I am not, however, here to spy on you.'

'And I'm supposed to believe that, am I? You knew who I was when you were here before. You knew the man you'd had in for questioning was my brother and you came here to find out whether I was using the lorinery to cover --'

'I came to see Collis, Buxton and Hayes,' said Eden, deciding that patience wasn't going to get him anywhere while she was in this mood. 'And I'm here now to offer my help.'

'We don't need help. We particularly don't need *yours*.' Lydia wasn't sure what infuriated her most; his iron control or his assumption that she'd believe anything he told her. 'But try explaining this to me. If you weren't here last month to determine whether or not the lorinery is what it seems, why didn't you tell me it was you who'd had Aubrey arrested?'

'Isn't it obvious? I didn't tell you because I assumed he wouldn't want you to know.' Eden sighed and, with deliberately provocative kindness, said, 'Perhaps you're not aware that men frequently do things of which they prefer their womenfolk to remain ignorant. I assumed that this was one such case and so, difficult though it may be for you to believe, I was actually doing your brother a favour.' He made a small dismissive gesture with one hand and added, 'It's hardly my fault if he couldn't keep his mouth shut.'

Lydia's own mouth opened and then closed again. Finally, 'Is that the truth?'

'I believe I just said so.'

'Oh.'

'Oh,' agreed Eden with only the merest suggestion of amusement.

'There's no need to be so patronising,' she muttered, aware that he'd cut the ground from beneath her feet but unwilling, as yet, to cede the point by apologising. 'He wouldn't have told me if he could have avoided it.'

'I'm sure. And now, since I have a number of other engagements today, might we discuss what happened this morning? If it helps, I'll admit that I don't take an interest in *every* fellow who falls from his ladder … just the ones who do so because the rungs have been sawn through.'

Lydia dropped abruptly into the foreman's chair. Now Colonel Maxwell had successfully deprived her of the self-righteous anger that had been keeping her on her feet, shock had its way with her knees. She swallowed hard and said, 'Sawn through? *Had* they?'

'Yes.' He frowned. 'You didn't know?'

'No. They … they finally told me about the dogs and the fish. But they let me assume what happened this morning was an accident. That's why I … why I thought --'

'That they had no business calling me in. Quite. Clearly, they're trying to protect you and equally clearly, they can't if you don't know what's going on.'

She drew a long, unsteady breath. This was worse, very much worse than she had thought. And that meant the Colonel was right. She *did* need help – if not for herself, then for the men who might get hurt if she didn't take measures to prevent it. Her voice tight with strain but perfectly steady, she said wryly, 'Perhaps you can tell them that. They might listen to you. Meanwhile, I'll arrange to put a padlock on the gate and --'

'It's done – or will be when my Major returns from buying one.'

'Oh. I see. How very *efficient* of you.'

'Wasn't it? We'll fix it before we leave.'

'I think my own men are more than capable of --'

'It will be more useful if you have your fellows check all the window-catches and mend any that appear weak. And, just in case the padlock doesn't keep your tormenters out and you want to be sure of avoiding further infestations of fish, you might think about affixing shutters on the ground floor.'

Her expression told him that she didn't like being managed.

Eden let his smile inform her that he didn't care and would do it anyway.

Lydia said grittily, 'What a good idea.'

'I have them sometimes,' replied Eden, enjoying the fact that, much as she'd like to throw him out, she was beginning to recognise that he probably had better knowledge of security than she did. 'You could also consider employing a night-watchman – preferably one with a well-trained dog.' He paused for a moment and then said bluntly, 'Someone wants to hurt you, Mistress Neville – and the only sure way to stop them is to find out who they are. Unfortunately, I don't have sufficient time to discuss ways of doing that today. My desk is piled high, I've a meeting with Major-General Lambert this afternoon and I promised to be home by six to meet my housekeeper's future husband. So attempting to identify your attacker will have to wait, I'm afraid.'

Lydia stood up and managed a coolly polite smile.

'I appreciate your advice, Colonel. It's been most helpful. But I am fully aware that your time is precious and don't believe that we need to take up any more of it. I'm sure we can manage matters ourselves from this point.'

'You'd like to think that, of course.' Eden uncoiled from the wall and reached for his hat. 'Or perhaps you already know who is persecuting you?'

'No.' *The whores in Strand Alley were one thing but surely even Margaret wouldn't stoop to something like this.* 'That is … no.'

'You don't sound very sure.'

'Well … I'd need to think about it.'

'Do that. And when you have, we'll talk again. Just in case it hasn't occurred to you, Mistress Neville, I'm in the business of uncovering secrets. Under the circumstances, you may find that useful. And now,' he concluded making a slight bow and replacing his hat, 'once I've seen to that padlock, I'll do the one thing you've been wanting me to do since you first clapped eyes on me.'

'What?'

'Leave,' he said succinctly. And smiled.

* * *

Lydia watched him go. She wondered if he ever got tired of being right all the time ... then concluded, rather sourly, that he probably didn't. She also wondered how he managed to make her feel angry, invigorated and unsettled all at the same time. A sly voice at the back of her mind suggested that the unsettled part might have something to do with that smile of his ... but she informed the voice that the damned smile wasn't to be trusted. As far as she could see, half the time, he used it as a weapon.

It was when she realised that her feet had unwittingly carried her to a window from which she could watch the Colonel at work on the gate that she started to wonder what on earth was the matter with her. He was an infuriating, over-bearing nuisance and she didn't need him poking about in her affairs. Indeed, she would be happy if she never saw him again.

Yes, she thought, relieved to have recovered her usual good sense. *That's more like it.*

At the back of her mind, the sly voice sniggered.

NINE

Dark, elegant and saturnine as ever, John Lambert said, 'General Monck is in Stirling from where he plans to block the enemies' passage to the lowlands. He says that the insurrection is more widespread than he was led to believe and has informed Oliver that he will advance into the highlands as soon as there is sufficient grass to feed his horses.'

Colonel Maxwell couldn't help grinning.

'He's waiting for the grass to grow?'

'Apparently. He is also waiting for money to pay his men, more cavalry and warships to assist him from the coast.' The Major-General paused and, sighing, added, 'Actually, the list of what he wants is endless. Surgeons, farriers and saddlers ... powder, shot and basic provisions; also a number of officers who should be on his strength but seem to be unaccountably missing. I am supposed to find them for him.'

'Can you?'

'Some of them. But since I assume the General would prefer to have his demands partially met quickly rather than fully met some months hence, I hope he will take the short-fall philosophically. Also, the Council of State has recently passed the ordinances for Scotland that he insists will be helpful – so there is compensation, of a sort.'

'You'll have to explain, I'm afraid,' said Eden. 'I've had no dealings with Council matters for some time and Secretary Thurloe is rarely communicative.'

'So I've noticed. Is that the principal reason you are so eager to quit your current position?'

'It's one of my reasons, certainly. Although I respect Thurloe's efficiency and his ability to keep numerous balls in the air whilst interlacing one thing with another, I don't find him easy to work with.' He had no intention of mentioning the two irate letters he'd recently received from his brother-in-law, Ralph Cochrane, berating him for failing to spend more than two days at Thorne Ash in the last six months. And so, returning to the point, 'But you were going to tell me about these Scottish ordinances.'

'Yes. The most important one unites Scotland with England and gives the Scots the right to send thirty members to Westminster when Parliament opens in September. The other is the Ordinance of Pardon and Grace – which is basically an act of oblivion and general pardon for any and all acts committed during the wars. There are exceptions, of course … but not so many that Monck shouldn't see a reduction in the opposition.'

'For which he'll be grateful, I'm sure. Do we know where General Middleton is?'

'The last report we had put him at Sutherland but, by now, he could be anywhere. That's the main problem. The Scots are leading our troops a merry dance up and down every mountain in the highlands. We had a couple of moderate successes at the head of the Cromerty Firth and Dunkeld last month but nothing big enough to stop them.'

Eden had started to wonder how he figured in all this – or even *if* he did. Deciding to bring matters to a head, he said, 'Exactly why did you want to see me, sir?'

'I'm going to put you in charge of General Monck's elusive officers and the supply train that will be going north with them.'

Hope sprang up as it had so many times now that Eden no longer dared trust it.

'Secretary Thurloe won't release me. There's a new possible murder threat.'

'Oliver?'

'Yes.' *Why do you look surprised? Cromwell's got more people wanting to kill him than the late King. They're just less well-placed to actually do it.* 'It may be nothing. But Thurloe's going to arrest people right, left and centre until he's sure. And, as you've said yourself many times, I'm … useful.'

'So are others,' came the cool reply. 'And the Army lists still show you as one of my officers. Consequently, although Secretary Thurloe has enjoyed the benefit of your talents for some time, I now need your services myself. Thus, he has no option but to release you.'

'I ... see.' *No I don't. If that's so, why couldn't you do this when I first asked – or at any time during the last year? Why wait till now?* 'Forgive me for asking, sir ... but you have any number of officers capable of seeing a supply train to Scotland. Why, suddenly, do I have some particular value?'

The Major-General eyed him thoughtfully and took his time about replying.

'You'll also be transporting a substantial amount of coin. Of the officers so far located that General Monck wants returned, I have failed to identify one I'd trust to keep hold of the change in his pockets – let alone a sum of this size. That, ostensibly at least, is why I need you.'

'Ostensibly?'

'Yes. Between ourselves, you'll be taking the opportunity to make a slight detour.'

Eden felt a faint quiver of wariness.

'I will?'

'Yes. I want you to visit Colonel Brandon.'

This was unexpected and Eden had to bite back an unwary reply.

'You look shocked,' observed Lambert. 'But I don't imagine you'll find it a chore.'

'No.' *It's what I've been wanting to do for months.* 'Far from it. But why?'

'I wrote to him some weeks since asking him to stand as member for his district in the forthcoming Parliament. Rather annoyingly, he hasn't deigned to reply. He may simply be undecided. If he is, I'm hoping that you are the one man who can persuade him.'

God. Don't you know Gabriel at all?

'I can try, sir. But he left both London and the Army more or less immediately after the execution of the late King. He was, as I'm sure you're aware, in total disagreement with the whole business.' *The truth is that he was bloody disgusted and wanted nothing more to do with anybody who had a hand in it.* 'He is also not particularly susceptible to persuasion.'

'I'm merely asking you to try, Colonel. Brandon's name still occasions respect in a good many quarters and he's the kind of sensible man we need filling the benches of Westminster. I hope he says yes ... but I won't blame you if he doesn't.' Lambert rose from his chair, indicating that the conversation was at an end. 'And look on the bright side. In two or three weeks from now, you'll be free of Secretary Thurloe.'

* * *

Mr Fisher proved to be quietly-spoken and pleasant-looking in an ordinary sort of way. He arrived bearing a posy of flowers for Deborah and, thanks to his trade, six bottles of extremely superior wine for his gentleman hosts. He was also clearly nervous.

Supper, which Deborah insisted on serving herself before sitting down to eat, was overlaid by a faint air of strain and the only person seemingly unaffected by it was Nicholas. Eden did his best to keep the conversation afloat but found it uphill work. Although Deborah smiled and was perfectly composed, she said very little ... and, as far as Fisher was concerned, Eden could virtually hear the wheels turning as the poor fellow weighed every word before he uttered it. Worst of all, Tobias spoke only in monosyllables whilst watching the visitor with something like predatory intent – which, considering his size, appeared decidedly threatening. Eden shot him a look that promised some sharp words later.

No one was sorry when the meal was over and, as soon as they rose from the table, Eden said pleasantly, 'A word with you, Mr Fisher, if I may?'

The vintner swallowed hard, cast a wary glance in Tobias's direction and then nodded.

Eden led him to the rarely-used back parlour and closed the door. He said, 'Don't take too much notice of my brother, Mr Fisher. He's feeling somewhat ill-used just at present – but he doesn't bite.'

'No? Oh – no. Of course not.' Fisher tugged at his collar and, summoning all of his courage, said, 'I was a little concerned. I wondered if ... if perhaps there was some attachment. Between your b-brother and Mistress Deborah, that is.'

Christ, Toby. You bloody idiot.

'No, no – nothing of the kind. You need have no fears about Toby. It's merely that Mistress Hart runs the house like clockwork which leaves him free to concentrate on his work. And then, of course, he is dreading the loss of her pies because he is convinced that no others could possibly be as good.' Eden managed a careless smile. 'Sad but true, I'm afraid.'

Relief rolled off Mr Fisher in waves and, for the first time, his answering smile was entirely natural.

'Thank you, Colonel. You have no idea ...' He stopped, groping for the words he needed and turning rather red. 'The thing is that I – I still can't believe my good fortune. That a woman like Mistress Deborah should choose an ordinary fellow like me seems almost too good to be true. For I *do* love her, you know.'

'I have no doubt of it.' *And I'm glad of it for Deborah's sake but sorry for yours. I know about loving a woman who wants another man. I hope you're lucky enough never to find out.* 'I had a reason for wishing to speak privately, Mr Fisher. Please accept that what I'm about to suggest is no reflection upon yourself or your ability to keep Deborah in comfort. But I'd like to arrange a small annual stipend in her name as a token of thanks for her service here. Would you be offended by that?'

'Offended? No, sir. How could I be? It's extremely generous of you.'

'Not at all. Call it a wedding gift. However, I know that if I mention this to Deborah, she'll refuse. Consequently, I thought that if I were to make the arrangements and have the necessary paperwork sent to you ... well, she need know nothing of it until the deed is done. If that is acceptable?'

'Perfectly acceptable, Colonel. Indeed, I hardly know what to say to you.'

Don't be grateful. Don't. I feel bad enough already.

'There's no need to say anything,' he said bracingly. 'Now that's settled, perhaps you'll join us upstairs for a glass of your excellent wine? And if Toby is still sulking, I'll send him to bed.'

Mr Fisher laughed. 'Please – not on my account. I have every sympathy with him. The lady's baking is indeed exceptional.'

As it turned out, Tobias was no longer glowering. Instead, he looked chastened and a little sheepish – thanks, presumably, to the martial glint in Deborah's eye.

'Ah,' said Eden. 'I see you've received a scolding. And deservedly so.'

Tobias crossed to Mr Fisher and held out his hand.

'I believe I owe you an apology, sir. Deborah says I was behaving rather badly.'

'That's not quite how she put it,' murmured Nicholas, his face alight with laughter.

'Shut up, Nick.' Tobias released Mr Fisher's hand and, with a deprecating shrug, said, 'If you'll allow me, I'd like to atone for it by making Deborah's wedding ring.'

Mr Fisher looked utterly taken aback.

'That is most generous, sir – but no atonement is necessary.'

'Yes, it is,' remarked Eden. 'Let him make the ring, Fisher. He's really quite good.'

'I'm *exceptionally* good,' corrected Tobias. And to Deborah, 'You'll let me, won't you? As a parting gift?'

'Put like that, how can I refuse?' Smiling was becoming uncommonly difficult but she managed it anyway. 'And for that I'll bake you one pie a week.'

'Two,' said Tobias promptly.

She shook her head, laughing. 'Very well. Two, then.'

'And I,' said Nicholas, rising from his chair, 'would beg the honour of offering my one good arm to escort you down the aisle. Unless there's someone you'd rather have?'

'There's no one,' she replied. *Oh God. Will this evening never be over?* 'And the honour would be mine.'

'In that case, I'd like to propose a toast,' said Eden, pouring wine and handing glasses to Mr Fisher and Deborah. 'To the future happiness of the bridal pair ... and to the hope that we three poor bachelors will not quite be forgotten.'

* * *

A little later, after Mr Fisher had left and Eden found himself alone with Nicholas, he said, 'Why did you offer to act in *loco parentis* at the wedding?'

Nicholas's expression suggested that this was a stupid question.

'*One* of us has to do it – but Toby won't and you can't.'

'No. I suppose not.' He re-filled both their glasses and dropped into a chair on the other side of the hearth. 'That was a hellish evening. I could cheerfully have *murdered* Toby. He managed to give Fisher the impression that he and Deborah might be in love with each other.'

'Oh. That's awkward.'

'*Awkward?*' Eden gave a harsh laugh. 'You have no idea.'

Nicholas eyed him thoughtfully for a moment. Then, he said bluntly, 'I'll save my sympathy for Deborah, if you don't mind.'

'Do you think I don't know how hard she's finding this – or that I don't care? Because, if so, rest assured that I do.'

'Good.'

'Oh for God's sake, Nick – leave it, will you?' Eden drained his glass and set it down with a force that nearly cracked it. 'This is Deborah's decision, not mine and I've had enough for one night. Also, I wanted to talk to you about Mistress Neville's lorinery.'

'What about it?'

'There have been further unwelcome developments.' And, in as few words as possible, he explained. Then, 'I intend to speak to Mistress Neville tomorrow with regard to anyone she knows of who might be behind all this. But if there aren't any obvious suspects, finding the culprit might take time and, in three weeks – possibly less – I'll be on the road to Scotland.'

Nicholas's eyes widened slightly.

'It's definite, then?'

'Yes. So I imagine you can see where this is leading.'

'I think so. You want me to take the lorinery under my single wing.' Nicholas grinned. 'Well, why not? At least I'll fit right in there.'

* * *

On the following morning, Eden and Nicholas got to the lorinery shortly after it began work for the day and earlier than Mistress Neville generally arrived.

'All quiet?' Colonel Maxwell asked Trooper Buxton.

'Yes, sir. Let's hope they've seen the padlock and taken the hint.'

'Hope, by all means. Just don't rely on it.' And then, glancing round at the hive of activity as workbenches began filling up with various tools and materials, 'Is Mr Potter here yet?'

'In his office, sir.'

'Excellent. Come on, Nick. Let's start by clearing your presence with the foreman before Mistress Neville gets here.'

Mr Potter accepted with relief the notion of Captain Austin helping to keep an eye on things for a while in case of further trouble but said, 'Mistress Neville will probably kick up a dust, Colonel.'

Eden grinned.

'There's no 'probably' about it. But don't worry – I'll stay to draw her fire. And, in the meantime, perhaps you wouldn't mind if the Captain introduces himself to your fellows while he and I take a look around the premises? There's a floor above this one, isn't there – and, presumably, also a cellar?'

'Yes. We use upstairs to store the more valuable stock – leather and metals, mostly. As to the cellar, it's damp. It even floods sometimes when there's heavy rain and the level in the Fleet rises. We don't need it so nobody ever goes down there.'

'We'll take a look anyway, if you can find us a lantern.'

Lydia arrived half an hour later to learn that Colonel Maxwell was in the cellar. She huffed an irritated breath and said, 'What is he doing down there? Come to that – why is he here at all?'

'I think he wants a word with you, Mistress – so I reckon he'll explain everything,' replied Mr Potter, carefully avoiding all mention of Captain Austin. 'Meantime, I've got to go round to Cotterells. There was a mistake in the last order that needs sorting out.' And he made good his escape.

Some minutes later, Eden emerged from the gloom of the cellar to find Mistress Neville standing at the top of the stairs with her arms folded. She said, 'Good morning, Colonel. I trust there aren't any nasty surprises lurking down there? No man-traps or barrels of gunpowder waiting to explode? No rotting corpses or hairy creatures with big teeth?'

'Fortunately, no,' he replied, arriving one step below her. 'Just spiders and mice.'

'Well that's comfort. You can't imagine how worried I've been.'

This time, Eden didn't resist the impulse to laugh but merely said, 'Do you think you might step aside? Aside from the chill, it smells down there.'

'Count yourself lucky,' said Lydia, moving so he could pass. 'I very nearly barred the door.' And then, seeing Nicholas, 'My goodness. Never say *you've* a fascination with cellars as well, Mr Austin?'

'Actually, it's Captain Sir Nicholas,' remarked Eden before Nicholas could respond. 'Best get it right – since you'll be seeing rather a lot of him.'

The silvery-blue eyes narrowed. 'Will I, indeed?'

'I'm afraid so,' said Nicholas cheerfully. 'But I'll try not to get in anybody's way. And I'm quite willing to lend a hand if there's ever a need for it.'

'Thank you.' Lydia drew a long, calming breath and avoided looking at Eden. 'Forgive me, Sir Nicholas ... but perhaps you could occupy yourself elsewhere while Colonel Maxwell explains to me precisely what he's done *this* time?'

'Immediately, Mistress.'

Nicholas grinned, bowed and strolled away in the direction of the yard, leaving Lydia to say flatly, 'Mr Potter's office, Colonel. *Again*.'

As before, Eden closed the door and leaned against it. He said concisely, 'I'll be leaving for Scotland in a week or two. If there are any further attacks and we haven't found the culprit before I leave, Nick can continue to offer some protection in my absence. He still has his sword-arm and, though his ability probably isn't quite what it was, it will certainly be adequate. Also, an occupation will hopefully keep him out of trouble.'

Of the many things she might have asked, Lydia heard herself say, 'What sort of trouble?'

'The same sort your brother got himself into.'

She stared at him, perplexed.

'Getting mixed up with the Cavaliers? Why on earth would he do that?'

Eden hesitated briefly and then said simply, 'Because he is one.'

'What? He's a *Royalist?*'

'Yes.'

'But – but you're an Army officer. You work in the Secretary of State's office.'

'I am and I do.'

'Then how …?' Lydia gave up and said, 'I don't understand.'

'Of course you don't. I don't myself, some days. But if you want chapter and verse, you can ask Nicholas. I daresay he'll tell you. And in the meantime, you and I have more important things to discuss … such as whether you've received any more threatening notes.'

'No. So you needn't --'

'Good. If you do, don't keep them to yourself and take the same precautions as before.'

Lydia eyed him forebodingly and didn't bother to keep the exasperation out of her voice.

'Colonel Maxwell … I don't know why you're making this your personal crusade. But --'

'Because I would be sorry to see this enterprise of yours fail. Also, I'll have a bone to pick with the fellow who hurt Dan Hayes when I catch up with him.'

'Oh. Well. Yes. That's quite … understandable, I'm sure.' *Blast the man. How can I argue with that?* 'However, I'd be obliged if you would please stop trying to arrange my life. I am more than capable of taking care of both my businesses and my person.'

'Since you don't know who wishes you ill or why, that is a singularly rash attitude,' he observed calmly. Then, 'And look on the bright side. The sooner we identify your anonymous enemy, the sooner you'll be free of me.'

Unable to help herself, Lydia smiled.

'You promise?'

Eden laughed. 'I promise. Now … have you thought of anyone who might want to harm either you or the lorinery?'

She sat down and frowned at her hands.

'No one I consider capable of wilfully injuring one of my workers.'

'That's an opinion – not an answer. To whom are you referring?'

She took her time about replying but eventually, she sighed and said, 'My late husband's son and daughter-in-law. And their cousin. They've all been badgering me to get rid of both this place and Strand Alley ever since the day we buried Stephen.'

For the first time, it occurred to Eden to wonder why Lydia had married a man forty years her senior. It wasn't unheard of ... but it was unusual enough for him to suspect there might have been a reason behind it. But rather than digress now, he decided to see if Nicholas knew and said merely, 'Strand Alley?'

She nodded. 'The women work there. They make lace and trimmings and so on.'

A vague recollection stirred but, again, he chose not to pursue it.

'And that business operates on the same lines as this one?'

'More or less. It's to benefit war-widows and the like – but they're not employed as the men are here. I just give them rent-free premises and help them sell what they make to the drapers and dress-makers. They're doing very well now and can barely keep up with demand.'

He heard the note of pride in her voice but refrained from commenting on it. Instead, he said, 'Why does your family object?'

'Oh – they think I should sit at home with my embroidery. In their view, widows ought to behave with more circumspection. They aren't supposed to involve themselves in sordid commerce.'

'That's nonsense.'

'I know. But Margaret insists on calling the sewing women whores and believing that the men who work here are all foul-mouthed drunkards.' Lydia hesitated and then, deciding the Colonel might as well know it all, told him about the two women recently dismissed from Strand Alley, adding, 'Of course, I can't prove it was Margaret. It just seems like the kind of scheme she and Joseph might dream up. The thing is that, if a case could be made that that the premises were also being used as a brothel, we'd lose our membership of the Haberdashers Guild – which would create untold problems.'

Eden considered this. Finally, he said, 'If your step-son and his wife would do that, what makes you so sure they're not involved in the damage here?'

'I suppose I'm *not* entirely sure,' replied Lydia truthfully. 'But I find it hard to believe they had anything to do with that business yesterday. Mr Hayes might have been killed.'

'He might indeed. And if your relatives have resorted to hiring assorted ruffians to cause damage but failed to specify just how far that damage should be allowed to go ...' He stopped and spread his hands. 'You see my point.'

'Yes.' She looked up at him, her eyes troubled. 'Unfortunately, I do. I'm just not sure what to do about it. I let them know that I suspected them of planting the whores in Strand Alley ... but that was before Mr Hayes nearly broke his neck. So if it *was* them, they haven't called off their hirelings. And if it *wasn't* and I say anything about what's been going on here, I'll have handed them another stick to beat me with.'

'And that would be worse than possibly stopping them in their tracks?'

'No. I suppose not. But you don't know what they're like. The constant criticism and nagging is either going to turn me into a gibbering wreck or make me take to drink.'

Eden smiled and shook his head.

'I doubt that. From what I've seen, you're made of sterner stuff. However ... would it help if I were to take a hand in my official capacity?'

'*Could* you?'

'Oh yes. A summons to the Secretary's office usually frightens people.'

'I'm sure.' A gleam of mischief appeared and she suddenly laughed. 'You have no idea how tempting that is.'

'But?'

'But, sadly, I suppose we should save the big guns until they are absolutely necessary.'

Eden raised one mocking brow. '*We*, Mistress Neville?'

'With the utmost reluctance, it would appear so.'

'Progress at last,' he breathed. Then, 'All right. Your family is a possibility. Are there any others?'

'I don't think so.' She thought for a moment. 'Oh – I had an offer to buy the lorinery from a gentleman who was prepared to pay a generous price. But that was made through his lawyer and mine so I doubt it has any connection to the current situation.'

'You refused to sell? No – don't bother to answer that. Of course you did.'

'Yes. I won't risk the men being turned off. And I *like* coming here.' She paused briefly. 'If you want the truth, this place and Strand Alley are the only things that give me either pleasure or purpose – so I'm damned if I'll give them up.'

Eden contemplated her in silence for a moment or two. He noted the determined set of her chin, the militant sparkle in her eyes and the oddly enticing brown curls that had escaped her cap to dance about her neck. The fact that he noticed the latter startled him slightly so he shoved it to the back of his mind for consideration later. He briefly wondered if her marriage to a man four decades her senior had provided either pleasure or purpose, then told himself that was no business of his. But there was no denying that he was beginning to realise that Lydia Neville was a mine of contradictions and surprises ... and that he enjoyed trading words with her, even when they clashed. No. *Particularly* when they clashed.

He said, 'Nick will be here most days, so find a use for him if you can – even if it's only escort duty. Should you need either one of us urgently, send a message to our home on the corner of Friday Street and Cheapside.'

Her brow wrinkled enquiringly. 'The goldsmith's shop?'

'Yes. The current proprietor is my younger brother, Tobias, and the previous one was the Italian brother-in-law who trained him. We Maxwells like keeping things in the family. And, to be fair, Toby has not only worked very hard but is also – according to Luciano, at any rate – extraordinarily talented.' He grinned suddenly. 'Visit the shop some time. Even if you don't want to buy, you'd enjoy looking at his work.'

Once again, that smile caused a strange little reaction in her chest and made her own mouth quiver in response. She said, 'You're proud of him.'

'And not a bit ashamed of it,' he agreed. Then, sighing, 'I should go – or I'll be working until midnight.'

Lydia came to her feet.

'When will you leave for Scotland?'

'As soon as Major-General Lambert gives me the order – which can't be soon enough for me. If I can't come myself, Nick will let you know.' Eden reached for his hat and bowed to her. 'Take care of yourself, Mistress Neville – and if you need help, ask for it.' He turned to go and then swung back to say, 'Oh – and try to keep Nick away from your brother. I happen to know that John Gerard and certain of his confederates are back in the country and that there's a possibility of further stirrings in that quarter. I don't want to return from the north to find Nick's been clapped in the Tower.'

TEN

At the meeting when Major Henshaw had announced that their main aim would be to assassinate the Lord Protector – and indeed all the other meetings thereafter – there had been a vast amount of discussion about the rights, wrongs and usefulness of such an extreme measure.

Some had argued that Cromwell's death would make little difference. The Army would remain in power and another officer – probably Lambert – would simply become Protector in his place. But most insisted that it was Cromwell who wanted to rule by the power of the sword and therefore that removing him would force a change. It was Cromwell, after all, who had cut off the late King's head and who had tossed out the Rump by force rather than constitutional means; it was Cromwell who had first sanctioned and then lost patience with the Barebones Parliament; and it was Cromwell who had assumed supreme power and was holding state at Whitehall, King in all but name. Cromwell, most of them agreed, was responsible for the fact that no workable form of government had so far been set in place and, since he was never going to step aside voluntarily, there was only one way to be rid of him.

Having swiftly discovered that they were united in their lack of enthusiasm, neither Sir Aubrey Durand nor Major Halsall threw themselves heart and soul into the business of recruiting. When, for the second time, they had to admit a joint catch of only one likely candidate, Major Henshaw said coldly, 'Is the City so bereft of loyal gentlemen, then? Or are the pair of you incapable of performing the duty you've been given?'

'You demanded caution,' replied Aubrey who had begun to realise that he didn't like the Major very much. 'So we can hardly go about sounding out fellows willy-nilly, can we? We might as well stick posters up on walls.'

Gerard's younger brother, Charles, who had been permitted to join their counsels for the first time and whose face reflected excitement and terror in equal measures, gave a nervous laugh.

Henshaw shot him a filthy look and then, turning back to Aubrey snapped, 'Idiot! You know as well as I do that there are certain taverns where His Majesty's friends can be found. Clearly, you are not trying – and *I* have to wonder why.'

'You're being too severe,' said Colonel Gerard pacifically. And to Aubrey, 'Try the Nag's Head in Fetter Lane and the Rose and Crown just off Tower Street. You might also, if you haven't already thought of it, put out some feelers to a few of the Levellers. They're still up in arms over Freeborn John's continued imprisonment and have been out of charity with Cromwell for years. The proprietor of *The Moderate* might be of some help there – a fellow by the name of Radford.' He stopped, smiling a little. 'And no, Henshaw – I'm *not* suggesting they ask Mr Radford to put a piece in his newspaper.'

Major Henshaw grunted and continued to scowl.

Colonel Aldridge attempted to change the subject.

'What are the latest numbers?'

'Three thousand and rising,' replied Henshaw. And only half under his breath, 'No thanks to *some* people.'

'Three thousand?' queried the Colonel, his tone one of mild disbelief. 'Really?'

'I just said so, didn't I?'

'I think we can count on roughly two hundred apprentices,' offered Somerset Fox, 'though they'll only have cudgels and brickbats.'

'The store of arms in Bermondsey is steadily growing – though not as fast as I'd like,' remarked Roger Whitley. 'Has anyone anything to contribute to it?'

'I've been trying to acquire more pistols,' said Peter Vowell, 'but it's not easy. On the other hand, I've enlisted a fellow to help seize the horses in Islington.'

'What fellow?' snapped Henshaw. 'Do we know him?'

'I doubt it. His name is Billingsley and he's a butcher by trade.'

'A *butcher?*' echoed Deane incredulously. Then, 'God help us. How many damned civilians are party to this business of ours?'

'Rather more than I'd like,' replied Gerard wryly. 'But beggars can't be choosers. And most things seem to be going according to plan.'

Colonel Deane said baldly, 'So what *is* the plan?'

Gerard hesitated for a moment, glancing round at his assembled troops. Then he said, 'As you all know, Cromwell's death must come first and everything else waits until we've received confirmation of that. The military elements remain unchanged and begin with the diversionary attack. After that, I'll secure Whitehall, Major Henshaw will take Horseguards and the Mews and Colonel Deane, St James's.'

'And the assassination?' asked Major Halsall. 'How is that to be accomplished?'

'Cromwell travels by coach from Whitehall to Hampton Court every Saturday morning to spend the day with his family. That habit is our opportunity – both because it *is* a habit and because, on those journeys, his coach is less heavily guarded than usual.' He paused but no one spoke. 'As has been said, Major Henshaw and I will lead a force of thirty armed men. Of those, the twenty-five I have approached – some of whom are here now – all know who they are. Major Henshaw wishes to include Mr Wiseman, Colonel Aldridge and Mr Tudor.'

'Tudor?' queried Deane. 'Who the hell is he?'

'An apothecary,' muttered Henshaw. And, recognising expressions of mingled disbelief and derision, added defensively, 'He's heart and soul for the King. And he can shoot.'

'Oh good,' muttered Aubrey not quite under his breath.

Frowning, Gerard shook his head slightly and picked up where he had left off before Deane's interruption.

'This combined force will attack the Protector's coach, overpower his guards and ... do the deed. Since Cromwell's route lies across to the bridge to the Surrey bank, Major Henshaw and I have agreed that the best place to carry out our attack is in Southwark where the road is quieter and there's less chance of untoward interference. Once Cromwell is dead, speed will be of the essence so I'll send riders to alert Colonels Haines and Deane – and Major Henshaw and I will get to our allotted stations as fast as possible. I hope matters don't go awry but, in case they do, I've also engaged the services of an expert marksman and ask you to trust my judgement in that.'

'We *do* trust it, John,' said Colonel Whitley. 'It's why we're here. But when is it to be? I'm assuming that a date has been set?'

'It's been set. We make our attempt on Saturday 13th.'

There was a long, airless silence. Then Aubrey said weakly, 'A week tomorrow?'

'Yes. We can be ready by then. And the longer we delay, the more chance there is that word will leak out and we'll all find ourselves behind bars.' Gerard stood up and raised his glass. 'Here's to His Majesty's health … and a successful blow on his behalf.'

The toast was drunk and, as everyone resumed their seats, Gerard said, 'And now, gentlemen, I suggest we all get busy.'

* * *

By the second week in May, the gossips in Westminster had once more turned their attention to the Franco-Spanish bidding war which was now into its third month. Cromwell had continued playing both sides against each other as he strove for additional concessions and as much money as he could wring out of them. But negotiations had disintegrated when Mazarin's ambassador told Cromwell to mind his own business regarding the French Huguenots – with the result that Protector immediately told the Spanish ambassador he'd send thirty men-of-war against France, along with a sizeable army of Horse and Foot. A good many of the Westminster clerks who'd laid wagers on the outcome toddled off to hedge their bets.

Meeting briefly with Lambert to find out how soon he would be departing for Scotland and at what point Thurloe was to be informed of this, Colonel Maxwell took the opportunity to ask the Major-General's opinion of the situation.

'In Council, it's a three-way struggle,' said Lambert irritably. 'The majority of us favour war with France – our need for money being great and the trade with Spain, lucrative. But a handful of fellows want a cosy French alliance. And Thurloe would like to reach an understanding with Mazarin in order to put an end to maritime warfare and presumably get Charles Stuart thrown out of Paris as well. Oliver is therefore in four minds over it and I've given up predicting which way he'll eventually jump.'

'Is there any point in having a Council,' asked Eden slowly, 'if Cromwell makes the decisions himself?'

'A question I've frequently asked myself. However, you wanted to know how soon you're likely to be leaving for Scotland. Unfortunately, your departure may be a week or so later than I'd hoped as we're awaiting delivery of the last of the powder and shot. I suggest you assume you'll be on the road by the last week of this month. Presumably that gives you sufficient time to arrange your own affairs?'

'It does. I've a wedding to attend on the 24th but will be free to leave the day after. When do you envisage giving the glad tidings to Secretary Thurloe?'

'As late as possible.' A hint of a smile accompanied the words. 'I want him to believe I'm only over-riding him because my need is urgent.'

Well, that will suit me, thought Eden. *The later he knows, the less time there'll be for him to have me working twenty hours a day.*

Rising, he said, 'I heard something about a price on General Middleton's head. Is it true?'

'Perfectly. We've empowered Monck to offer two hundred pounds to anyone who can bring Middleton in, dead or alive. I imagine there are men in Scotland who'd sell their grandmother for that.'

* * *

Back in his office, Eden found that a newly-delivered letter had been dropped on the pile of correspondence he'd been working his way through. He almost put it to one side but changed his mind when he noticed that it was addressed to Thomas Scot.

Ten minutes later he was in the Secretary's office and, not bothering to wait for Thurloe's full attention, said crisply, 'That assassination plot that we spoke of some weeks ago ...'

Thurloe looked up. 'Yes?'

'I've a letter here saying that it's real and already in hand. The writer claims to be a Royalist himself but be outraged by the notion of cold-blooded murder. The plan is to shoot the Protector *en route* between Whitehall and Hampton Court on one of his usual Saturday journeys. No specific date is given but the letter mentions John Gerard and a fellow by the name of Tudor who is either a surgeon or an apothecary.' Colonel Maxwell looked up from the paper in his hand. 'It's Wednesday today. I'm presuming you want to put some precautions in place?'

'Of course. I'll persuade His Highness to change either the day or his mode of travel.' Thurloe thought for a moment then said, 'Don't arrest Gerard for the time being. He's only one link in the chain. If we give them time to try and fail, we give ourselves time to find out who the other ringleaders are. I imagine you can probably predict most of them. Whitley, Halsall, Deane … possibly also Henshaw. All the usual suspects whom we know to be currently in England. I suggest you start making a list.'

'*Just* the ringleaders, sir?'

'No, no. Begin with them but list the small fry as well. I rather suspect that this time it will be necessary to make a few examples.' He turned back to his work. 'Thank you, Colonel. That will be all.'

Eden walked back through the corridors that separated him from Thurloe, thinking several things at once. Amongst the more serious was the hope that Sir Aubrey Durand's last experience of officialdom had been alarming enough to prevent him making the same mistake twice – because if the young idiot was arrested again, Eden had a strong feeling that Lydia Neville would expect him to do something about it. And at the other end of the spectrum lay the thought that, if Ellis Brandon was somewhere in the City, he'd arrest him just for the hell of it and to give Gabriel a laugh when they met.

For the rest, he chose not to delve too deeply. The only thing he was sure of was that the sooner he went to Scotland, the better … because he was becoming increasingly disenchanted with both the Lord Protector and everything he stood for.

Which meant, if taken to its logical conclusion, that he was more in sympathy with the Cavaliers than he'd ever expected to be.

*   *   *

At home, Tobias and Nicholas talked a great deal about Deborah's forthcoming wedding while the bride herself made quiet preparations but said very little on the subject. And because both Eden and Deborah knew that the future lay between them like a stone, they made a point of tacitly avoiding each other.

A third letter arrived from Ralph Cochrane. Terse and even more pointed than the previous two, it said simply, *Since it seems you've forgotten, I'll point out that you have children and a mother who misses you – and that London is not on another planet. Get your arse here, you uncaring bastard.*

Eden decided that a reply saying he'd come when he could wasn't going to help much. There would be no chance to visit Thorne Ash on the way to Scotland. The best he could do would be to go there on the way back – and since God alone knew when that would be, Ralph was likely to take a swing at him the minute he got off his horse. This wasn't a happy thought. His brother-in-law was even bigger than Toby and a mass of pure muscle.

Having been assured by Nicholas that there had been no further disturbances in Duck Lane, Eden took an hour the following afternoon to visit the shops in the Exchange. He'd arranged the annual stipend for Deborah with his man-of-law but wanted something tangible to give her on her wedding day. The trouble was that he had no idea what she would not only like but also find acceptable.

The hour he'd set aside slid fruitlessly by and then the one after it. Gifts of clothing would not be appropriate and, if he wanted jewellery, he could buy it from Tobias. He looked at books, at small paintings and ornaments but nothing seemed quite right. He was just staring at a lavish display of bolts of cloth at Howells when a familiar voice said, 'If you need a new coat, Colonel, you'd do better at Bennetts in Paternoster Row.'

And there, a large basket over her arm, stood the answer to his dilemma – disguised as Lydia Neville.

'Good day, Mistress,' he said with a smile. And, reaching out his hand, 'May I carry that for you?'

She shook her head. 'There's no need. I'm just delivering the shop's order from Strand Alley.' And, lifting the linen covering the basket, 'It's mostly lace because that's their speciality but there are some other trimmings as well and various bits of embroidery.'

'I see. I'm no judge of these things ... but it looks very fine work.'

'It is. They have customers for every yard they make and more enquiries than they can currently fulfil. But you'll have to excuse me, Colonel. Mistress Howell is waiting.'

And she hurried away.

Eden loitered in the doorway, hoping she wouldn't be long. Two ladies eyed him surreptitiously as they went by, then whispered to each other and giggled. A third conducted a frank appraisal and walked slowly past him, swinging her hips and sending him a provocative smile over her shoulder. Eden felt stupidly conspicuous.

Fortunately, Mistress Neville reappeared before embarrassment took over. She looked extremely pleased with herself until she caught sight of him and her expression turned to one of mingled surprise and suspicion.

'Still here, Colonel? Your devotion to duty is quite admirable – but I'm hardly likely to be attacked or abducted in broad daylight, am I?'

'One would certainly hope not. But I waited in the hope that you might help me with something.'

'Oh.' She felt a twinge of pleasure and mentally berated herself. 'I'll try. What is it?'

'As I think I told you, my housekeeper is shortly to be married and I want to buy a gift for her. But I've walked around here until I'm dizzy and all to no avail. I'd like the gift to be personal but not something that might be deemed ... unsuitable, if you see what I mean.'

'I think so. No cooking-pots or household linen ... but no jewellery, perfumes or items of clothing either.' Lydia wrinkled her brow and thought about it. 'Is she young?'

'Of a similar age to yourself, I imagine.'

'And how does she like to spend her leisure time?'

'I'm not sure.' *She used to spend it in bed with me.* 'She's always so busy I doubt she gets much.'

'Oh dear.' She frowned at him. 'Are you a tyrant or merely a domestic nightmare?'

'Neither, I hope,' replied Eden stiffly. 'I don't believe I'm particularly demanding and I've repeatedly offered to hire extra help but --' He stopped, as laughter flared in the light blue eyes. 'Ah. That was a low blow, Mistress.'

'I know. And you walked straight into it, didn't you?'

'I did. But I'll know better next time.'

'We'll see,' said Lydia cheerfully. 'Very well. We will go to Mr Holt's shop on Old Jewry where we will find a fine collection of decorative boxes.'

'Boxes?' he echoed dubiously.

'Yes. The sort a lady might use for jewellery or letters – or, indeed, anything of a valuable or sentimental nature.' She grinned up at him and slipped her hand through his arm. 'Trust me. I believe you'll find just the thing.'

As soon as they had left the crowds thronging the Exchange behind them, Lydia casually remarked that she'd had a long talk with Sir Nicholas.

So, as it happened, had Eden – and thus discovered the circumstances behind Lydia's marriage to Stephen Neville.

'Aubrey told me,' Nicholas had said. And, having related what he knew, added, *'The marriage seems to have been happy – or at least as happy as one might expect over such an age gap. But from Lydia's point of view, it can hardly have been ideal.'*

Thoughtfully non-committal, Eden had agreed with him.

Now, however, he merely looked at Lydia and said, 'You did?'

'Yes.' She hoped Nicholas wouldn't share the *whole* of that conversation – such as the fact she'd asked if Eden was married and, on learning that his wife had died, had put a knowing smile to Nicholas's face by saying *'Oh. Recently?'* 'He told me what you did for him.'

Eden shrugged, not really wanting to discuss it.

'I didn't do anything very much.'

'You saved his life.'

'No. It was Deb-- it was my housekeeper who did that.'

'Which wouldn't have been possible if you hadn't risked your own position to help a Catholic Royalist.' She glanced up at him. 'Don't pretend it was nothing, Colonel. It was a very great deal.'

'If you say so.' His slow, almost lazy smile dawned. 'Does this mean my other faults have become a little less unacceptable?'

'Perhaps,' she agreed. *That smile is dangerous. I wonder how many women have fallen into his lap because of it?* 'But I would strongly advise you not to count on that when you start dishing out your orders as if *everyone* were one of your troopers.'

'Yourself, you mean.'

'Exactly.'

* * *

Eden returned home with an exquisitely-carved and inlaid cedar box. Mistress Neville had been right. It was the perfect gift for Deborah. He'd even quite enjoyed buying it and had found his companion's delight in it rather touching. He wondered if she had such a box of her own ... and then told himself not to be an idiot.

He found Tobias in the parlour, scowling into space.

'What?' asked Eden, knowing what that look meant.

'Deborah's found us a housekeeper.'

'Oh.' His pleasure in the afternoon promptly dimmed. 'That's good. I suppose.'

'Not necessarily.'

'Meaning?'

'She's got the kind of chest that you just can't avoid looking at.'

In spite of himself, Eden laughed. 'I daresay you'll get used to it.'

'It's not me I'm worried about,' said Tobias darkly. 'She was here earlier and Deborah had her bake a pie. Matt Turner found no less than three reasons to leave the shop and the apprentices haven't stopped sniggering since they first clapped eyes on her.'

'Is she pretty?'

'I don't know. My eyes haven't travelled that far up yet.'

'That sounds serious.'

'It *is* bloody serious.' Tobias stood up and stretched his considerable frame. 'The pie was almost as good as one of Deborah's. So the bugger of it is that we'll have to hire her.'

ELEVEN

Saturday May 13th dawned overcast but dry, with a light wind blowing off the river. And lurking in the shadowy precincts behind St Saviour and St Mary Overie, thirty men waited to throw themselves into action.

Since Cromwell was known to leave Whitehall for Hampton Court early in the morning, Colonel Gerard's small troop had been in place from first light. The marksman, so Gerard said, had taken up his position in a deserted barn some little way further down the Clapham road from where – should the main attack fail – he expected to get a clear shot.

Everyone was edgy.

Aubrey's nerves were in shreds. He didn't want to be there at all but hadn't known how to get out of it without either pretending to be ill or being labelled a turncoat. Apparently Major Halsall had no such qualms – as he'd failed to turn up.

Time passed, the church clock chimed eight and everybody got restless.

'At what time does Cromwell normally pass this spot?' asked Mr Wiseman.

'Around now,' grunted Henshaw. 'We should mount up.'

Once their saddles were occupied but there was no sign that they were going anywhere, the horses became as fidgety as the men. Aubrey, striving to control a great hulking brute of a grey, hoped they got on the road before the damned horse dislocated his shoulders.

More time passed.

The Protector's coach didn't.

'How much longer do we wait?' asked young Charles Gerard.

'Another half-hour,' replied his brother. His voice remained perfectly level but worry lurked in his eyes. 'Ride back towards Whitehall and try to find out what's going on. But *don't* draw attention to yourself by careering through the streets – and don't ask questions that might be deemed suspicious. Clear?'

'Clear,' agreed Charles, plainly exhilarated at being given a task and wasting no time in setting about it.

'He's seventeen,' murmured Gerard to Aubrey, as if it explained everything.

'Yes.' The only coherent thought in Aubrey's head was that, if Cromwell didn't appear soon, the mission would have to be aborted. The possibility of a reprieve coupled with the equal possibility that the Protector wasn't there because the plot had been betrayed made him dizzy. He said, 'Perhaps he's been taken ill or something. Cromwell, I mean.'

'It could be any one of a dozen things. But if today doesn't go as planned, we'll need to find another way. And fast.'

Aubrey's stomach sank. 'Such as what?'

'Henshaw's idea of falling on Cromwell when he goes to chapel, probably.' Gerard stared bleakly between his horse's ears. 'But since we can't be ready by tomorrow, it will have to wait until next Sunday.'

Aubrey tried to make himself say, *"I'm sorry, John – I can't do this again. I'd like to – but I just can't."* But somehow the words stuck in his throat and he couldn't seem to force them out. Like Gerard and most of the other men, he relapsed into brooding silence.

Some twenty minutes later, Charles Gerard re-appeared, wild-eyed with agitation. Loud enough for everyone to hear, he said baldly, 'Cromwell's not coming. He went by boat from Whitehall two hours ago. Rob Harrison was at Millbank and saw him sail by. He'll be the other side of Chelsea by now. What are we going to do?'

'Calm down and stop bloody shouting!' snapped Henshaw with his usual charm. 'I need to think.'

* * *

Within twenty-four hours of the aborted Royalist plot, agents brought more names for Colonel Maxwell to add to the two he already had. Thomas Henshaw, John Wiseman and Somerset Fox were among the first; then, on Monday, came Peter Vowell, Charles Gerard and the Reverend Hudson ... and by Tuesday afternoon, Roger Whitley, Charles Finch and a fellow called Billingsly.

Eden frowned at the names, unsure what to make of them. He remembered Colonel Whitley from the Ship Tavern fiasco and Charles would be John Gerard's younger brother. As for Henshaw ... he wondered how much Gerard knew about him; whether, for example, he was aware that, like the fellow who'd drowned back in March, the Major had for some time now been keeping himself clear of arrest by furnishing Secretary Thurloe's office with snippets of largely useless information. Somehow, Eden doubted it.

The others on the growing list were unfamiliar. However, by the next morning, specific enquiries had yielded numerous bits of apparently unrelated information which Eden recorded alongside the names.

John Wiseman; brother-in-law to Thomas Henshaw
Peter Vowell; a schoolmaster from Islington
Edward Hudson; a blind cleric, also from Islington
Somerset Fox; one of the Gerards' numerous kinsmen
Mr Billingsly; given name unknown, a Smithfield butcher
Mr Tudor; given name unknown, an apothecary

Overall, decided Eden, it was probably the least likely collection of conspirators one could possibly imagine. A part-time informer, a schoolmaster, a blind vicar, a butcher and an apothecary; not exactly a group destined to strike fear into the heart of the establishment – even when one took into account a sprinkling of experienced soldiers like Whitley. The trouble was that this was the second such plot inside three months and Thurloe wasn't going to care that it might never have amounted to anything. *This* time, he was going to make sure the Cavaliers kept their heads down for the foreseeable future by putting the fear of God into them.

Then again – but for a timely fragment of information - I suppose it might have amounted to something.

Eden had little fondness for Cromwell these days ... but he favoured cold-blooded murder no more now than he had a year ago when he'd accidentally discovered a plot to assassinate Charles Stuart and his brother. Regardless of victim's identity, murder was still murder.

Sighing, he made his way to Thurloe's office and delivered his report.

'Bring one of them in for questioning,' said the Secretary. 'Do it quietly. Choose someone on the fringes of the plot but not so far from the centre that they won't know anything useful. And if you can pick a fellow who won't immediately be missed, so much the better.'

'Yes, sir.' *Is that all? You're sure you wouldn't like one with blue eyes or a limp?* 'Which one of them would you suggest?'

'I leave that to you, Colonel. Good day.'

Back in his office, Eden seethed quietly whilst devoting a few minutes to his own concerns. He scrawled a note to Lambert outlining the current situation and pointing out that, if the Major-General expected him to leave for Scotland on the 25th, he had only nine days left in which to convey the glad tidings to Secretary Thurloe and prevent Eden being chained to his desk for the duration of the current upheaval.

Then he settled down to address the task in hand.

For obvious reasons, the man he *wanted* to arrest was Henshaw ... but that would put Gerard and the rest on high alert, so he considered the apothecary instead. Tudor's name had been linked with Colonel Gerard's in that first letter – which suggested he'd been part of the conspiracy since its inception. The trouble was that the idea of an apothecary being either useful or neck-deep in a murder plot struck Eden as completely ludicrous. On the surface, the same seemed to be true of the schoolmaster, the butcher and the blind parson. And though Wiseman and Fox were probably key players, their disappearance – like that of Henshaw – would immediately set alarm bells ringing.

Damn.

Charles Gerard, then. He was a possibility. In Eden's view, though you might not keep your younger brother completely in the dark, you certainly didn't put him in the firing-line; and the fact that Charles lodged in Aldgate while John had rooms near the Temple, supported the notion that the brothers didn't necessarily meet every day.

Yes. That might work – for a while, at least. And if it stops a callow boy playing the kind of game that eventually leads to the scaffold, so much the better.

Colonel Maxwell got up and sent one of his clerks for Major Moulton.

'Arrest Charles Gerard – but discreetly. I'd rather there weren't any witnesses. And you can take your time. A day's delay will do no harm and might even be helpful.'

* * *

Major Moulton brought the young man to Westminster at dusk on Wednesday evening and installed him in a secure but comfortable chamber below stairs. Colonel Maxwell left the prisoner to stew overnight and conducted his first interview on the following morning. Since the lad – and, really, he was little more than that – was clearly terrified, Eden allowed him more latitude than he might normally have done and bore patiently with the usual stream of denials.

No, he knew nothing of any plot against the Protector.

No, he didn't believe his brother would ever countenance any such plot.

And no, he wasn't acquainted with Thomas Henshaw and didn't know any apothecaries or blind vicars.

'And what of Roger Whitley and Somerset Fox?' asked Eden, deceptively bland.

'Oh.' Charles froze and then stared down at his hands. 'Well, yes. They're relatives, so naturally ...' He stopped and then added rapidly, 'But we're not close. I hardly ever see them. In fact, I c-can't recall the last time I did.'

'Ah. Doubtless your brother knows them better.'

'He – he might. I don't know.'

Eden leaned back in his chair and contemplated the youth thoughtfully and in silence. Finally, when Charles started to fidget, he said gently, 'Mr Gerard ... if I didn't already have certain information, you wouldn't be here. You should try to bear that in mind. And though I sympathise with your reluctance to betray your brother, you might consider the fact that, as yet, he has done nothing irrevocable. Your best chance of keeping it that way is to tell me what you know.' He rose and summoned Ned Moulton with lift of his chin. 'I'll give you until tomorrow to think about it.'

In the event, it was Saturday before Charles started talking but, once he did, the words flowed like a torrent.

The plan to kill Cromwell had come from Henshaw. John hadn't liked it and the King hadn't sanctioned it. After the assassination, they'd intended to seize the Mews and other places and proclaim Charles the Second. Somerset Fox had been raising the apprentices and a schoolmaster from Islington had provided horses. And so it went … on and on and on.

By the time Charles stopped talking, Colonel Maxwell's list had grown by another dozen names and he suspected there were more to come. He was relieved that, so far, Sir Aubrey Durand was not among them and mildly disappointed that neither was Sir Ellis Brandon. Meanwhile, amongst what he had learned so far was one particular piece of information that wouldn't wait so he strode in on Thurloe and said, 'It's not certain – but there's a possibility they may try to cut Cromwell down tomorrow on his way to chapel. What are your orders?'

Frowning, the Secretary laid down his quill.

'Who are the ring-leaders?'

'Henshaw, Gerard and Wiseman. Also possibly Somerset Fox and Peter Vowell.'

'Arrest those five immediately, then set about rounding up the others. I'll see to the Protector's safety myself.'

'Very well.' Eden turned to go and then, looking back, said, 'Making the arrests simultaneously at dawn tomorrow, will give us our best chance of catching them all.'

Thurloe nodded and extracted a sheet of paper from amidst the neat heaps in front of him.

'Arrange matters as you see fit. And Colonel?'

'Sir?'

'I have a note here from Major-General Lambert requisitioning your services in a military capacity. His need appears to be urgent.' The cool, precise voice was laced with suspicion. 'Since he demands your release five days from now, I trust you can name someone capable of filling your shoes?'

Unable to believe that it could possibly be this easy and setting aside jubilation for later, Eden said expressionlessly, 'My chief clerk, Mr

Hollins, is able, efficient and fully briefed on all pertinent matters. I don't think you'd be disappointed.'

'Let us hope not, Colonel. Let us indeed hope not.'

Organising the co-ordinated arrests of five leading conspirators and planning the taking of twenty-five more from locations spread throughout the City and beyond was a feat of organisation which took most of the night. But at first light on Sunday morning, the operation went off without a hitch except in one not-insignificant particular.

Gerard, Wiseman, Fox, Vowell – and also the Reverend Hudson who'd been with the latter at the time – were all safely locked up. But Major Henshaw was nowhere to be found.

* * *

A crick in his neck and his eyes gritty with lack of sleep, Eden left Major Moulton to oversee the next wave of arrests and went back to Cheapside where he fell into bed for a well-deserved four hours. Then, recognising that time had been speeding by almost unnoticed and that Deborah's wedding was only three days away, he shaved, dressed and went in search of her.

She was in the small top-floor room, sewing something dark red and glowing which spilled from her lap to the floor. Something jerked at his nerves when he realised that it must be her wedding-gown.

Deborah stopped sewing and met his eyes. She said, 'I thought you might leave it to the eleventh hour. But do I take it that we are to have this conversation now?'

'Yes.' There was no point in pretending he didn't know what she meant. 'I think so.'

She pushed the gown aside to make room beside her on the settle. 'Then perhaps you'd better sit down.'

He did so, saying wryly, '*This* conversation? Am I so predictable?'

For a moment she said nothing; and then, 'I know you.'

Yes. You do – though that's not an answer.

'So you'll know I have to ask just one last time.' Eden reached out and took her hand. Then, waiting until her eyes met his, 'And you'll know why.'

'Yes.' A faint smile lingered in the night-dark depths. 'It means a great deal that you worry. But you must accept that there is no need. Jeremiah is a good man and he cares for me.'

'I know. But still --'

'*No*, Eden. I don't regret my decision. Indeed, during these last weeks, I've become more and more certain that it is right. And I'm at peace with it.'

His throat tightened and he said, 'That sounds very philosophical.'

'It's the product of a great deal of reflection,' she replied. 'For example ... if you think back to how our relationship started, it was I and not you who began it.'

'I don't recall putting up any great show of resistance.'

'No.' Her smile blossomed and then faded. 'But you never pretended. You didn't ask me to love you – or even want me to. And you never offered me forever.' She gave his fingers a slight squeeze and then withdrew her hand. 'These years with you have been a gift. One I never expected to have and one that many women *never* have ... and I'll treasure the memory of them. But from the moment Jeremiah puts a ring on my finger, a dear memory is all it will ever be. I will not repine and I won't look back, wishing things were different. He deserves better than that. And you need to go your way knowing I'm content to go mine.'

It was a long time before Eden spoke but finally he said, 'I hope you mean that and aren't still doing your damnedest to ease my mind – because there's something you should understand. It's true that I never offered you my whole heart. I'm not sure it's in me to offer it to any woman. But you carry a piece of it. And always will.'

Her eyes grew luminous with unshed tears.

'Thank you.'

'Don't! Don't thank me, for God's sake.' He put an arm around her and pulled her hard against his shoulder. 'Just promise that if there's ever a need ... if you're ever in trouble ... you'll come here. Not necessarily to me, perhaps. I'd understand that. But to Toby or Nick. Will you?'

'Yes.' *If that's what will comfort you.* 'Yes. I promise.'

* * *

A little later, meeting Nicholas entering the house just as he was leaving it, Eden took the opportunity to say, 'How are things in Duck Lane?'

'Still quiet – a fact probably more attributable to the padlock on the gate than to my distinguished presence.'

'Or both. But if you feel surplus to requirements and have better ways of spending your time --'

'I haven't. I enjoy going there and I like the company,' replied Nicholas simply. 'But I feel sorry for Lydia. That daughter-in-law of hers is worse than toothache.'

On first-name terms already, are you? thought Eden. But said, 'You've met her, then?'

'Once. I escorted Lydia home one day when there was a lot of unrest in the streets. Mistress Margaret looked down her nose at me and asked a lot of damned impertinent questions.' Nicholas grinned suddenly. 'I was forced to fall back on my title.'

'Dear me. She must have *really* annoyed you. So did it work?'

'Playing the baronet? Well enough. It took her by surprise and embarrassed her – which was all I wanted. There was another fellow there as well; a long-faced miserable cousin of some sort who clearly didn't take to me any better than the Toothache.' He paused and said, 'Will you find time to visit the workshop yourself before Thursday?'

'I doubt it. All hell is breaking loose today – and for some days to come, I suspect,' said Eden, stepping out through the door. 'If I get home at *all* tonight, I'll explain. Though I rather suspect that, by then, I won't need to.'

Arriving back at Westminster in the late afternoon, Colonel Maxwell found numerous officers and clerks busy transferring the more important prisoners to the Tower, the holding cells now being full to bursting. Scanning a list of those now in detention, Eden discovered two names he hadn't expected to see.

Looking up at Major Moulton, he raised enquiring brows and said, 'Sir Richard Wyllis and Colonel Villiers? Is there new information linking these two to the current conspiracy?'

'Not that I've heard. The Secretary just issued new orders adding them to the list. Actually, I don't even know who they are.'

'Edward Villiers is a highly-regarded and trusted member of the court-in-exile. He's related to just about everybody – including the Duke of Buckingham, the Earl of Suffolk and Ned Hyde. By contrast, Richard Wyllis – though an experienced soldier – has no connections worth mentioning. I'm just curious about why Thurloe wants them pulled in *now*.'

Ned shrugged this aside and bluntly changed the subject.

'There's a rumour that Lambert's sending you north with supplies for Monck. Is it true?'

'Yes.'

'I see. When were you thinking of mentioning that?'

Eden sighed. 'When I got the chance. Thurloe himself only found out a couple of days ago and it's been a mad-house here since then.'

'When do you leave?'

'On Thursday.' He looked sideways at the other man. 'Want to come?'

'What do you think?'

'Fine. Put your best Captain in temporary charge and I'll arrange it.' He grinned suddenly. 'After the Dunbar campaign, I didn't think you'd ever want to see Scotland again.'

'No. Neither did I.'

* * *

The morning of May 23rd brought forth a proclamation that all persons currently lodging in London, Westminster or Southwark were henceforth forbidden to change their abode without official permission. It also brought forth yet another surge of arrests until more than a hundred men were being held in custody. Both the proclamation and the continued arrests sent a wave of indignation through the City – the pot being deftly stirred by an inflammatory leaflet – and by the afternoon, placards declaring the plot to be a Government invention were fixed to walls everywhere.

After yet another day of chasing his tail in an atmosphere of near-chaos and wanting nothing more than food and his bed, Eden managed to get home just as Tobias and Nicholas were finishing supper.

'Is it true what people are saying?' asked Tobias before his brother had even taken off his coat. 'That this whole Gerard's Plot thing is nothing more than a ruse to enable Cromwell to crack down on the Royalists and anybody else that takes his fancy?'

'No.' Eden dropped into a chair and reached for the ale jug. 'The plot's real enough.'

'Folk in the street don't think so,' offered Nicholas, obligingly pushing the remains of a dish of collops across the table. 'You're saying they're wrong?'

'No.' Eden tipped some meat on to a platter. 'I'm saying I've had a hell of a day and I'd appreciate it if the inquisition could wait until I've had my supper.'

'So they're not wrong?' persisted Tobias.

'For God's sake!' Eden threw down his knife in disgust. 'The plot is real. The placards are wrong. The rumours were started by leaflets printed in Newgate Market. And I have nothing further to add other than the fact that I've to be in Westminster again tomorrow morning and will be lucky to escape in time for Deborah's wedding. Now ... may I please *eat*?'

TWELVE

'More names,' said Major Moulton resignedly as he handed a sheet of paper to Colonel Maxwell early the next morning. 'Some of those we've already arrested are trying to buy their way out of trouble.'

Eden scanned the sheet and went suddenly still.

'Have you sent troopers out after these yet?'

'No. I thought --'

'Don't. Drag your heels for an hour. In fact ...' Remaining on his feet, he scribbled a brief note. 'Get that to Nick Austin. At this hour, he's probably still in bed but don't let that stop you putting this in his hand. Tell him it's urgent. Go!'

Not unnaturally, Nicholas was more than a little alarmed to be shaken from slumber by a large, rather grim-faced Army officer. Rubbing sleep from his eyes and trying to assemble his brain, he said stupidly, 'What the – who – am I under arrest?'

'Read that,' said Major Moulton. 'And don't tell me what it says. I'd sooner not know. Just do whatever it says as fast as you can.' Upon which note, he stalked out.

For perhaps five seconds, Nicholas stared open-mouthed at the space where his surprise visitor had been. Then he broke the seal on Eden's note.

L. Neville's brother on list. Will delay arrest as long as possible. Get him to Shoreditch. Explain to Jack. Tell no one else.

And barely legible underneath, *Burn the note.*

Nicholas groaned and swung his legs out of bed.

He's risking his career. Again. And the wedding's at noon. Bloody hell!

* * *

Later, Eden would wonder why he was sticking his neck out for an idiot who plainly hadn't learned his lesson the first time. Now, however, he was too busy to think of it.

Aside from dealing with the large number of prisoners still held below stairs, he had also to ensure the smooth-running of the office after his departure on the morrow. This took the best part of two hours as he and Mr Hollins ploughed through a myriad of detail and the accompanying paperwork. At some point, Ned Moulton stuck his head around the door and gave him a brief nod before disappearing again.

Eden took a moment to hope rescuing Lydia Neville's brother from his folly wouldn't put Nicholas at risk and then restored his attention to the matter in hand.

At just before ten o'clock and with only two hours left before Deborah's wedding, a message arrived from Major-General Lambert requiring Colonel Maxwell to come to Whitehall at his earliest convenience to receive his marching orders and, Eden suspected, yet more paperwork. Realising that, unless he was prepared to grace the ceremony in his uniform, he was now cutting it extremely fine, he handed disposal of the prisoners over to the first Captain he met and took off at something close to a run.

Fortunately, Lambert didn't keep him waiting and was disposed to be brief. Eden accepted the various supply inventories he was handed along with a list of the troopers, officers and civilian artisans that General Monck had asked for. Then, sliding them into his coat, he said, 'Where is everything being assembled?'

'The Tower – on account of the gunpowder. Captain Grey has been dealing with all matters related and is already assembling the train in readiness for tomorrow. He's efficient, so you shouldn't need to do anything other than oversee the final stages in order to satisfy yourself that nothing has been overlooked.' Lambert gave his habitual ironic smile. 'You're scheduled to depart at eight … which means you may be on the road by eleven.'

Eden nodded, knowing only too well the truth of it.

'I commandeered the services of Major Moulton, by the way. Since, like me, he also served under Gabriel Brandon, I assumed that would be all right?'

'I'll make sure that it is.' Lambert rose from his chair. 'Do your best with Colonel Brandon. Judging by what I hear about him these days, I doubt he'd have any difficulty in getting elected. And if he's out of charity with the current form of government, remind him that he won't change that from Yorkshire.'

* * *

At around the time Colonel Maxwell was sitting with his chief clerk, Lydia Neville was woken by Nancy to the news that her brother had apparently left the house some two hours earlier, accompanied by a man with one arm.

'What?' Lydia yawned, sat up and pushed back her hair.

Nancy turned away to open the curtains.

'As best I can tell, Madge was just stoking the range when this one-armed fellow came in the back door, asking for Sir Aubrey. She pointed the way and he went off up the stairs. Then, no more'n ten minutes later, him and Sir Aubrey came back down in a hurry and went off together.'

Frowning, Lydia threw back the covers and got out of bed.

'They didn't say anything – or leave a note?'

'Not as I know of.'

'Did the one-armed man give Madge his name?'

'Don't think she asked. Can't describe him, neither. I reckon she was too flustered to take a proper look.'

Lydia thought about it.

A one-armed man suggested Mr Potter or someone else from the lorinery – though why they'd send for Aubrey rather than herself was a mystery. Unless ... unless it was something to do with the current wave of unrest sweeping through the City. She supposed it might be that. She *hoped* it was – because the other alternative was that it was something to do with Aubrey himself.

When the arrests had started, he'd told her not to worry and that he wasn't in any danger; but what he *hadn't* actually said was that he'd had nothing to do with the plot to kill Cromwell that everyone was talking about. As a consequence, she'd been living on a knife-edge for the last four days, frightened that every knock at the door heralded soldiers looking for her brother. It had therefore been a huge relief when people started saying that the only plot that existed had been formulated by Cromwell himself.

She dismissed her fears and started to dress. It was the lorinery. It had to be.

An hour later, Mr Potter stared at her in some confusion and shook his head.

'Sent for Sir Aubrey? No, Miss Lydia. There's been no trouble. And even if there had ... well, why would we be telling him and not you?'

'That's what I thought. But when Nancy said it was a one-armed man, someone from here seemed the most logical --' She stopped suddenly. 'Oh God. How stupid! It must have been Sir Nicholas. Why on earth didn't I think of that before?'

And without further ado, she whirled round and set off for Cheapside.

Since the main entrance to the house appeared to lie through the shop, the first person she encountered was a very large young man with a winning smile she found eerily familiar.

She said, 'Mr Maxwell?'

Tobias bowed. 'At your service, Mistress. How can I help you?'

'I – I need to speak with Sir Nicholas. Urgently.' And when he didn't immediately answer, she added rapidly, 'I'm Lydia Neville. My brother went off with Sir Nicholas early this morning and hasn't returned home. I was hoping to find out why.'

'Ah.' *The widow whose brother Eden arrested some while back. No wonder she's worried.* 'Unfortunately, Nick isn't here just now – and I've no idea where he's gone.'

'Oh. Then perhaps Colonel Maxwell might know something?'

'That's not beyond the realms of possibility,' agreed Tobias. 'But *he's* not here either. Both he and Nick will be back before noon but if you can't wait until then, Eden should be at Westminster – though finding him might be difficult.'

'Thank you,' said Lydia. 'You are the Colonel's brother, aren't you?'

'Guilty,' he grinned. And then, 'Mistress Neville, perhaps you should go home and see if your brother has returned. Meanwhile, when either Nicholas or Eden gets back, I'll tell them you need to speak with them.'

'Yes. That probably would be best – but I can't.' She dipped a small curtsy and added, 'I'm sorry to be so abrupt but I must go.'

Tobias watched her disappear amidst the crowds in the street and thought, *Oh dear, Nick. What have you got yourself mixed up in?*

Lydia arrived at Westminster just as the bells of St Margaret's chimed ten. After fruitlessly pursuing two sets of misguided directions she finally arrived at Colonel Maxwell's office to learn that he'd just left for an appointment at Whitehall.

Hot, dishevelled and tired, Mistress Neville sat down and dropped her head in her hands.

'You won't get into Whitehall, Miss,' said Mr Hollins kindly. 'Best let me get a chair to take you home.'

* * *

Freshly-shaved and dressed in his best coat and tawny silk sash, Eden got to St Matthew's on Friday Street just in time for the wedding but far later then he should have done since Nicholas was on the point of escorting Deborah into the church.

'Durand's in Shoreditch – and you're late,' hissed Nicholas crossly. 'Just get inside, will you?'

Eden nodded, smiled ruefully at Deborah and slid, as unobtrusively as possible, into one of the rear pews.

There were a handful of people present but not many. Near the front, Eden could see Tobias and, on the other side of the aisle, one row behind Mr Fisher and his groomsman, a soberly-dressed female sitting beside a pair of tow-headed youngsters who were presumably the vintner's children. Then he turned to watch Deborah make her entrance.

She looked stunning. Even in the shadowy light of the church, her skin glowed white against the blood-red of her gown and her hair was arranged in an elaborate cascade of curls guaranteed to entice a man's hands.

The vintner's hands, thought Eden, still not comfortable with the notion.

Deborah didn't look at him as she passed, but then he hadn't expected her to. She was approaching her wedding in the same frame of mind that she intended to approach her marriage; a scenario in which

Eden only existed as her former employer. He didn't relish that notion either.

The ceremony was simple and mercifully brief.

As they left the church, Nicholas leaned towards Eden and muttered, 'He's safe enough and I sent Lydia a note saying so.'

With which Eden was forced, for the time being, to be satisfied.

After lengthy deliberations, verging at times on argument, Deborah had allowed Eden, Tobias and Nicholas to host a wedding breakfast at the Lamb and Flag so everyone set off on the short walk to Foster Lane in moods varying from Mr Fisher's euphoria to Colonel Maxwell's grim determination to acquit himself properly.

Sensing his brother's unease, Tobias clapped him on the shoulder and murmured, 'You should try a smile that at least *looks* as if you mean it. After all, Deborah seems happy enough.'

Eden grunted and said nothing but thought, *Seems isn't the same as is*.

The soberly-dressed female turned out to be Mr Fisher's sister. The tow-headed children – a boy of roughly nine and a girl perhaps two years older – gravitated towards Deborah and regarded her with expressions not dissimilar to the one worn by their father. As Eden watched, the girl touched the taffeta of Deborah's gown with shy fingers and leaned up to whisper something. Deborah smiled, murmured a reply and held out the hand bearing the wedding ring. The girl looked from the ring to Tobias, eyes wide with something akin to awe. The boy, Eden noticed, stayed very close but said nothing.

The food was good and Nicholas ensured that wine and ale kept flowing.

When the time came – and only because it couldn't be avoided – Eden preceded a toast to the happy couple with a few graceful remarks about his household's loss being Mr Fisher's gain. And then, feeling that he'd done all that was required of him, he pulled Tobias to one side and said, 'Since your store of *joie de vivre* far exceeds my own and I've a lot to do if I'm to leave in the morning, you can take over now. But when they've finished with the syllabubs and tartlets, bring them back to

Cheapside. I'd like to say goodbye there rather than here,' replied Eden curtly.

And, having murmured a few words of excuse and apology in the bridegroom's ear, he left.

* * *

Walking into the shop, he narrowly avoided colliding with Lydia Neville who, after a startled gasp, rounded on him, saying, 'At last! *Where is my brother?*'

Eden hesitated, glancing at Mr Turner.

'*He* doesn't know,' she snapped, misreading his lack of response. 'If he did, I wouldn't still be here.'

'Perhaps we can discuss this in private,' said Eden, taking in her flushed face and the fact that her hair was making a creditable attempt to free itself from her cap. 'This way, if you please.'

Lydia didn't please. She just wanted answers. But since she plainly wasn't going to get them unless she did as he asked, she loosed an irritated breath and let him lead her upstairs.

As soon as the parlour door closed behind them, Colonel Maxwell said, 'I thought Nicholas sent you a note.'

'Oh yes. He did.' She eyed him witheringly over folded arms. 'He sent a note saying that Aubrey is quite safe and I'm not to worry. Oddly enough, I didn't find that helpful.'

'No,' began Eden, realising that Nicholas would have been wary about committing too much paper, 'but --'

'I'm aware that whatever Nick has done is something you told him to do ... but safe from *what* exactly?'

'Arrest. Surely you guessed as much?'

'No! Why should I? He hasn't done anything.'

'You mean,' remarked Eden aridly, 'that he hasn't done anything you know about.'

Lydia opened her mouth and then closed it again.

'Your brother's name appeared among half a dozen others on a list I was handed at a little after six o'clock this morning. The rest of them will have been rounded up by now. Indeed, I'm surprised *you* haven't had any troopers on the doorstep yet. But they'll come – make no mistake about that.'

'And when they do, the fact that Aubrey has vanished will make him look guilty.'

'He already *is* guilty – by association, if nothing else.'

She shook her head. 'I don't believe it. It's a mistake.'

'No. It isn't. Aubrey's name was supplied by one of the prisoners already in custody for complicity in the current plot,' replied Eden, his patience dwindling by the second. 'How do you think that happened if he had nothing to do with it?'

'I don't know.' Some of the colour drained from her face but she said stubbornly, 'It's a mistake or – or someone is lying. I don't know. But Aubrey *wouldn't* … he *can't* have … not after last time.'

'Unfortunately, the fact remains that he both would and did. And it's more serious this time. *This* time, they weren't planning a few riots. They were planning to kill Cromwell.'

'That's nonsense!' Pulling herself together, Lydia sniffed disparagingly and narrowly avoided stamping her foot. 'Haven't you heard what people are saying? There *wasn't* any assassination plot. It's all an excuse to allow the Protector to arrest anybody he likes. The only conspiracy was the one dreamed up in Whitehall.' She waited and when he didn't reply, added vehemently, 'There was no plot!'

Colonel Maxwell remained silent and it was that, rather than anything he might have said which suddenly filled her with dread. She said uncertainly, 'There wasn't, was there?'

'Yes.'

'To – to murder Cromwell?'

'Amongst other things. And by now, Secretary Thurloe has chapter and verse.'

'Oh.' Everything inside her seemed to collapse. 'And do you think that Aubrey …?'

'I imagine he knew of it, yes. For the rest, not having spoken to him, I couldn't say.' Trying to moderate his tone a little, Eden said, 'You'll appreciate that I can't be seen to have a hand in this? It's enough that I delayed matters this morning to give Nick time to get your brother out of harm's way.' He paused and then added, 'He's in Shoreditch, by the way, at the home of a good friend of mine. Nick knows where – but if you want Aubrey to stay safe, I'd suggest you don't visit. At least not until the dust settles which, on present showing, could take some time.'

'Will you go yourself? To question him?'

'No. By noon tomorrow I'll be on my way to Scotland.'

Something lurched in Lydia's stomach. 'Tomorrow?'

'Yes.'

'Oh. I see. And will you be gone long?'

'As long as is humanly possible,' he said with a sudden smile. 'But don't worry. Nicholas will still be here so --' He stopped, hearing sounds of arrival below. 'Ah. The wedding party. But please don't feel you have to leave. If you stay you'll be able to speak with Nick and receive whatever reassurances you need.'

Quickly and rather disjointedly, she said, 'I should ... I haven't thanked you.'

'And you need not.' He sensed that she was about to ask why he'd interfered and wasn't sure what the answer was. Fortunately, the sound of footsteps on the stairs enabled him to curtail the conversation. 'Enough, now. Stay and meet Deb – Mistress Fisher.'

Lydia noticed the slip; that and one look at the bride, with her masses of dark hair and enticing curves, inexplicably caused her spirits to sink even lower. Straightening her spine and pinning a smile on her face, she told herself not to be an idiot. Then she met the bride's eyes and had the awful feeling that the woman somehow *knew*.

During the course of the introductions and inevitable good wishes, Eden also thought he glimpsed an odd expression on Deborah's face but his mind was busy with the problem of how to achieve a few minutes in private with her without spoiling Fisher's day. Ten minutes later, when she excused herself to ensure that those of her belongings which hadn't already been sent to Southwark were ready for the carrier, he realised that, as usual, she had recognised his need and was taking care of it.

As soon as they were alone, he said, 'If you'll wait just a moment, I have something for you.' And ran smartly up to his chamber before she could reply. Then, returning with the carved box, 'This is neither inappropriate nor extravagant – though you must know I'd have liked to be both.'

Deborah's dark eyes looked down at the gift and then up into Eden's hazel ones.

'It's beautiful and I shall treasure it. Thank you.' She paused briefly. 'You'll take care of yourself in Scotland?'

'I always do. And you ... you'll remember your promise?'

'I'll remember. And of course, I'll call here from time to time.'

She didn't say, *It will be easier once you're gone* ... but he heard the words anyway.

'Of course. Two pies a week, wasn't it?'

'Yes.' Her smile was a trifle unsteady. 'You should re-join the others. The host shouldn't absent himself from his own party ... and Mistress Neville seems upset.'

'She's worried about her brother.'

'Oh?' *She is. But there's more to it than that. Only you don't see it, do you?* 'Why?'

'He should have been arrested this morning but I had Nicholas hide him in Shoreditch with the Morrells. I'm still trying to work out why.' And, shrugging it aside, 'But I don't want to waste these last minutes talking of that.'

'No.' *Why did I mention her? Knowing is one thing. Seeing – and on this of all days – is something else entirely.* 'I shall be all right, Eden. Go to Scotland and find yourself again. By the time you come back, everything will look different.'

'Will it? I don't know.' He took her hands, dropped a light kiss on each one and a third, slightly less chaste, on her lips. 'Be happy, Deborah. I shall pray that you are.'

* * *

When the wedding party had taken its leave, Eden bade another private but more business-like goodbye to Lydia Neville.

'I trust Nick has set your mind at rest?'

'He's done his best. And he says he'll take a letter to Aubrey.'

'That's fine. Just be careful what you put in it and destroy your brother's replies if they're not discreet. And now I'm afraid you'll have to forgive me. I've a number of things to attend to before the morning.'

'Of course.' Lydia hesitated, knowing she wanted to say something but not sure what it was. In the end, she said, 'Will there be fighting in Scotland?'

'Perhaps.' A slow smile dawned. 'One can but hope.'

That smile and the effect it had destroyed her usual caution.

'How can you say that? You could be *killed*.'

Eden looked at her, part surprised and part thoughtful.

'I'm a soldier. I could have been killed a good many times. But your concern is appreciated. And before you ask – yes, I shall be careful.'

* * *

His departure on the following morning was accomplished with the usual male *sangfroid* that hid some very real feeling.

Nicholas shook his hand, saying, 'Enjoy yourself but don't forget to come back.'

And, with a massive buffet on the shoulder, Tobias said, 'The poor Scots aren't going to know what's hit them. Then again, neither will General Monck. So give 'em all hell, Colonel ... and then go and see Mother.'

WINDS OF CHANGE
May to October, 1654

Dunbar field, resounds thy praises loud,
And Worcester's laureate wreath; yet much remains
To conquer still: peace hath her victories
No less renown'd than war. New foes arise ...

John Milton

ONE

Although due to the carts and wagons loaded down with supplies, the journey north was grindingly slow, Eden's spirits rose with every mile. The weather was changeable, alternating between bursts of brilliant sunshine and sudden downpours that left everyone sodden. Eden, feeling the weight of the last year gradually melting away, was as content when rain was dripping off his hat as when the sun warmed his skin. He simply took each day as it came and led his lengthy convoy onwards. By the time they reached Peterborough, he discovered that he was actually happy.

In many senses, this was fortunate because every day brought problems of one sort or another. A cart stuck in the mud or one with a broken wheel which always seemed to happen near the front of the column, thus bringing the entire train to a halt; horses going lame or needing to be re-shod which meant that one of the farriers had to get out his tools and set to work in less-than-ideal conditions; and difficulties with accommodation, fresh provisions and even, until Colonel Maxwell made it plain that his tolerance had a well-defined limit, discipline.

Then there was the endless grumbling of the civilians, none of whom were used to life on the march. The surgeons were the surliest and objected to every possible discomfort – particularly the frequent necessity of sleeping under canvas. The saddlers and farriers formed a little clique of their own and ignored everyone else as much as possible. And the armourers looked down on just about everybody.

As for General Monck's missing officers ... Eden swiftly found out what Lambert had meant when he'd declined to give any of them command of the supply train. Lieutenant Brady drank; Major West was both sly and slovenly; and Captains Foster and Beckett were just bone idle. Eden presumed that, to Monck, these men were merely names on a roster-sheet; if they weren't, God alone knew why he wanted them back.

'Do you think we can turn them into something resembling soldiers by the time we get to Scotland?' he asked Ned Moulton within twenty-four hours of leaving London.

'Not even if we were marching to Russia,' came the dour reply. 'But I don't mind knocking some of the cockiness out of them.'

'By all means,' grinned Eden. 'I'm all for making one's own entertainment.'

Three days later and approaching Wetherby, Monck's lost officers – though still far below the Major's exacting standards – had all progressed to a surly knowledge of how not to draw unwelcome attention to themselves.

'You see?' said Eden cheerfully. 'They've already acquired the in-born knowledge of every common trooper. In another couple of days, Foster and Beckett may even do a hand's turn once in a while. I'm sorry I'm going to miss it.'

'No you're not. You're delighted Lambert gave you an *official* reason to visit Colonel Brandon, rather than just having to simply absent yourself,' retorted Ned. Then, 'How long do you expect to be away?'

'Two nights at most. I'll leave early tomorrow and should be back the day after next. Meanwhile, you can carry on by easy marches. I'll catch up with you at Catterick, if not before. And don't worry – I'll give your regards to Gabriel.'

* * *

Colonel Maxwell rode to Brandon Lacey through intermittent drizzle and arrived to find his friend and former commanding officer in the stable, just about to saddle his horse.

After a second or two of frozen shock, Gabriel raised one quizzical brow and said, 'Nearly five years with scarcely a word and suddenly you're here? I must be hallucinating.'

'Oh – come now.' Eden dropped from the saddle. 'It's not that bad. I've written from time to time.'

'True. A grand total of half a dozen notes, each one less than three sentences long.'

'I didn't want to bore you.' And as their hands finally met and gripped, 'You shouldn't be too hard on me, you know. I've been trying to get here for the last year – and wouldn't be here now if Lambert hadn't picked me to command a supply train going north to Monck.'

'A supply train?' Gabriel turned to glance out into the yard. 'Please tell me you haven't brought it with you?'

Eden laughed. 'No. I've left Ned Moulton in charge of keeping it moving. At the rate we're going, Monck will be lucky to see his supplies by mid-summer.' He paused and then said, 'It's good to see you, Gabriel. You have no idea. And you look well.'

Actually, thought Eden, he looked exactly the same as when they'd last met ... as if the five years between hadn't existed. The near-black hair was untouched with silver, his face was lightly tanned and his body as lean and muscular as ever.

'I *am* well. But you look in need of a decent breakfast. Come into the house and we'll see what we can do.'

'But you were going somewhere,' protested Eden half-heartedly. 'If you're busy --'

'Don't be an idiot. I was only going to ride down to Scar Croft and that can wait. Do you honestly think that I'm going to waste the short time which I imagine is all you have? So come in and have something to eat – after which I'd guess you'd like a hot bath.'

'Please! We've been on the road for five days and I think the dust is now ingrained.'

As they entered the hall, a small hurricane hurled itself at Gabriel's legs, saying furiously, 'Where did you go? I looked and looked and you weren't *anywhere!*'

With a laugh, he swung the child up into his arms and said, 'Well, I'm somewhere now. And I've brought you a visitor.'

Dark grey eyes, the image of her father's, examined Eden briefly and with some suspicion.

'Who is it?' she demanded.

'He's Papa's friend. And if you're very good you can have him as an uncle. Eden ... allow me to present Mistress Rosamond Sophia Brandon – generally known as Rosie.'

Eden grinned at the child and bowed slightly.

'Delighted, Mistress Rosamond.'

'Rosie,' she corrected. And to Gabriel, 'If he's an uncle, has he brought presents? Uncle Tom always brings presents.'

Above her blonde curls, Gabriel exchanged a laughing glance with Eden but said, 'He's different sort of uncle and he'll bring presents next time if you don't tease him.' Then, setting his daughter on her feet, 'Go and find Mother. Tell her that Uncle Eden is here and ask her to confine the twins to barracks for an hour, if she can.'

'Eden?' Rosie examined her honorary uncle doubtfully. 'Like in the Bible story?'

'Exactly like the Bible story,' he agreed gravely.

She nodded, then added, 'Kit and Rob are only two and they're boys so they're noisy. Barracks means stay in the nursery.' And she ran off.

'God, Gabriel,' remarked Eden, watching her go. 'She's beautiful. By the time she's sixteen you'll be beating them off with sticks.'

'Yes. Well, I'm hoping her brothers will lend a hand with that.' He led the way to the dining parlour, where bread, cheese and cold meat were still laid out on the dresser. 'Help yourself. I'll get the ale.'

When Eden was sitting in front of a heaped platter, Gabriel dropped into a chair on the other side of the table, saying, 'So Lambert's got you acting as quartermaster, has he?'

His mouth full of ham, Eden nodded.

'An odd use for your talents, surely?'

'Perhaps. But I'd have jumped at anything that got me out of Thurloe's office. It was stifling me. And recently, we've done nothing but arrest people.' He looked up from his plate. 'I take it you've heard about the plot to kill Cromwell? The news-sheets have been full of it this past week.'

'We've heard,' remarked a voice from behind him, 'about a plot to *invent* a plot. But that's not quite the same thing, is it?'

'Venetia.' Eden rose to salute her hand and then her cheek. 'As beautiful and direct as ever, I see.'

She smiled at him, shaking her head.

'Not so much these days. But I wouldn't put anything past Cromwell and that sneaky spymaster of his. *Was* there an assassination plot?'

'Yes.'

'Which failed?'

'Again, yes. But --'

Seeing his wife open her mouth to demand details, Gabriel said, 'Let the man break his fast, Venetia. You can interrogate him later. Where's Rosie?'

'Upstairs. I left her explaining to Rob and Kit that they have a new uncle but he's not a *proper* one like Tom so they aren't to expect presents.' Her voice quivered slightly. 'She thinks this lack might be something to do with the not-a-real-uncle being out of the Bible.'

Gabriel gave a crack of laughter and waved Eden back into his seat. 'You can make up some ground next time. Speaking of which, how long can you stay?'

'Two nights – if you'll have me.'

'Do you need to ask?' Venetia turned to go. 'I'll have a chamber prepared. And a bath. After which you can tell me what's *really* been happening.'

When the door closed behind her, Gabriel said, 'How serious was it?'

'In the end, not very – though it might have been.' Eden explained briefly and then added, 'Cromwell's never been as unpopular as he is right now and death threats abound – so much so that he's taken to going about with a loaded pistol in his pocket.'

'Ah.' Gabriel grinned lazily. 'Now *there's* an accident waiting to happen.'

'I know. It doesn't bear thinking about, does it?' returned Eden cheerfully, once more attending to his plate. Then, as if struck by a random thought, 'Oh – you'll be interested to learn that I tripped across your half-brother back in February regarding what's commonly referred to as the Ship Tavern Plot. Cocksure sod, isn't he?'

'That's putting it mildly. I take it you arrested him?'

'Arrested him, questioned him and held him a lot longer than was strictly necessary just for the hell of it. His name hasn't come up in connection with the current fracas – or, at least, it hadn't when I left.' He paused and glanced around the room. 'And speaking of your relatives – I notice there aren't any animals. Doesn't Mistress Sophy live here any longer?'

'No. She married Venetia's Uncle Henry and they have a property near Boroughbridge. Venetia's sister, Elizabeth, and her husband, Tom Knightley also live nearby and have three boys. Phoebe, despite owning the family home and having her hand sought by half the county as a result, remains unmarried.' Gabriel leaned back in his chair. 'That was a nice try at turning the subject, by the way. But now, suppose you tell me why you're *really* here.'

Eden had been hoping to work up to that gradually so he said, 'The road brought me close by so I seized the opportunity. Isn't that enough?'

'No. Lambert chose you for nurse-maiding duty knowing it would bring you virtually to my gate. Do you want to tell me why – or shall I guess?'

Sighing, Eden laid down his knife and said, 'He wants you to stand for Parliament. I've a letter for you somewhere.'

'Of course you do. And no doubt you're supposed to persuade me.'

'That's the general idea.'

'You think you can?'

'No. I think you'll make up your own mind. But for what it's worth, I think Lambert's right in wanting you.'

'I'll let you justify that remark later.' Gabriel came to his feet. 'For now, finish your food, have some more ale and then go and get cleaned up. I'm going down to Scar Croft – thus leaving you to Venetia's tender mercies and Rosie's conviction that you've come here from Paradise. Enjoy yourself.'

* * *

By the time Venetia had finished with him Eden knew how the men he questioned felt. Oddly enough, giving her the facts about Colonel Gerard's plot to murder the Protector was the least difficult part of their conversation. Trickier to answer were the personal questions ... and then there were the references to her youngest sister and the subtle inference that he might like to renew their acquaintance.

Eden was dimly aware that Phoebe Clifford had developed an adolescent passion for him when she was seventeen years old. Had he thought about it, he'd have assumed that she'd grown out of that a long time ago. Something in the tenor of Venetia's conversation suggested that perhaps she hadn't. Either that or – if Phoebe had indeed rejected numerous proposals – Venetia was harbouring the notion that he might succeed where others had failed. Eden hoped that neither was true because, if Venetia *was* disposed towards matchmaking, he might end up pointing out that if he'd wanted another wife he'd have married his mistress. All in all, a meeting with Phoebe Clifford was best avoided and shouldn't, in the space of a mere two days, be too difficult to manage. He didn't, of course, know that Venetia had taken the matter out of his hands by sending a note to her sister.

Eden Maxwell is here with us briefly. His wife died some eighteen months ago. If you want to meet him again, sup with us tomorrow.

* * *

That evening while Venetia was reading Rosie her nightly story, Gabriel poured Eden a glass of wine and said, 'So tell me. Why should I consider standing for Parliament?'

'In the interests of creating some stability. You read the news-sheets so you must know as well as I do that nothing has gone right since we cut off the King's head. We've had a long, pointless and expensive war with the Dutch and, at home, new factions are springing up every day. It's not just the Levellers any more. Now we've got Ranters and Diggers and Fifth Monarchists all shouting from the pulpits. As for Worcester ... it was one of the bloodiest days I've ever seen.' Eden paused and took a large swallow of wine. Then, when Gabriel remained silent, he said, 'For the rest, Cromwell ejected the Rump at sword-point and replaced it with the so-called Barebones Parliament. Unsurprisingly, that didn't work – and mercifully, thanks to Lambert's discreet machinations, it didn't last either. So now Cromwell has become Lord Protector and is ostensibly governing jointly with the Council of State – except that, in reality, the Council is a mere cipher and Cromwell over-rides it at every turn, which means that, to all intents and purposes, what we have is a military dictatorship when what we *need* is a balance of power.'

'And you think Parliament can achieve that?'

'Don't you?'

'I have doubts,' returned Gabriel. 'I've read the *Instrument of Government* – which I assume will form the basis for whatever happens next. It says the Protector must call Parliament at least once every three years and that it should sit for a minimum of five months. From what you say and what I suspect, Cromwell can dissolve it at the first opportunity, if it's not dancing to his tune.' He smiled a little and added trenchantly, 'Where, exactly, does that differ from the late King's reign?'

'It doesn't. But what do you suggest? That next time we learn of an assassination plot, we shut our eyes and ears to it? Or we should depose Cromwell and invite Charles Stuart back?'

'At the end of the day, that might be the best thing you *can* do … assuming Lambert hasn't either the support or the will to stage a counter-coup and take over himself. But I suppose you have to begin by giving Cromwell the benefit of the doubt and waiting to see how matters go with his first Parliament. Personally, I don't hold out much hope. And even if I did, I hardly see my presence at Westminster making a shred of difference one way or the other.'

'If it was *just* you, neither do I,' agreed Eden. 'But Lambert is trying to pack the benches with as many men of experience and good sense as he can muster in order to give the House the best possible chance of reining Cromwell in.'

'And I wish him luck with it.' Gabriel's tone said that this particular topic was at an end and, for a few moments, there was silence. Then, reaching for his glass, he said, 'Enough of that. How is your family? In particular, your lovely mother and your children?'

'As far as I'm aware, everyone is well.'

'You mean you don't know?'

'As I think I told you, I've been busy.'

'That,' said Gabriel scathingly 'is just an excuse. I thought you overcame that problem some time ago.'

'I did,' replied Eden stiffly. 'And I'll visit Thorne Ash on my way south.'

'Do.' There was a brief silence. Then, 'Venetia told me about Celia but withheld the details.'

'I didn't give her any.'

'Ah. Then we'll change the subject.'

'Again?' asked Eden. And, on a small explosion of breath, 'She fell down the stairs and broke her neck. Francis wasn't convinced that it was an accident but couldn't prove that it wasn't. Since it happened in Paris, I've no idea either way.'

Gabriel nodded. 'And how is Francis?'

'Well enough, as far as I know. He married a French actress and is busy writing plays for some theatre or other.' Eden grinned suddenly. 'I imagine he's in his element.'

'Very likely. And what about you?'

'Me? I'm just happy to be away from London and free from paperwork. And if General Monck can use an extra sword for a few weeks, I'll be bloody ecstatic.'

* * *

On the following morning Eden accompanied Gabriel around the estate. They visited the cottages where the spinning and weaving was done, the fields planted with this year's flax and the sheds where the last of the lambing was still in progress. At the end of it, Gabriel said simply, 'This is my life now and, along with Venetia and the children, it keeps me extremely busy. The changes I put in place back in '48 are bearing fruit and we're finally – not merely solvent – but financially secure. Consequently, I have to ask myself why I'd want to leave it in order to spend five months sitting on my arse in Westminster ... and so far I haven't come up with a good answer.'

'Are you saying you won't even consider it?'

'I'll consider it. I'll even listen to any further persuasions you may wish to offer – but I'm making no promises. And in the meantime, I should probably drop a word of warning in your ear.'

'About what?'

'Venetia has invited Phoebe to supper.'

* * *

Colonel Maxwell bowed over Mistress Clifford's hand, his demeanour perfectly correct but faintly cautious. He noticed that, on the surface at least, she had changed very little from the girl she had been six years ago. To the best of his recollection, her figure was perhaps a little more rounded and her expression less easy to read … but the light brown hair and grey eyes were the same. On the other hand, she returned his greeting smoothly and without any of the obvious signs of delight she might once have shown. Eden was relieved.

Meanwhile, Phoebe conducted her own discreet appraisal and decided that he was still attractive – perhaps even more so than when she'd first met him. The mahogany hair, the hazel eyes, the easy way he carried himself … even the thin white line of the scar on his left cheek, now scarcely visible. Then there was that slow, bewitching smile which she remembered only too well but which hadn't so far made an appearance. Phoebe wondered how she'd feel if it did. Actually, wondering how she would feel was the only reason she'd accepted Venetia's invitation. Although her sister chose not to believe it, she hadn't rejected half a dozen suitors because she still hankered after Eden Maxwell. She'd rejected them because she suspected they all wanted her land more than they wanted her and because not one of them had made her pulse quicken. However, it would be comforting to know that Colonel Maxwell no longer had that power either … and so here she was, in her best blue taffeta, waiting to find out.

The talk throughout the meal hovered largely around the doings of the Gerard faction, the rumours that, due to Mazarin's desire to forge a military alliance with Cromwell, the king-in-exile was no longer welcome on French soil and Colonel Robert Lilburne's unsuccessful attempts to tame the Scots – all of which made it easy for Eden and Phoebe to avoid conversing directly with each other. But by the time the sweetmeats were being placed on the table and everyone seemed to be running out of suitably impersonal topics, Venetia said the first thing that came into her head in order to avoid an uncomfortable silence.

'Are you still living in Luciano's shop on Cheapside, Eden? Kate wrote that your younger brother was intending to set up his own sign there.'

'And he's done so – much to the delight of half the young women in the City. But yes, I still lodge with him. I've never got around to finding a house of my own – though I keep telling myself that I should. And the three of us rub along tolerably well.'

'Three?' asked Gabriel idly. 'Who's the third?'

Eden hesitated briefly and then said, 'Sir Nicholas Austin. He's a friend of Francis, though I didn't know that when I first met him. You might say that I ... acquired ... him after Worcester.'

Gabriel's amused, 'Acquired?' clashed with Venetia's immediate, 'He's a Royalist?'

'Yes. He was badly wounded in the battle. To be honest, I thought he'd die. But he didn't so I gave him house-room ... and now the arrangement seems to have become permanent.' For no apparent reason, he suddenly found himself thinking about Lydia Neville and wondering whether he'd return to London to find her betrothed to Nick. Then, shrugging aside the peculiar feeling the notion produced, added, 'He's the same age as Toby and has also struck up a friendship with Samuel Radford – which has its awkward moments.'

'I can imagine,' said Gabriel dryly.

'How *are* Sam and Bryony?' asked Phoebe. 'I haven't heard anything since she wrote to tell me about the baby.'

'I haven't seen a great deal of Samuel recently but Nick assures me that all three of them are well.' Forgetting the need for caution, Eden grinned at her across the table. 'Inevitably, they named the little boy John.'

Phoebe met that smile head-on and waited for the *coup de foudre*. It didn't come. All she saw was an attractive man with a spectacular smile. Dizzy with relief, she smiled back and said, 'I know. I'm only surprised they didn't go the whole way and call him John Free-born Radford.'

'Actually, I believe Sam did suggest that. Fortunately, however, Bryony decided that a line had to be drawn somewhere.'

* * *

On the following morning, Eden took his leave of Venetia, Rosie and the twins, then set about preparing his horse for departure. Pulling Lambert's letter from his saddle-bag, he handed it to Gabriel, saying, 'Read that before you make your final decision. I imagine it's pretty much what he told me to tell you.'

'Which was what?'

'That if you believe things are going wrong at Westminster, you won't put them right by staying in Yorkshire.'

'Profound.'

'But true,' countered Eden, swinging up into the saddle. 'I don't know what to expect in Scotland – whether Monck will want me on strength and, if he does, for how long. But if I'm heading south again by the beginning of August, would it be all right if I made a return visit?'

'To get my answer?'

'Well, there is that. But I was mostly thinking of trying to achieve *real* uncle status by bringing Rosie and the boys a present or two. What do you think?'

'I think you'd be better employed achieving real *father* status,' retorted Gabriel sardonically. 'But, as ever, the choice is yours.'

TWO

Colonel Maxwell caught up with the supply train at Catterick, just as it was settling down for the night.

'Any problems?' he asked Major Moulton.

'A wheel broke on one of the gunpowder carts which meant unloading the damned thing while it was repaired. It cost us a little time but nothing untoward. Aside from that, Foster reckons he has a fever and Beckett is complaining of boils on his backside.' Ned grinned suddenly. 'The surgeon gave Foster a powder which I think might have been an emetic; as for Beckett, I told him his arse would be less sore if he spent less time sitting on it and ordered him to spend a few days marching with the Foot. He was cured in no time. Miraculous, really.'

'So it would seem,' agreed Eden, amused. 'But the surgeon sounds a fellow to avoid.'

'As to that, I may have dropped a word in his ear.' Ned paused and then said, 'How was Colonel Brandon? Is he going to stand in the elections?'

'He's well and happy. For the rest, he says not but I'm hoping he'll change his mind. Time will tell, I suppose.'

Through the first days of June, the road to Scotland stretched endlessly ahead of them.

By starting each day's march at first light and continuing until an hour before dark, they usually managed an average of thirty miles, barring accidents. After Catterick, they exchanged the Great North Road for the old Roman one which led them eventually to Bowes. Then Eden took them over the Stainmore Pass to Brough ... a road he'd once travelled in the other direction during the second war in '48. The weather had been appalling, he recalled; he, Gabriel and the Army had slogged through mud virtually the whole way. This time the sun shone and he was able to appreciate the expanse of sky above a vast, bleak landscape populated only by sheep and the occasional croft.

From Brough, the column turned towards Appleby, then on to Penrith and finally, Carlisle. By this time, they had been on the road for twelve days and Colonel Maxwell calculated that, even without further delays, it would be another four before they reached Stirling.

Ecclefechan fell away behind them, then Locherbie and the heights of Beattock Summit. By the time they arrived in Lanark at around noon on June 7th everyone was tired, filthy and inclined to be snappish. Eden conferred briefly with Ned Moulton and then decreed a two day halt in order to rest the men and put a bit of spit and polish on their collective appearance. He had the junior officers find as many billets as possible at inns and private houses, left Major Moulton the task of getting the carts under cover and drawing up the usual roster of guard duty and, after taking a much needed bath, settled down to check the troop lists and inventories. Since the supplies had been guarded night and day throughout the march and couldn't be ticketed until they arrived at their final destination, he had to trust that nothing had been tampered with and that the original inventories had been correct. As to personnel, he'd got to Lanark without losing any of his forty troopers or their officers or any civilians – which was an achievement in itself.

Next morning, leaving Ned in charge, he rode to Colonel Lilburne's nearest lowland garrison at Glasgow in order to discover Monck's current whereabouts. Lambert had said he'd find the General at Stirling but that had been two weeks ago so it was logical to assume he'd moved on since then.

'Stirling?' said Lilburne with a sort of weary irritability. 'No. He's settled at Perth. You'll do it in a couple of days.' He paused and then, as if unable to help himself, 'I suppose you've brought him all the things I've been demanding for the last year?'

'I would think so.'

'Including money to pay the men?'

'Yes.'

'God damn,' breathed Lilburne bitterly. 'They left me with nothing yet still expected me to crush a rebellion in the north whilst keeping the lowlands secure. But Monck gets the whole weight of Westminster thrown behind him as soon as he lifts a finger.'

'I understood that the General was appointed at your suggestion,' said Eden mildly.

'He was.' The Colonel gave a brief, unamused laugh. 'Don't mind me. I'll just be glad to get the hell out of this benighted country. That is, assuming they'll let me.'

* * *

The final leg of their journey was accomplished on June 12th in driving rain. A few miles from their destination, Major Moulton paused to shake the drips from his hat and said, 'You know Monck, don't you?'

'I met him at Dunbar,' agreed Eden. 'It was after you were shipped out. But there was a lot going on at the time, so I doubt he'll remember me.'

'He's got a sound reputation. Deserved, do you think?'

'Yes. He got a wealth of experience abroad and stayed loyal to the King right through the first war even though it put him in the Tower. Then he came over to us and served in Ireland – which as we all know, is the graveyard of reputations. He fought with distinction through the Worcester campaign, then at sea against the Dutch. There can't be many officers with that kind of career history.' Eden grinned suddenly. 'Do you know what the Navy boys say of him?' And when Ned shook his head, 'They say that, in moments of crisis, he's likely to shout *Wheel right!* instead of *Hard to starboard!* In a way, that's rather endearing.'

When Colonel Maxwell finally stood before the General to make his report, the word 'endearing' seemed a lot less appropriate. In his mid-forties, Monck had a brusque, slightly gruff manner and plainly had little time for the usual courtesies. Eden didn't object to this. He was more than happy to discharge his mission with the least possible fuss. He did, however, take the time to speak his mind on the subject of Foster, Beckett and the rest.

Monck grunted an acknowledgement and then said, 'I'll send them to Colonel Morgan. If he can't do something with them, no one can. Meantime, what were Major-General Lambert's orders with regard to yourself and the men you've brought with you?'

'The troopers are to be added to your strength, sir. Major Moulton and I have discretionary leave and will also be happy to serve if you have a use for us.'

'I've a use for every man I can scrounge. Lord Glencairn is trying to gain ground in the western highlands and I've to rely on Argyll keeping him out; and General Middleton's somewhere near Loch Duich with between three and four thousand men. I've sent one of my officers to bring reinforcements from Ireland but I've no notion when they'll arrive. As to yourself ... aren't you the fellow who led the advance across the Brox Burn at Dunbar?'

Eden inclined his head. 'Yes, sir. I'm surprised you remember.'

'I remember it being a bastard of a job and Lambert singing your praises afterwards – so I'll be happy to have you on my staff, Colonel – even temporarily.'

* * *

Having sent Major Moulton to engage whatever lodgings he could find, Colonel Maxwell introduced himself to the other staff officers and listened while they explained their current problems. These, since Eden had fought in Scotland before, were by no means unfamiliar. The geography of the north, being almost solely composed of mountains, glens and lochs, made it ideal terrain for a small force of highlanders to make a lightning strike, vanish into the mist and then re-appear in the place least expected.

'For the moment, Glencairn's stuck near Dumbarton,' said someone gloomily, 'but Middleton's got Colonel Morgan running hither and yon like a chicken without its head. And when the General moves north, I reckon we'll all be doing the same.'

Eden relayed all this to Ned Moulton over supper in a noisy tavern on the High Street. They were just about to leave when a young officer strode in and, having sent a searching glance around the taproom, descended on their table saying, 'I'm looking for a Colonel Maxwell. Would that be you, sir?'

Nearby, in a shadowy corner, a man lifted his head and then sat very still.

'It would. What do you need, Captain?'

The fellow saluted and held out a sealed note.

'Message for you, Colonel Maxwell, sir. From the General.'

'Thank you.' Eden took the note and then, when the young man showed no sign of leaving, said, 'Was there anything else?'

'Wondered if you wanted to send a reply, sir.'

Eden sighed, broke the seal and scanned the brief contents. 'No reply,' he murmured. And to Ned, as the messenger took his leave, 'General Monck has suggested we spend tomorrow familiarising ourselves with the immediate area.'

'That's thoughtful of him. After nearly three weeks on the road, I was worried we wouldn't find anything to do once we got here.'

* * *

The two of them strolled to their lodgings, engaging in desultory conversation and had been back in their rooms for no longer than it took for Eden to discard his hat, sword and coat when there was a knock at the outer door. A few minutes later, Ned Moulton stuck his head into his Colonel's chamber and said, 'There's a fellow outside who insists on speaking to you. He says he has information that won't wait.'

'Has he given you a name?'

'No. He's the shy sort.'

Yawning, Eden reluctantly pulled his coat back on.

'All right. But if he's keeping me from my bed to no useful purpose, I may well kick him down the stairs.'

'Do you want me to stay within call?'

'No. If it comes to a fight, you'll hear it well enough. And if he pulls out a pistol and shoots me, it will be too late anyway. Just let the fellow in so I can get it over with.'

The man who presently appeared wraith-like on the threshold to close the door silently behind him wore a misshapen hat and was wrapped in an exceedingly shabby cloak. This, aside from his height, was all that could be seen of him.

For a handful of seconds, he surveyed Eden from beneath the brim of his hat and then said, 'Colonel Maxwell?'

'Yes. And you are?'

'Forgive me ... but I'd like to be sure exactly who I'm speaking to.' The voice was both beautifully-modulated and cultured. 'You are Colonel Eden Maxwell, originally from Oxfordshire?'

'Yes! What is this about? And who the hell are you?'

By way of answer, his visitor removed both hat and cloak to reveal long fair hair and clothes that, though serviceable and not new, were far from shabby. Finally he said, 'I have some news that may interest you. Your brother-in-law is about to become a father.'

Not surprisingly, it took Eden a moment to work this out. If Amy was pregnant and wanted him to know – which was unlikely – her husband could walk round to Cheapside and tell him; and this fellow was hardly likely to be bringing him news of this sort from either Ralph Cochrane or Luciano del Santi … which meant that it had to be …

'*Francis?*'

'Yes. I think he'd have liked you to stand sponsor to the child … but with him in Paris and you here, he'll probably have to make do with me.'

This was getting more peculiar by the minute.

'Who are you?' asked Eden again, just as the answer hit him. 'Oh God. *Colonel Peverell?*'

Ashley grinned and strolled forward, hand outstretched.

'Indeed. It's a pleasure to meet you, Colonel. Not something I expected or intended, of course – but when I heard your name mentioned, it seemed a pity to waste the opportunity.' And when Eden accepted his hand, 'The information you sent saved the King's life – and if he's ever restored to his throne, I'll ensure that he's made aware of it. But for now, since Charles is in no position to do it himself, I'd like to thank you on his behalf.'

Eden was still trying to come to terms with the fact that one of Charles Stuart's most trusted agents was wandering around loose in Perth, roughly three miles from Monck's headquarters. He said, 'Since you aren't here to break the news of Francis's impending fatherhood, what exactly *are* you doing?'

'You don't honestly expect me to answer that, do you?' returned Ashley with a glimmer of humour. 'Unless, of course, you plan to arrest me?'

'If anyone finds you here, I won't have a choice. *Is* anyone likely to do that?'

'Perish the thought. I'm better than that.'

'Modest too, I see.' Eden gave a sudden choke of laughter. 'This is one hell of a situation. Still, since we *are* both here you may as well sit down and take some ale.'

'Thank you. I'd be delighted.' Ashley took a chair near the empty hearth and said, 'If it helps, I'm willing to admit that I'm not doing anything that need concern you. His Majesty wants first-hand intelligence on Middleton's progress and evaluation of his chances of success. I'm here to provide it and deliver a few letters. That's all.'

'Really.' Eden handed his visitor a tankard of ale. 'So you're not passing information to General Middleton about Monck's numbers and movements?'

'No. He doesn't need me. The highlanders have spies in places that might surprise you.'

'Have they indeed? And how *do* you rate their chance of success?'

'The same as you, I imagine,' came the suddenly impatient reply. 'It's only a matter of time, after all.'

'That would be my view.' Eden sat down on the other side of the hearth and said gently, 'Where *is* Middleton?'

And, equally gently, Ashley said, 'I have no idea.'

'Clearly that isn't true.'

'On the contrary, it's perfectly true.' Amusement gleamed in the green eyes. 'I know where he was three days ago. But that wouldn't help you – even if I was prepared to tell you.'

'Which, of course, you're not.'

'No.' Colonel Peverell surveyed him reflectively for a moment and then said, 'Perhaps we should confine ourselves to less fraught topics. Francis is well, happy and his work continues to be successful. The baby is due in August and though Pauline is still capable of scaring the hell out of any sane man, Francis adores her for it. And now it's your turn. How is Nicholas?'

'Developing an interest in a widow who's making it her mission to provide work for disabled ex-soldiers,' replied Eden tersely.

The tone caused Ashley to shoot him an interested look but he said merely, 'Yes. That would appeal to Nick. He's always had a penchant for defending the weak. And presumably this is keeping him out of other sorts of trouble?'

'Yes – though I had concerns on that front for a time. Speaking of which – I take it you know about this recent plot to murder Cromwell?'

Colonel Peverell's mouth tightened.

'Yes. And in case you've been wondering, Charles flatly refused to sanction it and both he and Hyde are bloody furious that the Gerard faction went ahead anyway. The whole affair caused a massive argument between Charles and the Queen Dowager as well as deepening the rift between him and Rupert.'

'And the proclamation offering a reward to any who'd do the deed?'

'Edward Herbert. The man's an idiot. But he's shot his last bolt. Charles demanded that he render up the Great Seal and then told him to pack his bags.'

'Oh? Well, better late than never I suppose. He and the Gerards have certainly conjured up a storm. By the time I left London, we had at least a hundred men in custody and more still being arrested.'

'Including Richard Wyllis and Ned Villiers,' nodded Ashley. 'Yes. I heard.'

Eden said slowly, 'They wouldn't have had anything to do with the Gerard conspiracy?'

'Absolutely not.'

'What makes you so sure?'

'They're in Hyde's camp, not the Queen's. And Villiers isn't stupid.'

To give himself time, Eden reached for the ale and re-filled both their tankards.

'There are rumours of a highly secret elite committee having been formed by Hyde to oversee future conspiracies.'

'Really?' Ashley lounged easily in his chair. 'But there are rumours on every street corner.'

'So there are. But Villiers's name came up in connection with this one.'

'Hence his arrest?'

'That would be my guess.'

There was a long silence as each waited for the other to speak. Finally, Ashley said, 'This elite group wouldn't be very secret if every Tom, Dick and Harry knew of it, now would it?'

'No. But you aren't every Tom, Dick or Harry, are you?'

'Perhaps not.' The lash-shaded eyes narrowed slightly. 'What is it you want, Colonel? You know better than to expect me to give you privileged information – even supposing that I had it. So are you by any chance delivering a warning?'

'Now why on earth should you think that?' asked Eden smoothly. 'Indeed, if you'll pardon me for quoting your own words – perish the thought.'

Without any warning at all, Ashley suddenly grinned at him.

'Of course. My imagination must be running away with me.' He paused and then, with a touch of regret, added, 'I've enjoyed meeting you, Colonel – but I should go.'

'Probably. But, before you do ... tell me about Celia.'

'Ah.' The grin faded. 'You mean, did she fall or was she pushed?'

'That's exactly what I mean. Well?'

'I questioned everyone in the house at the time and could find no proof either way. My own opinion, for what it's worth, is that she fell and Verney didn't react quickly enough to save her. Read whatever you will into that. But if there had been a shred of evidence to suggest murder, you may be sure Francis wouldn't have let it lie.'

'No.' Eden's expression remained carefully enigmatic. 'No. I suppose not.' He allowed silence to linger for a few moments and then, on a completely different tack, said, 'And Honfleur? I take it that there actually *was* an attack?'

'There was. But sadly for the would-be assassins, not on the King and his brother.'

'Ah. Who took their places?'

'A French madman you're unlikely to have heard of ... and Francis.'

'*Francis?*' Eden gave a choke of incredulous laughter. 'Seriously?'

'Unlikely as it may sound, yes. But perhaps I'd better start at the beginning?'

'Do. This is starting to sound better than a play.'

THREE

On the day Colonel Maxwell left London, a sergeant and two troopers appeared on Mistress Neville's doorstep. Since Lydia was out, it was left to Margaret – who didn't appreciate the neighbours seeing soldiers at her door – to give them short shrift.

'Sir Aubrey isn't here – neither do I have any idea where he might be. You had best call again when his sister is at home. Good day.'

And she shut the door in their faces.

When Lydia returned, however, she showed no such reticence.

'Why has your brother got soldiers looking for him?' she demanded. 'Got himself mixed up in this plot to murder Cromwell, has he?'

Something curdled in Lydia's stomach but she managed a careless smile.

'No – though one of the officers warned me that this might happen. It seems Aubrey is acquainted with a man who has been arrested – which is enough, at present, to make the authorities want to question him.'

'You know one of the Army officers?'

'Yes. Moderately well, as it happens.'

'How come? And who is he?'

Margaret's suspiciously belligerent manner was beginning to grate but Lydia held on to both her easy tone and the recollection of Eden Maxwell saying he couldn't afford for his name to be linked with Aubrey's disappearance.

'He's a Colonel,' she sighed. 'And as to how I met him ... how do you think? Some of his old troopers work in Duck Lane and he occasionally passes the time of day with them.'

Margaret's expression was frankly scathing but she abandoned this tack in favour of another.

'Well, if we're to have soldiers knocking at the door, I'd like to know why Sir Aubrey isn't here to speak for himself. And *don't* give me that faradiddle about him visiting friends in the country because I don't believe a word of it.'

'That's up to you, Margaret. But as to the soldiers ... I'll go to Westminster tomorrow and straighten things out. And now, if you'll excuse me, I'd like to change my dress.'

As it turned out, the troopers came back an hour later. Her hands not quite steady and feeling slightly sick, Lydia pinned a smile on her face and ushered them into the back parlour. Then, since she was about to embark on a tissue of lies, she decided to let them think she was completely feather-brained and immediately launched into a long and extremely muddled speech in which Aubrey's whereabouts became inextricably entangled with the household accounts.

When she finally stopped talking, the sergeant in charge subjected her to a gimlet stare.

'Let me get this right, Mistress. You're saying your brother's been in the country for near on two weeks, visiting his young lady's family?'

'Yes. He left on a Saturday ... or it might have been a Sunday. No – it was *definitely* a Saturday because I remember I was adding up the bill for coal and it wouldn't come out right and of course I wouldn't have been doing that on a Sunday, would I? And that's when Aubrey told me all about Isabel and how her family wouldn't allow a betrothal until he'd met her brothers and uncles and her grandfather – which I *must* say I think is very small-minded of them. After all, my brother is a *baronet*. But they're a large family and quite wealthy and they live in Kent and Isabel's the only girl so naturally --'

'Where in Kent?' asked the sergeant.

'What? Oh dear. I'm not sure ... that is, Aubrey wrote it down for me and said to be careful not to lose it. Only somehow it got muddled with the bills and though I *know* it's here somewhere, I haven't been able to find it and Aubrey will be so *cross*. He's always telling me to be more careful and I *try*. I really do. Only there were bills we'd paid and bills we hadn't and I got confused. I was sure I'd paid the butcher but it turned out that I hadn't and he came to the door and was *most* unpleasant. So --'

Once again, the sergeant stopped the flow.

'Perhaps you could try *remembering* where Sir Aubrey said he was going.'

'Oh! Well, yes ... I suppose I could try.' Lydia screwed up her face in extreme and excruciating concentration. 'It may have begun with S. Er ... Sevenoaks? No. That's not it. Wait. Let me think.'

'Strood?' offered one of the troopers helpfully. 'Sittingbourne?'

She beamed at him. 'Yes! How clever of you!'

'Which?' asked the sergeant, testily. 'Strood or Sittingbourne?'

'I – I don't know. I'm so sorry.' Lydia wrung her hands. 'I'd help you if I could. Truly, I would. But I have the wretchedest memory. My l-late husband used to say I must have the worst memory in the world.' She whipped out a handkerchief and dabbed at her eyes. 'It m-made him laugh. But Aubrey doesn't laugh. He just g-gets annoyed.'

The sergeant's expression told her that Aubrey had his sympathy. He said, 'Is there anyone else who might know where your brother is?'

'No! Good *heavens*, no.' Lydia emerged from her handkerchief looking positively aghast. 'He had to keep his attachment secret or there'd have been no peace in the house. My step-daughter-in-law is the most *formidable* woman and she's set her heart on Aubrey marrying her eldest girl – for the title, you know. So --'

Seeing that another involved and unhelpful speech was forthcoming and recognising that he was getting precisely nowhere, the sergeant shoved his notes into the breast of his coat and said, 'Very well, Mistress Neville. We'll leave this for now. But if your brother returns or you remember where he's gone, you should let us know immediately.'

'Yes. Oh yes. Of course. Except that I'll have to tell Aubrey how silly I've been and he'll give me *such* a lecture – which I know is quite my own fault, of course! But still ...'

Lydia talked all the way to the door and watched them make a thankful escape.

Then she dropped exhaustedly on to a chair and stared desperately at the ceiling.

* * *

Next day she managed to have a brief, private conversation with Nicholas which ended with him saying, 'You did well and it might serve. But take Eden's advice and don't go anywhere near Shoreditch. Your brother is perfectly safe and the Morrells have made him very welcome.'

'So I gather from his last note. He certainly doesn't seem in any hurry to come home,' replied Lydia a shade tartly. 'And who exactly *are* these Morrells? All I've gleaned so far is that Mr Morrell is an armourer and that Colonel Maxwell apparently had no qualms about demanding a huge favour of him.'

'Eden knows he can rely on Jack. As to why your brother's enjoying his stay ... it might have something to do with Verity.' He grinned a trifle sheepishly. 'She's no relation to the Morrells but they took her in at the same time and in rather the same way Eden did me. She's twenty years old now and for a while, I think she hoped that she and I might ... you know.'

'But you won't.'

'No. She's a very sweet girl but she's like a sister.'

Lydia eyed him a shade caustically.

'I see. Well, hoping Aubrey may eclipse you is one thing; hoping he'll do more than flirt is quite another. I trust you've thought of that? Because if not – and however much it eases *your* mind – you are doing the poor girl an ill turn.'

* * *

At home, Cousin Geoffrey continued to call every other day and started to bring small gifts. Lydia avoided him as often as she could but found that the opportunities to do so were gradually shrinking. She realised that, in a few short weeks, she would be out of full mourning and when that happened, Geoffrey would waste no time in declaring himself. So she treated him with a chilly formality that would have had most men running for the hills and watched in despair when it simply bounced off the Reverend's thick skin.

Mercifully, no more troopers arrived in search of Aubrey and the unrest in the streets started to die down allowing Lydia to hope that the worst was over. Then, during the first week in June, Colonel Gerard and two other men she'd never heard of were put on trial for their part in the plot. Lydia felt slightly sick and was more than ever grateful to Colonel Maxwell for saving Aubrey from a similar fate.

A few days later, while she was enduring yet another irritating half-hour with Cousin Geoffrey, a tap at the door heralded Nancy who said, 'Beg pardon, Mistress Neville – but Sir Ellis Brandon has called. I've told him Sir Aubrey's from home and you have company but he's still hoping you'll receive him. What shall I say?'

For a second, Lydia merely stared at her.

Ellis Brandon? What on earth can he want? Please God let him not be looking for Aubrey. On the other hand, anything's better than listening to another twenty minutes of yesterday's sermon.

'Show him in, Nancy. Reverend Neville won't mind – will you Cousin?'

'No.' Geoffrey didn't sound very certain. 'No. Not at all.'

Nancy disappeared and Lydia took the opportunity to say quickly, 'He will be sorry to miss Aubrey, I'm sure. But I had rather not discuss my brother's business if it can be avoided.'

'As is entirely proper. And you need have no fears on *my* account, I can assure you.'

Lydia rewarded him with a cool smile, then rose to greet a man she didn't particularly like but intended to make the best use of.

'Sir Ellis – what an unexpected pleasure.'

Ellis took her hand and bowed over it with consummate grace.

'That is most kind, Mistress Neville – and more than I deserve. Had affairs not kept me from London these last two months, I would naturally have called before. But I must beg pardon for intruding upon you when you already have a visitor.'

Lydia retrieved her hand despite his apparent desire to hold on to it.

'That's not necessary, sir. Reverend Neville is family. Cousin Geoffrey ... allow me to introduce Sir Ellis Brandon.'

She'd very nearly said *only* family and knew that her tone implied it. She also noticed that Geoffrey was looking a little less self-satisfied – for which the reason was obvious. Elegant in well-cut claret broadcloth, his lovelocks curled and the inevitable ear-ring glinting in one ear, Ellis Brandon was the epitome of good looks and sophistication. She wondered if he was still looking to marry money and decided that, if his clothing was anything to go by, he probably was. If his visit today was less idle than it seemed, it was likely the last couple of months had failed to provide the kind of bride he needed ... and that being so, he must have come to the conclusion that the ordinary little widow would just have to do.

Someone else who's going to be disappointed, she thought.

Ellis acknowledged the introduction to Geoffrey and then made the mistake of asking about his parish. This enabled Geoffrey to pontificate at length on his many responsibilities, his needy parishioners and, eventually, the piety, virtue and generosity of his favourite patron. It was the kind of pompous speech Lydia had heard a hundred times and always found impossible to reply to. Sir Ellis apparently had no such problem.

'Lizzie Aylesbury?' he drawled. 'Really? Well, admittedly I haven't met her for a while. But I don't recall her being quite the paragon you describe, Reverend. Quite the opposite in fact.'

Oh Lord, thought Lydia, torn between terror and glee as a tide of red suffused the Reverend's face. *Geoffrey's going to have an apoplexy.*

Mercifully, he didn't. He stood up, every line of his body radiating furious disgust and delivered a sermon on vile and lewd insinuations in general and Sir Ellis's style of conversation in particular. Finally, spurred on by the mocking curl to Sir Ellis's mouth, he said, 'Cousin Lydia, I am alarmed that you should allow this – this *gentleman* into your presence. Alarmed and displeased. Indeed, I see no alternative but show him the door.'

Realising it was time to enter the fray, Lydia also rose and met his angry gaze with a firm one of her own. 'You take too much upon yourself, Geoffrey. This is not your house.'

'I am aware of that. But in the absence of your brother or my cousin, it is incumbent upon me to protect both your reputation and --'

'My reputation requires no protection and is, in any case, no concern of yours. Neither do you have the right to dictate which visitors I should receive. So let us put the subject aside - before you are left with no alternative but to go home.'

'And leave you alone with this – this --' Words failed him and he sat down with a bump. 'Never!'

'That's a pity,' murmured Ellis, not quite beneath his breath.

Lydia impaled him on a look that very clearly said, *Behave or go*. Ellis grinned and subsided. Nodding, Lydia resumed her seat and, as if nothing untoward had occurred, said composedly, 'They say that the Protector has doubled his guard and keeps a weapon at his side at all times. Do you think his life is really under threat?'

'All good Christians should pray that it is not,' said Geoffrey piously.

'Pray, by all means,' remarked Ellis. 'But these days, Cromwell has more enemies than friends … and those enemies aren't all Royalists. If I was him, I'd be worried too.'

* * *

A week later, four men sat in the Morrells' parlour in Shoreditch while in the next room, two women entertained the children and a third informed her cook that there would be three extra guests for supper.

'They can't *do* that!' said Aubrey Durand, aghast. 'Gerard doesn't deserve it. None of them do.'

'What they deserve is beside the point,' replied Samuel Radford flatly.

'But it wasn't even Gerard's idea! The whole plot was made by Thomas Henshaw.'

'Who would appear to have made himself scarce,' observed Jack Morrell, reaching for the ale jug.

'Yes. He would do, damn it,' said Aubrey bitterly. 'But it was he and Lord Gerard who pushed the scheme forward. John was never comfortable about going ahead with something the King hadn't sanctioned and wouldn't have done so if others hadn't chivvied him into it.'

Samuel eyed the other man with world-weary resignation.

'None of that matters. From the moment Thurloe learned of a credible plot to kill Cromwell, examples were always going to be made. That much was clear from the outset – and it's why they set up a special High Court of Justice. Cromwell wanted to be sure of the verdict.'

'Clearly,' said Nicholas Austin. 'But why did he think he wouldn't get it from a jury?'

'If a jury wouldn't convict Free-born John, there was no guarantee it would convict the members of a conspiracy that most people believe didn't happen. Cromwell didn't intend to take that risk and a High Court of Justice ensured the result.' Samuel paused and then added scathingly, 'It's iniquitous, of course. Everybody has a right to trial by jury under Magna Carta.'

'Clearly, Cromwell isn't letting that fact bother him,' remarked Nicholas.

'Neither that nor a good many other things. He's bending the law to suit his own ends. And when it won't bend, he simply ignores it. People are detained without trial virtually every day. Since they moved Free-born John to Jersey, I myself have been hauled in twice because I dared speak my mind in the editorial column of *The Moderate*. Nothing and nobody is allowed to stand in his way.'

'Parliament will,' said Jack, sitting back down after re-filling everyone's tankard. 'It must.'

'The *Instrument of Government* stipulates that Parliament must sit for five months out of every thirty-six,' replied Samuel impatiently. 'The way this trial has been handled shows fairly conclusively what's likely to happen the rest of the time.'

Aubrey stood up and swung away towards the window.

'Surely something can be done? Something to stop the executions?'

'No. If there was, I and others of like mind would be doing it.'

'But if the assassination scheme wasn't hatched by Gerard or the other two,' asked Nicholas reasonably, 'why are they the ones who are being made to pay?'

'That's what I'd like to know,' said Aubrey between his teeth.

'Did *nobody* read my report in the newspaper?' asked Samuel with a hint of annoyance.

'We all did,' soothed Jack. 'But we'd like the concluding paragraph you *didn't* write.'

Mr Radford sighed and set down his tankard.

'All right. Somerset Fox admitted his guilt on the first time of asking. In the end, that may save his neck – though there's been no word of that yet. Gerard and Vowell continued denying all knowledge – but their names came up too often to be ignored. Mostly, they came up in the evidence supplied by Charles Gerard.'

Nicholas sat up, eyes widening in shock.

'He gave witness against his own brother? Hell. What sort of man *is* he?'

'Seventeen years old and scared. I doubt he wanted to spill his guts – but presumably someone put the fear of God into him until he did,' shrugged Samuel. 'He's in the Tower now, along with a handful of others. But Cromwell wants to send a clear warning … so Fox and Vowell will hang and Gerard has been granted permission to die by the axe. His execution is to take place on July 10th.'

'It isn't right,' muttered Aubrey looking a little sick. 'None of us fired a shot.'

'But you meant to – and that's all Cromwell cares about,' remarked Nicholas. 'So just be grateful Eden got you out of the way or you might be sharing their fate.'

It was perhaps fortunate that Annis Morrell chose that moment to put her head around the door to say, 'If the four of you have finished putting the world to rights, we'd like to serve supper.'

Jack grinned at her. 'Excellent.'

'No,' she said, 'it isn't. Johnny is likely to put somebody's eye out with that dratted wooden sword you made him and Bryony can't get the baby to settle because he wants his father. As for you two …' She eyed Nicholas and Aubrey with mock severity. 'If you expect to eat, you can go and help Verity with the table.'

All four gentlemen rose as one. Despite being softly spoken and perpetually unruffled, when Annis gave an order, everyone obeyed instantly. Jack walked off to part his son from the favourite toy which he'd repeatedly been told not to brandish inside the house and Samuel went to relieve his wife of their nine-month-old baby – who instantly giggled and grabbed at his father's nose. Nicholas let Aubrey precede him and thus reach Verity first; and, not for the first time, Aubrey saw the girl's eyes slide over him to land on the other man.

But later that night when Aubrey found he couldn't sleep it wasn't Verity's glossy curls and heart-shaped face that kept him awake – nor even the depressing knowledge that she wanted Nicholas, not him. It was the notion that he'd let his friends down ... that he was as big a rat as Henshaw. And when nothing he told himself by way of comfort made him feel any better, he decided that – since he'd escaped with his own life – the least he could do was to bear witness to John Gerard losing his.

* * *

When she learned that Gerard and the others had been condemned to death, Lydia was thankful that Aubrey seemed content to remain in Shoreditch. From his rare scribbled notes, she got the impression that he was perfectly happy there. Mr Morell was educating him in the basic rudiments of sword-making, his wife kept a very good table and, despite being a Leveller, the editor of *The Moderate* was surprisingly good company. But if Aubrey was also enjoying a flirtation with Mistress Verity, he made no mention of it.

Aside from a few rude words being daubed on the gate, all remained quiet in Duck Lane and no more whores sought work in Strand Alley. But at home, Lydia found herself under hot pursuit from Ellis Brandon – which had the effect of forcing Cousin Geoffrey to compete. At times, this was funny; at others, it was just downright irritating. Margaret, of course, took Sir Ellis in profound dislike and tried, as Geoffrey had done, to make Lydia forbid him to visit.

'He's a Godless fribble,' she snapped. 'And he's only after your money.'

'Is he?' said Lydia, as if she didn't know. 'But then, so is Geoffrey. And even *you'd* have to agree that Sir Ellis is much better looking.'

Margaret turned scarlet and flounced off without a word.

* * *

Another week drifted by. From time to time and more often than was sensible, Lydia found herself wondering where Colonel Maxwell was and what he was doing. Nicholas said he and Tobias had heard nothing and didn't expect to.

'Quite apart from the Scottish rising, he's calling on his former Colonel in Yorkshire. And then, on the way back, Toby hopes he'll visit the family in Oxfordshire. He hasn't seen his children for months.'

'Children?' echoed Lydia weakly. 'Oh. I didn't realise. That is – you told me that his wife was dead but I didn't think …' She stopped and managed a careless shrug. 'Stupid of me, I suppose. But if the Colonel is at home so rarely, who takes care of the children?'

'Their grandmother – together with Toby's twin sister and her husband.' As when they'd spoken of Celia, a knowing glint appeared in Nicholas's eyes. 'The boy is fourteen and the girl, some four years younger I think. Of course, I've never met them but Toby visits pretty regularly.' He hesitated and then added, 'You'd be wise not to ask Eden about them, though. If you catch him at the wrong moment, he won't respond well to it.'

'Really?' She stared at him, nonplussed. 'Why not?'

'There are … reasons. And although Eden is one of the best fellows I ever met, he has depths that are best left undisturbed.'

* * *

On a day at the end of the month, Lydia returned home from an afternoon spent in Strand Alley to find Nancy lying in wait for her in the hall.

'There's a fellow here to see you, Miss Lydia,' she whispered. 'Not that Sir Ellis – *another* one. And he's *gorgeous*. Tall and dark-haired, with beautiful clothes and *lovely* manners.'

Lydia grinned but said merely, 'His name?'

'Mr Wakefield.'

'Wakefield?' She thought for a moment, then shook her head. 'I don't know him.'

'He said you wouldn't. But Janet and Kitty were here when he arrived and now they've got him trapped in the parlour.'

'Oh God. I'd better go in, then.'

Nancy looked disapproving.

'Yes. But don't you think you should change your gown first?'

'Not if the gorgeous Mr Wakefield isn't to run screaming from the house before I get to meet him.'

And she walked in to the parlour.

The gentleman who immediately rose to greet her was everything Nancy had said. Tall and perfectly proportioned with long dark hair and impossibly blue eyes, he made a graceful bow and said, 'Mistress Neville? I hope you'll forgive me for taking the liberty of calling on you despite the fact that we've never previously met. But my father was a long-standing friend of your late husband and I know he would have wished me to pay my respects and offer our family's condolences on your sad loss.'

'That is most civil of you ... Mr Wakefield, I believe?'

He inclined his head but before he could speak, Janet said, 'Mr Wakefield's brother is a viscount, Lydia – not a paltry baronet, like *your* brother.'

'Thank you for pointing that out, Janet.'

'Well, it's true,' she insisted. 'A viscount is *proper* nobility.'

'I don't see why you're getting so fussy all of a sudden' objected Kitty. 'You'd be happy enough if Aubrey looked your way – not that he's ever likely to.'

'Nor yours, either,' retorted Janet heatedly. 'And anyway, I --'

'That's enough,' interposed Lydia quietly. 'I believe we can dispense with your presence. Both of you.'

'Why?' demanded Kitty. 'We can stay if we want to.'

'And continue making an exhibition of yourselves? I don't think so. I doubt if Mr Wakefield wants to listen to your squabbles any more than I do. And since your manners belong in the nursery, I suggest you take them there.'

Mr Wakefield looked down at his hands, a small smile curling his mouth.

Her face rather red, Janet said, 'You can't talk to us like that.'

'Actually,' replied Lydia, 'I can. Now please remove yourselves and leave the adults in peace.'

Just for a second, she thought they were going to defy her. Then, in a manner reminiscent of their mother, both girls stormed from the room, slamming the door behind them.

Lydia looked across at her guest and, inviting him to sit with a small gesture of one hand, said, 'I'd like to say they don't always behave like that – but I'd be lying.'

The gentleman waited until she was seated before taking the chair she'd indicated.

'I imagine that is extremely wearing.'

'That's putting it mildly,' she agreed. 'Moreover, if their mother had been here we'd never have got rid of them. But now that we *have* ... you said that Stephen knew your father?'

'Actually, he knew both my parents. I believe he had business dealings with my father from time to time – though I'm not entirely sure about the nature of them. And recently I discovered that he knew my mother when she was a young woman, more than thirty years ago.' He paused briefly and added, 'Ah. I should perhaps have mentioned that, like your husband, both of my parents are also deceased. Father passed away almost two years ago and Mother followed him just before Christmas.'

'I'm sorry,' said Lydia automatically. A small frown creased her brow. 'Forgive me but I'm a little confused. Stephen died last July. So why --?'

'Why wait till now? You might call it a coincidence. My brother, Edmund – the Viscount, you know?' He paused to give her a swift, mischievous grin. 'Well, having little interest in such things, he left me to sort through our parents' letters and papers – of which there are a great many. Stephen Neville's name appeared often enough for me to realise that he must, at one time, have been a close family friend. I decided I'd like to meet him – only then, on making enquiries, I learned of his death.' He looked across at her, his deep blue eyes somewhat anxious. 'I hope I haven't caused any offence or distress. If you'd rather I hadn't come, you have only to say and I'll leave immediately.'

'Please don't. It was a kind thought and I appreciate you taking the trouble. It's just that I don't recall the name Wakefield featuring in any of Stephen's paperwork and I thought I'd been through all of it quite carefully.'

He shook his head.

'Your husband would have referred to my father by his title.'

'Which was what?'

'I'm sorry. Didn't I say? He was Lord Northcote. As for my mother, it's possible that – having known her for so long – Mr Neville might have used her given name. Arabella.'

'I see.' Lydia thought for a moment and then shook her head. 'No. I can't say I recall those names either.'

'Oh. That's disappointing. I'd thought perhaps ... but it's of no consequence.'

'You hoped I might be able help you with something in particular?'

'It was a wild idea I had,' he returned wryly. 'Unlikely as it may seem, I began to wonder if our two families might be related in some way but could find nothing that confirmed it. You'll think me foolish ... but the handful of blood-kin that Edmund and I have left are scattered across Europe, so the possibility that we had relatives we knew nothing about was an attractive one.'

Lydia experienced a sudden wave of sympathy. She said, 'I don't think you foolish at all, Mr Wakefield. Indeed, since my brother and I are similarly bereft, I understand completely.' She smiled suddenly. 'But I should warn you that the members of the Neville family you haven't met aren't much better than the ones you have – and that consequently, you might want to think twice about claiming kinship.'

He returned her smile with a very charming one of his own.

'And so I might have done, Mistress Neville ... except that I'd be delighted to acquire *you* as a cousin – however distant the connection might be.'

FOUR

Despite the difficulties in finding General Middleton's will-of-the-wisp army and the fact that, after an abnormally dry spring, the highland weather was now composed of either mist or drizzle, Eden decided that he enjoyed staff-work. Being largely a matter of relaying orders and information between Monck and the senior officers, it didn't compare with commanding a regiment ... but it was a damned sight more fun than being at Secretary Thurloe's beck and call in Westminster. And the scenery, even in the rain, was outstanding.

Deciding that the grass was now sufficiently long, General Monck advanced into the highlands during the second week in June and set about securing the line of the Tay. Having overcome garrisons at Weem Castle and Balloch, he settled briefly at Ruthven Castle until word came that General Middleton's four thousand-strong army was at Kintail – and then they were on the march again towards the southern end of Loch Ness.

There, Colonel Maxwell got the task of liaising with Colonel Brayne and the newly-arrived reinforcements he'd brought from Ireland; and General Monck received the Marquis of Argyll's repeated assurances that he was keeping the Royalists out of his domain – despite the fact that his eldest son had been fighting with them for the best part of a year.

Leaving Colonel Brayne at Inverlochy, Monck despatched Colonel Morgan to the head of Loch Ness in the hope of trapping Middleton between them. It didn't happen. Somehow, Middleton winnowed through which, given a terrain bereft of roads and broken up by lochs, Eden didn't find particularly surprising. Monck had blocked the south-bound passes and thus prevented the Royalists from descending into the lowlands; but keeping watch over the myriad of tracks snaking their way through the mountains was a sheer impossibility.

Having lost Middleton in the mist and thoroughly displeased as a result, General Monck led the remainder of his force to Inverness and, during the course of a Council of War, said bluntly, 'We need provisions. If we're going to end up playing grandmother's footsteps up hill and down dale for any length of time, we'll need as many basic supplies as we can carry. Meanwhile, I want an accurate picture of Middleton's movements. I want to know, not just where he is *now* but where the hell he'll go *next*. Major Chard, Colonel Maxwell; take a dozen men and find out. You have three days.'

'The words *needle* and *haystack* come to mind,' remarked Harry Chard to Eden. 'Any suggestions as to where we should start? With a map, perhaps?'

'The maps are less than useless,' replied Eden. 'The big lochs are marked but the smaller ones aren't and neither are the majority of the passes. A *map* gives you the idea that you can march from Balgowan to Invergarry in a day. You can't.' He paused and looked doubtfully at the other man. 'If you've been relying on maps --'

'I haven't. I've two troopers who act as guides. One is from Loch Tummel and the other hails from Newbigging. Between the two of them, we generally manage to stay on the right path.' He grinned. 'I know the maps are useless. I just wanted to know if *you* did.'

While Major Chard hunted the area between Loch Lochy and Loch Druich, Colonel Maxwell – assisted by a highlander whose accent he could barely understand – scoured eastern Lochaber.

At some point on the second day, Major Moulton said, 'Since everybody seems to spend all their time chasing Middleton, I've been wondering what's happened to Lord Glencairn. You know ... it being him who started this whole thing in the first place.'

Eden shrugged.

'Presumably *somebody* knows where he is – though at the moment nobody particularly cares. But if Monck manages to defeat Middleton, no doubt the Earl's turn will come.'

The rest of that day and all of the next was spent riding up and down narrow tracks in the mountains. It was exhausting and largely unrewarding. Eden caught not a whiff of their quarry; Chard missed them by half a day in Glen Urquart, then lost their trail altogether.

General Monck was less than impressed.

'Very well,' he snapped in the ensuing Council of War. 'If we can't even *find* the enemy – let alone overtake him – we'll make damned sure the land won't sustain his Horse. I'll burn every seed, stalk and croft between here and Dunkeld, if I have to. Get ready to march, gentlemen. We're heading for Locheil and Glenmoriston at first light.'

* * *

As June became July, Eden's pleasure in his new-found freedom dimmed. They stormed through the lands of the Camerons, the Macdonalds and the Mackenzies, burning as they went. Although he understood Monck's determination not to let the campaign drag on into a second winter, he wasn't comfortable with wholesale destruction. The ordinary clansmen who lived in these remote reaches of the kingdom weren't rich. They scraped a living from an inhospitable landscape and owned little more than the roof over their heads ... so the sight of blazing thatches wasn't something he thought anyone could rejoice in. Indeed, the only good thing about those weeks was the fact that every single croft and cottage was deserted. During the whole nasty business they never found a man, woman or child ... all having taken whatever livestock they owned and fled to even more inaccessible regions.

News from England became a thing of the past and even letters from the lowland garrisons took days to find them. And throughout it all, they never once caught a glimpse of General Middleton's army – though at Loch Alsh they found all the powder, shot and supplies that the Cavaliers had abandoned in the course of a hasty retreat. It began to feel, remarked Eden moodily to Ned Moulton, that they were chasing a will-o'-the-wisp.

After they'd been running fruitlessly around the highlands for a month, a report came in that Middleton had ferried his infantry over to the Isle of Skye but that his cavalry, now severely reduced in number, were still on the move. His expression even blacker than ever, General Monck sent a rider ordering Colonel Morgan to move to Caithness and take possession of all the food and gunpowder stored there. Then he led his own weary force back to Inverness for a brief rest while they re-provisioned.

Three days later and once more back on the road, the Governor of Blair Atholl brought them the first positive news of Middleton's whereabouts that they'd had for some time.

'Damn it!' snarled General Monck. 'He's not heading north at all. He's turned south towards Dunkeld and the lowlands. Colonel Maxwell – take yourself off to Caithness. Tell Tom Morgan what's happening and that he's to get to Braemar with all possible speed in case Middleton tries to get through that way. And you might as well stay with him because I'll need to force Middleton to double back – and don't know where the hell that will take us.'

'Thank you, sir,' murmured Eden. And thought, *Does he* know *how many miles it is to Caithness from here and how many more from there to Braemar? Or does he just think I've got wings?*

When informed of their orders, Major Moulton said laconically, 'Look on the bright side. By the time this is over, you'll be able to draw your *own* maps.'

'By the time this is over,' retorted Eden, 'nobody will want them.'

* * *

It took two long days of hard riding to reach Caithness and when they got there, Colonel Morgan's reaction was much as Eden had expected.

'Bloody hell,' he groaned. 'We've only been here four days. It's going to take at least five to get to Aberdeenshire. And do you know what's going to happen when we get there, Colonel? The General will have received fresh intelligence which requires my presence on the opposite side of the country. My arse has barely been out of the saddle for a month or more … and my horse has begun to hate me.'

'Ah,' said Eden gravely. 'It's bad news when they do that.'

'Isn't it?' Morgan stood up and stretched. Then, musingly, 'Why Braemar? Monck can't seriously think Middleton might make it to the lowlands. And even if he did … what then? By now, his force must be half what it was.'

'Less,' agreed Eden. 'The Governor at Blair Atholl put his current strength at no more than fifteen hundred.'

'Well, if that's so and we can only *find* him, this whole ridiculous business is as good as over.' He grinned suddenly. 'Unfortunately, finding him has been the crux of the problem all along. I'll swear the damned man's a ghost.'

* * *

On July 10th Sir Aubrey stood under an overcast sky on Tower Hill. The crowd around him was large and tightly-packed but Aubrey had taken the precaution of tucking his hair inside a broad-brimmed hat which he wore low over his face and shrouding his person in a shabby black cloak. He hoped he looked suitably nondescript and little different from those around him.

On the previous day word had leaked out around the City that Somerset Fox's sentence had been commuted to life imprisonment or transportation to Barbados. Peter Vowell was due to be hanged at Tyburn within the next few hours. And the noisy jostling crowd in which Aubrey now stood was waiting to see not one but two men lose their heads. It seemed that the government – perhaps in a fit of economy – had decided that John Gerard's execution should be immediately followed by that of Dom Pantaleon Sa; the Portuguese gentleman who, the previous November, had mistaken some poor fellow for Gerard and murdered him. Aubrey wondered if John appreciated the irony of the situation ... then decided that it was unlikely. He couldn't even appreciate it himself. He just felt sick and, never having watched an execution before, hoped that he didn't disgrace himself.

The headsman was already on the scaffold, along with a cleric and two Army officers and there were soldiers all around to hold back the crowd in the event of trouble. From what Aubrey could see, there wouldn't be any. Of the people nearest to him, most seemed to be in a mood of cheerful anticipation – as if seeing someone decapitated fell into the same category as a puppet show or a wrestling match. Some of them were even *eating*. The scents of meat and pastry and onions flavoured the air. Something unpleasant rose in Aubrey's throat and he had to swallow hard to rid himself of it. Then there was a collective stirring amongst the spectators ... and John Gerard was led up the steps of the scaffold.

He looked exactly as he'd done the last time Aubrey had seen him. His clothes unostentatious but neat, his expression calm, his posture relaxed.

How can he do it? Aubrey wondered. *How can he climb those steps so steadily, without any hesitation, knowing what awaits him at the top? I don't think I could. I think they'd have to carry me. Oh God, John ... you never did anything to merit this.*

Gerard was holding some sheets of paper. An Army officer stepped forward and said something, Gerard replied and the officer shook his head. With an air of regretful resignation, Gerard slid the papers into the breast of his coat.

Then, stepping to the edge of the platform, he waited for the crowd to fall silent and said, 'I'm not permitted to read my last words to you – though I hope that, in time, they may find their way into print so that my brother may know that I whole-heartedly forgive him for testifying against me. For now, however, I would say just this.' He stopped, seeming to take a breath. 'I die a faithful subject and servant to King Charles the Second, whom I pray God to bless and restore to his rights. And had I ten thousand lives, I would gladly lay them all down thus for his service.'

Tears stung the back of Aubrey's eyes and he blinked them away.

He's only twenty-two years old, for God's sake. Just twenty-two – three years younger than I am myself. How can they do this?

Gerard knelt briefly before the clergyman, before rising to unlace and remove his coat. Although he didn't seem to hurry, there was an eagerness about him now ... as if what lay ahead was something to be accomplished without undue delay. On his knees before the block, he paused for perhaps a minute, hands clasped and eyes closed. Then he laid his head down and spread out his hands.

The axe came down hard, cleanly and with a sound that Aubrey hoped he never heard again. Forcing himself not to look away, he watched the executioner hold up his friend's bloody head and say the words. Then, he swung round and started pushing his way through the crowd. It was done. Over. John was dead. Let the rest of them stay to watch Dom Pantaleon being butchered if they would. Aubrey merely wanted to get as far away from this hellish place as he possibly could.

* * *

Six days after Colonel Gerard went to the block, Colonel Morgan's troops arrived at Granton-on-Spey to be met by one of General Monck's gallopers with a message.

Having read it, Morgan looked around at his fellow Colonels and said, 'Change of plan, gentlemen. Middleton has doubled-back and is apparently still in Perthshire, so the General wants us to make for Ruthven – where we may or may not, depending upon the circumstances, rendezvous with him. Since, from here, our route lies along the banks of the Spey, we should be able to complete it in two days' march. In fact, I fear that we must.'

The following day took them as far as Kincraig which meant another night under canvas. Over supper with the other officers, Eden said, 'What do you think our chances are?'

'Of catching up with Middleton?' Tom Morgan toyed idly with his tankard of ale. 'Failing fresh and useful intelligence, much the same as they've always been, I imagine.'

'Oh. In other words, I shouldn't get my hopes up.'

'Or hold your breath,' remarked a Captain from the far end of the table. 'Wild geese are easier any day of the week.'

They didn't find General Monck at Ruthven. They did, however, receive a message from him saying that Middleton's Horse now stood at a mere twelve hundred or so; that he was still in the region of Loch Rannoch and that, if he was now heading north again, the only route open to him was the pass linking the upper reaches of the River Garry with that of the Spey.

'Assuming Monck's intelligence is correct, Middleton is moving more or less directly towards us,' said Eden. 'Shall Major Moulton and I try finding them?'

'By all means,' came Morgan's laconic reply. 'The rest of us will continue along the Spey, before turning into Glen Garry. There's a place near the loch called Dalnaspidal – not, since you're unlikely to meet any friendly locals, that there's anything to tell you that. But you'll recognise it because it's just about the only piece of level ground suitable for making camp. If you haven't already re-joined us with news, you'll find us there.'

Setting out at first light on the following morning, Colonel Maxwell and Major Moulton rode on through Kingussie to comb the area around Dalwhinnie and the most northerly reaches of Loch Ericht. They found precisely nothing.

'Damn,' breathed Eden, when they stopped at around noon to eat some bread and cheese and rest the horses. 'Morgan thought this would their easiest route northwards from Loch Rannoch but, if that's so, we'd have seen some sign of them by now. The fact that we haven't is beginning to suggest that Middleton may be heading due north towards Loch Garry.' He stopped and fixed Ned with a grim stare. 'Oh hell.'

Ned opened his mouth, closed it again and then said, 'If he does that, Morgan will meet him head on.'

'Yes.' Eden was already swinging himself back into the saddle. 'Let's go.'

They finally caught sight of the Royalist army half-way down Loch Garry. Examining it through his perspective glass, Eden said, 'They're getting ready to move. I'd say Middleton's Horse numbers a lot less than we thought ... but on the other hand, he has got some Foot with him.' He folded the glass. 'Right. Back to warn Morgan.'

When they reached the main force, it had barely arrived at Dalnaspidal and most of the men were just beginning to unsaddle their horses. Hurling himself from his own saddle and tossing his reins to Ned Moulton, Eden ran through the troop shouting, 'Stop – stand! Where's Colonel Morgan?'

'Here,' said the Colonel, emerging from a knot of officers. 'What is it?'

'They're no distance away – probably with the same idea you had about camping here. Roughly eight hundred Horse and the Foot following some distance behind. If you advance now, you can take them.'

Morgan wasted no time but immediately began issuing orders. In less than ten minutes, the entire troop was once more on the move and at a smart pace. Riding alongside Morgan, Eden rapidly supplied such information about the terrain as seemed useful and then fell silent, his eyes searching for the first sign of the enemy.

They came upon them even sooner than he'd expected, approaching from the western side of the loch. Taking in the situation at a glance, Colonel Morgan spared a second to cast a triumphant glance at the sky and breathe, 'Oh my God. Finally.'

Then he issued the order to charge.

Thundering onwards with the rest, Eden recognised the exact moment when General Middleton saw disaster staring him in the face and attempted to avert it. In the last critical minutes before Morgan's force reached his own, he must have barked an order to retreat – whilst already knowing that it was too late. His infantry were far enough back to turn and run. But his Horse, attempting now to wheel about, had run out of time. As Morgan's troops hurtled down on them, the Royalist van found itself abruptly transformed into the rear and thus was left with no choice but to meet the attack as best it could, unsupported by the rest of their fleeing army.

Christ, thought Eden grimly, as no more than a hundred fellows turned back to meet the onslaught, *it's going to be a bloody massacre.*

And then the two forces collided and for a brief time, wielding his sword for the first time since Worcester, Eden let instinct and physical reflex take over. Shots were fired, swords sang and scraped, voices screamed over the din; he was surrounded by all the familiar sounds of battle and for a few minutes he almost enjoyed it.

But despite the chaos in their ranks as those trying to flee hampered those determined to do battle, the little troop of Cavaliers fought hard and with a wild sort of gallantry born of desperation. Travel-weary and severely outnumbered as they were and with hope of nothing save defeat, still they offered the kind of resistance that Eden couldn't help but respect. He even felt sorry for the poor bastards.

The action was brief and bloody.

Eden started fighting to disarm rather than kill and shouting at the enemy to surrender. Some of them listened and followed his advice, dropping from their saddles to drive their swords into the moist peaty ground. Others, when the sheer hopelessness of their position could no longer be denied and further resistance was clearly futile, abandoned their horses and started escaping into the bogs in the wake of the Foot.

Gradually the field cleared, leaving behind the dead and injured. Eden looked on it without pleasure and then turned to await Colonel Morgan's instructions, hoping he wouldn't order a pursuit.

He didn't. Instead, he said, 'Let them go – but round up their horses. They're irreplaceable hereabouts and, without them, Middleton's finished.' And with a sudden sharp-edged smile, 'Well done, gentlemen. Let's send the glad tidings to General Monck.'

* * *

Colonel Maxwell and Major Moulton remained in the highlands for two more weeks, grimly assisting with what could only be called a mopping-up operation.

Monck turned his attention to the Earl of Glencairn, now lurking in the region of Aberfoyle, and Colonel Morgan marched off to drag Middleton from his lair in Caithness. Of the numerous prisoners taken, many bowed to the inevitable and bent the knee. The highland rising was over; and just to make certain, a campaign of the torch rather than the sword destroyed places where the insurgents had once sheltered and hostages were taken to ensure good behaviour. No more enamoured with burning the countryside than he'd ever been, Eden was relieved when his term of service came to its natural end.

* * *

Retracing their steps southwards through the first days of August and in increasingly fine weather, Eden and Ned arrived at Brandon Lacey late one afternoon to an initially warm welcome from Venetia which cooled considerably when she saw what Eden had brought for the twins.

'A drum and a penny whistle?' she said. And then, acidly, 'It's clear how little you know of small children. The boys can make quite enough noise without this kind of help.'

Eden grinned and said, 'The choices were limited. But at least Rosie's doll isn't noisy. Where is she, by the way?'

'Out with Gabriel. And as usual I expect he'll bring her back far later than he should and too full of curd tart to eat her supper.' She finished pouring ale for both men and said, 'I take it he hasn't written to you?'

'If he has, his letter is somewhere in the wilds of Scotland. We've been moving around rather a lot.'

'The rising is over?'

'Yes. We defeated what was left of Middleton's army on the 19th of last month. And though neither he nor Glencairn have been taken yet, neither is in any position to fight on.'

Venetia sat down, her expression resigned.

'It was never going to work, was it?'

'If by that you mean could it ever have resulted in the restoration of Charles Stuart — no. It couldn't.'

Major Moulton said, 'In York we heard that, aside from the widowed Queen, the entire Stuart faction had been thrown out of Paris. If that's true, it means the Protector has decided to get into bed with Mazarin rather than Philip of Spain.'

'I don't know *what* he's decided. But the rest is true enough. Charles left Paris at the end of June and is staying with his sister, the Princess of Orange at Spa.' Fixing Eden with a very direct gaze, she said, 'I'm surprised at you, you know. I'd have thought that you'd be done with Cromwell by now. How much further does he have to go before you realise that he's a bigger tyrant than the man whose head he cut off?'

'I know what Cromwell is,' came the even, if ambiguous reply. 'Like the rest of the country, I'm waiting to see what happens once Parliament is sitting.'

'Oh — so am I. In fact, I'm looking forward to it.' She smiled sardonically. 'Would you like to know where Gabriel is right now?' And then, without waiting for an answer, 'He's doing what he's been doing every day for the last two weeks. He's out taking ale with every man in the hundred who has a vote.'

Eden eyes widened. 'He's going to stand?'

'He's going to stand,' agreed Venetia, 'and has written to Lambert saying so. As to *why* ... I'll leave him to explain that to you himself.'

* * *

The twins' delight in their gifts coupled with their father's slightly sore head resulted in them being banished to the nursery almost immediately. Rosie, by contrast, settled happily on Uncle Eden's knee clutching her doll and informing him that her name was Araminta. It was therefore some time before Gabriel was alone with his two guests and able to ask about the Scottish campaign.

'All in good time,' replied Eden. 'First, I want to know what made you change your mind about standing for Parliament.'

'Three trials for treason conducted by a High Court of Justice,' said Gabriel crisply. 'In short, I had a letter from Sam Radford.'

'The editor of the *Moderate*?' asked Ned, surprised. 'He's a friend of yours?'

Gabriel exchanged an amused glance with Eden.

'I suppose you could call him that. We've certainly had dealings with each other from time to time and his wife is my foster-brother's niece – which makes him a relative of sorts.'

'And what,' asked Eden politely, 'did Sam say that carried more weight than anything Lambert or I said?'

'He told me what the newsheets had told me already. That John Gerard, Peter Vowell and Somerset Fox were found guilty of treason by a High Court of Justice. He also pointed out – just in case I didn't already know – that treason cases are supposed to be tried by a jury and that therefore the use of a High Court indicates a determination to secure a guilty verdict.'

'And that annoyed you enough to make you decide to stand?'

'Not *just* that – or not entirely. Sam has apparently had the opportunity to interrogate a fellow who was in the assassination plot and is currently lying low in Shoreditch. The same opportunity, one might say, that Cromwell's people must have had with numerous other fellows. Yet according to Sam's informant, the plot wasn't hatched by Gerard at all; Vowell's involvement amounted to rounding up a few horses; and Fox was supposedly encouraging apprentices to riot. It doesn't sound like something deserving death, does it?'

'Not when you put it like that,' agreed Ned. 'But perhaps Radford was misinformed.'

Gabriel looked at Eden, his expression gently enquiring.

'Do you think that likely?'

Eden huffed a resigned breath. 'No. But I'd rather not discuss it.'

'Ah,' was all Gabriel said.

There was a short slightly tricky silence while Major Moulton looked from one to the other of them. Finally, he said, 'All right. Clearly, Radford got his information from Lydia Neville's brother … which makes me wonder just how stupid you think I am.'

'It's not that,' said Eden quickly. 'Recently I seem to have been finding myself on the wrong side of the line rather frequently. And if my actions with regard to Aubrey Durand come to light, you would be the first person they'd question. I didn't want that.'

'Then, with all due respect, Colonel – you're a bloody idiot.'

'Thank you.'

'Don't mention it.' Ned turned back to Gabriel. 'What happened to them, the three who were tried?'

'Fox pleaded guilty and is to be transported, Vowell was hanged and Gerard went to the block.'

'Dire retribution,' breathed Eden.

'Exactly. I always said that removing the late King's head was a mistake and that, if Parliament was dissolved, there would be nothing left to balance the power of the Army. But I used to think Cromwell would try to maintain the existing order to some degree or other – instead of which he's turned military dictator. If the Council of State had any say in his recent actions at all, I'd be surprised to learn of it.' Gabriel stood up and stretched. 'And so, gentlemen, I intend to be elected as member for this district. And then I'm going to take my seat in Westminster and try to bring the Lord Protector to heel … in which, one hopes, I shall not be labouring alone or in vain.'

***

Eden spent three nights at Brandon Lacey. At Gabriel's invitation, Ned Moulton remained for a further week, thus leaving his Colonel free to visit his family in Oxfordshire alone.

In the stable yard and once more on the point of departure, Eden looked at Gabriel and said, 'I'll see you in London, then.'

'Yes. By the end of this month, since Parliament's due to open on September 3rd. Venetia will stay behind until after the harvest and then join me. She may or may not bring Phoebe with her. I don't know.'

'Phoebe,' said Eden cheerfully, 'has got over me. I don't know why everyone seems to have thought she wouldn't.'

'Speaking for myself, I gave up predicting women a long time ago.' There was a pause; and then, 'You *are* going to Thorne Ash, I hope?'

Eden's jaw tightened. 'Yes.'

'And staying more than twenty-four hours?'

'Again – yes.'

'Good.' Gabriel smiled and offered his hand. 'Please give my warmest regards to your mother.'

FIVE

When it was too late to do anything about it, it occurred to Eden that perhaps he ought to have let his family know he was coming. As it was, he rode into Thorne Ash's courtyard feeling unsure of his welcome and, as a result, distinctly edgy.

The first person he saw was his brother-in-law.

Ralph Cochrane, blond and massive as a Viking, was engaged in fixing a new wheel to a cart. When he spied Eden, he summoned a stableman to take his place and then slowly straightened his back and stood up.

'Well,' he said coolly. 'Finally.'

Eden dropped to the cobbles but held on to his horse's reins as if intending to unsaddle her himself.

Seeing it, Ralph said, 'Leave that.' And over his shoulder as he advanced towards Eden, 'Harris ... go into the house and have somebody tell the ladies that Colonel Maxwell has arrived and will be with them shortly – then see to the Colonel's horse.'

'Sir.' The man nodded and walked off.

Ralph looked unsmilingly back at Eden.

'A word or two in private, if you wouldn't mind.'

Eden suspected that he *was* going to mind but decided he might as well get it over with. Following his brother-in-law inside the shadowy quiet of the stable, he said, 'I'm sorry I've taken so long to get here. But Lambert --'

And that was as far as he got before a fist like Thor's hammer knocked him off his feet. Head ringing and pain roaring through his jaw, it took a moment to reassemble his wits and come to the conclusion that it would be stupid to stand up just yet.

'That,' snapped Ralph, 'was for not managing to get here in time to mark the tenth anniversary of your father's death. Everyone else came – even Kate and Luciano from Genoa – but not you. And you can save your excuses. I've heard too many of them already. So just shut your mouth and listen. I don't mind being a father to your children – in fact, since Tab and I still haven't any of our own, I wouldn't be without them. But I *do* mind you behaving as if they don't exist.'

'I don't --' began Eden weakly.

'You bloody well do! You haven't been near them for nearly seven sodding months, Eden – and the last time you *did* come, you only stayed forty-eight hours. Mary, of course, doesn't expect anything else. But Jude is fourteen years old and starting to wonder why his *real* father has no time for him.' Ralph stopped, ran a furious hand through his already wildly disordered hair and said, 'You won't have noticed – but he's a son any man would be proud of. So what the hell is the *matter* with you?'

'Quite a lot, obviously.' Hoping it was now safe to do so, Eden stopped massaging his jaw and got to his feet. 'I'm sorry.'

'It's not me you need to apologise to.'

'I know. I'll --'

'Try explaining yourself to your mother.'

'I will as soon as --'

'And don't expect anybody to fall on your neck. They won't.'

Eden decided he'd had enough.

'I don't expect it – though I hope nobody else feels inclined to break my jaw. I'm sorry it's been seven months. I'm sorry I couldn't be here last month for Father. I'm sorry that previous visits have been short. I'm even sorry I can't meet everybody's expectations. But I'm here now – contrite and prepared to stay for at least a week if you think you can put up with me for that long. And now do you think I might be allowed inside the house?'

* * *

Mr Cochrane let him go into the house alone – where, in fact, Dorothy Maxwell *did* fall on her elder son's neck, saying, 'Oh Eden – my dear. What a wonderful surprise!'

Kissing her cheek and then each of her hands, Eden smiled ruefully and said, 'I'm sorry. By the time I realised that I should have sent word, it was too late to do it.'

'Sent word? Why on earth would you need to do that? This is your home.' Stepping back a little, Dorothy touched the bruise that was already forming on the side of his jaw. 'No sooner here than fighting?'

'No. Just taking my punishment like a man. Father would be proud. Or then again, maybe not.' He looked past her to where his sister stood, flanked by Jude and Mary. 'If anybody else wants to hit me, now would be the time.'

Tabitha smiled, shook her head. 'Ralph has been a little annoyed with you.'

'I noticed.' Eden strolled forward, to give and receive a swift hug and then immediately turned to his son, saying, 'Good Lord, Jude ... you're nearly as tall as I am. What on earth is your Aunt Tab feeding you?'

The boy, red-haired as his father and still lanky as a new colt, gave a brief and clearly involuntary grin. 'Scraps, mostly.' Then, holding out his hand, said self-consciously, 'How are you, sir? Uncle Toby wrote that you'd been sent to end the Scottish rising.'

Eden took the proffered hand and, knowing that he only had himself to blame, hid how being addressed as 'sir' felt like a punch to the stomach. 'Well, I lent a hand, certainly. But I actually went north to deliver much-needed supplies to General Monck.'

'And are the Scots defeated now?' asked Jude quickly.

'All bar the shouting,' agreed his father with a slight smile. Then, keeping every nerve and muscle under rigid control, he turned to Jude's ten-year-old sister. 'And Mary ... you've grown too, I see.'

'Yes, sir.' The girl dropped a slight curtsy and, without meeting his eyes, said in a colourless little voice, 'Thank you.'

'She can ride her pony nearly as well as me,' announced Jude with a hint of challenge.

'Is that so?'

'It is indeed,' interposed Dorothy smoothly, seeing pitfalls ahead. 'In that respect, she's just like Kate at the same age. But all this can wait. No doubt you're eager to get rid of the dust of the road and change your clothes. Your room is waiting and Flossie has sent up hot water. Then, when you're ready, you can come down and tell us all your news.'

Eden sent her a fleeting smile and gratefully accepted the reprieve.

Perhaps, he thought, *now the first moments are out of the way, it will be easier.*

* * *

When he went back downstairs, he found his mother waiting in the parlour. She was alone. Gesturing for him to sit beside her, she said simply, 'I told everyone that I wanted you to myself for a little while. I didn't think you'd mind.'

'No. Of course not.' He absorbed the threads of silver in the rich, dark red hair and the small lines around the still-lovely green eyes. 'I believe I'm glad of it.'

'Yes. It's been a while, hasn't it? I expect you're finding it difficult to adjust.'

Eden swallowed and heard himself say baldly, 'It ... I shouldn't find it difficult. Not now. I don't know why I still do.'

'Of course you do. It's because you're never here often enough – or long enough – to become accustomed and remember who you are.'

'I know who I am.'

'No, Eden. You only know *part* of yourself. The rest is shut away in a box that you refuse to open.' She patted his hand. 'But we needn't speak of that now. Tell me what you've been doing these last months. I know from Toby that you've been kept exceptionally busy.

Toby said that, did he? It's more than he's ever admitted to me.

But he put that thought aside and began giving her a carefully edited picture of his working life since Cromwell had made himself Lord Protector. Dorothy listened carefully for a time and then said, 'Is that *all* you've been doing? Working?'

'Yes. All too often, there's no time for anything else.'

She surveyed him thoughtfully.

'To all intents and purposes, you've been single for a decade and free to re-marry for the last year and a half. I'd have thought that, by now, some lady might have engaged your ... interest.'

Eden opened his mouth to say no, then closed it again as an image of Lydia Neville hauling him over the coals in that tiny office came to mind. Resolutely banishing it, he said evasively, 'I rarely meet any ladies.'

Dorothy noticed that he'd side-stepped the question but chose not to pursue it. She said, 'That's a shame. I don't like to think of you spending the rest of your life alone. But perhaps you have a mistress?'

Eden's jaw slackened in surprise and then he laughed.

'What sort of question is that for a mother to ask her son?'

'A perfectly natural one when the son in question is thirty-five years old and free to take his pleasures where he chooses,' came the composed reply. 'However ... you needn't answer if you'd rather not.'

'Thank you.' He realised he'd forgotten how acute his mother could be. Amusement rippling through his tone, he said, 'You shouldn't confuse me with Toby, you know. He's the one with women tripping over themselves and each other in order to catch his eye.'

'I know about Toby,' replied his mother calmly. 'Tabitha only tells me half of it, of course, but I'm adept at reading between the lines. Ah ... and speaking of Tabitha ... nothing has been said yet but I think you must make allowances if Ralph is particularly tense at the moment.'

'I don't follow,' began Eden. And then, 'Oh. Yes. I see.'

Ralph and his sister had been married for six years. During that time, Tabitha had conceived twice and miscarried both babes around the start of the fourth month. The second time had been especially bad and there had been fears for her life. If Tabitha was in the early stages of pregnancy now, it was no wonder Ralph's nerves were at full stretch.

'Does Toby know?' asked Eden.

'I imagine so – though I doubt Tabitha has actually told him.'

He nodded, aware of the peculiar bond between the twins.

'I imagine we can expect him to arrive any day, then.'

'Yes.' She paused and, looking down at her hands, added carefully, 'He came at the end of June, of course, and brought Amy with him. Kate was here, too.'

'Ralph told me.' *The last day of June. The day after the battle of Cropredy Bridge in '44. The day Father died. Do they think I don't remember? That I don't mark the occasion in my own way and as best I can?* 'I'm sorry I couldn't be here as well but it ... wasn't possible. We were still chasing General Middleton from glen to glen in the highlands.'

Dorothy looked up at him then and said quietly, 'You needn't explain. I know you loved your father and haven't forgotten. But it's time to put aside the other memories of that day. Not just for yourself – but for the children. Particularly Jude.' She stood up and said, 'He is unlikely to make it easy for you ... but if you don't forge a relationship with him now, you'll lose him forever. It's up to you.'

* * *

Supper with everyone at the table together was less awkward than he'd expected. Due largely to Dorothy and Tabitha, conversation flowed relatively easily; Ralph showed no sign of wanting to hit him again; and though Mary said very little, Jude occasionally whispered something in her ear that made her giggle. Gradually, Eden relaxed.

It was the following morning before the rest of the family conspired to leave him alone with his son. Jude immediately suggested that they ride out together.

'I thought,' he said politely, 'that you might like to see the changes and improvements that Uncle Ralph has made here and there.'

'Yes. I'd like that very much.'

They spent an hour or more touring the home farm and surrounding land while Jude pointed out various things, casually expounding on subjects which Eden realised he'd once known all about himself but now recalled very little. After a while, he said, 'I'm impressed. You obviously take a lot of interest in the running of the estate.'

Jude shoved a recalcitrant lock of red hair back from his face.

'When I'm not at lessons, I go around with Uncle Ralph most of the time. He explains things and sometimes asks what I think and then we discuss it.' He paused and then said, 'Of course, soon I'll be going to university and I won't be here as much. So I want to learn everything I can before I go.'

'Are you looking forward to Oxford?'

'I think so. Did you enjoy it when you went?'

'Yes. But it was a little different for me, I suppose. Your Uncle Francis and I went there together.' Eden hesitated briefly. Then, 'He's in Paris, by the way – Francis. He's married to a French actress and he writes plays for the theatre where she performs.'

Jude nodded. There was a long silence but finally he said expressionlessly, 'I know Mother didn't die when they said. That she just ... left. And I know she's really dead now. But no one says what happened to her. Do you know?'

Eden swallowed and worked hard at keeping his voice perfectly neutral.

'She tripped on the stairs and fell. It was an accident.'

Another nod, another silence and another unexpected question.

'Are you going to get married again?'

'I don't plan to do so.' He shot his son a sideways glance. 'Do you mind either way?'

Jude hunched one shoulder and reined his horse to a stop, forcing Eden to follow suit.

'Not for myself. But ... if you chose the right kind of lady, I think it might be nice for Mary. It's not that she needs anybody really. She's got Aunt Tab and Uncle Ralph and Grandmother. But if you were married, your wife might like her.' He turned an austere, faintly accusing and very adult stare on his father. 'She knows that *you* don't.'

Once again, Eden felt as if he'd been kicked in the stomach.

'That isn't true. I --'

'Yes it is. You can barely look at her. She knows that. She just doesn't understand why.'

Christ. This is getting worse by the minute.

Eden didn't want to ask but couldn't see any way of avoiding it. To give himself a few second's grace, he dismounted and turned to look unseeingly across a field of corn.

Finally, forcing the words out, he said, 'And you think you do?'

'I *know* I do.' Jude also dismounted and studied the soon-to-be-harvested field. 'At first I thought it was because she looks like Mother but it isn't. It's because --' He stopped abruptly and then went on bluntly, 'It's because you don't think you're her real father.'

Eden felt the ground sliding away from beneath him.

'What makes you suppose that?'

'Something Aunt Tab said to Grandmother. I didn't mean to listen but ... well, it's what they think.' He turned, waiting until his father looked him in the eye. 'If it's true, I wanted to hear it from you. Is it?'

Knowing what his answer would unleash, Eden shut his eyes for a moment and then opened them again. 'Yes.'

Jude drew a sharp breath and loosed it. He didn't immediately say anything but when he did, his words were unexpected.

'I thought you'd lie. I'm glad you didn't.'

A small, harsh laugh scraped Eden's throat.

'So am I.'

'You don't have to tell me the rest if you don't want to. After all, if it's true, it's pretty obvious that Mother had … that she was … well, you know.' Another pause. 'I suppose you're sure?'

'As sure as I can be – though perhaps not entirely.'

Jude considered this.

'Then why can't you give Mary the benefit of the doubt? Even if you're right and it *is* true, it's not her fault, is it? And – and she's still my sister.'

'I know. And I'll try harder.'

'And visit more often?'

'That, too.' Eden thought for a moment and then said, 'Or if, like the last few months it becomes impossible, perhaps you could spend a few weeks with Uncle Toby and me in London.'

The boy's face lit up.

'Really?'

'Of course.' Eden smiled, ridiculously pleased at his son's reaction. 'You'd like that?'

'Yes. I've never been to London. Neither of us has.'

Us?

Pleasure dimmed and the solid ground Eden thought he'd found turned back into a swamp.

Meanwhile, Jude was rushing on.

'We could see the lions at the Tower and London Bridge. And you could show us Westminster and Whitehall and we might even be able to see the Lord Protector. And --'

'Wait. Jude – just wait a minute. Mary could come with you if it was possible – but it isn't. My household in London is a bachelor establishment and, though that would be all right for you, it isn't remotely suitable for a little girl.'

Instantly, Jude looked suspicious.

'You're just making excuses.'

'No. I'm not. There's Toby, my friend Sir Nicholas, a kitchen-maid and a new housekeeper I've barely met yet. Your grandmother would have a fit if I even suggested it.' He ran a hand through his hair, thinking furiously. 'I suppose ... I suppose it might be possible for you to stay with me and for Mary to go to Aunt Amy but --'

'No.'

'No?'

'Aunt Tab asked Aunt Amy to invite us last year but she wouldn't. She said she has enough to do looking after her own children without taking on yours as well. And even if she changed her mind, Mary wouldn't go.'

'Let me guess. She doesn't like Amy?'

'Neither of us do.'

'Why does that not surprise me?' murmured Eden with a sigh. His younger sister's pretensions meant that contact between them had become as near to non-existent as made no difference. Then, 'It's not an excuse, Jude. Mary could stay in Cheapside if there was a suitable female to look after her – but there isn't. Unless that changes --'

'It would change if you got married.'

This time, Eden's laughter was perfectly genuine.

'You don't let go, do you? All right. No promises ... but I'll bear it in mind. Meanwhile, you'll have to make a decision. It's London without Mary or not at all. Think it over.'

* * *

Certain elements of this conversation cropped up with Tabitha the following afternoon. He found his sister in the rose garden, helping Mary with her embroidery and, mindful of his promise to Jude, Eden leaned over the child's shoulder to admire her work. Mary looked as shocked as if a camel had just sauntered out of the shrubbery ... which made it easy for him to smile.

'That's very pretty,' he remarked. 'Are those roses?'

'P-peonies,' she stammered and bent her head over her work again.

Having no idea what to say next, Eden looked helplessly at his sister who immediately filled the void by saying lightly, 'Mary likes to make her own designs. But she'll probably monogram a handkerchief for you if you ask very nicely.'

'Would you?' he asked, once more looking down at the girl. 'Please?'

She shot him a lightning sideways glance. 'I – I suppose.'

'Thank you.' *God. Why am I so bad at this?* 'I'd like that.'

Once again, Tabitha took pity on him.

'You look hot, Mary. Why don't you go inside and see if Flossie has something cool to drink? Oh – and ask her if Uncle Ralph has left any of last night's bread-and-butter pudding. I don't suppose he did but one never knows.'

Mary nodded, scrambled to her feet and made a rapid escape.

Tabitha grinned at her brother. 'Well done.'

'Was it?'

'Not particularly. But it's a start.' She continued with her own sewing and, when Eden neither advanced nor retreated, said, 'If you're staying, why don't you sit down? We haven't had a moment to talk properly yet, have we?'

'No.' He dropped neatly on the grass as her feet and searched her face. 'How are you, Tab?'

'I'm well. Don't I look it?'

'Yes. But Ralph's twitchy and Mother thinks she knows why.'

'I'm aware of what Mother thinks,' she replied tranquilly. Then, seemingly apropos of nothing, 'Toby says your housekeeper has got married.'

The pause before the word 'housekeeper' was infinitesimal but Eden heard it anyway. He sighed. 'Toby has always had a big mouth where you're concerned. But I'll bet he doesn't tell you everything he gets up to himself.'

'He tells me enough for me to guess the rest.' She set her work aside and gave him her full attention. 'Women like him.'

'They certainly do. But he doesn't have to say yes to all of them.'

'What are you saying? That he's a rakehell?'

'No. But it's borderline.' Eden grinned suddenly. 'Take no notice of me, Tab. I'm just jealous. The girls never swarmed over me even when I was young.'

'You never gave them a chance, did you? You didn't look beyond Celia and you married her when you were only twenty-one. Then the war came.' The grey eyes, so like those of her twin regarded him with disconcerting clarity. 'As to *'when you were young'*, you're not exactly in your dotage. Yet.'

'Thank you,' he murmured.

'Then there's Deborah Hart. Yes – of course I know her name. Toby said she was in love with you.' She paused invitingly and then, when he said nothing, 'He also said she was your mistress.'

Damn Toby. I'll have a few things to say to him myself in due course.

'As I said – a big mouth.'

Tabitha shrugged impatiently.

'Oh for heaven's sake, Eden! You know Toby and I don't have secrets with each other.'

'And Ralph? And Mother? No secrets there either?'

'Not from Ralph in the things that matter – of which, oddly enough, your love-life isn't one. As for Mother … how stupid do you think I am? Not that she'd mind, of course. But what she *really* wants is to see you happily married. As do we all.'

'Oh God – not that again!' he groaned. 'I'm fully aware of that fact, thanks to Jude.'

'Really?' Her brows rose. 'That's interesting. What did he say?'

'He thinks I ought to consider providing Mary with a step-mother.'

'Ah. And will you?'

Eden got to his feet in one fluid movement.

'Let's say it's about as likely as hell freezing over and leave it at that, shall we?'

* * *

The week wore on and grew increasingly comfortable. Eden made a conscious effort to forget Mary's probable parentage and to treat her like any other child. She still never spoke to him unless he addressed her first … but his efforts were rewarded by the approval he read in Jude's eyes.

His relationship with Ralph also slid back into its usual rhythm and, on the night before he planned to leave, the two of them sat up late over a deck of cards and a couple of bottles of claret.

For a time, they talked about nothing in particular. But eventually Ralph said, 'Jude tells me you invited him to London for a visit. Did you mean it?'

'Does he think I didn't?'

There was a pause while Mr Cochrane stared intently at the cards in his hand.

'It's not him that's asking.'

'Hell's teeth!' Eden threw his own cards down. 'I realise I haven't been much of a parent – but give me a little credit, can't you?'

'All right.' Ralph looked up. 'I apologise. You meant it. But why now?'

'Why *not* now?'

'That's what I asked.'

Eden stared at him, somewhere between fury and grim laughter. He said, 'I think I preferred it when you just hit me. However. If you must know …because it's high time I made the effort to get to know him properly and I realise that I'm lucky he's still willing to let me. He's old enough to enjoy the sights and he'll like spending time with Toby in the workshop when work prevents me being there myself.'

Ralph nodded. 'And?'

'That's not enough?'

'It's enough. It's just not the whole story. If it was, you could have suggested this a year ago, couldn't you?'

Since I wasn't about to have my son under the same roof as my mistress, no. I couldn't.

'Circumstances have changed since then,' said Eden curtly. 'And much though I appreciate everything you and Tabitha have done for the children, I'm damned if I'm going to either excuse or explain my life to you.' He stood up. 'This is quite possibly a pointless conversation anyway. Jude hasn't said he wants to come to London.'

'Because Mary can't go too,' agreed Ralph calmly. 'And, of course, she can't. Tab has reiterated pretty much what I gather you said yourself – so I think it's only a matter of time before he accepts your invitation.' He rose and stretched. 'And since Toby will almost certainly turn up in the next few days, Jude doesn't need to travel with you tomorrow.'

Eden's expression changed.

'It's true, then? Tabitha's pregnant?'

'Yes. Since everybody appears to know anyway, we might as well just have admitted it.'

'How far along is she?'

'Just over three months.'

'You must be worried sick.'

'Worried?' grunted Ralph. And then, 'Eden … you have no bloody idea.'

SIX

In London, meanwhile, when the first weeks of August brought no more troopers to the door in search of Aubrey, Nicholas suggested that it was probably safe for Lydia to visit Shoreditch. She agreed with alacrity and the two of them set off from Duck Lane in a cart so that any casual observer would suppose them merely going to collect supplies for the lorinery.

Annis Morell greeted her guest warmly and sent Nicholas to find Aubrey.

'It was extremely good of you to take my brother in,' said Lydia. 'I hope he's been no trouble and is as grateful to you as I am.'

'Oh – he's quite one of the family now. Jack is always happy when he finds somebody who has as much fun with a tub of grease and a grinding wheel as he does himself.'

Lydia stared at her. '*Aubrey?* Dirtying his hands with manual *work*?'

'At every opportunity.'

'Good God.'

Annis laughed but, before she could reply, the door opened on a young woman engaged in drying her hands on her apron and who immediately halted on the threshold to say, 'I beg your pardon, Annis. I didn't realise you had company.'

'Come in, Verity. This is Aubrey's sister. Mistress Neville – allow me to present Verity Marriott, another member of our extended family.'

Ah. The girl who hoped to marry Nicholas, thought Lydia, murmuring the usual response whilst absorbing dark curls and big, brown eyes. *Pretty, too. How strange that Aubrey has never mentioned her in his letters.*

Verity sat down and said politely, 'Have there been no more attempts to arrest Sir Aubrey?'

'No, thank goodness – and I'm hoping that the danger is now behind us.'

'So he'll be able to return home?'

'He probably could,' agreed Lydia. And exchanging amused glances with Annis, 'Whether or not he *will* is another matter. I suppose it all depends on how long Mr Morrell is prepared to put up with him.'

It was a further ten minutes before Aubrey arrived to sweep his sister into a hard hug, saying, 'Lyd – at last! I could hardly believe it when Nick said you were here. You look wonderful – though I'd have thought you'd have put off your blacks by now.'

'I'll do it soon,' she said, returning his embrace. 'But happy as I am to see you, I could positively *murder* you for getting yourself into this position.'

Aubrey released her and grinned.

'Oh well ... it's an ill wind, as they say.'

Annis rose, beckoning Verity to follow her.

'Let's leave Mistress Neville and Aubrey to themselves for a little while.'

'Yes, of course,' said Verity. And, to Aubrey, 'Is Nick here now?'

Her tone was eager and it caused Aubrey's expression to tighten fractionally.

'He's in the yard with Jack. I'm sure you can catch him if you try.'

Verity coloured a little and followed Annis out of the room.

Drawing certain conclusions, Lydia decided to test the water.

'Oh dear. If Mistress Marriott is still living in hope, it's high time Nicholas did some plain speaking.'

Aubrey spun round, frowning. 'What do you mean?'

'I mean that Nicholas isn't interested in her in the way he suspects that she would like.'

'He *told* you that?'

'Yes.' She lifted one enquiring brow. 'Obviously that information is of some interest to you.'

'It might be.'

She sat down again and eyed him thoughtfully.

'Do you want to come home?'

He grimaced and leaned one elbow against the mantelpiece.

'Not especially. But that's got nothing to do with Verity.' He paused and smiled wryly. 'Well a bit, perhaps – but it's more to do with working alongside Jack and the other fellows. I enjoy it.'

'So I've gathered.'

'I hated working at Neville's. I tried because I owed it to Stephen but I always loathed it. This is different. And although I've already learned a lot, it's only a fraction of what Jack can teach me if I stay.' He hesitated and then said, 'I know I ought not to leave you on your own with bloody Margaret and the rest of them but --'

'But you want to.'

'Yes.'

'Will staying keep you out of further trouble of the kind that landed you here in the first place?'

'God, yes.'

'Then stay.'

Aubrey stared at her. 'Do you ... that is, are you sure?'

'Yes.' Lydia smoothed her black bombazine skirts and said, 'I promised to continue living in Stephen's house for my year of full mourning. That's over now and I've already begun looking at alternatives. There's a house near St Botolph's in Bishopsgate that might suit. It's a pleasant property and not too far from here, which means you could live with me but still continue your work with Mr Morrell. What do you think?'

'That, after my reckless stupidity, it's a damned sight more than I deserve,' came the candid reply. 'You're a good sister, Lyd.'

'I know. There is just one condition, however ...'

'Name it.'

'Will you please for the love of God stop calling me *Lyd*?'

* * *

Within days of her visit to Shoreditch Lydia had agreed terms and signed a lease on the house in Bishopsgate. Then she employed a small army of relatives from both her work-forces to clean it from top to bottom and deal with any necessary minor repairs. She decided there was no need to mention any of this to the Nevilles until she was ready to move.

She also decided that there was no further excuse to cling to her widow's weeds. Stephen had been gone for over a year now and, aside from the fact that it would bring Cousin Geoffrey to the point, Lydia realised that she actually *wanted* to wear colours again. Black didn't suit her and never had; news from the north said the Scottish rising was at an end which meant that Colonel Maxwell might presently re-appear in London; and then there was Gilbert Wakefield.

Mr Wakefield called every third or fourth day, as did Sir Ellis Brandon. Inevitably, the Reverend Neville came even more often. Sometimes these visits collided and those occasions were usually entertaining – not just to Lydia herself but also, judging from the gleam in his eyes, to Gilbert Wakefield. Geoffrey bristled like a cat in the face of his rivals and resorted to being more than usually pompous; Ellis lounged in his seat and maintained his usual air of world-weary cynicism; and Gilbert simply sat back to enjoy the show. Lydia admired his tactics – if tactics they were. Although he took obvious pleasure in her company, he gave no sign of wanting to court her. He did, however, take an enormous interest in Stephen's private correspondence, some of which Lydia allowed him to read after he showed her a handful of letters Mr Neville had written to Gilbert's mother nearly thirty years since.

These were quite brief and were apparently replies to letters Lady Northcote had written to Stephen. The only thing that struck Lydia as odd was that there wasn't even one note from her ladyship amongst the plethora of correspondence Stephen had left. Since meeting Gilbert and in the hope of finding the connection he sought, Lydia had gone through all of Stephen's papers again and come up empty-handed save for two scrawled notes from the late Viscount relating to some unspecified business matter. For the rest, Stephen's replies to the Viscountess suggested that her letters to him had been no more than rambling descriptions of life within her family which focussed mostly on the doings of her children.

'It's peculiar, isn't it?' mused Gilbert. 'Why would Mr Neville dispose of Mother's letters when he seems to have kept everything else? Then again, perhaps he *didn't* get rid of them ... just kept them somewhere else.'

'There's nowhere else he *could* have kept them. He never left private papers in his office at the pewter workshop. It was all in his desk here in the house.'

'Are you sure? Maybe he had other premises --'

'That I didn't know about?' asked Lydia sharply. 'Hardly.'

'No? No, of course not.' He gave her a ruefully charming smile. 'I'm sorry. That was stupid of me and now I've offended you.'

'Not at all.'

'Yes, I have. I let my hopes get the better of me and started clutching at straws. I'm an idiot. Forgive me?'

Lydia thawed a little, though her answering smile remained cool.

'There's nothing to forgive. May I offer you a glass of wine?'

* * *

She continued wearing black until the items of furniture she had purchased started to arrive in Bishopsgate and the house was virtually ready for occupation. Then, on the first evening she went down in a gown of lavender damask trimmed with violet ribbons, everything came to a head when she entered the parlour to find it occupied only by Cousin Geoffrey.

For a few seconds, he stared at her. Then he surged across the room, grasped her hands and said enthusiastically, 'Lydia, my dear! You look delightful. Exactly the right note of discretion, if I may say so.'

'You can't imagine how relieved I am that you think so, Cousin,' she replied sardonically, trying without success to tug her hands from his slightly clammy grip.

'I do. I do indeed. The sincerity with which you have mourned Stephen is a great credit to you. A *very* great credit, when one considers your youth. But it is an enormous pleasure to see you finally feeling ready to face life again.'

She yanked her hands free and nobly refrained from remarking that she'd been facing life quite successfully for the last year. Instead, she said, 'I have been considering the future and made certain decisions. This,' she gestured to her gown, 'is just one of them.'

'And a very good place to start.' Then, his tone growing decidedly arch, 'But decisions, Cousin? How can that be? Is it possible you have been unaware that I have only been waiting for your mourning period to end before offering you my hand?'

Lydia's heart sank. She'd been hoping that this might be avoided but, since it couldn't, her best course was to speak very plainly so that there could be no misunderstanding.

'No. Your intentions have been clear enough but I have never given you any encouragement. Quite the reverse, in fact.'

Geoffrey brushed this airily to one side.

'I can assure you that I did not heed that, Cousin. I understood your position completely and admired both your modesty and your dedication to Stephen's memory. But now ... surely *now* I may speak?'

'Well, I can hardly stop you,' sighed Lydia, 'but I would very much rather you didn't.'

His expression grew a little less assured.

'What you mean is that you would prefer I didn't pay my addresses just *yet*?'

'No. I mean that I'd prefer you didn't pay them at all.' She drew a bracing breath and said, 'I'm sorry, Geoffrey. I don't wish to be rude or to wound your feelings. But I'm afraid that I have absolutely no intention of marrying you – either now or at any time in the future. And, to be honest, I can't imagine why you ever thought I would.'

'But we ... we had an understanding,' he spluttered.

'No. We didn't. *You* had an understanding with Margaret and Joseph that was less to do with me personally than about keeping Stephen's money in the family. Somehow, the three of you persuaded yourselves that I'd meekly do as you wished. It was a mistake.' Softening her tone a little and managing something vaguely akin to a smile, she said, 'I'm sorry if you are disappointed. But there's no point in continuing this conversation because my mind is quite made up. So perhaps --'

She stopped speaking as Margaret sailed into the room, closely followed by Joseph.

'My goodness, Lydia – colours at last. And not before time, in my opinion.'

'Earning your good opinion is naturally one of my foremost priorities, Margaret,' came the dulcet reply. 'But now we are all here ... perhaps this would be a good time to tell you of my future plans and to clear away any misconceptions.'

Joseph blinked. 'What are you talking about?'

'Two things. Firstly, Cousin Geoffrey has made me an offer of marriage which I have refused. And secondly --'

'Refused?' gasped Margaret incredulously. 'What do you mean – you *refused*?'

'I said no. How much clearer must I make it?'

'But you *can't* say no. You have a – a duty to the family and --'

'I don't know what gives you that idea, Margaret. You are my step-daughter-in-law – not my mother and neither you nor Joseph is related to me by blood. I shall not marry Geoffrey and no amount of blustering or arguing the point is ever going to make me. Furthermore, I have taken a lease on another house and --'

'*What?*'

'And will be moving there next week,' continued Lydia calmly ignoring the interruption. 'Nancy and Tam will be coming with me – also little Madge from the kitchen. Since you never wanted me to employ them, I feel sure you'll be happier choosing their replacements yourself.' She smiled, aware that she'd finally deprived them all of words. 'And now I think it might be best if I took supper in my room so that the three of you can damn my intransigence to your hearts' content.'

Upon which note, she walked out – for once to the sound of nothing but her own footsteps.

Upstairs, Nancy took one look at her face and said, 'Oh my! You told 'em, didn't you?'

'Yes. I'd hoped to put it off for another day or two but events overtook me. Basically, the Reverend Neville proposed, I said no and Margaret embarked on one of her tirades. So I decided to get everything over in one go and told them I was leaving.' She grinned. 'I imagine they're still trying to work out a way of stopping me.'

'Can they?' asked Nancy.

'No. Ah – I told them that you would be coming with me, so you needn't take any nonsense from Margaret. In fact, it might not be such a bad idea to install Tam and Madge in the new house right away … and you can begin packing.'

'I've already started.' Nancy hesitated and then said, 'I'm sorry if I've done wrong, Miss Lydia but I reckon Mistress Pyke must've over-heard something I said to Tam. She asked if you might have a place for her as well.'

Lydia's eyes widened and then she burst out laughing.

'Cook wants to come too? My God. Margaret will have an apoplexy.'

* * *

Two days later, Lydia had just left the house when Mr Wakefield hailed her from across the street. Winnowing swiftly through a press of carts and drays, to catch up with her, he said, 'This is fortunate. I was just about to call on you.'

You don't know how *fortunate*, thought Lydia.

Since she'd made her Grand Announcement, Margaret had taken to lying in wait in the hall to continue haranguing her about her decision to live elsewhere and her refusal of Cousin Geoffrey's proposal. Needless to say, it had taken no time at all for Margaret to blame the latter on Sir Ellis Brandon and Mr Wakefield and the secret hopes she was convinced Lydia cherished about one or both of these gentlemen.

'You've abandoned your widow's weeds,' remarked Gilbert, eyeing her forest green gown with approval. And, offering his arm, 'May I escort you to wherever it is you're going?'

'If you don't mind braving Duck Lane.'

'Duck Lane?' he repeated. And wrinkling his brow slightly, 'I can't say I know it.'

'No. You wouldn't. It's off St Martin's, just north of Newgate Market. Not, I am sure, an area you'd normally frequent.'

'But you do?'

She nodded. 'I have business premises there.'

'Really?' He looked surprised. 'I had no idea. What sort of business?'

'A lorinery,' said Lydia. And briefly explained, adding, 'I go there most days for an hour or so – mostly, I admit, to escape Margaret.'

Mr Wakefield laughed.

'For which no one could blame you. But your lorinery sounds interesting. Can I see it?'

'If you wish.' Having reached the end of John Street to cross Long Lane, Lydia lifted her skirts well clear of the ground as they prepared to circumnavigate the meat market at Smithfield where the gutters were always full of accumulated filth. 'You should understand that I employ men from both sides in the recent conflicts – so if you have any strong political views, I would be glad if you kept them to yourself.'

'Of course.' He grasped her arm when her foot slipped on something resembling rotting offal. 'Forgive me ... but do you usually walk through this area alone? It isn't very pleasant – or even safe, I would have thought.'

'It's safe enough. Most of the meat traders know who I am. But I agree that the smell takes some getting used to.'

Leaving the worst of the stench behind them at the turning to Duck Lane, they arrived at the lorinery to find Nicholas helping to load an order on to the cart. Lydia smiled a greeting and said, 'Isn't that Jem Buxton's job?'

'He's finishing the packing so I thought I'd make a start.'

Nicholas looked at Mr Wakefield and then back to Lydia with an air of mild enquiry.

Lydia made the necessary introductions, gave the two gentlemen a moment to acknowledge each other and then promptly ushered her guest inside.

Gilbert said, '*Sir* Nicholas? He can't work for you, surely?'

'He doesn't. He ... I suppose you might call him a volunteer.' Lydia saw no need to explain exactly how and why Nicholas had somehow become a permanent member of the lorinery team. 'I have a few things to discuss with my foreman. But you are welcome to look around and the men will answer any questions you may have. However, please don't wait for me. I have other calls to make and Nicholas will probably accompany me as I need to speak with him anyway.' She smiled and offered her hand. 'But thank you for this morning.'

He bowed over her fingers. 'It was my pleasure.'

* * *

A little later, walking beside Nicholas to Strand Alley, Lydia said, 'How long did Mr Wakefield stay?'

'Quite a while. He wandered around the workshop – even went upstairs – and spoke to a few of the fellows, though he didn't seem that interested in them. Who is he?'

'A relatively recent acquaintance. His late parents seem to have known Stephen and he's convinced there is some family connection.'

Nicholas shot her a curious glance. 'And is there?'

'I don't believe so.' Lydia paused and then said, 'Since I revealed my plans, Margaret has become even more objectionable than usual. I didn't intend to move to Bishopsgate until next Friday but I don't think I can stand much more of her. Could you spare the time to help transfer my things on Tuesday, do you think?'

'Tomorrow if you like,' he replied readily. 'Since you're hardly taking any furniture – which, by the way, doesn't seem right to me – one cart-load should be sufficient.'

'I'm not prepared to fight over every cupboard or chair,' she shrugged. 'It's not worth the effort. I've bought enough to make the house habitable and can purchase anything else I need later.' She gave a tiny gurgle of laughter. 'Did I tell you that, as well as my own servants, Margaret's cook wants to work for me? You can't *imagine* the furore that caused. I honestly thought Margaret would explode.'

'You mean,' he grinned, 'that you hoped she would.'

They strolled on in companionable silence for a few minutes until Lydia said casually, 'Have you had any word from Colonel Maxwell?'

'Oh. Didn't I say?' Nicholas's artless tone was at variance with the gleam of laughter in his eyes. 'He got back last night.'

The unexpectedness of it caused Lydia's breath to hitch. She took a moment to ensure that her voice was level and that she didn't blurt out anything stupid. Then she said, 'Safe and sound, I trust?'

'Aside from a nasty bruise on his jaw that Toby and I reckon he probably got some time in the last week – yes. If an extra pair of hands is needed on Tuesday, I daresay he'd help. He's reporting to Major-General Lambert today but is trying to avoid coming to Secretary Thurloe's attention.'

'He doesn't want to resume his previous duties?'
'That's one way of putting it,' responded Nicholas cheerfully.
'Another is to say he'd sooner have some lingering disease with boils.'

SEVEN

'My congratulations,' said Major-General Lambert. 'Naturally, I hoped you would succeed where I failed ... but knowing Colonel Brandon, I didn't dare count on it.'

'The credit isn't all mine, sir,' replied Eden. 'Gabriel's change of heart had more to do with the manner in which Gerard and the others were tried for treason than anything I said.'

'Yes. And one sees his point, of course.'

'But you're pleased it had at least one positive outcome.'

'Quite.' Lambert toyed idly with a quill, running it back and forth through his fingers. 'The outcome in Scotland is equally pleasing. General Monck did well.'

'He did. But if Colonel Morgan hadn't got lucky at Dalnaspidal, General Monck would still be chasing Middleton from Perth to Caithness and back,' observed Eden bluntly. Then, 'However ... I know some of what has been happening here during my absence, but by no means all of it. With Parliament due to open in less than a fortnight, is there anything I ought to be aware of?'

'Nothing particularly significant. The treaty with Portugal was signed on the same day Dom Pantaleon was executed. But the French ambassador, was implicated in an Anabaptist plot to murder Oliver and immediately ordered to leave the country.'

'That's unfortunate. Are we still speaking to France?'

'We are. Thanks to the muddled and seemingly endless negotiations between ourselves and both Spain and France, the Protector indicated his willingness to continue talking to King Louis with the result that a new ambassador has been sent.' Lambert leaned back in his chair, his expression enigmatic as ever. 'In a nutshell, Oliver has continued playing the game from both ends. He asked Spain to give him Dunkirk until it could be exchanged for Calais. Then, before he received Spain's reply, he asked France to cede Brest until Dunkirk could be wrested from Spain. Unsurprisingly, France said no. More recently, Oliver has decided on a commercial treaty with the French rather than a military alliance and he's currently preparing to attack Spanish colonies in the West Indies.'

Eden took a moment to assimilate this barrage of information. Then, frowning a little, he said, 'Naval warfare? Again?'

'Just so. They're calling it the Western Design and I fear it's going to cost as much – or quite possibly more – than the Dutch War.'

'I wouldn't have thought the Treasury could stand it.'

'It can't – though the optimists think our ships will return laden with Spanish gold.'

'Not impossible, I suppose.' Another moment's thought, and then, 'Shouldn't some of these decisions have waited until Parliament is in session? Or to put it another way, how many of them had anything to do with the Council of State?'

'I feel sure Colonel Brandon would say not enough. But Oliver has the bit between his teeth, you see.'

'And you think Parliament can halt that?'

'I live in hope. For the rest, Charles Fleetwood has been made Lord-Deputy of Ireland and, in his usual immoderate fashion, is pursuing the policy of clearances.'

'I thought we'd stopped doing that.'

'We had. Fleetwood doesn't believe we went far enough and is busily consigning the Irish Catholics to Connaught. I believe Oliver has written asking him to curb his enthusiasm … but, knowing Charles, I doubt it will have much effect.' Lambert tossed the quill down and eyed Colonel Maxwell meditatively. 'Would I be right in assuming that you've no burning desire to return to Secretary Thurloe's office?'

'Do you really need to ask?'

'Probably not – though I generally prefer not to make assumptions. Do you think you might feel inclined to continue working for me?'

'Something else you needn't have asked,' returned Eden lightly. 'But doing what?'

'Officially, commanding some of the guard details at Whitehall. It needn't take up more than a few hours a week and, when Major Moulton returns to London, you can add him to the strength.'

'And unofficially?'

'Something more covert. Recently, I've been hearing whispers. Doubtless Thurloe has heard them too. We know that, due to an outbreak of smallpox in Spa, Charles Stuart has moved his court to Aachen in the Netherlands. He's also made Sir Edward Nicholas his Secretary of State – which may or may not be pertinent.'

'And the whispers?'

'That an organisation calling itself the Sealed Knot exists – its function being to authorise and control Royalist activity. Yes – I'm aware that Thurloe has been on the trail of this for some time. But now there are rumours of another, more militant group that is seeking support among disaffected Presbyterians and even some radical elements such as the Fifth Monarchists and Levellers.' Lambert paused. 'I know Thurloe's attitude to the Royalists and also his methods. Spies, agents provocateur and multiple arrests – all effective enough, I grant you. Personally, I'd like to try a more subtle and less unforgiving approach but, as you'll appreciate, I can't do it openly.'

'Meaning,' said Eden slowly, 'that you want me to do it for you.'

'Yes. Correct me if I'm mistaken but I sense that you have no more wish to see all the Cavaliers either dead or behind bars than I do myself.'

'No. You're not mistaken. We'll never heal the country that way.'

'My own opinion precisely. Furthermore, I've seen the list of incoming members for the new Parliament. There are more Moderates than anyone anticipated and even a number of known Royalist sympathisers. This, coupled with a reasonable approach to some of the less hot-headed Cavaliers might be turned to good effect.'

'Who did you have in mind?'

'Edward Villiers. He's a sensible man. And he's both trusted and highly-regarded by the court-in-exile.'

'He's also still in the Tower. Or so I thought.'

'He is – but not for much longer. Both he and Willys have petitioned for their liberty and Thurloe knows he hasn't any reason to continue holding them. I suspect they'll be out by the end of the month.' Lambert's gaze became speculative. 'There's also Sir William Compton.

Another level-headed fellow ... with whom I thought you might already be acquainted.'

Eden laughed and shook his head.

'We've met. He was in the Tower after Colchester in '48 at the time I was posted there. Not, you'll agree, the kind of circumstances likely to foster friendship.'

'You hadn't come across him before that?'

'When he was holding Banbury Castle, you mean? No. And since he's six or seven years younger than me, our paths never crossed before the war either. On the other hand,' he continued reflectively, 'he's neither stupid nor, I would imagine, one to hold a grudge.'

'So you'll do it?'

'Yes.' Eden got to his feet and grinned wryly. 'Let me know when Villiers is released and where I can find Compton and I'll do my best.'

* * *

Back in Cheapside, Eden found Mr Turner explaining to no less than three disconsolate young ladies that Mr Maxwell was currently unavailable and would be so for several days. Colonel Maxwell didn't need to ask where his brother had gone. En route for London two days before, he'd half-expected to meet Tobias riding *ventre à terre* in the other direction and had only been surprised by finding him still at his work-bench.

Upstairs, Nicholas was about to sit down to a very belated noon-day meal. Tossing his hat on to a chair, Eden said, 'Gone to Thorne Ash, has he?'

Nicholas swallowed a mouthful of cold beef.

'Apparently. I wasn't here. He says his sister is pregnant. Did you tell him that?'

'I didn't need to. Toby and Tabitha communicate in ways that pass all understanding. Or ways, at least, that are beyond mine.' He sat down and reached for a clean platter and a slice of game pie. 'Tell me Nick ... speaking as a Royalist, how would you feel about an approach from the other side of the fence?'

'What sort of approach?'

'The sort aimed at finding some middle ground that might lead to a less hostile relationship.'

Nicholas took his time about answering. Finally he said, 'I'd listen.'

'And then?'

'That would depend on whether or not I considered the person who'd approached me to be honest and trustworthy.'

'And assuming you were satisfied that he was both these things?'

'Assuming that ... I'd probably pass what he'd said to other men I thought might be receptive.'

Eden nodded.

'Good. That's what I hoped you'd say.'

'I gather that this is your next task. Your idea or Lambert's?'

'Lambert's. It might work or it might not – but it's worth a try.' He paused and took a bite of pie. Then, 'I don't suppose you know either Edward Villiers or William Compton?'

'No.'

'Pity. An introduction and having someone to vouch for me would have been helpful.'

'Shouldn't saving the King and the Duke of York from assassination be sufficient recommendation?'

'It would be if anyone knew I'd done it – ah. I almost forgot. I met your friend Colonel Peverell while I was in Perth.'

'Ashley?' Nicholas stared at him. 'What was he doing there?'

'Gathering information for Charles Stuart. Coincidentally, he heard my name and took the opportunity to seek me out. He asked after you, of course and told me that Francis is about to become a father ... after which we had quite an interesting conversation.' Eden grinned. 'Cordial, too – in case you were wondering.'

'I wasn't. I always thought you'd like him.'

Silence fell for a few minutes as both of them returned to their food. Then Eden said casually, 'Have you seen Deborah recently?'

'Yes. I call on her from time to time. She's perfectly well and seems happy. Fisher's still besotted and his children plainly adore her.'

'She doesn't come here?'

'No. She sends a servant with Toby's pies – oh. I ought to tell her he's away. I'll go tomorrow. So if you wanted to send her a message, I could --'

'No. No message. Just tell her I asked after her.' Eden helped himself to another slice of meat and changed the subject. 'How are things going with Mistress Neville?'

Nicholas flicked him a brief, considering glance.

'There's been no further trouble at the lorinery and Aubrey is still in Shoreditch – though from choice rather than necessity.'

'No one came looking for him?'

'They came but Lydia sent them away no wiser and probably with a headache.' Nicholas laid down his knife and pushed his platter aside. 'As for Lydia herself, between the appalling step-daughter-in-law and the oily cousin who won't take no for an answer, she's --'

'Stop,' interposed Eden. 'What cousin?'

'There's only one. The Reverend Geoffrey Neville. The family want her to marry him and are driving her demented over it – so she's moving into a house of her own tomorrow. About time, too, if you ask me.' He paused. 'I gather Sir Ellis Brandon is still sniffing around.'

Eden frowned.

'Brandon isn't to be trusted. Does she know that?'

'I think so – though she hasn't said as much. And now there's this fellow, Wakefield. I don't know what to make of him but there's no denying he's a good-looking charmer of the sort women generally like.'

Eden leaned back in his chair and kept his expression perfectly bland.

'Too much competition for you, Nick?'

'Hardly.' Nicholas finally decided to answer the question he was fairly sure Eden had been asking in the first place. 'I like Lydia. I even admire her. But that's all. Did you think there was more to it?'

'I ... wondered.'

Yes. I rather thought you did.

'Well, there isn't. And it wouldn't do me much good if there was.' Nicholas pushed back his chair and stood up. 'Lydia Neville isn't interested in me. I rather suspect her eye has been drawn in quite another direction.' He smiled a little and added, 'Of course, I could be wrong. Either way, it's not for me to give away a lady's secrets.'

* * *

On the following day Nicholas and Trooper Buxton took a cart to John Street to collect Lydia's belongings and also those of her brother. Margaret, Joseph and their two bickering daughters eddied around them carping, demanding to know what was being taken and generally getting in the way. Just when the noise level was reaching its peak and Lydia felt like screaming, a voice pitched to keep fifty troopers in order said blightingly, 'Enough! This bear-garden can be heard half-way down the street.'

Instant silence as everyone turned to face the speaker.

'Thank you,' said Colonel Maxwell, stepping through the open doorway. 'Good morning, Mistress Neville. If the behaviour I've just witnessed is normal in this household, I understand your desire to leave it.'

Lydia flushed, remembered to curtsy and opened her mouth to reply but, before she could do so, Joseph said belligerently, 'And who the devil might you be?'

'Eden Maxwell, Colonel and senior aide to Major-General Lambert,' snapped Eden. Then, pointedly ignoring him, 'Trooper Buxton – perhaps you'd escort Mistress Neville to Bishopsgate while I take your place here.' He smiled briefly at Lydia, adding, 'I think we'll get on quicker without you. And, since it's likely to be a busy day, you won't want to start it with a headache.'

She managed not to laugh but couldn't resist saying softly, 'I'm happy to see you safe and well, Colonel. And thank you.'

Eden shook his head. 'Just go. Doubtless we'll talk later.'

Margaret stepped squarely between Lydia and the door. She said spitefully, 'Do you think I don't know what you're up to? You just want somewhere you can consort with all your men whenever you like. I always knew you'd turn out to be no better than you should be – what with your fondness for trollops and gutter-scum. Like calls to like. That's what I --'

''Scuse me, Miss Lydia.' Trooper Buxton stepped in front of her and looked down at Margaret with an expression of utter disgust. 'I reckon you've said enough, you old cat. Move – or I'll make you.'

Margaret spluttered incoherently but allowed her husband to pull her aside.

Lydia smiled at her with lethal sweetness.

'Goodbye, Margaret. I shan't expect you to visit.'

And she walked out into the sunshine.

* * *

It was, as Eden had said, a busy day.

Aubrey turned up shortly after the laden cart and joined the others in carrying chests, boxes and a few small items of furniture to the appropriate rooms. Then, when the opportunity for a private word presented itself, he said, 'Colonel Maxwell?'

'Yes?'

'I – I wanted to thank you,' he mumbled awkwardly. 'You needn't have helped me get away and I know you took a risk in doing so.'

'Yes,' agreed Eden coolly. 'I did – and won't do it twice. Try remembering that next time.'

'There won't *be* a next time. God knows I was uncomfortable enough with the whole business – and only got sucked into it because I liked John Gerard. Now he's gone ... well, I'm done with such things.'

'Good. And now that's said, you can give me a hand with this clothes chest.'

By the late afternoon, the house – though still sparsely furnished – was beginning to resemble a home and enticing smells were coming from the kitchen where Mistress Pyke was preparing a hearty meal for the workers.

Lydia seized a moment to tidy her hair and remove the voluminous apron she'd worn to protect her gown. Then she went looking for the Colonel and was lucky enough to find him alone in the room she'd chosen as her office. Shutting the door behind her, she said, 'This is uncommonly good of you, Colonel. I'm sure you have many other more important matters demanding your attention.'

'Not today.' Engaged in transferring books from packing cases to shelves, Eden barely glanced round. 'You'll probably want to re-organise these when you have the time but I thought you'd prefer to be rid of the boxes.'

'Yes.' She perched on the edge of a chair, wanting to talk to him but unsure what to say. 'How was Scotland?'

'Wet, chilly, exhausting ... and, for the most part, enjoyable.' He stopped what he was doing to look across at her and was belatedly aware of the fact that she had dispensed with the ugly widow's cap and was no longer wearing black. The dark brown hair contained hints of bronze and the cornflower-coloured gown intensified the winter-sky blue of her eyes. Previously, he'd thought her almost plain. She wasn't. Surprised at himself, he pushed the thought aside and said, 'Tell me something. Did that unpleasant female *always* speak to you like that?'

'Most of the time, yes.'

'Then I'm surprised you didn't take the opportunity to slip some henbane into her syllabub.'

'The temptation was almost over-whelming but I managed to resist it.'

'I commend your will-power.'

'Thank you.' Lydia hesitated and blurted out, 'It wasn't true – what Margaret said. I don't – I haven't --'

'I never thought you had,' he interrupted, calmly obviating her need to find the right words. And with a swift, slanting grin, 'Although, from what Nick tells me, you're quite sought-after.'

'Don't!' she groaned. 'If you'd met Cousin Geoffrey, you wouldn't tease me.'

'Oh dear. That bad, is he?'

'Worse!'

'Ah. And Ellis Brandon and ... Mr Wakefield, is it?'

'Nicholas *has* been busy,' remarked Lydia trenchantly. 'He'd have you believe every man I meet falls victim to my fatal charm and that I'm surrounded by suitors.'

'And aren't you?'

'Not unless *you'd* like to court me as well?' She stopped, aghast at having let her tongue run away with her. A tide of colour washed over her face and she said abruptly, 'That was a joke. I wouldn't want you to think that I ... that I ...'

'I don't think it.' *Or do I? Is this what Nick was hinting at? And if it is, what – if anything – do I want to do about it?* Deciding that, until he knew the answer to that question, the safest course was to change the subject, he went back to work and said easily, 'Your brother has promised me he'll stay out of further trouble. I trust he's made you the same promise?'

'Yes. He's been working with Mr Morrell and wants to go on doing so – which I'm extremely glad about.' She picked up a cloth and began dusting the books Eden had piled up on the desk. 'It's time he grew up – and this may be just what he needs.'

'Very probably, I should think. If Jack's prepared to train him, it's presumably because he sees an aptitude worth nurturing. You may not know it – but he's considered the foremost armourer in the country.'

'Is that how you came to know him? Through his work?'

'No. My former commanding officer is Jack's foster-brother.' Eden pulled out the last of the books. 'Gabriel left London after the King's execution and hasn't been back since. But he's going to be sitting in the forthcoming Parliament so I imagine he'll visit Shoreditch at the first opportunity. And that reminds me of something I wanted to say to you, if I may?'

'Of course. What is it?'

'I once warned Aubrey to be wary of Ellis Brandon. For different reasons, I'd like to say the same to you. He's sly, he manipulates the truth and he attracts trouble – usually for other people.'

'You know him?'

'We've met. But I know a great deal about him – and none of it good.'

'How come?'

'Because he's Gabriel's half-brother.'

She blinked. 'Now I'm confused.'

'Yes. It's complicated. But my point is that, if Ellis asks for your hand, you should think very carefully before accepting him.'

'I shan't need to think at all,' said Lydia candidly. 'In truth, I don't like him very much. And even if I did, I'm perfectly well-aware that he's only interested in me because Aubrey was idiot enough to tell him that Stephen left me well-provided for.' She smiled wryly. 'I know money is my main attraction. Since it was the same with Cousin Geoffrey, I can hardly *fail* to know it.'

Eden surveyed her thoughtfully. Her hair was escaping its pins to form tiny curls around her face and he recognised that there was something very appealing about her ... something that had stuck in his mind all the time he'd been away and culminated in the way he'd thought of her when he'd been at Thorne Ash. Now he realised that he'd rather like to sample that soft pink mouth – and, if he was honest with himself, quite a few other things as well. Moreover, he *liked* her; liked her enough to contemplate attempting to form a relationship – except that he knew he couldn't. She was a respectable woman and was no more likely to take a lover than he was a wife ... all of which meant that the only possible relationship they could ever have was that of friendship. And a cautious friendship, at that – so her reputation didn't suffer and he didn't raise expectations he couldn't meet.

A voice at the back of his mind told him to be careful. He tried. Then he let a slow smile dawn and said, 'You do yourself an injustice, Mistress Neville. You've also been unfortunate in meeting the wrong men. We're not all so cold-blooded and venal, you know.'

Caught unawares by his smile and the disturbing way his eyes had lingered on her mouth, it took time for his words to penetrate the fog in Lydia's brain. When they did, she said stupidly, 'Yes. I mean, no. Of course. I know that.' And, attempting to pull herself together, 'I'm sorry. I should go. The food is probably ready and I doubt if Nancy has set the table. Excuse me.'

And she fled.

Eden watched her go.

Damn, he thought ruefully. *Was that embarrassment – or something else? How the hell does one ever know?* And then, *I wonder what she'd have done if I'd kissed her? Screamed? Slapped my face? Or just possibly ... no. Best not to think of that.*

* * *

By the time her team of helpers were assembled around the table, Lydia had recovered her composure though she was still furious with herself for behaving like a witless ninny. Really, that smile of his had a lot to answer for. He probably had women falling over him in droves. Fortunately, she was too sensible to allow herself to be one of them.

During the course of conversation over a substantial supper, Eden referred in passing to the imminent arrival of Colonel Brandon and then, glancing at Nicholas and Aubrey, immediately added, 'But do *not* tell Jack. Give Gabriel the chance to surprise him.'

Trooper Buxton said wistfully, 'Colonel Brandon. Now *there* was a good officer, for all he could scare the hell out of you. One of the best, he was – present company excepted.'

'Present company included, if you like,' shrugged Eden. 'I wouldn't dispute it.'

'Think he'd come to Duck Lane one day, sir? I'd like to pay my respects – and I daresay Dan Hayes would an' all.'

Eden shook his head.

'I'm sure the Colonel would enjoy sharing a jug of ale with you and the others – but not at the lorinery. Leave it with me, Buxton and I'll arrange something.' Eden stood up and reached for his hat. 'Thank you for supper, Mistress Neville. Both the food and the company were excellent but it's time I left.'

'Yes. That is – of course.'

Despite knowing that she ought to avoid being alone with him again, Lydia found herself rising to show him out. He inclined his head, stood back to let her precede him and, once out of earshot of the others, said simply, 'If I embarrassed you earlier, I apologise.'

Lydia's nerves promptly went into spasm.

You didn't embarrass me. I embarrassed myself – but we'll let it pass or I'll probably do it again.

'There's no need, Colonel. I was ... I suppose I was just surprised. It's of no consequence at all – so please forget about it.' She gave him a determined smile. 'Thank you again for your help today. I'm very grateful.'

'No need for that either,' remarked Eden, putting on his hat. 'I enjoyed myself. Perhaps I could call again in a few days to see how you and Aubrey are settling in?'

'Yes. Of course. I don't yet know what hours Aubrey spends in Shoreditch but I am assuming he will usually be home for supper. I – we would be happy if you cared to join us one evening.'

'Thank you. I'd be delighted.' He took a step through the front door and then half-turned back, tilting his head slightly. 'Surprised, Mistress Neville? By a very tepid compliment? You really *do* know the wrong men.'

And he was gone.

EIGHT

The following morning brought Eden two notes. The first was from Major-General Lambert stating that Edward Villiers and Richard Willys were to be released from the Tower later that day and would be required to provide an address. The second was from Colonel Brandon announcing that he had just arrived in London and could be found at a house in Cockspur Street near the Tiltyard.

Eden threw on his sword, grabbed his hat and strode out.

He was admitted to a pleasant three-storey house by a fellow with a broad Yorkshire accent, who said, 'If you'll give me a minute, sir, I'll tell Colonel you're here.'

Eden shook his head. 'Where is he?'

'Front parlour, sir. Upstairs – second door on right. But I ought to --'

'Don't worry. He won't mind. And if he does, I'll shoulder the blame,' returned Eden, already taking the stairs. And, reaching the landing, he called out, 'Stand to, Colonel!'

'What the --?' A door jerked open and Gabriel stepped through it, cursing when he banged his head on the lintel. Then, seeing Eden, 'Oh – very funny.'

Eden grinned and held out his hand.

'Did you doubt I'd come to welcome you back? How are you?'

'I'll be a damned sight better when I get used to low ceilings. I've cracked my skull three times this morning alone.' But he gripped Eden's hand and smiled back. 'It's good to see you. Come in and take some ale. Venetia's not here – but Moulton travelled down with me. Doubtless you'll trip over him soon enough.'

'Doubtless,' agreed Eden. Then, 'Since you're a temporary bachelor, why don't you leave the servants to get this house ready for Venetia and come and stay with us? As you're aware, there's plenty of room and you won't need to duck every time you go through a doorway.'

Gabriel gestured to a chair and turned away to pour ale.

'That's extraordinarily tempting and I certainly wouldn't mind imposing on you for the next few days until the House convenes. But once it does so, this place is more conveniently situated.'

Eden accepted the mug he was offered and said, 'Come to Cheapside and see how it goes.'

'Thank you. If your brother won't mind?'

'Toby's hot-footed it off to Thorne Ash because Tabitha's pregnant.' He paused briefly. 'She's lost two already and the last time was bad. So Toby won't be able to settle to anything until he's sure she'll be all right. The price of being a twin, I suppose.'

Gabriel nodded and dropped into a chair.

'Young as they are, we see it occasionally with Kit and Rob. Rather unnerving, actually.' He took a sip of ale. 'How did you get on at Thorne Ash?'

'After Ralph knocked me on my backside? Better than previously. I spent time with Jude and found him surprisingly mature for his age. I even asked if he'd like to come and stay with me for a few weeks – though I'm not sure that will happen unless I can somehow make provision for Mary to come as well.' Eden drew a long breath and expelled it. 'The worst moment was when he told me he'd worked out the truth about Celia and challenged me to confirm it.'

'And did you?'

'Yes.'

'About his sister's paternity as well?'

'Yes.'

'Good.' Gabriel frowned slightly. 'Does the girl know?'

'Jude says not – and naturally enough, he doesn't want her to.' He stared into his ale. 'I made more of an effort with her than I've done in the past ... but she still looks at me as if I'd got two heads.'

'What did you expect? It will take time.' Gabriel leaned back in his chair and decided to change the subject. 'And what have you been doing since you got back from Scotland? More skulduggery in the Intelligence Office? Or are you temporarily unemployed?'

'That will be the day. Lambert has a new bee in his bonnet,' replied Eden. And, after describing his current mission, added, 'I'm hoping to catch up with Edward Villiers later today – which should provide some indication of the kind of reception I can expect.'

Colonel Brandon took his time about answering but finally he said, 'I never met Villiers. But I suspect I'm better-acquainted with Will Compton than you.' He grinned suddenly. 'We used to take the air together while we were both lodged in the Tower. You, of course, were just the fellow with the keys.'

'I haven't forgotten that.'

'Neither have I, as it happens. So if you think I can help, you need only ask.'

* * *

Back in Cheapside a further note from Lambert revealed that Colonel Villiers had been duly released and could be found at the Rose and Crown on Fleet Street. Leaving Gabriel to settle into the spare bedchamber whilst getting over his first glimpse of Mistress Wilkes's bosom – the magnitude of which had actually stopped him in his tracks for an instant – Eden changed out of his uniform and set off to try his hand at diplomacy.

He found Edward Villiers in a corner of the tap-room with another fellow he assumed must be Sir Richard Willys. Villiers was a lightly-built man of roughly Eden's own age and height. Willys was both older and stockier. Eden repressed a sigh. He knew a great deal about Villiers. Of Sir Richard, he knew only that he'd earned his knighthood on the battlefield and had briefly served as Governor of Newark. Eden wondered if he'd be allowed to speak to Villiers privately but suspected that he wouldn't – which meant being doubly careful what he said.

'Colonel Villiers?' he asked, holding out his hand. And, when the other man rose looking mildly surprised, 'We haven't met – but I was hoping you might spare me a few minutes of your time.'

Villiers accepted his hand but said, 'And you are?'

'My name is Maxwell.'

Villiers shook his head slightly, indicating that the name meant nothing to him. Willys, by contrast, came to his feet saying forcefully, 'I know who you are. You were at Newbury with Waller. So you're not plain *Mister*, are you?'

'Your memory is excellent, Sir Richard,' agreed Eden smoothly. 'No. I currently hold the rank of Colonel. But the fact that I'm not in uniform should suggest that I'm not here in any military capacity now.'

'Then why *are* you here?'

'Richard,' said Edward Villiers quietly. 'Perhaps you might allow Colonel Maxwell to state his business as he sees fit?'

Sir Richard grunted and subsided into a chair.

'And in private ... if you don't mind.'

Willys's expression said he minded very much but he stood up, gestured to the other side of the room and said gruffly, 'I'll be over there.'

Smiling faintly, Colonel Villiers watched him go and then, turning to Eden, said, 'You're aware, I'm sure, that Richard and I were released from the Tower only hours ago.'

'I am – and can fully appreciate Sir Richard's reservations.' Eden sat down, signalled to a pot-boy for more ale and, with a hint of humour, said, 'This role is new to me, Colonel so I'll trust you to make allowances.'

'I imagine that will depend on what you have to say. My impression so far is that the matter is delicate and you are unsure how best to proceed. May I suggest you do so directly?'

'Thank you. I'd be delighted.' Eden waited for the pot-boy to pour the ale and go. 'I don't know how much you know of Charles Stuart's recent movements or shifts in policy, but --'

'As much as you do, I daresay. Word leaks into the Tower through every crack.'

'Good. Then you'll know that Charles is at Aachen and that some of the men he's been talking to recently have been cultivating fellows like Wildman and Sexby. Royalists who believe alliances with Presbyterians and sundry Radicals may prove beneficial.'

'Yes. I'm somewhat alarmed, however, to find that you know it too.'

'Very little escapes Secretary Thurloe,' returned Eden flatly. 'But that's not why I'm here. I've been asked to speak with you for two reasons. Firstly because, quite aside from your kinship with Sir Edward

Hyde and his Grace of Buckingham, you have influence with other Royalists of stature ... and, I believe, the ear of Charles Stuart.'

'Since you feel able to refer to both Ned and George by their correct titles, it would be a courtesy to refer to His Majesty the King by his,' observed the Colonel dryly. 'However, I suppose I must accept that you can't ... so let us move on. The second reason?'

'The fact that I can't and therefore don't doesn't necessarily mean I'm averse to doing so. But by all means let us stick to the matter in hand ... and that is that the list of Members for the new Parliament suggests that the composition of the House will be significantly more Moderate than had been expected.'

'Really? That must be a cause for concern in certain quarters.'

'Very likely. But in others, there's a feeling that a degree of reasonable communication between Westminster and the court-in-exile might lead to some middle-ground ... or at least to a reduction of the current levels of hostility.'

Colonel Villiers regarded him steadily over the rim of his ale-pot. After what seemed a very long time, he finally said, 'Who sent you to me?'

'You know I can't tell you that.'

'No. If he or they could do this openly, they wouldn't need you. But I'll require more than vague hints if you want me to take this to the gentlemen best-placed to consider it – with a view, eventually, to placing it before Ned Hyde and the King. I know nothing about you, Colonel. For all I know to the contrary, you might be one of Thurloe's agents provocateur.'

'I'm not – though, as you'll find out easily enough, I worked in his office for a time. But the man who sent me to you is of a very different persuasion – as am I. Neither of us believe the country's divisions can be healed by simply tossing every Royalist-sympathiser into a cell.' Eden hesitated briefly and then said, 'I'm speaking on behalf of someone with both influence and principle. You may well guess who that is ... but I can't confirm it. I can, however, offer you a gesture of good intent on my own behalf – though I'd prefer you didn't reveal where you got the information.'

Villiers nodded. 'You have my word.'

'Very well.' Eden lowered his voice a little more. 'Secretary Thurloe has known for some time of the existence of an organisation which he believes is called the Sealed Knot. But so far as I'm aware, he doesn't yet have the names of any of its members.' He pushed his ale aside and stood up. 'You may want to drop a word of warning in the appropriate quarters.'

A slightly arrested smile, lit the Colonel's grey eyes.

'Yes. I believe I might indeed want to do that. Thank you.' He also rose and held out his hand. 'This has been ... interesting. If I wished to contact you, how might I do so?'

'Send a message to Sir Nicholas Austin at Neville's lorinery in Duck Lane. He'll make sure I get it.'

'Sir Nicholas is to be trusted?'

'He lost an arm fighting for Charles Stuart at Worcester,' replied Eden with a grim smile. 'What do you think?'

* * *

On the following day, Lydia returned from her routine visits to both Duck Lane and Strand Alley to learn visitors were lying in wait in the front parlour.

She stared at Nancy.

'Oh God. All three of them? Here? At the same time?'

Nancy grinned.

'Yes, Miss Lydia. Sir Ellis got here first, then Mr Wakefield turned up and, not ten minutes ago, the Reverend Neville was on the doorstep.' The grin became a laugh. 'What's more, they've all brought flowers.'

'It's not funny,' hissed Lydia. 'Why didn't you send them away?'

'I tried. I said you wasn't at home and I didn't know when you'd be back – but none of 'em took the hint. So I put 'em all in the best parlour so they could set about trying to get rid of each other. Only they haven't.'

Lydia drew a bracing breath and straightened her spine.

'Right. Give me ten minutes. If they haven't left by then, come and call me away. Any excuse will do. Tam's got the plague – the kitchen is on fire – anything. I don't care. Just bring me an escape route.'

And she stalked purposefully into the ominously silent parlour.

All three gentlemen immediately got to their feet and spoke at once.

'Please!' said Lydia, stemming the tide with one upraised hand. 'One at a time, if you wouldn't mind.'

Gilbert Wakefield grinned ruefully and gave a deprecating shrug.

Ellis Brandon raised one brow and made her an extravagant bow.

Geoffrey Neville stormed forward brandishing a bunch of wilting roses and said fulsomely, 'Cousin Lydia! I have been so worried about you. Indeed, since you left John Street I have scarcely been able to sleep. By this morning, I felt I could bear it no longer.' He shoved the flowers virtually into her face. 'I *had* to know how you were!'

'And as you now see, I am perfectly well,' replied Lydia, retreating a step and taking the roses from him with due deference to the many thorns. Then, placing them to one side and turning to Sir Ellis, 'And you, sir? To what do I owe the honour of *your* visit?'

Ellis sauntered forward, kissed her hand with consummate grace and then wrapped her fingers about an exquisitely-tied bunch of white lilies.

Funeral flowers, thought Lydia immediately, pasting an expression of pleasure on her face whilst holding the bouquet at arms' length.

'I merely called to ask if you would care to take a stroll about the Exchange with me one day.'

'I'm sure that would be delightful when I have time – which, at present, I'm afraid I don't. But I thank you for the thought and the flowers.' Placing the lilies beside Geoffrey's roses, she smiled more warmly at Mr Wakefield. 'And Gilbert? What brings you here today?'

He smiled back and held out a simple posy of lavender and larkspur.

'I wanted to wish you joy in your new home and to ask if you needed help of any kind.' He glanced around the still only partly-furnished parlour and added, 'It's a pleasant house and you appear to be very comfortable here.'

'I am – though there is still a great deal to be done.' Lydia breathed in the scent of the flowers. 'As to needing help – it's kind of you to offer but my brother has returned to live with me now so I have him to call upon.'

'Aubrey is back?' drawled Sir Ellis. 'May one ask where he's been all this time?'

'Taking up a new trade. No doubt he'll tell you all about it when you meet.'

Geoffrey scowled. '*What* trade?'

'One that is more to his taste than the pewter business,' replied Lydia unhelpfully. Then, with a swift apologetic smile, 'You must forgive me for not inviting you to stay and take wine, gentlemen. As you'll appreciate, we're not ready to receive visitors yet. My cook is still in the midst of ordering the kitchen to her liking and --'

Her words were punctuated by the pealing of the doorbell.

Oh God. Now what?

Reading her expression without any difficulty, Gilbert Wakefield laughed.

A tap at the door heralded Nancy, her eyes brimming with wicked enjoyment.

'It's the Colonel, Mistress Neville. Shall I show him in?'

The air froze in Lydia's lungs. She didn't know whether she was relieved or worried.

'Of course, Nancy. Please do.'

Eden walked in, his glance taking in the assembled company before settling with the merest suspicion of a smile on Lydia.

'Mistress Neville.' He bowed, hat in hand. 'You're very popular today.'

'So it would seem.'

'Ah ... and Sir Ellis. This is a coincidence. Your brother is currently staying with me for a few days prior to taking his seat at Westminster.'

Some of Ellis's customary swagger evaporated but he managed a harsh laugh.

'Another bastard in Parliament? That *will* make a change!'

Eden tutted. 'You are forgetting your manners, sir. There is a lady present.'

Ellis flushed a little and made Lydia a curt bow.

'My apologies.' Then, 'I wasn't aware that you were acquainted with Colonel Maxwell.'

'Why should you be?' she replied blandly. 'But now *I'm* forgetting my manners. Colonel Maxwell ... you won't have met my cousin-by-marriage, the Reverend Neville. And this is Mr Gilbert Wakefield.'

Geoffrey scowled at the Colonel and muttered something indistinguishable. Gilbert held out his hand and said pleasantly, 'A pleasure, Colonel – but since I suspect that we have already outstayed our welcome, I'll take my leave and hope to run into you again at some other time. Lydia?' He bowed over her hand. 'Send for me if you have need. Failing that, I'll call again in a few days.'

Then he was gone.

Colonel Maxwell eyed Cousin Geoffrey and Sir Ellis expectantly but in a way that made the Reverend fidget and take a sulky and protracted leave involving many exhortations and pieces of extraneous advice. Finally only Ellis was left, his face hard and set and his hands gripping the brim of his hat to damaging effect.

Meeting the other man's stare with an equally challenging one of his own, Eden said, 'You have something you wished to add? A message for Gabriel, perhaps? If so, I'd advise you to be careful how you phrase it.'

'I have nothing to say to either him or you.' Ellis swung round to face Lydia. 'Please excuse me, Mistress Neville. As you'll have gathered, there is a deal of animosity between the Colonel and myself – as a result of which you should apply more than a pinch of salt to anything he says with regard to myself.'

'And *vice versa*,' murmured Eden. Then, helpfully, 'If you were thinking of leaving, Mistress Neville's maid appears to be waiting to show you out.'

Ellis narrowly avoided grinding his teeth and, with a curt bow, strode from the room.

Eden shut the door behind him and eyed Lydia enquiringly.

'Is it a case of there being safety in numbers – or do you just enjoy seeing them glare at one another?'

'Neither.' She dropped into a chair, her hands curled into fists in her lap. 'They were all already here when I got back. I was --'

'Wait.' He frowned. 'Are you saying they arrived in your absence and your servants *let them in?*'

'Yes. Of course, there's only Nancy at the moment. She tried to send them away --'

'Get a man. Someone with the ability and authority to oversee the household and deal with anyone who thinks they can just invade your privacy without so much as a by your leave.'

'Yes. I probably will. There's been no time yet to --'

'Make it a priority.'

Lydia stood up again, pink with annoyance

'Colonel Maxwell,' she snapped. 'I've already had a very trying half-hour with three gentlemen – two of whom I'd have been happy not to see. If, on top of that, you're going prevent me finishing every blasted sentence, I shall probably become extremely ...' She stopped.

'Extremely what?' Eden asked hopefully.

'Uncivil.'

He gave a choke of laughter.

Lydia scowled at him. 'It's not funny!'

'Forgive me – but it is. *Uncivil?* You can do better than that, surely?'

'Of course I can – but after your help on Tuesday, I'd sooner not be rude.'

'Don't let that hold you back. I can take it.' He grinned. 'I can even be fairly uncivil myself when the occasion warrants it.'

'So I've noticed,' she said waspishly, wishing he'd stop smiling at her and holding tight to her annoyance because it was better than behaving like a complete imbecile.

'That's more like it,' he encouraged. And then, when she sealed her lips tightly together refusing the provocation, 'I know what it is. I didn't bring flowers.'

'I didn't *want* you to bring flowers. I didn't want *them* to bring flowers either. And anyway – just look at them! The roses are half-dead, I can't abide lilies and I doubt there's a single vase in the house.' She let out a huff of exasperation. 'This is a ridiculous conversation.'

'But effective.'

'*What?*'

'When I arrived, you were angry, weren't you? Angry that they were here uninvited – or indeed at all – and angry because you wanted to tell them so but good manners wouldn't let you.'

'Perhaps,' she admitted grudgingly. 'I suppose so.'

'Good. And now you've vented some of that anger snarling at me --'

'I did not *snarl* at you.'

'Oh you did. Fortunately, I enjoyed it. We didn't argue at all the other day and I quite missed it.'

Lydia drew a steadying breath and, in a tone which even to her own ears sounded sulky, said, 'Now you're calling me argumentative.'

'And so you are,' came the maddening reply.

'I am not!'

Eden folded his arms and grinned at her, saying nothing. And suddenly Lydia felt laughter bubbling up. She said unsteadily, 'Colonel Maxwell, you are atrocious.'

'Eden,' he replied unexpectedly. 'My given name is Eden. I don't think using it will lead you into a life of vice, do you?'

'No.' Laughter died as quickly as it had come. She liked him far too well already and he was making it all too easy for that liking to slide into something more. She cleared her throat and said, 'Despite appearances to the contrary, I was glad to see you earlier. But you haven't told me why you came … that is, if you had any particular reason?'

'I had, as it happens.' *Just not the one I'm going to admit to.* 'Troopers Buxton and Hayes and one or two of your other workers want to meet Colonel Brandon so I'm arranging for them to do so tomorrow evening over a meal in a tavern. But Gabriel is interested in the lorinery and would like to visit. He knows about your rule and will abide by it. In fact, I suspect he'll take a look around and then cross-question you on your general organisation.'

Lydia gave the merest suggestion of a shrug.

'He's welcome to visit and I'm happy to answer any questions he may have – though I don't see why he'd want to know.'

'It's because he does something not entirely dissimilar himself,' replied Eden. 'I'll leave Gabriel to explain it properly – but basically he's encouraged the tenants on his estate to form a sort of co-operative which benefits everybody and keeps the rents low.'

'Really? I've never heard of anything like that.'

'Neither have I. Come to that, I don't suppose Gabriel had either until he realised he had to find a way of making Brandon Lacey solvent without also making his people worse off than they already were.'

She eyed him thoughtfully.

'The Colonel doesn't sound much like Sir Ellis.'

'He's *nothing* like Sir Ellis. The only thing they share is a father. Ah.' Eden stopped. 'I should have asked. Does illegitimacy bother you?'

'Of course not. Why should it?'

'Excellent. Then will the day after tomorrow suit you?'

* * *

Colonel Brandon's visit to the lorinery was a huge success all round. The men were delighted to see him and he responded to their quips with terse ones of his own that had everyone laughing. He peppered Lydia with questions on every aspect of the business as well as her hopes for its future and listened intently to the answers. Then he explained how things worked at Brandon Lacey and why changing the status quo had been necessary.

At the end of two hours when he was about to leave, Lydia looked curiously up into eyes the colour of storm-clouds and said, 'Not that I'm not *glad* you're doing it ... but, after everything you've told me, I'm a little surprised you're willing to sacrifice five months of the year to sit in the Parliament.'

'It's an extremely reluctant sacrifice,' he replied. 'But in the end I realised it had to be made because if the entire country descends into either political chaos or the rule of the sword, there'll come a point when Brandon Lacey won't be immune. As for the rest, I've known Oliver Cromwell for a number of years and there was a time when, had I been told that one day he'd assume the mantle of kingship, I wouldn't have believed it. Now, however, I merely remember and worry about something he once said.'

'What was it?'

'Nobody rises so high as he who doesn't know where he's going.'

NINE

When Cromwell had chosen to open the first Parliament of the Protectorate on the anniversary of his victories at Dunbar and Worcester, thought Gabriel Brandon sardonically, he had plainly not taken account of the fact that September 3rd would fall on a Sunday. The result was that the Godly set up an immediate clamour against not keeping the Sabbath day holy – which, in turn, meant that none of the four-hundred-and-sixty elected members could take their seats until the religious services of the day were over.

The chamber was noisy, the benches crowded and no one seemed to know what was happening. In short, it was no better than Gabriel had expected. He passed the time mentally putting names to faces, which drew him to the conclusion that there were two main groups. One was composed of men who'd still been sitting in the Rump at the time Cromwell had dissolved it the previous year; men like Haselrig, Whitelock and Lenthall. The other was the presence of the Army; a plethora of senior officers such as Desborough, Harrison, Skippon … and Lambert.

Gabriel met the latter's eyes and received a nod of acknowledgement. It was just as well, decided the Colonel sourly, that they were too far away from each other to speak.

Eventually, in the middle of the afternoon, came a summons for the members to attend the Lord Protector in the Painted Chamber.

There was a sudden shout of, 'Sit still! Do not stir!' and the call was immediately taken up by a dozen or so other voices.

Gabriel looked across at the instigator, still stubbornly seated and recognised him as John Bradshaw – the fellow who had presided over the late King's trial.

Holy hell, he thought grimly. *Is this how it's to be?*

Fortunately, virtually everyone ignored Bradshaw and got to their feet, grumbling.

Crammed like herrings in a barrel inside the Painted Chamber, it was fortunate that, for once, Cromwell was disposed to be brief. Having begged the members to embrace a spirit of unity and reason, he asked them to reassemble the following morning – first to listen to a sermon in Westminster Abbey and then to hear his own address.

An hour later, Gabriel was back in the parlour at Cheapside.

'What happened?' asked Eden.

'What do you think?' came the irritable reply. 'Nothing.'

'Ah. Well, if you've found today annoying, I can't wait to hear what you make of tomorrow.'

'Why?'

Eden smiled acidly. 'He's having a procession. I know because I'm in it.'

* * *

Colonel Brandon had no intention of attending the service in the Abbey. He'd had more than enough of wasting time with endless prayer meetings during the Army debates at Putney back in '47. So he leaned against a wall by Palace Yard and watched the approach of something not far short of a royal progress.

The coach bearing Cromwell, his son, Henry, and John Lambert was large, heavily ornamented and very clearly new. Around and behind it, hats in hand, marched a hundred officers and soldiers; as much a demonstration of power and status as it was a guard of honour. Amongst the watching crowd around him, Gabriel heard rumbles of disgust. He wondered whether Cromwell didn't know or simply didn't care how much public opinion was turning against him.

Inside the Painted Chamber it got worse. They'd erected a damned throne. A great carved and gilded thing, set two steps above the assembled company.

They might as well put a crown on his head and have done with it.

The Lord Protector was accompanied with all due pomp and ceremony to his appointed place and a hush fell over the chamber.

Over in the far corner, Gabriel could see Samuel Radford – poised to record events as close to verbatim as made no matter in his extremely accomplished short-hand. Although Gabriel had twice taken supper with Jack and Annis during the last week he hadn't yet come across the young Leveller. Idly, whilst waiting for Cromwell to begin, he wondered if Sam had changed at all ... and then, with wry amusement, decided that it was unlikely.

Finally, after gazing for a few moments over his waiting audience, Cromwell spoke.

'Gentlemen ... you are met here on the greatest occasion that I believe England ever saw; having upon your shoulders the interests of three great nations with the territories belonging to them. And truly, I believe I may say that you have upon your shoulders the interests of *all* the Christian people in the world.'

Gabriel's expression became openly sardonic.

Does he honestly believe that? If so, Louis of France and Philip of Spain might have something to say on the subject. But then, as we all know, God is an Englishman.

The speech gathered momentum. Today, Cromwell was plainly prepared to make up for yesterday's brevity and speak at some length. He generously chose to pass over those past events which might *"set the wound fresh a-bleeding"* rather than achieve the *"healing and settling"* he hoped for. Since these events presumably included the King's execution as well as three civil wars, Gabriel conceded that this omission was probably wise. But the Protector had no hesitation in blaming the Levellers for stirring unrest with their foolhardy attempts to overturn *"the ranks and orders of men, whereby England hath been known for hundreds of years"*. And he denounced the Fifth Monarchists for believing themselves to be the only ones to both understand and properly protect God's will.

Gabriel folded his arms and leaned against the wall.

Why the hell can't he just give us his blessing and send us off to start work?

But of course that was too much to hope for. First he had to indulge in self-congratulation regarding the achievements of his Protectorate thus far; law reform, regulation of the Church, peace with the Dutch and foreign treaties with Denmark and Portugal. It was therefore some time before he finally he came to the only thing which, in Gabriel's opinion, needed to be said at all.

'I have not spoken these things as one who assumes to himself dominion over you --'

Oh really?

'-- but as one who does resolve to be a fellow-servant with you in the interest of these great affairs and of the people of these nations. I shall trouble you no longer; but desire you to repair to your House and to exercise your own liberty in the choice of a Speaker, that you may lose no time in carrying on your work.'

Gabriel lingered outside the chamber until Mr Radford appeared.

'Well, Sam,' he said, extending his hand. 'Still keeping the public informed, I see.'

Samuel grinned, gripped the proffered hand and said, 'Somebody has to. How are you, Colonel? It's good to see you.'

'Likewise – though I'm due at the House and can't, unfortunately, stay to talk with you now. However … briefly, what did you make of that?'

'Hard to say. He was less fervent and Godly than when he addressed the Barebones Assembly. I suspect a grain or two of disillusion. But whether he's seriously looking for Presbyterian support is anybody's guess. Personally, I doubt it.' Samuel hugged his papers to his chest and said rapidly, 'The first two or three days should be a fair indication of how things will go – so I'll catch up with you then.'

By the time everybody was back on their benches in Westminster Hall the day was already well-advanced with the result that the House conducted only two pieces of business.

It chose a Speaker; and it ordained a fast day to be held on September 13th.

Hell and the devil, thought Colonel Brandon. And left the chamber before anybody could engage him in conversation.

* * *

Having spent the afternoon arranging duty rosters with Ned Moulton at Whitehall, Eden came home to find Gabriel scowling into a tankard of ale. Since this did not bode well, Eden filled a tankard of his own, sat down and said, 'All right. I can see that the day has left you unable to contain your enthusiasm. So tell me.'

'Cromwell,' said Gabriel bitingly, 'addressed us from a bloody throne – or at least the next best thing to one – and talked for what felt like an eternity.'

'Of course. He's always liked the sound of his own voice. What else?'

'He instructed us to sod off to the House and elect a Speaker.'

'Not, I presume, in those exact words?'

'No. Some fool proposed Bradshaw.'

Eden stopped being facetious and groaned. 'Tell me they didn't choose him.'

'They didn't. They just did something equally crass. They elected William Lenthall.'

There was a long silence. Then, 'You're not joking, are you?'

'Do I look as though I'm joking?'

'No. Unfortunately.'

'They elected the same Speaker who served the House from 1640 to the day, thirteen years later, when Cromwell tossed it out. I don't know what that tells you ... but it tells *me* that the relationship between this Parliament and the Protector is likely to prove similar to the Long Parliament's relationship with King Charles. In other words – stormy.'

'Well, we expected that ... even wanted it.'

'No. What we *wanted* was to ease Cromwell into working *with* Parliament – not alienate him from the outset. With a bit of give-and-take on both sides, we might expect to effect some change – such as a return to constitutional government and a respect for the letter of the law; and, in time, even some diminution of Cromwell's power. But I've a feeling that this House is so hide-bound and full of past grievances that it's likely to plunge straight into confrontation. Oh, Oliver's packed it with a large – some might say overly-large – Army presence in addition to the members of the Council. But my impression is that disgruntled Rumpers and Presbyterians out-number it.'

'If that's so, the House should be able to make some impression with or without the Protector's co-operation.'

'Not necessarily. The *Instrument of Government* clearly grants the Protector and Parliament equal power to rule jointly. If that doesn't happen ... if the House blocks Cromwell at every turn ... we may see Parliament being dissolved at the first opportunity. After all, since Oliver's following in the late King's footsteps in so many other ways, why not that one as well?'

'Hell,' muttered Eden. Then, 'He can't, surely? If, after the fiasco of the Barebones Assembly, he shows himself unable or unwilling to work with Parliament either, he'll make himself a laughing-stock. And if he *did* dissolve the House – what the hell can he replace it with this time?'

'Precisely. So we'd better hope it doesn't come to that.'

* * *

On Tuesday, Gabriel sat through numerous complaints from the Republicans about Cromwell's kingly arrogance in summoning them to his presence instead of attending them in the House as tradition dictated. No sooner was this over than another member demanded to know whether the House was prepared to hand over control of the law to a single man; then Arthur Haselrig made an impassioned appeal for establishing one form of religion and suppressing all the sects. But before any of these questions could result in a vote, a suggestion that the first order of business ought to be ratifying the *Instrument,* sent discussion off at a tangent again.

Wednesday was supposed to have been devoted to a serious study of the *Instrument* itself. Instead, Cromwell's Treason Ordinance of the previous January raised its ugly head. Since this prohibited any attack on the Protector's actions or title, many members saw it as a muzzle – effectively removing their right to freedom of speech within the House. It took a great deal of persuasion from Thurloe, Desborough and some of the other Councillors to convince the doubters that the ordinance did not apply to proceedings within Parliament and avert a motion to declare the said ordinance invalid. Gabriel supposed there was satisfaction of a sort in the fact that they'd finally had a vote on anything at all.

On Thursday, instead of simply endorsing the *Instrument* – as the Protector had clearly expected – they began picking it apart clause by clause. Realising that this was likely to take some time, Gabriel resigned himself to several days of tedious, long-winded argument combined with a numb back-side.

* * *

Eden, meanwhile, spent a pleasant hour with Jack Morrell while his sword was given a new edge. Then, telling himself he was only doing it because he had nothing more pressing to do, he paid a call on Mistress Neville.

The door was opened by a muscular fellow with an air of courteous implacability which defied anybody to suppose they might get past him if he didn't choose to let them. Eden smiled to himself.

He was made to wait in the hall, then shown into the parlour where he found Lydia sitting, quill in hand, in front of neat columns of figures. He said, 'You took my advice, then.'

'Henry?' She rose, alarmed at just how pleased she was to see him and grateful that she'd had a moment's warning. 'Yes. He's remarkable.'

'He's certainly large.' He gestured to the ledgers. 'Am I interrupting?'

'Thankfully, yes.' She closed the books and rose. 'Mr Potter's record-keeping is meticulous to the point of obsession which makes arriving at the quarterly totals a time-consuming business. But please sit down, Colonel.'

'I thought we'd agreed you were to call me Eden?' He took a seat by the hearth, noticing that the room now boasted a large carved dresser, side-tables and a fire-screen. None of it was new but everything spoke of comfort and quality. Although he tried not to, he also noticed that several locks of hair were drifting tantalisingly round Mistress Neville's neck and that the décolletage of the dark blue gown was just low enough to tempt him to look. 'You're making this room very welcoming.'

'It takes time – but I hope so.' Lydia moved to the dresser, poured two glasses of wine and set one down beside him. 'Is this a casual visit – or was there something in particular that you wanted to talk about?'

'I've been to Shoreditch where your brother made a fairly decent job of beating the dents out of my back-and-breast. Jack says he learns fast.' He paused. 'Jack also says that Annis thinks he's more than a little attracted to young Verity.'

'He hasn't said as much – but I think so, too. Unfortunately, Verity only has eyes for Nick and hasn't yet accepted that nothing will come of it. A problem easily solved if Nick would be honest with the poor girl.'

'Have you told him that?'

'I ... hinted at it.'

'Ah. Perhaps – if you think Nick should speak plainly – you ought to do the same.'

Lydia's eyes narrowed and she sat up a little straighter.

'Is that another attempt to lure me into argument? Because if so --'

'It isn't.' Eden threw up one hand in a gesture of surrender. 'It isn't – and I apologise. The truth is that it wouldn't do any good if you *did* spell it out. Nick isn't capable of hurting Verity with open rejection. It's not that he's weak. But he has an overpowering instinct to protect the helpless. Children, small animals ... that sort of thing.'

'And Verity?'

'And Verity,' he agreed. 'When he first met her she was being bullied at home. She needed a little kindness, Nick supplied it and she repaid him by searching for him among the wounded after Worcester. If she hadn't done that – and persuaded me to help – he'd be dead. So you see ...?'

'Yes. She believes herself in love with him and Nicholas believes he owes her something – quite possibly his life.'

'In a nutshell, yes.' Eden looked at Lydia thoughtfully. 'May I ask you something?'

'What?' she asked cautiously.

'You married Stephen Neville when you were what ... twenty-two?'

She nodded, unsure where this was going.

'Was there no one before that? No young man you might have married had things been different?'

'No.' She shrugged, trying to look careless. 'I suppose I never met a man who inspired more than liking.' *But I've met one now and it's tying me in knots.*

'I imagine you will re-marry, though?'

'Perhaps. Will you?'

His face closed up tight in a way she'd never seen before. 'No.'

He must have loved his dead wife very much.

The instant conclusion clenched painfully in her chest ... while the tone of his voice and every line of his body shouted that this was a thing best left alone. On the other hand, he'd been prying into her life in one way or another since the day she'd first met him, so perhaps she was entitled to just a *little* prying of her own.

'You seem very sure.'

'Yes.' Another monosyllabic warning.

'You have children, I believe?'

Eden drew an explosive breath and, when he spoke, his voice was like splinters of ice.

'My son is fourteen and his sister is ten. They have an aunt, an uncle and a grandmother – and I visit when I can. Was there anything else you wanted to know?'

Yes. Why this is such dangerous ground ... and why you referred to your daughter as your son's sister? However, I can see that I'd better not ask.

'Yes. *Now* who's snarling? And please don't say you're not. You look furious.'

Eden clenched his hand hard on the arm of the chair and took a moment to force the worst of his tension away. Then he said stiffly, 'I'm sorry. It's not a comfortable subject.'

'I gathered that.'

He reached for his wine but, instead of drinking, merely stared into the glass.

Without warning and without looking up, he said rapidly, 'I'll say this now so that you'll never enquire further. My late wife eloped with her lover in 1644. Jude was four years old and Mary, just a few months. No doubt you can draw the obvious conclusion from that. As for Celia ... I never saw her again. I trust that makes the position plain?'

'Yes.' *Oh God. Why did I start this? No wonder he won't speak of it.* 'Yes. Perfectly plain. I – I'm sorry. I had no idea or I wouldn't have ...'

She hesitated, spreading her hands. 'And now I don't know what to say to you.'

'No one ever does.' Eden set the glass aside and stood up. 'You might, however, have some inkling as to why I don't plan to re-marry. And now – having snarled at you – I should probably go.'

'No – please don't.' Lydia shot to her feet, the words tumbling out before she could stop them. 'If you leave now, you'll feel awkward about coming here again. And – and I'd regret that even if you wouldn't.' She stopped, appalled not just at what she'd said but at what she'd *nearly* said.

He looked at her oddly for a moment. Then that lethally attractive smiled dawned and he said ruefully, 'I would, actually. Regret it, that is. I enjoy our conversations.'

She swallowed hard. It wasn't much but it was more than she'd expected.

'As do I. So you'll stay and drink your wine?'

'Yes. And I thank you for asking.'

* * *

Later, when he had gone, Lydia sat for a long time in contemplation of what he'd told her. Try as she would, she couldn't begin to understand how any woman lucky enough to be Eden Maxwell's wife could look elsewhere even for a moment. It certainly wasn't because he hadn't loved her. That was as clear as day. If he hadn't given her every bit of his heart, there wouldn't be a part of it that, even after ten years, still hadn't healed.

Then there was the not-insignificant fact of her having left him with a child he suspected – or perhaps even knew for certain – wasn't his. That was betrayal of the worst kind. No man deserved that. And what kind of woman could do it?

She realised after a time that her cheeks were wet. And that was when she knew.

She'd fallen stupidly, ridiculously in love with a beautiful, intelligent, honourable man who had no intention of every re-marrying ...but who enjoyed her conversation.

* * *

Unaware of what he'd left behind him, Eden sat down to supper with Nicholas, half-inclined to broach the subject of Verity Marriott. He was just working up to a subtle enquiry when the door opened and Gabriel walked in.

Tossing his hat and coat aside, Colonel Brandon dropped into a chair and said, 'Tell me that some of this food is still hot.'

'More or less.' Eden pushed various dishes and platters towards him, then went to pour some ale. 'Or I can ask Mistress Wilkes if she'll --'

'No. Don't get that woman up here, for God's sake.'

'Why not?'

'Because I find myself staring. It's embarrassing.' He stopped putting food on his plate and looked up. 'It's all very well for you to laugh. You're both used to it.'

'I don't think,' remarked Nicholas, 'that it's something a man ever gets used to. So much natural bounty in one place.'

'That's one way of putting it.' Gabriel cut a slice of pie. 'I can think of others.'

'I see what it is,' said Eden. 'You're missing your conjugal pleasures. We --'

'If you are wise, you'll stop right there.'

'-- don't have that problem,' finished Eden. 'Nick ... when was the last time you had a --'

'I can't remember,' said Nicholas firmly, 'and we are *not* having this conversation.'

'No,' agreed Gabriel, refusing to laugh. 'We are not.'

A little later, having given Colonel Brandon time to eat, Eden said, 'So ... another scintillating day in the House?'

'Oh yes. The excitement is crippling.'

'Share it, then,' invited Nicholas. 'As Eden has just kindly pointed out, I could do with a little excitement – no matter how vicarious.'

'You can't be that desperate – though we did receive word that the Earl of Glencairn has finally surrendered to General Monck. A relief to our fellows in Scotland, no doubt.'

'Most certainly,' agreed Eden. 'What else?'

'Cromwell has presented the House with a list of no less than eighty-two ordinances he wants ratified; everything from financial and legal reform to highway repair and traffic laws. Meanwhile, my esteemed colleagues have voted to nominate an Assembly of Divines, aimed at creating a single religion and suppressing all minority sects.'

Amusement vanished from his listeners' faces and Eden said tightly, 'Cromwell's been trying for toleration. It's about the only thing he's got right. So whose idea was that?'

'Arthur Haselrig's. But it might not have passed if Harrison hadn't threatened to deliver an Anabaptist petition calling on Parliament to rise up against tyranny – and boasted that he'd have twenty thousand men at his back to support it. I daresay you see the trend. For the rest, we've spent the last three days battling back and forth over the same ground. Oliver's friends – now becoming known as the Court Party – want the *Instrument* accepted as it stands. The Opposition wants changes restricting the Protector's power to act independently – mainly to avert summary dissolution; words suggesting that the office of Protector be *'limited and restrained as the Parliament should think fit'* are being bandied about. The problem with *that*, of course, is that the elections were based on Clause One of the *Instrument* – which makes changing it now a legal and electoral nightmare. They also want members of the Council of State to face re-election every three years ... and they're asking Cromwell to surrender command of the Army to another officer.'

'Lambert?' guessed Eden.

'His name has been mentioned.' Gabriel paused. 'Naturally enough, Cromwell isn't about to simply give way so, much to everybody's surprise and backed by the Council, he's offered a compromise. He'll allow some alterations to the *Instrument* if the House will guarantee three key points. That the 'single person' – in this case Oliver himself – has the authority to prevent Parliament sitting till Doomsday; that control of the Militia be shared between Protector and Parliament; and that religious freedom be maintained.'

'That doesn't sound too unreasonable,' observed Nicholas. 'Will they do it?'

'Ask me tomorrow,' replied Gabriel. 'That's when we vote.'

* * *

In the event, there was no vote because the Protector had decided not to risk it going against him. Arriving at the entrance to the House, Gabriel and his fellow members found the doors barred and guarded by soldiers who directed them again to the Painted Chamber.

There, after speaking at some considerable length, Cromwell informed them that he required only one thing. Their signatures on what he called the *Recognition*.

It was brief and, though coercive, not unreasonable.

I do hereby freely promise and engage to be true and faithful to the Lord Protector and the Commonwealth of England, Scotland and Ireland and shall not, according to the tenor of the indentures whereby I am returned to serve in this present Parliament, propose or give my consent to alter the Government as it is settled in a single person and Parliament.

The terms that accompanied this were also brief – and very straightforward.

Only those members who signed would be permitted to resume their seats in the House.

Gabriel was one of the first hundred or so who put their hands to it. Bradshaw and Haselrig, he was pleased to discover, led the exodus of those who wouldn't

TEN

Quite suddenly in the days following the hiatus at Westminster, Lydia found herself beset with a mixture of minor irritations and very real problems. In one sense, this was good as it gave her little time to brood over Eden Maxwell. In another, she started to wonder why troubles never came singly.

A note reminding her of his invitation to stroll in the Exchange arrived from Sir Ellis Brandon. Lydia replied, saying that unfortunately she was still far too busy and also managing to include a seemingly casual reference to her meeting with Colonel Brandon which she rather suspected would put an end to Sir Ellis's attempted courtship.

In Strand Alley, Lily Carter informed her that no less than five destitute widows of the recent Dutch War had applied for places.

'The Navy doesn't do anything for them at all,' she said in disgust, 'and I'd like to take them on but we don't have room.'

'Then we'll find it,' responded Lydia. 'Actually, it might not be that difficult. The rooms on the floor above these are free at present. I'll speak to my man-of-law about leasing them. But, in the meantime, give places to the widows and, if necessary, send some of the others to work at my house until I've made the necessary arrangements.'

'*Your* house, Mistress Neville?' asked Lily, startled. 'But won't Sir Aubrey mind?'

'Since he spends all his daylight hours in Shoreditch, I doubt he'll even notice.'

* * *

Lydia went home and wrote a note to Lawyer Hetherington about leasing the entire house in Strand Alley. She was just asking Nancy to pay a boy to deliver it when Henry announced the arrival of a visitor.

'Are you at home to the Reverend Neville, Madam?'

She groaned. 'I suppose I'll have to be.'

Henry bowed and withdrew to usher Geoffrey in. Lydia noticed with some amusement that he did not quite close the parlour door behind him.

'Cousin!' The Reverend surged across the room with his usual gushing enthusiasm. 'What a joy to find you at home – and alone. A rare privilege.'

'And a brief one, I'm afraid because I have an appointment in an hour on Cheapside.' It wasn't true. She intended to spend the afternoon finishing the accounts for the lorinery. But the excuse would serve to speed Geoffrey on his way. 'What can I do for you?'

'Really, Lydia! It's impossible to rush into what I wish to say. I cannot do it.'

'Try,' she said. And then, sensing the onset of one of his long, usually pointless speeches, 'Or, if you can't, perhaps I can say it for you.'

'You? No. How could you possibly know --'

'At a guess, you're here to ask me to reconsider your proposal of marriage.'

Geoffrey turned rather red and spluttered incoherently.

'I'll assume that means I'm right.' Folding her arms, Lydia spoke with slow and deliberate clarity. 'I will not change my mind. I will *never* change it. How much clearer can I be? I am not going to marry you, Geoffrey – not ever. And, if you are wise, you will stop asking – before I'm forced to be even more uncivil than I'm being right now.'

He stared at her, completely at a loss for words.

'Good.' With a decisive nod, Lydia went to the door and, as she'd expected, found Henry just on the other side of it. She said, 'Reverend Neville is leaving, Henry. In future, if he wants to see me he can request an appointment.'

'Certainly, Madam.' Henry bowed. 'Sir? Allow me to show you out.'

His complexion turning from red to puce, Geoffrey hesitated for a moment. Then, seeing defeat staring him in the face, he stalked out.

* * *

Next day in Duck Lane, she found Dan Hayes – still on light duties due to his weakened arm – slapping whitewash on the front gate and muttering to himself.

'Daniel? Why are you doing that?'

Trooper Hayes spun round, an arc of white flying from his brush and missing Lydia's skirts by a hairsbreadth. 'Oh Gawd, Miss Lydia! Didn't know you was there. I've not got this dratted stuff on you, have I?'

'No. Just explain why you are painting the gate. It was fine two days ago.'

'Bloody apprentices – begging your pardon, Miss. Out for a lark and daubing daft slogans everywhere. Sir Nicholas said to paint over 'em.'

Frowning a little, Lydia walked inside and found Nicholas checking an order-sheet while two of the men packed goods into a crate.

'Apprentices, Nick? Or something else?'

He froze, meeting her gaze with a frowning one of his own. Then, handing his lists to the nearest man, walked over to her and said curtly, 'Obscenities. You don't want to know.'

'Were you going to tell me about it?'

'Not unless it became a regular occurrence. And as of this morning, we have more important problems. Belcher's have cancelled their order.'

Lydia drew a sharp breath. 'Why?'

'They claim that a number of harnesses in the last batch we sent them were faulty. Since I processed the order myself, I know that they weren't. Mr Potter's gone round there now to try and straighten it out. If he can't, I'll go myself.'

She thought for a moment.

'It's odd, don't you think? Nothing since the incident with the ladder – and now two things in one day?'

'Yes. It could be coincidence ... but a little extra vigilance won't go amiss.'

Lydia nodded and, as casually as she could, said, 'Mention it to Colonel Maxwell, if you think it worthwhile. He usually has a suggestion.'

Nicholas grinned suddenly.

'Yes. And it would be a shame to waste the opportunity.'

She felt her cheeks grow hot.

'What is that supposed to mean?'

'I think you know. I also think that if you simply invited Eden to supper, he'd come.'

* * *

The afternoon brought a note from Mr Hetherington that had Lydia running hot-foot round to his office.

'What do you mean – the deeds to Duck Lane are missing? How *can* they be?'

'I don't know, Mistress Neville. I have had no occasion to look for them since your husband died and it was purely by chance that I noticed their absence yesterday when I took out your file to remind myself of the terms on which you lease Strand Alley.' Mr Hetherington pursed his lips and tapped a quill against his fingers. 'It is possible that the deeds were never in my possession and were somehow left amongst Mr Stephen's other papers.'

'They weren't. I've been through everything twice. If the deeds were there, I'd know. And I'm as sure as I can be that I gave them to you along with everything else of a similar nature. Is it possible that they have been misplaced – perhaps put in the wrong file?'

The lawyer drew himself stiffly to his feet.

'Are you accusing my office of inefficiency, Mistress Neville?'

'No. But if I was, that would be better than negligence, wouldn't it?'

He stared down on her.

'I will instigate a thorough search – though I do not expect it to yield results. Fortunately, since you are resolute in your refusal to sell, the absence of those particular documents need present no immediate problem.'

Lydia also rose.

'Wrong, Mr Hetherington. They present a *massive* problem. For if *I* don't have them and *you* don't have them, it means that someone else does. And neither of us has the faintest idea who that person is – or to what use they may choose to put them.'

* * *

While Lydia was tearing the house apart looking for papers she already knew she wasn't going to find, Colonel Maxwell ran into Major-General Lambert outside Westminster Hall.

'Any progress?' asked Lambert quietly.

'No. I'm still waiting – as, presumably, are Colonel Villiers and his friends. I doubt I'll hear anything until they've got what they believe is a true indication of the feeling within the House. And so far, I'd be surprised if even *you* know what that is.'

'Things are gradually settling down. Aside from the most determined Radicals, the majority of members have now signed the *Recognition* and resumed their seats.'

'So Gabriel has said. And that being the case, perhaps the Protector should have allowed matters to take their course instead of forcing Parliament's hand.'

Lambert sighed. 'Possibly. But Oliver wasn't prepared to risk what he considers to be vital issues. And events have now moved on. A committee has been formed to consider the *Instrument* with a view, possibly, to replacing it with a civil constitution – so I have hopes of achieving some workable balance.'

'As do we all. But first you'll have to end the tug-of-war between Westminster and Whitehall ... and I wish you luck with that.'

* * *

That evening whilst waiting for Nicholas to join them for supper, Gabriel announced that he was moving back into the house near the Tiltyard.

'Not that I haven't enjoyed your hospitality,' he explained, 'because it's been a pleasure. But the house is more convenient for Westminster and I'm expecting Venetia to join me in the next couple of weeks ... certainly, I hope, by the end of the month.'

Eden nodded. 'Well, until she arrives, you can still sup here any time you like. Or any time you have a need to air the frustrations of your day.'

'Thank you. I'll remember it.'

The door opened and Nicholas came in saying, 'I'm sorry. Have I kept you waiting?'

'It's of no consequence,' shrugged Eden. And, as they took their seats at the table, 'You're not usually as late home as this.'

'No. It's been a peculiar day. You might say, fraught.'

'Something's happened? At the lorinery?'

Nicholas nodded, busy piling his platter with pickled cabbage and slices of roast pork.

'This morning we found rude messages daubed all over the gate. And an hour later --'

'What messages?' asked Eden tersely.

'The sort calling Lydia the kind of names I'd rather not repeat and accusing her of various perversions involving cripples.'

'Hell,' said Gabriel, surprised. And then, reading Eden's face, 'This has happened before?'

'That – and worse.' And to Nicholas, 'What else?'

'One of our regular customers cancelled an order – faulty workmanship, they said. I thought it was just an excuse to delay payment because I'd overseen the packing of that consignment myself and there was nothing wrong with it. Only when I went round there, Hal Belcher showed me the evidence. Bridles coming undone ... bits bent out of shape and with roughened edges and so forth.' Nicholas drew an exasperated breath. 'I think I talked Belcher into giving us another chance. I hope so, anyway.'

'Does Lydia know?'

'Everything except the damage to the harnesses. Potter was still at Belcher's when she came and I didn't see it myself until later.'

'Is she worried?'

Whatever Nicholas might suspect and whatever he'd said to Lydia, he wasn't about to betray her to Eden so he said smoothly, 'Enough to ask me to mention it to you.'

Eden glanced at the clock, a fancy gilded thing Tobias had brought back from Genoa. *Too late to go calling on a respectable woman – widow or not.* He said, 'I wish you'd let me know earlier, Nick. You could have sent me a message.'

'Sent a message to you *where*, exactly?'

'All right.' He'd been on the move for most of the day. 'Point taken.'

'You'll see her tomorrow morning?'

'Yes. Early – before she sets out for Duck Lane.'

'Good,' said Nicholas. And restored his attention to his supper.

Gabriel, having listened to the conversation with interest and drawn certain conclusions as a result, said reflectively, 'The little widow's an unusual woman. I like her. Why would anyone want to hurt her?'

'Good question.' Eden frowned at his plate as if it held the answer. 'Today may merely have been coincidence ... but I wouldn't like to rely on it. *Damn*.'

Amusement and speculation lurking in his eyes, Gabriel said, 'The world can be a tricky place for a woman alone. I gather the husband was a good deal older – but she must miss his protection, nevertheless.' He paused and then added casually, 'Still ... she'll be able to choose a younger man this time. I don't imagine there'll be any shortage of volunteers.'

'There aren't.' Eden looked up, his face hard. 'Your bloody half-brother being one of them.'

* * *

The next morning, Colonel Maxwell was hammering on Mistress Neville's door at a few minutes past eight o'clock. With his usual urbane impassivity, Henry Padgett opened the door but, before he could speak, Eden said, 'I know it's early but will you ask if Mistress Neville can see me?'

Although Mr Padgett had only been occupying his current position for a short time, he had enough experience to know which were privileged visitors and which were not. He was also aware that Mistress Neville had been up half the night turning the parlour into a sea of papers and that she had virtually screamed at Nancy when the maid offered to help tidy up. Consequently, he bowed slightly and said, 'I'm sure Madam will be happy to do so, Colonel – if you would but give me a moment?'

Eden nodded and waited, tapping his gloves against his thigh until the major-domo returned and ushered him into the parlour. And then he stopped dead, staring at the chaos before him.

'What on earth happened here?' he demanded crisply. 'Have you been burgled?'

'No.' Lydia looked up from where she knelt on the floor. 'I was looking for something.'

Her face was pale, her eyes strained and her hair was hanging down her back, tied in a ribbon. In contrast to her usual composure, she looked almost distraught.

Eden walked over to her and held out his hand.

'Come and sit down.' And when she was perching, rigid with tension, on the edge of a chair, 'Now take a deep breath and tell me about it.'

'I can't find the deeds to the lorinery. Mr Hetherington ought to have them – I'm *sure* he had them – but he says not. He promised to look but --'

'Stop a moment. Who is Mr Hetherington?'

'My lawyer. He dealt with Stephen's will and everything. But I saw him yesterday and he said he'd noticed the deeds were missing but he wasn't concerned because he thought *I* had them. But I don't. I knew I didn't and I told him that. I'd already been through Stephen's papers more than once and I *knew* the deeds weren't there. Only I couldn't help looking – hoping I'd been mistaken and they'd turn up. But they haven't.'

Eden sat down facing her.

'Then the lawyer will find they've been in his office all along,' he said calmly.

'Perhaps. But what if he doesn't?'

'He will.' In all the time he'd known her, Eden had never seen Lydia Neville looking even remotely fragile ... but she did so now. Frightened, strained and somehow smaller. He reached out and took her hands, feeling her fingers cling to his. 'And worrying yourself silly won't help.'

'I know. But somehow – on top of everything else yesterday – it all seemed too much.'

'That's understandable. Nick told me what happened and we'll come to that later. But first we need to address the matter of the deeds – systematically and logically. Yes?'

She nodded, grateful for the warmth of his hands and the feeling of relief his presence brought. She drew a long, unsteady breath and, attempting to recover some self-control, said, 'Yes. You're right, of course. I'm sorry. I don't usually panic.'

'I think I may be said to be aware of that fact,' he smiled. Then, releasing her hands, 'Have you had breakfast?'

Lydia blinked. 'No. I couldn't face it.'

'Neither have I – and I most definitely *could* face it.'

'Oh!' She stood up. 'I'll order food immediately – though not, perhaps, in here.'

'Definitely not in here. But if you'll be good enough to feed me, I'll help you restore order.'

He watched her go, his easy expression slipping away. In truth, he wasn't particularly hungry but recognised that giving her something to do would help. If those deeds really *were* lost ... if, God forbid, they had fallen into the wrong hands and Lydia's ownership of the premises was ever challenged, she was going to be faced with a well-nigh insoluble problem.

And that wasn't the only thing bothering him. All the time he'd been holding her hands and those wide, anxious eyes had been gazing into his, he'd had the devil's own time not pulling her on to his lap and folding his arms round her. In truth, he'd wanted to kiss her ... and not, as should have been the case, merely to give her comfort. He'd wanted it for himself. What worried him was how *much* he'd wanted it.

While he watched her pick at some bread and cheese, he talked about other things; the news from Westminster; the surrender of Glencairn in Scotland ... and finally, the imminent arrival of Colonel Brandon's wife and children.

'You should meet Venetia,' he said thoughtfully. 'She's as direct as you are. God alone knows how she managed to pass muster at Whitehall where lies and flattery were the order of the day. Ah.' He stopped. 'I should probably warn you of a couple of things. Venetia was once one of the Queen's ladies and, despite being married to Gabriel, she's still a Royalist at heart. Don't ask me how that works – I only know that, between them, it does. She's also exceptionally beautiful.'

'Oh. That sounds rather ... daunting.'

'To you? Perish the thought.' Eden grinned at her. 'But enough of that. With regard to the situation at Duck Lane ... Nick has seen the goods your customer claimed were faulty and, from what he told me, all the signs are that they were tampered with after leaving the lorinery. That is something that can be investigated and prevented in future. The daubings on your gate are another matter. Nick will be on the alert for further incursions and so, on a personal level, should you be. Have you told Aubrey about it?'

She shook her head.

'He stayed at Shoreditch last night. He does that sometimes.'

'Then he'd better *stop* doing it,' came the inflexible reply. 'As for the mystery of the missing deeds ...we'll go and tidy up your papers and, while we do, we'll formulate a plan. How does that sound?'

'Sensible.' Without quite being sure why, Lydia felt suddenly shy; then shyness became embarrassment when she recalled how she'd clutched at his hands as if she was drowning. 'Thank you for coming this morning and for – for being so kind. You've made me feel much better. But you don't need to help clear up the mess. I can do it.'

'I'm sure you can. And if you'd rather deal with it in private, then --'

'It isn't that. It's just that I've no business taking up your time when I know how busy you must be.'

'As it happens, I'm not busy at all right now. I'm still assigned to Major-General Lambert – on paper, at least – and all he requires of me at the moment is that I talk to a few people on his behalf.' *Men who Venetia might know. Now there's a thought worth pursuing. Or then again, maybe not. Involving Venetia in nefarious Cavalier activities is likely to result in Gabriel putting my head through the wall.* 'I have nothing pressing to do this morning so I can stay – or not. As you wish.'

Lydia stared at him, helpless to deny what she felt and praying it didn't show.

If you knew what I really wish, you'd be half-way to Scotland by now. 'Then I'd be grateful for your help. Thank you.'

Standing once more amidst the sea of papers, Eden said, 'Is this as random as it looks?'

'Almost,' she sighed. 'Everything falls into one of four basic categories and I began by trying to keep them separate but then panic set in and I forgot.' She looked down a little sadly on the mess she'd made. 'In truth, I could have got rid of most of it months ago. I don't really know why I haven't.'

'Presumably, because you weren't ready. So, for now, I suggest we just sort it into the various piles and you can go through it properly at a later date. Agreed?'

'Yes. Agreed.'

For a time the silence was only broken by the rustle of paper while Lydia tried not to notice the tanned, well-shaped hands systematically sifting and sorting. Then, as areas of the floor once more became visible, Eden held out a heavy brass object some six inches long.

'What's this?'

'Oh.' She gave a wry laugh. 'I'd forgotten about that. It's a key of some sort – though it doesn't fit any lock I know of. But Stephen thought it important and made me promise to keep it safe – so I have. There's a box for it somewhere.'

Eden had already found the box and the scrap of paper lying at the bottom of it.

'And these?' he held out several sheets covered in apparently random groupings of numbers and letters.

'I don't know. Stephen was good with numbers. For example, he could reconcile a ledger in less than half the time it takes me. But he liked mathematical puzzles as well and during the last few months when he was bedridden, he covered endless pages with that sort of thing. I never had the faintest idea what he was doing.'

Eden had a fair idea of what the late Mr Neville had been doing but, keeping his tone casual, he said merely, 'I like playing with puzzles, too. If I promise to return them, would you mind if I took these away to look at them?'

Her brows rose in mild surprise.

'Not at all. Do you think they actually mean something?'

'They obviously meant something to your husband,' he replied. 'So that makes them of interest, wouldn't you say?'

And even more interesting is why the late Mr Neville spent the last weeks of his life devising and perfecting ciphers.

ELEVEN

Over the next few days, a number of things happened.

Six women from Strand Alley, all of them well-known to Lydia, moved into the room she'd prepared – bringing with them a great deal of laughter and numerous baskets filled with the tools of their trade.

Gilbert Wakefield called one afternoon armed with a bunch of Michaelmas daisies, a slim volume of poetry he thought Lydia might like and, for the first time, a quantity of flirtatious banter. On some superficial level, she enjoyed all three. So when Aubrey arrived home early just as Gilbert was leaving, she invited him to stay for supper ... and watched the two men striking up an immediate friendship.

At the lorinery, Nicholas collected the damaged merchandise and supplied replacements which he insisted on unloading himself in the presence of Hal Belcher. This, he informed Mr Potter, was to be their new system. To remove any possibility of tampering, they would make all deliveries in their own carts and insist that goods were checked on arrival in their presence.

Colonel Maxwell sat down to study what he swiftly recognised were three entirely different codes. On first glance, one of them looked so straightforward that he expected to unlock it in a matter of minutes. An hour later he realised he had made completely the wrong assumption and had, in fact, fallen into a neatly laid trap. Eden sat back, smiling.

Very clever, Mr Neville. I'm going to enjoy doing battle with you.

* * *

On the following day, having received word from Lydia that she'd heard nothing from the lawyer, Colonel Maxwell put on his uniform and paid Mr Hetherington a visit.

Forced to admit that he hadn't exactly taken his office apart in a search for the missing documents the gentleman found himself subjected to the Colonel's most forbidding stare and said defensively, 'I was sure Mistress Neville would discover the deeds in her own possession.'

'She didn't. Furthermore, she told you at the outset that she wouldn't,' snapped Eden. Then, 'Can it have escaped your attention that this is a very serious matter? Or that your professional reputation will scarcely be enhanced by a charge of negligence?'

Mr Hetherington blanched.

'I'll set both my clerks on to it immediately, sir,' he promised. 'If the deeds are here, I can assure you that we will find them.'

'See that you do. And keep Mistress Neville informed – or I'll be paying you another visit.'

Mr Hetherington shuddered at the thought.

Eden left the office hiding a grim smile.

* * *

On September 28th, a cavalcade of two coaches accompanied by a groom and two outriders pulled up in the Tiltyard. Venetia had arrived ... along with her younger sister, her maid, all three children, their nursemaid and a mountain of luggage. Regardless of the chaos and grinning stares around them, Gabriel swept his wife off her feet and kissed her until she was dizzy. Then, aware that three pairs of small arms were clutching what bits of him they could reach, he knelt down to hug his children, directed a lazy grin over their heads at his sister-in-law and said, 'Hello, Phoebe.'

While this was going on, a complete stranger sought Nicholas out at the lorinery and handed him a sealed missive addressed to Colonel Maxwell. Since he'd been expecting something of the sort for a while now, Nicholas wasted no time in passing it on to Eden.

'Villiers?' he asked.

'Yes. Finally.' Eden looked up. 'Don't delay supper on my account. I may be late.'

The note directed him to a tavern in Doctors Commons. Eden arrived there early but found Colonel Villiers already ensconced in a corner, partially hidden from the main room by a pair of stout beams. Moreover, he had two companions with him – one of whom Eden instantly recognised.

Eden removed his hat and made all three a courteous bow of acknowledgement.

'Colonel Villiers ... and Sir William.'

Edward Villiers rose and offered his hand, swiftly followed by Sir William Compton who smiled faintly and said, 'I remember you, Colonel.'

'Yes. I imagine one tends to remember one's gaolers.'

'What I primarily recall is being treated with a good deal of civility while you were in command of the Tower – and much less after you were posted elsewhere.'

'Mother always insisted that good manners cost nothing.' Eden sat down and glanced enquiringly at the third man, 'Perhaps someone could introduce me?'

'Henry Wilmot, Earl of Rochester,' murmured Villiers.

Eden narrowly avoided revealing his shock.

Hell, he thought. *Rochester? In England? Why? I hope nobody's going to pretend he's here just to meet me.*

But he bowed to the man who'd got Charles Stuart away after Worcester, shared his subsequent wanderings and worked tirelessly for him ever since as envoy to all the courts in Europe, and said, 'A pleasure, my lord.'

Rochester inclined his head. 'I hope so. Ned, William ... would you allow the Colonel and myself a moment's privacy?'

Surprise registered on both their faces but they immediately rose and moved away.

The Earl said, 'I am placing a great deal of faith in your discretion. You will realise, I am sure, that if my presence in England comes to the attention of either the Secretary of State or *any* of the Army leaders, I face immediate arrest.'

'Yes.' Eden had realised that quickly enough, aware that it made his own position decidedly tricky.

It was about to get trickier still.

'Your name,' remarked Rochester calmly, 'has come up in Paris.'

Although he hadn't previously thought about it, Eden realised that his approach to Villiers had made this almost inevitable. Deliberately flippant, he said, 'Nothing bad, I hope?'

'No.' There was a long, meditative silence. 'I discovered that you and I have a mutual acquaintance. The gentleman in question doesn't share information lightly – or, indeed, at all if he can help it. But in order to convince me that I might trust you ... and without supplying any details whatsoever, he managed to convey the impression that you once performed some far-from-insignificant service for the King.'

The air froze in Eden's lungs.

Had Ashley sodding Peverell lost his mind?

Since there was nothing he could usefully say, he said nothing at all.

'I only mention this, Colonel, so that you will see the possible ramifications.'

Oh I see them well enough.

'Are you threatening me?' asked Eden softly. 'If so, allow me to inform you that it is neither wise nor necessary.'

The older man smiled and shook his head.

'If I'd wanted to threaten you, I wouldn't be keeping what I know from Ned and Will. I merely dislike playing without holding at least one good card.'

'And letting your opponent see it?'

'In certain instances. There is no point to it otherwise.' Rochester leaned back in his chair and toyed idly with his tankard of ale. 'What are you doing here, Colonel? What do you hope these talks may achieve?'

'A more reasonable attitude,' returned Eden. 'On both sides.'

'And that is all?'

'Isn't it enough? Without the constant threat of Royalist-led insurrection, you and your friends wouldn't be facing arrest on a daily basis. That's worth something, surely?'

'To some of us, less than you might think. You're asking us to give up.'

'Give up *what* exactly?' asked Eden impatiently. 'Hope of seeing Charles occupy his father's place? You can go on *hoping* for it. What you *can't* do is continue trying to achieve it by force. The recent rising in Scotland was a waste of time, money and lives on both sides. You must know that. And you must *also* know that the country is sick of bloodshed and upheaval. It's been going on for thirteen years, for God's sake! Time to make an end.'

Rochester sighed. 'I can't argue with that – much as I might like to. Unfortunately, the murder of the late King and personal loyalty to his son aren't lightly set aside. Also, Charles is not quite twenty-five years old and can't exist purely on hope. If there was the slightest chance of a change through negotiation, he'd take it. He is a pragmatist. He knows compromise is essential and will do it. But there *is* no such chance, is there?'

'Of him regaining the throne? No. Cromwell may be unpopular but he has a firm grip on the reins. He isn't going to relinquish it voluntarily and putting him in the ground won't help. In fact, it's likely to put Charles further from the throne than ever because there would finally be some chance of constitutional government.' Eden paused and then, rising said bluntly, 'Personally, I consider the King's execution a lamentable and unnecessary mistake – in which I'm not alone. But it can't be undone. And the opposite side of the coin says that any move towards restoring Charles would leave a lot of currently powerful men wondering just how far his spirit of compromise will actually stretch ... and how many of them would end up entertaining the crowds at Tyburn.'

Rochester also rose. 'Your point being?'

'Accept the hand that is being held out to you. It may not give you everything you want but it offers something. And if, my lord, you are in England to ferment yet another abortive rebellion, I'd advise you to think again.'

* * *

On the following day an event occurred which caused consternation in a few quarters and gales of laughter in a good many others.

Accompanied by Secretary Thurloe, the Protector took a drive in Hyde Park to try out the team of six horses recently bestowed upon him by the Duke of Oldenburg. Part-way through the ride, Cromwell apparently took it into his head to drive the coach himself. This turned out to have been a mistake. Deciding to test the horses' speed, he whipped them up a bit too enthusiastically – upon which the horses tried to bolt, jolting Cromwell from his seat, on to the pole and from there to the ground. Unfortunately, his foot remained entangled in the reins. Even more unfortunately, while he was being dragged along the loaded pistol in his pocket discharged itself.

At this point, Thurloe took a wild leap from the coach, landed badly and wrenched his ankle. Cromwell, unnerved and mildly singed, managed to extricate himself and roll out of the way; and the coachman was finally able to bring the excited beasts to a standstill.

The tale spiralled like a tornado from tavern to tavern, gathering momentum as it went. Secretary Thurloe had screamed like a girl as he flew through the air; he'd broken his ankle and the surgeon had advised amputation. Cromwell had been dragged half the length of the park and shot himself in the arse. The coachman had lost his job and was being charged with treason; so too, for having provided the horses, was the Duke of Oldenburg.

By the time Colonel Brandon made a flying visit to Cheapside an hour or so before supper, saucy verses were already being set to music.

Grinning at Eden, Gabriel said, 'I always felt that loaded pistol was a mistake.'

And Eden, who had only heard rumours, said, 'I assume he *didn't* shoot himself?'

'No. But that ruins the story, doesn't it? And people are having so much fun. I've just heard a fellow remark that he hoped the Protector's next ride would be in a cart to Tyburn.'

'I imagine quite a few others think the same. If you're staying, I'll fetch the ale.'

'No. I'm going home. I only came to issue an invitation. Venetia suggested that you might like to sup with us tomorrow evening.'

'Thank you. I'd be delighted.'

'Good,' said Gabriel, picking up his hat and turning towards the door. Then, as if it was an afterthought, 'I've asked Nicholas as well, by the way. And the widow. You'll arrange to escort her, won't you?'

And was gone before Eden could answer.

* * *

If Colonel Maxwell had doubts about the forthcoming evening, Lydia had more of them. Nicholas had somehow guessed that she liked Eden more than a little; Colonel Brandon was far from stupid; and the Colonel's wife, as well as being beautiful, was probably also a pattern-card of manners, deportment and sartorial elegance. So the most serious question facing Lydia was what on earth she was going to wear.

All her clothes pre-dated Stephen's death and some, thanks to his failing health in the last few months, were even older. Telling herself that it didn't matter and couldn't be helped, she began pulling gowns from the clothes-press. One of them would do. One of them *had* to.

By the time Nancy walked in, the bed was piled high and Lydia was no nearer making a decision. Gesturing to the mess, she said, 'This is hopeless.'

'No it's not. Sit down and leave it to me. Where's that dusky-pink taffeta?' Nancy started sorting through the heap and finally found what she sought at the bottom of it. 'Yes. This one. Now let's get busy.'

An hour later, Lydia stood before the mirror, twisting her hands together. She looked at the low, sweeping neckline and embroidered bodice of the rose-coloured gown. She hadn't worn anything like this for so long she didn't know whether to be elated or alarmed. She said, 'I'm sure widows aren't supposed to show quite so much flesh. I should add the lace collar.'

'Over my dead body. You're fine as you are.'

'And my hair.' Her fingers strayed to the clever tumble of curls piled high on her head. 'It's lovely, Nancy ... but perhaps a little young for me?'

'Stop this minute!' scolded the maid. 'You will *not* go out looking as if you was fifty. And there's the doorbell. That'll be the Colonel.'

'And Sir Nicholas,' Lydia reminded her a fraction too quickly.

'I reckon.' Nancy dropped a light cloak over her shoulders and fastened the ties. 'Sir Nicholas is all right. More than all right, as it happens. But I know which one I'd pick, given the choice. Now – off with you.'

Eden waited in the hall, hat in hand and impeccably neat as ever in moss green broadcloth, against which his hair glowed like dark fire.

Lydia hesitated at the turn of the stairs and then, swallowing hard, continued her descent.

'Good evening, Colonel.

'Mistress Neville.' He bowed politely. 'I congratulate you. In my experience, ladies are rarely so punctual.' And offering his arm, 'Shall we go? The carriage is waiting.'

'Carriage?' It hadn't previously occurred to Lydia to wonder how they were getting to the Tiltyard which lay on the far side of the City. Then, seeing the smart equipage at the door and feeling suddenly guilty, 'Oh. Did you hire this because of me?'

Eden helped her up, waited for her to settle in the seat facing Nicholas and climbed in after her. 'Not at all. Nick and I tossed a coin to see which of us should have the pleasure of taking you up before us on horseback – but then it looked like rain and Nick was worried about his new hat.'

Nicholas grinned and shook his head.

'Ignore him, Lydia. He's been like this ever since he heard this tale about Cromwell shooting himself in the ...' He stopped. 'Well, shooting himself.'

Her eyes widened. '*Did* he?'

'Nearly. You hadn't heard?'

'No. Tell me.'

'Since Nicholas has apparently turned too finicky to use the word 'backside', *I'll* tell you,' said Eden. And proceeded to do so.

By the time he had finished Lydia was pink with laughter, her misgivings forgotten. Then the carriage came to a halt and her skin prickled with nerves again.

Ten minutes later, she wondered what she'd been worrying about. Colonel Brandon welcomed them, his small daughter balanced comfortably on his hip and said, 'Venetia will be down in a minute. The twins are creating a storm. Eden – take Mistress Neville's cloak, will you? I seem to have my hands full.'

And just like that, Lydia knew it was going to be all right.

Inside the parlour, Phoebe Clifford rose to smile cheerfully at her brother-in-law's friends.

Then, when the introductions had been made and Gabriel had put Rosie down in order to pour wine for his guests, the child said clearly, 'Aunt Phoebe ... where is that man's other arm?'

Gabriel communed briefly with the ceiling; Eden turned a laugh into a cough; and Phoebe, turning scarlet, whispered, 'Hush, darling. That isn't a – a polite thing to say.'

'Why?' Rosie continued to gaze at Nicholas in apparent fascination. 'Can I ask him?'

'No!' said Gabriel and Phoebe in unison.

'Yes,' said Nicholas, easily. And dropping on his knees beside Rosie, he said gravely, 'I only have one arm because I lost the other one.'

Her expression said that she didn't find this explanation convincing. 'Didn't you look for it?'

'I did. But it was quite badly hurt, you see ... and it wouldn't ever have worked again.'

The big grey eyes grew worried. 'Couldn't the doctor make it better?'

'No. He tried but he couldn't so I have to manage with just the other one.' Nicholas smiled at her. 'Don't worry, sweetheart. It doesn't hurt.'

'Can ... can I touch where it was?'

'Do you want to?'

She nodded and stretched out her hand. Around them, everyone else in the room held their breath. Then very gently she stroked his shoulder over and over. And returned Nicholas's smile with a beaming one of her own.

Lydia found herself blinking back tears and saw that Eden had turned away, clearing his throat. Mistress Clifford, while biting hard on her bottom lip, was staring at Nicholas with an expression that defied interpretation.

Then the spell was broken as the door opened and the loveliest woman Lydia had ever seen walked into the room; a vision of alabaster skin, silver-gilt hair and pansy-blue eyes.

As though he wasn't aware of doing it, Nicholas stood up, his jaw going slack.

And Lydia saw Phoebe Clifford's gaze drop to her lap, a tiny resigned smile touching her mouth.

'I'm so sorry,' said Venetia. 'I swear the boys deliberately turn into imps from hell every time we have company. And now the cook is telling me that supper will be served in exactly twenty minutes – whether I like it or not, apparently. Sir Nicholas, Mistress Neville ... welcome to the bear-pit. But first,' she turned to her daughter, 'it's past your bed time and Molly is waiting.'

'Sit down, Venetia,' said Phoebe. 'I'll take her.'

Nicholas felt the child slip her hand into his and give a little tug. She said, 'I want you to come, too.'

He looked down at her. 'You do?'

'Yes. I want you to help me with something.' She looked up at him soulfully. 'Please.'

Knowing that look and trying not to smile, Gabriel said, 'Sir Nicholas is a guest, Rosie. If you need help, I'm sure Aunt Phoebe can --'

'It's all right, Colonel,' interposed Nicholas. 'When a young lady asks so nicely, how could I refuse?'

'That's just the trouble,' sighed Venetia. 'No one ever does. And in no time at all, you'll be an uncle. She collects them, you know.'

'Then I'll be honoured,' said Nicholas with a bow. And, accompanied by Mistress Clifford, he allowed Rosie to tow him out of the room.

Accepting a glass of wine from her husband, Venetia immediately sat beside Lydia and asked a stream of questions about the business in Strand Alley; and gradually Lydia recognised that what Colonel Maxwell had said was true. Venetia Brandon was a woman she could imagine becoming a friend.

On the far side of the room and under cover of a desultory conversation with Gabriel, Eden watched the little widow and wondered whether the expanse of décolletage exposed by that rather nice pink gown was as satiny as it looked.

Nicholas and Phoebe re-appeared, laughing.

'Well?' asked Gabriel. 'What did Major-General Rosie want?'

'Her favourite doll had become a casualty of war in a battle between Captains Kit and Rob. She ... I'm sorry to say that she'd l-lost an arm in the conflict.'

Venetia exchanged a despairing glance with Lydia. Gabriel and Eden dissolved into laughter. Phoebe continued unsteadily, 'Rosie felt that Sir Nicholas was the person best suited to – to putting Araminta to rights because he would know how she f-felt.'

'As a reward for which service,' added Nicholas, 'I am now a *sort*-of-uncle.'

'Only Rosie's against sharing him with the twins because they're too rough.'

'Well, since there's no arguing with that,' remarked Gabriel, 'I suggest we eat.'

Supper was a cheerful affair. Lydia noticed how often Mistress Phoebe's eyes strayed to Nicholas but failed to be aware of how often a pair of hazel eyes rested upon herself. Gabriel, of course, noticed both.

The evening flew by and suddenly the coach was at the door.

Venetia kissed Lydia's cheek and said, 'May I visit you? And perhaps also meet your sewing women?'

'Of course, if you wish. They'd be delighted, I'm sure.'

'Good. Tomorrow Phoebe and I are going to Shoreditch. But perhaps the day after …?'

'The day after,' said Phoebe firmly, 'I want to see Bryony and Sam. But you don't need to come with me if you don't want to, Venetia. I can take a chair.'

'Not,' decreed Gabriel firmly, 'on your own.'

'Why not? I'll be perfectly all right.'

'The Colonel is right, Mistress Clifford,' said Nicholas. 'Sam's lodgings aren't in the most salubrious part of the City.'

She stared at him. 'You know Sam?'

'He's a friend I haven't seen for a while – so I could escort you, if you wish.'

'Oh! That's extremely kind.' Phoebe flushed becomingly. 'If you're sure it would be no trouble?'

'Not at all,' replied Nicholas politely. 'The day after tomorrow, then.'

Once inside the coach, silence fell for a few minutes. Then Eden said idly, 'You did well with Rosie, Nick.'

He laughed. 'Who wouldn't? The child is a little charmer and promises to rival her mother in looks one day. Speaking of which – you might have warned me.'

'I enjoyed seeing you gawp like a fish. I don't believe there's a man born who doesn't do that the first time he sees Venetia.'

Lydia said thoughtfully, 'It can't have been easy for Phoebe, growing up with a sister who looks like that.'

'Two,' said Eden succinctly. 'I believe there's another one almost equally stunning. But these days Phoebe is the most sought-after girl in the county. She owns the family estate – and runs it, too. Rather efficiently, I believe.' He shrugged. 'Cats to catmint, I imagine.'

'That's not as much fun as you'd think,' muttered Lydia.

'No. I suppose not.' Eden paused and then said, 'Before I forget – if you don't hear from Hetherington by noon tomorrow, let me know and I'll pay him another visit.'

'You don't need to do that. I can deal with it.'

'*You* don't frighten him,' returned Eden with a grin. 'Nick …since we'll be passing the door, I'll let you out there. Then, once I've taken Mistress Neville home, I'll walk back so the driver can return the coach.'

Nicholas smiled in the darkness … but said nothing.

* * *

Back in Bishopsgate, Colonel Maxwell handed Lydia down from the coach, passed the driver a few coins and sent him on his way.

Giving Henry her cloak, Lydia said, 'Is my brother at home?'

'Sir Aubrey took supper and then retired. I believe Nancy found him asleep over the fruit tart,' he replied with the suggestion of a smile. 'I have taken the liberty of placing wine in the parlour, Madam. Will there be anything else?'

'Oh. No. Thank you, Henry.' Lydia looked at the Eden, feeling suddenly awkward and wondering what the correct etiquette was when entertaining a gentleman alone after ten o'clock at night. 'Would you care for wine, Colonel?'

He hadn't planned to stay. He'd intended to see her safely inside the house and then leave. But now the offer was there, he found himself accepting it.

Once inside the parlour, with candles lit, curtains drawn and the door closed behind them, Lydia busied herself pouring wine and tried to think of something to say that wouldn't make the moment seem any more intimate than it already did. But before anything suitable occurred to her, Eden said slowly, 'Please tell me that Henry wouldn't leave you alone with just *any* fellow at such an hour?'

'No.' She put the wine down beside him. 'He regards you as a special case.'

'Why? He knows virtually nothing about me. I could be a dangerous lunatic.'

'If you were, I think both he and I would have noticed it by now.'

'I keep my depravity well-hidden.'

She laughed. 'Of course you do.'

'And you've dismissed your only protection.'

Lydia looked at him, trying to fathom this rather odd conversation.

'Yes,' she agreed calmly, 'But fortunately I have a very loud scream.'

'Ah. And assuming that I gave you the opportunity to use it – which, as a dangerous lunatic, I wouldn't – how long would it take Henry or your brother to come to your rescue?'

'Heavens – *I* don't know. Two minutes? Three?'

'Shall we find out?' asked Eden. His tone was pleasant, his eyes curiously intent. He took a step towards her and then another. And when she merely stood her ground, staring at him, he said helpfully, 'You're supposed to be alarmed.'

'Well, I'm not. I know you're not going to attack me. The notion is ridiculous. And --'

'Have you not realised yet that attacking you isn't *all* I might do?'

Another step brought him to within easy touching distance but it was the sudden darkening of his voice that made Lydia want to step back. Forcing herself to stand still, she said a shade irritably, 'Why are you doing this?'

It was a good question. Why *was* he doing it? He'd begun it because he didn't like the idea of her being alone with any man other than himself ... but she'd already said that didn't happen. So at what point had his focus turned into something quite different? Something he ought to resist but suspected he wasn't going to.

'I told you. I want to see how long it takes Henry to get here after you scream.'

'But I'm not *going* to scream. Now ... please sit down and drink your wine and let us talk of something else. I thought Mistress Clifford was rather taken with Nicholas, didn't you?'

'Perhaps. At the moment, I'm not particularly interested either way.'

Without warning, Eden stretched out a hand and ran the back of his curved fingers down her cheek. This time, taken unawares by the gesture, Lydia *did* retreat, her eyes flying wide. He smiled and advanced again. 'Ah. *Now* you're alarmed.'

'No. I'm not.'

'Not even a little bit?' Another step towards her.

And another one back. 'No.'

'Liar.'

This time he stepped right up to her, sliding an arm about her waist and using his other hand to tilt her chin. Lydia promptly forgot to breathe.

'This,' he whispered, his breath hot against her ear, 'is where you're supposed to fight me off and shout for help.'

She dragged some air into her lungs and said unevenly, 'If I ... if I simply asked you to let me go ... would you?'

'Normally, yes. But not, I think, tonight. Because you wouldn't mean it, would you?'

'That would depend on – on what you have in mind.'

'Ah.' He smiled slowly, deep into her eyes. 'Just one thing.'

And he kissed her.

It was no more than a butterfly brush of his lips but it still made Lydia gasp – which was all the encouragement he needed to pull her a little closer and tease her mouth open with his own. All through the evening – and probably for much longer than that – something at the back of his mind had been telling him that he wanted this. So he took his time, savouring the taste of her and enjoying the way her body seemed designed to melt into his own.

Lydia had stopped thinking at all. This moment was everything she'd imagined and never dared hope for. Somehow her hands shifted from the hard muscles of his arms, to his shoulders and finally into his hair. His mouth invited, tempted, offered. And her body responded with a growing wave of unfamiliar sensations that made her hot and dizzy.

Eden wasn't sure when the knowledge that she wasn't going to fight him off filtered hazily through his brain ... but, when it did, he realised that it was up to him to call a halt before things went further than they should. Regretfully, he released her mouth and stepped back.

Lydia looked at him, her skin flushed and her eyes wide and confused. She said nothing.

Eden cleared his throat. Finally, because he already knew that giving way to temptation had been a mistake, he said, 'Well. Delightful as that was, I suppose I should apologise.'

'For what?' Her voice sounded odd, as if she hadn't used it in a long time.

'For becoming distracted. I meant to demonstrate what can – and usually will – happen when a man has the opportunity. I didn't intend to be quite so ... thorough.'

A cold, hard lump formed in Lydia's chest.

'You're telling me that you were making some sort of point?'

No. God, no. 'That was the original intention, yes.'

'I see.' She drew herself up very straight. 'Just how naïve do you think I am? No. Don't answer that. You've already made it very clear.' She managed a chillingly sweet smile. 'Should I thank you for the lesson? As you said, it was ... pleasant.'

Pleasant? That stung every bit as much as he suspected she meant it to.

Forcing another stupid impulse back where it belonged, he picked up his hat and said blandly, 'You're angry. I should probably go. Unless you'd like to slap my face first?'

'No. But next time you decide to treat me like an imbecile, I suggest you do it from a distance. And yes – you should definitely go. Now, if you wouldn't mind.'

Now, before I humiliate myself more than I already have.

Eden hesitated for a moment, suddenly unsure. Then he bowed, wished her good night … and left. Outside on the steps, he hesitated again. He'd done something monumentally stupid and then compounded it by lying. The quickest way to mend that was to walk back inside and admit it – which would probably end with him kissing her again. But even as he turned on his heel, he heard the sound of the bolt being slammed home with unnecessary force.

Ah, he thought ruefully. *Too late, then. And I can't honestly blame her.*

SHADOW DWELLERS
October 1654 to January 1655

'Weeds and nettles, briars and thorns have thriven under your shadow; dissettlement and division, discontent and dissatisfaction, together with real danger to the whole.'

Oliver Cromwell to Parliament

ONE

Lydia slept hardly at all. He'd kissed her and, for the space of a few precious moments, she had actually dared to hope. Then he'd ruined it and left her feeling as though the ground had crumbled beneath her feet.

Idiot, she told herself, furious and miserable. *You ought to have known it meant nothing to him. He kissed you because he could. That's all. Then he regretted it and that stupid, insulting excuse was just his way of stopping you taking it too seriously. Worse ... he knows now. He knows you want him.* She groaned, shoving her head under the pillow. *Oh God. How am I ever going to face him again?*

Next morning, heavy-eyed and listless, she went downstairs to find Aubrey finishing breakfast. Looking up, he said, 'This is a rarity. Am I late – or are you early?'

'I couldn't sleep. And Lily's girls will be here in another hour or so.'

'What?'

'We need more space at Strand Alley so some of the women are working in one of our spare rooms until I arrange it,' she said impatiently. 'Since they're never here at the same time as you, I knew you wouldn't notice.'

Aubrey eyed her narrowly.

'Are you all right? You look a bit out of sorts. Was your supper-party not enjoyable?'

Out of sorts? Lydia had a crazy impulse to laugh at the euphemism. Instead, she said, 'Supper was fine and so am I. Go to work. Colonel Brandon's wife and her sister will be visiting the Morrells today. Try not to stare.'

'You're not making much sense this morning, Lyd. Why would I stare?'

'You'll see. And for the love of God, *stop* calling me *Lyd!*'

Aubrey left the house and, in due course, the women arrived with their usual cheerful bustle. Lydia found the effort of trying to look and behave as normal despite the lead weight in her chest, exhausting. She was just contemplating locking herself in her room, away from the rest of the household, when Henry announced that she had a visitor.

It was Lawyer Hetherington, clutching his hat and looking extremely red-faced.

He said, 'Mistress Neville – I cannot apologise sufficiently. Such a thing has never happened in my office before. In truth, I cannot conceive how such an occurrence could --'

'Mr Hetherington,' cut in Lydia crisply. 'Could you please come to the point. Have you located my deeds or not?'

'We have. My junior clerk found them this morning. They had slipped from their bindings and got wedged in the side of the drawer. I deeply regret the inconvenience this has caused – quite unforgivable, of course. But all is now well and order has been restored.'

'Good.' Lydia wondered why she didn't feel more relieved. It should be a weight off her shoulders – yet somehow it wasn't. Attempting to pull herself together, she said, 'I hope you'll ensure that nothing of the kind happens again?'

'Indeed, Mistress Neville. Indeed I will. And on a happier note, I have reached a favourable agreement regarding the Strand Alley premises, based on the assumption that your requirements will be long-term.'

'Good,' said Lydia again. And when he continued to turn his hat in his hands, 'Was there anything else?'

'I hoped,' he said hesitantly, 'you might inform Colonel Maxwell that the other matter has been satisfactorily resolved.'

'Oh yes,' she replied flatly. 'I'll tell him. Don't worry about that.'

* * *

Eden read the curt little note and cursed under his breath. At some point in the darkest hours of the night it had occurred to him that the problem might be worse than he'd first thought. It wasn't simply that she objected to being treated like some foolish little ingénue. She was also insulted and perhaps even slightly hurt that he hadn't kissed her purely because he wanted to. Except that he had. Only she didn't know that because he'd lied about it. He suspected that an apology, no matter how sincere, wasn't going to fix this. The only thing that might was telling her the complete truth.

There was no ulterior motive. I wanted to kiss you and I'd like to do it again. Hell, I'd like to do a lot more than kiss you. But I won't because marriage is out of the question and you need a husband, not a lover.

Yes, he could say that. She was a reasonable woman so she'd understand and accept it. But if he believed that, why had he lied in the first place?

Damned if I do and damned if I don't, he thought, thoroughly annoyed with himself. Then, looking back at the note, *Convenient – the deeds turning up like that. Lydia seems to believe it. I'd believe it myself but for everything else; though it has to be said that stealing the documents, then putting them back seems a pointless exercise. I wonder …'*

His ruminations stopped abruptly at the sound of someone taking the stairs two at a time. Then Tobias strode in grinning and said, 'Missed me?'

'We noticed that the rations went further,' responded Eden, rising to take his brother's hand. 'How is Tabitha?'

'Fine. She's fine.' Tobias dropped into a chair. 'She has to rest a lot, of course – but, God willing, it's going to be all right this time.'

'I'm glad. If that's so, your time won't have been wasted.'

'She needed me there,' came the shrugging reply. 'So … what have I missed? Turner says business has been steady. You're still here – not dashing off on some new quest. And I suppose Nick is busy chasing his widow … so what's new?'

'Parliament is in session. I'm engaged in what you might call diplomatic work for Lambert. And Nick is most emphatically *not* chasing Lydia Neville.'

'No? Changed his mind, has he?'

'No. We were mistaken,' said Eden. And, firmly changing the subject, 'Do you know if Jude has decided whether or not to pay us a visit?'

'I don't.' He fished in his pockets. 'But he's sent you a letter. Here it is.'

Eden took it and spread it open. After a few moments, he looked up smiling and said, 'He says he'd like to come after Yule.'

'Good. He can travel back here with me. You as well, if you care to spend the festive season at home for once.'

'That will depend on a few things – but I'll see.' He stood up. 'Doubtless you've already ordered food. Unfortunately, I've got to give Lambert a progress report and won't be able to join you – but I'll see you at supper.'

Actually, I've got to give Lambert a report that omits all mention of Rochester and the fact that I've now met the man twice. This assignment is turning into a knife-edge.

* * *

Nicholas duly escorted Mistress Clifford to the small house in Botolph Lane to which Samuel Radford had moved his family upon the discovery that a second child was on the way. For the hour during which Phoebe and Bryony scarcely stopped talking, Nicholas took a mug of ale with Samuel and said, 'How are things at the newspaper?'

'We're scraping by. Leveller politics aren't fashionable, these days.'

'And Free-born John?'

'Still in prison on Jersey. None of the petitions have borne fruit. And though I have hopes of the new Parliament, it's too early yet to expect anything.' Samuel smiled wryly. 'I have to be more circumspect in my activities now that I have a family to think of. Making sure I won't be arrested is rather limiting. Not,' he added, looking across the room at his wife, still chattering animatedly to Phoebe, 'that I'd have it any other way. Marriage and children have their own rewards.'

'I'll have to take your word for that.'

'Your turn will come. Meanwhile, thank you for bringing Phoebe – and don't hesitate to do it again, if you have the time. As always, she brings the sunshine with her.'

Later, conveying his charge back to the Tiltyard, Nicholas said curiously, 'Eden says you own your family's lands. That's rather unusual, isn't it?'

'Yes. But Father is dead, Mother doesn't like dirtying her hands, Venetia and Elizabeth are both married and my only living brother is a Jesuit priest. So that just left me.'

He blinked. 'I ... see. That sounds a heavy responsibility.'

'It is – and at first I found it overwhelming. But Venetia was near enough to advise and Gabriel taught me to treat it as a challenge.' She cast him a sideways glance. 'I imagine you know all about challenges. If it's all right to ask …when did you lose your arm?'

'Three years ago.'

'Oh. Worcester?'

'Yes.'

She nodded, part sympathetic and part matter-of-fact.

'Then afterwards … learning to manage. I can't imagine how you did that.'

Her voice was full of candid admiration. Slightly taken aback by it, Nicholas said tersely, 'One gradually finds ways to adapt.'

'And now you help Mistress Neville at her lorinery?'

'Where there are a good many men in far worse case than I am. Men with families who, but for Lydia, would be begging on the streets. Thanks to Eden I was never in that position.'

'Do you not … have you no family of your own to go back to?'

'Not one that would welcome me.'

For a moment, he thought she was going to ask why not. Instead, however, a frown entered the grey eyes and she said seriously, 'I understand how politics and religion and war can create divisions with families. But what I've *never* understood is why those divisions are allowed to become permanent; why people can't put them to one side and agree to differ. Even now, Mother can barely bring herself to be civil to Gabriel because she's never looked past his birth and the colour of his sash to who he actually *is*. It's quite maddening.'

Nicholas looked at her, recalling what Samuel had said. *She brings the sunshine with her.* He hadn't understood that at the time. Now, however, he was beginning to.

'You obviously think a lot of the Colonel.'

'*No* one could have a better brother,' she said firmly. And with a slight, rueful smile, 'Gabriel's wonderful – and I'm profoundly envious of Venetia. Her marriage isn't just a loving one – it's also a genuine partnership. And, from what I can see, that is *truly* rare.'

'And what you'd like for yourself?'

'Ideally, yes. But sooner or later I expect I'll have to accept something less.' She laughed wryly and rolled her eyes. 'Mother is driving me demented on the subject of marriage. A daughter of hers, unwed at the advanced age of twenty-four? God forbid!'

'God forbid, indeed,' grinned Nicholas, as they arrived outside Gabriel's door.

'Will you come in?' asked Phoebe.

He shook his head. 'I promised to oversee some consignments at the lorinery.'

'Then thank you for taking me to see Bryony and Sam – and for your company. I've enjoyed it.'

'So have I,' replied Nicholas. And surprised himself by adding, 'If you wish, we could do it again.'

* * *

The first week of October drifted by, then the second.

Venetia Brandon visited Mistress Neville at her home, met the women currently making lace and other folderols in the spare room and pronounced the quality of their work excellent. Then she insisted on bearing her hostess off to the Exchange to do some shopping.

'If you've had nothing new since well before your husband died,' said Venetia, in a tone that brooked no argument, 'it's high time you did.'

The result was that Lydia went home with a length of sapphire watered taffeta and another of shell-pink shot-silk – and an instruction from Mistress Brandon to have the latter trimmed with 'that exquisite pearl beading Jenny Sutton is making'.

Two days later, Lydia signed the lease on the entire building in Strand Alley and spent the next week purchasing the necessary additional furniture. On the day the rooms were finally ready, Venetia and Phoebe arrived with baskets of food and wine so that everyone could celebrate. The rooms rang with eager voices and laughter and, for a time at least, Lydia's spirits rose.

It didn't last. By the time she got home, she was feeling lonely and a little forlorn. She'd seen nothing of Colonel Maxwell for a fortnight and was beginning to wonder if she ever would again. So when, on the following morning, Mr Wakefield arrived on the doorstep in time to escort her to Duck Lane, she found she was glad of the distraction.

* * *

In fact, though he'd decided to allow time for Lydia's temper to cool, Eden hadn't intended to stay away for quite so long and wouldn't have done so had Major-General Lambert not asked him to investigate rumours of discontent within the Army.

Eden reflected that, having spent years fighting the King in the name of Parliament, it was hardly surprising that some officers might consider the Protectorate equally undesirable. But he said merely, 'Anyone in particular?'

'No – though I suspect that John Wildman may be stirring the pot.'

No surprises there, either. Wildman has a number of talents – most of them nefarious.

'There is already trouble brewing in Portsmouth,' Lambert went on. 'Sailors petitioning for everything from the end of impressment to pensions for widows – which, since Admiral Penn's fleet is due to sail for the Caribbean, we could well do without.'

'Pay the sailors. It will quiet down quickly enough.'

'I daresay. But it's a bad time to be facing rumblings in the Army as well.'

'When is it not?' asked Eden, getting to his feet. Then, 'With regard to the other matter you entrusted to me, neither Villiers nor Compton are currently in London. But even if they were, there'll be no progress until they see signs of conciliation from Westminster … for which, on present showing, they're unlikely to be holding their breath.'

Several days later, Eden was back in Lambert's office with the required information.

'Colonels Okey, Saunders and Alured have been holding meetings with Wildman – who has drafted a petition asking for complete liberty of conscience which they intend to circulate through the Army. Robert Overton's name has also been mentioned …but since he's still in Scotland, his involvement seems unlikely.'

'We can but hope,' sighed Lambert. 'Meanwhile, I'd better arrest the three Colonels. I don't suppose Wildman has written something inflammatory enough for me to arrest him as well, has he?'

'No. He's too wily for that.'

'Ah. Pity.'

Very soon after this meeting, Eden suspected that the Major-General was regretting his restraint. He arrested the Colonels. And Wildman retaliated by having the *Humble Petition* printed. Within twenty-four hours, copies of it were everywhere.

* * *

With this mission accomplished and no other pressing business, Eden recognised that he ought to try mending his fences with Lydia before their friendship was past saving. Circumstances, as it turned out, were against him. The first time he called in Bishopsgate, Henry regarded him with mild reproof and informed him that Mistress Neville was at the lorinery; and when he tried again on the following day, Henry announced that Madam was shopping in the Exchange.

'I believe Mr Wakefield offered his escort,' he added in such an approving tone that Eden wanted to grind his teeth. 'He has been quite a frequent visitor of late.'

Walking back towards Cheapside, Eden reminded himself that Lydia was free to do as she pleased and that he had no right to feel aggrieved. It didn't help very much.

Fortunately, a note from Annis Morrell inviting him to supper the following evening arrived in time to improve his mood. She suggested that Tobias might like to join them and added that, in addition to Gabriel, Venetia and Phoebe, Nicholas would also be present – as would Aubrey and his sister.

Eden thought about this. Meeting Lydia in company for the first time since he'd behaved like a prize ass might either be a good thing or a very bad one. The only certainty was that he didn't need Tobias watching him try not to make an ever bigger fool of himself than he already had – and also, knowing his brother, quite possibly interfering. Consequently, he told Toby of the invitation and, without giving him chance to reply, added, 'Unfortunately, you are otherwise engaged.'

Tobias's brows rose. He said, 'No. I don't think so.'

'Think again,' advised Eden. 'There will be two susceptible, unmarried females present. One of them is being sought by Aubrey Durand and the other seems to have taken to Nicholas. Neither of them needs to end the evening drooling pointlessly over you.'

'Can I help it if women find me irresistible?' grinned Tobias. And then, meditatively, 'Actually, I wouldn't mind furthering my acquaintance with the little widow.'

'No.'

'No? Why not?'

'Because you're not coming,' said Eden flatly.

And turned away before he was stupid enough to try wiping the knowing expression from his brother's face.

* * *

The only thing that dissuaded Lydia from sending Annis her excuses was the knowledge – somewhat smugly conveyed by Henry – that Colonel Maxwell had paid not one but two abortive calls at her house. She assumed from this that he wanted to put the damned kiss behind them ... in which she was perfectly prepared to meet him half-way.

The fact that the sapphire gown had just been delivered from the dressmaker, she told herself firmly, had nothing at all to do with it.

Eden would have disagreed with her on that point. When she walked into the Morrells' parlour on Aubrey's arm, his brain turned fuzzy at the edges. The dark watered-taffeta reduced her waist to a hand-span and its décolletage formed a calyx for fine-boned shoulders and creamy skin. She wasn't precisely beautiful ... but by God there was something about her that made a man want to touch.

Lydia avoided looking at Colonel Maxwell for as long as possible but had the odd – and patently ridiculous – feeling that he was staring. In an attempt to rid herself of the sensation, she watched Aubrey watching Verity watching Nicholas, as he and Phoebe talked animatedly together on the opposite side of the room.

'I haven't seen Phoebe glow like this since the first time Eden Maxwell smiled at her,' remarked Venetia, arriving at her side. 'I only hope she doesn't make the same mistakes.'

Lydia took a breath, tried not to ask ... and failed.

'Mistakes?'

'She was seventeen and wore her heart on her sleeve for a while. Eden didn't handle it with a great deal of finesse – though to be fair, he was still reeling from his travesty of a marriage – oh.' She stopped abruptly. 'I don't suppose you know about that.'

'Actually, I do. He told me.'

The violet eyes widened.

'He did? *Really?* Heavens! Did you use thumbscrews or red hot pincers?'

'Neither – though he behaved as though I had,' admitted Lydia with a wry smile. 'He used as few words as possible, none of them being specifically about his wife.'

'He could describe Celia in one word if he didn't mind using it.'

Venetia's tone gave a fair indication of what that word might be and also suggested something else. Lydia said, 'Did you know her?'

'Celia? Yes. Not well – but as well as one would want to. Eden's sister, Kate, couldn't abide her and his parents had doubts but ... well, he was twenty years old and dazzled by the outside.'

'She was beautiful?'

'Very. One of those curvy brunettes with big blue eyes and lashes constantly a-flutter. She was also vain, selfish and rather stupid. According to Kate, the wretched girl was making Eden miserable even before she ran off with Hugo Verney. Everyone who cared for Eden, thought he was well rid of her.'

Lydia nodded but said slowly, 'And yet he's still not over it, is he?'

'Perhaps not ... but I think that's less to do with Celia herself than the probability that Mary isn't his child,' returned Venetia dispassionately. 'Also I think something else happened the day he found Celia with Hugo; something that made everything much worse – if that's possible. But I don't know what it was and I'm not sure Gabriel does either.'

A few minutes later, Eden finally managed to trap Lydia in a quiet corner and, coming directly to the point, said, 'I behaved atrociously and then made bad, worse. I'm sorry. I'm also sorry it's taken me until now to tell you so.'

She looked back at him, keeping her expression carefully neutral. 'Presumably you've been busy.'

'Yes – but that doesn't excuse it. If I promise to behave like a gentleman in future, do you think you might forgive me?'

'Probably.' *Though I'd much rather you behaved badly and meant it.* 'Henry said you'd called. I wondered if it was because you'd made sense of Stephen's strange jottings.'

'Not yet – but I will.' Eden hesitated briefly and then said, 'They aren't just random collections of numbers, Lydia. Your husband was creating codes.'

'Codes?' she echoed, disbelievingly. 'Are you *sure*?'

'Perfectly.'

'But *why*? Why would he do that?'

'For fun?' Eden grinned at her expression. 'It may sound odd but the ciphers on those papers are the best I've seen for a very long time and I'm going to enjoy breaking them.'

'You know how to do that?' she began. And then, 'Oh. Of course. It's what you were doing for Secretary Thurloe, wasn't it?'

'Yes.' He glanced round, aware that Annis was summoning everyone to the table and that any chance of private conversation was at an end. 'I really *am* sorry, you know – about what happened.'

Lydia's spine stiffened and she started to turn away.

'So you said. There's really no need to go on about it.'

Oh I think there is. But if I tell you I lied, we'll find ourselves in a situation that neither of us will know how to deal with. And that would do more harm than good. Damn.

Annis had arranged matters so that Aubrey was sitting beside Verity at one end of the table, while Nicholas and Phoebe occupied places at the other. Lydia had Jack on one hand and Gabriel on the other ... and Colonel Maxwell directly opposite which meant that virtually every time she raised her eyes from her plate, they met his. She wondered whose idea *that* had been. It was ruining her appetite.

'What news from Westminster?' Eden asked Gabriel.

'We've paid the sailors and peace now reigns in Portsmouth.'

'And that's all?' asked Jack.

'We've also – despite the point already having been laid down in the *Instrument* – been debating the succession of the Protectorate,' replied Gabriel dryly. 'For some reason best known to himself, Lambert proposed making it hereditary. I need hardly say that the vote went overwhelmingly against him.'

'Thank God for that,' muttered Eden. 'Have you *met* Richard Cromwell?'

'No. Have you?'

'Yes. He's weak; he's certainly no soldier; and rumour says he's up to his neck in debt.'

'Not much like his father, then,' observed Jack. 'So --'

'Please stop.' Annis's quiet voice checked their conversation. 'We do not argue politics over supper.'

'We're not arguing,' Jack pointed out, smiling.

'Yet,' observed Annis, calmly. 'Meanwhile, you're ignoring Mistress Neville.'

'It's all right,' said Lydia quickly. 'I don't mind.'

'But I do,' said Annis. And turned back to the conversation she'd been trying to promote between Aubrey and Verity.

Jack sighed; Gabriel sent a slanting grin at Lydia; and Eden looked as if he wanted to laugh.

Phoebe bent her head closer to Nicholas's and whispered, 'Annis is quite right, you know. Sooner or later, it always turns into an argument. It seems that you men can't help yourselves.'

'Not me,' he objected. 'And of course, you *never* argue.'

'No. I don't.'

'So what was all that about with Bryony yesterday?' It had been the third time he'd escorted her to Botolph Lane and she and Bryony had spent at least twenty minutes wrangling amicably over baby names.

'That was different.'

'If you say so.'

She eyed him sternly. 'I do.'

'Right.' Nicholas took his last bite of pie and laid down his knife. Then, shaking his head, 'Archibald? Really? Poor, poor child.'

Phoebe giggled. 'It could be a girl.'

'One can but hope.' He took a sip of wine and then said, 'Do you still want to visit the lorinery?'

'*Yes*!' She'd been trying to persuade him for days. 'Can I?'

'Tomorrow. I'll come for you around noon. But don't wear your best gown.'

'As if I would.' Phoebe beamed at him and got an answering smile in return. 'Thank you.'

At the other end of the table, Verity came abruptly to her feet.

'I'll start clearing for the puddings, Annis.'

'You don't need to. Polly will do it.'

'No – I'd rather.' And she began gathering platters and dishes.

Aubrey also rose. 'Let me help.'

'No! That is – thank you but I can manage.'

'Verity,' said Annis gently. 'Let him.'

Aubrey picked up the massive meat platter and followed the girl into the kitchen.

Annis and Venetia exchanged glances.

'He should kiss her,' murmured Venetia. 'Then they might both stop being miserable.'

'And what a mercy *that* would be,' sighed Annis.

Later, when the meal was over and everyone had risen from the table, Colonel Maxwell bore Nicholas off into the hall for a few very direct words. Then, pouring two glasses of wine, he carried one to Lydia and said, 'I've told Nick to resolve the situation with Verity at the first opportunity. Letting it drag on isn't fair to either her or Phoebe – if that's where his interest truly lies. Or your brother either, come to that. Though to be honest, I can only admire Aubrey's fortitude. Faced with a girl who mopes with such dedication, most men – myself included – would have abandoned the chase weeks ago.'

An elusive smile crept into Lydia's eyes.

'Did you talk to Nicholas by way of a peace offering?'

'I won't deny that the idea had occurred to me. Did it work?'

'It didn't need to. I wasn't still angry.'

The hazel gaze grew suddenly serious.

'Yes,' said Eden. 'You were. And rightly so.'

TWO

Nicholas didn't sleep very well and got up with a lead weight in his chest at the thought of what had to be done.

'Everybody's sick of watching Verity eat her heart out over you – so do the girl a favour and tell her what you told me,' Eden had said bluntly. 'This has gone on long enough.'

Hell, thought Nicholas dismally. *He's right ... but it's going to be awful.*

Suspecting that if he ate anything it wasn't likely to stay down, he set off for Shoreditch as soon as he was dressed and, walking in through the back door, found Annis in the kitchen conferring with her cook. Although she smiled at him, her brows rose a little and she said, 'If you were looking for Jack, you've just missed him.'

He shook his head.

'I came to see Verity. I – I need to speak with her privately.'

'Ah.' Annis's gaze sharpened but she merely nodded and said, 'Wait in the front parlour and I'll find her for you. And Nick ... I'll be here afterwards, if you need me.'

He swallowed. 'That would be kind. Thank you.'

While he waited, he stared sightlessly through the window and tried to find the words he needed. They wouldn't come. Then hearing the rustle of Verity's skirts as she entered the room, he turned and tried to smile. Judging by the uncertain look in her eyes, he was making a poor job of it.

She said, 'Nicholas? Is something wrong?'

'No. That is – not exactly.' He hesitated and then, gesturing to the settle by the hearth, 'Will you sit down? There's something we need to talk about.'

Verity sat down leaving space for him to sit beside her.

He didn't. Instead, frowning down at his boots, he said, 'I'm not sure how to begin – except by saying that we should have had this conversation some time ago. Not that it's your fault we didn't,' he added quickly. 'It was up to me to raise the subject, not you. And I ought to have done so as soon as I realised how I ... how matters stood.' *Only I hoped I wouldn't need to. I hoped it would resolve itself on its own.* 'I delayed because I thought I might be mistaken in – in your feelings.'

A hint of colour crept up under her skin and the uncertain expression changed to one of confusion mingled with a tiny glimmer of hope.

She said softly, 'Oh. Do you think you were?'

No, more's the pity. And please don't look at me like that.

'No. It seems not.' Nicholas drew a bracing breath, loosed it and then said rapidly, 'You know how grateful I am for what you did for me at Worcester. And you also know that I'm very fond of you. But if you thought ... if I've given the impression that one day fondness might become something more, then I – I was at fault and I'm more sorry than I can say.'

Verity stared at him as if he'd spoken in a foreign language. Then she whispered, 'I don't think I – I quite understand.'

Christ. Do I really have to spell it out?

'I'm saying that I care for you but – but not in the way I would hope to care for my wife. I'm sorry.'

The colour drained slowly from her cheeks and the brown eyes were suddenly luminous with tears. She said, 'I can wait. I don't mind waiting.'

'Then you should,' he said bitterly. 'I certainly mind for you.'

'You needn't. I understand that you're not ready to marry yet. But in time that will change and then --'

'It may change – or it may not.' He clenched his hand at his side and added, 'The thing that *won't* change is the fact that you're like my sister. I know that isn't --'

'Your *sister?*' She stood up and took a step towards him. 'No. You don't mean it.'

'Yes, Verity. I do.'

'You don't. You can't.' She hurled herself at him and grabbed the front of his coat. Then, when he merely stood very still, saying nothing,

'But I *love* you. I've always loved you! Right from the very first. I – I thought you knew that.'

I did. God damn it – I did know it. I just tried not to believe it.

He put a comforting arm about her waist and guided her back to the settle. The tears were coming in earnest now and he didn't know how to stop them. His own throat felt raw and his stomach was in knots. When she subsided on to his shoulder, he said desperately, 'It's not the end of the world, you know. And you can do better than me ... such as a fellow with two arms to put round you.'

'I don't care about that,' she sobbed. 'I don't *care*!'

'One day you will. When you meet --'

She sat up and pushed away from him. 'It's Ph-Phoebe Clifford. Isn't it?'

Since his arm was now free, he took the opportunity to pull out a handkerchief and put it into her hand whilst simultaneously taking a second to think. Then, because he wasn't sure of the truthful answer, he said carefully, 'No ... and that's not what this is about. I don't want you to go on hoping for something that isn't going to happen. I want you to be *happy*. And you won't be as long as you sit around waiting for me.'

Verity mopped her face. Falling silent for a time, she stared down at the damp linen between her fingers. And finally she said dully, 'You never promised me anything. I know that. But I truly thought that one day ...'

'I know. And I'm very sorry.'

'Yes. You said.' She stood up and turned away from him. 'That doesn't stop it hurting.'

'No. I know that too.' Nicholas also rose, unsure what to do. 'Perhaps I should go?'

'Yes.' Her voice was thick with tears and hopelessness. 'Go. You might as well.'

* * *

Although he was grateful that the ordeal was behind him, Nicholas arrived at Duck Lane still feeling less than cheerful and wishing he hadn't promised to go and fetch Phoebe. But, since he had, he exchanged a few words with Mr Potter and then walked down to Paul's Wharf to take a boat as far as Suffolk House.

It was perhaps fortunate that after being admitted to the house near the Tiltyard, the first person he saw was Rosie. Instantly, her small face lit up and she cried, 'Uncle Nick!'

It was impossible not to smile back and, as he always did, drop down for her to climb on to his knee, so he could scoop her up into his arm.

'And how is my best girl today?'

'Upstairs getting her cloak.'

The child's assumption gave him a jolt but he managed a weak laugh and said, 'I thought *you* were my best girl.'

She snuggled against his neck. 'Where are you and Aunt Phoebe going?'

'We're going,' announced Phoebe, pulling on her gloves as she descended the stairs, 'to see some men who used to be soldiers. And no – you can't come.'

'Why can't I? I'll be good.'

'I know that, darling. But it's not really a place for little girls.'

'Also,' remarked Venetia, from the parlour door, 'you promised to help Betty make fruit tarts this morning.'

'Oh. I forgot.' The child turned back to Nicholas and said, 'Can I come another day?'

'Perhaps,' he replied, dropping a quick kiss on the silver-fair curls before setting her back on her feet. 'If your father says it's all right.'

'Good.' Rosie nodded and ran happily away to the kitchen.

His smile instantly becoming more forced, Nicholas turned to Phoebe and said, 'Shall we go? The tide's about to turn and the boat-man won't want to miss it.'

Once they were settled in the boat and on their way downstream, Phoebe said bluntly, 'What's the matter?'

His nerves snarled.

'With me? Nothing. What makes you think there is?'

'I've got eyes,' she replied. 'But you don't have to say if you don't want to.'

Suddenly, contrarily, Nicholas realised that he did want to tell her at least part of it.

'I had to hurt someone's feelings this morning and it was ... difficult.'

'Oh.' Phoebe picked at the cuff of her glove. 'Like saying no when the person wants you to say yes?'

Nicholas's gaze sharpened 'Yes. Rather like that.'

'Horrible, isn't it? If you're kind and tactful, they don't think you mean it. So you have to be blunt and it leaves you all churned up inside.'

'Yes. That's exactly it. I didn't do it well because I hated doing it at all.'

For a moment or two, silence punctuated only by the usual sounds of the river, fell between them. Then Phoebe said abruptly, 'Five men have asked me to marry them so far. All perfectly nice men in their way except that I don't think any of them cared a fig for me.'

Her matter-of-fact tone stirred something inside Nicholas's chest. He said, 'Their loss, then. And you can't marry a fellow who doesn't look beyond the end of his nose, can you?'

'That's a very kind way of putting it,' said Phoebe with the merest suggestion of a sigh. 'However, the truth is that they looked but didn't find the view all that inspiring.' And then, as if deciding she'd said too much, 'Ah. We're nearly there. Are you sure the men at the lorinery won't mind me visiting?'

'They'll enjoy it.' Nicholas grinned at her. 'The truth is that they'd have enjoyed Rosie, too. But it might be best not to tell her that.'

Two hours later, he stood at the side of the work-room with Mr Potter and watched Phoebe sitting at a bench and chattering happily with Will Collis as she tried to fit a bridle together. During the time she'd been there, she'd made a complete circuit of the room and talked to every man in it. She'd bubbled over with questions about their work and their families; and she'd listened and smiled that wide, genuinely friendly smile and *cared*.

'You know ... I wasn't sure about bringing her.'

'Glad you did, sir,' said Mr Potter. 'Breath of fresh air, she is.'

'Yes. Isn't she?'

Nicholas pushed the thought and what it suggested aside and instead listened to Phoebe telling Mr Collis that her niece had wanted to come with her.

'Colonel Brandon's daughter, you know. I wish now that I'd let her.'

'Best not, Miss. This is no place for a little 'un – and us with all our injuries. Give her nightmares, it would.'

She shook her head. 'Rosie's an odd little thing. She wants to make everyone better. And even when she knows it isn't possible, she still tries.'

Rather like her aunt, thought Nicholas. And put that thought aside as well.

It was when he was escorting her home again that she said, 'Thank you for today.'

'I'm glad you enjoyed it.'

'I did. Very much.' *Almost as much as I liked watching you laughing with the men and joining in their work ... or sitting with Sam over a tankard of ale ... or being so heart-wrenchingly sweet with Rosie. In fact, I like you altogether too much. And suspect I'm going to miss you.* The last thought bred another and, on a slight sigh, she said, 'Venetia and I ought to think about going home.'

'Oh.' A hollow feeling settled in his chest. 'Soon?'

She nodded. 'We've been away nearly two months and, though we both have excellent land stewards, there'll be decisions to be made. Obviously, Gabriel will be here as long as Parliament sits ... but he'll feel better about that if Venetia is at Brandon Lacey dealing with day-to-day matters.'

'Of course.' In order to avoid saying something he thought he shouldn't, he said, 'Tell me about your home and how your time is spent there. It sounds interesting.'

'That's one way of describing it,' laughed Phoebe. And launched into an animated account of life at Ford Edge which lasted them all the way back to the Tiltyard.

* * *

While her sister was in Duck Lane with Sir Nicholas, Venetia sent a note to Annis Morrell suggesting an hour in the Exchange and received a regretful refusal. *Verity,* wrote Annis despairingly, *is still in floods of tears.*

Venetia eyed the note thoughtfully and decided it would serve as an excuse to call on Lydia Neville. Smiling to herself, she summoned a chair.

Lydia, wearing her oldest gown while she toiled over the lorinery ledgers, entertained a fleeting wish she'd had some warning and then forgot about it when, almost before the parlour door had closed behind her, Venetia said, 'Annis says that Nicholas has finally put an end to Verity's expectations.'

'Already?'

'You knew he was going to?'

'No. Not exactly. But Colonel Maxwell had a word with him about it last night.'

'Successfully, it would seem.' Venetia set aside her gloves and considered asking Lydia why she persisted in referring to Eden formally when it was clear that the two of them knew each other better than might have been supposed. Then, deciding to work round to that, she said instead, 'Nicholas has taken Phoebe to your lorinery this morning. And I'd hope that, by the time he brings her home again, he'll be looking a little less bleak.'

A tap at the door heralded Nancy with a tray of wine and small cakes. When she had gone, Lydia said carefully, 'Would you mind if I asked you something?'

'Not at all – so long as it's reciprocal.'

'How well do you know Colonel Maxwell's family? He rarely mentions them.'

Refraining from asking why Lydia wanted to know, Venetia shrugged.

'I've met them all but Kate's the one I know best. She was betrothed to my brother for a time until the man she eventually married took a hand and the arrangement was terminated. Then Kit died and I ... well, truthfully, I found it hard to forgive her for sending him back to the war, hurt and angry. But these things pass and now we correspond on a regular basis.'

'She's married to an Italian gentleman?'

'Luciano del Santi. Yes. Now *there's* the kind of man you don't meet every day. Clever, skilled, ruthless – and sinfully good-looking. Not to mention being disgustingly rich and, I suspect, rather powerful.'

'He sounds ... formidable.'

'He is. But he and Kate don't travel to England very often. The last time I saw them was six years ago at Toby's twin sister's wedding.' She smiled and appeared to concentrate on choosing a cake. 'So I imagine the *next* time will likely be at Eden's.'

'He says he won't re-marry,' blurted out Lydia. And immediately regretted it.

Venetia licked some sugar from her fingers.

'He's been saying that for years. If you ask me, it's become a habit he doesn't know how to break. But if a woman wanted to take a little trouble ... well, I don't imagine it would be too difficult to rid him of it.'

There was a long silence broken only by the crackling of the fire and a knife-grinder crying his trade in the street outside. Finally and with a good deal of trepidation, Lydia said baldly, 'You mean me, don't you?'

'Yes.' The lovely eyes were suddenly alarmingly direct. 'You like him, don't you?'

'Yes. But --'

'*More* than like him, unless I'm much mistaken.'

'Perhaps. But that --'

'Good. And it must be mutual – or he wouldn't be telling you things he's avoided talking about to anyone else. So why on earth don't you stop calling him *Colonel* Maxwell and start making him sit up and take notice? You're a widow. You're free to re-marry ... or follow any other inclination you may have.'

Lydia's colour rose. 'For God's sake, Venetia!'

'Oh don't look so shocked. You must have thought about it.'

Lydia started to laugh.

'All right. I won't pretend the idea hasn't occurred to me. But it isn't that simple. Aside from the fact that Col--' She stopped, checking herself. 'That *Eden* is dead set against marrying again and therefore likely to avoid potential risks, *you* didn't see his former housekeeper.'

'Housekeeper?' Venetia blinked. 'What does she have to do with anything?'

'More than you'd suppose. More than *I'd* supposed until you told me his late wife was exactly the same type,' replied Lydia gloomily. 'I only saw them together once and then for just a few minutes but I'm fairly sure that Deborah Hart was his mistress.'

'There are only two words of any significance there. *Was* and *mistress*.'

'Only a woman who looks like you could believe that. I doubt there's a man alive who wouldn't come to heel if you snapped your fingers.'

'There is one,' admitted Venetia with a smile. 'I married him.' And then, catching Lydia's expression, 'Gabriel and I didn't start out as you see us now, you know. But that's a story for another day. I need to go home and make sure Rosie hasn't set fire to the kitchen. Meantime, consider what I've said. I think you could make Eden happy. But you won't do it without taking a few risks ... so you'll need to decide if you think them worth it.'

THREE

October drifted into November and the weather turned foggy and damp.

Lydia thought a great deal about her conversation with Venetia but failed to decide what, if anything, she wanted to do as a result of it ... and would have been hard-pressed to do anything anyway since Colonel Maxwell's visits had decreased in frequency.

Mr Wakefield, on the other hand, visited Bishopsgate every other day, finally giving Lydia the distinct impression that she was being slowly courted. He was young, charming and good-looking; he was also pleasant company and brother to a viscount. But beyond that, she realised that she knew very little about him ... and when she tried asking questions, she emerged little wiser.

Eden, with time on his hands while he waited for either Ned Villiers or Will Compton to renew communications, bent his brain to the task of cracking Stephen Neville's codes but disciplined himself to call on Lydia less often than he might have liked.

There were two reasons for this.

The first was that he was not only physically attracted to Lydia Neville; he actually *liked* her. He liked talking with her and listening to her. He enjoyed the sharpness of her mind and their occasional verbal sparring. And those things, combined with the fact that he was drawn to her on the most primal level, made a dangerous combination.

The other reason was that, having tripped over Gilbert Wakefield twice – first at the lorinery and then in Bishopsgate – he discovered another primal desire; that of planting his fist in the fellow's face. This was largely to do with finding Wakefield very much at home in Lydia's parlour at a time when he himself wanted to show her the progress he'd made with the first two of Stephen's codes. Since he had no intention of revealing this in Wakefield's presence, he was forced to leave his neatly transcribed sheets in his pocket and cut his visit short. He left feeling angry, confused and stupidly disappointed ... at which point he started to realise that, unless he wanted to find himself in the kind of trouble he was determined to avoid, he ought to get the hell out of Mistress Neville's life before it was too late.

Since his mood was decidedly uncertain, it was probably as well that both Tobias and Nicholas were supping elsewhere that evening ... Tobias with his latest woman and Nicholas with the Brandons. Eden brooded over a glass of wine and decided he envied the ease with which his brother seemed to manage his numerous affairs. In his own experience, nothing was ever that straightforward.

The arrival of Colonel Brandon saved him from further depressing ruminations.

'I've had a bloody awful day on top of a bloody awful week,' said Gabriel, tossing his hat aside. 'So I thought I'd come and share it with you.'

'How thoughtful.' Eden rose to pour wine for his unexpected guest. 'But aren't you supposed to be at home entertaining Nick?'

'I sent Venetia a note. I'm sure she'll manage.' He accepted the glass and sat down on the far side of the hearth. 'Unless I'm mistaken, you don't look in the best of humours yourself.'

'Nothing that a night's sleep and some mature reflection won't cure,' said Eden evasively. 'So ... what is it now? Surely the House can't *still* be nit-picking its way through the *Instrument*?'

'Yes and no. The current bone of contention is the size of the Army.'

'Ah. Let me guess. Your esteemed colleagues want it reduced – Cromwell and the Army chiefs don't.'

'That's part of it.'

'And the rest?'

'Is all to do with money,' said Gabriel wearily. 'The *Instrument* specifies a standing army of twenty thousand Foot and ten thousand Horse to be funded by a level of taxation mutually agreed between the Protector and the Council without involvement from Parliament. But additional forces necessitated by war are to be paid for with money raised *by consent of Parliament and not otherwise.* It's the 'not otherwise' bit that's causing the problem.'

Eden frowned a little. 'Go on.'

'The fleets under Admirals Blake and Penn are sailing with some twenty-seven thousand soldiers between them. Those additional forces necessitated by war, I just mentioned ... if, that is, one regards these Naval missions as being necessary at all.'

There was a long silence, broken only by the crackling of the fire.

'You're saying,' remarked Eden at length, 'that the Army currently has a fighting strength of fifty-seven thousand men?'

'Yes.'

'That can't be allowed to last.'

'Quite. At present, the monthly assessment stands at £90,000. Parliament feels it should be reduced by a third. But the Army is nearly twice the size anticipated in the *Instrument* ... and the House is baulking at authorising the extra cost – not least because it's fair to assume that Penn's activities in the West Indies will almost certainly result in war with Spain, thus occasioning even *more* expense.'

'So what is the solution?'

'As yet, there isn't one. A committee has been holding discussions with Army officers personally selected by Cromwell but all that's come out of that so far is a suggestion to discharge half a dozen garrisons – which would be a mere drop in the ocean. But with twenty-seven thousand troopers sailing the seven seas for God alone knows how long, it's hard to see how to make any substantial reduction in numbers here at home without leaving the country insufficiently-defended.'

'Not to mention that the common troopers aren't going to take disbandment lying down.'

Gabriel nodded and drained his glass.

'Shades of '47 all over again ... and my feelings on the matter are no different. I accept that some disbandment is necessary on financial grounds. Cromwell doesn't. He's against losing even *one* man, while the House wants to shed roughly ten thousand. If Cromwell has his way, *nobody* is going to get paid. If the House has theirs, we'll see men just tossed away indiscriminately – probably without their back-pay. Either one is a disaster.'

'And you'll fight against both in the hope of finding some middle ground.'

'Yes.'

'Well, this should be one battle you won't have to fight alone.'

'I certainly hope not.' He paused, staring into his empty glass. 'And there's more.'

'Really?' Eden rose, reached for the bottle. 'It's good to know that the nation's representatives are keeping busy.'

Gabriel gave him a sour look.

'Their *mouths* are exceptionally busy,' he said acidly. 'It's exactly what I expected and exactly why I didn't want to stand. In the eleven weeks we've been in session, I can count on one hand the number of times anything has got as far as a vote and if you don't know how bloody frustrating that is --'

'All right, all right!' Having re-filled their glasses and set the bottle aside, Eden held up one hand in a gesture of surrender. 'I take it back. So what else?'

'As you're aware, Oliver's friends – the so-called Court Party – are outnumbered by the rest; radicals, republicans, Presbyterians, Royalist sympathisers and God knows who else. So the House wants to limit the Protector's power and has been talking about assuming total control of matters relating to taxation by removing his right to veto. It's also considering a recommendation that control of the military be limited to the lifetime of the present Protector. And I think, from where Cromwell's sitting, these two things will look like the thin end of a wedge which will eventually lead to Parliament relieving him of any control over anything.' The dark grey eyes fixed Eden with dispassionate clarity. 'If I'm right, it's also the wedge that will drive Parliament and Protector asunder. And you know where that will end.'

'Dissolution?'

'Dissolution. After which I shall wash my hands of the whole sorry mess and go back to normal life.' Gabriel leaned back in his chair, his mouth curling in a half-smile. 'And upon that happy note, perhaps we might have supper and talk of other things.'

They sat down to a substantial meal of Dutch pudding with mustard sauce and Scotch collops fried in butter, accompanied by a dish of mixed parsnip and carrots. Gabriel, whose stomach had been rumbling, groaned appreciatively over the beef pudding and said, 'If your cook wants new employment, tell her I'll pay her double.'

'Firstly,' laughed Eden, 'my cook is the female whose bounteous pulchritude embarrasses the hell out of you. And secondly, if you tried to lure her away Toby would come for you with a hatchet.'

'Oh. Well, in that case …' He took another bite. 'Where *is* Toby, by the way?'

'God knows. In bed with somebody, I should imagine.'

'Somebody? You don't know who?'

'No. He has so many offers that I stopped trying to keep track some time ago.'

Gabriel looked up, grinning. 'Jealous?'

'In the sense that he manages to keep it all so uncomplicated – yes.' Eden fell silent for a while, toying with his food. Then he said, 'Nick wasn't the only refugee I acquired at Worcester. The other was the woman a foul little magistrate was trying for witch-craft. I removed her and she was my house-keeper until she married in May of this year.'

The dark brows rose.

'I'm assuming that she wasn't a witch?'

'No.' *She was … something. But I never wanted to know quite what.* 'Actually, she was … more than my house-keeper. But things grew complicated in the ways Toby manages to avoid. Deborah knew I'd never re-marry but she still fell in love with me.' He shrugged. 'She deserved more out of life than that. And I'm hoping that she has it now.'

Gabriel reached for another collop and a helping of vegetables. His expression perfectly bland, he said, 'And you? Are you really determined not to marry again?'

'Yes.'

'Why?' And when Eden didn't immediately reply, 'You don't have to answer. It's simply that one would think you'd have got over Celia by now.'

'Of course I've bloody got over her,' snapped Eden, tossing down his knife. 'It's not that.'

'Well, if you're not nursing a broken heart --'

'I'm not. But after the debacle of my first marriage I'm not sure I trust my judgement to make a better job of it next time. Neither do I place any great reliance on the lasting qualities of the kind of grand passion that stops your brain working.'

'Oh my God. A cynic.'

'Yes. Once bitten, twice shy has that effect.'

'That merely sounds craven. It also suggests that you never look around you,' said Gabriel calmly. 'How many examples of a good marriage do you need? Your parents? Kate and her Italian? Myself and Venetia? Love *can* last, Eden – for you, as much as for anyone else. But you have to let go of the past and give it a chance.'

It was a long time before Eden spoke but finally he said, 'I don't know if I can.'

'The place to start is *wanting* to. And from the way I saw you looking at Lydia Neville the other night, I thought you'd finally found the right incentive.'

A hint of colour touched Eden's cheekbones.

'I like her,' he admitted reluctantly.

'So do I,' came the amused reply. 'But in case you haven't noticed, *I* don't look at her as if I'd like to throw her over my shoulder and carry her off to bed.'

'Neither do I, damn it!'

'You've no idea, have you?' Gabriel shook his head sadly. 'Tragic, really.'

'Oh – for God's sake!' Feeling in serious need of a drink, Eden rose from the table and crossed the room in search of a bottle of brandy. 'All right. I *more* than like her. And yes – I'd happily bed her. But I won't because she's not a light-skirt. And unlike Toby, I don't have a compulsion to bed every woman who engages my body's attention.'

'Does she?'

'I'm not answering that.' He slapped two glasses on the table and half-filled them with amber liquid. Then, downing a hefty mouthful, 'There's a limit to what I'll discuss – even with you.'

'Point taken.' Gabriel took a sip of brandy and eyed Eden reflectively over the rim of his glass. 'Of course, there's no saying the little widow would have you even if you *did* feel inclined to --'

'Take the bloody hint, can't you?'

The dark eyes filled with laughter. 'Or what? No – don't answer that either. Very well, then. Let's talk about Nicholas Austin.'

Eden blinked. 'What about him?'

'Unless I'm mistaken, Phoebe's falling in love with him. I want to know if that should worry me.'

'If you're asking whether Nick feels the same, I've no idea.'

'He hasn't said anything to you?'

'No. And I haven't asked. We're not all as fond of prying as you are.'

'This isn't prying. This is me protecting Phoebe,' said Gabriel flatly. 'She and Nicholas have been spending a lot of time together. But if he's no more interested in her than he was in that child in Shoreditch, I'll put a stop to it before any more damage is done.'

'Phoebe might have something to say about that. Also, to be fair to Nick, Verity's expectations weren't his fault.'

'So Annis has said. She's also said that he's dealt with the situation. But that doesn't necessarily mean that he's serious about Phoebe. And then there's the other side of the coin. He is – or was – a Royalist. He's also Catholic. Aside from that, I know nothing about him.'

'If you're talking about family and whether or not he can lay claim to money of his own, I don't know either. I've assumed he inherited his baronetcy but he rarely uses the title that goes with it. For the rest, he prefers not to talk about himself and I respect his wishes. Everyone's entitled to some privacy, after all,' remarked Eden with a sly glance. 'But I'm more than willing to speak for his character. He's loyal, trustworthy and too soft-hearted for his own good. He's also not stupid enough to make the same mistake twice and has too much integrity to court Phoebe for her money. Does that set your mind at rest?'

'It certainly helps.'

'Good. And here's something else you might consider. He and Phoebe have known each other for less than two months. *She* may be capable of falling in love between the game pie and the syllabub ... but most people take longer. At least,' he finished bitterly, 'they do if they don't want to end up with a marriage like mine.'

* * *

Much of what Gabriel had said with regard to Lydia preyed on Eden's mind. It left him feeling restless and confused. The only thing he was sure of was that he had to guard his expression when Lydia was around since it wouldn't do for anyone else to guess what was uppermost in his mind when he looked at her. This new need for caution was ultimately responsible for him staying away from Bishopsgate for almost a week. And because he found this more difficult than it ought to have been, it was fortunate that a handful of events served as a distraction.

Having been arrested, the three colonels involved in the *Humble Petition* had now to face the music. One confessed and was grudgingly restored to his command; one was forced to resign; and the third – also accused of encouraging the Irish army to mutiny – was cashiered and imprisoned.

The whole episode might have been of little consequence had not copies of the damned petition been all over London and being read by every Tom, Dick or Harry both inside the Army and out. The prospect of further unrest in the ranks coupled with Parliament's unceasing attempts to alter the *Instrument of Government* spawned two meetings in which the senior officers swore to *live and die to maintain the government as it is now settled*.

Although summoned to attend, Eden avoided both of them and hoped that no one noticed.

* * *

He finally allowed himself to visit Lydia on the last day of the month but this time took the precaution of asking Henry whether Mistress Neville had other company.

'No, Colonel. And though I believe she plans to visit her sewing women this morning, she is at present in the back parlour attending to some correspondence. In your case, sir, I feel sure that Madam would have no objection if you went straight in.'

Eden looked Henry in the eye but could detect no hint of anything untoward if one discounted that vaguely avuncular expression. Handing over his hat and sword, he said, 'If you say so – and on your head be it.'

With her back to the door and her head bent over the letter she was writing, Lydia murmured, 'Yes, Henry? Who is it?'

'Not Henry,' said Eden, strolling towards her and seeing surprise cause her pen to splutter ink across the hitherto neatly written page in front of her. 'I'm sorry. That was my fault. Next time Henry gives me permission to walk in unannounced, I'll obey the same rules as everyone else.'

Lydia laid down her pen and stood up.

'Since it isn't Henry's job to decide who I'll receive and who I won't,' she said crisply, trying to ignore the surge of pleasure his presence created, 'there won't *be* a next time.'

'Oh dear. Poor Henry.'

Lydia made a small huffing sound that might have been either annoyance or amusement.

'Since you and he are such good friends, perhaps you should call on him instead.'

'Damn,' said Eden cheerfully. 'And we thought we'd been so discreet.'

She gave a tiny choke of laughter but said, 'You're outrageous!'

'Not generally. There must be something about you that--'

'Don't you *dare* blame me!'

'—makes me want to provoke you,' he finished, his eyes at complete variance with his innocent tone. 'What did you think I was going to say?'

'You know perfectly well. And you *were* going to say it.'

He smiled. 'Yes.' Then, having successfully deprived her of words, he reached into the breast of his coat and drew out some folded sheets of paper. 'I've something to show you.'

Her face brightened with interest.

'Stephen's codes? You've managed to work them out?'

'Yes.' He spread the papers out on the table, gestured to a chair and said, 'May I?'

'Of course.' She managed to avoid starting another flippant conversation by remarking that it was a bit late to begin observing the courtesies and instead sat down beside him. Then, frowning at the uppermost sheet, 'I hope you're going to explain.'

'Yes. Stephen created three quite different codes and wrote out an example of each of them; a sample which reveals its own key. My personal favourite is this one because it looks incredibly simple but isn't.' Eden placed Stephen's original beside his own work. 'It's also the only one that doesn't use number substitution. After some fairly laborious trial-and-error, I eventually worked out that A is now M, B becomes N – and so on. So that first line which reads AGD RMFTQD ITA MDF UZ TQMHQZ translates to Our Father who art in heaven.' He directed a slanting smile at her. 'Simple, wouldn't you say?'

'So the next bit says 'Hallowed be thy name?'

'Does it?'

Lydia squinted at the first group of letters, trying to figure it out. Finally, she said, 'I don't know. The A in hallowed should be M but it's not.'

'No. In the second line, A has become P; in the third line it becomes C and, in the fourth, V. Thankfully, the fifth line uses the same key as the first. This isn't just one code – it's a combination of four different ones. And you'll appreciate that if it was an ordinary message ... if we didn't already know what it says ... every line would have to be worked out from scratch.' He leaned back in his chair. 'It's quite impressive.'

She shook her head. 'You really think Stephen did this purely to pass the time?'

'Unless you can suggest any practical application – yes.' He reached for the next two papers. 'These are number substitutions – the most common method of cryptography – and they took me a lot longer because they translate into Shakespearean speeches with which I am absolutely not familiar. This one is complicated by setting three numbers to each consonant and four to each vowel. And in this, numbers of less than a hundred represent single letters while larger numbers are either syllables or sometimes names of people or places. I've written out the keys of both but thought you might like to do the transposition yourself when you've nothing better to do – which I know doesn't often happen.'

Lydia looked from the neat tables of highly complex-looking figures to the fine-boned face beside her. She said, 'I can't believe you did all this. It must have taken hours.'

'And a good deal of wasted paper,' Eden agreed. Realising he was becoming far too aware of just how close she was and what he'd like to do about it, he resisted temptation by standing up. 'And now I should probably go. Aside from having to re-write your letter, Henry said you were going out. Strand Alley, is it?'

'Yes. If you wished, you could --' She stopped abruptly. 'Or no. Of course not. I daresay you've other things to do.'

'Nothing in particular. And I'd be interested to see the other half of your enterprise.'

'Really?' Lydia beamed at him. 'Then just give me a moment to get my cloak.'

Watching her whirl from the room, Eden wondered which was responsible for that wide uninhibited smile; the prospect of his company or that he'd expressed interest in the sewing women. Somewhat ruefully, he decided that it was probably the latter.

A little while later, walking along with her hand on the Colonel's arm, Lydia tried very hard to stop the big bubble of happiness inside her from manifesting itself by grinning like an idiot or constantly looking up into his face. It was important, she decided, not to get carried away with the idea he might actually *want* to walk with her when the truth was that he was genuinely interested in the female branch of her business. She just hoped that Lily and the other women would put her flushed cheeks down to the near-freezing temperature rather than the man at her side.

As it turned out, she needn't have worried. An air of rare gloom clung to the rooms and, though the women greeted her politely enough and took long, appreciative looks at Eden, nobody smiled.

'What's wrong?' asked Lydia immediately.

'It's Jenny,' sighed Lily Carter. 'When she didn't come in this morning, Betty went round to see if she was ill.'

'And is she?'

'No. That idle lump of a father said she'd got another position. One that pays better. Only he wouldn't tell Betty what it was or where.'

'Wouldn't he?' A martial gleam lit Lydia's eyes. 'Well, he'll tell *me*. Where does she live?'

'Bridewell. Three doors down from the bridge. But --'

'Good.'

She spun round and was heading for the door when Eden's hand closed round her wrist. He said, 'Wait. Before you go storming into one of the most sordid parts of the City, you should recognise that though this girl worked for you, you don't have the right to interfere in either her life or her family.'

'You don't understand,' replied Lydia impatiently. 'Jenny was widowed almost before she was a wife and went back to live with her father so she could look after her younger brother and sisters. Her father is a lazy, bullying drunk.'

'That's as may be. But --'

'Jenny wouldn't just go,' said one of the women suddenly. 'She'd never up and leave without a word.'

There were murmurs of agreement but Lily said regretfully, 'That's true enough. But what the gentleman says is also true, Miss Lydia. It won't do you no good to interfere. And even supposing you *do* find out where Jenny's gone ... what then?'

'I'll know she's all right,' came the stubborn reply.

'What makes you suppose that she might not be?' asked Eden. 'She may have been given an unexpected opportunity but had no time to tell you about it. At least wait for a couple of days to see if she sends a message.'

'And if she doesn't?'

'If she doesn't, I'll track her down for you,' he sighed. 'But only on condition you don't go wandering about Bridewell on your own. Do we have an agreement?'

Glancing around, Lydia saw that a few smiles were breaking out ... one or two of which contained more than a hint of sly speculation about the exact nature of her relationship with Colonel Maxwell. She said grudgingly, 'Yes. All right. I suppose so.'

'Excellent,' said Eden. 'So now perhaps you'll introduce me to these ladies.'

* * *

Three days later, Lydia was just scribbling a note to tell the Colonel that there had been no word from Jenny when a hammering on the front door followed by frantic voices in the hall drew her out to discover what was going on.

'It's Rachel this time,' said Lily Carter breathlessly. 'And Mary. They've vanished.'

FOUR

'Stop. Sit down, take a breath and start at the beginning,' said Eden when Lydia arrived white-faced in Cheapside. 'And full names would be helpful. The first girl was Jenny ...?'

'Sutton. Jenny Sutton.' Lydia folded her hands tightly together to stop them shaking.

'Good.' He wrote it down, added the girl's direction and then looked up, his expression calm and attentive. 'And the others?'

'Rachel Walker and M-Mary Dawson.'

'And neither of these women went home last night?'

She shook her head and said distractedly, 'Mary's mother must be frantic. I've sent Nancy but --'

'Who is Nancy?'

'My maid. She's Mary's sister.' Unable to sit still any longer, Lydia stood up and said wildly, 'Why is this happening? Are women being seized off the street all over London – or is it just the ones at Strand Alley? And where *is* Jenny? You can't still think she went off of her own free will!'

'I don't think it. Please sit down again, Lydia.'

'I can't!' She felt sick and her brain wouldn't work. She'd come running to Colonel Maxwell without thinking, throwing incoherent words at him like a mad woman. And he was being *reasonable* which somehow felt like the last thing she wanted. 'Something terrible could be happening to them and I have to stop it!'

'No. You have to leave it to me,' he said, gentle but firm. 'Now sit down and tell me where Rachel and Mary live.'

She settled back on the edge of the chair and gave him the information he asked for. Then, abruptly, 'Do you think they might have been taken to a brothel?'

'It's a possibility.' *The most obvious one. But it doesn't explain why these particular women were chosen. And three inside a week?*

'Leaving Jenny aside for a moment ... did either Rachel or Mary have a young man? Someone they might have spent the night with?'

'No! Rachel's a married woman whose husband has been bed-ridden since Worcester. And Mary's mother would skin her alive if she thought she was up to no good. Somebody has them and – and this is wasting time.' She stood up again. 'I'm going to see Jenny's father. He must know something!'

'I agree.' Eden also rose and closed his hands over her shoulders. 'And this is what we're going to do. *I'll* visit Mr Sutton. *You* are going to apply your mind to keeping yourself and the other women safe. That is an absolute priority. And if you can't promise to let me deal with this and follow my instructions to the letter, I'll have Henry lock you in the attic until I've found out what the hell is going on. Clear?'

'Yes. But I need to go to Strand Alley --'

'Presently – and by way of your home. Now, if you don't want to waste yet more time, you'll stop arguing,' he said crisply. 'Let's go.'

In Bishopsgate, Colonel Maxwell apprised Henry of the situation and then asked him to find a young, stalwart footman to dog Mistress Neville's every step.

'And make sure he's able to handle himself in a fight,' he added.

'Certainly, Colonel. You may safely leave it to me,' replied Henry. 'I shall also take extra measures here in the house. I believe it is wholly secure ... but one can never be too careful.'

'No. One can't. And one more thing.' Eden lowered his voice. 'It's possible there'll be a letter. If there is, I want to see it first.' And, turning to where Lydia was pacing up and down. 'Now I'll escort you to Strand Alley. But I want your word that you'll stay there until either I or someone I send arrives to bring you home again.'

'I can't promise that! I --'

'Henry and the attic or a few hours with your women,' he said implacably. 'Your choice.'

'I can't – oh! This is ridiculous! I --'

Without further ado, Eden seized her elbow, marched her into the parlour and pinned her to the closed door.

'This is neither a game nor me being magisterial. I'm trying to keep you safe, you stubborn, idiotic woman! Hasn't it occurred to you yet that, if someone can abduct your girls at will, they can also abduct you? I know you want to know where they are – but that would be a damned silly way to find out.' He dropped a fleeting kiss on her brow. 'Now will you please stop being bloody difficult and just do as you're told so that I can go and shake some information out of Sutton?'

Lydia stood perfectly still, staring into a pair of irritable hazel eyes. That kiss had made her want to cry. Swallowing hard, she said, 'Yes. I'm sorry. You're right, of course.'

'Thank God you've finally realised it,' he snapped. 'Now let's go.'

* * *

Leaving Lydia in Strand Alley with numerous admonitions, Colonel Maxwell strode south down Old Bailey, crossed Ludgate Hill and plunged into the labyrinthine alleyways of Bridewell. Here the Fleet River flowed sluggishly on its way to the Thames at Blackfriars. The houses were jostled together, overshadowing the streets and the air stank.

Random thoughts and possibilities about the situation occurred to him as he walked. Had someone turned their attention from the lorinery to the haberdashery? And if so, why? Were the women being taken for the obvious reason that sprang to mind in such cases or were they bargaining chips in a hand yet to be played? He couldn't, he realised, answer any of these questions with certainty. His only concrete thought was, *What the bloody hell does somebody want with Lydia?*

He couldn't answer that question either but it was better than letting his mind drift back to the moment she'd half-run into Cheapside, white-faced and shaking. Something had cracked in his chest then and he'd wanted to wrap his arms about her and stroke her hair and tell her not to worry because, whatever was wrong, he would mend it for her. He'd almost done it ... and still didn't know how he'd stopped himself. Or why.

Because he knew Bridewell well from days long gone by, he found the house he sought without difficulty. Aside from the fact that someone had made an effort to sweep the filth from the step, it looked little different from the others around it. Eventually, his peremptory knock caused the door to open a crack and the scared face of a girl peered around it.

Eden did his best to look unthreatening.

'Is Jenny Sutton your sister?' he asked. And, when the girl nodded, 'And your father is at home?' Another nod. 'Good. I want to speak to him.'

'He – he's asleep,' she whispered. Then, 'Where's Jenny?'

'I don't know yet. I'm going to find her but I need to ask your father some questions first. Will you let me come in?'

'I – I dursn't, sir.'

'I won't hurt you, I promise.' And then, 'Mistress Neville sent me.'

This did the trick.

'Miss Lydia?' She opened the door wide enough for Eden to step through. 'Really?'

'Yes.'

Eden glanced around the gloomy sparsely-furnished room and landed on the man snoring beside the hearth. The wine-bottles littering the floor around him told their own story. The fellow was dead drunk; and households as poor as this one couldn't normally afford wine.

Eden looked back at the girl and said, 'What's your name?'

'Becky, sir.'

'Well, Becky … did your father buy the wine after Jenny went away?'

She nodded, twisting her hands together.

'Someone gave him money?'

'I don't know. I think so.' She hesitated and then added, 'But he didn't give me any for market so Polly and Walter ain't eaten since yesterday.'

Eden's temper had been simmering gently. Now it started to boil. But he merely said, 'Nor you either, I imagine.' And when she stared down at her hands, 'Where are Polly and Walter now?'

'Upstairs.'

'Good. Go and stay with them and don't come down until I call.'

Her eyes were wide with alarm. 'But sir … what'll you do?'

'I'm going to wake your father so we can have a little chat. Now go.'

He waited until Becky had vanished up the narrow twist of the stairs. Then he advanced on her stinking stertorous lump of a father and hauled him out of the chair. The fellow didn't stir. Grunting, Eden heaved him over his shoulder, grateful that the bastard was of spare build. Then he went outside to the banks of the Fleet and tipped Mr Sutton face-down into it.

Fortunately, the river wasn't deep. Less fortunate was what was in it.

Sutton shuddered, inhaled a lungful of filthy water and dissolved into a fit of coughing whilst trying to push himself on to his hands and knees. Eden let him right himself and then, mastering his own disgust, stepped into the river to kick Sutton's arms from under him and plant one boot on his neck.

A handful of neighbours came out to watch. Colonel Maxwell barked an order for them to mind their own business and they melted back into the shadows. When Sutton started to thrash wildly, Eden removed his foot and gave him a moment to breathe before repeating the process. Not until Sutton began cursing volubly between duckings did Eden let him clamber to his feet. Then, regaining dry ground and in a tone that could have cut bread, he said, 'Out. And shut your mouth. You'll have plenty of time to talk in a moment – but not here.'

Dripping and rank as a midden, Sutton lurched to the bank. He knelt for a moment to recover his breath, then he pushed to his feet and took a stumbling dive at Eden.

Having expected something of the sort, Eden stepped to one side and stuck out his foot. Sutton went down like a sack of meal.

'I wouldn't try that again if I were you. I don't mind hurting you. In fact, I'd enjoy it. But if you want me to refrain from reducing you to pulp, you're going to answer my questions – privately, in your own yard. Now move.'

Foolishly, Sutton told him to bugger off. Eden hit him; hard enough to take him down but not hard enough to knock him out. Somebody watching from one of the doorways applauded and shouted, 'Want a hand, Captain? He's a useless piece of shit so there's a few of us here who'd be happy to help.'

Eden looked round at them and shrugged.

'Why not? If you want a share of the fun, feel free.'

Two burly men emerged grinning and set about man-handling Sutton through his own house to the yard behind it and drop him unceremoniously in the dirt. One of them delivered a half-hearted kick.

Flicking a couple of coins their way, Eden said, 'Do either of you know what happened to his eldest girl?'

'Jenny? No. She was here – then she wasn't. And he's been drunk ever since. You looking for her?'

'Yes.'

'Good luck with that. The youngsters won't fare well without Jen.'

Eden waited until they'd gone and Sutton was on his feet again, eyeing him with surly mistrust. 'Where is Jenny?'

'Dunno.'

'I think you do. What have you done?'

'I ain't done nothing. Jen got offered work what pays better'n sewing – so she took it.'

'Really?' Eden advanced on him slowly. 'If that's true, you'll be able to tell me where and with whom, won't you?'

'Don't see why I should. Ain't no business of yourn.'

'I'm making it my business, Mr Sutton.' He took another step forward, his mouth curling in a disquieting smile. 'And this is the last time I'll ask politely. Where is Jenny?'

Sutton told him to do something anatomically impossible. Eden smashed one fist into his jaw and the other to his gut. The air rushed out of him and he fell to the ground again.

Without wasting a second, Eden rolled him over on to his stomach, wrenched his right arm high and flat against his spine and dropped a knee in the small of his back. Sutton whimpered and discovered that he couldn't move without making everything worse.

'I'm not wasting all day over gutter-scum like you,' remarked Eden coldly. 'But here is a thought for you to ponder. Who's going to look after you when I break your arm?'

'You – you won't,' grunted Sutton. 'Not a – a fancy cove like you.'

'Sure of that, are you?' asked Eden, fractionally shifting his grip and making Sutton yelp. 'Let's start again, shall we? Where's Jenny?'

'Dunno,' Sutton panted. Then, hurriedly, 'No, stop – I dunno *exactly*.'

'What's that supposed to mean?'

'A – a fellow come for her. Some gent's servant. He had a rattler waiting at the top of the lane. Said ... said the gent's wife wanted our Jen for her maid.'

'Christ!' muttered Eden. 'If you believed that you're even more stupid than I thought. But you *didn't* believe it, did you?'

'Why wouldn't I? He said Jen'd get twenty pounds a year and her keep. Clothes an all. He give me six months' wages and said he'd bring the rest in a week or two if Jen ... if she worked out all right.'

Eden found *he* had to work hard at not smashing Sutton's face into the ground.

'You mean,' he said, 'if Jenny lifted her skirts any time the *gentleman* asked.'

'No! It weren't that. She was to be a lady's maid. That's what was said.' He groaned. 'Let me go, will you? You're crippling me.'

'Not yet, by any means. So Jenny agreed to this, did she?'

'Yes.' The knee in his back increased its pressure. 'N-no! Not at first. Only when the fellow said the Widow Neville wouldn't be carrying on much longer --'

'*He what?*'

'It's what he said. So Jen agreed.'

Eden thought, rapidly sifting lies from truth.

'I don't believe that. In fact, I don't believe three-quarters of what you've just said. But here are the things I *do* believe. You were willing – even eager – to sell your own flesh and blood for a handful of coins and you then spent the bulk of those coins in the wine-shop, not caring that your other three children were going hungry. But what you did *not* do was to let a complete stranger take Jenny away when there was more money owing and no guarantee that you'd get it.' He dragged Sutton's head up by his hair and brought his hold on the man's arm to the brink of agony. 'You should think about your next answer very carefully. The man who came here was no stranger to you. Who was he?'

Sutton gasped, spluttered and finally managed to say, 'I – I dunno his name.'

'The vast array of what you *don't* know is becoming tedious,' snapped Eden. 'Talk. And make it count – before my patience snaps and your arm with it.'

'He – I think he's one of Quinn's crew. Seen him once or twice at the Three Cranes.'

'Who's Quinn?'

'Somebody you don't cross. He – his bullies'll do whatever you want. For a price. Thieving. Moving on stolen goods. Making folks disappear.'

'And brothels?'

'M-maybe. Owns all the knives and dark cribs between Blackfriars and Wapping, does Quinn.'

'And you let one of his men have your daughter?' Eden slammed Sutton's face down into the dirt. 'Your neighbours are right. You're a piece of shit.' And yanking him up again, 'Where can I find Quinn?'

'D-Dowgate. Or the Steelyard. Got a place somewhere thereabouts. That's it. All I know. His men don't talk. Scared of getting their tongues cut out. Now ... let me up, will you?'

In one lithe, economic movement, Eden rose to his feet dragging Sutton up with him. More than anything, he wanted to plough his fists into this useless mass of flesh. But temporarily curbing the impulse, he said, 'Pray that I find Jenny safe and sound. Pray that I don't come here again and find your children unfed. And pray, Mr Sutton, that when I find Quinn I don't tell him it was you who told me about him.'

And finally giving way to temptation, he delivered a massive punch to the man's jaw ... watched him career off the wall and collapse unconscious on the ground.

Back in the house, he called Becky downstairs and folded her hand around some coins.

'Take that and get your little brother and sister to the cook-shop for a meal – then hide whatever money is left where your father won't find it.'

Tears filled the girl's eyes. She said, 'You'll bring Jenny home, won't you, sir?'

'I'll try, Becky. I promise I'll do my very best.'

* * *

He felt filthy. Contaminated. Moreover, his boots were wet and stank of Fleet effluvia. He needed to wash and change before returning to either Bishopsgate or Strand Alley. But first, because it wasn't far away, he turned east along Thames Street towards the wharves. Since it would hardly be sensible to go around asking about someone who was some kind of arch-criminal, he didn't really know what he hoped this might achieve ... but he decided to do it anyway.

From Puddle Wharf to the bridge, the riverside was crowded with warehouses, lock-ups and boat-yards, any one of which could be hiding Jenny and the other girls. Eden bought a mug of ale in the Three Cranes and drank it slowly while he discreetly surveyed the other customers. Eventually, forced to conclude that Quinn might be any or none of them, he abandoned his ale and strode back to Cheapside.

Tobias was in the shop, talking to Matthew Turner. Fortunately, for once, there weren't any doting ladies.

'God,' said Tobias, staring at him. 'What the hell have you been doing? Aside from how you look, you smell like a – a --'

'I know how I smell, thank you,' replied Eden. And, taking the stairs at a run, shouted over his shoulder, 'Have some hot water sent up, will you? I've got to go out again.'

* * *

It was mid-afternoon by the time he got to Strand Alley. As soon as he walked through the door, conversations stopped, hands were stilled and every eye became fixed on him.

Lydia took several hurried steps towards him and then stopped, as if realising what she was doing. She said, 'Did you see Jenny's father?'

'Yes.' *And you were right to be worried.*

'So you know where she is?'

'No. Not yet – though I've a thread worth following.'

'She didn't go to a new position,' said Lily Carter slowly. 'Did she?'

'No.' Eden looked at Lydia. 'Do you really want the details now?'

'Yes. Everyone sticks together here. So they should all know.'

'Fine,' he sighed. And gave them the gist of his conversation with Jenny's father but took care to omit all mention of Quinn and the Steelyard. Then he said crisply, 'Revile Jenny's father all you like – then forget him. He's not worth a spit. What matters is that I suspect all three women are now in the same place and, though I've an idea of how to resolve this, it may take a few days. In the meantime, let's not lose anyone else.'

'We've made plans,' said Lydia. 'No one is to be out after dark or, if possible, alone.'

Eden nodded. 'Yes. That will help. Another thing you might consider is varying the route between your homes and here. In addition, I'll arrange for a couple of troopers to watch the street. If anyone is loitering outside on a regular basis, I'll know. And now, ladies, if Mistress Neville is ready, I really have to go.'

Walking back to Bishopsgate with her hand once more on the Colonel's arm, Lydia said, 'What was it you weren't telling them?'

'The same things I'm not telling you.'

'But I need to know!'

'No. You don't. Firstly, I've further enquiries to make. And secondly, there's nothing whatsoever that you can do.' He smiled down at her. 'If and when either of those things change, you may be sure I'll tell you.'

She opened her mouth as if to argue, then thought better of it. She fell silent for a moment and then said, 'I haven't thanked you for helping. You didn't have to.'

'But you knew I would.'

'Yes.'

'Good. Then you'll trust me to do what's best.'

Back in Bishopsgate, Henry greeted them with his usual dignified aplomb and introduced a strapping young fellow with a mop of black curls.

'This is Peter. He is my nephew. He is also a pugilist.'

Lydia looked up and then up some more.

'Goodness,' she said weakly.

Laughing at her, Eden offered his hand to Peter who took it in a bone-crushing grip.

'Uncle Henry says the lady needs guarding,' he said simply. And, with some pride, 'Nobody'll get to her through me. And that's a promise.'

'I believe you,' said Eden, flexing his fingers to check they still worked. 'Your main problem may be keeping Mistress Neville under your eye. She's quite slippery.'

'I am not!' protested Lydia.

'And difficult,' confided Eden. 'You'll have your work cut out.'

Peter grinned. 'I'll bear that in mind, sir.'

'Do.' Eden turned to Lydia, laughter fading from his eyes. 'You should sit by the fire and get warm. I'll call tomorrow – though I can't say when. Meanwhile, try not to worry.'

'That's easier said than done,' she replied ruefully.

'I know. But for what it's worth, I don't think the women will be hurt.' *Not to begin with, anyway.* 'And now,' dropping a kiss on her hand, 'I have to go.'

He took his time descending the front steps and had barely reached the road when Peter materialised behind him holding out a sealed missive.

'Uncle Henry said to give you this, sir – and to say thank you.'

And he vanished back into the house.

* * *

Eden contained his impatience to read the letter until he was sitting by his own hearth. Then he broke the seal and unfolded the paper. The message, written in an educated hand, was brief and to the point.

If you want your women returned to you – soon and in good order – you will follow my instructions implicitly.

I require that you find and return to me certain records secretly held by your late husband.

It may be that you have not yet found them. If this is so, I suggest you do so without delay.

You will not make copies of these documents. Neither will you speak of them to any other person.

In due course, I shall communicate the means by which you will deliver what I ask for.

If you are foolish enough to either refuse or procrastinate, the women will suffer the consequences.
You have one week.

Eden was still perusing it and considering both its implications and his own options when Tobias walked in, resplendent in beautifully-cut Italian velvet. Looking up, Eden contemplated his brother thoughtfully for a moment. Finally, he said, 'Toby ... where might I obtain a suit of clothes of the kind that would make me look like a fashionable fop with more money than sense?'

Tobias stared at him. 'You? Fashionable? It can't be done.'

'Thank you for your opinion. Now ... where do I get the clothes.'

'From a tailor. Where else?'

'I haven't time for that. I need them tomorrow evening.'

'Why?'

'So I can look like a fashionable --'

'Yes. I got that bit. But why?'

'Because, in order to save three women I've never met from God knows what, I've got to cultivate the acquaintance of a criminal who, amongst other things, kills people for money. And much as I'd like to, I can't do it with half a regiment at my back ... hence the need to seem fatuous, harmless and plump in the pocket. In short, a pigeon ripe for plucking.'

'Holy hell,' breathed Tobias. 'I think you'd better start at the beginning. But first, I need a drink – as, by the look of you, do you.'

'You were on your way out.'

'Later. Or not. It doesn't matter.' Tobias filled two glasses, handed one to Eden and sat down facing him. 'Now. What's this about?'

Eden told him and watched his brother's normally good-humoured countenance darken.

'Bastard,' said Tobias succinctly.

'Which one?'

'All of them.' He took a drink. 'So. You don't know who sent the letter. You say Mistress Neville hasn't found any secret papers. But you think Quinn's been employed by whoever wrote the letter and that he's got the women in whatever hole he hides in – only you don't know where that is. You can't go asking questions from Queenhithe to the bridge, so you want to tempt him out with the prospect of a well-paid job.'

Eden nodded. 'A wealthy fop with a grudge against someone or other ought to do it.'

'Maybe. But tell me something, will you? Were you planning on dealing with this all on your own? Storming in on your white charger like bloody Galahad and riding out with three women over your saddle-bow?'

'I'm neither suicidal nor an idiot,' came the impatient reply. 'Once I'm as sure as I can be where the women are being held, I'll be enlisting help ... including yours.'

'You'd better.' Tobias frowned into his glass for a moment, then set it aside with a decisive snap and stood up. 'Give me a moment. I think I've an idea.'

He left the room and ran downstairs to the workshop. When he returned to the parlour, he said, 'Forget playing the fop. You'd never get away with it. Instead, play the out-of-work soldier who's down on his luck. If that terrible green coat is still in your closet you've already got the wardrobe for that. Pretend you've turned to crime ... and tempt Quinn out with these instead.'

And he dropped a handful of gem-encrusted jewellery on the table.

Eden picked up a gold necklace inset with rubies and pearls, then a sapphire-studded bracelet.

'It's a good idea,' he admitted. 'But there's no guarantee you'll get these things back.'

'If I don't, I don't,' shrugged Tobias. 'The workmanship's inferior so I'd intended to remove the stones and melt the rest. In truth, I only bought it to help a certain lady. But it's worth a fair bit. Enough, I'd think, to interest somebody who doesn't mind stolen goods.' He paused and then added, 'Take it and welcome – but on one condition. You don't go wandering round the Steelyard with this in your pocket and nobody watching your back. Let Nick and me share the fun.'

'Fun? That's the last thing it's likely to be.'

'You think I don't know that? So try this for size. If it goes wrong, someone needs to get you out. Or who the hell do you think is going to look after the little widow *then*?'

FIVE

Although, between two hours at Whitehall and devoting a good deal of thought to how best to approach matters in the Steelyard that evening, Eden did find time to call on Lydia, he elected not to mention the letter. She already had enough to worry about. And if he managed to retrieve Jenny, Rachel and Mary, the anonymous demands would become redundant; better yet, if he got his hands on Quinn, he ought to be able to find out who was behind the entire thing and deal with the bastard.

Inevitably, Lydia made another attempt to get him to divulge his plans.

Equally inevitably and with a smile specifically designed to be infuriating, Eden refused.

'The men at the lorinery know about Jenny and the others,' she said, trying a different tack. 'They all want to help.'

Eden already knew that. Nicholas had arrived home full of both the men's indignation and questions of his own. He'd also volunteered for rear-guard duty before either Eden or Tobias could ask him.

'Their offer is appreciated. At present, however, there's nothing they can do.'

She eyed him suspiciously.

'And you wouldn't involve them even if there was, would you?'

'Not,' he agreed, 'if I thought it put them at risk. You ought to approve of that.'

'I do. Of course I do.' Lydia drew a long breath and then loosed it. 'But I don't want *you* to be at risk either. And I'm very much afraid that you're going to be.'

Warmed by her concern but unwilling to show it, Eden shrugged.

'I'm used to it.'

'I know you are. But I'm not.'

* * *

Afterwards, he couldn't help wondering how deep her concern went and whether it stemmed from guilt for involving him in something potentially dangerous or from something more personal. He was still wondering it when he, Tobias and Nicholas prepared to depart for the Steelyard.

Eden wore the ancient green coat, a pair of boots he'd intended to throw away but forgotten about and carried the plain, serviceable blade he kept for occasional bouts of practice. Nicholas and Tobias were much better dressed, though not ostentatiously so. Nicholas was unarmed but Tobias slid a slender, evil-looking knife up his sleeve.

'Genoese back-streets,' he said by way of response to his brother's enquiring gaze.

'Ever used it?'

'Yes.'

'Jesus,' muttered Eden.

It was a little after six o'clock and fully dark. Trade at the Three Cranes was already fairly brisk and promised to get busier as the evening wore on. Nicholas and Tobias arrived first and settled down in a corner with a bottle of wine and a dice-box. Eden slouched in some ten minutes later, leaned against the counter and let the bar-keep watch him count out a few precious coins to pay for a small pot of ale.

He drank it slowly, the very picture of a man who couldn't afford another. He also glanced frequently about the tap-room, looking nervous. Eventually, just when he was beginning to think he'd have to initiate the conversation himself, the inn-keeper paused beside him and said, 'Looking for someone?'

Eden grunted an assent, hesitated and then mumbled, 'I heard there's a man hereabouts who … buys things.'

'There's a few of 'em, soldier.' The man gave him an appraising look, then grinned and shook his head. 'No offence – but I don't reckon you've got much worth selling.'

Eden slid his hand from his pocket. His little finger sported a diamond ring.

The landlord's eyes widened a bit and Eden shoved the hand back in his pocket. He said, 'I've got more. But I …' He stopped as if afraid of saying too much. 'I've been told this fellow Quinn doesn't ask questions.'

'Oh. Like that, is it?'

Eden nodded and took another sip of ale.

'You wouldn't know where I can find him, would you? Only ... well, I can't hang on to the stuff much longer.'

'Burning a hole in your pocket?'

'Something like that.'

Caution warred with greed in the fellow's face. Finally, he said, 'If I was to point you in the right direction, let's say ... what would be in it for me?'

The possibility that he might achieve his objective so quickly had Eden reminding himself not to take anything for granted. He'd expected to have to do this twice, if not three times before it bore fruit.

Knowing he shouldn't appear too eager, he hesitated again and then said reluctantly, 'The ring I showed you ... if Quinn buys the rest.'

A crafty gleam lit the landlord's eye. He said, 'Quinn don't like uninvited guests but there's a fellow in the back room who could introduce you. Give me the ring and I'll take you to him.'

Eden shook his head.

'Take me to him first. Then, if he can do what you say, the ring's yours.'

'Cautious one, ain't you?'

'Yes. I learned it the hard way. But my word's worth something.'

There was a long uncomfortable pause and then the landlord gave a gruff laugh.

'Come on, then. But don't blame me if Quinn robs you blind and slits your throat for good measure.'

Eden followed the landlord to a door on the far side of the room. As he passed their table, he caught his brother's eye and gave an almost imperceptible nod.

In the back room, the four men playing cards instantly impaled Eden on four very hard stares. One of them, a pock-marked fellow whose nose looked as if it had been broken more than once, slapped his hand face-down on the table and stood up, scowling.

'Ben? Who the sodding hell is this?'

'He's looking for Quinn. Lone wolf and a first-timer, I reckon. Says he's got some fancy gew-gaws to sell.' He nudged Eden. 'Show 'em.'

Slowly, Eden withdrew his hand from his pocket and let the diamond catch the light.

The man on his feet held out his hand. 'Give.'

Eden closed his fist and shook his head. 'No.'

Pock-face grinned and suddenly there was a knife in his hand.

'Rather I took your finger with it, would you?'

Seeing no alternative, Eden pulled the ring free and tossed it towards Pock-face, hoping he'd drop the knife. He didn't. He caught the ring neatly in his left hand and took a good long look at it. Then, tossing it back so suddenly that Eden nearly failed to catch it, he said, 'Looks real enough – but I ain't no expert. Got any more like it?'

'Some. I heard Quinn would be interested.'

'Might be. Where d'you lift it? And how long since?'

'Does it matter?'

'Don't know much about Quinn, do you?'

'No. I just --' Eden stopped and then said rapidly, 'All right. I took it from a – a lady just two days ago. She won't have missed it yet. But when she does, she – '

'When she does, she'll know who took it. And you want enough ready to disappear before she comes looking. That it?'

'Yes. Look – I don't want any trouble. I never stole anything before and wouldn't have this time if I hadn't been desperate. Now I just want to get rid of the stuff and be on my way. So if you think Quinn might be interested, for God's sake just take me to him.'

Pock-face stared at him for a long moment, toying gently with the knife. Then, the blade vanishing as swiftly as it had appeared, he turned to the seated man on his right and said, 'Reckon he's on the level?'

'Looks to be,' came the laconic reply. Then, derisively, 'Sodding rabbit.'

Pock-face laughed.

'Come on, then. Let's see what the boss makes of him.'

The other three men promptly stood up.

Wonderful, thought Eden. *They're all bloody coming.*

The landlord grabbed his arm. 'We had a deal. The ring.'

With a resigned shrug, Eden gave it to him.

A door from the room led into a yard, linked to other yards and finally to an alley. Surrounded by his silent escort, Eden found himself being led down towards the river in the general direction of the bridge.

Nick and Toby ... I hope to God one of you has this covered. I don't fancy taking on all four of these bruisers if they decide to bounce me off the wall and take what's in my pockets for themselves.

They crossed Old Swan Lane into the Steelyard, skirted All Hallows the Less and turned down to the dock-side. Then, at a large warehouse with no lights showing, they knocked, waited and knocked again. A small grille opened briefly and then was slammed shut. From inside came sounds of bolts being withdrawn. Nerves tingled in Eden's hands and he forced himself to breathe evenly, glad that he'd got this far in one piece.

Inside was a great barn of a place that appeared to have been adapted to suit whatever business was conducted there. A narrow wooden staircase led to a galleried upper floor supported by massive timbers. Five doors up there, Eden noted. The section below it had been closed off, presumably to provide a private office. And around where he stood, a good many crates and barrels suggested that a delivery of some sort had just arrived and was being sorted for onward travel. Three men worked on this and a fourth sat to one side, smoking a pipe.

How many others that I can't see?

Pock-face sauntered over to the smoker and nodded. 'Bones.'

'Skinner.'

'Boss in tonight?'

'Aye. Rooster's with him.'

'Ah.' Skinner alias Pock-face grinned at his three companions. 'Won't need you, then. I'll see you back at the Cranes in a bit.'

With a few rumblings of discontent about wasted time, the trio turned and left.

The pipe-stem pointed at Eden. 'What you got here, Skinner?'

'Rabbit selling some shiny stuff the boss might like.'

'Seen it?'

'Some.' He grinned and jerked his head towards Eden. 'Didn't want to scare him off. Nerves on the snap all the way here in case we jumped him. Reckon nobody told him Quinn's crew knows better than cross him. Ever.'

Grateful though he was that Quinn's apparent vice-like discipline had spared him a mauling in an alley, Eden recognised that, on other levels, it was likely to present a problem. He was also getting tired of being treated like a deaf-mute, so he said, 'Can I see Mr Quinn?'

'Impatient, ain't he?' Bones heaved himself to his feet and turning to a door behind him, rapped on the panels. Then, sticking his head round it, he said, 'Skinner's here. Got something for you.'

A voice from within said something Eden couldn't hear but which made Bones laugh. Then he pushed the door wide and said, 'Go on, then. But your sword stays here with me.'

Having expected as much, Eden pulled off his sash and handed the weapon over. Then, obeying a shove from Skinner, he entered the lair of the man who he was beginning to suspect ruled half of the City's criminal underbelly.

There were three people in the room. A massive fellow with a shock of ginger hair, leaning against the wall, picking his teeth; a very pretty blonde reclining on a sofa in a state of semi-undress; and a man perched on the edge of a carved oak desk.

Eden didn't know what he'd expected Quinn to be like ... but it certainly wasn't this.

Of roughly his own age, dark-haired and slender, Quinn wouldn't have appeared out of place on the benches at Westminster. Perfectly groomed and plainly dressed, he looked like a successful lawyer. He did not look like someone who made money from every vice known to man and murdered to order; or not, that was, until you caught that dark, empty gaze. Then, thought Eden feeling oddly chilled, you became aware of a reptilian quality that told you to be ready to move fast.

The door closed behind him. Skinner leaned against it and, presumably with the intention of making Eden nervous, set about cleaning his fingernails with the point of his knife.

Quinn looked at him in silence for a moment, then said, 'And you are?'

The voice was flat, cold and untainted by any discernible accent.

'Is my name really necessary?'

'No. I asked who you *are*.'

'I am – I *was* – a soldier.'

'Your regiment was reduced?'

'No.' Eden stared at the floor. 'I was cashiered.'

'Why?'

'For striking a superior officer.'

Silence; unnecessarily lingering and deliberately enervating; the kind of silence Eden had often used himself because it made people want to break it – or at the very least, fidget. With an inward sigh, he obligingly fiddled with the brim of his hat.

Still Quinn took his time. Then, finally, 'You have a problem with authority?'

'Not when it knows what it's doing.'

'And you are the best arbiter of that, are you?'

Eden shrugged and said nothing.

'I,' remarked Quinn coming unhurriedly to his feet, 'am not an admirer of independent thought. However. Why are you here?'

'I've something to sell that I can't sell elsewhere.'

'Ah. Of course.' His tone was one of mingled boredom and contempt. 'Show me.'

Finally. I thought he was going to ask to count my teeth.

Without speaking, Eden pulled the jumble of jewellery from his pocket and dropped it into Quinn's outstretched palm. Then he waited for what seemed like an age while the fellow laid it out on the desk, piece by piece.

'Not the best workmanship,' said Quinn at length. 'Rather crude, in fact. But pretty enough.' And beckoning to the blonde, 'Come and see, Angel. Is there anything you like?'

Angel slid from the couch and undulated across the room.

'Yes.' She touched each item with considering fingers and clasped the sapphire bracelet on her wrist. 'All of it. But I'll settle for this.'

He tapped her cheek and was just about to speak when a series of thuds and bangs sounded from one of the rooms above. Angel scowled and sighed. 'God damn. The bloody trulls are at it again. Don't they *never* stay quiet? I've been up and down them stairs more times than I can count.'

'Rooster.' Quinn spoke to the big, silent red-headed man. 'Go and shut them up. Do *not* use your fists. I need them unmarked. Just make further disturbance impossible. Skinner will remain here with me.'

When the door closed again, Quinn resumed his examination of the jewellery. He said, 'I will give you forty pounds for it.'

Tobias had said market value was roughly a hundred and fifty.

'It's worth more than that,' protested Eden.

'Not to me. And not to you – unless you can take it to a legitimate jeweller. Can you?'

'No.'

'No. If you could do that, you wouldn't be here, would you?' An almost imperceptible but definitely unpleasant smile curled the corners of Quinn's mouth but didn't get as far as those curiously vacant eyes. 'Forty. Take it or leave it.'

Eden hesitated as long as he dared. Then, managing an expression of hopelessness, he said, 'What choice do I have? I'll take it.'

'That is wise.' Quinn walked round his desk, opened a drawer and counted out coins. He dropped them in a small, cloth bag and tossed it to Eden. Then he said unexpectedly, 'The next time you're desperate, come to me. It's possible I could find a use for a man like you.'

Eden felt an insane desire to laugh. He said, 'You'd give me work?'

'Of a sort. Not, perhaps, the kind you're used to ... though I imagine you've killed your fair share over the years. And you've already said goodbye to honour, haven't you?' He paused. 'Forty pounds won't last forever. Give some thought to your future. But if you decide to come back here, know two things. I demand implicit loyalty and absolute obedience – and reward both generously. But men who adapt their orders because they feel they know better than I ... men who disappoint me ... don't live to do it a second time. I trust I make myself clear?'

'Very.'

'Good. Then we are done. You may go.'

* * *

As previously agreed, Tobias and Nicholas shadowed Eden from a safe distance all the way back to Cheapside in case Quinn decided to have him followed. Eden only knew they were there when he rounded a corner, paused and then looked back in time to see Tobias's distinctive figure emerging at the end of Watling Street.

Once back by the fire, Eden shed the despised green coat and went in search of brandy. If he was cold just from the walk home, the others – after their long vigil by the river – must be downright freezing. They came in bringing gusts of bitter air with them.

'Please tell me,' said Nicholas, through chattering teeth, 'that we don't have to do that again.'

'You don't.' Eden handed him a glass and passed the other to his brother. 'For which I'm as relieved as you are.'

Tobias downed a large gulp of brandy, then threw off his coat.

'You found Quinn?'

'Yes.'

'And he took the bait?'

'Yes.' Eden tossed him the purse. 'Forty pounds.'

'*Forty*? He must have taken you for a complete flat.'

'Very likely. But I got to leave with all my body parts intact so I'm not complaining. In case you hadn't realised, these aren't people you want to barter with.'

'Has he got the women?' asked Nicholas.

'I think so. He's certainly got *some* females locked up upstairs.'

'Must be them,' yawned Tobias. 'What's he like, this Quinn?'

'Not your everyday throat-cutting villain.' Eden paused and allowed the amusement he'd previously suppressed to surface. 'He offered me a job.'

Tobias choked on his brandy. 'As what?'

'I rather think ... as a professional assassin.'

SIX

On the following evening, six men sat around the table in Cheapside. In addition to Tobias and Nicholas, Eden had also summoned Colonel Brandon, Major Moulton and Sir Aubrey Durand. For the benefit of these three, he explained the situation thus far and then said flatly, 'There is no need for Mistress Neville to know any of this. Time enough to tell her when we've got her women back.'

'*If* we get them back,' muttered Aubrey.

'Quite,' agreed Eden coolly. 'Though a more positive attitude would be helpful.'

Aubrey flushed and subsided.

Gabriel said, 'You're proposing the six of us break into Quinn's premises?'

'Unless anyone's got a better idea – yes.'

'Assuming you're correct about him having abducted these women, the man is probably also responsible for half the crime in the City. Why not inform the appropriate authorities and let them send a troop of Militia in?'

'I thought of that,' replied Eden. 'At least, I considered going to Lambert and asking for official help. But I've no proof ... and there's always the chance that I'm wrong and the women are being held elsewhere.'

'That doesn't alter the fact that Quinn's a criminal,' remarked Ned Moulton. 'Lambert would probably consider it a risk worth taking.'

'Possibly. But *I* can't risk losing Quinn – which might very well happen if Militia go storming in there.'

'Under *your* command?' murmured Gabriel.

'All right – point taken,' agreed Eden with a faint smile. 'But Quinn is the key to unlocking this whole mess. I doubt he confides in his underlings. And if that's so, he's the only one who knows who's paying him and *also* the only one who can tell that man that he's lost the bargaining tool he was paid to obtain.'

'That,' observed Nicholas thoughtfully, 'alters the case somewhat. If Quinn slips the net, you lose more than the opportunity to question him. Once his employer finds out that the women are gone, he'll disappear back into the woodwork and we'll have no way of tracing him until he tries something else.'

'As,' nodded Eden, 'he most assuredly will. I don't know what these supposed secret documents are ... in truth, I'm not sure they even exist. But someone is willing to go to any lengths to get them – which means that Lydia won't be safe until he's found and stopped.'

Tobias stood up and stretched.

'God, Eden – why not just admit that you don't want the Militia involved because, as far as you're concerned, it's bloody personal.'

'Hardly,' snapped his brother. 'Since I've never laid eyes on any of the missing women --'

'Not them,' grinned Tobias. 'The widow.'

Aubrey sat up suddenly and frowned at Eden.

'Oh. I didn't ... that is, are Lydia and you --?'

'No,' came the thoroughly exasperated reply. 'There is no Lydia and me. As usual, Toby is doing his damnedest to be annoying.' Eden drew a sharp breath and loosed it. 'Do you think we might stick to the business in hand?'

'By all means,' agreed Gabriel, banishing the glint of amusement in his eyes. 'So ... no Militia. But if it's just to be the six of us, I think we'd all like some idea of how many we're likely to be up against. Presumably you counted the men you saw?'

'Yes. Four men in the warehouse, a ginger-haired giant in Quinn's office and a fellow called Skinner who accompanied me there. But I don't think we can assume there won't be others. Skinner's gaming cronies in the Three Cranes are also Quinn's men and I daresay they're not the only ones.'

'So we could be tangling with at least ten or even more?' asked Major Moulton.

'It's possible. I imagine their numbers fluctuate.'

'In that case – and since you plainly want this kept to men you trust – I'll have a word with Sergeant Trotter. You know him. And as it's for you, he won't need asking twice.' Ned looked around. 'Anybody got any other suggestions?'

There was silence for a moment and then Aubrey said tentatively, 'Peter? Lydia's new footman? He's something of a pugilist, I believe – and he's certainly built like one.'

Eden nodded. 'Ask him – but make sure your sister doesn't catch wind of it. If he agrees, that brings our strength up to eight – which, since five of us are trained soldiers, ought to be enough. Aubrey ... I'm assuming you can handle a sword and know how to fire a pistol. Find out what Peter's weapon of choice is, will you?' Then, when the other man nodded, 'Very well, gentlemen. I'd like to do this tomorrow night so now we'd best formulate a plan. And the first hurdle we need to negotiate is how – since the door will be barred and bolted and there aren't any windows – we are to get inside.'

* * *

On the following evening under a clear sky lit by only the merest sliver of a moon, Eden's little army made its way to the Steelyard. In order not to draw undue attention – since everyone was armed to the teeth – they did this in three separate groups. Colonel Brandon, Nicholas and Aubrey approached from the shadows of the Fishmongers' Hall; Major Moulton led Sergeant Trotter and Peter down from Thames Street, between the two All Hallows churches; and Tobias, hands shoved carelessly into his pockets, trailed Colonel Maxwell along the wharves from Dowgate, whistling.

Eden could hear that light-hearted whistling even though Tobias was several hundred yards behind him. In one sense, this was a comfort. In another, he wondered where the hell his brother got his ability to sound so damned cheerful.

They'd spent a lot of time debating the various ways of getting into the warehouse.

Ned had suggested creating a disturbance that would have Quinn's men opening the door to investigate. A small fire on the wharf, he said, should be sufficient. Gabriel had pointed out that such a disturbance wouldn't only bring out Quinn's men but God knew how many others as well. Also, considering the amount of flammable material along the riverside and the fact that they didn't want to risk burning down half of the Steelyard, starting even the smallest fire probably wasn't very wise.

Tobias had asked why they didn't just hammer on the door and shout 'Fire!' anyway.

Nicholas had reminded him that, since the door had a hatch they could squint through, they'd know there wasn't a fire without bothering to step outside.

So, in the end, they'd agreed on the simplest solution of all.

'Quinn offered me a job,' Eden had said at length. 'I'll let them think I've come to accept it. Once the door is open, I can hold it while the rest of you come up.'

'On your own?' demanded Tobias. 'Bugger that!'

Which was why Tobias was now closing the gap between himself and his brother and letting the knife slide smoothly from his sleeve to his hand.

Eden risked a glance over his shoulder and then banged on the door, keeping the pistol hidden at his side. Although he couldn't see them, he trusted that Gabriel and Ned had their troops in position. There were a number of problems with what they were doing, of which overpowering an unknown number of men and getting the women to safety were the most obvious. Another complication was that they'd agreed not to kill anyone if it could be avoided. But the thing that was bothering Eden the most was the gnawing possibility that Quinn himself might not currently be inside.

The small grille in front of him opened and Bones peered out at him.

'Oh,' he said. 'You again.'

'Me again,' Eden agreed amicably. 'Is Quinn about?'

'Might be. What do you want with him?'

'That's between me and him.'

'Not if you want this door opening, it's not.'

'If you *must* know, he offered me work and I reckon I could do worse than take it.' Eden stamped his feet and wrapped his arms around himself. 'Are you going to let me in or not? It's colder than a witch's tit out here.'

Bones gave a bark of laughter. The grille slammed shut and there were sounds of bolts being withdrawn. Toby arrived wraithlike at Eden's shoulder and the faces of Gabriel and Major Moulton materialised from the shadows at either side of the building.

Eden barely had time to make a tiny gesture, telling the others to wait before the door swung open. Easing through it, he paused almost imperceptibly but just long enough to establish that three men were busy stacking crates in the far corner. Then, without further hesitation, he smashed his fist into the doorkeeper's jaw.

Tobias caught Bones and lowered him soundlessly to the floor as Gabriel and the others ran past him.

'Nice punch,' he murmured. 'But witches' tits? I'm shocked.'

Eden ignored him as a number of things happened at once.

Behind him, Sergeant Trotter re-barred the door. Quinn's workers slammed down their loads, pulled out knives and swung to face the intruders as if ready to charge; but before they could do so they found themselves facing Colonel Brandon and Major Moulton, swords in one hand and pistols in the other, at uncomfortably close quarters.

'Not a sound,' said Gabriel softly. 'And if you want to see tomorrow, lay down your weapons.'

For an instant they froze, their eyes flickering from Eden's troops to each other and back again. Then with obvious reluctance, they dropped the knives. A nod from Gabriel sent Peter to gather them up.

Tossing coils of rope to Ned and the sergeant, Tobias strolled forward saying, 'On the floor, boys. Be sensible and no one need get hurt.'

A few steps away, Sergeant Trotter peered into a still-open crate and said, 'Come and see this, Major. Must be two dozen pistols in here – all nice and shiny-like.'

Ned looked and muttered, 'Bloody hell. Where are these going?'

Aubrey and Nicholas, meanwhile, were making their way quietly up the stairs with Peter, having put the knives out of harm's way, following in their wake.

Good, thought Eden. *Everyone's sticking to the plan. If the women are upstairs, we can be out of here in less than ten minutes ... which is somehow beginning to seem too easy.*

Leaving Ned and Tobias to truss and gag the workers, Gabriel emerged at Eden's elbow and said, 'Time to find Quinn?'

'Yes.' He pointed. 'In there.'

Gabriel nodded and the two of them made their way to the door. Unsurprisingly, it was locked. Eden knocked with seeming politeness. Then, when nothing happened, he took a step back and put his foot to it. It shuddered but remained stubbornly closed.

Gabriel raised his pistol, preparing to shoot the lock but Eden shook his head.

'Bolted,' he said. 'Which means someone's inside and they know --'

Without warning, the door swung wide revealing the Rooster ... grinning and wielding a claymore in a two-handed grip.

'—we're here,' finished Eden. Then, 'I want to see Quinn.'

'Aye? But mebbe he doesna want tae see ye.'

'And maybe I'm not giving him the choice. Is he here?'

'He isna, no.'

'No? Then you won't mind us taking a look.'

'Och, I'll mind fine ... and ye'll no be coming in here.'

'Think again,' said Eden. And launched an immediate attack.

His blade was met with a force that nearly dislocated his shoulder. He grunted a curse and fell back a step, hoping the massive Scotsman would advance on him and thus leave the doorway clear for Gabriel. The Rooster stood his ground, laughed and beckoned.

'Ye'll no get tae Quinn that way, ma wee laddie. Ye'll have tae take me first.'

'Fine,' snapped Eden, advancing again with a deceptive sweep that suddenly became a lunge.

Once again, the long reach of the claymore blocked him. The blades hissed and slithered to a disengage and the Rooster remained firmly planted in the doorway. From upstairs came the sound of someone kicking a door in and a woman's muffled scream.

'Oh for God's sake, Eden,' said Gabriel irritably. 'Just get out of the way.'

And when Eden did so, he pointed his pistol at the Scotsman's heart and said, 'Lay down your sword and step aside. A few words with Quinn and we're gone with no harm done.'

'Och no.' The Rooster shook his head. 'I dinna think so.'

'Don't be a fool, man. You can't argue with a bullet.'

'I ken ma duty.' His hands gripped the hilt of the massive sword more tightly. 'Ye'll no get in while I've breath in ma body.'

'Your choice,' shrugged Gabriel. And fired.

The claymore went clattering to the ground as the shot took the Rooster in his right shoulder, causing him to grunt and drop to his knees. Eden wasted no time in kicking the blade aside and, with a brief, muttered apology, used the hilt of his own sword to knock the big Scotsman unconscious.

'Good,' remarked Gabriel, competently re-loading his pistol as he strode past into Quinn's office. And then, 'Ah. Perhaps not.'

Eden spun round, looked – and swore.

The room was empty.

'Where the hell has he gone?'

'Perhaps he was never here,' Gabriel suggested.

'He was here. That hulking brute is his personal body-guard.' Already on the move, Eden started scouring the room for a possible exit. The walls were lined with rough shelving crammed with boxes and ledgers. 'There's another way out of here. Has to be.'

'Very possibly. But we won't --' He stopped when Eden began yanking at the shelves, dislodging a miscellaneous avalanche of paperwork, assorted objects and dust. 'Eden. We don't have time for this. The man's gone and finding out how he managed it is the least of our worries.' Turning back to the doorway, Gabriel looked up to the galleried landing. 'Nick and the others are bringing the women down now. We need to go. If Quinn *did* get out of here --'

'I know.' Abandoning his attempts to discover if a door was hidden behind the shelves, Eden flew across to Quinn's desk. 'Take charge, will you? I'll be there in a minute.'

Gabriel cursed under his breath and strode away.

Nothing of interest lay on the incongruously polished surface of the desk and the drawers opened at a touch. All, that is, save one. Without hesitation, Eden shot the lock and pulled it wide. Inside, lay a heavy pouch of coin ... and a thick, leather-bound book. He snatched up the book and shoved it in the breast of his coat. Then, jumping over the Rooster's recumbent form, he ran back into the warehouse.

Hemmed in by Nick, Aubrey and Peter, three wild-eyed and dishevelled women stared at him. The youngest of them was clinging to Peter as if her legs wouldn't support her. The other two stood shoulder to shoulder, their backs straight and their jaws set.

Eden shot them a swift, reassuring grin and, swiftly re-loading his pistol, said, 'We're going to get you home, ladies. Are any of you hurt?'

'Not so as you'd notice,' said a very pretty blonde. 'Tired, hungry and full of pins and needles from being tied up – but we'll get out of here if we have to bloody crawl.'

'It shouldn't come to that.' He turned to Gabriel. 'All set?'

'Yes,' grunted Colonel Brandon. 'Let's go. Ned, Nick, Sergeant – to me, if you please. Colonel Maxwell will doubtless join us at his convenience.'

'Sarcastic bugger,' muttered Eden. Then, 'All right, Toby. Unbar the door – but be careful.'

Tobias slid the bar back, eased the door open and peered through the gap.

'Looks quiet enough,' he said. 'Now?'

'Yes. Stick to the plan and move fast.'

Tobias pulled the door wide and stood back to let Gabriel and the others past him, followed by Eden and the detail guarding the women. Then, as Tobias stepped out in their wake, figures rushed from the shadows towards them.

There was no time to think or weigh up the scale of the opposition. With a mixture of brief, colourful curses, Gabriel, Eden, Ned and Sergeant Trotter reacted instinctively, surging forward to meet Quinn's bully-boys while, behind them, Nicholas volunteered to get the women back inside.

'*No!*' shouted Eden over his shoulder as he dodged a vicious cudgel blow to his head, disarmed its owner and then knocked him out with the butt of his pistol. 'Not safe. There's another entrance.'

Gradually he began to see what they were up against. Nine or ten men, muscled like dock-workers and bearing an assortment of clubs, metal bars and knives. Away to his left, Gabriel had put down another of them with a sword-thrust to the thigh; Ned and the sergeant were grappling with two others while Peter sent a third staggering back with a punch like a sledgehammer; and, knife in hand, Tobias was circling a fellow who was trying to gut him with a bill-hook.

'Nick – Aubrey,' said Eden as he spun to face another attacker. 'Get the women away. We'll hold here.'

'Get Mary away,' said one of the women grimly as she snatched up a fallen cudgel. 'Jenny and me'll fight.'

Nicholas pushed Mary into Aubrey's arms. He said, '*You* take her. I'll stay.' And he threw himself into the mêlée.

For a few minutes, the fight became messy, confusing and noisy. Jenny and Rachel screeched angry insults at their former captors and hit out at anything they could reach. A couple of Quinn's fellows laughed ... and then stopped laughing when one of them went down, howling from a well-placed kick to the groin.

Another five men poured in from Dowgate.

Finding himself briefly back-to-back with Gabriel, Eden said breathlessly, 'Sod it. We're going to have to shoot a couple of them to end this before any more turn up.'

'Pick whichever you like. I'll take the one annoying Ned.'

Eden glanced across to where Nicholas was struggling with a fellow wielding a heavy crowbar. He raised his pistol and fired, a mere heartbeat before Gabriel felled his own target. Suddenly the odds looked manageable again.

Tobias had despatched the fellow with the bill-hook and was now dancing about an overweight rotundity with yellow hair and a hefty length of lead pipe. He was laughing.

'Stop playing and take him down, Toby,' yelled Eden. 'We don't want to be at this all bloody night!'

'Speak for yourself,' sang out Tobias cheerfully. But the wicked Genoese knife made a lightening sweep at the fat man's wrist and the lead pipe clattered to the cobbles. 'Happy now?'

'Idiot!'

Almost before the word was out, something crashed hard against his shoulder, sending him reeling and a second blow to the back of his thigh forced him down on one knee. Swivelling, he was just in time to see a cudgel swinging at his head with murderous intent. With no time to gain his feet, he ducked and made an inevitably clumsy slash with his sword. His blade met empty air but his attacker screamed, dropped his cudgel and backed off clutching his rear.

Tobias grinned down on his brother and held out his free hand.

'Stuck him in the arse,' he grinned, as he pulled Eden to his feet, 'You can thank me later.'

A few yards away, Gabriel, Ned and Sergeant Trotter had isolated the women from the main thrust of the fight and were driving the opposition back across the quayside towards the river. Behind them, Peter was gasping for breath and clutching his side with blood welling steadily through his fingers while Nicholas, limping badly from a savage blow to his knee, struggled to fend off the blows of a beefy fellow wielding what looked like half an oar. Tobias swung back to help him.

Pivoting on his heel, Eden found himself face to face with Skinner and wondered, briefly, where the hell he'd come from.

Bad teeth and a pair of long knives gleaming in the fitful light, Skinner said, 'Well, well. If it ain't the bleeding rabbit. Didn't think you was this stupid.'

'Your mistake, then.' Eden swept his blade round in a murderous arc that sent Skinner hopping back a couple of paces. 'Call your men off. So far, we haven't killed anybody – but that stops now. Call them off.'

'Give us the women and I might.' He stepped across, circling like an animal waiting to pounce. 'Mr Quinn wants them, see.'

'Where is he?'

'Ah. Like to know that, wouldn't you?'

Skinner made a sudden feint to his left, then swiftly reversed it whilst nodding at someone Eden couldn't see. A second later, something heavy and sharp slammed into Eden's kidneys sending pain roaring through him and causing him to stumble. Skinner raised both knives, his intentions clear. Then, before he could drive them into Eden's body, another blade arched through the air and buried itself in Skinner's throat. He gave an unpleasant gurgle and went down in a fountain of blood.

Summoning his resources as best he could, Eden turned to deal with the man who'd hit him whilst five paces beyond and looking anything but cheerful, Tobias strode towards his handiwork. He dragged his knife from Skinner's throat and immediately swung round to guard Eden's back. There was a moment or two of scuffling confusion … and then a shot rang out. Tobias grunted, jerked oddly and doubled up, clutching his arm. Without hesitation, Eden drove his sword into his attacker's heart and lurched towards his brother. Gabriel and Ned, meanwhile, both shot at the shadowy figure wreathed in smoke.

For the space of perhaps half a dozen heartbeats, everything froze. Then a single word punctuated the abrupt silence.

'Retreat.'

And without further ado, Quinn's men turned and melted swiftly back into the darkness.

Eden found the suddenness of it unnerving. One arm around Tobias's shoulders, he said, 'Where are you hit?'

'Arm,' mumbled Tobias, hauling himself upright on a hiss of pain, holding his knife in one hand and his left arm in the other. 'It's nothing.'

Eden rose, still holding on to him. 'Liar.'

'All right. It sodding hurts. But it won't kill me.'

Gabriel arrived beside them.

Eden looked up. 'Did you get him?'

'I doubt it. Ned and I both fired at the smoke from his pistol. He'd have been an idiot if he just stood there waiting for it.'

'What's our situation?'

'They've gone – but Ned and Trotter are checking,' replied Gabriel concisely. 'The women are unhurt, Peter has a nasty gash to his ribs and Nicholas, an injured knee. The rest of us merely have a collection of cuts and bruises. If the two of you can walk, we should go.'

'Yes,' agreed Tobias faintly. 'Let's. It's been fun ... but now I could use a drink.'

* * *

By the time they got back to Cheapside, Nicholas could barely hobble, Peter was white from loss of blood, the women were ready to drop with fatigue and Tobias was sounding a good deal less jaunty. It was a few minutes short of midnight.

In the hallway, arms folded beneath her magnificent bosom, Mistress Wilkes eyed them all with something akin to exasperation and said briskly, 'The young lord and the girl are in the best parlour. And I'll say now that if this kind of thing is to happen again, I'd appreciate some warning.'

'Of course,' replied Eden. 'But at the moment, we need --'

'I can see well enough what you need, Colonel. Food and drink; hot water, bandages, salves – and probably a doctor. So go on upstairs – and try not to bleed on the furniture.' Upon which note, she sailed away in the direction of the kitchen.

For a moment, everyone simply stared at her retreating back. Then Rachel muttered, 'Soddin' hell. Whichever one of you is married to *her* is even braver'n I thought.'

Upstairs, Aubrey stood by the hearth and Mary was sitting bolt upright in a nearby chair. But as soon as the door opened, she rose and, stumbling towards her friends, said, 'Oh thank the good Lord you got away all right. I was so afeared you wouldn't.' And then all three of them were talking at once, while Aubrey tried to ask questions of his own.

Ignoring the hiatus around them and leaving Gabriel and Ned to see to Nicholas and Peter, Eden settled Tobias into a chair by the fire and, moving very stiffly thanks to the agony in his back, went in search of brandy. Then, sloshing the amber liquid into whatever glasses he could find, he snapped, 'Will you all just *stop talking*?'

Immediate silence.

'Thank you. Now. One of you ladies see how badly Peter is hurt, if you please. Aubrey – go home and stay there. Tell Henry what's happened and that Peter won't be back tonight. If your sister's still awake – which I doubt – you can assure her that the women are safe and that I'll call on her tomorrow.' Without waiting to see if Aubrey did as he was told, Eden turned back to his brother. 'Toby – I want that coat off you before you pass out.'

'I'm not going to pass out,' grumbled Tobias, reaching half-heartedly for his laces. 'What do you think I am – a bloody daisy?'

'Yes. That's *exactly* what I think you are. Now shut up and let Gabriel see the damage. If, in the absence of a doctor, one of us has to dig holes in you, he's the one likely to make the best job of it.'

SEVEN

'Wait! Just stop for a moment!' said Lydia, holding up both hands to stem her brother's flow of words. 'Let me get this straight. You're saying Colonel Maxwell assembled a small army and that, last night, you went storming into the Steelyard to rescue Jenny and Rachel and Mary. Is that right?'

'Yes. More or less.'

It was the following morning and Aubrey was attempting to explain everything across the breakfast table. He'd expected Lydia to be delighted. Her expression suggested that she wasn't – or at least, not entirely.

'So – discounting Colonel Maxwell and Nicholas for a moment – both you and Peter knew this was planned. For how long?'

'A couple of days,' he said uneasily.

Lydia folded her arms and fixed him with a darkening gaze.

'And Henry. Henry must also have known.'

'Well, yes. Naturally, he had to be told --'

'Oh – naturally! *Henry* had to be told. But I, apparently, did not.'

'Colonel Maxwell's orders. I suppose he didn't want to get your hopes up in case something went wrong.' Sighing, Aubrey offered her a placating smile. 'Stop quibbling, Lyd. Surely the important thing is that the women are safe?'

'Of course it is,' she snapped, exasperatedly. 'But I object to being treated like some frail, hand-wringing female who can't be trusted not to succumb to the vapours. And I object even *more* to being kept in the dark about something that is very much my own concern.'

'Fine.' Aubrey pushed his half-empty platter aside and stood up. 'Tell that to the Colonel. He said he'd call today.'

'How nice of him to spare the time,' she muttered. Then, 'Wait. *Did* anything go wrong? Were you hurt?'

'Not even a scratch. Peter has a nasty cut and --'

'Will he be all right?'

'Good as new in a few days,' he assured her. 'The only thing that didn't go according to plan was catching that fellow Quinn ... but I daresay the Colonel will find another way of getting answers.'

Lydia also rose, frowning a little.

'Answers? *What* answers?'

Aubrey realised he should have kept his mouth shut. In Lydia's current mood, he didn't want to be the one to reveal that there had also been a blackmail letter she knew nothing about. Deciding to place this thorny issue squarely on the shoulders of the person whose decision it had been, he said evasively, 'Colonel Maxwell could explain it all much better than me. I suggest you ask him.'

'I will,' she replied. 'Oh - I will. And what is more, I don't intend to wait on his convenience.'

'Good. Then I'll leave you to it and take myself off to Shoreditch. Jack has promised to teach me how to construct a basket-grip,' he added, heading for the door. Then, half-turning, 'Oh – and don't bother to thank me or anyone else for last night. Just carry on carping, why don't you?'

* * *

On her way through the chilly streets to Cheapside, Lydia acknowledged the justice of her brother's parting shot. He was right, damn it. The only thing that really mattered was having her women back, safe and sound; that and the fact that no one had been seriously injured during the rescue. So she would thank the Colonel nicely ... and then tell him what she thought of his high-handed methods.

Mr Maxwell's assistant was in the shop, trying to serve one lady whilst fending off enquiries about his employer from two others. Glancing over at Lydia, he said, 'Go up, Mistress Neville. Things are a bit chaotic this morning and Mistress Wilkes is somewhat occupied – but I believe you know the way.'

'Indeed,' she nodded. 'Thank you.' And walked through to the stairs.

The parlour into which she'd been shown on her previous visit was occupied by Nicholas, sitting by the hearth, one leg propped on a footstool and Peter, his wound currently being re-dressed by the housekeeper. Of Jenny, Rachel and Mary, there was no sign.

Before either man could rise, Lydia said quickly, 'Don't get up. How are you both?'

'A trifle battered but we'll mend,' replied Nicholas with a tight grin. 'I suppose Aubrey gave you the glad tidings?'

'Some of them, certainly. Where are my women?'

'Major Moulton and Sergeant Trotter escorted them all home a little while ago. Don't worry. They're tired – and shocked, of course – but otherwise unhurt.'

'Unlike the two of you.' She turned to the housekeeper. 'They've put you to some trouble, it seems.'

'And not a word of warning, either,' came the terse reply. Then, leaving Peter to replace his shirt, Mistress Wilkes dropped a slight curtsy and said, 'These two will heal fast enough. My concern is for Mr Tobias. The wound's clean but I've a suspicion he's developing a fever – so you'll excuse me going back up to him. Meantime, since I daresay you've come to speak to the Colonel, I'll let him know you're here.'

'Thank you. I'd appreciate it.'

Mistress Wilkes – nobody's fool – correctly interpreted both Lydia's tone and the slightly martial gleam in her eye.

'If you want to be private, you'd best wait in the back parlour.'

'Yes. I believe I will.' As the housekeeper bustled from the room, Lydia looked sternly back at Nicholas and Peter. 'And if either of you even *think* of working until you're well enough, I'll have something to say about it.'

'There's a surprise,' breathed Nicholas.

Peter merely grinned.

Lydia paced the meagre width of the rear parlour for a full ten minutes before Eden appeared. He had plainly pulled on his coat in a hurry and a frown lurked behind his eyes but he greeted her pleasantly, if a trifle briskly, saying, 'I intended to call on you later. Didn't Aubrey explain?'

'He did. But I decided you'd already been put to enough trouble on my behalf.'

'You mean you were too impatient to wait.'

'That, too.' She took a breath and reminded herself to be reasonable. 'How is your brother? The housekeeper seems concerned about him.'

'So am I. At present, our biggest problem is keeping the stubborn idiot in bed – and I'm hoping it doesn't get any worse than that.' He gestured to a chair, wincing slightly as the movement sent a spear of pain slicing through him. Then, with something approaching a sardonic smile, 'But don't feel you have to hold back on Toby's account. I'm sure you've a number of things you want to say to me.'

'Yes.' She took the chair he'd indicated and sat very straight. 'Yes. I do. Obviously, I'm immensely relieved that the women are safe and deeply grateful to you for everything you and the others have done.'

'Obviously,' he said dryly, slowly taking the chair facing her. 'But?'

'But I don't appreciate you deciding I shouldn't be told what you were about. Those women are *my* responsibility. So although I appreciate your help and recognise that I couldn't have managed without it, I had a right to know what was going on.'

'And now you do know.'

'*Now*, yes. But you should have told me before. Didn't it occur to you that I was half out of my mind with worry? That I might have felt better knowing something was being done?'

'I could have been wrong, Lydia. If I had been --'

'But you weren't! My God – it comes to something when my brother, my footman and even my *major-domo* know more than I do myself!'

'Aubrey, Peter and Henry knew because I needed their help – the same being true of Nick, Toby and Gabriel. Since there was nothing for you to do – other than sit fidgeting on a knife-edge – I don't see how telling you in advance could possibly have been helpful. If *you* can, feel free to enlighten me.'

'You're deliberately missing the point,' said Lydia, frustratedly.

'So are you. The *point*,' stated Eden unequivocally, 'was to rescue the women – which we did ... and to get out of it with whole skins – which we almost did. Anything else is completely irrelevant.' He stood up with due care for his back. 'Mistress Wilkes is doubtless busy upstairs. But if you'd care for some refreshment, I'll --'

Lydia's eyes narrowed. She said curtly, 'Thank you – I wouldn't. Where are you hurt?'

'I'm not,' he began. And then, when she continued to regard him with patent disbelief, 'It's merely a little bruising and some muscular stiffness. Nothing a hot bath won't cure.' *I hope. Right now it's bloody agony.* He paused and then added reprehensibly, 'Mistress Wilkes wasn't inclined to kiss it better. But if you feel differently ...?'

A little colour crept across her cheekbones but she said accusingly, 'You're just trying to change the subject.'

'Yes.' He smiled hopefully. 'Did it work?'

Yes. All too well.

'No. You should go and take that bath, then have Mistress Wilkes make you up a bran poultice.'

Amusement stirred in his eyes. 'Lydia ... I am not a horse.'

'I know – but the principle is the same. First, however, I'd like to hear about this fellow Quinn. Aubrey said you wanted to question him. About what, exactly?'

'Ah.' With resignation, Eden sat down again. 'How much did Aubrey tell you about Quinn?'

'Aside from the fact he's some sort of criminal, virtually nothing.'

'He's a powerful, ruthless and very dangerous criminal with an army of assorted killers at his disposal,' agreed Eden, meeting her gaze with a level one of his own. 'Amongst other things, he does other people's dirty work. And he's not stupid.'

Lydia digested this in silence for a moment. Then, 'You think he was paid to take my women?'

'I know he was. And I was hoping to discover the name of his client. Unfortunately, I didn't manage to lay hands on him.'

'You say you know ... but how can you be so certain?'

He'd known it would come to this. He'd just hoped to put it off for a time but, given the lady's current mood, clearly that wasn't going to be possible. Reaching into his pocket, he wordlessly handed her the note.

She read it ... and then read it again. Finally, she said, 'How long have you had this?'

'Since the day Rachel and Mary disappeared.'

'I see. *Another* little thing you elected not to mention.'

Eden sighed.

'Do you know anything about any secret papers Stephen may have had?'

'No.'

'Then there was nothing to be gained by alarming you.'

'There you go *again!*' she said hotly, coming abruptly to her feet. 'Making assumptions and decisions on my behalf – when nobody gave you the right. It – it's maddening!'

'So I see.'

She heard the almost imperceptible tremor in his voice.

'And not remotely funny!'

Eden inclined his head politely but wisely kept his mouth shut.

Aware that she would never win this particular battle, Lydia dropped back into her chair.

'The note says a week. When does it expire?'

'Tomorrow. But the question is redundant. By now, whoever employed Quinn will know your women are gone and that he therefore lacks the means to coerce you into giving him what he wants.'

'Whatever *that* is.'

'Precisely.' He let a brief silence develop and then said, 'Presumably you can see the ramifications of this.'

'Oh I think so. Somebody we can't put a name to thinks I've got something I haven't and is prepared to go to any lengths to get it. And, aside from trying to find this thing I don't believe I've got, there's nothing we can do about it until he tries again.'

'I couldn't have put it better myself.'

'Goodness! I didn't think there was *anything* you couldn't do better yourself.' She scowled moodily down at her hands and thus missed the flare of laughter in his face. 'So what do you suggest I do?'

The laughter vanished as swiftly as it had come, leaving Eden's expression rather grim. He said flatly, 'Search everywhere you can think of for something of Stephen's that you might have over-looked. And be very careful. This isn't over. Until it is, you can't afford to let your guard drop for a minute – neither you nor anyone who works for you. In the meantime, I'm going to ask Lambert to authorise a troop of Militia to find Quinn and arrest him.'

Seeing a point she thought she *could* win, Lydia pounced.

'You could have done that in the first place. It would have spared your brother his injury and you a pain in the – in your back.'

He surveyed her under raised brows until he saw her fidget. Then he said mildly, 'I do not have a pain in my arse. But if what you actually wanted to say was that I *am* one ... why didn't you?'

For a second, she looked completely flummoxed. Then, without warning, she gave him a dazzling smile and said primly, 'Because one of us ought to remember our manners.'

And the other can't afford to get distracted. Damn.

'Very true. I apologise. As to the Militia – no, I couldn't have done that in the first place because I might have been wrong. *Now*, however, I have proof that Quinn was holding your women against their will. If I can question him, I have some chance of finding the man behind him. A small chance, admittedly, because I imagine Quinn will lie and go on lying. But, at present, it's all we've got.' He stood up. 'Did you walk here?'

'Yes.'

'Alone?'

'Yes. But --'

'That was stupid. If Peter isn't fit to escort you home, I'll come with you myself.'

Lydia also rose. 'No. You'll have a bath and a poultice.'

Eden shut his eyes briefly and then said the one thing guaranteed to end the conversation.

'Be careful, darling. You sound like a wife.'

This time her cheeks burned scarlet.

'I beg your pardon. That wasn't ... I didn't mean ... I was trying to be helpful.'

'No. You were being stubborn and argumentative. And normally, I enjoy it. But not today, Lydia. Today, I've neither the time nor, I fear, the patience. I need to see Lambert; I want to ensure that you and your workers are safe from attack; and I'm worried about Toby. So if you could see your way clear to not making my life any more difficult than it already is, I'd appreciate it.'

EIGHT

Since Peter declared himself well enough to see Mistress Neville home and protect her *en route*, Colonel Maxwell took himself off to Whitehall in search of the Major-General.

Lambert heard him out in silence, scribbled an order to the Captain of Militia at the Tower which included the information that there was a concealed exit somewhere at the rear of the building and then said, 'Next time, come to me first. It will save you both time and trouble. Have you had any word from Villiers or Compton?'

Eden shook his head. 'They're both still out of London.'

'Let me know when they return.'

Eden nodded and left. Back in Cheapside, he discovered that Mistress Wilkes' suspicions had proved correct that that Tobias was growing increasingly feverish.

She said, 'The doctor has been – for all the good he did. I showed him and his leeches the door, then I got Mr Toby to swallow a little elderberry tea and put a poultice of echinacea root on his wound.'

'Not a bran poultice?' Eden couldn't help asking.

Alice Wilkes looked at him pityingly.

'He has a bullet-hole, not a strained hock, Colonel. Echinacea root to draw out any infection and the tea to encourage sweats. We'll see how he fares in a few hours' time. Meanwhile, with the weather near freezing and the cost of ice being what it is, I've got enough water chilling in the yard to make compresses for Sir Nicholas's knee as well as keeping Mr Toby sponged down. And Joan is heating water for your bath.' She paused, head tilted consideringly. 'Come to think of it, a bran poultice might ease your back. We'll see when you've had a good, long soak. Now ... is there anything else?'

'No. You appear to have thought of everything. Thank you.'

'No need for thanks, Colonel. Just don't bring everybody home in this state again.'

Upstairs, he found Nicholas sitting beside Tobias's bed and his brother, flushed, over-heated and restless.

Seeing the question in Eden's face, Nicholas said, 'I can sit here as well as anywhere and I want to help. As for Toby ... he's got slightly worse in the last hour but Mistress Wilkes seems to know what she's doing.'

Eden laid a hand on Tobias's brow. It was burning up. Tobias knocked Eden impatiently aside. Nicholas reached for a cool, damp cloth imbued with lavender and laid it where Eden's hand had been. Tobias sighed and appeared to settle.

'The relief is temporary,' said Nicholas. 'But it's all we can do for now. So go and see to your own hurts before you're as crippled as I am.'

* * *

By the time Eden got out of the bath, the skin of his fingers and toes was wrinkled as prunes but his back felt somewhat easier. This, as it turned out, was fortunate because he barely had time to dress before Mistress Wilkes came to tell him he had a visitor.

Captain Forbes of the Tower Militia saluted smartly and said, 'I'm sorry, Colonel. We've brought in five fellows but none of them are Quinn. As far as I can make out, he hasn't been in the building since some time last night – and, if any of the ones we've arrested know where to find him, they're not saying. Not so far, anyway.'

Eden cursed under his breath.

'Quite,' agreed the Captain. Then, 'Orders, sir?'

'Hold them overnight – separately and somewhere not too comfortable. Major Moulton and I will question them tomorrow. Though I doubt,' he finished bitterly, 'that we'll get any more out of them than you have. They'll be more frightened of Quinn than anything we can do to them.'

* * *

Sitting beside Tobias's bed through the long hours of the night, Eden managed to take a brief look at the book he'd taken from Quinn's desk but was kept too busy sponging down his brother's body to study it properly so he put it to one side and concentrated on the task in hand.

At around six in the morning, Mistress Wilkes changed the dressing on the bullet-wound and pronounced it clear of infection. But in general terms, Tobias's condition was gradually worsening.

'It's to be expected,' she said calmly. 'I've never seen a fever break in less than twenty-four hours. But Mr Toby is strong and healthy so there's no need to fear for his heart. We'll continue with the sponge-baths and the elderberry tea for a while yet and see how he does. If there's no improvement by this evening, I'll consider dandelion and lobelia – though it's not a remedy I like. In the meantime, Colonel, you can leave your brother to Sir Nick and me and seek your bed.'

'Can't,' yawned Eden, shoving a hand through his hair and trying to ease the cramp in his back. 'Duty calls – which means a shave and a clean shirt. I'll be back as soon as I can. If you need me before then, send to the Tower.'

Precisely as he had expected, in hour upon hour of questioning, the five men Captain Forbes had in custody refused to talk and when Eden tried offering protection from Quinn in return for information, three of them actually laughed.

'Think you can stop him cutting off me privates afore he slits me throat?' said one. 'Maybe you don't know Quinn or maybe you're just bloody stupid. But *I* know 'im and I ain't. And that's all I'm saying.'

In the end, Eden was forced to admit defeat. Leaving Ned to see the prisoners back to their cells, he walked out into the fading light and incipient frost of the late afternoon and decided he'd better go home via Bishopsgate – purely, he told himself, in order to make sure that Mistress Neville wasn't doing anything stupid.

When she'd parted from the Colonel on the previous day, Lydia hadn't known who she was more annoyed with; him for saying she sounded like a wife – or herself for giving him the opportunity. Then she'd visited Strand Alley and, after falling on her neck, Jenny and Rachel recounted what had happened in the Steelyard ... and her previous thoughts seemed suddenly very trivial.

Aghast, Lydia couldn't believe how *stupid* she'd been. She'd let herself drift into argument and complaint when what she *should* have been doing was asking for details – such as the nature of Tobias

Maxwell's injury, for example. And then, having let the moment go by, she'd continued to behave as though Eden and his friends hadn't done much more than throw a few punches – which clearly couldn't have been further from the truth

Oh God. If what Jenny says is right, they had to fight tooth and nail to get both my women and themselves away safely, Eden must think I'm the most ungrateful, self-centred idiot alive. And if something happens to his brother, he's never going to forgive me.

Next morning, she sent Nancy to Cheapside to enquire after the invalid and received a brief note from Nicholas informing her that Toby wasn't improving but that Mistress Wilkes saw no cause for real anxiety as yet. This brought a new thought.

How are they managing? The housekeeper seems very efficient ... but how can she nurse Mr Maxwell and keep the house running all at the same time? I should have offered to help. Given the circumstances, it's the very least *I can do.*

By the time she decided to send Mistress Wilkes a note rather than risk offending her by simply turning up on the doorstep, darkness was falling and she was just about to send Tam to Cheapside rather than Nancy when she heard sounds of someone arriving. Three minutes later, Colonel Maxwell walked in looking tired and faintly irritable.

He said, 'I won't stay. I just came to let you know that I've spent most of the day interrogating five of Quinn's men and got precisely nowhere. So I wanted to make sure you remembered what I said about being careful.'

'After everything that's happened, I'm hardly likely to forget, am I?'

'You're likely to do whatever comes into your head and damn the consequences,' he replied tersely. Then, 'Henry tells me that Peter is recovering. How are the women?'

'Astonishingly resilient.'

'Not to mention handy with a blunt instrument.'

He turned as if to go, causing Lydia to say quickly, 'Please – wait a moment. How is your brother? And why didn't you tell me he'd been shot?'

'No reason other than that you didn't ask.' Eden hesitated, turning his hat in his hands. 'If you must know, he took a bullet that was meant for me.'

'Oh. I see.' And because she was fairly sure she did, added, 'But you'd have done the same for him, wouldn't you?'

'That's hardly the point,' shrugged Eden impatiently. 'I'm sorry. Toby was acutely feverish throughout the night and I'm eager to get home in the hope he's doing better. If and when I have any other news for you, I'll --'

'Let me help,' blurted Lydia. And snatching up the folded note beside her, 'I've just written to Mistress Wilkes asking if there is anything I can do. She must be run off her feet – and you look exhausted. I could at least share the load a little. Please?'

He surveyed her thoughtfully and then said, 'If you're sure ... some help would be appreciated. Perhaps tomorrow, if --'

'No. I'll come now.' She stopped and then, her words tumbling over each other, said, 'I'm ashamed I didn't ask what happened or properly appreciate what you did and I'm sorry I didn't offer help sooner. So I'll come with you now and do what I can. And if that sounds like a wife – I'm sorry about that, too.'

* * *

Cheapside, when they got there, proved to be full of surprises. Informed by Mistress Wilkes that he had visitors – but not who they were or even how many – Eden led Lydia upstairs, saying, 'I admire economy as much as the next man. But just occasionally I wish that woman would spare a few additional words.'

Then he opened the parlour door and stopped dead.

Gabriel stood before the hearth talking to Ralph Cochrane; Phoebe Clifford sat in a corner holding Nicholas's hand; and sitting at the table, wrapping himself round a large slice of meat pie, was Eden's son.

For a second, everyone stopped talking ... and then immediately started again.

Eden threw up a hand and said, 'It's an invasion. Why wasn't I warned? Not that it matters. You're all welcome. Jude – happy as I am to see you, I can wait to embrace you until you've finished eating. Ralph ... what the hell brings you here?'

'Tab,' said Ralph succinctly, holding out his hand. 'The night before last she woke in a sweat, saying something had happened to Toby. And after that – since there's absolutely no way I was going to let her travel – nothing would do but that I came in her place. Jude offered to keep me company – so here we are. I didn't think you'd mind.'

'Mind? Far from it.' Eden looked around. 'Gabriel?'

'Venetia's leaving for home tomorrow before the weather breaks and the roads turn into mud,' replied Colonel Brandon. 'I was coming to ask after Toby and Phoebe insisted she couldn't leave without saying goodbye to Nick.'

Phoebe stood up, her colour rising.

'That's not what I said!'

'It's what you meant.' Giving Eden a moment to greet his son, Gabriel strolled over to Lydia. 'Mistress Neville ... a pleasure. I believe Venetia has sent you a note. She wanted to call but, between the children and the packing, she hasn't had a spare moment.'

'I can imagine. Please wish her a safe journey from me and tell her I'll write.'

'I will. And now, if Phoebe can tear herself away ... we'll take our leave. With Toby ill upstairs, Eden must be wishing us at Jericho.'

There were a few more moments of confusion while Nicholas struggled to his feet, kissed Phoebe's hand and whispered something in her ear that made her nod vigorously and brought a beaming smile to her face. Eden hugged his son and briefly introduced both Jude and Ralph to Lydia ... and Gabriel and Phoebe finally took their leave. Then Eden said, 'If everyone will excuse me, I want to look in on Toby.' He frowned slightly. 'I take it somebody's sitting with him?'

'Yes,' said Nicholas. 'I thought --'

'Good.' Eden relieved Lydia of her cloak and said, 'Perhaps you'd care to come with me? If you're going to help, you may as well see what you're up against.'

They left the room and Nicholas dropped his head in his hands.

'Oh God,' he muttered.

'What?' asked Ralph and Jude more or less in unison.

'Something I really *should* have warned him about.'

With Lydia on his heels, Eden opened the door to his brother's room and, for the second time in ten minutes, came to an abrupt halt.

Standing beside the bed, one hand resting lightly on Tobias's brow, was Deborah. Slowly, she turned a fathomless gaze, dipped a slight curtsy and said, 'Nicholas sent for me. I hope I'm not unwelcome?'

Eden swallowed his shock, distantly aware that he shouldn't be shocked at all and acutely conscious of Lydia standing just behind him.

'Unwelcome? No. How could you be? I know how skilled you are ... and if you can help Toby, I'll be more than grateful.'

'I've done what I can.' The dark eyes drifted over Lydia and then returned to Tobias, now lying peacefully beneath orderly sheets. Deborah pointed to the small pouch hanging about his neck and said, 'Leave that where it is until you see a marked improvement in his condition. For the rest, I've dosed him with an infusion of my own and left more with Alice. She knows how much and how often.'

'Thank you,' said Eden. And then, moving aside, 'I'm sorry. Lydia ... you'll remember Mistress Fisher, of course.'

'Indeed.' Lydia smiled and stepped forward. 'I know a little of herbs, Mistress Fisher – but not nearly as much as you, it seems. What do you recommend for fevers such as this?'

'Blackthorn and feverfew, of course ... with a little ginger and some fenigreek seeds.'

For the first time, Deborah turned away, allowing a glimpse of her profile and the clearly discernible rounding of her belly. Standing so close to him, Lydia was aware of the hitch in Eden's breathing and wondered afresh how deep a bond had existed between him and this exotic woman. In order to give him time, she said randomly, 'Ginger? I wouldn't have thought of that.'

'Few people do.' Deborah reached for her cloak. 'I should go. My husband has been meeting with a supplier in the Lamb and Flag while he waits to escort me home. It was a pleasure to see you again, Mistress Neville. And Colonel ... I don't think you need worry. Toby is as strong as an ox and will therefore recover more quickly than most.'

'I hope so.' Eden managed a smile. 'Thank you for coming.'

'I was happy to do so,' came the serene reply. Then, 'Please don't trouble to show me out. I remember the way – and you have other guests.' And, with another tiny curtsy, she left the room.

Eden wanted to follow her. He wanted to ask if she was well and happy and glad of the coming baby and a dozen other things. But he knew he shouldn't and that Deborah wouldn't welcome it. So he watched her go and hoped Lydia Neville wasn't reading things in his face that he'd rather she didn't.

Lydia was very carefully *not* looking at his face. Head bent over her cuffs as she unfastened them in order to push back her sleeves, she said, 'I'll sit with Mr Maxwell tonight if Mistress Wilkes will tell me what he is to be given and how often.'

He nodded but said, 'Part of the night only. Either she or I will take over from you later.'

'No. She has enough to do and you need to sleep. Meanwhile, you should go back to your son. He's very like you, isn't he? She paused and hiding a smile, added, 'He has very good manners.'

As clearly as if she'd said it, Eden heard the 'but' hiding between the two last sentences. He started to laugh and then realised that what he actually wanted to do was sweep her off her feet and kiss until neither of them knew what day it was. It was a ridiculous impulse; totally and utterly illogical. And it told him something he'd half suspected before. It told him that he was already in a lot deeper than was wise.

He said, 'Jude owes his looks to me and his manners to my mother. And before you say it – yes, she tried just as hard with me but, as you're aware, with a signal lack of success.'

Lydia looked up at him gravely.

'In some things, perhaps. But, taken all in all, I don't imagine she's disappointed.'

Hazel eyes locked with silvery-blue ones and the silence between the two of them grew charged. Finally, breaking the thread before it could tighten further, Eden said, 'I'll go, then. And ... thank you.'

She shook her head and tried, despite the hiatus in her chest, to speak in her usual tone.

'But for me, your brother wouldn't be ill. So the thanks are mine.'

When the door closed behind him, she sank into a chair and stared down at her hands. They were shaking a little. She thought, *I have to stop this. Somehow I have to stop feeling like this before he notices. But when he looks at me so intensely ... in truth, when he looks at me at all ... nothing in the world exists except him. And I don't know how to deal with it.*

Tobias slept on, stirring slightly from time to time. At regular intervals, Lydia wiped the sweat from his face and neck with cold, lavender-scented water; and while she watched and tended him, her thoughts scuttled round like mice in a cage, each raising its own unanswerable question.

A little after the bells of St Matthew's chimed nine, Mistress Wilkes appeared with a tray containing supper and the tincture Deborah Fisher had made for Tobias. Having told Lydia the dosage and that it could be exceeded if necessary, she said, 'It's good of you to help and I appreciate it. But don't hesitate to wake me if you've cause. My room is directly above this one.' For a second, she stared at the pouch resting on Tobias's chest. Then, as she turned towards the door, she said abruptly, 'Oh – and you'd best call me Alice.'

Shortly after that, Tobias started shifting restlessly and muttering under his breath. Lydia abandoned her supper, coaxed him into swallowing some of Deborah's mixture and sat beside him, holding a cool cloth to his brow while she waited for the potion to take effect. He was just beginning to settle when the door opened to admit Colonel Maxwell bearing a glass of wine.

Taking in the scene, Eden said quietly, 'Finish your meal. I'll take over there for a while.'

'There's no need. He's quieting again.' She dipped the cloth to cool it, then wrung it out and replaced it. 'Thank you for the wine, though. I'll be glad of it later.'

He sat down in her vacated chair and, realising something, said, 'I imagine you've some experience of sick-rooms.'

'With Stephen? Yes – though that was different. His heart was failing.' She shot him a reassuring smile. 'From the little I've seen of him, I doubt your brother has ever ailed a day in his life before.'

'Not to my knowledge.' He paused, feeling he ought to say something about Deborah but not knowing quite what. Finally he said, 'Mistress Fisher's potion seems to be working.'

'Yes.' Lydia touched the mysterious pouch. 'But what is this?'

'I don't know. She did the same thing when Nick lost his arm and seemed likely to die. Medical care after a battle is never good and Worcester was even worse than usual. Miraculously, the amputation hadn't killed him and there was no infection but he wasn't getting better. Deborah changed that – though I never knew precisely how. She has ... you might say she has some unusual skills. It's why Nick sent for her.'

'I see.' There were at least a dozen other questions she wanted to ask but suspected that – if he actually answered any of them – she'd end up feeling more inferior than she already did. So she said, 'I'm so sorry about this. I feel ... responsible.'

'Don't. It isn't your fault.' Eden paused and then added abruptly, 'I'll continue doing my damnedest to find Quinn though I don't hold out much hope since I imagine he has numerous bolt-holes.' He reached for the leather-bound book from where he'd left it on the window-ledge. 'I took this from his desk but haven't had the opportunity to examine it properly yet. It appears to be lists of transactions along with money paid or still owing but Quinn's clients – if that's what they are – are only referred to by their initials. Look through it and see if anything strikes a chord.'

Lydia accepted the book, surprised that he hadn't kept this to himself as well but said merely, 'I will. Now go to bed, Colonel. If I'm worried, I'll call Alice. And if *she's* worried, we'll call you. But in the meantime, you should sleep.'

He stood up, only too aware that his brain was sluggish with exhaustion. Perhaps it was this that made him say baldly, 'My name is Eden. Why won't you use it? God knows I've been using yours long enough.'

'It doesn't have to be reciprocal.'

'Yes. I think it does – but I'm too tired to argue with you now. So I'll bid you goodnight, Mistress Neville.'

And he walked out, leaving Lydia not sure whether she wanted to laugh or kick herself.

Time passed. The intervals when Tobias seemed to be sleeping peacefully grew gradually longer and it seemed to Lydia that he was sweating less. During the times he was quiet, she turned the pages of Quinn's book, squinting at the cramped writing and learning precisely nothing. By the time dawn had grown into day, her muscles were protesting from the long night's vigil but she felt a sense of satisfaction. Both Eden and Alice had enjoyed an unbroken night's rest and young Mr Maxwell was definitely on the mend.

When St Matthew's told her it was seven in the morning, the door opened again and a face framed by tousled mahogany hair peered around it.

'Good morning, Mistress Neville,' said Jude politely. 'Is it all right for me to come in?'

'Of course.' She watched him cross to take long, serious look at the patient and said, 'You needn't worry. Your uncle is a great deal better this morning.'

'I wasn't worried really. Uncle Toby is like Father. Pretty hard to kill.'

Lydia heard the note of pride and repressed a smile.

'True. So what has you up so early?'

'Uncle Ralph. I'm sharing a room with him and there wasn't much point trying to sleep once he got up. He's gone off to the tavern where we stabled the horses to check they're being cared for properly. But nobody else is up except the girl in the kitchen so I thought you might not mind me sitting with you for a bit.'

'I don't mind at all. In fact, I'm glad of your company.' She grinned. 'As you may imagine, your uncle hasn't been doing much talking. And I doubt your father will be up for a little while yet. Last night is the first sleep he's had in the last forty-eight hours.'

'Yes. He said something about that.' Jude hesitated briefly. 'It's nice of you to help look after Uncle Toby. Is ... is he a particular friend of yours?'

'No. Actually, I don't know him very well at all but he helped your father rescue my ladies so I'm in his debt. And your father's too, of course.'

'Oh.' He appeared to turn this over in his mind and then said, 'Why were the women abducted?'

'We don't know exactly.'

An expression of resigned impatience crossed his face.

'You mean you're not telling me.'

'No. I mean I really don't know. We think someone took them in order to make me hand over some papers belonging to my late husband but we don't know who that person is or what the papers are. Your father is hoping to find out – but it won't be easy because I've searched high and low for something that might give us a clue but haven't discovered anything remotely useful.'

Jude suddenly grinned at her.

'Thank you.'

'For what?'

'Not treating me like a child too young to understand.'

Lydia laughed.

'Well, I know how it feels. Most of the time, no one tells *me* anything either because I'm a poor wilting female. And it's downright infuriating.'

'What is?' asked Colonel Maxwell from the doorway. And, with a yawn, 'Or is that a silly question?'

'Yes.' Lydia and Jude spoke more or less in unison, then exchanged a startled glance and laughed.

Eden's brows rose and he looked from one to the other of them.

'I see it behoves me to be careful,' he said mildly. 'Jude ... see if anything is being done about breakfast while Mistress Neville tells me how your uncle is doing.'

'His uncle,' said a raspy, reproachful voice from the bed, 'wants to know why he's being starved ... and who's responsible.'

NINE

By the following day, Tobias was sufficiently recovered to insist – against all advice to the contrary – on leaving his bed.

Ralph said, 'Get up, then. If you can stay on your feet more than ten minutes, I'll go home and tell Tabitha you're back to being your usual stubborn self.'

'Go anyway,' returned Tobias. 'Tell her to stop fretting about me and look after herself instead. I'll see her at Yule.'

While this conversation was taking place, Jude was in Duck Lane with Nicholas – now able to walk without wanting to swear – and being introduced to the fascinating skill of harness-making. Until Lydia walked in unexpectedly, he was also enjoying previously unheard tales of his father's military exploits – the comic as well as the heroic. So when he arrived back in Cheapside to learn that Ralph was getting ready to leave on the following morning, he said flatly, 'Oh. Can't I stay?'

'Do you want to?'

'Yes. I could come home with Uncle Toby at Christmas. It's only another three weeks, after all.'

Ralph shrugged. 'Well, it's all right with me. But you'd best ask your father.'

'Ask me what?'

Eden threw his hat and gloves on a chair and advanced gratefully on the fire. He'd spent the last two hours combing the dockside for any trace of Quinn and, unsurprisingly, had no success whatsoever. The man seemed to have vanished into thin air. Likewise, the book he'd purloined from the locked drawer had so far failed to yield anything useful and Eden had come home hoping for a couple of quiet hours to spend studying it in greater detail.

'If I can stay here with you until Yule,' Jude replied. 'I wanted to go to the lorinery again when Mistress Neville *isn't* there so Troopers Buxton and Hayes can tell me more about what you did in the war. And I hoped you'd take me to Westminster and Whitehall and the Tower.' He stopped and added, 'If you've the time, that is. I know you have to work.'

Eden felt a glow that had nothing to do with the cheerful blaze in the hearth.

'Aside from trying to discover who is persecuting Mistress Neville and keeping my distance from the latest Army petitions, I'm not even remotely busy at present. So stay, by all means and I'll take you anywhere you want to go.'

Jude's face lit up. 'Really?'

'Really. In fact, I'd like it very much.' He grinned at his son's evident pleasure. 'Where do you want to start?'

'The Tower, I think. Oh – and I'd like to visit the shops and buy gifts for Grandmother and Aunt Tab and Mary. There's never much choice in Banbury but there are hundreds of shops in London, aren't there?'

'Hundreds,' agreed Eden somewhat hollowly. He'd never understood the fascination for trailing round the Exchange. Then memory of the last time he'd done so brought a cunning notion in its wake and he said, 'But if you want gifts for the ladies, I suggest you enlist the help of Mistress Neville. She knows more about these things than I do.'

Behind his back, he heard Ralph give a tiny snort of laughter – and ignored it. Eden wasn't sure precisely where Ralph had come by the idea that he liked Lydia Neville rather more than he wanted to admit but he suspected he had Gabriel to thank for it. What he *didn't* want to do was allow the idea to take root elsewhere. Then he caught the thoughtful gleam in his son's eyes and thought, *Oh hell. Too late*.

His tone one of limpid innocence, Jude said slowly, 'That's a good idea. But perhaps *you* should ask her. I mean ... after you rescuing her women and Uncle Toby getting shot and everything, she's bound to say yes, isn't she?'

* * *

In Duck Lane, in Strand Alley and at home in Bishopsgate, Lydia started to feel that life had settled back into its usual rhythm. During those few, terrible days when she'd been cold with fear about the possible fate of her women, she'd given Henry instructions to admit nobody but Colonel Maxwell with the result that Gilbert Wakefield had been turned from the door three times. Now, she relaxed her embargo ... and Mr Wakefield arrived more or less within the hour.

Striding across the room to grasp her hands, he said, 'Lydia – what has been going on? I've been so worried about you!'

'That's kind of you and I'm sorry to have caused concern.' She tried to free her hands then gave up and let him continue to hold them. 'There was a – a crisis involving my sewing women. A couple of them went missing for a time.'

'Missing?' His grip on her fingers tightened and something she couldn't interpret shifted in his face. 'How? What happened to them?'

Lydia decided she'd already said quite enough and wasn't about to add to it.

'In the end, nothing. They're back safe and sound now and the panic is over.' She paused. 'Gilbert ... you are crushing my fingers.'

'Oh. I beg your pardon.' He released her immediately and managed a smile. 'But why didn't you let me help? You know I would have done anything in my power.'

'Of course. But there really wasn't anything you *could* have done.'

'I might have at least lent you my support – perhaps given you advice. I believed that we were cl-- ... that we were good enough friends for that.'

Close was what he had been going to say. She was glad he'd thought better of it.

For perhaps the first time his proprietorial attitude grated just a little. She said carefully, 'As, indeed, we are. But I am very used to managing my own life, you know.'

Fortunately, he seemed to realise that perhaps he had over-stepped the mark. A rueful expression crossed his face and he said, 'Forgive me. I didn't mean to sound over-bearing. It's just ... well, it's just that you mean a great deal to me and I hoped that, by now, you trusted me enough to feel you could turn to me in times of trouble.'

'And I do. You're a very good friend, Gilbert. But on this occasion there wasn't a great deal that you could have --' She stopped, hearing the pealing of the door-bell and feeling half-thankful for it.

Mr Wakefield looked less happy. And when the door opened on Colonel Maxwell and his son, he had to banish a frown.

Lydia directed a beaming smile at Jude and said, 'This is a nice surprise. I thought you might have gone home with Mr Cochrane.'

'No. I'm staying with Father for a little while.'

'Oh? That will be enjoyable for both of you, I daresay.' She turned and said smoothly, 'Gilbert ...you already know Colonel Maxwell and this young man is his son. Jude – my friend, Mr Wakefield.'

Eden watched Jude politely acknowledging the introduction and silently told himself not to be an ass. He hadn't any right to be annoyed at finding that fellow here yet again. All right. So Wakefield was younger than him, better-looking than him, taller than him and probably a whole lot more charming than him. Why should any of that matter? And as for being annoyed with himself for *feeling* annoyed ... that was downright bloody stupid. Unfortunately, knowing it didn't help.

Putting both face and voice under strict control, he said, 'I'm sorry if we've arrived at an inconvenient time but Jude wanted to ask a favour. More than one, actually.'

Lydia's swift, 'It isn't inconvenient at all,' clashed with Gilbert's rather stiff, 'Please don't mind me. I was about to take my leave.'

Recognising that he had meant well and that she hadn't really been very kind, Lydia said, 'Perhaps you'd care to join Aubrey and me for supper one evening, Gilbert?'

'Thank you,' he bowed, thawing a little. 'I'd be delighted.'

'Good. I'll send a note when I'm sure Aubrey will be at home. He still stays overnight in Shoreditch as often as not – but I'll arrange something soon. And thank you again for worrying about me.'

When everyone had said the right things and Mr Wakefield had taken his leave, Eden eyed Lydia with the impenetrable expression he usually reserved for interrogating suspects and said, 'So. He worries about you, does he?'

'Apparently.'

'And is he wholly in your confidence?'

She folded her arms and stared back at him.

'Not entirely, no.'

'Meaning what?'

'Meaning he doesn't know a half – or even a quarter of what you know. But if he did ... I didn't realise I needed your permission on what I might say and to whom I might say it.'

'You don't.' *Good. She's as annoyed as I am – just not for the same reason.* 'But until we know who wishes you ill, you'd be wise to be wary of sharing your troubles with anyone you're not completely sure of.'

Lydia smiled at him with lethal sweetness.

'That sounds as if I shouldn't share them with anyone but *you*.'

'Not at all,' he snapped. 'I merely meant that you should be careful.'

'Oh. That refrain again. We really should set it to music.'

Jude, who had said nothing throughout this, suddenly startled them by laughing.

'What?' asked his father tetchily.

'Nothing. It's just quite funny watching the two of you arguing.'

'Yes? Well, we've had a lot of practice,' grumbled Eden. And then, bathing Lydia in a slow, reluctant smile, 'But this time was my fault.'

That smile had its usual effect and Lydia couldn't help responding to it.

'I know. On the other hand, a true gentleman would have merely admitted being at fault but missed out the words "this time".' And to Jude, 'What do you think?'

'It might have been more tactful,' he agreed gravely.

'Ignore him,' said Eden, buffeting the boy's shoulder. 'He just wants you to let him loose in the lorinery and help him choose Yuletide gifts for his sister, his aunt, his grandmother and the Lord knows who else. Of course, you can say no to either one.'

'Why would I do that?' Lydia grinned at Jude, unable to hide her pleasure. 'Of *course* you may visit the lorinery – though if you want more stories like *How Colonel Maxwell Crossed the Bridge at Upton* or *The Day Colonel Maxwell Led the Charge at Dunbar*, I'd be grateful if you did it outside the workshop.'

'Good Lord,' muttered Eden. '*Is* that the kind of thing you've been listening to?'

Jude flushed. 'Yes. It's all true, isn't it?' And when his father didn't immediately answer, '*Isn't* it?'

'Yes,' sighed Eden. 'It just wasn't as heroic as Buxton and Hayes probably make it sound. It was more to do with mud, sweat and knowing when to duck.'

'Then why don't you tell Jude about it yourself?' suggested Lydia. And without waiting for him to reply, she turned back to the boy and said, 'Meanwhile, I'd be honoured to help you find gifts for the ladies in your family. And since gentlemen usually find shopping a tedious exercise, I suspect the Colonel would be happy to be spared that particular task.'

'He would,' agreed Eden promptly.

Lydia laughed. But Jude, with a smugness that his father found deeply suspicious, said, 'You can't. Mistress Neville can help find the right gifts for *me* – but you can't expect her to do it for you as well. So you'll have to come with us, won't you?'

* * *

After that, the days flew by. Jude spent hours at the lorinery or standing in rapt fascination beside Tobias's work-bench. And, in between, his father took him to Westminster Hall and the Painted Chamber; to Inigo Jones' piazza in Covent Garden; and to watch the troops drilling on Tothill Fields. They toured the maze of chambers, galleries and courtyards that comprised the Palace of Whitehall where, without troubling to conceal his pride, Colonel Maxwell presented his son to Major-General Lambert; then they took a boat from Westminster Stairs to the massive bulk of the Tower with its forbidding history and arsenal of weapons.

Despite all of this, they still somehow managed to spend more time with Lydia Neville than Eden thought wise. What he'd considered the one unavoidable shopping expedition became two and then three – throughout which alarm bells rang loud and clear. He watched her laughing with his son and looking like the girl she must have been before her life was turned upside down; and he saw the two of them forming a bond … one he almost envied because she achieved it so easily and because it contained none of the reservations from which he, the absentee father, still suffered. Familiarity with Lydia was only breeding a desire for even more familiarity. Day by day, he found himself wanting what he shouldn't. And worst of all, he occasionally caught himself imagining the kind of future that, for ten years, he'd been convinced was the very last thing he wanted – which suggested that his wits were becoming addled.

And yet he couldn't regret any of it because Jude was clearly having the time of his life. Eden wondered why he'd never done this before ... and wished that he had.

* * *

With no wife to go home to, Gabriel once more took to supping in Cheapside on a regular basis. On these occasions, the conversation was inevitably dominated by progress – or more usually the lack of it – made in the House.

'It's one step forward and two steps back,' remarked Gabriel, one evening towards the middle of the month. 'Nothing ever arrives at completion. For example, last week we adjourned discussions about reducing the size of the army because Cromwell gave the impression that, though he didn't agree with it, he wouldn't necessarily stand against it ... so the House decided to wait and see if we might find a compromise.'

'And have you?' asked Nicholas.

'No – because I doubt very much that it's possible. And within twenty-four hours, we were in deep waters of a completely different kind that resulted in a vote that *the true reformed Protestant religion and no other shall be maintained* – which in turn brought up the thorny question of toleration. We spent two whole days on *that,* while everyone said all the same things they said six weeks ago.' Gabriel drained his glass and set it down. 'In the end, they managed to agree that there would be no Bill compelling attendance at established church services and that those with *tender consciences* would be left alone so long as they didn't cause any trouble. In addition, Parliament wants the right to pass Bills against atheism, blasphemy, popery, licentiousness and the like on its own authority – the Court Party failing to get *damnable heresies* made an exception.'

Eden pushed the bottle across the table in Colonel Brandon's direction.

'Cromwell's still for toleration, then?'

'Yes. He was recently heard to say that everyone wants liberty but no one will give it – a statement hard to argue with. As to the Army … it sees what's happening in the House as a step back to repression rather than slow progress in the right direction. And as I imagine you know only too well – it wants liberty of conscience for everybody except the Catholics.'

'The folks who hate Catholics can't have met the likes of Jonas Radford,' volunteered Jude absently from the corner where he was systematically beating Tobias at cribbage.

'That would be Sam Radford's brother, would it?' asked Gabriel.

'The very one.' Eden glanced across at his son. 'Still as big a zealot as ever, I presume?'

Jude nodded, his eyes on his cards.

'Uncle Ralph won't go near him for fear he'll punch him in the face. It's a shame really.'

Nicholas laughed but said, 'Leaving my fellow Catholics out of it for a moment … is the House likely to consider liberty of conscience?'

'Not a chance.' Gabriel re-filled his glass. 'It's ploughing ahead with its right to legislate on religion without consulting Oliver.'

'Ah.' Eden's brows rose. 'He won't like that.'

'No. He won't. Still less will he like the fact that, with the current assessment about to expire on what used to be known as Christmas Day, the House will be forced to come to a decision about the size of the Army – because if it doesn't and no fresh taxes are levied, the soldiers are going to be living at free quarter. And *nobody* will like that.'

'Meaning that the situation has to be resolved quickly.'

'In the next few days,' agreed Gabriel. 'The last report put Blake's fleet at Naples, currently in pursuit of the Duc de Guise. Meanwhile, the so-called Western Design under Penn is assembling at Portsmouth and due to sail before the end of the month.'

'Its strength?' asked Eden.

'Eighteen men-of-war, twenty transports and three thousand troopers under Robert Venables. The cost is enormous – despite which I think the House will still vote to reduce the monthly assessment by the same thirty thousand pounds it discussed before. And if I'm right, a corresponding reduction in the size of the Army is inevitable.'

'As, therefore, is a battle-royal with Cromwell.'

'Yes.'

'There'll be a battle-royal right here in a minute,' remarked Tobias, running a baffled hand through his hair. 'Eden – your son is a Captain Sharp.'

'Yes? Well, it takes one to know one, doesn't it?' retorted Eden. And with a grin, 'Have at him, Jude. He can afford it. God knows he's won enough money from me in the past.'

'And me.' Nicholas wandered over to perch on the arm of Jude's chair.

Gabriel watched them with a sudden air of speculation.

'I wonder if that's it?' he mused. 'Gaming is severely frowned upon these days but men still do it ... some of them, presumably, to excess.'

'What are you talking about?' Eden asked.

'Alderman Roger Frost of the victualling office. He's a respectable fellow with a young wife and family and no reason I can see to be so desperate for money that he'd risk stealing it. And yet he was arrested yesterday for embezzlement.'

'He took money from the victualling office?'

'Yes. Apparently, he's been appropriating small amounts for some time. But a few weeks ago, he seems to have become either greedier or bolder and falsified the books to cover a withdrawal of two hundred pounds. Unfortunately for him, the chief clerk is a meticulous fellow who lives for his work and he discovered the entire fraudulent trail.' Gabriel frowned slightly. 'What strikes me as odd is that it's the third similar case in the last two months.'

'Who were the others?'

'George Pettigrew – a pillar of the established church – was defrauding the Army by paying a dozen non-existent soldiers scattered through different regiments. And Sir John Seldon, chairman of the committee in charge of supplying Venables' three thousand troopers with arms. He hasn't been charged with embezzlement ... but two consignments of small arms have inexplicably gone missing.'

For a moment, Eden went very still. Then he said, 'Pistols?'

'Yes. Why?'

'Ned Moulton saw an open crate containing new pistols in Quinn's warehouse.'

Hazel eyes locked with storm-grey.

'Ah,' said Gabriel gently. 'It could be nothing or just a coincidence. But I think one of us needs to have a little talk with Sir John.'

'I'll do it. Where's he being held?'

'Newgate. Let me know what you find out.' He paused. 'And speaking of Quinn ... how are your enquiries regarding Mistress Neville's situation progressing?'

'They're not.' Eden frowned into his glass. 'I've turned over every stone I can think of, all to no avail. We're still holding five of Quinn's fellows in custody – who I'll question again about the pistols – but there's no trace of the man himself. The warehouse where he held the women is now empty so I can only assume he has other premises elsewhere – probably several of them. And the ledger I took from his desk has yielded nothing of use so far. For the rest, there have been no further attacks on either Lydia or her people and no more attempts at blackmail.'

'So you and everyone else are on a state of high alert.'

'That's putting it mildly. I *think* I've managed to ingrain a sense of caution into Lydia but I daren't rely on it – especially now.'

'Meaning?'

'Jude. He likes visiting the lorinery and he likes *her*, damn it. If anybody's watching and is looking for new leverage, he'd be the perfect target.'

'That can't be a comfortable thought. How soon is he going back to Thorne Ash?'

'Toby wants to leave a week today. Originally, I'd intended to go with them – but now I'm not so sure.' Eden paused for a moment or two and then added, 'Lydia can't find anything among her husband's papers that anyone might want and is therefore convinced that such a thing doesn't exist. I have my doubts. The late Mr Neville dabbled in cryptography.'

Gabriel stared. 'Did he indeed?'

'Yes. Actually, he did more than dabble. He was bloody good at it. So I can't help wondering if he had more use for his skill than merely passing the time. But unless Lydia trips across coded documents other than the samples I've already seen – which are little more than amusing demonstrations that eventually lead one to the key – we'll never know.'

'You've become remarkably involved in the widow's affairs,' observed Gabriel meditatively. 'And, one would think, with the widow herself by now.'

'Oh God. Don't start that again.'

'Start what?'

'Delving into my personal life and putting your own construction on it.' Eden lowered his voice and said, 'My relationship with Lydia is the same as it was last time you refused to let the subject drop and I'm not discussing it again – now or ever. Am I making myself clear?'

'Extremely.'

'Good. She needed help and I supplied it. Any other involvement is purely coincidental.'

'Of course.'

Eden cast him a dirty look. 'Stop smiling, damn you. It's true.'

'I'm sure it is – though that's not how it looks. And you say that Jude likes her.'

'He does,' said Eden, irritably wishing that just sometimes Gabriel would mind his own business or that they didn't know each other quite so well. 'But don't read too much into it. He likes Alice Wilkes as well.'

Laughing, Colonel Brandon got to his feet.

'I daresay he does.' And with a deliberately infuriating grin, 'But I doubt he's looking at her in the light of a potential step-mother.'

* * *

Next morning, Eden sent Major Moulton to start a new round of questioning with Quinn's five bully-boys while he braved the filth and stench of Newgate in search of Sir John Seldon. It was a relief to find that, having the means to pay for private accommodation, Seldon was not in the general ward. He was less relieved when the surly turn-key unlocked the door of the cell to reveal its inmate hanging from the bars of the window by means of his own belt ... and quite dead.

'Suicide?' asked Colonel Brandon later. 'Why? Unless there was some proof that he sold the pistols for personal gain, he'd have squirmed out of the charges. So why kill himself?'

'Good question. He had a visitor earlier in the day – a servant delivering fresh linen. The turn-key insisted Seldon was alive when the fellow left but eventually admitted that he hadn't actually *seen* him,' replied Eden grimly. 'There are two possibilities. One is that Sir John's visitor murdered him; the other is that he brought some news or made some threat that caused Sir John to hang himself. Either one of these might lead back to Quinn ... but now, of course, we'll never know.'

'What about the men you have in custody? Anything useful there?'

'No. It's the same story as before. None of them know anything about any pistols – or anything else, for that matter.'

'That might actually be true,' mused Gabriel. 'I doubt anyone in Quinn's empire knows more than they need to. And if the fellows you've got are mere muscle ...'

'Yes. I realise that. And since I've no positive reason for holding them, sooner or later I'm going to have to let them go,' agreed Eden frustratedly. 'The whole thing is just another bloody dead end. And I'm seriously beginning to wonder if I'm ever going to find a way past it.'

TEN

As things turned out, the decision on whether or not to spend Yule at Thorne Ash was taken out of Eden's hands on December 20th when an urgent summons arrived from Major-General Lambert.

'The trouble stirred up by Wildman's petition rumbles on,' he said. 'Aside from the three colonels, there are rumours of seditious meetings involving Lord Grey, Sir Arthur Haselrig, Colonel Hacker and John Bradshaw. Worse still, we've received word from General Monck of a plot fermenting in Scotland, involving all these gentlemen and others.'

'To do what?'

'According to Monck's information, disaffected officers are to meet in Edinburgh on New Year's Day. Their plan appears to involve seizing Monck himself and giving command to Major-General Overton who will then march south with three thousand Foot and an undisclosed number of Horse. Once in England, he'll join other forces assembled by Bradshaw and Haselrig.'

'I'm surprised that Rob Overton would lend himself to something like this,' remarked Eden, frowning. 'But presumably since Monck now knows about it – and Overton and his co-conspirators *know* that he knows – nothing will come of it.'

'So one would hope. But the fact that Wildman is somewhere at the heart of it suggests other, more worrying possibilities. If the Levellers and certain discontented members of the House decide that their grievances and those of the Royalists are one and the same, the situation becomes potentially explosive. And that being so, Oliver feels that some preventative measures need to be taken now, before talk boils over into action.'

Eden was beginning to have a shrewd idea of where this might be going. Managing not to sigh, he said, 'I see. And I fit into these measures where precisely?'

'For the immediate future, at the Tower. We want to raise the strength of the current garrison to nine hundred and, since you've served there before, you and such members of your old regiment who are still on the Army lists are an obvious choice. I'm assuming you'll want Major Moulton as your second-in-command?'

'Yes.'

'Good. Then I suggest you make arrangements to commence duty there immediately.'

Eden rose, saluted and said, 'Sir.'

And thought, *I suppose it could have been worse. At least he's not asking me to arrest Ned Villiers or Will Compton. But neither Toby nor Jude is going to be happy.*

* * *

Eden spent the rest of the morning introducing himself to the Lieutenant of the Tower, visiting the barracks in the Mews, sending a note to Ned Moulton and generally attending to everything that would enable him to take up his new post on the following day. Then he went home to break the glad tidings to his son and his brother.

Jude wasn't there and Tobias was downstairs in the workshop.

Pausing for a moment to watch the dexterity with which his not-so-little brother set rubies into a circlet of twisted gold, he recalled the day long ago when Tobias himself had stood on the same spot and become instantly enthralled as Luciano del Santi worked on the exquisite lattice that was designed to hold an amber chalice. The image became even clearer when, without looking up and very much as Luciano had done, Tobias said, 'Give me a minute, will you?'

Eden smiled and waited. Finally, Tobias laid down his tools and said, 'This must be important. The last time you came down here was the day we buried Luciano's loot.'

'I remember. And yes, it is important. I won't be coming to Thorne Ash with you.'

Tobias fixed him with a level grey gaze.

'I never supposed that you would. So what's the excuse this time? I hope it's more than your reluctance to leave Lydia Neville.'

'It is.' *Though that is also alarmingly true.* 'Lambert's assigned me to guard duty at the Tower. They want the garrison strengthened and I've done that particular job before, so ...' He stopped, shrugging. 'I'm sorry.'

'Apologise to Jude, not me.'

'I would if I could find him.'

'He's with your widow in Bishopsgate.'

'She's not *my* widow,' began Eden. Then, 'What is he doing there?'

'I've no idea. He just said he was helping her with something and would be back later.' Tobias turned back to his bench and picked up a minute pair of pincers. 'Why don't you go and find out? Or no. What am I saying? Of course you'll bloody go.'

Eden turned on his heel and went out before he said something he'd probably regret.

Henry admitted him to Lydia's house with the information that Madam was busy in the kitchen but that if the Colonel cared to wait in the parlour, she would doubtless be with him directly.

'Is my son here?' asked Eden.

'Yes, Colonel. He is also in the kitchen.' Henry permitted himself a small smile. 'In fact, saving only myself, the entire *household* is in the kitchen.'

'Then I may as well join it.' And he walked off without waiting for an answer.

The door to the large kitchen stood open and Eden remained there unnoticed for a time, observing the hive of industry within. Tables and counters were laden with various kinds of foodstuffs and on the floor all around the edges of the room were numerous large baskets, each bearing a label. In the midst of all this, Mistress Pyke, Nancy, Tam, Madge and Jude were stocking the baskets in response to Lydia's instructions. It looked like utter chaos. Knowing Lydia, Eden suspected it wasn't.

Jude was the first person to notice him. He said, 'Father! Have you come to help?'

'I'm not sure.' He strolled towards Lydia, observing the sheaf of lists in her hands and the fact that the thick, glossy hair was escaping its pins. 'I might if I knew what you are doing.'

She looked at him, her expression faintly harassed and, as if it was perfectly obvious, said, 'It's the Yule baskets.'

'Ah. The Yule baskets. Of course.'

Lydia shook her head, dislodging yet another lock of hair which she shoved impatiently behind her ear. 'For the Duck Lane and Strand Alley families.'

'I see.' He looked around him again. 'It looks … complicated.'

'It is,' Jude told him eagerly. 'They're nearly all different so Mistress Neville has special lists for what goes in them.'

'Yes,' agreed Eden, his eyes still on Lydia. 'Mistress Neville would have.'

She smiled at him then. 'If you want to help, nobody's taken charge of the pickles yet. They're on the counter over there.'

'So I see. And they go where?'

'A pot in each basket. It's one of the few things that everyone gets.'

'You don't think I can manage anything more complex?'

Her smile grew and gathered a note of mischief.

'It's your first time. We wouldn't want to tax you.'

'How thoughtful.' He looked at his son. 'It's your first time, as well. Presumably, you're not being taxed either?' And when Jude grinned, 'No. Don't tell me. I'm demoralised enough already.'

It was a further two hours before the baskets were filled to Lydia's satisfaction and, leaving Mistress Pyke to organise the tidying of the kitchen, she led Eden and Jude up to the parlour for some well-earned refreshment.

Sipping a glass of wine while his son demolished a dish of small pastries, Eden said, 'How are the baskets delivered?'

'Peter will hire a cart and take them in two separate loads.'

'And you do this every year?'

'Yes. I know we're not supposed to celebrate Christmas any more but, to a greater or lesser degree, most people still mark the occasion. The baskets help.' She turned to Jude and said, 'I'll be sending them out tomorrow. If you'd like to give Peter a hand, I'm sure he'd appreciate it.'

The boy nodded. 'We're not leaving till the next day – so yes, please. I'd like to.'

'About that,' said Eden reluctantly. 'Leaving, I mean. I know I said I'd come with you if I could ... but it turns out that I can't.'

'Oh.' The hazel eyes, so like his own, reflected resignation rather than disappointment. 'Why not?'

'Major-General Lambert has other plans for me, I'm afraid. I'm sorry.' He paused and then, hoping it might help, said, 'I've been ordered to join the Tower garrison for a time.'

Resignation was replaced with interest. 'Really?'

'Really. And past experience tells me it's not likely to be nearly as much fun as you might think.'

Lydia tried not to be glad that the Colonel would be spending Yule in London rather than in Oxfordshire with his family. She failed. Keeping her voice perfectly neutral, she said, 'Will that mean lodging in the Tower?'

'No, thank God. My off-duty hours – whatever they may be – will remain my own.'

A thought occurred to her but she put it to one side, deciding that this wasn't the best time to suggest it. Instead, for want of something better, she said, 'Is your brother fully recovered now?'

'He is – and I think I preferred him enfeebled.' Eden watched Jude eat the last of the pastries and, with devious intent, said mildly, 'I recognise that you're still growing – but I was looking forward to trying one of those.'

'Oh.' A half-guilty grin. 'Sorry.'

'There are more in the kitchen,' offered Lydia. 'Go and ask Mistress Pyke.'

He nodded and, clutching the empty plate, hastened from the room.

'I can only apologise for him,' sighed Eden. 'Clearly, he has his Uncle Toby's appetite.'

'He's a delight,' replied Lydia without thinking. And narrowly avoided adding, *And more like you than I think you realise.* 'You'll miss him, I daresay.'

'Yes.' He hadn't really wanted a pastry. He'd hoped for a few minutes alone with her but stupidly, now he had them, he didn't know what to do with them – since pulling the remaining pins from her hair and filling his hands with the heavy silk of it wasn't an option. So he said, 'I'm not sorry, however, to be staying in London at this time.'

'Oh,' she said again, trying not to hope it meant what she'd like it to mean. 'You're not?'

He held her gaze with his own.

'No. If there are any further incidents – and I think we can be sure that sooner or later there will be – I know you'll send me word. But, that matter aside, I wondered if our friendship is now such that – like Mr Wakefield – I, too, might be invited to supper one evening?'

The silvery-blue eyes widened and colour bloomed in her cheeks.

'Of course. You may come whenever you wish.' She hesitated and then said impetuously, 'And, unlike Mr Wakefield, I won't feel it necessary to engage Aubrey's services as a chaperone.'

'Won't you?' Eden stood up and gave her a decidedly wicked smile. 'Dear me. I don't know whether to be flattered or insulted.'

Lydia stared back at him, uncertain and flustered.

'I don't understand.'

'Well, either I'm a dull, staid fellow who would never dream of taking advantage ... or I'm not and you don't mind. Upon which note,' he finished blandly, 'I should probably rescue your cook from my son and take my leave.'

* * *

Two days later, Tobias and Jude left for Thorne Ash, their saddle-bags bulging with Yuletide gifts and Colonel Maxwell prepared for another eight hours of tedium kicking his heels with Ned Moulton at the Tower.

The day improved when he arrived home and Nicholas handed him a note from Lydia.

Perhaps, she wrote, *having been prevented from joining your family for Yule, you would care to spend the day with Aubrey and me – if your work permits it, of course. Wassail may be in short supply but we can guarantee a good dinner*. And below her signature, as if in afterthought,

I should add that, since you are clearly a dashing fellow with whom no woman is safe, Nicholas and Colonel Brandon are also invited.

Eden didn't know how many sheets of paper Lydia had ruined in the writing of this – or that, as soon as Nicholas had pocketed it and set off for Cheapside, she'd wanted to run after him and demand it back. Neither did he know that she'd spent the rest of the day worrying about whether she'd embarrassed him as well as herself. He merely read her words again and grinned. He recognised the joke, of course. But he wondered if *she* recognised the challenge implicit within it.

Still smiling, he dashed off a reply.

Thank you for your kind invitation which I will be delighted to accept. Your care for my reputation is also much appreciated.

* * *

The fact that Christmas had been banned by Act of Parliament ten years ago and anyone caught celebrating it was liable to be arrested had merely driven the festival underground. There was much surreptitious gathering of greenery and secret boiling of plum puddings. Some people even risked quietly humming carols. Lydia, Nancy and Mistress Pyke were three of them as they toiled in the steamy kitchen preparing the feast, safe in the knowledge that Henry was upstairs in the hall ready to repel any chance visitors.

On the day itself, Lydia rose at first light and laid out her newest gown. Then, clad in her night-rail and wrapper, she set about putting the finishing touches to the garlands Aubrey and Peter had hung in the dining-parlour, laid the table with the best candlesticks and pewter and checked on progress in the kitchen. Finally, when she was satisfied that everything that could be done *had* been done, she went up to her chamber with Nancy and set about readying herself for the occasion.

'Do you think,' she asked later, standing in front of the mirror, 'that I may have over-done it a trifle?'

Nancy subjected her to a critical stare which encompassed the cunningly-piled hair and the gown of shell-pink shot-silk, trimmed with pearl beading.

'No. I think you'll make the Colonel's mouth water. But if that's not what you want and you don't mind still being up here dithering when your guests arrive, I can always dig out your old grey damask. That hides pretty much everything. So what's it to be?'

There was a brief, indecisive silence. Then, 'I'll go down,' Lydia muttered.

'Good. And stay out of the kitchen. Mistress Pyke has everything under control and splashes of goose fat won't improve that gown.'

When she entered the parlour, Aubrey subjected her to a gaze every bit as critical as Nancy's had been. Finally, he said, 'Is it true, then?'

'Is what true?'

'That there's something going on between you and Colonel Maxwell. Is there?'

'No.' Her colour rose a little. 'What on earth gave you that idea?'

'Something his brother said.' He shrugged. 'The Colonel denied it, of course – but then I suppose he'd do that even if it was true.'

'Well, it isn't. Just because I'm wearing a new gown doesn't mean --' Her words were cut off by the pealing of the door-bell. 'They're here. Please try not to say anything idiotic.'

In fact, only Nicholas and Colonel Brandon had arrived. Nicholas handed her a box of candied fruit tied in red ribbon while Gabriel set down a small crate holding an assortment of bottles, saying, 'Don't worry. This is neither an insult to your hospitality nor an indication that we intend to get utterly cupshot – merely that we felt a small contribution was in order.'

'Thank you. That was thoughtful.' She swallowed the obvious question and said, 'Come in to the fire. We have mulled some wine, if you'd care for it.'

'Perfect,' grinned Nicholas. 'Eden will be here as soon as he's put in what he hopes will only be a token appearance at the Tower.'

'Of course.' She busied herself pouring the wine. 'Is there really a threat?'

'No. There's merely the vague possibility of one,' returned Gabriel. 'The idea of anyone attacking the Tower is frankly ludicrous. Eden will be bored witless.'

Lydia handed all three gentlemen a glass before taking a seat herself so they could do likewise. She said, 'He's been posted there before, I think?'

'We both were after the war in '48. Eden managed to stay on the right side of the bars – which was fortunate since I didn't.'

Aubrey stared at him. '*You* were locked up in the Tower?'

'Yes.'

'May we know why?' asked Nicholas, looking interested.

'I crossed Henry Ireton once too often,' replied Gabriel lightly. 'The charges were never going to amount to much but the timing was unfortunate. They let me out the day they cut off the King's head.'

There was a brief, thoughtful silence.

Then, 'You'd spoken against it?' asked Lydia.

'Yes.' In truth, he'd done more than merely speak against it. Also, other memories of that time still cut deep so he said, 'Forgive me – but I think a change of subject is called for.'

She nodded. 'And I have been remiss. I haven't yet thanked you for your part in rescuing my women. It was --'

'Since it was the most fun I've had since leaving Yorkshire, no thanks are necessary,' he replied calmly. 'My hours in the House are no more entertaining than Eden's ones at the Tower. Ah ... and speaking of Eden ...'

Lydia had also heard sounds betokening another arrival. She stood up without thinking and was equally unaware of the change in her expression.

Colonel Maxwell walked in wearing a faint frown which melted away the instant he saw her. *God. She shouldn't look at me like that. I might forget to be sensible.* But he bowed and said, 'Forgive me. I'd hoped to be here before this but, as usual, someone had other ideas.'

She shook her head. 'It doesn't matter. You're here now and can hopefully stay?'

'I can and I will. Major Moulton knows where I am – but will keep the information to himself if he knows what's good for him.' He glanced round. 'I see the rest of you decided to start without me. Is that spiced wine I smell?'

'Yes.' Lydia filled another glass and handed it to him.

His fingers slid against hers, though whether by accident or design, she couldn't tell because, having thanked her, he immediately turned to Colonel Brandon and said, 'They've increased the size of the garrison. Again.'

'Today? By how many?'

'A further three hundred. And they're planting cannon in Whitehall.'

'Ah. Doubtless you have the feeling there's something they're not telling you?'

'Either that or Cromwell's nerves are completely shot. Whatever the cause, I'm not aware of any new arrests ... for which I and numerous other people can be duly grateful.' Looking back at Lydia, he said, 'And that, you will be glad to hear, is the end of politics for today.'

The mood, once everyone was assembled around the table, became increasingly relaxed and convivial. Over roasted goose, ham glazed with honey and studded with cloves, buttered parsnips, leeks extravagantly flavoured with ginger and half a dozen other dishes, all washed down with Mr Fisher's excellent wine, conversation eddied and flowed in a myriad of directions. And throughout it all, Lydia fought to stop her eyes straying towards Eden more often than was seemly ... and had no idea he was fighting a similar battle himself.

He felt oddly unsettled. He watched her conversing easily with Gabriel or laughing at something Nicholas said or moving gracefully about the room, seeing to everyone's needs. Judging by the distant sounds drifting up from below stairs, Henry and the rest of them were having their own celebration which Lydia had no intention of marring by allowing them to do their usual work. He realised he shouldn't be surprised. The business with the Yule baskets ought to have been sufficient to teach him that she never did anything by halves. Anyone else – assuming they'd thought of sending baskets at all – would have been content simply to put the same items in all of them. Lydia hadn't. She made each one personal for the family in question. Truly, the better he got to know her, the more remarkable she became.

Inevitably, looking at her now, her shoulders revealed by the pale pink gown, he wanted to touch her. Naturally. Any man would. But more than that he wanted to have her to himself; to talk to her as he couldn't do in company ... to make her laugh for him alone. And he found himself wishing Gabriel and the rest of them at the devil.

Lydia glanced across the room and encountered a gaze so intense she found herself unable to look away until Colonel Brandon broke the spell by asking an apparently casual question about Major-General Lambert's passion for tulips.

A few minutes later, while Lydia was obligingly hunting for a pack of cards for Aubrey and Nicholas, Gabriel said quietly, 'Be careful, Eden. If you've no intentions in that direction --'

'I've no intentions in *any* direction,' came the irritable reply, 'and you're imagining things. I was merely thinking of something else.'

'Yes. That much was apparent.' Gabriel fell silent for a moment and then said, 'Very well. Since we have a moment to ourselves, the latest debates in the House are leaning towards reducing the cost of the Army by disbanding twenty-seven thousand men.'

'That's nonsense. With so many troops overseas, it can't be done.'

'It can if the resulting shortfall is made up by the Militia – which, as you may imagine is a very attractive idea to the Puritan country gentlemen in Parliament who control those forces.'

'Cromwell won't let it happen.'

'The way things are going, he may be left with only one way of stopping it. And the day is fast approaching when he can use it.'

'Meaning?'

'Parliament has to sit for a minimum of five months ... and it was convened on the third of September. Do I really need to spell it out?' Gabriel broke off as Lydia left Nicholas and Aubrey to their game and crossed the room towards himself and Eden. Rising, he said, 'This has been an extremely enjoyable day, Mistress Neville and I thank you for letting me share it. Unfortunately, I must go. There's an early sitting of the House tomorrow and I have a quantity of paperwork to complete before then. I hope you'll forgive me.'

Smiling, she held out her hand and said, 'Of course. And the pleasure has been mine.' Then, 'I'm sure Venetia must have missed having you at home – just as you must have regretted not being there.'

'My dear,' sighed Gabriel, 'you have no idea.'

In the absence of Henry, Lydia saw the Colonel to the door herself. When it closed behind him, she turned round to find Eden standing four paces away. He said simply, 'I have been thinking how delightful you look.'

'Oh.' The unexpectedness of it plucked at her nerves and caused her to tumble into rapid speech. 'Thank you. It – the gown is new. Venetia helped choose the material and the beading was made by Jenny Sutton. It's pretty, isn't it?'

'Very. But it wasn't the gown I was looking at.' *Hell. Did I just say that out loud? Yes. It seems I did.* He smiled and advanced a couple of paces. 'You look shocked. Why?'

Lydia swallowed hard and concentrated on trying to sound light-hearted.

'I suppose because it sounded … flirtatious. And you're not. Flirtatious, I mean.'

Another step brought him perilously close and this time, when he spoke, his voice was darkly enticing.

'That's a damning indictment. Am I truly so lacking in charm?'

'No!' Silently cursing her vehemence for what it revealed, she decided it was time to fight back. 'You're doing it again, aren't you? Playing games to see what I'll do. And if that's it, you can stop right now.'

'Or what?' *She's right. I should stop. I should stop and step back. This isn't being careful. It's the ultimate degree of stupidity. And yet …* 'Time was when the twelve days of Christmas permitted a little licence.'

'But n-not any more.'

'Sadly, no.' He smiled and reached out to touch her cheek very lightly with his fingertips. 'I always wanted to be the Lord of Misrule.'

She shook her head. 'I don't know what to make of you.'

'No.' He stepped right up to her, sliding one arm about her waist to pull her close. 'No. And, odd as it may seem, that makes two of us.'

This time the kiss was different … still seductive but less tentative; *this* time his mouth told her what he wanted from the very beginning. And it was neither mild nor flirtatious. He kissed her with an intensity and hunger that suggested that this was no momentary impulse but something very much deeper.

Lydia, with virtually no experience to guide her, understood none of this. She only knew that his arms were holding her close, that his body was hard against hers, that his mouth sent sensation flooding through her and promised untold delights. She forgot they were in the hall and that anyone could walk in at any moment and discover them. She just wanted more.

Eden wanted more as well – a great deal more – but there was still just enough sense at the back of his mind to tell him he couldn't have it. Not here, not now ... probably not at all. On the other hand, that small core of reason wasn't enough to make him break the kiss and let her go.

Not yet. Not just yet.

The parlour door opened and Nicholas stepped through it. For the space of a heartbeat, he simply froze; then, as Eden slowly released Lydia, he shook his head swiftly and turned back into the room saying clearly, 'Damn. I forgot. Stupid of me. I left it at home ...' And his voice faded as the door closed firmly behind him.

Eden looked at Lydia. Her cheeks were flushed, her breathing, rapid and uneven. Taking her hands in his to toy with her fingers, he said, 'That was unfortunate. And entirely my fault.'

'Not – not entirely, perhaps.' She cleared her throat and tried to sound blasé. 'And it could have been worse. At least it wasn't Aubrey.'

'No. Nicholas will be discreet.' He frowned down at his hands and hers. 'Do you still think I kissed you to make a point?'

'I don't know what to think,' she replied truthfully.

'No. Neither do I.' He released her and created a space between them. 'So this shouldn't happen again until we do.'

* * *

Later, walking back through the frosty streets to Cheapside, Eden waited for Nicholas to refer to what he'd seen. Eventually, when the younger man remained stubbornly silent, he said, 'I suppose you are shocked?'

'*Shocked?*' echoed Nicholas, unlocking his jaws. 'Don't be a bloody fool. It's been brewing for weeks – if not months. The only question is not where *you* imagine it's going, but where Lydia *thinks* it is.'

Eden blinked. 'I don't know. I doubt she does either.'

'So stop playing fast and loose with her affections. If --'

'I don't believe I am.'

'Then you're a bigger idiot than I thought – and blind into the bargain.' Nicholas stopped walking and swung Eden round to face him. 'That being so, I'll put this into very simple words. If you break her heart, I'll do my damnedest to put your head through a wall.'

ELEVEN

The last days of December saw a flurry of loosely-related activity. Thomas Harrison was arrested, then immediately released when he promised to behave; a proposal to offer Cromwell the Crown was made and then withdrawn; and, precisely as Colonel Brandon had feared, Parliament gave itself authority to pass future Bills without the consent of the Lord Protector.

January arrived, bringing flurries of snow. And two days into the month, Eden learned something he rather felt he should have been told in advance and which sent him hot-foot to Lambert's office.

'Just when,' he asked crisply, 'were you intending to tell me about these new measures against the Royalists?'

'Ah.' The Major-General laid down his quill and met his Colonel's thoroughly annoyed stare. 'My apologies. That was remiss of me.'

'Considering you sent me off to gain the trust of Edward Villiers and the rest of them, I think *that's* an understatement.'

Lambert's expression became a little less friendly.

'I believe I may be said to have gathered that. If you will sit down and master your temper, I'll apprise you of the situation.'

Having little choice in the matter and wisely keeping his mouth shut, Eden removed his hat and sat.

'Towards the end of last month there were reports of relatively large quantities of gunpowder leaving London for the country. Further enquiries revealed that sales of muskets and pistols have also increased. Three days ago, two Worcestershire gentlemen were arrested for receiving consignments of arms. Yesterday, other arrests followed on similar charges; one Major Norwood, for example, who we know has been received at the court-in-exile ... also gentlemen from Caernarvonshire and Anglesey. The matter, you will appreciate, is already quite widespread – hence the need to prevent it getting out of hand.'

'And so?' Eden already knew what was being done. He just wanted to hear Lambert say it.

'So a regulation has been issued stating that any Royalist found amassing arms and powder will be arrested.' The Major-General leaned back in his chair. 'I realise that this will complicate your talks with Villiers but --'

'*Complicate* them?' echoed Eden incredulously. 'It will *bury* them – and my integrity, as well.'

'What did you expect, Colonel? That national security would take second-place to your reputation?'

'No. I merely assumed that this was the kind of information of which I might reasonably have expected to have been kept abreast. It may interest you to know that Will Compton is back in the City. I had a meeting set up with him for tomorrow which is now a less likely occurrence than that someone will try to stave my skull in.' He rose and snatched up his hat. 'I'll make sure you find out which.'

* * *

Eden had made no attempt to see Lydia for a week – neither had she contacted him. Although he tried to deny it, he knew that this was taking its toll on his temper. A voice at the back of his mind that he couldn't seem to silence whispered that he was leaving the field clear for Gilbert Wakefield. Common sense asserted that this didn't – couldn't – matter. If Wakefield offered marriage and Lydia accepted, both the situation and any questions in his own mind would be resolved. Unfortunately, knowing this and being comfortable with it were two different things.

On the following evening, he went to the Dolphin Tavern in Tower Street and sat down with a tankard of ale he didn't want. An hour later, he pushed it to one side and walked out into the dark. The fact that he'd never expected Sir William to keep their appointment didn't really make it any better. He felt like hitting someone.

Ironically enough, someone was about to give him the chance.

Later, he realised that if he'd been paying attention he'd have had some warning. As it was, however, he'd just turned into Walbrook Street in the direction of the Poultry, when three figures erupted from one of the narrow alleys to his left. The largest of them cannoned into him, sending him crashing into the wall while the other two closed in behind. Then they were on him.

A blow to his jaw sent him careening back into the arms of the first man who promptly punched him so hard in the stomach that the breath left him. Another swift, vicious blow pushed him into the black mouth of the alleyway; and then all three set about the business of beating him to a pulp.

It all happened so fast, there was no time to think, let alone use his training. Years ago, his father had taught him how to ride a blow so it hurt less but there was no possibility of doing that now and the confined space made drawing his sword an impossibility. So he fought back as best he could and mostly on the defensive, using every dirty trick he knew while three pairs of fists pounded into him. Because he knew what would happen once they got him on the ground, he stayed on his feet until it was no longer an option. But eventually a particularly brutal blow to the jaw, resulting in another collision with the wall, put him on his knees and a kick sent him sprawling on the cobbles.

His breath came in raw, useless gasps. His mouth was full of blood, one cheek felt numb and most of his body hurt. Then a booted foot slammed hard into his side and his pain level ratcheted up from merely agonising to beyond excruciating. Instinctively, he rolled – trying to prevent another blow in the same place. And that was when a hand shoved his face into the ground while a knee pinioned the small of his back and a voice said, 'You're a busy fellow, aren't you? Got a finger in all manner of pies. And some of 'em sod all to do with you. Pity that. This is what you get for sticking your beak in where it's not wanted.'

Any vague notion Eden might have had that this was anything to do with his business for Lambert promptly evaporated. This was to do with Lydia. Somebody wanted him out of the picture and thought they could scare him off. Well, he was scared all right – just not on his own account.

He managed to make his mouth work well enough to say, 'Quinn sent you?'

This earned him a buffet that made his head ring.

'See ... there you go again, asking questions. Don't make any odds to you who sent us, does it? Could be Old Noll himself and you'd still be where you are now.'

The hand at his nape, grabbed a fistful of hair and yanked his head up. The movement drove the sickening pain in his ribs ricocheting through the rest of him.

'Now you're going to listen very careful-like and you're going to remember what I say. You've gone past being a nuisance. A long way past it. So if you want to stay in good health, you'd better stop poking about in things what don't concern you. That clear enough for you?'

Eden spat blood and grunted two words that caused the fellow kneeling on his back to slam his head down, then immediately drag it back up again. A chipped cobble scraped the cheek that wasn't already numb and his ribs screamed again. Then a boot settled on the wrist of his outflung hand and pressed down hard, barely shy of the point where he expected to feel his bones cracking. It was his sword-hand and he thought distantly, *Oh Christ. Not that.*

'There's not a lot of point being a hero when there's nobody to see,' said the voice in his ear, 'and we can carry on hurting you as long as you like. Up to you. But try and grasp that this is just a warning and there won't be another. Next time we'll put you in the ground – and, seeing as you enjoy pain, it doesn't have to be quick. Then there's that stubborn bitch in Bishopsgate ...' Something must have given Eden away because the man holding him down gave a short laugh and said, 'So that's the way of it. Got your attention now, have I?'

'Yes.' The sound was a mere breath.

'What was that?'

'Yes, damn you.' Making just those three words audible nearly caused him to pass out but he fought on. 'Touch her and ... better kill me first.'

Laughter erupted, vibrating through Eden's body and making him clamp his teeth together in an effort to hide just how badly he was hurting.

'He's got a sense of humour,' remarked the fellow standing on his wrist. 'Got to give him that.'

'I,' remarked a new and very different voice from behind him, 'am not entertained.' And then, coldly, 'You have caused me a lot of inconvenience, Colonel. The women removed, my ledger stolen, one of my best men incapacitated and another dead – not to mention five others in custody thanks to a visit from the Militia. Did you really think I wouldn't find you?'

Eden spat more blood and, his voice no more than a thread, said, 'Quinn. What do you want?'

'Several things. To begin with, my fellows out of prison; since, as I imagine you already know, they won't talk, there is no point in continuing to hold them. I also require the return of the book you stole. It may interest you to learn that it is those things – and *only* those – that are keeping you alive at this moment. Finally and most importantly, I want the records Stephen Neville kept about matters that didn't concern him.'

'Why?'

'You are in no position to ask questions,' returned Quinn, sounding bored. 'Tell the widow to find the papers and surrender them next time she is asked. Then all this will be over.'

Eden heaved in a breath. 'She can't. She doesn't ... have them.'

'She is either lying or mistaken. I know she has them. And this will not stop until she gives them up. I trust I'm making myself quite clear?'

He struggled to think, then to force out the words.

'Your men ... the book ... yes. But you don't ... touch Lydia.'

For a moment, there was silence. Finally, Quinn said dispassionately, 'My men, my book and no further prying by you or visits from the Militia ... and I will allow the woman some time. That is all you get, Colonel.' Then, from what sounded to Eden like a few steps further away, 'Finish it, Packer. I doubt he's in any state to follow but you may make sure of it, if you wish.'

Somebody grunted an assent and two things happened at once. The weight increased on his lumbar region but the foot left his wrist. There was a split second of acute relief and before his right arm was grabbed and savagely twisted against his spine. This time the world swam around him and a sound of pure agony forced its way past his lips.

'You heard the man. Be sensible and take notice.'

Then, without bothering to force a reply, he gave Eden's arm one final wrench followed by a savage blow to the side of the head ... and was gone.

For the space of several heartbeats, Eden just lay there listening to retreating footsteps while he struggled to breathe and fought to retain consciousness. Finally, he gritted his teeth and slowly set about trying to get himself upright. Bit by excruciating bit, he managed to heave himself first on to hands and knees and eventually, by degrees and using the wall for support, to his feet. By that time, he was drenched in sweat and nausea was threatening to overwhelm him so he just leaned thankfully against the wall and shut his eyes while he took an inventory of his injuries.

The pain in his left side was severe and it hurt to breathe; so ... a cracked rib or, if he was really unlucky, a broken one. Cautiously, he flexed his sword-hand. That hurt, too, but mercifully didn't appear to be broken. Just bruising, then; nothing that wouldn't mend in a few days. For the rest ... his lip was split, his right eye beginning to close and his entire body was protesting from the pummelling he'd received. Basically, he felt like hell but had somehow to find the strength to haul his miserable carcass home.

He tried telling himself he'd had worse ... but since he couldn't remember when, this didn't help much. Further thought suggested that he was no more than a third of a mile from home; just a hundred yards to Cheapside, then a few hundred more to the junction with Friday Street. No distance, really.

I can do this, he thought. *I can. It just may take a while.*

As it turned out, he had no idea how long it took – only that it felt like hours, with pain increasing every gruelling step of the way. When he finally got inside the house, the relief was so acute that he simply slid down the wall and sat on the floor, looking at the seemingly insurmountable obstacle of the stairs.

A white apron over brown skirts swam into his line of sight, causing him to look up at its owner.

'What *now*?' asked Mistress Wilkes, her concern well-hidden behind a mask of annoyance.

'Sorry,' replied Eden hazily. 'I'll get up. In a minute.'

'You'll stay where you are and wait for Sir Nicholas and me to help you,' she snapped. And vanished.

He shut his eyes, glad that he didn't have to move just yet. And slid imperceptibly into welcome oblivion.

* * *

'Holy hell!' said Colonel Brandon. 'I thought Nick was exaggerating.'

It was the following afternoon and, despite his various injuries having been attended to, Eden wasn't feeling much better. Mistress Wilkes had dealt with all the superficial cuts and scrapes and made him drink something vile to ease the pain; and the doctor, having pronounced his ribs cracked but not broken, had strapped him up so tightly that a deep breath – even if he'd fancied taking one – was impossible.

'It looks worse than it is.'

'One would certainly hope so.'

'And at least I still have all my teeth.' He'd been worried about that for a time.

'By all means let's look on the bright side.' Gabriel pulled a chair up to the bed and sat down. 'What happened?'

'Three men helping Quinn to deliver a message.'

'Quinn? He was *there*?'

'I didn't see him – but yes. He wants his men back and his ledger.' Eden took a moment to breathe and repeated what had been said. 'And he wants Stephen Neville's thrice-blasted and seemingly non-existent papers.'

'Yes.' Gabriel frowned thoughtfully. 'What precautions have you taken?'

'I've ordered the prisoners released and sent the ledger back with them – so, if Quinn keeps his word, Lydia should be safe for a while. But Nick has warned Henry and Peter to be extra vigilant and I've sent to Ned, asking for a couple of troopers to keep an eye on the women and the lorinery.' Another pause. 'But without anything further to go on, I don't know what else I can do.'

'At the moment, you're in no fit state to do anything,' said Gabriel flatly.

'I can be up by tomorrow.' *I hope so, anyway.*

'Don't be a bloody fool. You may haul yourself out of bed – but what possible use do you think you'll be?' He waited and, when Eden said nothing, asked abruptly, 'Does Lydia know this happened?'

'No. And I don't want her to.'

'Then she'd best not see you.'

'I realise that.' Eden didn't need a mirror to know that he had a spectacular black eye, a split lip, a miscellany of cuts and that his jaw was bruised and swollen. And those were just the marks clothes wouldn't hide. 'Nick has told her I've got extra duties at the Tower. That should buy me a few days unless she starts to wonder why there are troopers loitering around her premises – in which case she'll be hammering on my door wanting to know what I haven't told her *this* time.'

Gabriel's opinion was that he'd need more than a few days but he merely said, 'Leave her to me. Fortunately, a letter arrived from Venetia enclosing a note – so I've an excuse to call. I don't suppose it will turn up anything new but I'll find a way of getting her to talk about these mysterious papers while I'm there.' He leaned back in his chair. 'And now you can explain how three hired bravos managed to jump you without you having the least warning. At the risk of sounding unsympathetic, I thought you were better than that. Well?'

* * *

Having slept most of the afternoon, Eden woke with an appetite and asked Mistress Wilkes very politely for some solid food. She told him that he could have calves foot jelly, a little mutton broth and a custard. Rather less politely, Eden demanded some chops and a mug of ale. Mistress Wilkes folded her arms beneath her more-than-ample bosom and said, 'No. Tomorrow, perhaps – if I'm satisfied it'll stay down. Today you get what you're given.'

As a consequence of this, Eden was not in the best of moods when Nicholas stuck his head round the door later that evening and said, 'If you're feeling up to it, can I talk to you?'

'That depends. Get me some ale and a slice of pie and I'll think about it.'

Nicholas grinned and shut the door behind him.

'Alice would have my head on a spike.'

Eden grunted and, in one very terse sentence, said what he thought of Alice.

'Say that to her face – I dare you.'

Eden sighed in defeat and let his head fall back.

'Prisoners in the Tower get better treatment than this,' he muttered. Then, 'All right. What do you want?'

Nicholas pulled up a chair and sat astride it, facing the bed. The amusement faded from his face and he said slowly, 'You know I've been corresponding with Phoebe Clifford?'

'I didn't – though I daresay I might have guessed.'

'She ... she writes exactly as she *is,* if you know what I mean. So it's almost as if she's standing next to me. Only, of course, she isn't. And I wish she was.'

'I see. And how does Phoebe feel?'

Nicholas coloured a little and traced the chair-back with one finger.

'I think she may possibly feel the same ... but I'm not sure.'

'Then go to Yorkshire and find out.'

The brown eyes rose, frowning a little. 'It's not that simple.'

'Yes,' said Eden. 'It is.'

'No. There's all this trouble surrounding Lydia – and now this.' He waved his hand to encompass Eden's injuries. 'I can't just walk away from the two of you.'

'I agree that Lydia would miss you. But between us, I'm sure Henry and I could find a way to cover your absence for a while. And as for me ... I'm not your responsibility and neither do I need a nursemaid.'

'Maybe not. But you *do* need help,' replied Nicholas flatly. 'The whole situation's getting out of hand and, with Toby still away --'

'Oh for God's sake, Nick – if you want to go to Yorkshire, *go* to bloody Yorkshire. Are you in love with the girl or not?'

'I ... yes. I think so.'

'Then you'd better tell her, hadn't you? Or at the very least, write something that gives her a clue and ask her permission to visit.'

Nicholas took his time about answering but finally he said, 'There's something else.'

'Naturally,' muttered Eden. Then, 'What?'

'This.' Nicholas touched his empty sleeve. 'On top of everything else, it hardly makes me the ideal suitor. From what Phoebe's told me, her mother would have a fit at the mere thought of acquiring me as a son-in-law. And I can't imagine what Colonel Brandon would think.'

'Gabriel merely wants to see Phoebe married to a man who will make her happy. But the only thing that truly matters is what Phoebe thinks.' Eden paused and then said bluntly, 'What's the *real* problem, Nick? Frightened she'll be horrified when she sees you without your shirt?'

This time the silence lapped the edges of the room.

Then Nicholas's mouth twisted and he said, 'Wouldn't you be?'

'Yes. Probably.' Eden tried to envision it and felt his insides curdle. 'Unfortunately, there's only one way to find out. And, for what it's worth, I don't think Phoebe would recoil or even think less of you ... not if she's already come to care for the man you are. She's not that shallow.'

'No.' A faint smile dawned. 'She isn't, is she?'

'Can I give you a couple of other pieces of advice – one of which may not be palatable?'

'Of course.'

'Talk to Gabriel. And visit a decent brothel.'

* * *

On the following afternoon, Eden decided it was time to test his abilities. He was just heaving himself out of bed, stark naked, when the door opened unexpectedly causing him to snatch belatedly at the sheet.

'Shy, aren't you?' said Tobias cheerfully. Then absorbing the state of his brother's face and the multi-coloured patterning on what could be seen of his torso, 'God. Did somebody put you through the meat-grinder?'

'Something like that. And I thought you were Mistress Wilkes. She's in and out of here like a bird with twigs in its beak.'

'Hoping to catch you in the buff, no doubt.'

'Very funny. When did you get back?'

'Just now. And I suspect I've beaten the snow by little more than a day.' Tobias put a hand on Eden's shoulder and gently pushed him back down on the bed. 'Sit before you fall – and tell me. Lydia again? Or is a jealous husband on your trail?'

'Lydia,' replied Eden, more grateful to be seated again than he cared to admit. And, in as few words as possible, told his brother what had happened.

Tobias listened in silence and then said, 'What are you doing about it?'

'Right now? There's not a lot I *can* do.'

'You can start taking your own advice and stop wandering about the City at night unaccompanied. They know who you are, Eden – and probably a lot of other things as well.'

'Thank you. That thought had occurred to me. But I'm not going about my business with a bodyguard in tow. And they wouldn't have been able to give me such a mauling if I'd been paying attention – as, in future, I will be. So stop trying to be Mother and tell me how things are at home.'

* * *

Lydia had been worried about facing Nicholas after what he'd witnessed on Christmas Day but, in the event, he behaved as though nothing had happened. Inevitably, this left her free to worry about Colonel Maxwell instead … what he had thought, what he might do, what the mood of their next meeting might be. Then, as one week became two and there was no meeting at all, worry turned to faint resentment. After all, she thought, he had no business leading her into temptation like that and then, for the second time, calmly walking away as if nothing of any great consequence had happened.

Nicholas had said Eden was exceptionally busy and Colonel Brandon, when he came to deliver Venetia's note, had echoed this. Difficult though it had been, Lydia congratulated herself on not appearing unduly interested in Colonel Maxwell's doings during the course of either conversation. That she had fooled neither gentleman mercifully did not occur to her.

'Fretting about why you've not been near since that night we won't speak of,' was Nicholas's verdict.

And, 'She's careful about what she says but less good at guarding her expression,' shrugged Gabriel. 'I sensed confusion – but you'd know better than me, I daresay.'

* * *

It took over a week for the worst of the marks on Eden's face and hands to fade and during it the promised snow arrived and various events took place in Westminster and elsewhere. In defiance of the Army, Parliament abolished the extended franchise created by the *Instrument* and restored the old, narrower system of forty-shilling freeholders, hedged about with numerous religious and moral restrictions. This done, it confirmed the vote on 'damnable heresies' and, amidst a fresh wave of arrests, moved on to financial matters. These, according to Colonel Brandon, were the subject of much on-going argument and resulted in a temporary Act granting the Protector a woefully inadequate sum to cover both domestic and foreign policy. And finally, adding insult to injury as Gabriel put it, the House re-affirmed its earlier decision to have the final say on what Cromwell was or was not allowed to veto.

The cracks were not only showing but getting wider by the day and through them emerged the fanatics and the mildly deranged. In Lambeth, Thomas Taney – or Theoro-John as he called himself – lived in a tent. To Eden's knowledge, he had been doing this long enough for most passers-by to be accustomed to him. Now, as the mutterings of discontent grew ever louder, he decided to get their attention. He lit a bonfire into which he tossed a Bible, a saddle, a sword and a pistol and announced to his baffled audience that these were the Gods of England. Then, blade in hand, he marched off to Westminster and swung wildly at all and sundry until guards restrained him and hauled him off to prison.

'Time was,' observed Colonel Maxwell to Colonel Brandon, 'when that might have been funny. I'd have thought that this wasn't one of them ... and yet here you are looking unaccustomedly cheerful.'

'That's nothing to do with Theoro-John,' returned Gabriel. 'There are finally signs of common-sense emerging. The House has back-tracked on the question of the so-called damnable heresies and agreed that the Protector be consulted on those exempted from toleration. Better and more encouraging yet, we've formed a coalition comprising both Court Party members and some of the less-radical Opposition MPs.'

'Of which I imagine you are one?'

'I am. And our first priority is to increase the stupidly impractical sum previously awarded to the Protector. The proposal under discussion is to add a further hundred thousand pounds to the original grant for domestic government, plus substantial amounts to fund the Army and Navy.'

'Well that should keep both the Council of Officers and Cromwell happy – though one has to wonder where the money is coming from.'

'There'll be a deficit,' admitted Gabriel. 'But that's something that can be remedied. The current deadlock between the Protector and the House, on the other hand, is stifling progress of any kind and *must* be resolved. Money, at this stage, is the least of our worries.'

* * *

In the event, Colonel Brandon's optimistic mood didn't survive the next twenty-four hours. The following evening, he hurled his snow-covered hat and gloves across the room and sent a stream of invective flying after them.

'Ah,' said Eden. 'A less than successful day, I gather?'

'It needn't have been,' ground out Gabriel. 'We'd voted seven hundred thousand for the Army over the next four years. Everything was going well and, barring the usual extremists, everyone was happy.'

'Until?'

'Until the Court Party couldn't resist pushing its luck and pressing for the *Instrument* to remain in force and in its original form if Cromwell wouldn't sanction the changes to the franchise contained in the Constitutional Bill. That sent the Opposition members of the coalition scurrying back to their own side of the House – and put the Opposition as a whole back in the majority. So now we're no further forward and I'm bloody sick of the whole thing.'

Eden handed him a glass of wine.

'So what now?'

'I don't know.' He pushed a weary hand through his hair. 'The rumblings in the streets are getting ever louder and the gulf between Protector and Parliament remains as wide as ever. Not one of the eighty-two ordinances Cromwell laid before the House has been ratified – not even one as a good-will token. I wanted to see his power reduced but the House is cutting too much ground from beneath his feet and doing it far too fast because it fears the influence of the Army. The result is that men like myself are voting with the Court Party more often than not in the frail hope of holding back the tide – which is not something any of us anticipated and which clearly isn't working. We've gone from Cromwell having the bit between his teeth to the honourable members having it between theirs and any possibility of reasonable compromise is as far away as ever. In short, nothing either useful or lasting has been achieved and the whole thing is a mess.'

'How long before Cromwell loses patience?'

'Not long. I think he'll dissolve Parliament as soon as the terms of the *Instrument* entitle him to do so.'

'The third of February?'

'The third of February,' agreed Gabriel, raising his glass. 'And here's to it.'

'I can see,' remarked Eden, shifting his position which the strapping round his ribs was beginning to make uncomfortable, 'that you're looking forward to it. Still ... it's an ill wind, I suppose.'

'Quite.' Gabriel fell silent for a moment. Then, 'What are you going to do about Lydia?'

'What would you suggest?'

'You might start by watching your back.'

'Oh Christ – not you as well!' snapped Eden. 'First Nicholas, then Toby and now you. What do you all think I am? No. On second thoughts – don't tell me. I doubt I'll like it.'

TWELVE

At around the time Colonel Brandon was tearing his hair out over matters at Westminster, Mistress Neville received an unexpected visitor.

'Lord Northcote, Madam,' said Henry – looking, for the first time that Lydia could remember, slightly worried.

She frowned.

'Northcote? I don't … oh. It must be Mr Wakefield's brother.'

'Ah.' Henry's brow cleared. 'Then you'll receive him?'

'Yes.' *I can't very well refuse – though goodness only knows what he wants with me.* 'Yes. And ask Nancy to bring wine, please.'

The gentleman who entered the room was dark-haired, slender and dressed in the height of fashion. In fact, for the first few moments, all Lydia really noticed were the wine-red velvet coat, the extravagant scalloped-lace collar and the jewels winking on his hands.

He made her an exquisite bow and said, 'Mistress Neville. You will forgive me, I hope, for calling without prior arrangement but affairs keep me frequently from London – which means it is often a case of seizing an opportunity when it presents itself.'

'Of course, my lord.' Lydia made her curtsy and wondered afresh why he'd come. 'Please sit down.'

'Thank you.' He laid his hat to one side, waited until she was seated and then took a chair facing her. 'I felt it was time I made your acquaintance.'

Something about his tone and the way he said it was time *he* made *her* acquaintance rather than that *they* became acquainted, ruffled Lydia's feathers.

So she smiled and said, 'Oh? Then you must forgive *me*, sir, if I ask why that should be.'

His lordship's brows rose.

'Do not be unnecessarily disingenuous, Mistress. I should have thought my reason rather obvious. I understand that my younger brother is making you the object of his attentions. His very *marked* attentions, if my information is correct.'

'I'm not convinced that it is. It's true that Mr Wakefield and I have become friends but --'

'It is a little more than that, is it not? He visits this house often and the two of you have been seen together in public on numerous occasions. I believe I may be excused if that speaks less of friendship than courtship.' The Viscount crossed one beautifully-clad leg over the other. 'If Gilbert has not yet made you an offer of marriage, the indications are that such an offer cannot be far distant.'

Lydia was prevented from replying by the arrival of Nancy with refreshments. Swallowing her annoyance, she waited until the maid had left the room and then, whilst busying herself with the wine, said coolly, 'I have no idea – and would imagine that you know your brother's intentions better than I. But if --'

'In fact, I don't,' said Lord Northcote, interrupting her for the second time inside five minutes. 'Gilbert and I have been at odds for some time now and, in recent months, rarely speak. This, however, does not mean that I do not interest myself in his doings ... and, in particular, with his possible choice of a wife.'

'Then perhaps,' said Lydia, setting the glass down at his side with a little snap, 'you should mend whatever rift is between you and speak to him directly. However --'

'Sadly, that is unlikely.'

'Do you think,' she asked glacially, 'that you might do me the courtesy of allowing me to finish?'

'Of course. I beg your pardon.'

'Thank you. I was about to inform you that if the sole reason for your visit was to establish whether or not Gilbert has asked me to marry him, I can set your mind at rest. He hasn't.'

'He will.'

'Since by your own admission you and he don't communicate, you can't possibly know that.'

'I can and do.' Northcote took a sip of his wine. 'I can also see that you might be tempted to accept. It would be better, however, if you did not.'

'Better for whom?'

'Everyone. It is not my intention to insult you, Mistress Neville ... but our family is an old and distinguished one. I would therefore prefer my brother to look a little higher than a tradesman's widow – even one as attractive and well-provided-for as yourself.'

'What would *you* know of my financial circumstances?' snapped Lydia. 'That is absolutely none of your affair!'

'It becomes very much my affair if you are to become my sister,' he replied smoothly. 'As for knowing ... the scope of my knowledge would undoubtedly surprise you. There is very little I can't discover if I choose to do so. But let us return to Gilbert. I am sure he is very taken with you – but that is by no means the whole story.'

Lydia was by now more than half-inclined to have Henry show his lordship the door. He was rude, arrogant and patronising and she disliked him more every minute. There was also something naggingly familiar about him ... something she could only put down to him being Gilbert's brother even though, in most respects, the two men couldn't be more dissimilar.

She said, 'Then what is? I'd be obliged if you would come to the point, sir.'

'The point, Mistress Neville, is that my brother has a number of wild and fantastical notions ... one might even call them obsessions ... in which you have quite unwittingly become embroiled. Family loyalty and respect for my name forbids me to give you details. But it seemed unfair to allow you to fall blindly victim to Gilbert's charm without realising that you do not have a complete picture.'

'Considering you don't want a tradesman's widow in the family, that is exceedingly thoughtful of you.' Lydia stood up and waited for the Viscount to do the same. He didn't. Her brows rose and she said, 'I think this conversation is at an end, don't you?'

'Not entirely.' He took another sip of wine, set down his glass and finally came unhurriedly to his feet. 'I am aware of your twin charitable enterprises. I even applaud them. But you should understand that marriage with my family would preclude your continued involvement in them.' His mouth curled slightly but his eyes remained chilly and expressionless. 'You may think I could not prevent you. You would be wrong.' He reached for his hat and added, 'I suggest you consider what I have said. It was well-intentioned.'

'Pardon me for observing that it didn't seem so,' responded Lydia tartly. 'And there appears to be one little thing you have over-looked.'

'Indeed?'

'Yes.' She rang the bell that would summon Henry. 'You don't seem to have considered the possibility that you need not have told me any of this; that, if your brother *were* to propose marriage, I might simply refuse.'

'And would you?'

'I think Gilbert deserves to know that before you do,' said Lydia sweetly. And then, as the door opened. 'Henry. Lord Northcote is leaving. Please show him out.'

* * *

Twenty-four hours later, Lydia was still quietly fuming. Inevitably, she'd spent a large part of the night thinking of all the things she *could* have said to his infuriating lordship and wishing they'd occurred to her at the time. As a consequence, when Gilbert Wakefield arrived just as she was about to set off for Duck Lane, she was still in no mood to be tactful.

Removing her cloak and tossing it over a chair, she said, 'Come into the parlour. I'd like a word.'

His brows rose slightly but he followed her and, closing the door behind him, said, 'Has something happened to vex you?'

'Yes. Your brother.'

'Edmund?' he said blankly. And then, 'He came here? *Why?*'

'To let me know that should you offer me marriage, he'd like me to refuse.'

For a long moment, Gilbert simply stared at her. But finally, in the coldest tone she had ever heard him use, he said, 'Damn him! How *dare* he? That is no business of his.'

'My thoughts exactly.'

'What else did he say?'

'Quite a lot. Enough – and in such a way that I've told Henry not to admit him in future.'

He nodded distractedly. 'Yes. But what did he actually *say*?'

'Does it matter?'

'I don't know. It might. And don't worry about offending me – you won't. I know precisely what he can be like.'

'Very well. He said you can do better than a tradesman's widow. He inferred that he knows more than he should about my financial status. He accused you of having wild, fantastic obsessions which are in some way related to myself. And he finished by informing me that if I married you, he'd see to it that what he called my 'charitable enterprises' came to an end. All this despite my having already told him you hadn't proposed to me at *all*.' She drew an unsteady breath and added, 'I'm sorry. As you can see, I'm still furious.'

'I don't blame you and it's I who should apologise to you.' A note of worry mingled oddly with his initial anger. 'There are times when Edmund takes far too much upon himself ... and other times when he gets completely inexplicable ideas.'

'So these wild fancies he spoke of have nothing to do with what you said to me when we first met? That you hoped to find some connection between Stephen's family and yours?'

'No! Not at all.' He hesitated. 'I don't suppose you've come across anything since --'

'No – and I've been through Stephen's papers more times than I can count,' she replied tersely. Then, refusing to be side-tracked, 'So your brother was either making it up or imagining things?'

'Yes. He didn't explain what he meant?'

'No. Pride and loyalty apparently forbade it. Personally, I'd have thought a man with such reverence for his family name would have better manners but --'

'He thinks his title and influence obviate the need for them.'

Lydia eyed him narrowly.

'*Does* he have a great deal of influence?'

'It would seem so. He knows a good many powerful men and has various business interests, the nature of which he doesn't discuss – at least, not with me. And of course he's one of the members for Kent, along with Thomas Kelsey and a couple of others.'

'He sits in the Parliament?'

'He has a seat – though I believe he rarely occupies it. Didn't I mention it?'

'No.' Lydia eyed him thoughtfully. 'Actually, you scarcely ever speak of him at all.'

'What would I say?' asked Gilbert uncomfortably. 'You've met him. It must be fairly clear that we don't get on with each other.'

'I suppose so.' Lydia thought for a moment and then said, 'At the risk of embarrassing us both, I think we have to address the real point of his visit. You didn't appear particularly surprised that he spoke of a possible marriage between you and I. Angry at his presumption, yes – but not surprised. Why was that?'

He coloured slightly and when he spoke, his voice was leaden.

'Because it's true. I was ... working my way up to making you an offer. But after this, you're hardly likely to say yes, are you?'

Lydia tried to find a kind way of being honest and, when she couldn't think of one, settled for the simple truth.

'I'm sorry, Gilbert but I'd have said no anyway.'

'Oh. I see.'

'No. I doubt if you do. I like you and I value your friendship a great deal but I don't think that's enough. I know that marriage is supposed to be about mutual gain rather than mutual affection ... but I can't look at it that way. I married Stephen out of necessity and was incredibly lucky that we grew fond of one another and were happy. But if and when I marry again, I'm hoping for something more. Can you understand?'

'Yes.' He smiled wryly. 'Unfortunately, I can. It's Colonel Maxwell, I suppose?'

It was Lydia's turn to flush.

'Not at all! Colonel Maxwell is completely beside the point.'

'Of course. Forgive me.' He stopped, looking vaguely at a loss. And then, 'Am I also to be barred from your door?'

'By no means! How could you think it?'

'Then may I escort you wherever you were going? The snow has stopped but the streets are icy and treacherous. I'd be happy to give you my arm.'

'And I'd be happy to take it,' said Lydia truthfully. 'But since your objectionable brother seems to have been spying on one or both of us, I think it might be sensible not to give him further ammunition.'

* * *

Later, when she had the leisure to think about it, Lydia wondered just how foolishly transparent she actually was when it came to Eden Maxwell. Venetia had guessed – as had Nicholas, long before having his suspicions confirmed on Christmas Day. But Gilbert? How had that happened? As far as she could recall, he'd only seen her with the Colonel on two extremely brief occasions. So if *he* knew ... was there anyone left who didn't?

It was an acutely embarrassing thought and she hadn't even begun to get over it when the Colonel arrived in person; the first time she'd laid eyes on him in over three weeks.

Unsure whether pleasure or pique was uppermost, she eyed him coolly and said, 'Goodness. I thought you'd taken to the heather.'

Eden looked back, trying to gauge her mood and said cautiously, 'Why would I do that?'

'I've no idea.' Realising how pettish she sounded, she sought to mend it. 'Nicholas said you'd been given additional duties at the Tower.' And then she ruined the effect by adding, 'Obviously, they were extremely time-consuming.'

'Yes.' Feeling on much safer ground, he smiled. 'You sound cross. Have I called at a bad time – or did you miss me?'

'Neither. And don't flatter yourself.'

'I wasn't.' Catching the flash of annoyance in her eyes, Eden decided further provocation might be unwise. 'I'm sorry. I'd neither wanted nor intended to disappear for so long but, as things turned out, it was unavoidable. Please believe that I'd have come if I could – indeed, I'd have come regardless, if you'd needed me.'

'Then it's lucky I didn't, isn't it?'

'Probably.' *It wasn't luck. I had you surrounded with every wall I could build.* 'Am I forgiven?'

'There's nothing to forgive.' *Yes. All right. I missed you. And missed you - and missed you - and missed you. And now you're here and I sound like a shrew.* She made a small helpless gesture and said abruptly, 'I'm sorry, too. It's just that I've had ... an odd couple of days.'

'Odd?'

'Unsettling – though not really of any great consequence.' She paused and then, with a swift smile, said, 'You're allowed to sit down – if you have time to stay, that is.'

'I've time enough.' Eden waited until she was seated before taking the chair facing her. 'Do you want to tell me about these odd things of little consequence?'

'Not especially.' Lydia decided it wouldn't be fair to reveal that Mr Wakefield had almost made her a proposal of marriage. 'None of it is anything to do with my other difficulties – so I'd sooner hear your news. You're still at the Tower?'

'Yes. I'd like to say that tensions are easing but unfortunately there's scant sign of that as yet.' In fact, he'd just taken delivery of Major-General Overton – sent south under guard for his part in the plot to relieve General Monck of command in Scotland. 'And according to Gabriel, things are no better at Westminster. He's anticipating dissolution early next month.'

'Even earlier than that, if Mr Radford's newspaper is to be believed.'

Eden's brows rose and he grinned.

'I didn't know you read the *Moderate* ... though I suppose I shouldn't be surprised. I can see how Leveller principles might appeal to you.'

'Some of them,' she agreed. 'But that's not why I buy the news-sheet.'

'Why, then?'

'Nicholas says Mr Radford is struggling to make ends meet and I'm working on the assumption that every copy he sells will help.'

He laughed and shook his head.

'Of course. Why did I need to ask?

'I don't know. Why did you?' And then, without waiting for an answer, 'Is your brother back from Oxfordshire yet?'

'Yes. He returned just after Twelfth Night – though with Tabitha's baby due towards the end of February, I imagine he'll be dashing off again around then.' He hesitated briefly and then said, 'Has Nicholas talked to you at all?'

Lydia stiffened, praying he wasn't going to refer to what Nicholas had seen at Yule.

'He talks to me nearly every day.'

'Yes – but about himself.'

She relaxed. 'No. Should he have done?'

'No. I just thought he might. As I imagine you've guessed, he's formed an attachment for Phoebe Clifford but, for obvious reasons, is nervous about declaring himself.'

Lydia stared at him blankly.

'Obvious reasons?'

'Exactly. That's why I hoped he'd speak to you.'

'Well, he hasn't. *What* reasons?'

'His arm ... or rather, the lack of it.' And when she continued to look baffled, 'He's worrying about his physical appearance. Clearly, you think he needn't.'

'No. I understand why he *would* of course, but not why he considers it an obstacle.'

Eden sighed. 'I knew you'd say that. If I'd thought of it earlier, I might have given him better advice.'

'Why? What advice did you give him?'

A slow smile dawned, half-rueful and half-wicked.

'I don't think I'd better tell you.'

Lydia swallowed hard and tried to think past that smile. Then, eyes widening, she said, 'Oh my God. You told him to find a sympathetic whore. Didn't you?'

Laughter flared in his face.

'Mistress Neville! What a thing to say! I'm shocked!'

'Don't prevaricate. Did you or didn't you?'

'Yes ... though not in those exact words. Was it such a bad idea?'

'That would depend.' She thought for a moment and then shook her head. 'I doubt he'll do it anyway.'

'So do I.' He continued to regard her with lazy amusement. 'You know ... with the possible exception of my mother, I don't think I've ever met another lady who could use the word 'whore' without blushing – or indeed, use it at all.'

Belatedly and not for the reason he'd just mentioned, Lydia felt her cheeks grow warm.

'Most gentlemen wouldn't consider that a recommendation.'

'I'm not most gentlemen.'

'So I've noticed.'

Oh well done, darling. You don't give an inch, do you?

He had become almost accustomed to his body responding to her when he least expected it. Usually it happened when her hair was threatening to fall around her neck or when she was wearing a gown that displayed inches of soft, creamy skin. Right now, her hair was neatly pinned and the dark grey up-to-the-neck, down-to-the-wrist gown ought to have been about as enticing as a shroud ... except that it wasn't. It made him think of unfastening it to reveal first the parts of her he'd seen and then the parts he hadn't. But the reason he was thinking that way right now was because she was warm and acerbic and clever; and because something unexpectedly tempting flowered in his chest at the certainty that she'd missed him.

Realising she was waiting for him to speak, he cleared his throat and said, 'Is that why I've not been offered wine?'

'No.' *But it's why I can't marry Gilbert Wakefield.* 'I just didn't think you'd be here long enough to drink it.'

* * *

During the next five days, Gabriel reported that things in Westminster were going from bad to worse. On the 17th, Parliament declared that the Protector must either accept or reject their changes to the franchise; on the 18th, it set up a committee to supervise partial disbandment of the Army; and on the 20th, it voted to take complete control of the Militia into its own hands.

This proved to be the final straw.

On the morning of January 22nd, members of the House found themselves summoned once more to presence of the Lord Protector in the Painted Chamber.

His complaints were many and varied and, as ever, lengthy.

He had hoped they might leave the *Instrument* as it stood in favour of dealing with at least *some* of his eighty-two ordinances; he objected to having been omitted from discussion on the Constitutional Bill; and he launched with passion into the "division, discontent and dissatisfaction" that had multiplied during the five months the House had been sitting.

'Foundations,' he accused, 'have also been laid for the future renewing of the troubles of these nations by all the enemies of them abroad and at home – these have nourished themselves under your shadow. The Cavalier party has been designing and preparing to put this nation into blood again. They have been making great preparations of arms; commissions for regiments of Horse and Foot have been likewise given from Charles Stuart – all since your sitting.'

Next came the Army which he claimed had been "starved and put upon free quarter despite the current peril." And finally, the crux of the matter.

'I think myself bound, as in my duty to God and to the people of these nations for their safety and good in every respect. I think it my duty to tell you that it is not for the profit of these nations, nor for common and public good, for you to continue here any longer. And therefore I do declare unto you that I do dissolve this Parliament.'

Inevitably, the Protector's announcement called up a storm of argument and protest. Colonel Brandon let it wash over him and walked through fresh flurries of snow to break the news to Colonel Maxwell.

For a moment or two Eden regarded him speechlessly. Then he said, 'But he can't *do* that. Can he? Until the five months are up, surely it's not legal?'

'That would depend on your reckoning. Oliver has decided to reckon the life of the Parliament in lunar months, rather than calendar ones. And really, what difference does it make? Having achieved nothing useful in five months, another ten days is hardly going to matter one way or the other. Speaking for myself, I'm grateful to him because, as soon as the weather permits, I'm going home to my wife, my children and my own bed.'

'Well, I can't blame you for that. But aren't you even the smallest bit worried that, if Cromwell sticks to the letter of the *Instrument*, he doesn't have to call Parliament again for three years?'

'After the roaring success of this one? Hardly. And I really hope,' returned Gabriel with a grimly sardonic smile, 'that no-one is foolish enough to suggest that I stand for the next – because I fear my response may be somewhat less than polite.'

* * *

The snow continued for another three days, thus delaying Colonel Brandon's departure for Yorkshire and finally persuading Nicholas to pluck up the courage to take what might well be his last chance to speak privately with him.

Gabriel listened without interrupting and, when Nicholas finally stopped speaking, said, 'I'd tell you that all this ought to be addressed to Phoebe – except that listing all your failings isn't the best way to make a proposal of marriage if you want the girl to accept.'

'I know that.' Nicholas smiled ruefully. 'But it can't be denied that I'm not a very good bargain.'

'You're a better bargain than any she's been offered so far – in as much as it's Phoebe herself you want, not Ford Edge.'

'Does that mean I'd have your approval to ask her?'

'You don't need my approval, Nick.'

'Perhaps not. But I'd be more comfortable if I had it.'

'Then it's yours,' shrugged Gabriel. 'But don't count on it weighing with Phoebe. She'll make up her own mind – the same as she's been doing for the last five years.' He paused and then said, 'Do you want to travel north with me?'

'More than anything – but I can't. Not yet. Not while Lydia's still in trouble and Eden needs all the help he can get. I owe him more than that,' said Nicholas resolutely. 'If I wrote a letter explaining everything and asking leave to visit her as soon as I can get away, I think Phoebe would understand.'

'I'm sure she would.' Amusement lurked in the Colonel's eyes. 'Write your letter and I'll deliver it for you. I've never seen myself as Cupid …but I suppose there's a first time for everything.'

THE GOLDEN KEY
London, February to April, 1655

I did not live until this time
Crowned in my felicity
When I could say without a crime
I am not thine, but thee.
No bridegroom's nor crown-conqueror's mirth
To mine compared can be;
They have but pieces of this earth
I've all the world in thee.

Katherine Phillips (1631-1664)

ONE

Snow stopped falling and it froze.

Gabriel left for Yorkshire with Nicholas's letter in his pocket and Eden received a message summoning him to a discreet corner of the Blue Boar's Head in King Street. Two men awaited him there. One was Edward Villiers; the other, looking disapproving as ever, was Sir Richard Willys.

'I imagine you were surprised to hear from us,' remarked Colonel Villiers when ale had been brought and the pot-boy withdrew.

'Astonished,' agreed Eden. 'Sir William failed to keep our last appointment – which was not unexpected and for which I don't blame him.'

'I'm sure that'll be a relief to him,' muttered Sir Richard.

Villiers ignored this and came directly to the point.

'The recent Parliament proved a disappointment to us in a variety of ways. Since future government will be by Protector and Council, I have been asked to seek your opinion on whether Lambert's views on moderation may now carry more weight ... or indeed any weight at all.'

'I don't believe,' said Eden delicately, 'that I ever named Lambert.'

'You didn't. But logic dictates that the approach couldn't have come from anyone else.'

This, reflected Eden, was unfortunately true. He said, 'With regard to what's likely to happen next, it's too early to say. Certainly, Cromwell has serious concerns about you and your fellows finding common ground with other disaffected parties – in particular those within the Army; concerns which rumours of forthcoming insurrections have naturally strengthened.'

'That's no doing of ours,' snapped Sir Richard.

'Isn't it?' asked Eden, interest mingling with a subtle hint of disbelief.

'No.' Villiers laid a hand on his companion's arm to prevent him speaking. 'There are other forces at work these days. Gentlemen who are determined to take the initiative without sufficient thought to their chances of success or the possible consequences. Rather like the Gerard faction of last year, in fact. It isn't helpful.'

'And would these unhelpful gentlemen be the ones responsible for the consignments of arms, powder and shot leaving London last month?'

'Yes.'

Eden allowed himself a small flicker of hope.

'I have a purely non-professional interest in some of those consignments.'

'Do you?'

'Yes. More specifically, in where they originated and who supplied them.'

Villiers shook his head.

'I can't help you there.'

And wouldn't even if you could? thought Eden cynically. But said only, 'I'll tell the Major-General that you've opened the door to further talks and that you and your colleagues aren't responsible for recent events. As for the other matter ... I appreciate your reluctance to give me the names of anyone who might be able to answer my questions. But perhaps it would help if I said that I don't care who ordered the arms or where they were going or for what purpose. I only want to get my hands on the supplier.' He paused and then added, 'Odd as it may sound, the matter involves a lady's safety.'

Villiers and Willys exchanged glances.

Finally and against all expectation, Willys said, 'You don't need names. Thurloe's already arrested two men who'd have the answers you want. Go and talk to them, why don't you?'

* * *

It didn't take Eden long to find out that the men he needed to speak to were currently lodging in the Tower. Two hours later, he was facing Major Henry Norwood across the meagre width of his cell and offering him a more comfortable stay in return for information.

Norwood shrugged and said cautiously, 'Have you asked Richard Thornhill?'

'I tried. The man's drunk.'

'Yes. He generally is – though it's a mystery how he manages it in here.'

It was a mystery to Eden as well but not one he had any interest in pursuing. He said, 'I'm here purely on my own behalf and will happily give you my word that nothing you tell me will result in repercussions you might find undesirable. I want to trace the fellow who acquired the arms on your behalf. That's all.'

'Your word, you say?'

'Yes.'

'And a few home comforts in return?'

'Again, yes.'

The Major considered it for a moment and then, apparently deciding it could do no harm, said, 'All right. But the truth is that I never had any dealings with the man who got hold of the pistols and neither did Richard. There was a go-between.'

Of course. There bloody would be.

'And who was that?'

'His name is Ellis Brandon. But I doubt you'll find him,' said Norwood, his tone one of pure disgust. 'The minute things started to unravel, we didn't see him for dust. He's probably on the other side of the channel by now.'

'Ellis Brandon,' echoed Eden flatly. *It just had to be him, didn't it?*

'Yes. Going to ground when there's a hint that his hide might be in danger is the only thing he's any good at.'

Eden left Newgate for Westminster and a few private words with his one-time clerk, Mr Hollins, which resulted in two letters being added to the day's outgoing post. One was to an agent still working in Paris; the other was destined for the gentleman currently reporting on the court-in-exile in Cologne. Both gave the same instruction.

Find Sir Ellis Brandon; arrest him and put him on the next boat.

In truth, Eden didn't expect anything to come of it. But it would be stupid, since he had the required connections, not to try.

* * *

February brought a welcome thaw and a few days of less bitter weather. Accompanied by Peter – without whom Henry never let her leave the house – Lydia visited the Loriners' and Haberdashers' Guilds and paid the annual dues. Then, after a couple of hours in Duck Lane going through the order book with Mr Potter, she decided she deserved a little leisure time and debated the various ways in which she might spend it.

Of the many things she might have chosen, the only one that had any appeal was the one she knew she absolutely should not do. She made a mental list of all the reasons why this was so … and then she ignored them and set off for Cheapside.

Luck was on her side. Mr Maxwell was in the shop watching with a critical eye while his assistant added several new pieces to the small display that was always kept on hand during business hours. He grinned easily at Lydia and said, 'This is a pleasant surprise – and very welcome. Our morning thus far has been one of unparalleled dullness.'

'What he means,' murmured Mr Turner gently, 'is that no pretty ladies have wandered in to ogle him yet.'

'The day is young,' retorted Tobias. 'Mistress Neville … allow me to offer you some refreshment.'

'That's very kind but I didn't come … that is I merely called to ask if you're fully recovered now. And to collect a recipe Alice promised me.'

'You mean you don't want to see my wares? That's disappointing. I have a necklace that might have been designed especially for you. However … yes, thank you. I'm fully recovered and fighting fit – though I generally prefer to leave the fighting to Eden because he's better at it and enjoys it more. Not that I suspect he enjoyed his most recent bout very much but the things you like aren't always good for you, are they?' Tobias noticed the way those rather extraordinary silver-blue eyes sharpened and, smiling to himself, sailed blithely on. 'Are you sure you won't join me upstairs for a glass of wine? As you can see, there are no customers and I'm staying out of the workshop for an hour or so. I've set my apprentices a tricky little task – and though they work quicker when I stand over them, they work better when I don't.'

'Well,' said Lydia hesitantly, as if allowing herself to be persuaded, 'if you're sure I'm not interrupting your work …?'

'Not in the least.' He began ushering her up to the parlour. 'Ah. I should probably admit that Eden's not here. It's impossible to keep track of his movements these days.'

Lydia sat down, folded her hands in her lap and, while Mr Maxwell was busy pouring wine, said, 'What did you mean when you said "his most recent bout"?'

Tobias swung round, glass in hand. '*Did* I say that?'

'You know you did.'

He sighed. 'Yes. I was hoping you hadn't noticed. Eden will have my head on a pike.'

'Because I'm not supposed to know about it?'

'He seemed to think that would be best.'

'He *always* seems to think that would be best,' muttered Lydia, almost but not quite beneath her breath. Then, 'Since you've said this much, you might as well tell me the rest. What happened?'

'He took a bit of a battering,' said Tobias rather more cheerfully than Lydia thought was warranted. 'It was ... getting on for a month ago, now. Two or three ruffians set on him in the street one night.' He set the glass of claret at her elbow. 'Nasty business at the time – but no permanent damage.'

Despite the heat of the fire, Lydia felt suddenly rather cold. *Nearly a month ago* would coincide with the three weeks in which Eden hadn't come near her. Gripping her fingers together, she said, '*How* nasty precisely?'

'Cuts and bruises mostly – though the cracked ribs were a bit more serious.' He watched with interest as the colour seeped slowly from her skin and added gently, 'You've seen him quite recently, haven't you? So you know there's nothing to worry about.'

'I'm not worried. I think I'm about to be furious.'

Tobias shook his head, laughing a little. 'He's suffered enough – trust me.'

She fixed him with a stricken but very direct gaze.

'He was attacked because of me, wasn't he? Because he got my women out.'

Having discovered what he'd wanted to know, Tobias decided not to be drawn into even deeper waters.

'You'd better take that point up with Eden. I've already said a good deal more than I should and will be up to my neck in trouble as a result.' He grinned at her again. 'My only consolation is that, when you catch up with him, Eden will be too.'

* * *

'You might want to make yourself scarce for a time when Eden comes in,' suggested Tobias to Nicholas a short while before supper. 'I've something to confess and he's going to rip my head off.'

'Why? What have you done?'

'I've told Lydia Neville about Quinn's fellows knocking the stuffing out of him.'

Nicholas stared at him. 'Why in God's name did you do that?'

'Call it a slip of the tongue.'

'Was it?'

'No. But it's what I'll be telling Eden.'

'Good luck with that,' replied Nicholas dryly. 'Just don't involve me.'

Tobias made up the fire, told Mistress Wilkes to delay supper for half-an-hour or so and poured two glasses of wine. Then he sat down to wait.

Eden came in as he always did, tossing his gloves aside and heading straight for the fire. He said, 'It's sleeting again and the wind's got up. It must be nice to have the kind of job that doesn't necessitate braving the elements on a daily basis.'

'Yes. Well, you know what a tender plant I am.' Tobias handed his brother one of the glasses, indicated the most comfortable chair which was also the one nearest to the fire and said, 'I won't ask if you had a pleasant day because you never do.'

'I've had worse.' Eden sat down, sipped the wine and eyed Tobias over the rim of his glass. 'Why do I get the feeling you're up to something?'

'Your naturally suspicious nature.' Taking the chair on the other side of the hearth, Toby drained half his glass and said, 'I had a visitor today. Lydia Neville.'

'Oh? What did she want?'

You, actually – though of course she didn't admit it.

'I don't think she wanted anything in particular – though she did say something about a recipe from Alice. She didn't stay long. But we talked and one thing led to another the way it does and the upshot was that I did something you won't like.'

Given his brother's spectacular success with women, Eden's immediate assumption made him want to grab Tobias by the throat.

'What, exactly?'

'Not what you're thinking,' came the blunt reply. 'I inadvertently let something slip about recent events. It was hardly anything really. But the lady's like a terrier, isn't she? Once she has her teeth into something she doesn't let go.'

There was a long, uncomfortable silence.

'You told her I was attacked last month?'

'Yes. I'm afraid so. It --'

Slamming his glass down with a force which cracked it, Eden stood up and let fly string of curses, culminating in, 'You thrice-damned bloody interfering fool. Why the sodding hell did you do it?'

'It was an accident. I --'

'Liar. It was no accident. I know you, Toby. You did it deliberately and for some God-knows-what reason of your own.' He shoved a furious hand through his hair. 'Did you ever consider the consequences of telling her something she never needed to know? No. Of course you didn't. You just went wading in the way you always do – indulging in a bit of mischief to pass a dull Tuesday.'

'That's not --'

'I specifically said she wasn't to know. You knew that. I didn't want her told because I knew how she'd react. You, it seems, didn't give a four-penny damn about making her feel as guilty about me as she already felt about you. You just don't bloody *think*!'

'Have you finished?' asked Tobias mildly. 'If so --'

'No. I know you did it on purpose. I'm waiting to hear *why*.'

'All right.' Tobias rose to his full, impressive height and faced his brother impassively. 'If you'll let me finish a sentence, I'll tell you.'

Eden stared back over folded arms. 'Well?'

'I told her because I wanted to find something out.'

'What?'

'I wanted to know how she feels about you. Whether you're just the useful fellow who solves her problems … or something more.'

If he had been angry before, Eden now looked ripe for murder.

'What the *hell* has that to do with you?'

'The way I see it, quite a lot,' returned Tobias, his own gaze turning a lot cooler. 'I don't remember how it was with you and Celia in the beginning because I was rarely there. But I saw your relationship with Deborah clearly enough to know that what's going on now between you and Lydia Neville is very different. You'd bleed to death sooner than admit it, I daresay, but I think you're in love with her in a way that's unlikely to prove transient. Until today, all I've seen is you risking your neck for her and her letting you do it. I decided to find out if there was more than that.'

'I repeat – my relationship with Lydia is none of your business.'

'If you think that, you're being even more dense than usual. It's my business because you're my brother … and I love you.'

To which, of course, there was no answer whatsoever.

* * *

Realising there was no point in putting off the inevitable, the following morning saw Colonel Maxwell being shown into Mistress Neville's parlour.

Lydia looked across at him – for once, not seeming to know what to say. And so, having let an awkward silence linger for a few seconds, Eden said baldly, 'It wasn't your fault. It was mine. If I'd been paying attention, my attackers would never have got as close as they did without me being ready to meet them. Unfortunately, I'd let my mind wander.' *To you, as it happens.* 'Toby should never have told you.'

She shook her head but managed a faint smile.

'He said you'd put his head on a pike.'

'I almost did.'

'How are your ribs?'

'Sore but mending.' He looked at her. 'What else did Toby tell you?'

'Not very much. What did they want? Aside from hurting you, that is?'

'Quinn's ledger; the release of his men from prison; and Stephen's mythical papers. I've given him the first two --'

'Him?' she asked sharply. 'You mean Quinn was there? In person?'

'Yes. The good news is that, in return for the book and his men, he agreed to allow us a little time.' *Most of which has now elapsed, with no progress to show for it.* 'The bad news is that he is unshakeably convinced that these papers exist and that you have them.' He sighed. 'The *really* bad news is that he won't give up.'

Lydia sat very straight, her hands gripped tightly in her lap.

'So what can we do?'

'There's one thing we can try. It should stall Quinn for a while until he figures out that he's been cheated.' *At which point the situation is likely to become a whole lot worse.* 'It would help if we knew what the papers are about. Since we don't, I'll just have to make something up ... and put it into one of Stephen's ciphers. As I said to you, one of them is fiendishly difficult if you don't know what to look for.'

A little colour came back into her face but she said, 'It's a good idea. But buying more time won't solve the problem if we can't find the real papers.'

'I know. But it might enable me to get to Quinn and end this another way.' Eden thought for a moment. 'I'll need Stephen's original coded sheets so I can copy his style of writing.'

'I'll get them.' Lydia stood up and then said hesitantly, 'Is there ... can I help at all?'

He ought to say no. He ought to take the codes and go. Sitting here, working beside her would just brew more temptation and he had to stop that manifesting itself. He drew a long, slightly painful breath and said, 'You could help with the script. That way we can get it done quicker.'

Her smile lit up the room and made the risks worthwhile. Nevertheless, in the short time she was away he dropped his brow on his hand and tried, with no more success than he'd ever done, to make sense of himself.

Lydia returned with everything they needed to begin work, sat down on the opposite side of the table and then said, 'What sort of thing should we write?'

'Since somebody is willing to go to inordinate lengths to get hold of whatever they think Stephen knew, we should assume it's extremely damaging. My guess is that we're dealing with an apparently respectable man who has the kind of dirty secrets which might lead to the pillory, prison – even the noose.' Eden stopped, shaking his head. 'I'm asking you to do the impossible, aren't I?'

'No – though I'll probably need help.' She wrinkled her nose, consideringly. 'Brothels, do you think?'

'Almost certainly.'

'I'll look to you for seedy details, then.'

He couldn't help himself. 'What makes you think I know any?'

'Don't you?'

'More than you, I daresay.'

'That's what I thought,' she said, her tone perfectly matter-of-fact. 'I imagine you'll want to add the seediness later rather than risk shocking me.'

Eden grinned at her.

'Lydia ... I'm no longer sure that shocking you is possible. It's much more likely that I'll be the one to be embarrassed.'

'I know,' she replied calmly. 'So what else has he done?'

'Theft, extortion, fraud; threatening widows, cheating at cards, kicking dogs.'

Lydia shook her head at him and then looked suddenly less cheerful. 'Murder?'

'Yes.'

She fell silent for a moment. Then, 'He's a particularly nasty specimen, isn't he?'

'Indeed. Ridding the world of him would be a public service.' *And, given the chance, I'll do it.* 'Let's make a start. No names or dates that might immediately reveal it isn't what it's supposed to be; and it might be best to set it out like a sort of journal. Since it's the obvious choice, we might as well begin with his fondness for brothels.' He stopped and then, as carelessly as he was able, added, 'Speaking of which ... I should probably admit that my knowledge and experience are several years out of date.'

'Oh.' Lydia's colour rose a little and she busied herself sharpening a quill. 'I don't suppose that matters. Those places probably don't change much.'

They settled down to work, scribbling notes and exchanging ideas. After an hour, Lydia asked Henry to bring refreshments and then, meditatively watching Colonel Maxwell demolish a slice of game pie, said half-regretfully, 'It's a shame our villain gets Quinn to kill people for him. I've always thought poison sounded more interesting.'

Eden managed not to choke on a mouthful of pie. 'Have you now?'

'Yes. I thought about it quite a lot while I was living with Margaret.'

'That's understandable. Forgivable, even.'

Concentrating on the bit of pastry she was crumbling in her fingers, she said, 'Oddly enough, I've never thought about it before ... but you must have killed people.'

'In battle, yes. Not in cold blood. The nearest I came to that was --' He stopped abruptly.

'Was when?' she prompted. And then, looking up and seeing his face, realised that she shouldn't have asked.

Jaw set and frowning down at the knife in his hand, Eden remained silent so long she thought he wasn't going to answer. But finally, his voice tight and cold, he said, 'It was when I found Celia in bed with Hugo Verney ... only an hour or so after having to tell my mother that she was a widow.'

Lydia dragged in a shocked breath. If there were words, she didn't know what they were.

After a moment, he added, 'I'd had no idea about Celia up till then, you see. So I fought Verney with the intention of killing him ... and very nearly did.'

Her throat aching for him, she managed to say, 'Eden ... that wasn't in cold blood. Given the circumstances, most men *would* have killed him. The fact that you didn't says a great deal about you.'

'Perhaps. I don't know.' He stopped, seeming to come back from wherever he'd been. Then he smiled and said, 'That's the first time you've ever used my name.'

'Yes.'

'If I'd known baring my soul would achieve that, I might have tried it before.'

'No. You wouldn't.'

His expression changed to one she couldn't interpret and he said, 'No. Probably not.' Then, returning his attention to the evidence of their labours, 'Shall we continue? There's no saying when Quinn's patience will wear out … so the sooner we have this ready, the better. And Lydia …?'

'Yes?'

'With luck, the next demand will come by letter rather than in person. I hope Quinn will send it to me. If he doesn't and it comes to you, I want to know. Immediately.'

She picked up her quill and reached for the ink-pot.

'Of course. And *vice* very definitely *versa*.'

TWO

The second week of February brought prolonged driving rain. It also brought the long-debated reduction of the Monthly Assessment, the arrest of John Wildman for plotting against the Protectorate and finally, after Secretary Thurloe intercepted letters containing details of an imminent Royalist rising in the City, a direct order from Cromwell for the seizure of every horse in London.

Although aware of all these things, Eden was too busy to dwell on them. Every spare waking minute was devoted to coding the lengthy fiction he and Lydia had devised between them. The encryption itself was complicated; the need to also write it in a fair imitation of Stephen Neville's oddly spiky hand made it laboriously time-consuming. And then there was the fact that in all his years working in the Intelligence Office he had rarely seen a perfectly clean report from any of his agents. There were always scratchings out or corrections. In Eden's view, perfection meant one of two things; either the agent had re-written his report, in which case another copy might conceivably fall into hands other than his own – or the report itself was of suspicious origins. He therefore included a few random crossings-out in his pages and the occasional scrambled word.

It all took hours of burning the midnight oil but eventually he subjected his work to careful scrutiny and decided it would do. He just prayed Quinn didn't have an expert cryptographer on hand because if he did, this whole exercise would prove an immense waste of time.

A brief communication from Lambert informed him that one Daniel O'Neill had been detained at Dover. At their last meeting, the Major-General had been interested but not particularly surprised to learn that a more militant group of Royalists was currently at work. The recent arrests of Sir Humphrey Bennett and Colonel Grey had apparently led him to guess as much. *Now* he pointed out that O'Neill was a Royalist agent of some standing and reputedly Charles Stuart's personal envoy.

Within hours of Lambert's message, Eden received a note from Edward Villiers. The King, said Villiers, had sent Mr O'Neill to act as both mediator and a calming influence; and the rising that the authorities were seemingly convinced would take place February 13th was merely a rumour. With more important things on his mind, Colonel Maxwell re-sealed Villiers' note and sent it on to the Major-General.

On the following evening, walking back to Cheapside through the incessant deluge, Eden became aware that he was being followed. He slowed his steps, loosened his sword in its scabbard and then halted in a darkened doorway, well distant from any narrow alleys.

The footsteps hesitated a short distance away and then resumed. When they arrived at the point where he wanted them, Eden stepped forward, blade in hand.

'Looking for me?' he asked.

The fellow started and then, on seeing the naked sword, backed off.

'Bloody'ell! Ain't no need for that, mister.'

'After last time, you'll pardon my caution. You were following me. Why?'

'Got something for you.' He moved to reach inside his coat and then, with another glance at the sword, thought better of it. 'No need to get twitchy, is there?'

'That would depend on whether you're about to produce a letter or a knife. If it's the latter, I suggest you leave it where it is. I'm not so fond of Quinn that I'll mind despatching another of his minions.'

'Never said Quinn sent me, did I?'

'Since no one else sends fellows skulking after me, you didn't have to. Now ... show me what you're here to deliver.'

Slowly, the man pulled a sealed missive from his coat and held it out.

'See? All above board and no trouble.'

Eden took the letter and shoved it in his pocket.

'Well done. Now go.'

Gratefully, the fellow took to his heels.

Still with his sword in hand, Eden continued on his way.

Back in Cheapside, he read Quinn's note.

Time has run out, Colonel. One of my employees will meet you tomorrow evening an hour after dusk in the churchyard of St Dunstan's in the East. If you fail to appear or arrive empty-handed, the widow will suffer some extremely unfortunate consequences.

Needless to say, it was unsigned.

* * *

Early next morning, Eden paid a fleeting call on Lydia. He said, 'It's set for tonight. The pages are ready but I think we should add a note in your own hand. Something along the lines of this being the only thing you can find that looks as if it might be the document they want – but of course you've been unable to read it. If we get away with this, I don't want to leave Quinn with the idea that you might need silencing.'

'No. I'd rather he didn't think that either.' She wrote what he'd suggested virtually word for word and then said, 'Will I see you after it's done?'

'If you wish. But since I'll simply be handing over the thing they're expecting, there won't be much to tell.'

'All the same,' said Lydia firmly. 'I'd like you to come.'

He understood what she was asking. She wanted to see for herself that he'd come to no harm. The knowledge created a warmth inside him that nothing in the rest of that long, wet and dismal day managed to dispel.

He deliberately arrived at St Dunstan's early and chose his spot; a place that offered the best protection from both the weather and whoever came to meet him. Then he leaned against the wall and waited.

The man who eventually sauntered into view was the same one he'd met the night before. He said breezily, 'Have to stop meeting like this, mister.'

'I'll be more than happy to do so.'

'Ah. Brought something for me, have you?'

Wordlessly, Eden handed over the sealed packet. Quinn's runner stowed it inside his jacket against the rain, raised his hand in a mock salute and walked off back the way he'd come.

It was almost, Eden thought, an anti-climax. Almost ... but not quite.

He found Lydia pacing anxiously back and forth in her parlour.

The moment he came through the door, she half-flew across the room then stopped a couple of steps away, looking him over.

Eden smiled and spread his hands.

'As you can see – wet but undamaged.'

'Thank God,' she said. 'Did the person you met say anything?'

'Nothing of any consequence.'

'So what do we do now?'

'You could offer me a glass of wine and supper,' he suggested.

'No! Well – yes, of course. But I meant --'

'I know what you meant.' He took her hand and led her to a chair. 'You carry on being every bit as careful as before. And you wait.'

'To see what happens next? Yes. I suppose so. And while I'm waiting, what will *you* be doing?'

'The same thing I've been doing since before Yule. I carry on trying to find Quinn – whilst praying that our deception lasts long enough for me to do so. I also pray for more success than I've had so far.'

* * *

Eden had worked on the assumption that, if the deception hadn't worked at all, they'd know very quickly. So when two days had gone by without repercussions, he set Ned Moulton and half a dozen troopers scouring the City for any sign of either Quinn or someone belonging to him. Not unexpectedly, a further three days went by without bringing any result. Nor was there any response from the agents in either Paris or Cologne.

The rain continued and as the Thames gradually started to rise, people began worrying about the possibility of flooding. Eden worried only about how much time he had left before Quinn realised he'd been cheated. He re-emphasised his safety instructions to Henry and Peter as well as to Lydia herself and he told Nicholas to watch out for anything unusual in Duck Lane. He even wrote to Jack Morrell telling him to send Aubrey Durand home at night. It still didn't seem enough but he didn't know what else he could do.

Lydia worried much less than Colonel Maxwell – mainly because two rather vital points had floated by her unnoticed. Unlike the Colonel, she hadn't realised that if and when something happened, it would happen without warning. And she'd also failed to fully understand that, once Quinn knew they'd tried to fool him, his response was likely to be swift and vicious.

So she went about her daily concerns exactly as she always did. She spent time in Duck Lane where business was now flourishing; she found two new outlets for the women's embroidery and trimmings; and she visited the Exchange where she bought lace-trimmed chemises, petticoats threaded through with ribbons and a more than usually pretty corset. At no point during this did she allow herself to think why she was doing it.

She did, however, think a great deal about Eden Maxwell. What he'd said about the day he'd first discovered his wife's infidelity explained a great deal and was probably the missing link that Venetia Brandon had referred to. She wondered why he'd told her and whether his reason was significant. She'd wondered the same thing about those two kisses; the kisses she'd thought he wanted and liked as much as she had but to which he'd never subsequently referred. More than anything else, she wished she knew where, if anywhere, their relationship was going.

She knew where she wanted it to go. She'd known that for a long time. It hadn't needed Venetia to point out that – as a mature woman and a widow – marriage wasn't the only option; that when one finally met the only man one had ever wanted or *would* ever want, half a loaf was definitely better than no bread. The only problem, when one had absolutely no carnal experience, was how to go about getting it.

Lydia suspected that her inexperience was likely to be a stumbling-block in more ways than one. At what point, for example, was she supposed to admit she was a virgin? Before they got as far as the bed? At the crucial moment? She didn't know whether to laugh or cringe at the image that brought to mind. What she *did* know was that afterwards, he wasn't going to need telling ... and letting him find out for himself might not be the best idea.

And so the days went by while the rain continued to fall. In Duck Lane, Mr Potter said the level of the Fleet had risen sufficiently to put the cellar floor under a couple of inches of water.

'And it'll likely get worse pretty quick now it's started,' he said gloomily. 'Even if the rain lets up, the water's got nowhere else to go.'

As a result of this conversation, Lydia wasn't as surprised as she might otherwise have been when one of the street boys who earned the odd coin running errands and delivering messages appeared at the door with the news that there was a problem in Duck Lane her head-man thought she ought to see.

'What problem?' asked Lydia. 'It's Sunday. No one should be working.'

'Dunno about that, Miss. 'E just said to bring you word – and I brung it.'

She dropped a groat into the outstretched palm and the child took off like a bullet. Turning to Henry, she said, 'I'd better go. Tell Peter I'll need him, will you?'

'Perhaps, Madam, it might be better to have Peter ascertain what this problem is?' Henry suggested. 'It's already dark outside and Colonel Maxwell's instructions regarding your safety were very explicit.'

'I know. But Mr Potter has been concerned about the cellar and it's more than likely he went in this afternoon to check and found it had got worse. The premises are my responsibility, not his – so I'll have to go.' She smiled, noting his obvious concern. 'If I'm not back by supper, send word to the Colonel … but I should be home long before then.'

Outside, the rain had slackened to a light drizzle but the streets were running with water in which floated all kinds of assorted filth. Lydia clutched her hood in one hand and her skirts in the other as she tried to avoid the worst puddles. Nevertheless, by the time she reached Duck Lane her feet and hem were completely sodden.

There were lights inside and the door was unlocked. Pushing it open and realising Peter was even wetter than she was, Lydia said, 'I'm sorry to drag you out like this. If you'd like to leave me here for an hour and go to get warm in the tavern --'

And that was as far as she got before hands grabbed her and something heavy and evil-smelling was cast over her head. An involuntary scream tore from her throat, only to be abruptly cut off as an arm was clamped about her waist, trapping her inside her cloak and driving the breath from her body. Shocked, blind and disorientated, she felt herself being dragged into the workshop, whilst from somewhere behind her came a rapid series of dull thuds and grunts.

She tried to call Peter's name but all that came out was a strangled whisper.

Someone spoke, his voice muffled by the thing over her head.

'Take her cloak, tie her hands and put her there.'

Hands were at her throat, yanking loose the ties of her cloak. Instinct made her twist violently, trying to get free. The fellow holding her merely laughed ... and her cloak dropped to the floor, leaving her feeling as vulnerable as if she'd been stripped naked. Fear turned into sheer panic, drying her mouth and sending her heart pounding so hard she thought she was going to faint. She froze into absolute stillness, fighting to breathe and stay conscious. Her arms were hauled behind her back and her wrists swiftly tied with some kind of twine that bit into her flesh. Then someone shoved her down on a stool.

'Good,' said the voice. 'Bring me a lock of her hair. There are shears on that bench. Do *not* remove the hood.'

The thing over her head pressed against her face as unseen hands fumbled at her hair, randomly pulling out pins until it tumbled down her back. Lydia's breath came in rapid little gasps. The blindness was beginning to terrify her more than anything else, making her want to scream and go on screaming. She didn't. She sat, huddled and still as any trapped animal while the scissors sliced through her hair.

All around her was silence. Then the voice spoke again.

'Take that and go. You know what to do.'

'Aye. All's in place, just as you ordered.'

'Of course. Should anything have been over-looked, I shall be ... displeased.' There was a pause, then, 'And now, Mistress Neville, you and I will have a little talk.'

Lydia tried to moisten her mouth so she could speak. She said, 'Who are you? What have you d-done with Peter?'

'Your guard-dog is still breathing. How long he continues to do so rather depends on you. And so far you've been extremely stupid. Did you really expect that farrago of nonsense to deceive me for long?'

'I d-don't know what you mean.'

'Don't be tiresome, Mistress Neville. You have already put me to the considerable inconvenience of finding a man capable of de-coding the sheets you sent me ... not to mention the time it then took him to decipher enough to reveal their utter uselessness. You would be wise not to try my patience any further.'

'I didn't m-mean to try it at all or – or to deceive you.'

'And yet you have done both.'

'I don't know what you want!' she cried desperately. 'I've searched everywhere a dozen t-times and eventually f-found those sheets hidden inside the cover of an old l-ledger. I thought ... they were in code and I couldn't read them, so I thought they must be what you wanted. If they're n-not --'

'They are most definitely not.'

'Then I don't *have* the thing you want!'

'I am very sure you do.'

'No! Please – I don't even know what I'm supposed to be looking for. I've been through all Stephen's papers at home and at the pewtery. The lawyer doesn't have --'

'I'm aware of that. I searched his office myself.'

The hood was beginning to stifle her and her face felt wet.

'If I'd found what you want, you could have it. But I *d-don't!*'

The owner of the voice sighed.

'This is not getting us anywhere, is it?'

'Because I can't help you! Why won't you *believe* me? Do you think I'd have let it get this far if I could have stopped it?'

'Perhaps. Perhaps not. We'll see what happens when Colonel Maxwell arrives.' A note in the smooth voice conveyed cold and implacable anticipation and a deliberate pause gave time for his words to sink in. 'He should be here soon.'

* * *

When Quinn's note arrived, Eden was alone in the house but for Mistress Wilkes and the kitchen-maid. Tobias had an engagement with his latest *innamorata* and Nicholas was supping in the Lamb and Flag with Troopers Collis and Buxton.

Since there was no superscription, Eden had no warning of what lay ahead. He merely broke the seal, opened up the page and then stopped breathing when a lock of soft, dark brown hair fell on to his lap. Ice invaded his veins and shock made his fingers clumsy as he reached down to pick it up. Forcing his lungs to start functioning again, he read the words.

Come to Duck Lane and come alone. I have watchers posted everywhere. One sign of Militia; one sign that you are being followed by a man who is not mine and the next thing I cut will not be the lady's hair.

Equal parts of murderous rage and mind-numbing fear darkened Eden's vision for a moment until he willed them away in order to make his brain function properly. He couldn't – wouldn't – risk Lydia. He had to do as Quinn said or at least *appear* to do so. Was there a way around that? Could he summon help to arrive once he was already in the lorinery? Not if someone was watching the house; and, in any case, who could he send? Alice? Hardly. And if he left the note for either Tobias or Nicholas to find – what then? It was only a little past six o'clock so Nicholas wouldn't be back for hours and Tobias might not come home at all. Also, what would that achieve other than possibly getting them both killed? Two men couldn't help him now. He needed a bloody army.

Thinking furiously, he threw on his coat, then took the stairs two at a time to his chamber. No point in taking sword or pistol. They'd disarm him – though perhaps not completely. Where was his damned knife? He found it lying at the back of the closet and slipped it into his boot. What else? A much smaller blade used for sharpening quills lay on the table. He spent precious minutes inserting it into the lining of his jacket beneath his collar, all the time racking his brains for some other preparation that might help. Five minutes later, unable to think of anything else he could do, he ran back downstairs and out of the house.

Outside the pools of light cast by the lanterns over-hanging doorways, the street was black as sin. Eden didn't stop to find out if someone was following him. He knew they would be. He tore along Cheapside, swerved into St Martin's Lane and then raced the length of Duck Lane in the direction of the Holborn Conduit. Then, with the lorinery in front of him, he stopped to gather both his breath and his wits before he shoved the door wide and walked inside.

The first thing he saw was Peter – bound, gagged and barely conscious – lying a couple of yards from where he himself stood. The second thing was Lydia ... and the sight of her made his heart stop for a second.

She was sitting on a stool, her hands presumably tied behind her and a thick hessian bag over her bowed head, below which her hair spilled out in wild disorder. No one was near her – though Eden was aware of a number of men standing idle around the edges of the room. She looked small and helpless and alarmingly fragile. Eden couldn't allow himself to think just how terrified she must be. Instead, he turned to look at Quinn.

'Well?' he snapped. And in a tone any of his troopers would have recognised, 'What the hell do you think you're doing?'

Lydia's head came up and she said, 'Eden?' Her voice was little more than a strained whisper. 'Is that you?'

'Yes. I'm here. Have they hurt you?'

'No.'

Someone materialised behind Eden, breathing heavily but managing to say, 'Ran all the way here, he did. Had a ... job keeping up.'

'So I see,' said Quinn coolly. Then, 'Hatcher, Repton ... check that the Colonel has not been followed and, assuming that he has not, tell the men to remain at their stations for a further hour. Rooster ... disarm our guest but don't hurt him. I want him fully functional for the time being.' The empty dark gaze encompassed Eden. 'I hope you have not been stupid enough to disobey my instructions, Colonel.' A snap of his fingers sent one of his men to stand behind Lydia, toying suggestively with a slender knife. 'I'm sure you wouldn't wish the lady to suffer for your mistakes.'

Eden made himself remain perfectly still while the big Scotsman checked his pockets and body for firearms. Then, in the hope of retaining his coat and his boots, he said, 'I'm here and no one will follow me. Now let Mistress Neville go. You don't need her.'

'I disagree.'

'Then for God's sake, at least get that bloody thing off her head!'

'In the event that she survives the night – which as yet is by no means certain – that bloody thing on her head, as you so eloquently put it, is there for her own protection.' An almost imperceptible gesture brought one of his men forward. 'Tie his hands.'

Eden instantly swung round and slammed his elbow into the fellow's throat, causing him to double up retching.

'That was foolish. Rooster ... give the Colonel a lesson in manners, then restrain him.'

Without any warning, Rooster smashed one fist into Eden's face and the other into his stomach. Then, before Eden could recover, his arms were wrenched behind him and held there in a vice-like grip while the other man lashed his wrists together.

Hearing both the blows and Eden's grunt of pain, Lydia cried, 'Stop it! I'm sorry you didn't get what you wanted but hurting him won't help!'

'That is a matter of opinion,' said Quinn, his tone verging on boredom. 'Rooster ... again.'

Two more blows which, being expected, Eden managed to make marginally less painful.

'*Don't!*' Lydia stood up but was rammed back down by the unseen hands behind her.

'There's an easy way to make this stop, Mistress Neville. Give me what I want.'

'I *can't!*'

'I remain unconvinced. Again.'

This time the blow landed on Eden's barely-healed ribs and he had to clamp his teeth together so Lydia wouldn't know how badly it hurt. Quinn, of course, noticed.

He said wearily, 'Very heroic, Colonel. Let us see if you can remain silent while Rubens carves patterns on your chest.'

Lydia gave a small, sobbing gasp. Without removing his eyes from Eden, Quinn said, 'He's quite the artist, Mistress Neville – hence the name. Perhaps I should give you time to reflect on that. Chaff ... put her below.'

The fellow with the knife grinned and hauled Lydia to her feet but the man leaning against the cellar door said, 'Down there, Mr Quinn? There's a good foot of water now – and it's rising.'

'So? She won't drown, will she?' came the careless reply. Then, to Chaff, 'Once she is inside, you may remove the hood but leave her hands bound.'

Eden didn't like the sound of that. But then he didn't like her sitting here, blind and frightened, with a knife-happy killer standing at her shoulder either. He said quickly, 'It's all right, Lydia. Stay on the stairs. And don't worry.'

Most of Quinn's men sniggered. As always, Quinn's own expression remained unchanged. He waited until the cellar door was bolted behind Lydia and then said, 'I am going to enjoy watching my employees hurt you, Colonel. You damned yourself when you tried to cheat me with those forged pages.'

'What the hell is it with you, Quinn?' demanded Eden savagely. 'Are you deaf or so completely bone-headed that you don't recognise the truth when you hear it?'

An indrawn breath echoed around the workshop.

'Again?' asked the Rooster hopefully.

'Presently. First – while he is still able to speak – I want to hear Colonel Maxwell admit what he did.'

'Admit what? The pages I gave you were so well-hidden it took Lydia weeks to find them. They were also in Neville's own hand and in codes he'd devised himself; so, in the absence of anything else, it was reasonable to assume they contained the information you were looking for. It's hardly the fault of either Lydia or myself that they didn't.'

'But you *knew* they didn't.' For the first time, Quinn moved and strolled across the intervening space to look Eden in the eye from no more than two steps away. 'The gentleman I persuaded to decipher them is a former colleague of yours from the Intelligence Office and he was most informative. He couldn't identify the hand-writing as yours but he was very definite about your ability to construct those pages.'

This was a blow Eden hadn't expected and it was a bad one but he shrugged it off.

'It's true that, given time, I *could* have done it. But time was in short supply – which is why I didn't waste it breaking the codes. Since I've no more idea what was on those sheets than I have of what the ones you want contain – how the hell was I supposed to know they were wrong?' He drew a steadying breath and tried to stop his mind racing. 'If I had the bloody papers, you could have them with my blessing the second you let Lydia walk safely out of here. But I don't have them and neither does she. Sooner or later you're going to have to recognise that you're asking the impossible. Meanwhile you're clutching at straws, Quinn – and dangerous straws, at that. If anything happens to Lydia or me, there are plenty of people who will know in which direction to look.'

'Don't threaten me, Colonel. It is unproductive.'

'I wasn't. I'm giving you good advice. And for what it's worth, here's some more. If these papers exist at all – and, personally, I'm beginning to doubt it – there's only one place they might possibly be. The same place, unless I'm completely mistaken, that you've been targeting since this whole mess began. Right here in the lorinery.'

Nothing shifted in the cold, expressionless face.

'Do you think I haven't looked?'

'How the hell would I know what you've done? At a guess, you suspected they were here and tried to drive Lydia out of business so that you could take the place apart brick by brick if you had to. But you made the mistake of thinking you were dealing with a meek little widow ... and instead you found yourself up against a woman with steel in her spine and a personal crusade. If your thrice-damned papers are anywhere, they're here. So if you've already searched the place, either you missed something or you're chasing a myth.' Eden paused and then, both eyes and voice expressing derision, 'If you still think beating me to a pulp is going to provide what you want, then do it. I can't stop you. But if I was you I'd be praying that Neville didn't bury his secrets under the cellar floor.'

THREE

Sick with terror, Lydia sat on the stairs, three steps from the top and strained her ears for any sounds that might tell her what was happening. She heard nothing; just the echo of that spine-chillingly calm voice saying, *"Let's see if you can remain silent while Rubens carves patterns on your chest."*

Horror welled up inside her until she thought she might vomit.

He won't do it, ran the refrain in her head. *It was just a threat – a vile threat to frighten me. He won't actually do it. Oh God, oh God –* please *don't let him do it.* And then, *This is my fault. If I'd stayed at home, none of this would be happening.*

It was a relief to be free of the hood, but the cellar was nearly as dark. The only light came from beneath the door at the top of the stairs behind her. She couldn't see the water but smell and faint sounds told her it was there. The man had said it was over a foot deep. That meant it must be above the bottom step ... maybe nearly at the second one. Since she'd never actually been in the cellar before, she didn't know how many steps there were and therefore how long it might be before the water reached her feet. Eden had been down here, she recalled. He'd probably know. But Eden wasn't here now. He was upstairs suffering God knew what.

Don't think of it. If you let yourself imagine it you'll go to pieces completely and that isn't going to help. Think about whether there's any way to get out of here. There might be one of those trap-doors to the street. Lots of cellars have them for taking in coal and such-like. If there is and if I could find it ...

But finding it meant descending the stairs and braving the water when she was already shivering with cold. And in the dark, with her hands tied behind her how was she going to find anything? The thought brought the blackness tightening around her. Panic crept several steps closer, closing her throat. She pushed it back and forced herself to take slow, calming breaths. She could feel her fingers going numb so she concentrated on clenching and unclenching them to restore the circulation, doing her best not to cause the twine on her wrists to tighten any further as she did so.

Time passed. She didn't know how long – only that the cold was seeping so deep into her bones that she was literally shaking with it. She refused to recognise that terror of what might be happening over her head was worse than the cold, the dark and the rising water all put together. From time to time, she felt a scream forming inside her chest; a scream she didn't dare let out because she suspected that if she once started, she might not stop.

When the door opened, releasing a sudden stream of light, she nearly jumped out of her skin. The next second, Eden was shoved through it with a force that would have sent him down on top of her if he hadn't managed to right himself in time. Then the door slammed shut again, leaving her temporarily blinded.

'Eden,' she said, teeth chattering with cold and shock. She tried to stand up but her knees refused to co-operate. 'Oh God ... Eden. What d-did they do? Have they hurt you?'

'No. Stay still while I feel my way down to you. I can't see a damned thing.'

'It's too dark to see m-much anyway.' The tears she'd been holding back through all this horrible time of waiting started to slide, silent and unchecked, down her cheeks. For the first time, she was grateful for the darkness that hid them from him. 'I'm so glad you're here. Are you sure you're n-not hurt?'

'Yes. I'm sure.' Eden lowered himself to the step above hers, his knee against her shoulder. He knew she needed comfort but, at present, that couldn't be his priority. His voice low and rapid, he said, 'Listen to me. I don't know how much time we have and we're going to need every second of it if we're to have any chance of getting out of here. They haven't finished with us yet. Aside from four fellows left in the workshop, Quinn's got the rest of them dismantling the top floor and the attics but if they don't find what they're looking for, you and I will be in for a lot worse than happened earlier. How high is the water?'

'I d-don't know.'

'Well, we'll have to find out. But the first thing is to get our hands free. Slide over to the wall. I want to squeeze past you.'

It was an awkward manoeuvre but as soon as it was accomplished, Eden said, 'Good. I'm going to lower myself one more step and you're going to twist so that your back is to me. Yes – that's it. Try to touch me.' Icy hands bumped clumsily against his face. 'God. You're freezing. Can you feel your fingers?'

'N-not very well,' she admitted.

'You're going to need to use them. Put them against my mouth.'

Lydia did as he suggested and felt his breath on her skin ... hot and vital. She nearly groaned with the relief it brought. After a minute or two, he leaned back and said, 'Better?'

'Yes. I think so.'

'Then feel your way down to my left shoulder.' Although he knew that it would be easier to reach the knife in his boot, circumstances made the smaller blade more suited to the task. 'There's a small pen-knife in the lining of my coat about a hand-span from my throat. The tip of the handle is protruding slightly so you should be able to find it. When you do, pull it out – and for God's sake, don't drop it.'

Lydia gritted her teeth and tried to follow his instructions. He'd made it sound easy. Instead, it was immensely difficult and seemed to take forever; but eventually she located the rounded end of the bone handle and slowly, gradually she slid the little knife free.

'Got it,' she said.

Eden turned his back on her and hoisted himself up a step.

'Saw through the bonds on my wrists.'

'I can't. I'll cut you.'

'That doesn't matter. Getting my hands free does. Do it.'

Lydia's first attempt to use the blade met empty air and the second one, the back of Eden's hand.

'I'm sorry – I'm sorry.'

'You're wasting time. Try again.' And when she made a more successful attempt, 'Yes – there. Well done. Now keep going.' When the point of the blade nicked the side of his palm, he kept the fact to himself; and again when she scraped the inside of his wrist. And when the rope finally started to slacken he said, 'Stop. I can break it.'

As the rope gave way a huge weight fell from Eden's shoulders. They weren't out of trouble by any means but at least they now had a fighting chance. He turned, told Lydia to stay quite still and to give him the knife. Two minutes later, her hands were free as well.

Shoving the blade back roughly where it had come from, he hauled off his coat and gave it to her. Then, rising to pull up the tops of his boots, 'Put that on and stay where you are. I'm going to try opening the old coal-chute.'

'I wasn't sure there was one.'

'There is – but the bolts are probably corroded to hell. Still ... we'll see.' As he set off down the stairs a series of bangs and thuds came from somewhere far above. 'Good. The din they're making should cover any noises of ours. Ah. Here's the water.'

It was almost at the third step. By the time Eden reached the cellar floor, the level was just below his knees. He waded across to the far wall and started hunting by touch for the old double wooden doors and the bolt that held them. He tried to remember what he'd seen when he'd been down here before and wished he'd paid more attention. Then his fingers encountered metal. One of the hinges and, exactly as he'd feared, it was heavily encrusted with rust. The heavy foot-long bolt, when he found it, was worse.

This, he thought grimly, *isn't going to be easy.*

Exerting all his strength, he tried shifting it with his hands. It wouldn't budge.

Hell. I wish I could see what I'm doing.

He tried again, this time attempting to twist the head of the bolt to loosen it. After a few moments he thought he detected a hint of movement. Encouraged, he drew a bracing breath and re-doubled his efforts. Yes. The thing was definitely beginning to turn.

Her voice disembodied in the blackness, Lydia said, 'What are you doing?'

'Struggling,' grunted Eden.

'Can I help?'

'Yes.' He continued trying to force the thing to swivel in its brackets. 'Stop ... asking ... questions.'

Lydia huddled deeper into the warmth of his coat and fell obediently silent.

Finally, squealing in protest, the bolt showed signs of co-operating. Eden lowered his arms and gave himself a brief respite. Then he tried again. He managed to move it an inch before it stuck.

I'm never going to do it like this. I don't have the time.

He investigated with his fingers, seeking out the worst of the corrosion and finding it beside the right-hand bracket. Pulling the knife from his boot, he set grimly about hacking at those parts he thought were causing the problem. Flakes of rust rained down on his face and hair. He tried the bolt again, still to no avail. Wondering if he might have more success with the bracket itself, he inserted the knife-point and used it as leverage. Despite the fact that the cold was seeping through his boots to his feet, sweat was beginning to bead his face and neck. He heaved as hard as he could, thanking God that the blade was sturdy. One side of the bracket started to yield.

Yes! Another massive heave. *Come on, you bastard. Give way.*

The thing groaned and fell loose in another shower of rust. Eden jammed the knife above the bolt and levered downwards so that it strained on the other bracket. Then, as soon as the gap became viable, he shoved the knife back in his boot and grasped the bolt with his hands and hung on it, using the whole weight of his body. For a moment or two he didn't think it was going to work. Then, without warning, the remaining bracket came away from its moorings and the bolt fell loose into his hands.

Thank you, God.

The chute door, however, remained stubbornly closed.

Eden tossed the bolt aside and, raising his arms, began trying to weaken the point where the two parts of the door met with a series of hard, rapid pushes. His shoulders began to ache with the strain but he didn't stop. Finally, just when he was beginning to despair, the thing gave one tremendous creak ... and dropped open, narrowly missing his head.

Light. Not much, it was true ... but shadowy light from a lantern outside. Eden didn't think he'd ever seen a more welcome sight.

'You did it,' said Lydia, her voice unsteady and almost awestruck. 'You really did it.'

'Yes.' His breathing was laboured and he'd have liked to rest just for a moment – but he didn't dare. 'Time for you to get wet. But first, take off your petticoats.'

'What?'

'Just do it!' he snapped. 'I'm going to have to lift you out of here and I don't need the added weight of a dozen ells of wet cambric. Get rid of them. Now. And come down here.'

Lydia hoisted her skirts and fumbled clumsily for the tapes of her petticoats. Then, stepping out of them, she kicked them to one side, held her dress up about her knees and prepared to walk down into the water.

'Oh!' The first shock of it took her breath. 'It's freezing!'

Eden didn't answer. He was already hoisting himself up awkwardly through the chute, his arms and shoulders screaming with the effort. Once he had his torso out, he scrambled over the top into a crouch and looked around, hoping against hope Quinn hadn't left any of his men on this side of the building.

He hadn't. The lane was silent and deserted. Wasting no time, Eden got on his knees and bent double to lower his upper body back into the cellar. He reached down towards Lydia, saying, 'Take my wrists and hold on.' Her hands found his and he wrapped his fingers round her forearms. 'Ready? Now!'

Lydia found herself hauled out of the water in one violent tug and then, more gradually, pulled up and forwards over the ledge until she was almost nose to nose with Eden. One final heave had her rolling with him away from the chute.

For a second, they both lay there breathing hard. Then Eden pushed to his feet, snatched the knife from his boot and, grabbing her arm, said quietly, 'Up. We need to move fast – the other way through Newgate Market. Let's go.'

He set a smart pace which had Lydia, still clutching her dripping skirts in one hand, half-running to keep up. He didn't speak so neither did she. Silently, they fled past the church of Saint Sepulchre ... past Pie Corner and down the northern edge of the market. When they got to the top of Old Change, Eden pushed her into a doorway and said, 'Wait. I want to see if the house is being watched.' And he left her.

Having been too concerned with running, Lydia hadn't so far given any thought about where they were running *to*. Now, she realised he was taking her to his home rather than hers.

When Eden returned, she said, 'Cheapside?'

'Yes. It's nearer. Come on.'

The door was unlocked – a fact that left Eden both annoyed and grateful. Pulling Lydia inside, he bolted it behind him and then shouted for the housekeeper.

Alice appeared, hands on hips. 'I'm not deaf, Colonel.' Then, taking in the state of the pair of them, 'Not *again*. What *this* time?'

'Later,' said Eden, retrieving his coat from Lydia. 'The lady needs a hot bath and dry clothes. Use my room until there's a fire lit in the spare bedchamber – and leave the water. I'll need it later. Are either Toby or Nick back yet?'

'Both of them,' said Alice. She took a hasty step back so the Colonel could take the stairs two at a time ahead of her. Then, shepherding Lydia in his wake, she muttered, 'Whatever next? These men! I never saw the like.'

Eden shot into the parlour and without bothering to explain, said, 'Get your boots on and load every pistol we have. I need you.'

* * *

Lydia, meanwhile, found herself summarily stripped of her wet clothes and wrapped in a voluminous chamber-robe while Alice and the kitchen-maid toiled back and forth with pails of hot water. The bath, when she finally sank into it, felt utterly blissful. For a little while she allowed herself to stop thinking and merely gave herself up to warmth and comfort.

Of course, the bliss didn't last.

Peter! How could I forget about Peter?

Abruptly, she sat up in the water, dislodging her hair which had been left hanging over the rim of the tub. But before she could get out, Alice walked in with a steaming mug and said, 'Whatever are you doing, Mistress Neville? Stay where you are and drink this.'

Lydia shook her head. 'I can't. I have to speak to Colonel Maxwell.'

'Well, you can't. He's gone out again. All three of them have.'

'Gone out? Where?'

'How would *I* know? No one ever tells me anything. They just come back trailing muddy footprints over my floors and, often as not, bleeding as well.' She pushed the mug into Lydia's hands. 'It's hot spiced wine. Drink it. You coming down with a fever won't help anybody.' She waited until she saw Lydia take an obedient sip. 'Good. Stay there and finish it. The towels are here and your shift is airing by the fire but you'll have to put my wrap back on because I've got your gown drying downstairs – not that it's ever going to be the same again. Then, when you're ready, there's a fire lit in the next room so the Colonel can clean himself up in here when he gets back.' She paused, looking into the white, strained face and added more gently 'Whatever happened is over.'

'It isn't,' said Lydia miserably. And thought, *It isn't and he's gone back there. If they catch him again, they'll kill him.*

Later, with her hair still damp and Mistress Wilkes' wrapper over her shift, she left Eden's bedchamber for the one next to it and settled down to wait. Her thoughts were unpleasant companions, sending her mind scrambling back and forth and arriving over and over again at a single inescapable conclusion. Those horrible hours in Duck Lane were entirely her fault. And if something happened to Eden or the others now ... that would be her fault, too.

By the time an hour had passed she was becoming frantic.

Where is he? Why doesn't he come back? What is happening?

Minutes continued ticking silently by with maddening slowness. Alice returned with a tray of food. Lydia thanked her politely and, as soon as she was alone again, set it to one side, inwardly shuddering. Unable to sit still any longer, she took to pacing up and down the room, half-tripping every now and then over the too-long robe. Finally, just when she thought she couldn't stand it any longer, she heard voices and footsteps on the stairs. Wrenching open the door, she came face to face with Eden and said, 'Oh thank God! I thought – I thought --'

'Yes. But do you mind if we leave this until I've at least put on a clean shirt?' he replied tersely. 'Go back to the fire. I'll join you presently.'

And he walked away into his own room, leaving her staring after him.

The shock of relief almost overwhelmed her. Then, as five minutes became ten and ten, fifteen, she grew agitated again ... and from there, illogically angry with him for putting himself at risk a second time.

The result was that by the time, Eden – clean and in fresh clothes – rapped brusquely at her door and walked in, Lydia was beyond rational thought. She threw herself at him, stumbled over the robe and fell into his chest to pound at him with her fists.

'You went back, didn't you? *Didn't* you? You went back – knowing they might *kill* you.'

He caught her wrists and held them still.

'Of course I went back. What *else* was I going to do? Did you want me to leave Peter trussed up on the bloody floor?'

'I – no. But --'

'I didn't think so.' He gave her a little shake. 'If you'll sit down, I'll tell you.'

Lydia subsided back into her chair. Her face was wet and she dabbed surreptitiously at it with her sleeve. 'I'm sorry – I'm sorry. I was just so worried.'

'So I see.' His glance took in the untouched tray. 'You should eat something.'

'I can't.'

'Well, I can.' He picked up a plate of bread and cold meat and carried it over to the stool by the hearth. 'I went back with Toby and Nick – and we met Aubrey by the gate. Henry had sent him in search of you. By that time, Quinn and his entourage had gone – though whether he'd found what he was looking for is debatable. At any rate, they'd left Peter where he was, every door unlocked and an unholy mess upstairs.' He took a bite of ham, chewed and swallowed. 'Potter and the rest of them will have their work cut out tomorrow.'

Lydia stared, watching him eat. She said, 'How can you be so calm?'

'*One* of us should be, don't you think?'

She shook her head.

'I don't understand how you can just sit there eating as if nothing had happened.'

Eden demolished another mouthful.

'I'm hungry. And even if I had the energy to lose my temper – which I don't – it wouldn't do much good, would it? What's done is done.'

She caught a hard, gleaming look and swallowed, recognising the justice of it.

'Yes. I know … I'm aware it was all my fault and I'm sorry.'

'Good. Perhaps next time you'll think first.'

'Yes.'

Without appearing to do so, Eden absorbed her bent head and tightly-clasped fingers. He saw the hair tumbling wildly down her back over the awful green thing that half-buried her and her bare toes peeping out from under its hem. She well and truly deserved the rough edge of his tongue … but he hadn't the heart to inflict any more distress on her, so he said, 'Cheer up. We got out of it with whole skins – more or less, anyway. And you did well when it mattered.'

'Oh.' She looked up. 'I did?'

'Yes. You followed orders and managed not to have hysterics. I was grateful for that.'

There was a long silence, during which Eden carried on with his meal. Finally, Lydia said, 'I don't know what to say to you. Thank you doesn't seem enough.'

'It will do.' He rose and returned his empty plate to the tray. 'Peter went back with Aubrey and they'll tell Henry you'll be staying here tonight.'

Lydia also came awkwardly to her feet.

'I could go home once my gown is dry.'

'You could. But since there is no way on God's earth that I am going out again tonight, you won't,' he replied pleasantly. 'I see that Alice has made up the bed for you.'

'Yes.'

Suddenly the room seemed inexplicably warmer and smaller than it had a minute ago.

Lydia summoned what was left of her courage and walked over to lay a hand on his arm.

'Thank you,' she said softly.

She reached up to place a brief kiss on his jaw ... and somehow managed to brush his lips instead. Eden remained perfectly still, his eyes locked with hers.

He realised that, after the hellish evening they'd both had, he shouldn't be thinking what he was thinking ... but, equally, he knew exactly why he *was* thinking it. Not because she was standing so close that the faint elusive scent of lavender was clouding his reason or even because they were alone and, although decently covered, he suspected she wasn't wearing a great deal. No. This was more – so very much more – than simple lust. Indeed, if he was honest with himself, this moment had been inevitable for a long time. Perhaps, he thought distantly, it was time to surrender to it. He was still wondering that when he heard himself murmur, 'Is that all my heroics deserve?'

Her breath snared. 'No. But I – I wouldn't want to embarrass you. Or myself.'

That sounded like an invitation. He decided to take it as one.

His drew her up against him and said, 'You won't. But you're welcome to try.'

And then his mouth came down on hers.

FOUR

In the space of an instant Eden stopped thinking about what was wise and sensible ... what he should or should not do. In fact, he stopped thinking about anything at all. Miraculously, his shoulders – sore and aching from his earlier activities – seemed to stop hurting; or if they hadn't, he was no longer aware of it. All he knew was the intoxicating sweetness of her mouth and the fact that, beneath the green wrapper, the body pressed against his own was wearing little or nothing; that every lovely slender curve was there within reach, awaiting the discovery of his hands. And the knowledge was enough to drive out any possibility of sensible thought ... or, indeed, anything at all.

He began with the slight indentation of her spine; that indomitable spine that was at the core of everything she was but which felt so fragile beneath his fingertips.

The merest ghost of a thought drifted by.

So delicate ... so soft and pliant; and yet I've known men with less resilience.

He moved on to the line of her waist and hip, pressing lightly against her pelvis with his thumb whilst teasing her mouth with his own. She trembled a little, clutching the front of his shirt. Fisting one hand in the thick mass of her hair, he released her mouth in favour of her throat. Immediately she let her head fall back in invitation. Eden took advantage of the offer. He nipped and tasted his way down to the vulnerable place where her neck met her shoulder and, feeling her fingers tangling in his hair, loitered there. Then, gathering her closer, he kissed her again and encouraged the wrapper to slide from one shoulder so that he could trace her collar-bone beneath that warm, soft skin.

Lydia explored the muscles of his shoulders and back; she kissed his throat and jaw, wanting to take as much – to give as much – as these brief, transient moments allowed.

He'll stop. It will be like before. Any minute now, he'll end it. But please ... not quite yet. Please ... this time give me just a little longer.

His hand in the small of her back encouraged her to press even closer. Heat sped through her veins and odd little pulses of sensation flicked along her nerves. When he pushed the wrapper aside, she instinctively shrugged so that it slipped a bit further and sensed rather than saw his smile. He murmured, 'This garment belongs to Alice?'

'Yes.'

'It's horrible.'

'I know.' Her face hidden against his neck, she said, 'I could take it off. Or you could.'

For a moment, he said nothing. Then, as if the words were being wrenched from him, he said, 'I could. But first you should consider where that would be leading us ... and whether it is somewhere you want to go.'

Unable to believe he seemed to be offering what she so badly wanted, she whispered, 'I have. And it is.'

Eden took a moment to control the surge of exultation that surged through him. Then he kissed her with a sort of fierce hunger and managed to send Alice's despised wrapper slithering to the floor. Wasting no time, his hand blazed a slow lingering trail from shoulder to waist, skimming her breast through the flimsy lawn chemise and sending a new pleasure streaking through her. Lydia gasped and clung.

He felt so good ... so *right*; but his shirt was in the way. Her hands tingled with the need to touch his skin, so she tugged impatiently at the annoying thing until Eden realised what she wanted and pulled it off over his head.

'Oh.'

She slid her palms over and over warm firm flesh and its underlying muscle. There were a few old scars ... as old, perhaps, as the one on his cheek ... and some bruising still showed from the more recent injury to his ribs. Lydia stroked that gently before linking her arms about his waist and laying her mouth against a scar on his shoulder.

Eden drew a sharp breath, causing her to look up at him in sudden doubt.

'I'm sorry. Should I not do that?'

'Yes. Oh yes. You most certainly should.'

He gazed into her eyes for a moment longer, wondering if he should ask just once more if she was sure and then realising, from her expression that it was unnecessary. He'd been determined to take this slowly but suddenly doubted his ability to do so. It had been a long time ... and he wanted her more than he could remember ever wanting anything.

In an effort to reclaim some self-control, he stepped back and, reaching out to brush her cheek with light, insubstantial fingers, said huskily, 'Darling, you may do anything you wish and be quite sure that I'll like it.'

Her colour rose. Somewhere at the back of her mind a disturbing little voice reminded her that she had something to tell him but she ignored it rather than spoil the moment and, instead, moved back into his arms. They closed about her, enveloping her in the heat and scent of him

Eden guided her to the bed and sat down beside her, his eyes on her face and one hand finding its way beneath her shift to caress her thigh.

Fire licked her skin, a pulse throbbed insistently low in her body and her breathing grew uneven.

Still struggling for control, he gestured to the shift and said, 'May I?'

A small tremor shook her and she nodded. Then he was looking at her, his eyes dark and intent and, so softly that she barely heard it, he said, 'Oh God. Even lovelier than I expected,' before pushing her gently back against the pillows.

Slowly, savouring each new discovery, he explored her body ... first with his hands and then with his mouth. Lydia gave a sobbing moan of delight, oddly mingled with a species of impatience she didn't understand. Everything inside her was melting in the inferno created by those clever, seductive fingers which seemed to know exactly where to touch her and how. Her own hands raced over him; seeking, worshipping and telling him that whatever he wanted, he could have. By the time he left her to shed the rest of his clothes, nothing in the entire universe existed but him and the wild demands his body was arousing in hers.

She gazed at him now ... at that intelligent, fine-boned face and lean, compact, perfectly-proportioned body ... both of them a true reflection of the incredible man inside. Her heart swelled with love for him and she forgot everything else. She even forgot the small but vital piece of information she ought, by now to have given him. Words were beyond her so she held out her hands in mute appeal.

That and the exquisite sweetness of her response almost undid him but he held fast to the dwindling threads of his will-power.

Not yet, he ordered himself. *Not ... quite ... yet.*

He returned to her, his caresses growing ever more intimate and his own desire blazing to almost impossible heights. And only when she could no longer remain still against him ... when he knew she was burning up in the same fires that consumed him ... only then did he permit himself the ultimate pleasure.

He knew she was ready; more than ready. So although he took her slowly and with infinite care, he didn't hesitate ... with the result that he was through the unexpected barrier in the exact same instant he detected it. Suddenly very still, he thought, *Christ Almighty. Did I really feel that?* And looking sharply into her face, now tense with a discomfort she was trying to hide, knew that he had.

He said, 'Lydia?'

'Yes.' She shut her eyes, 'I'm sorry.'

He supposed that he was, too; but right now, surrounded by the tight heat of her body with sensation taking over again, he couldn't think properly – or even at all. He wanted – was becoming desperate – to move inside her but tried to hold back for fear of hurting her. Then her eyes opened again, their expression changing gradually to one of confused wonder and, in a very different tone, she said, 'Oh. I – oh. Yes.'

And after that, it was easy; easy and astoundingly wonderful, watching her pleasure build again along with his own; feeling her climb with him and fall into ecstasy only a second before he did so himself.

Too easy, he soon realised when his brain started sluggishly functioning again.

He'd meant to take one simple precaution. He hadn't.

He was suddenly and very unpleasantly alert. He moved away from her and sat on the edge of the bed. A glance over his shoulder showed her curling on to her side, watching him warily out of wide, dilated eyes. He knew he ought to say something. He just didn't know where to start.

There were two issues here. He'd unwittingly bedded a virgin and felt, not unreasonably, that she might have acquainted him with that fact in advance. But worse yet, he'd failed to minimise the risk of pregnancy outside wedlock – a fault that was entirely his own.

The only words that formed in his throat were *'Hell and damnation'* but he managed to swallow them. He knew what she wanted right now. She wanted him to take her in his arms and kiss her hair and murmur something comforting. He wanted that, too.

He couldn't do it. Not yet, at any rate. Rising, he dragged on his breeches and said, 'Forgive me. I know this isn't …' He stopped and tried again. 'I'm aware we should talk – and we will. Just not right now.' Crossing to the wash-stand, he dipped a cloth in the water, wrung it out and walked back to put it her hand. In other circumstances, he'd have handled that differently but right now he wasn't capable of such an intimate gesture; nor, given the fact that she'd never been with a man before, did he think she would welcome it. He found his shirt on the floor and, seeing her shift lying nearby, picked it up to place it within her reach. 'I'll see if your gown is dry and – and …' He stopped for the second time. 'I'm sorry. I won't be long.'

Once outside the door, he merely leaned against it for a moment, trying to order his breathing and ease the turmoil inside him. Then he went downstairs, hoping he didn't meet his mischievous, inquisitive brother on the way.

Lydia stayed where she was, listening first to the stillness and then to his retreating footsteps. Tears stung her eyes and burned in her throat. After the incredible beauty of what had just passed between them, his coldness was more hurtful than she would have believed possible. She knew she ought to have told him. She'd known he might be annoyed that she hadn't … but she'd never expected this chilly, impersonal withdrawal.

She stared blankly at the cloth he'd placed in her hand and the purpose for which it was intended finally dawned on her, bringing wave upon wave of mortification in its wake. Was that what happened afterwards? Practicality without warmth or kindness? She doubted it. And the fact that Eden had treated her that way left her unsure whether she wanted to cry or vomit.

But she wouldn't do either. She had some pride, after all and there had been humiliation enough for one night. She didn't know how long he'd be away and she would *not* let him come back and find her helpless and broken.

I won't cry. I'm stronger than that. So he's angrier than I expected. Well, I don't see why he should be but I can be angry too, if it comes to that. I will not cry.

She used the damned cloth, then hurled it across the room. She dragged her shift over her head and clambered from the bed to wash her hands and face. Finally, once more swaddled in Alice's wrapper, she sat down by the fire to wait … her back straight and her chin up so that there would be no sign of the gaping hole of misery in her chest.

Eden returned bearing a bottle of wine and two glasses.

His mind was calmer but not particularly clearer and his guts were still churning – both with anger at his own lack of control and the knowledge that he'd walked away leaving her hurt. She'd just given herself for the first time – something she wouldn't have done lightly – and he'd walked out as if it meant nothing. He prayed he wouldn't find his brave, stubborn girl in tears. He'd much rather she threw something at his head. At least he'd be able to deal with that.

Inevitably, being Lydia, she did neither. She sat like an icy, disdainful statue and didn't even look at him. Eden didn't know whether to be relieved or worried.

Setting the glasses down and filling them, he said neutrally, 'I'm afraid your gown isn't dry yet. Alice says she'll have it ready for you in the morning – or she can send the girl to your house for fresh clothes.'

She didn't reply. Indeed, she gave absolutely no sign of having heard him. Eden offered her a glass and then, when she ignored that as well, he placed it nearby and sat down facing her.

'I apologise for the way I left you earlier. I'm aware of how it must have looked. But I just ... I needed a moment.'

The blue eyes, drained of all expression in a way he'd never previously seen, drifted over and past him. She said, 'I see. And now?'

'And now we should talk.'

'So you said. About what?'

He sighed. Plainly, she wasn't inclined to make this any less difficult than it already was. He supposed he couldn't really blame her.

'I think you know the answer to that.'

She raised one inimically enquiring brow but said nothing.

Eden kept his tone gentle and persevered.

'Why did you not tell me that you were a virgin?'

She shrugged. 'I didn't *not* tell you. I just didn't *tell* you.'

'Isn't that splitting hairs?'

'I don't think so. And anyway ... it seems to me that *why* isn't the right question. However, if it helps, I've never told anyone else either. I'm sure you can work out why that was necessary.'

He could. An unconsummated marriage could be overset. So if Neville's son or the daughter-in-law from hell had found out, the consequences for Lydia didn't bear thinking about. What puzzled him, however, was *why* the marriage had remained incomplete ... but he knew he'd better not ask. Or, at least, not just yet.

'Yes. I can see that. So what is the question you believe I ought to be asking?'

'When,' she said succinctly. 'Just *when* do you imagine I was supposed to tell you? Over the supper table? In the middle of one of our many discussions about my various troubles?'

'No. But --'

'No. The words *'Oh – by the way I'm a virgin'* don't exactly trip off the tongue in the midst of ordinary conversation, do they? Especially when, until tonight, there was never any question of you needing to know.' Lydia paused but this time Eden didn't speak so she added consideringly, 'I suppose I *might* have mentioned it while we were stuck in the cellar. You know. Something along the lines of *'Just in case, when we get out of here, you were hoping I'd reward your heroic endeavours with my body --'*

'That's enough!' snapped Eden. 'What happened between us earlier had bugger all to do with that – and you damned well know it!'

'If you say so. Though it's not what you said before.'

'That, as you know perfectly well, was a joke.'

She managed to look subtly sceptical and it sent his temper soaring. Controlling his voice with an effort, he said, 'I have never expected – or wanted – payment from you of any kind. And I don't bed women just because they happen to be grateful.'

She knew he didn't just as she knew he'd been joking; but because some perverse piece of logic was prompting her to ensure he was as miserably off-balance as she was herself, she chose not to admit it. Instead, as if the matter were of little of no consequence, she said, 'I never said you did.'

'You implied it.' She'd implied it and the implication made him utterly furious. *How dared she?* Was she goading him on *purpose*?

His brain froze for a second and then became suddenly very clear indeed.

Yes. Of course she bloody is. Well, two can play at that game, darling.

He folded his arms and looked her over with seemingly lazy curiosity. 'Ah. Is that why you decided to sacrifice your long-guarded virtue? I must admit that the possibility hadn't occurred to me – though I'm sure you're going to tell me it should have done. I thought, you see, that we came together out of mutual desire. If that wasn't so ... well, let's just say it must be galling for you to realise your sacrifice wasn't necessary.'

Too shocked, as yet, to recognise she'd just been hoist with her own petard, Lydia stared back at him feeling as if the breath had been knocked out of her. It was several moments before she had any idea what to say or was actually capable of saying anything at all but eventually she managed to mutter weakly, 'That's not true. None of it is.'

'No? I'm relieved to hear it. Odd as it may seem, we men like to believe our conquests are owed solely to our good looks and charm.' Having recovered his temper, Eden felt mildly ashamed of himself. Not too much, however ... because now at least there was some chance of clearing the air once and for all. He said quietly, 'What was it, Lydia? Did you think I'd mind?'

This time she had the sense not to ask what he meant.

'Yes. Didn't you?'

'Not in the way you may have thought. And the real issue, as you must surely have realised, was not that you were a virgin but that I didn't *know* you were. However, I can understand your difficulties in broaching the subject.'

'I doubt it,' mumbled Lydia.

He hid a smile. 'It's just that it would have been better if I'd known.'

'Better for whom?'

'You,' he said simply.

'Oh.' She searched through her disordered thoughts – now, thanks to him neatly turning the tables on her, more confused than ever – and said awkwardly, 'But afterwards you were ... different. Cold and distant. Angry, even. I thought that's why you walked out.'

It was Eden's turn to struggle for the right words. He frowned down into the untouched glass of wine in his hands and, deciding that he needed it, took a hefty swallow. Then he said baldly, 'It was. And yes, I was angry. But with myself – not you.'

'I don't understand.'

'No. I suppose not.' He drained the glass and set it aside. Partly because he was curious and partly to evade what was obviously going to be her next question, he said, 'May I ask something? It's not my business and you don't have to answer if you'd rather not ... but why didn't Stephen consummate your marriage?'

Lydia stared into the fire for a long moment.

'He said that, at his age, he didn't need a second wife but that marriage would give me standing and security. He also said that I deserved a young lover, not an old man. He even hinted that if I were to meet someone and ... well, he wouldn't mind very much so long as I was discreet.' She sighed and then said meditatively, 'At first I thought he preferred to remain faithful to his wife's memory or that perhaps he simply didn't want to sire more children. Later, I wondered if there hadn't been someone else in his life ... a woman circumstances prevented him being with. Either way, he made it clear from the beginning that he'd no intention of lying with me. I didn't mind. We were happy as we were.'

'And you were never tempted to take advantage of his offer?'

She looked puzzled. 'His offer?'

'Yes. You said he more or less gave you permission to take a lover.'

'No!' She sat up very straight. 'I mean – yes, he did. But I'd never have done so – *never*! After his kindness to Aubrey and me ... *God!* How can you even *ask* that?'

'Ah.' Eden looked down at his hands. 'You're insulted.'

'Of *course* I'm insulted!' she began. And then stopped, remembering. 'Oh. How stupid of me. I'm sorry.'

'Don't be.' The hazel eyes rose to meet hers, their expression enigmatic. 'The fault was mine for being crass enough to ask a question to which I already knew the answer.'

'You like blaming yourself, don't you?'

'I don't believe so. What makes you think it?'

'You said you were angry with yourself earlier,' she replied simply. 'Why?'

Eden suppressed a groan.

Damn. I hoped I'd got away with that.

He said baldly, 'I'd intended to reduce the chances of getting you with child. I didn't.'

Lydia stared at him. 'I don't understand. How is that possible?'

Hell. He really didn't want to explain this but could see that he was going to have to.

'It's done by withdrawing at – at the optimum moment.'

He watched her trying to figure this out and finally doing so. Tilting her head and in a perfectly matter-of-fact tone, she said, 'That sounds ... awkward.'

Awkward? He wanted to laugh and tell her she had no idea. He wondered how she'd take it if he said, *It's not awkward, darling. It's bloody murder. But after Jude was born it was the only way Celia ever let me near her so I got fairly good at it.*

No. He wouldn't say that. She didn't need to know and it demeaned him. So he merely said, 'It's ... difficult ... but not impossible. I should have done it. Having discovered it was your first time, there was even more reason to be careful. But I wasn't. I'm sorry.'

'Is that really why you ...?' She stopped and waved a hand in the direction of the door.

'Fled? Yes. And for what it's worth, I apologise for that as well. It's hardly surprising that you wanted to flay me. I deserved it.'

Lydia smiled for the first time since he'd re-entered the room.

'I forgive you. And as for the other thing ... there's very little chance I'll conceive. It – it was only once, after all.'

'It only takes once,' he replied a shade grimly. 'You must know that.'

'Yes. I suppose so.' She swiftly suppressed the foolish quiver of warmth at the notion of having Eden's baby. 'However, I still think it unlikely enough not to be worth worrying about. We'll know in a couple of weeks, anyway.'

Eden finally looked into the heart of the truth that had been hovering about him since he'd first left her bed. He didn't want to wait two weeks. Neither did he want it to be 'only once'. He wanted it to be as often as they both felt inclined. He also wanted *her* ... in his life, every day, in every sense there was. And there was only one way he could have that.

He cleared his throat and said slowly, 'You could marry me.'

Lydia stared at him, struck dumb with shock and feeling something painful twisting inside her chest at the certain knowledge that he couldn't really mean it – or, at least not for the right reasons. He'd always been very clear about his views on re-marriage; understandably so. And though as Venetia had said, that might have become a habit, it wasn't one Lydia could see him breaking without a struggle. She wished he hadn't said it. She *particularly* wished he hadn't said it in that odd tone of voice.

Managing something resembling a tiny laugh, she said, 'That's a bit extreme isn't it?'

'Is it?'

'Purely on the remote possibility I may have conceived? Yes. I think so.'

'It isn't ...' He stopped, wondering why it suddenly seemed so difficult. 'It wouldn't be *purely* for that.'

'Wouldn't it?' The sceptical note was back again but, before he could respond, another thought occurred and she said impatiently, 'Oh for heaven's sake! *Please* don't tell me it's because you've deflowered me. That sounds so ridiculous I can barely bring myself to say it.'

'I know. And that's not --'

'I'm a *widow*, Eden. No one expects a widow to be a virgin. *You* certainly didn't.'

'No. But it isn't --'

'So if you've some muddle-headed ideas about honour and making an honest woman of me, you can forget them. I can share my body with anyone I like – and I didn't share it with you out of any notion of entrapping you into matrimony.'

'I know that,' he said irritably, a part of what she'd said stabbing through him like a knife. 'And none of this is why I asked you.'

'Actually,' she said acidly, 'you didn't. Ask, I mean. It sounded more like a suggestion – and a reluctant one at that.'

It was at this point that Eden realised that exhaustion was robbing him of the ability to think and reducing him to the point of bumbling idiocy. It was just a pity that the same wasn't true of Lydia who, it seemed, was still fully capable of tying him in verbal knots.

An experienced campaigner always knows when to make a tactical retreat and how to do it in good order. Eden decided that this was that time.

Coming to his feet, he said, 'Perhaps we can resume this tomorrow. Meanwhile, if you're half as tired as I am, you need to sleep.' Crossing to her side, he kissed each of her hands in turn and added, 'Goodnight, my dear. Everything will be clearer in the morning.'

I hope.

FIVE

Shutting his own door behind him, Eden crossed the room shedding his clothes as he went. He told himself he'd been sensible. If he'd stayed any longer with Lydia firing broadsides at him, he'd probably have done something both stupid and unhelpful ... such as grabbing her by the shoulders and telling her to stop ripping up at him and listen. As it was, if she was left alone perhaps the night would bring, not just counsel, but a grain or two of tolerance.

He'd expected to fall into oblivion as soon as his head touched the pillow. Instead, his mind was awash with images of everything the last few hours had brought. His fear when the note had arrived; the sight of Lydia, bound and blind, with a knife-wielding killer at her shoulder; the fight to get out of that bloody cellar; and later, joy greater than any he could ever recall.

Dwelling on the memory of Lydia lying naked in his arms was not going to let him sleep. Unfortunately, neither was dissecting the conversation that had followed. He began by framing things he might have said or should have said ... from whence it was a short step to searching for the words he'd need in the morning. He could only think of three.

Three words didn't seem very much. Perhaps it was all in the way one said them?

* * *

He finally slept like the dead and didn't wake until the morning was well-advanced. He washed, shaved and dressed as quickly as he could, then tapped on Lydia's door in the hope she might still be there. She wasn't – but, given the hour, that wasn't so surprising. Eden ran smartly down to the parlour, expecting to find her at breakfast. Instead, the room was occupied only by his brother, sitting at the table attending to some paperwork.

'Where's Lydia?'

'Gone,' replied Tobias absently.

There was a moment of dangerous silence.

'Gone?' said Eden flatly. And then on a note of incipient temper, 'She left ... and you *let* her?'

'Yes.' Tobias cast Eden an oblique considering glance. 'What was I supposed to do? Keep her prisoner here until you heaved yourself out of bed?'

'After what happened yesterday, you were supposed to keep her safe, damn it!'

'Me? Perhaps you ought to keep better track of your women.'

Eden's fists clenched and he swung away towards the door.

'Go to hell.'

'Stop.' Tobias laid down his quill and turned round. 'She's perfectly safe. According to Alice, she was up while the fires were still being lit and determined to leave. Fortunately, her maid and a clutch of other women arrived bearing the usual female paraphernalia without which a woman can't set foot outside the house. They were accompanied by Sir Aubrey and that young footman.'

'Oh,' said Eden, weak with relief. 'I see. Good.'

'The women clucked round Lydia like mother-hens and made enough noise to wake the dead – though it obviously didn't disturb *you*. And then the whole tribe left.' He stood up and smiled invitingly. 'I don't know what went on between the two of you last night ... but whatever it was seems to have sent Lydia running for the hills. If you need some advice for next time, I'll be happy to help.'

Not without difficulty, Eden ignored this provocation. He said curtly, 'Where did she go?'

'How would I know?' Tobias shrugged and resumed his seat. 'Home? The lorinery? One of them, I suppose. I'm sure you'll manage to find her.'

Eden swallowed a curse and strode out.

* * *

Lydia had decided her first priority was to assess the damage at the lorinery. Before that, however, she needed to dismiss her protection squad. Assuring everyone that, in broad daylight, Peter was sufficient protection, she told Nancy to go home and sent Mary, Lily and Rachel off to their work, promising to visit later and tell them the whole story.

Aubrey was less easy to dismiss.

He frowned at her and said, 'I should have thought that, after what happened, you'd be content to stay at home today. In fact,' he added disapprovingly, 'I don't see why you couldn't have returned home last night. I'd have come for you.'

'I know – but my clothes were wet.' Lydia turned away before he saw that she was blushing. 'And Colonel Maxwell didn't want anybody at risk out there in the dark when Quinn's men might have been anywhere.'

Aubrey huffed a little. 'Well, I still think you could leave the men to the clearing up.'

'I probably will once I've seen the state of the place. Now stop worrying and get yourself off to Shoreditch. Mr Morrell is probably wondering where you are.'

He was finally persuaded to leave and, sighing with relief, Lydia turned towards Duck Lane ... aware that Peter was shadowing her a step or two closer than before.

Mr Potter met her in the workshop, looking both worried and harassed.

'Miss Lydia – thank God you're safe! We were all that worried when we got here this morning and saw the state of things – what with your cloak on the floor and your petticoats on the cellar steps. But Sir Nicholas told us what happened.' He shook his head. 'It's a mercy the Colonel was here. If he hadn't been there's no telling *what* might have become of you.'

'No. He was very ... resourceful. Now tell me – how bad is the damage?'

'Nothing to speak of in here but the office is a mess. Papers everywhere. And I've got Cooper and Hayes outside sealing up the coal-chute as best they can. There's no working on it from inside yet – the water's up to about four feet. Worst it's ever been.'

Lydia swallowed, grateful it hadn't been that deep last evening.

'And upstairs?'

'Best go and see for yourself, Miss Lydia – but watch your step. They've ripped up half the floorboards and Sir Nicholas is up there now trying to sort out what's best to do.'

At the top of the stairs, Lydia stopped dead and stared. The crates normally stored tidily, section by section depending on their contents, had been shoved against the back wall. Between them and where she stood, the space was largely bereft of floorboards – except where a few had been laid back down to allow access. Amongst all this, Nicholas was directing his immediate attention to the crates containing partly made-up orders while some men – those in possession of two good legs – gathered up the items Quinn's crew had let fall into the gaps between the joists and others started attempting to re-laying the foot-wide oak planks.

All these immediately stopped work to express both their pleasure in seeing her safe and their fury at what had happened to her. Lydia smiled, answered as best she could and was about to step into the room when Nicholas said, 'Stay where you are, Lydia. Moving around is tricky if we're not to have somebody putting their foot through the ceiling. We'll get as much of the floor back as we can – but perhaps not all of it, thanks to the amount of damage.'

'Do you think they got what they came for?'

'Maybe – maybe not. It's impossible to say.' He shrugged slightly in his usual lop-sided fashion. 'We can but hope. Meanwhile, are you all right? They didn't hurt you?'

'No. It was just very frightening. And if Eden hadn't got us out ...' She stopped and then said, 'I don't know how on earth he managed it – yet somehow I just knew he would.'

Nicholas suspected it was a fairly safe bet that Eden hadn't been so confident. But he said merely, 'I imagine he had something to say to you afterwards about having come here at all.'

'Less than I deserved.' She looked around her. 'There doesn't seem much that I can do here apart from get in the way. I'll go and see if I can restore order in the office so Mr Potter's free to do other things.'

An hour later and still up to her elbows in a muddle of loose pages, Lydia heard a familiar voice say crisply, 'Where is she, Mr Potter?'

'In the office, Colonel. And if I may, I'd like to shake you by the hand. That was a remarkable thing you did last night.'

'Not especially. It was mostly brute force and ignorance.'

Lydia had barely got up off her knees before Eden was in the doorway. He said, 'Why are you here? And where's Peter?'

'Why do you *think* I'm here?' she retorted, keeping her eyes firmly fixed on the pages in her hand in an attempt to stem the tide of feeling the mere sound of his voice sent rushing through her. 'And Peter's upstairs helping Nick and the rest of them put the floor-boards back. If you've nothing better to do, you could lend a hand – though I'd have thought you've work of your own.'

'Delegation,' said Eden, shutting the door behind him, 'is one of the advantages of being a Colonel. Why did you run away without seeing me?'

'I didn't. You weren't up and Nancy had brought me some clothes, so --'

'You ran away,' he said blandly, 'leaving behind unfinished business. And now you won't look at me. Why?'

She looked at him then and immediately wished she hadn't. He was smiling at her with an expression she'd never seen before and which made her body remember things for which this very definitely wasn't the time.

She said feebly, 'Surely there's no more to be said about – about last night.'

'There is ... though not here and now.' He paused and stepped back from her. 'I'll join Nick's team, then. But tell me when you're ready to leave and I'll walk home with you.' At the door, he turned back and added, 'Don't ask me to forget it happened, Lydia. I can't.'

As soon as the door closed behind him, Lydia dropped abruptly into Mr Potter's chair.

I can't either, she thought. *That's just the trouble.*

Upstairs, Eden was met with a barrage of questions about how he'd got Miss Lydia and himself out of the flooding cellar in the dark. He answered them briefly and with grim humour while he absorbed the progress that had been already made on the devastation he'd seen the previous night. Then, pulling off his coat, he asked Trooper Buxton how he could help and set to with the rest of them.

For a time he and Buxton worked largely in silence, nailing down the oak planks. But after a while the trooper said, 'What do they want to go and hurt Miss Lydia for, Colonel? She's never done nobody an ill turn – nor ever would. Why won't they leave her alone?'

'They're being paid to find something.'

'And they think Miss Lydia's got it?'

'Yes.' Eden hammered down one corner and reached for another nail. 'So let's hope they found it and that this bloody mess won't have been for nothing.'

Buxton finished nailing down his end of the plank and sat back on his heels. He said mournfully, 'It'll sound daft ... but it's a shame about the old cupboard. It wasn't locked and there was nothing in it apart from a few old ledgers – but look what the buggers done to it.'

Eden glanced across at the cupboard in question. It was a big, ugly thing resembling a dresser; narrower above than it was below and built into the wall. Now, those of its doors which hadn't been wrenched off completely hung drunkenly from their hinges and much of its heavy, black oak frame bore signs of someone having taken a hatchet to it.

He shrugged slightly and went back to work.

'The doors can be replaced, I imagine.'

Buxton grunted an assent and said, 'I know it don't look much, Colonel. But Mr Stephen was fond of it. Said it must have been built along with the house. Even gave it a name, he did.'

The back of Eden's neck prickled and he laid down his hammer. Rising, he picked his way across the beams to take a closer look at the monstrosity. It looked perfectly ordinary. He ran his hands over it, he tapped each section for secret compartments and he investigated the crude, lumpy carving for anything that moved. He found nothing. Stepping back, he scrutinised it bit by bit. Eventually he noticed a pair of irregularly shaped insets, one at either end. He peered at these more closely, pushing his index finger inside and encountering nothing but years of accumulated dust. Finally, he gave up. Just for a moment, he'd hoped ... but no. He really should have known better. And for all he knew, the late Mr Neville might have had an affection for a dozen of pieces of furniture.

'Called it Old Job,' muttered Trooper Buxton, more to himself than to Eden. 'Never did understand why.'

* * *

Lydia worked until the office was once more restored to order and then, reluctantly sent word upstairs that she was ready to go home. She'd expected Peter to materialise alongside the Colonel but he didn't. Eden came down alone and blithely informed her that the young man wanted to finish what he was doing and would follow later.

Out in the street with her hand on his arm, he said mildly, 'Are you feeling awkward because things have changed between us or because you're wondering what happens next?'

'I'm not --' she began and then stopped, sighing. 'I don't know. Both, I think.'

He nodded. 'Then let me clear up at least one point. Much as I'd like to lie with you again, I'm making no assumptions ... and I won't. Does that help?'

Since this sounded very much as if he was leaving the nature of their future relationship up to her, Lydia wasn't sure whether it did or not. His admission brought a flush of pleasure. But finding a way of hinting that she wanted the same thing and didn't require a wedding band seemed as difficult as telling him she was a virgin. However, she murmured politely, 'Yes. Thank you.'

Eden shot her an amused smile but, realising that this wasn't a conversation to be having in the street, changed the subject to the one still niggling at the back of his mind.

'Tell me about the cupboard upstairs.'

Lydia gave a tiny puff of amusement. 'Old Job?'

'That's the one. Did Stephen make a habit of naming articles of furniture?'

'No. Just that one.'

'Why? And why Old Job?'

She tutted. 'Don't you remember your Bible? *"Job lived an hundred and forty years ... and died being old and full of days."* That's roughly the age of the building.'

Eden, frowned a little. There was something odd about that and it increased the annoying feeling that he was missing something. However, since whatever it was wouldn't come into focus, he restored his attention to Lydia, chatting easily about the damage in Duck Lane.

Back at home and having laid aside her cloak, tidied her hair and ordered a meal to be served in the dining parlour, Lydia joined Eden by the fireside and said, 'Do you think there's any chance we've seen the last of Quinn?'

'It's not impossible.'

'But you don't feel inclined to rely on it.'

'No.'

'No.' She sighed. 'Neither do I.'

'Good. Then you'll be more careful than you were yesterday, I hope.'

'You can rely on it. I know what happened was my fault. If I'd listened to Henry --'

'Listen to him next time,' said Eden crisply. And then, with a smile, 'And increase Peter's wages. God knows, he's earned it.'

'I already tried. He got rather annoyed and said the only reward he wanted was a chance to get his hands round Quinn's throat.'

'A man after my own heart, then.'

Lydia eyed him thoughtfully.

'If you had the opportunity ... would you kill him?'

'Yes.'

It was perhaps fortunate that Henry chose that moment to tap on the door and announce that food awaited them. Eden who – aside from the bread and meat that should have been Lydia's supper – had eaten nothing for twenty-four hours, decided that he might make a better job of asking Lydia to marry him when his stomach had stopped growling. It also occurred to him that he was likely to meet with more encouragement if he kept the mood light and worked on re-establishing their previous easy relationship.

Consequently, while they dined off mutton stew and peppery mashed swede, he spoke only of trivialities and watched Lydia gradually slip back into her usual manner.

However, the meal done and once more settled beside the fire, he knew he couldn't put it off any longer; didn't, in fact, *want* to put it off any longer. So he said, 'I need to rectify some omissions. Things I neglected to say last night. Do you think you might bear with me?'

Instantly, she looked wary. 'Is it important?'

'I think so. Yes.'

'Then I suppose I'll have to, won't I?'

'There's no need to look so worried,' said Eden, as casually as he was able. 'I merely wanted to clarify a few things.'

'Such as what?'

'Such as the fact that I don't take what happened between us lightly. I recognise that you gave me a great gift and one I'm honoured to have received.'

'That sounds very formal,' said Lydia. And thought, *Please don't ask me why I did it; why I chose you in particular. I shan't know what to say.* 'Grandiloquent, even.'

'It isn't meant to. Does "thank you for trusting me" sound better?'

'Yes.' A swift, unexpected and slightly wry smile dawned. 'Though it seems a small thing to trust you with – considering that my life has been in your hands for quite some time now.'

'I disagree ... but we won't pursue it.' Eden paused, trying to assemble the right words. 'Last night I made what you called a suggestion and which you dismissed out of hand for a whole barrage of assumed reasons – none of which were correct. It's true that I hope I have some honour and know *how* to behave like a gentleman even if I don't always do it. But, given my personal history, you must surely admit that my having ... how did you put it? Yes. My having *deflowered* you is hardly enough to make me plunge into matrimony.'

At some point during a sleepless night, Lydia had finally realised that. What she *hadn't* done was come up with any other credible reason. She said, 'When you put it like that ... no. Probably not.'

'*Definitely* not.' He hesitated again and then said, 'Of course, you weren't the only one making assumptions. I took it for granted that, if … if you liked me well enough to go to bed with me, you might like me well enough to live with me. That may have been foolish. Was it?'

'I – no.' She wasn't entirely sure what he was asking so she said cautiously, 'It was a reasonable enough thing to think.'

'I'm aware. But was it *true*?'

Lydia was beginning to feel as if she was picking her way through a bog in the dark. He seemed to be skirting around something but she didn't know what it was – which meant she could as easily say the wrong thing as the right one.

Had she but known it, Eden felt worse. The more he tried to put his thoughts in order, the more muddled they became. Having embarked on this conversation, he'd suddenly recognised that the only thing that mattered was whether or not she loved him. If she didn't, his only sane course was to walk away … because he was fairly sure that marriage to another woman who didn't truly want him would destroy him. He'd do it – he'd *have* to do it if there was to be a child; not just for Lydia but because no child of his was going to be branded a bastard. But otherwise? He didn't think he could. More fully perhaps than ever before, he understood how Deborah must have felt and wondered where she'd found the strength not only to live with him knowing he didn't love her but also, in the end, to set him free.

Lydia was no Celia. He knew that. She was honest, loyal and incapable of betrayal. But love didn't wait for an invitation. It arrived unbidden. So if, by now, she felt nothing more than friendship, the likelihood was that she never would. Or not for him. And therein lay the rub. She would never betray him. But the time might come when she'd want to.

That thought ripped through him like a knife. He couldn't do anything about his own feelings. He'd fallen completely and irrevocably in love with her longer ago than he'd been prepared to admit; but he *could* spare himself a lifetime of waiting for something that might never happen or, worse still, watching her face light up for some other man.

So he had to know ... had to ask; but still couldn't quite bring himself to lay his heart at her feet and risk having her reject it.

He realised she hadn't answered him. Clearing his throat, he said, 'Perhaps I'm not making myself clear.'

'Not entirely, no.'

'Then I'll be blunt. Will you marry me?' He paused, absorbing her expression of utter shock and then added, 'You'll notice that *wasn't* a suggestion.'

'Yes.'

'Yes, you'll marry me – or yes, you noticed it was a question?'

'The I-latter. I haven't come to terms with the first bit yet.' Everything inside her was in turmoil. Despite what he'd said last night, she'd never thought he'd actually propose to her; unless, of course, she was with child. He'd definitely ask her then and probably refuse to take no for an answer. But he wasn't waiting for that. He was asking her *now*. And though she didn't understand what his motives might be, she wanted to simply say yes more, she thought, than she'd ever wanted anything in her life. Drawing a slightly ragged breath and preparing to speak as bluntly as he'd done, she said, 'You've always been adamant that you wouldn't marry again.'

'Perhaps I've changed my mind.'

And perhaps you haven't.

'Why would you do that? You don't need to marry me. If there should be a child ... things might be different. But as it is --'

'Are you refusing me?' The words felt like razors in his throat.

'No. I'm saying you've no reason to – to feel obligated to do anything you don't want to. I thought ... I wondered if we might ...' She stopped, feeling her cheeks grow hot and thinking, *What am I doing? If he says no ... worse still, if he laughs - I'll die of mortification.*

'You wondered if we might ... what?' he prompted.

'Carry on from where – from where we left off last night,' she blurted out. 'Marriage isn't a necessity.'

It was Eden's turn to be shocked into silence. Finally he said slowly, 'Are you ... did you just offer to become my mistress?'

'Yes.'

'Rather than marry me?'

'Yes – no. Not exactly. That would be insulting.'

'Just a little,' he agreed. 'And so?'

'I'm honoured and f-flattered that you should offer. Of course I am.'

'Thank you.' Inexplicably, the weight that had been pressing down on him lifted and was followed by a surge of hope so strong it made him dizzy. She wasn't saying no ... though quite what she *was* saying and, moreover why she was saying it, still eluded him. 'As, indeed, I am by your own offer. Were you serious about that, by the way?'

'Perfectly serious.' *It would be more than I dared hope for. God knows I'd like to marry you; but I can't if there's even the slightest chance you'll end up feeling trapped.* 'Yes.'

'That is extraordinarily tempting. But I interrupted you ... just at the point I suspected you were about to add the word *but*.'

Lydia nodded.

'But I didn't expect it. How could I? And it seems so – so sudden.' *God help me, I sound like a ninny.* 'Especially on the heels of what happened last night. With Quinn, I mean,' she added hurriedly, in case he thought she meant something else. 'Really, you ought to consider whether or not you're being over-hasty. It's only been a day, after all.'

No, darling. It's been a lot longer than that.

'You think I might regret it?'

'Yes. I want to be sure you're sure.' *That you're not just doing it because you think you should.* 'And I need time to think as well. But in the meantime ...' She stopped again.

'In the meantime – while all this considering is going on,' supplied Eden helpfully, 'you thought we might enjoy a love affair.'

'Yes.' She shot him an acute glance, suspicious that he might be laughing at her after all and relieved to see he looked perfectly serious. 'As I said, we don't have to be married to – to be together.'

'I see.'

And suddenly he did. She was just being so *Lydia*. Simultaneously arguing him out of offering his hand, and herself out of accepting it; because she *would* accept it. He was confident of that now. A woman like Lydia didn't suggest sharing a man's bed out of wedlock unless her heart was engaged. Joy exploded through every vein and along every nerve and sinew. He wanted laugh, to cry, to sweep her up into his arms and pour out everything that was in his heart. The only thing that stopped him doing so was the fact that it seemed she wasn't quite ready to hear it ... or had possibly not fully explored her own feelings as yet. So he'd wait. He could do that now. He could do *anything* now.

'Perhaps you don't think it's a good idea,' he heard her murmur doubtfully.

No, love. I think it's positively hare-brained – and if I wasn't sure it would end in marriage, I'd have some very serious objections to it. As it is, have you really *not recognised that you're giving me the chance to remove your options with a week or two of love-making?*

Shrugging, he said, 'I'm a man, Lydia – so naturally I think it's an excellent idea. I only hesitate because I'm just not entirely sure how this liaison is to be managed.'

She stared at him, clearly nonplussed. 'Managed? I don't ...'

'Well, were you thinking of visiting my bed – or do I visit yours?' Eden frowned thoughtfully to hide the fact that, against all expectation, he was enjoying himself. 'It's just that I can't imagine Aubrey being very happy with the situation – or with me. And it really wouldn't do for the pair of us to end up fighting each other, would it?'

'Oh. No.' Her heart sank. 'I hadn't thought of that.'

'No. So perhaps we should take a little time to work out the best course of action. For example, I could take a room in a tavern ... but that seems rather sordid.'

'Yes. Yes, it does.' It was also beginning to sound a lot more complicated than she'd imagined it would be. Suspicion stirred afresh and she said, 'Are you trying to put me off the idea? Because if you are ... if you don't want to – to --'

'Of course I want to. But the thing about illicit love affairs,' he confided blandly, 'is that they inevitably involve a good deal of subterfuge. In one sense, that might add an extra frisson of excitement – but in another, it doesn't seem very romantic.'

'No. I can see that.' Lydia eyed him with a glimmer of resentment. 'How fortunate it is that you know so much about all this.'

'Isn't it?' said Eden, leaving his chair to advance on her with predatory intent. And pulling her easily to her feet and into his arms, 'Leave it with me, sweetheart. It may take a few days but I'm sure I can work something out. And while we're waiting, there's always this.'

He kissed her with everything that was in his heart and soul. He'd withheld the words for the time being but he wanted her to know, on some level, what she had. So he kissed her long and deeply and with undisguised passion; and when he was fairly sure that the only thing holding her up was himself, he released her mouth briefly to murmur, 'Convinced yet?'

The long silky lashes fluttered open revealing dazed blue eyes. 'I – what?'

Eden smiled down at her, knowing the answer.

'Good,' he said. And kissed her again.

SIX

On the following morning, Eden – still trying to stop grinning like an idiot – walked into the parlour and narrowly avoided tripping over his brother's saddle-bags, full to bursting and lying just inside the door as a trap for the unwary.

Tobias himself was standing up, hastily consuming some bread and a lump of cheese. Reading these signs without any particular difficulty, Eden, 'I gather Tabitha's having the baby.'

Tobias grunted, swallowed and said, 'Yes. It started about two hours ago or at least that's when I woke up. I don't know how long I'll be away – maybe no more than four or five days. Turner will keep the shop open. Try not to get beaten up or locked in any more flooding cellars will you, there's a good fellow?'

'Don't worry about me. Just go and hold Tab's hand and tell Ralph he's not supposed to break out the brandy until *after* the birth.'

'Yes, Colonel.' Tobias strode across the room to sling his bags over one broad shoulder. 'You're looking remarkably cheerful this morning. Is that Lydia's doing – or have you finally found the key to catching Quinn?'

'Neither. I spent a large part of yesterday nailing down floorboards, if you must know. And now I need to show my face at the Tower before I'm cashiered for dereliction of duty.'

'That won't happen,' said Tobias over his shoulder as he descended the stairs. 'How on earth would Old Noll and the rest of them manage without you?'

And was gone before Eden could summon up a retort.

* * *

At the Tower, he explained his absence of the previous day by giving Ned Moulton a brief account of his and Lydia's recent brush with Quinn.

'Do you think you'll ever catch him?' asked the Major, after he'd been assured of Lydia's well-being. 'Slippery as an eel, isn't he?'

'Very – but I persevere. Is there anything urgent here?'

'No. Just the usual paperwork. And we've got a few new temporary guests.'

'Who?'

'Thomas Harrison and three of his Fifth Monarchist friends. They stood in front of the Council and said that when the Protector dissolved the Barebones Parliament he took the crown off Christ's head and put it on his own. They also said that religious matters should be left in the hands of the Saints --'

'Meaning themselves,' said Eden.

'Meaning themselves,' agreed Major Moulton. 'And they accused the government of being, not just anti-Christian, but also a usurped authority against which it was lawful to take up arms.'

'Bloody idiots. Harrison may be one of Cromwell's pets but he must have known that kind of provocation would land him in here.' He paused. 'Temporarily, did you say?'

'Yes. One of them – Nathaniel Rich – has been given liberty to attend his wife's death-bed but the others are being despatched to separate prisons. Exactly which ones, I haven't yet been told. But I'll be glad to speed Harrison on his way. The man gives me gut-ache.'

'He has that effect on a lot of people,' said Eden. 'Give me the paperwork. I'll take it with me and get it done when I can. But first I need to speak to someone at Whitehall.'

* * *

Colonel Maxwell found his erstwhile head clerk, Augustus Hollins, privately and without difficulty. He came directly to the point.

'Has anything come in from Paris or Cologne regarding that matter we spoke of?'

'Nothing from Paris. But our man in Cologne reports that Sir Ellis Brandon has been hovering around the periphery of the court-in-exile for the last three months and has recently married a wealthy Flemish widow. Consequently, bundling him on to a boat back to England isn't viable. I have however,' finished Mr Hollins primly, 'taken the liberty of instructing our agent to pay Sir Ellis a visit and obtain, by any means necessary, whatever information he can regarding the provenance of the pistols. I hope I did right, Colonel.'

'You did exactly right, Mr Hollins – and thank you.'

'It is always a pleasure to assist you, sir.'

'Are there any other developments you think I might like to know about?'

'The recent abortive rendezvous in Salisbury resulted in the arrest of a few Royalist gentlemen – none being of any note. But due to the existence of that near-insurrection, there is now to be a new commission to regulate the Militia in defence of the City ... and a proclamation banning race meetings for the next six months is currently being prepared.' The clerk's mouth curled wryly. 'Daniel O'Neill has managed to escape from Dover Castle – from which one must suppose him to be blessed with the luck of the Irish. And there is a rumour, as yet unconfirmed, that the Earl of Rochester and Sir Joseph Wagstaffe landed at Margate a few days ago.'

Eden nearly groaned. Rochester ... *again*. He hoped the bloody man wasn't careless enough to get himself picked up. Or if he was, that he'd keep what he knew to himself.

'Interesting. If you hear anything further on those last two, let me know.' He turned towards the door and then, as if it was a vague and not particularly important after-thought, said, 'Ah. Do you happen to know if any of my former colleagues have been absent in the last week or two?'

Mr Hollins brows rose in surprise.

'Why, yes. Isaac Scrope – Mr Samuel Morland's chief assistant. Bad oysters, he said. I believe he was house-bound for three or four days. How did you – ? No. Of course. A foolish question.'

'Not so foolish,' murmured Eden. 'Is he in the building now?'

'Indeed, Colonel. Did you want to speak to him?'

'Yes. Discreetly.'

'Naturally. If you will wait here, I'll send him along to you.'

'Thank you. And Mr Hollins ... there will be no need to mention my name.'

His expression admirably impervious, the clerk nodded and left. Then, in due course, Isaac Scrope entered the room to stop dead and turn deathly white.

He stammered, 'C-Colonel Maxwell. I d-don't understand.'

'You understand perfectly, Mr Scrope,' said Eden pleasantly. 'Those bad oysters of yours were actually a few unpleasant days with a fellow named Quinn. I could sympathise with you about that had you not seen fit to gossip about me.'

'I didn't! It was him – Quinn – who first mentioned you. He knew about you already.'

'I doubt he already knew that you and I had been in the same line of work.'

The man's face crumpled.

'I'm sorry – I'm *sorry*! But he was threatening my wife and daughters. What was I to do? The man is evil and – and powerful enough to do anything he wants. If I hadn't done what he told me, he said ... he said he'd put my girls in a brothel and I'd never see them again. How could I risk that?'

'You couldn't,' agreed Eden wearily. 'You couldn't, Mr Scrope. And, for what it's worth, I'm sorry you were dragged into something that had nothing to do with you.'

'That's – that's generous of you, Colonel,' came the faintly startled reply. And then, with a small and very tentative smile, 'Had the circumstances been different, I might have had some pleasure in the decrypting. They were very good codes.'

* * *

In an attempt to stop his mind straying to Lydia – which it was very prone to do – Eden decided to go back to Duck Lane for another look at Old Job. Lydia, he knew, would not be there. When she'd finally been capable of saying anything ... and it gave him immense satisfaction to know how completely he could scramble her wits ... she had said that she'd be spending most of the day with the women. Since she would have Peter in attendance and had promised not to be out after dark, he reasoned she should be safe enough. And meanwhile he could try to work out just what it was about that bloody cupboard that was pricking at the back of his brain.

Neville had given it a name. Why? Why would anybody in their right mind do that? Eden could only think that it had some significance that had so far eluded him. Talking to the men who had known Neville might yield some clue. But failing that, he'd risk reducing Buxton to tears by taking the damned thing apart if he had to.

Normal work had now been largely resumed on the ground floor but Nicholas and two or three others were still restoring order above. Eden spoke to Mr Potter and half a dozen fellows, all of whom had been at the lorinery since its early days and who had therefore known Stephen Neville best. All agreed that Mr Stephen had a soft spot for Old Job; all laughed at the name he'd given it as a joke; none of them knew anything remotely useful.

Eden thanked them all for their time and went upstairs to stare broodingly at the cupboard over folded arms.

From his work on the far side of the room, Nicholas said, 'I take it Lydia's no worse for her ordeal? No delayed reaction?'

'No. Any other female would have had hysterics at the time and taken to her bed immediately after. But with Lydia, it's business as usual.' Eden glanced round. 'Do you know anything about this cupboard – aside from the ridiculous name?'

'No.' Nicholas walked across to join him. 'As far as I can see it's a perfectly ordinary example of its type – built into the wall along with the house. Why do you ask?'

'I don't know. It's just a feeling I have.'

'Based on what?'

'To begin with, why would Stephen Neville – who, as far as I'm aware, wasn't any more eccentric than you or I – give the thing a name? Then there's the fact that the lorinery has been at the heart of this business with Quinn right from the beginning; as if he, or perhaps the man who's paying him, knew the thing he wanted would be here. And finally, I have the aggravating feeling that my eyes have seen something my brain hasn't understood.' He shook his head. 'I went all over this thing yesterday, looking for hidden compartments and the like – and if it *is* holding a secret, I couldn't find it. But I still can't shake off the feeling that I'm missing something.'

'If you *are* and if there is more to Old Job than meets the eye,' said Nicholas musingly, 'the chances are Quinn missed it as well.'

'Thank you. Yes. I had realised that – and don't find it comforting.'

'No. So what are you going to do now?'

'Go over it again. Then rip it out, if necessary.' Eden sighed. 'Just leave me to it. You might as well. If and when I need help, I'll let you know.'

He started at the top, doing all the same things he'd done yesterday but approaching the problem more systematically. Inch by laborious inch, he worked his way from top to bottom, then from right to left ... and found nothing. The thing was as solid as it looked. There were no places where it sounded hollow; no double-skinning to the shelves or doors; nothing concealed in the carving. In fact, thought Eden, sitting down to glare at the frustrating thing, the only interesting feature Old Job possessed were those two oddly-shaped and apparently functionless tubular cavities.

Oddly-shaped and useless? Why?

The openings of both were wide enough for him to insert two fingers comfortably but too deep for him to touch their backs.

Assuming, of course, that they have one, he thought suddenly.

'Nick – is there any kind of narrow blade up here? And more light would help.'

Nicholas handed him and knife and sent Dan Hayes downstairs for a lantern.

'Found something?'

'Probably not. But since my last resort involves demolishing the blasted thing completely and not necessarily to any good purpose ...'

Eden knelt on the floor and slid the knife into the left-hand cavity. It disappeared to a depth of some five inches and then hit a barrier. He moved over to the right and did the same thing again. This time the entire blade – a good eight inches of it – disappeared before it found resistance. He gently rotated the blade in the cavity and, feeling what might be an uneven surface, withdrew the knife to try again with his fingers. *Yes.* At the furthest point of his reach was some kind of groove or channel. Eden sat back on his heels and started scraping at the rim of it. He'd originally taken it for wood – the same nearly black oak that the rest of the cupboard was made of – but some unreasoning instinct told him he'd been wrong. Flakes of something dropped to the floor and he detected a hint of shine.

'Where's the bloody lantern?' he demanded.

'Here.' Trooper Hayes materialised at his shoulder and, seeing what the Colonel was doing, held the lantern where it would shed most light. 'All right, sir?'

Eden didn't answer but simply went on scraping until the entire rim was revealed.

It was brass. Bright, shiny, golden brass.

An image appeared in Eden's mind ... along with the echo of Toby's voice that morning.

And, without warning, the penny finally dropped.

'Christ,' he breathed. His heart was beating like an urgent drum-roll. 'Oh my God. That's it, isn't it?'

'What is?' asked Nicholas and Trooper Hayes more or less in unison.

Eden came swiftly to his feet.

'I'll tell you when I'm sure. But for now ... Nick. Get some of the men to stay on after their shift and *don't* under any circumstances let this place be left unattended even for a second. I'll be back as soon as I can.'

'But what --?' began Nicholas.

'Later,' snapped Eden. And took off at a run.

* * *

There was no real need for haste. But the possibility that, after all their months of searching, he might finally have found Stephen Neville's hiding-place, sent him hurtling in search of Lydia. Fortunately, he knew where to look.

Since the day he'd rescued three of their number, Lydia's women had sighed over him in solo and chorus – a phenomenon which his recent rescue of Lydia herself had only intensified. Consequently his unexpected appearance in their midst caused a flurry of feminine excitement.

Lydia watched them clustering round him and watched him reply with his usual courtesy and that slow, dazzling smile. He looked windswept, purposeful and to her eyes, even more attractive than usual.

'Gawd, Miss Lydia,' sighed young Betsy beside her. 'He's lovely. You ain't 'arf lucky.'

Oh. *Not* just to her eyes, then.

As he forged a path towards her through the admiring throng, he said, 'I'm so sorry, ladies. I'd be delighted to sit with you all for a time and taste Mistress Carter's cake – but I'm afraid it will have to wait for another day. Just now I'm in something of a hurry and have urgent need of Mistress Neville.'

Lydia stood up. 'Is something wrong?'

'Not at all.' He made her a small but perfectly correct bow. 'But something has arisen that I believe you may be able to help me with.'

'Of course. I'll get my cloak.' Feeling her colour rising and hoping to hide it from him, she turned to the senior seamstress. 'Lily ... I'll call on Mistress Howell in the morning and attempt to reach an agreement about price on such a large quantity of lace. If I can't get back here myself, Nancy will come and let you know what's been decided.'

Lily Carter curtsied. 'Thank you, Mistress Neville. That'd be a help.'

Once out in the street with her hand on Eden's arm, Lydia shot a brief sideways glance up at him and said, 'What is it? Where are we going?'

'We're going to your house,' he replied, a note of suppressed excitement filtering into his tone. 'I want that brass thing Stephen told you to look after; the thing you thought was a key.'

'Oh.' For a second, she felt stupidly deflated. Of *course* he hadn't swooped in to carry her off to an assignation. What on earth had she been thinking? 'What do you want it for?'

'It's a theory I have. I'll explain if and when I'm sure it's correct.' And swiftly changing the subject before she could enquire further, 'Your women are a touch overwhelming, you know. Do they swarm on every man who strays through the door?'

'No. Just you.'

'*Me*?' He turned to stare down at her. 'Why?'

He sounded so genuinely baffled that Lydia couldn't help laughing even though she knew she was being side-tracked.

'Why do you think? You're the daring rescuer of distressed maidens. You're their hero; their real-life knight in shining armour; their flesh-and-blood, dragon-slaying Saint George. And as if that wasn't enough, you charm them and treat them like ladies and make shameless use of that smile of yours – so of *course* most of them are half besotted with you.'

A faint tinge of colour that had nothing to do with the biting wind touched his face.

He said, 'What do you mean – that smile of mine? I smile the same as anyone else.'

'No,' said Lydia patiently. 'You don't. You do it in a way that is dangerous to any female within ten paces.'

'It doesn't seem to have any effect on you,' he observed.

It does. Every time. It always has.

'Ah but *I* have the advantage of knowing you better,' she replied cheerfully. 'I'm wise to your underhand ways. I know, for example, when I'm being offered a red herring. Tell me why you want the brass thing.'

'No.'

'Why not?' Then, when he merely shook his head and said nothing, '*Is* it a key?'

'Possibly.'

'To what?' Again he didn't answer but merely smiled. 'Eden. Tell me.'

'I'll tell you when I'm sure. For now, I merely want to borrow it for an hour or so.'

'And take it where?'

Eden looked at her with amused exasperation.

'Will you stop? You'll know everything in due course. Just give me a little lee-way.'

Lydia muttered something under her breath and, much to Eden's relief, fell silent for the rest of the way. As soon as they arrived in her hall, he realised he should have known better.

'Thank you, Henry – but I won't need you to take my cloak. I'll be going out again shortly.' Then, turning a bright determined smile on

Eden, she said, 'You want the brass key. Tell me why and you may have it.'

The hazel eyes narrowed. 'Lydia --'

'No. Those are my terms. Take them or leave them. Well?'

He bundled her into the parlour away from Henry's eyes and ears and trapped her between his body and the closed door.

'Now listen to me, you maddeningly stubborn woman! I'm not --'

And there he stopped, losing his thread completely when she laughed up at him.

'Not what, Colonel?' she asked in a meek tone that he knew wasn't meek at all.

'God,' he muttered, torn between shaking or kissing her and simultaneously realising something. She thought this was a battle of wills but it was more than that; this, whether Lydia knew it or not, was about testing her power over him. And given the delicate stage of their relationship, it would be foolish of him to pretend she didn't have any.

Dropping a hard, swift kiss on her mouth, he said, 'All right. I think I may have found a hiding-place we didn't know existed. But it's just a guess and I might --'

'You might be wrong. Yes. I got that bit.' Her expression was as eager and glowing as that of a child. 'Equally, you might be right. So tell me.'

He was enjoying the feel of her body against his and, as it always did, the scent of her hair lured him so he leaned a little closer and, the words no more than a warm breath against her ear, whispered, 'Not ... just ... yet.'

Despite liking their proximity as much as Eden did, Lydia clung to her argument.

'No key, then.'

'Key?' he murmured absently, nuzzling her hair. 'What key?'

'Oh.' Her knees were starting to go weak so she put her hands against his shoulders and gave him a push. 'That was a low trick.'

Eden stepped back, grinning. 'It nearly worked though, didn't it?'

She shook her head. 'Tell me more. Where do you think the key fits?'

'At the lorinery. And that's enough for now. May I please have it?'

Since she'd already decided that he wasn't leaving this house alone to test his theory, Lydia decided it was time to give him what he wanted. Crossing to the large carved dresser, she searched in one of the lower cupboards and eventually emerged with the leather box Eden had seen once before.

'One moment,' he said, taking it from her. 'I seem to recall ... yes.' He produced the slip of paper lying beneath the large brass object. 'The only scrap of Stephen's codes I never decrypted. Let us hope it's one of the ones I recognise.'

It was and it was very brief. Five minutes later, Eden laughed and looking at Lydia, said, 'You're not going to sit quietly by the fire and wait, are you?'

'Did you honestly expect me to?'

'No. Truthfully, I don't think I even hoped for it. So put your hood up and get ready to brave the cold again, Mistress Neville. We're going to Duck Lane ... where we will hopefully find some answers.'

Lydia all but danced over to kiss his cheek. Then, almost as an afterthought, 'What was written on the paper?'

'Exactly what you said yesterday,' he replied. 'Job lived an hundred and forty years--'

'And died being old and full of days!' she declaimed with him. '*Yes!*'

* * *

Lanterns still burned in the lorinery against the gathering gloom of the late afternoon. Inside, about half the men were still busy at their benches ... the rest, said Mr Potter wryly, were all upstairs keeping watch over Old Job as though they expected it to walk off on its own. Everyone, he added, was refusing to go home until they knew what was afoot.

'That,' demurred Eden, 'isn't a good idea. There can't be any talk of this outside.'

'Won't be, Colonel,' said Will Collis flatly. 'I reckon after everything that's gone on, we all know about keeping our mouths shut. And there ain't one man here who'd risk bringing further trouble to Miss Lydia. Not one.'

Eden was happy to take Collis's word ... and those of Buxton and Hayes and a couple of others come to that. It was the remaining fifteen that worried him. However, since Lydia was now half-way up the stairs, he didn't see what could be done about it. So he sighed and said softly, 'Mr Potter ... you know all these men much better than I. Is Trooper Collis right? *Can* I rely on everybody's discretion?'

'Absolutely, Colonel. No question.'

Upstairs, Lydia was talking animatedly to Nicholas but as soon as Eden appeared, she said, 'Where do you think it fits? And what will it do?'

'Patience,' replied Eden. He gestured for everyone to step back and give him room and then hesitated. He hadn't intended to turn this into a whole five-act drama; but then he hadn't intended on doing it before an audience either. So he said, 'Gentlemen ... Mr Potter and Trooper Collis have assured me that none of you will breathe a word of this. I don't doubt that they are right – but, since it's a matter of Mistress Neville's safety, I'd be more comfortable hearing it from you. Like me, you are all fighting men of one sort or another; men who understand the nature and value of a sworn oath. Who will swear an oath of union and secrecy now?'

It seemed to Lydia that something in what he'd said made every man there stand taller. Slowly but without hesitation, she watched every one of them raise a hand. Then Mr Potter said solemnly, 'Let all who accept the oath say aye.'

'Aye,' they said, loudly and firmly.

For a moment, there was silence. Then Eden said simply, 'Thank you. I'm sure that means as much to Mistress Neville as it does to me. And so ... time to find out whether or not I'm clutching at straws.' He took the big brass key from his pocket, 'This belonged to Stephen Neville. With it, he kept a scrap of paper bearing the words of Job 42:16-17. I think it fits here.'

And he pushed it into the right-hand cavity.

His audience gasped.

'As for what it does ... well, let's find out.' He took a firm grip on the shank of the key and tried to turn it. It didn't budge. 'Damn. That serves me right for being dramatic, doesn't it?'

This provoked some laughter and bits of helpful advice. One man offered to fetch some oil and another told the Colonel to put his back into it. The Colonel, still straining over the immoveable key, muttered something extremely rude which produced even more laughter. Then the oil arrived and Eden yanked the key out in order to lubricate both it and the lock.

'Right,' he said, shoving his hair back out of his face. 'Here goes.'

This time, in response to a good deal of effort and accompanied by a roar of encouragement, the key grudgingly turned in the lock. Eden heard it click home.

Thank you, God. Now please give me something more than spiders.

Bracing himself, he gripped the edges of the frame and pulled. With a groan of protest, one whole section of the cupboard came away from the wall ... revealing a shallow recess, lined with shelves.

And on the shelves were just two small brass-bound boxes.

SEVEN

An hour later, Eden, Lydia and Nicholas were half-way back to Cheapside.

Once Old Job had finally given up its secret, the mood inside the lorinery had become almost euphoric and the Colonel had endured a good deal of back-slapping. Aware that, until he knew what was inside those boxes, congratulations were premature, he'd merely smiled and asked if anyone knew how to pick a lock. Luckily, it turned out that Trooper Buxton did. Eden hadn't wanted to know how and why.

The boxes held numerous folded sheets of paper. With Lydia at his shoulder but refusing to satisfy her curiosity there and then, Eden had gathered them all up and thrust them inside his coat. Then he asked Mr Potter for redundant lorinery correspondence to replace what he'd taken and told Buxton to re-lock the boxes, put them back where they were and return Old Job to its usual state.

Finally, he'd glanced round at the expectant faces and said, 'I'm not going to read what we've found here right now. First, there's too much of it – and secondly, the sooner it's away from here, the better for everyone. But I *do* thank you, gentlemen. If there are answers ... and if I find I need further assistance, I'll know where to look for it.'

Tripping along with her hand on his arm and a dozen questions hovering on her tongue, Lydia said, 'Why are we going to Cheapside?'

'Because – even though I don't yet know what we've found – I am not risking it being kept anywhere near you.'

'But you *are* going to let me read whatever it is, aren't you?'

'Is there any way of stopping you?'

She smiled up at him. 'No.'

'That's what I thought,' grumbled Eden. 'I don't know how you've won the hearts of those fellows back there – because you frighten the hell out of me.'

'I do not.'

'You do. Right now, you'd be sitting snug at home instead of out here in the cold if you hadn't bullied me into bringing you.'

'I didn't bully you,' objected Lydia, despite being on the edge of laughter.

'No. I suppose *blackmailed* is a more apt description.'

'When the two of you have finished bickering,' remarked Nicholas, hiding his own smile, 'what are we hoping to find?'

A name, thought Eden.

'At the moment, I'm trying not to hope too much for anything – except perhaps that everything inside my coat isn't in code. If it is, I'll be slaving over it for a week.'

Since darkness had now fallen and it was beginning to freeze, all three of them were heartily grateful for the roaring fire that greeted them in Cheapside and the hot, spiced wine Mistress Wilkes produced within minutes of their arrival.

Then, without further ado, Eden laid the twin bundles neatly on the table.

'Since Stephen kept these separate from each other, I suggest we do the same. It would appear that this pile consists of letters and the other, of dated notes.' Looking round, he said, 'Lydia ... you take the letters. I suspect you'll find them more interesting. Nick and I will make a start on the other stuff. Mercifully, nothing I've seen so far is encrypted.'

Nodding, Lydia took the heap of letters away to the fireside settle while Eden and Nicholas faced each across the table. For a long time there was silence, broken only by the crackling of the fire and the rustle of paper. Then Nicholas said, 'Hell!'

'What?' asked Lydia.

He stared across at Eden and it was a moment before he answered. Then, 'Is yours the same as this? Notes and theories about somebody he refers to as Daemon?'

'Yes – though mostly what I have here are questions about the clients of an organisation he calls the Sabura.'

'It's not an organisation,' said Nicholas grimly.

'I know. Mr Neville's choice of name told me that.'

'Will one of you please explain?' demanded Lydia.

'In ancient Rome, the Sabura district was known for housing depravity of every kind. The natural conclusion is that Stephen's talking about the worst kind of brothel.'

'*Are* some worse than others?'

'Yes,' replied Eden. 'Trust me, Lydia ... you don't want details.'

'Mr Neville did,' said Nicholas. 'It appears to have taken him a long time to get them but they're all listed here. Meticulously.'

'Does he say where it is?'

'Not precisely. But there's a reference to St Olave's ... and something I don't understand that's apparently seething.'

Eden looked up. 'St Olave's is on Crutched Friars – just around the corner from Seething Lane, just below Tower Hill. If that's it, we can find it – though I hope it doesn't become necessary.'

'Does this man Daemon own it?' asked Lydia.

'I think it's safe to assume so, yes. What are the letters?'

'The history of a love affair – and all from the same woman. I've put them in order. The earliest one is dated March 1620 and the last, May 1649 – though the correspondence isn't continuous. There are gaps, sometimes of years.' She looked up, her eyes expressionless. 'Stephen's first wife died in childbed in the summer of 1618 and he married me in the autumn of '48. I suspected there might be someone in his past but not that it might have gone on for nearly thirty years.'

'Does she sign her name?'

'No. That would make everything far too simple, wouldn't it? Besides, she's married – so she calls herself Persephone. And even *I* know who that is.'

'Then read on and hope you find a clue,' said Eden. 'All these classical allusions must fall apart somewhere.'

Silence fell again. And the next time, it was Lydia who broke it.

'Here's something. It's August 1621 and she's expecting a baby.'

Eden laid down the list he was currently perusing.

'Don't tell me,' he said dryly. 'The child is Stephen's but she's going to pass it off as her husband's?'

'She doesn't say so – but we can't discount the possibility.' She shot him a worried look and then, relieved to see that he merely looked sardonic, turned quickly to the next letter and said, 'It was a boy, born in February 1622.'

It was Nicholas's turn to look mildly shocked.

'Her husband's heir was sired by Stephen Neville?'

'Not necessarily. We don't know he was her first child.' She scanned the next letter. 'Two years on, she's had another son ... but there are no clues to this one's paternity either. The trouble is that sometimes she writes retrospectively which means any dates she gives don't tell us much.' She sighed and looked up. 'I don't see how this is helping.'

'It might not be,' agreed Eden, 'or it might turn out to be crucial. At this stage, it's impossible to say – so I suggest we all lay anything we think may be even vaguely significant to one side for consideration later.'

'You haven't told us what you've got,' remarked Nicholas absently.

'A list of clients of the Sabura that Stephen believed Daemon was blackmailing. These gentlemen are only identified by their initials or, in some cases, by their position. Three are MPs which means they had to have been members of the Rump. One is an under-secretary to what I believe may be the Army Council; another works in the victualling office and a third is an alderman. With a little effort, I imagine we could put names to all of them – but it's likely to be a waste of time. If they've been paying someone to keep their dark secrets, they're hardly going to admit it to us, are they?'

The three of them went back to work. After a while, Nicholas announced that Stephen now suspected Daemon of other unspecified crimes; and a little later, Lydia remarked that Persephone was becoming concerned about the behaviour and character of one of her sons.

'It's 1636 and she writes that *"At times, young as he is, I glimpse something in him that I do not know how to name but which alarms me. Behind the charm, something quite different seems to look out of his eyes. And yet my husband sees no fault in him and, indeed, indulges him beyond all good sense, to the detriment of the other".*' Lydia looked up, frowning. 'Which son is she talking about, do you think?'

'Don't ask me.' Nicholas put down the paper he'd been holding. 'I'm past thinking at all. It's late, Eden. My concentration is slipping and I'm for bed. We can't possibly get through all this tonight anyway.'

Eden glanced at the clock. It was a quarter after eleven. He stood up and said quickly, 'Lydia – I'm so sorry. I ought to have taken you home hours ago.'

'It doesn't matter.'

'It does. It was damned thoughtless of me.' He turned, saying, 'Go to bed, Nick. I won't need you.'

'You're sure?'

'Yes. I'll go armed.' And when Nicholas had bidden them both a sleepy 'goodnight' and set off upstairs, he said, 'Get your cloak and we'll go now. Unless ...'

'Unless what?'

'The chamber you used the other night should still be made up and it will take no time at all to light a fire there. But if you'd rather go home, we should set off immediately.'

Lydia thought of the cold, dark streets. In particular, she thought of Eden walking back through those streets alone. And finally she thought something else she refused to acknowledge. She said, 'I think I'd prefer to stay – if that would be all right.'

'It would be a relief,' he admitted. 'I don't relish the idea of going out again tonight any more than you must do. Help yourself to wine and stay here in the warm. I'm not disturbing Alice at this time of night so I'll see to the fire myself.'

When he had gone, Lydia sat by the hearth cradling a glass in her hands and staring into the flames, half excited and half nervous. Would he share her bed or wouldn't he? The fact that there was nothing to stop him doing so suggested that he might; but the fact that he clearly didn't intend her to spend the night in his own chamber suggested otherwise. The only thing she was certain of was that it wasn't up to her to offer; it was up to him to ask.

Eden returned and joined her at the fireside.

'By the time you've finished your wine it should be reasonably warm up there. You must be exhausted.'

'No. Oddly enough, I'm not. I think it's the excitement of finally finding Stephen's papers. How did you guess there was a hiding place behind Old Job?'

'Purely by chance,' he shrugged. 'Something I hope you've realised – and the main reason we're not walking to Bishopsgate right now – is that, since *we* have the papers, Quinn is still on the hunt.'

'I'd realised it,' she sighed, 'but not really thought about it.'

'Then do so now. From this point on, you follow my rules to the letter. And if you're tempted to risk your own safety by deviating from them in any way, try to remember that you'll be risking my neck as well as your own.'

'I know – and I won't. I promise.'

'Good. Now drink your wine and tell me what you make of Persephone.'

'I think she loved Stephen very much. The terms in which she mourns their long partings and the knowledge that they can never be together are ... very moving. And since the relationship out-lasted the love affair by many years, along with the fact that he kept her letters, suggests that Stephen felt the same.'

He nodded. 'Go on. What about their son?'

'Well, it was natural that she should send Stephen news of him, wasn't it? I just wish she wrote more clearly so we knew whether it was his son she had concerns about or the other.' She took a sip of wine. 'However, I *am* beginning to wonder if the presence of the letters isn't just coincidence.'

'You're saying that Stephen hid them for purely sentimental reasons and that they have nothing to do with the ill-doings of Daemon?'

'Yes. Don't you think so?'

'As yet, I haven't decided what I think ... aside from the fact it's time you were in bed.' He rose and reached for a candle. 'Come on. I'll light you upstairs.'

Once in her bedchamber, Eden lit more candles and banked up the fire. He'd already decided about what would – or rather wouldn't – happen next; his difficulty was in knowing how best to manage it.

Rising and dusting off his hands, he said, 'Is there anything else you need?'

Yes.

'No. Thank you.'

Eden had heard her thought as clearly as if she'd spoken it.

Placing his hands on her shoulders with the intention of keeping them there, he gave her a long, sweet kiss. Then he lifted his head and smiled ruefully at her.

Lydia said huskily, 'You're not going to stay with me, are you?'

'No. Not tonight.' *Nor hopefully any night unless you refuse to marry me – in which case I'll have no choice but to be grateful for whatever you're willing to give.* 'But not because I don't want to.'

'Then why?' She tried not to let it sound either disappointed or pleading.

'Those papers downstairs have put you in danger long enough. I want it finished – and for that I need a name or some sliver of information that will lead me to one. Since it won't simply leap out and present itself, I'm going back to do a few more hours work.'

'Oh.' Lydia laid a hand against his cheek, her eyes worried. 'But you need sleep.'

'I'm a soldier, love. I'm used to sleeping when I can.' He allowed himself to slide his arms around her in a brief embrace and then, dropping one last kiss on her brow, stepped back. 'Go to bed, Lydia. I'll see you in the morning.'

She stood quite still watching the door close behind him. And a little later, curled up beneath the covers while her mind flew round in circles, two new thoughts occurred to her.

Had he ever truly intended to take her as his mistress? And if he hadn't, might that be because, contrary to all her assumptions, he actually *wanted* to marry her?

It was a possibility too dizzying to contemplate … but she fell asleep contemplating it anyway.

Downstairs in the parlour, it took Eden a little time to stop his body wanting what it wasn't going to have and focus on the task in hand. But finally, drawing a long determined breath, he sat down and pulled the next stack of papers in front of him.

* * *

Having worked on until four in the morning by which time his eyes felt full of grit, Eden allowed himself a couple of hours' sleep and then rose again to resume his efforts.

Stephen Neville had gone to a lot of trouble to discover and document information about the man he called Daemon. Clearly, he must have had a particular reason for doing so and Eden was beginning to suspect that reason had been a personal one. Unlike Lydia, he didn't think that Stephen had put his one-time lover's letters alongside the Daemon file by chance. He'd done it because he either believed or knew that Daemon was one of Persephone's sons. The question, of course, was which? One legitimate, one not; one spoiled by a man who might or might not be his father and the other seemingly passed over; and one of the two growing up in a way that was making his mother fear for the man he might become.

More and more, Eden was convinced that the answer, if there was one, would be found in Persephone's letters. Lydia had ordered these according to date and had been reading from the beginning of the correspondence. Eden flipped the pile and started from the other end.

By the time Mistress Wilkes walked in bringing breakfast only to scowl at the litter covering the table, he had a page full of scribblings. Glancing briefly up at the housekeeper, he said absently, 'Put it in the back parlour, please.' And failed to hear her grumble of disapproval.

Nicholas appeared, yawning. He said, 'You're a busy soul, aren't you? Anything?'

'Plenty – but nothing that connects yet.' Eden sat up and stretched. 'I've concentrated on the letters. Lots of references to one of the sons being away a great deal, of being secretive and spending money he shouldn't have … and a couple of allusions to mysterious night-time visitors. In the later letters, she started calling him Janus.'

'The two-faced god of gates? That sounds appropriate.'

'Bloody annoying is what it is. The other son is Mother's comfort and joy. She calls *him* Gaius.' He threw down his quill. 'I'm beginning to hate mythology.'

Nicholas grinned at him. 'Come and eat. You'll feel better after some food.' And when Eden rose and followed him, 'Did you get Lydia home safely?'

'No. She's in the spare bedchamber. At least, I *hope* she damned well is. If she's gone wandering off on her own, I may well strangle her.'

'Strangle who?' asked an amused voice from behind him. And, dipping an apparently respectful curtsy when he wheeled to face her, 'You see? All present and correct and reporting for duty, sir.'

Despite himself, a gleam of laughter appeared in Eden's eyes.

'Colonel,' he corrected pleasantly, 'is the correct form of address from subordinates.'

'Of which,' she said blithely, 'I am not one.' Then, differently, 'Did you get any sleep at all?'

'A couple of hours.' He pulled out a chair for her and when they were all seated, explained again and in slightly more detail, what he'd been doing. Then, pausing to consume a slice of cheese, he said, 'I think ... indeed, I'm fairly sure that Stephen's Daemon is Persephone's Janus. I found a letter dated December '48 where she says she is *consumed with the darkest suspicions* which she will confide to Stephen separately *when Janus is away and I can be sure my letter will be seen by you and you alone*. She insists Stephen must burn that letter immediately on receipt of it – and, since it isn't there, he must have done so. Despite this, her next letter sounds frightened. She says *I think he knows. What shall I do?*'

'Knows what?' asked Nicholas, reaching for the bread. 'It's a great shame we haven't got the other half of the correspondence. It might solve everything.'

Lydia was suddenly very still. Eyes wide and turning a little pale, she thought, *No. No – it can't be. Can it?* Realising that Eden was looking questioningly at her, she said slowly, 'I – I've had an idea. It's probably preposterous and I'm completely wrong but ...'

'But what?' he asked. 'At this stage, no idea can be too preposterous.' And when she continued to stare at him, a frown of concentration marking her brow, 'Lydia ... what is it?'

'I think I may know who Persephone is,' she said flatly.

The breath hissed between Eden's teeth and Nicholas laid down his knife. Neither of them said anything, leaving her words to echo on in the silence.

Finally Lydia said slowly, 'I don't know why I didn't see it before. The two sons, the long correspondence with Stephen ... the only thing that doesn't fit is one of the sons being Daemon. That's just not – not possible.'

'Do you think you could just give us a name?' asked Nicholas.

'Yes. I'm sorry.' She sat up very straight. 'I think Persephone is – was – Arabella Wakefield, Viscountess Northcote. She's dead.'

'*Wakefield?*' snapped Eden.

'Yes. She was Gilbert's mother.'

'I see. And what makes you think she was also Stephen's paramour?'

'When Gilbert first introduced himself, he said he'd wanted to inform Stephen of his mother's death but had discovered that Stephen had predeceased her. Apparently, he'd been going through his mother's papers and found numerous letters from Stephen and so wondered if *I* had the ones written by his mother. I hadn't, of course ... but he always seemed convinced that I'd eventually stumble across them.' She paused slightly. 'He was quite persistent about it. I remember finding it rather irritating.'

I found a lot of things about him irritating, thought Eden darkly; but said, 'You've never mentioned anything of this.'

'Why would I? It wasn't important before. But it's different now; a lot of things fit. Gilbert's older brother is now Viscount Northcote. *He's* arrogant, patronising and rude – but so full of his own consequence that I can't imagine him --'

'Wait!' snapped Eden. 'You've *met* his lordship?'

'Once – and that was enough. I virtually threw him out and told Henry not to --'

'What did he want with you?'

Lydia concentrated on crumbling a piece of bread and said reluctantly, 'He called to tell me I wasn't good enough for his brother and that if Gilbert offered me marriage, it was in my own best interests to decline.'

Eden's face became perfectly expressionless.

'I see. And *did* Gilbert propose to you?'

'Yes.'

'Ah. Something else you didn't mention.'

This time the silence was deafening. Nicholas glanced from one to the other of them and wisely kept his mouth shut.

Lydia lifted her chin and looked him defiantly in the eye.

'Again – why would I? But, if you really want to know, I told Gilbert what I might have told his obnoxious brother had he not made me so furious. I said that I valued his friendship but that marriage was and always would be out of the question.'

Eden leaned back and folded his arms. 'When was this?'

'About six weeks ago.' She thought about it. 'Shortly before Parliament was dissolved.'

'So ... after we retrieved your women from the Steelyard but before our interlude in the cellar?'

'Yes.'

'Interesting.'

'And a possibility worth looking into, wouldn't you say?' asked Nicholas carefully.

'Yes.' The hazel eyes didn't move from Lydia's face. 'Let us be quite clear. Although you think Persephone may be the late Lady Northcote, you don't believe that either of her sons could be Daemon. This, I gather, is because you like one of them and think the other too high in the instep to run a brothel.'

'In a nutshell, yes,' she replied a shade uneasily. 'Is something wrong with that?'

'I think so. Assuming you're right about Lady Northcote – and I agree that you may be – one of her sons is illegitimate and one is not. If either of them knows this, he'll want any proof of it in his own hands; the one to keep it hidden, the other to make it public. Both of them have equally good reasons for hunting for it. Especially in Gilbert's case if he thinks a title which ought, by rights to be his, has gone to an elder brother born on the wrong side of the blanket.'

Lydia shook her head.

'I can't believe Gilbert is responsible for any of the things that have happened. He isn't ... I just don't think he's capable of it.'

'Not everyone is what they seem,' returned Eden uncompromisingly. 'As for the Daemon question ... Stephen didn't go to so much effort just to pass a dull Tuesday. He had a reason. And the only reason I can think of is personal. But if either of you has a better idea, I'm listening.'

Lydia said nothing. But after a few moments Nicholas asked, 'All right. So where does this leave us?'

'If you can bear the thought, I'd like the two of you to continue sifting through Old Job's harvest. Look for anything that supports the theories we've just been discussing – but don't discount anything else.'

'And while we're doing that,' asked Lydia with misgiving, 'what will *you* be doing?'

'Paying a call on Mr Wakefield. I presume you know where he lodges?'

Lydia didn't like the sound of this. She said, 'No. I don't --' And then stopped, not sure how best to phrase an objection.

The implication and timing of her words proved unfortunate. Eden's expression turned ice-cold and he said softly, 'Don't lie to me.'

'I wasn't going to!' she protested, realising that – with this man in particular – any impression of deceit would be catastrophic. 'He has rooms over the White Hart, near the Temple. I was only going to say that I don't think you should go – that it would be better if I sent a note inviting him to Bishopsgate.'

'Delightfully cosy as that sounds,' replied Eden pushing his platter aside and standing up, 'I think we will do this my way.'

'Wait!' Lydia also rose. 'If you must do this – I'll come with you.'

'No. This time you most certainly will not. *This* time,' said Colonel Maxwell grimly, 'you will do as I ask and stay here with Nicholas. And I'd further appreciate it if, just for once, you could do it without arguing.'

EIGHT

Finding Mr Wakefield's lodgings was not difficult. Colonel Maxwell ran up the stairs, emptying his mind of personal feelings in order to concentrate on what mattered. The door was opened by a servant, who eyed him blankly and said, 'Yes?'

'Colonel Maxwell to see Mr Wakefield. Is he here?'

The servant quailed under the Colonel's eye. 'Y-yes. But he isn't dressed yet.'

'That is easily remedied. I don't mind waiting – though not on the landing.'

'No.' The man stepped back to let him enter the comfortably furnished parlour. 'Of course. If you'd care to t-take a seat, I'll tell Mr Wakefield you're here.'

Eden nodded, removed his hat and, instead of sitting down, strolled across to the window.

The servant disappeared into an adjoining room from whence, in due course, came sounds of voices and hurried activity. Eden smiled sourly to himself.

Of course. I might have known the fellow would have somebody to brush his coats and fasten his breeches for him. And then, wearily, *Forget you don't like him. Forget that Lydia does. Do what you came to do.*

Gilbert Wakefield appeared quicker than Eden had thought he might. He eyed his unexpected visitor with unease bordering on confusion and said, 'Colonel? I'm surprised to see you here. Is this an official visit ... or something other?'

Eden subjected him to a long, trying stare and finally said, 'You may wish to give your man an errand that will take him elsewhere for a time.'

'The matter you wish to discuss is ... confidential?' And then, when the disconcerting hazel gaze remained fixed on his face, 'Very well. If you think it necessary.'

'I imagine that it is *you* who will think it necessary. But it amounts to the same thing.'

He waited again while Gilbert sent his servant out to buy half a dozen assorted items. Then, when the door closed behind him leaving them alone, he said, 'I understand from Mistress Neville that your late mother corresponded with the equally late Stephen Neville.'

'Yes. But --'

'I also understand that you showed great interest in seeing and possibly also possessing your mother's letters.'

'Again, yes. But I don't understand how that can be any concern of yours.'

'You will.' Eden produced one of Persephone's letters from his pocket. 'Is this your mother's handwriting?'

Gilbert took the paper, stared at it. His hand shook a little and he said, 'Yes. How --?'

'Read it.' The letter had been deliberately chosen to contain the names of both Janus and Gaius but no mention of either being the lady's son. 'Then tell me what you make of it.'

Gilbert walked away to the light of the window. He read the dozen or so lines and then apparently read them again. Finally he turned back to Eden and, sounding genuinely bewildered, said, 'What is this is about? It doesn't make sense.'

'It does when you read some of the others.'

'You have more?'

'I believe I have all that exist. But rid your mind of any idea that I've come here with the intention of making you a present of them. I haven't. Neither are they for sale.'

'What then? Why *are* you here?'

Colonel Maxwell continued to watch him in silence.

Mr Wakefield began to feel inexplicably nervous. It wasn't that the Colonel was a particularly big man – indeed, he was an inch or two shorter than he was himself. And though the compact frame beneath that plain russet coat hinted at well-honed muscles and physical strength, the real cause of Gilbert's inner disquiet lay elsewhere. It was due to the intimidating quality of the man's expression and the fact that, when he chose to exert it, Colonel Maxwell had a truly formidable presence.

Eventually, Eden said dispassionately, 'I'm here because the existence of your mother's letters has caused Mistress Neville a great deal of pain, worry and inconvenience. Obscenities daubed on her walls ... her workmen put at risk of lethal injury ... three of her women abducted for the purpose of extortion; and finally, an attack upon Mistress Neville herself. I'd like to hear what you know about all this.'

'*Me?*' Mr Wakefield stared back as if Eden had been speaking in a foreign language. 'Nothing! What do you think I am, damn it? I like Lydia – more than like her, if you want the truth. I hoped to see the letters, yes. But if you think I'd go to any lengths to get them, you must be deranged!'

'Are you saying you didn't?'

'Yes! How many times must I say it?'

'As often as it takes to convince me,' came the cold reply.

'I don't know what the hell you're talking about! Is that clear enough for you?' Gilbert ran a distracted hand through his hair. 'I don't know where you came by this insane idea – but this is the first I've heard of any of it.'

Eden had had a lot of practice in telling lies from truth and, if this was a performance, it was a very convincing one. He was not, however, prepared to accept it just yet. He said, 'Sit down, Mr Wakefield.'

'Thank you – but I don't think I will.'

'Sit down.' The quiet implacability of the command was more effective than a parade-ground bark. Gilbert sat. 'Good. I am aware that you didn't commit any of these acts personally. They were performed under the auspices of a powerful and dangerous criminal who accepts commissions like these for payment. Are you acquainted with such a person?'

'No. And I wouldn't know where to start looking for one. Look ... none of this is anything to do with me and I can't see why you think it is.'

'I'm coming to that.' Eden let another silence develop before saying, 'Why do you want your mother's letters to Stephen Neville?'

'Why do you think? If it was your mother, wouldn't *you* want them?'

'You're saying you wanted them for purely sentimental reasons.'
'Yes.'

This time Eden detected a difference. It was very possibly the first lie.

'I see,' he said mildly. 'So ... not because you have reason to question either your own or your brother's legitimacy?'

The blood drained slowly from Mr Wakefield's skin and his hands clenched on the carved arms of his chair. He said, 'No. Not at all.'

Ah, thought Eden. *The second lie. And now I know how bad he is at it.*

'Try again,' he said mildly. 'We both know that isn't true.'

'Do we?' muttered Gilbert. 'I'm beginning to wonder what the hell you *do* know.'

'The same thing you do. I know that one of you – I'd guess your brother – was sired by Stephen Neville.'

Gilbert sucked in a raw breath and sagged against the chair-back. Finally he said, 'So. It's true, then.'

'Weren't you already sure that it was?'

'No.' He paused, plainly struggling to master both thoughts and words. 'Mother whispered something of the sort. But she was dying, semi-delirious and ... and Edmund hadn't been treating her kindly for quite a long time. She said it, yes – but, as much as I wanted it to be true, I didn't dare rely on it.'

'So you needed the letters to find proof. That's understandable. And supposing you found them and they supplied it – what then?'

'I don't know.' Seemingly unable to sit still any longer, Gilbert surged to his feet and swept away across the room. Then he said jerkily, 'Edmund and I don't get on. No. That's an understatement. There've been times in recent years when I've hated him and he me.' He gave a harsh laugh. 'Needless to say, I'd like to take the title from him – but, since my father accepted him, that's a damned sight easier said than done. In truth, I don't know *what* I'd do or even if I could do anything. I just felt I had to *know*.' He stopped and then, as if the words were being wrenched from him, said, 'Hell. Since you know so much, I may as well tell you. Mother was dying and it was near the end. I'd been sitting with her and that's when she told me about Edmund. There was something else she seemed to want to say but she drifted off to sleep.

A servant called me downstairs on some foolish pretext. I wasn't away more than ten minutes but when I went back, she'd gone. She'd gone … and Edmund was there, holding her hand and smiling fondly at her in a way I'd never seen before.'

The inference was plain enough. Eden said slowly, 'You think he … hastened her end?'

'I suspected it. I still do,' replied Gilbert bitterly. 'That's a terrible thing to think of one's brother, isn't it? But not quite as terrible as not being sure.'

'No. No, I can see that.' Eden continued to survey the other man while he debated the various courses of action. Then, making up his mind, he said slowly, 'You'd better come and see the rest of what Mistress Neville and I have found. If my own suspicions are correct, there is a great deal more to your brother than meets the eye. And from what you've just told me, I doubt any of it will come as a shock.'

* * *

When the door slammed behind Eden, Lydia remained quite still staring at the food on her plate. Her appetite had gone and, even if it hadn't, she didn't think she could swallow past the foolish lump in her throat. Last night's rosy dreams evaporated without a trace and, trying to replace misery with resentment, she said, 'He didn't have to jump to conclusions quite so readily.'

Nicholas continued placidly eating. 'No?'

'No. I wasn't going to lie to him. He ought to have known that.'

This time Nicholas said nothing.

'He was just being deliberately difficult. He's good at that. And he always has to know best. At times he – he can be positively infuriating.'

'Because he's usually right,' said Nicholas finally. 'In instances like these, he *does* know best. And when you stop sulking, I hope to hear you admit it. Meanwhile – if you're not going to eat that – I suggest we go and do what he asked us to.'

Lydia watched him leave the room, her vision slightly blurred. Then, dashing an irritable hand across her eyes, she got up and followed him.

For perhaps an hour, they worked in silence. Then, unable to help herself, Lydia said, 'What do you think he will do?'

'What will who do?' asked Nicholas abstractedly. And when she didn't immediately answer, 'I can't speak for your Mr Wakefield but --'

'He's not *my* Mr Wakefield!'

'Oh. Well, if you say so. As for Eden, he doesn't kill people unless he has to. I thought you'd already know that.'

'I *do* know it! Nick – will you stop being so angry? It – it just came out wrong.'

He shrugged. 'It's not me with whom you need to make it right. But just for future reference and in case you don't appreciate what he's already gone through on your account ... do you *know* about his wife?'

'Yes.' She hated how small her voice sounded.

'Then you'll know why he reacted as he did. Given the circumstances, any man alive would have done the same.'

Lydia opened her mouth, then closed it again as a startling possibility dawned. She said slowly, 'What circumstances, Nick? Are you saying he ... that Eden ...?'

'I'm not saying anything. I'm trying,' said Nicholas, hiding his smile behind the document he was currently perusing, 'to get on with this. So do you think we might stop talking?'

It was a further hour before the sound of the shop door followed by footfalls on the stairs had Lydia shooting to her feet, one hand clenched hard over the other. Then the parlour door opened and Eden was ushering Gilbert Wakefield through it. She froze and had to remember to close her mouth.

'As you can no doubt see,' announced Colonel Maxwell coolly and without preamble, 'Mr Wakefield and I managed to reach an understanding without recourse to violence. Since it seems he is Gaius, not Janus, and he has his own reasons for wanting the answers we are currently seeking, it seems reasonable to pool our resources.'

Seeing that this speech had left Lydia lost for words, Nicholas stood up and offered his hand to the newcomer. 'What we've learned so far, suggests this isn't going to be much fun for you.'

'Perhaps not,' replied Mr Wakefield, taking it. 'But I'm sick of wondering.'

When everyone was seated around the table, Eden picked up the fruits of his night's work, gave a prosaic précis of their discoveries and then, with Gilbert's permission, related that gentleman's suspicion about his mother's death. Throughout all of this, he avoided making eye contact with Lydia – who, in turn, avoided looking directly at Mr Wakefield. Nicholas started to feel as if pitfalls were lying in wait all around them.

At the end, Eden said, 'And now to progress. Mr Wakefield ... you will doubtless wish to read some of the letters and we've laid to one side those of most interest so I suggest you begin with them. Lydia ... there are still some here we've yet to look at. And Nick ... I thought you might check that all is well at the lorinery, set Henry's mind at rest concerning Lydia's safety and ask him to send Peter here to escort her home later this afternoon.'

Nicholas came gratefully to his feet.

'I'll see to it. But before I go, there's something I want to show you. I found it this morning.' And he handed over a single sheet of paper.

Eden glanced at the tightly-scripted sheet and then sharply into Nicholas's face.

'Hallelujah. I think. Are there any others like this?'

'No. After I found that one, I went through all the rest.' He grinned. 'Enjoy yourself.' And he walked out, leaving Eden once more staring at the page in his hand.

'What is it?' asked Lydia tentatively.

'My morning's work,' he returned with a brief, impersonal smile, 'It's in code. A new one, unfortunately – so, since I work quicker in complete silence, I'll take it into the back parlour. But do feel free to tell me if you find anything new.' And following Nicholas from the room, he closed the door behind him.

It was at that moment that Lydia felt she could cheerfully have hit him. She stalked to the door and jerked it open again, muttering not quite under her breath, 'Stupid, *stupid* man!'

Eden heard it and continued into the back parlour, smiling a little.

Since Gilbert was sitting by the hearth, already immersed in reading, Lydia took the remaining letters to the window-seat on the far side of the room. The fact that it was decidedly chilly there served only to deepen her black mood. After a while, Gilbert lifted his head, his expression completely bemused and said, 'This is ... I don't know. Mother seems to have suspected Edmund of all manner of things for years. I had no idea.'

'No. I suppose you wouldn't.'

He looked at her. 'I had no idea about the rest of it, either. Of the trouble and danger to you and yours for which the Colonel believes him responsible. I'm exceedingly sorry for it. Until today, I honestly thought the secret of his birth was mine alone. Obviously, he's known for as long – if not longer – than I have.'

'Obviously.'

Gilbert laid aside the letters and walked over to her.

'Lydia ... have I offended you in some way?'

She drew an impatient breath and finally met his eyes.

'No. It isn't your fault. I did something stupid earlier and am still kicking myself.' She paused and made a small helpless gesture. 'Do you really suspect your brother of murdering your mother?'

'Yes. To be brutally frank, I think he put a pillow over her face. But I can't prove it.'

'If he could do that,' said Lydia slowly, 'he's capable of anything.'

'Yes. That's what I'm beginning to realise.'

Lydia turned back at the letter in her hand and realised that, since she hadn't absorbed a single word she'd read since Eden left the room, continuing was pointless. Rising, she said abruptly, 'I'm sorry. Please go on reading, Gilbert. I need to speak to Colonel Maxwell.'

She entered the neighbouring room and shut the door behind her. Eden remained hunched over his work as if he hadn't heard her come in. Lydia cleared her throat and waited. Finally, without looking around, he said, 'You've found something?'

'No. I wanted to talk to you.'

'Oh?'

'Yes. I'm sorry if I gave a mistaken impression before. I wasn't going to lie to you. I've never done that and I never will.'

Eden laid down his quill and swivelled to face her, his own expression unreadable. In the last hour, he'd come to the conclusion that enough was enough. It was time to clear away any misconceptions ... and with Lydia the quickest way of doing so was to be inflammatory.

'You don't need to either explain or apologise. It was unreasonable of me to take offence. After all, it isn't as though you and I have any definite understanding, is it?'

That caught her unprepared. She stammered, 'I – I thought we had.'

'Well, come to that, I suppose I did, too,' he said pensively. 'I thought you were considering my offer of marriage. But perhaps you were *re*considering Mr Wakefield's similar offer?'

'No!' Lydia stared at him in utter horror. 'How can you *think* that?'

He shrugged. 'Since, until this morning, I was entirely ignorant of the nature of your relationship with him, it's a possibility that can't be discounted.'

'Then discount it now. I told you I'd refused him.'

'So you did.' He waited and when she continued to stare at him without speaking, 'Was there anything else?'

'Yes.' She sat down with a bump on the nearest chair and without stopping to think, said rapidly, 'I can't do this any more. I just can't. I still don't know whether you actually *want* to marry me or just think you should – but it ought to be perfectly plain what my answer was always going to be.'

'Odd as it may seem, I don't find this a subject for guesswork, intuition or assumptions.'

His apparent nonchalance added intensity to the maelstrom of thoughts and emotions boiling inside her and, unrecognised at the back of them, was a determination to splinter his infuriating composure. She snapped, 'Why not? Any one of those would have told you the truth – unless you thought I fell into bed with you on a whim because you happened to be handy. Did you?'

Eden had to repress a flicker of involuntary amusement. 'No.'

'No. I lay with you because I'd wanted you for weeks but never thought it would actually happen. And suddenly you gave me the chance of something I'd only dared dream of and it – it was ...' She stopped and shook her head, breathing rather fast. 'Then immediately afterwards you asked me to marry you. *You* – the man who'd always sworn he'd never re-marry. What was I to think? I'd never expected you to offer and couldn't account for it except in one way. So it didn't matter how badly I wanted to say yes; that I'd have sold my soul for the privilege of being your wife. I couldn't risk you wanting to change your mind but feeling you couldn't do so – or regretting it once the deed was done. Because that would have hurt worse than giving you up.'

'You don't seem to --'

Lydia cut him off. 'Stop. You wanted the truth and you'll damned well sit there and let me finish.'

'I beg your pardon.' *Oh sweetheart. Only you could approach a moment like this as if it was a cavalry charge.* 'Please go on.'

'I'm in love with you.' she said baldly and without emphasis. 'I've probably been in love with you throughout virtually our entire acquaintance. Perhaps you'll think I should have said so before – but I didn't know if you'd welcome it so I didn't. Instead, I prevaricated and said I needed to think but that we could be l-lovers, if you'd like. That alone should have told you that it was you I wanted; *just* you – with no conditions attached.' Lydia swallowed hard and added, 'And it hasn't changed.' She stood up. 'Well then, now you know where you stand and I've made a complete idiot of myself, I'll l-let you get on with what you were doing.'

'Wait.' Eden also rose. 'Don't I get a turn?'

His tone was plaintive but the look in his eyes was something very different.

'Yes. Of course.'

'Thank you. For the time being, I'm going to keep this very simple. I didn't ask you to be my mistress. I asked you to marry me and I have been waiting, not very patiently, for you to say that you will. I didn't offer marriage out of any sense of duty or obligation. I offered it because I want, with every fibre of my being, to spend the rest of my life with you. In short, I love you.' His smile, as he held out his hand to her, was slightly crooked. 'I just ... love you.'

Something unbelievably beautiful seemed to fill her chest; something too vast for her to immediately comprehend. Tears filled her eyes and, reaching out to grasp his fingers, she said, 'Oh. That is ... I ... oh. I don't know what to say to you.'

'Good. Then don't say anything,' he replied. And, unable to wait any longer, pulled her hard against his body and folded his arms about her. 'In fact, stop thinking as well. I've been wanting this for the last hour and more.'

Later, curled up on his knee with her mouth against his jaw and her hands tangled in the long, mahogany hair, she managed to murmur ruefully, 'I made a mess of it, didn't I?'

'Did you?' He traced her clavicle with one teasing finger.

'Yes. It didn't come out at all the way I'd imagined.'

'That's a shame.'

Lydia tried to concentrate. 'You don't know what I'm talking about, do you?'

'No, darling – and at the moment I don't much care.' His fingers trailed down to the disappointingly modest neckline of her gown and he felt her breath hitch. 'Ah. That's encouraging. I was beginning to worry.'

'You weren't.'

'How would you know? My *amour-propre* is very frail.'

She laughed against his mouth and then sighed as one finger dipped inside her bodice.

'I think you always knew I'd marry you.'

'Let's say I felt there were reasonable grounds for hope. And before you ask,' he said, his voice becoming slightly unsteady, 'that was because I knew you hadn't fallen into bed with me just because I happened to be handy.'

Lydia hid her face against his neck and mumbled, 'That might have been better put.'

'It might. But your turn of phrase is a constant delight to me. As is your warmth, your obstinacy, your intellect ... and your delectable body.' He cuddled her a little closer and said, 'You can think of compliments to shower on me later. Don't trouble your head right now.'

Silence fell between them while she kissed her way up his throat. But after a while, she said, 'Now we're officially betrothed ...'

'Mm?'

'I thought ... that is I wondered ...'

'Yes?' Eden knew what she'd wondered – or at least hoped that he did. 'What?'

'Well, when Peter comes I thought I could go home for a change of clothes.' *For a nicer gown and my pretty new petticoats and corset.* 'Then perhaps I could ... come back?' She felt his body's immediate reaction to the implication of her words and couldn't resist adding innocently, 'After all, once you've broken Stephen's code, we might have new information.'

'Witch,' he grumbled into her hair. 'Yes. Come back. But if you think I'm spending the night poring over bloody codes, you've another think coming.'

* * *

After Lydia went back to Bishopsgate escorted by Peter, Eden poured every ounce of skill and concentration he had into revealing the contents of the encrypted page. He'd already established that the code was a variation on one of the previous ones in that it used three numbers to each consonant, four to each vowel and larger numbers to denote names. But all the combinations were different and, even beginning with those which, due to their repetition, he believed to be names, it still took him well over an hour to decipher the first one. Until that moment, he'd been increasingly conscious of how tired he was and had needed to continually remind himself that he was doing this for Lydia. After it, triumph sent renewed energy surging through him, making it easy to re-double his efforts.

He was vaguely aware that, from time to time, someone came in to light candles, make up the fire or bring food ... but he had eyes only for the task in front of him. So the broth went cold and the ale remained untouched. By the time he had the whole page laid out in plain English, his shoulders and neck were aching and his fingers, stiff with cramp but he didn't care. Tossing down the quill, he stood up and stretched his arms to loosen his protesting muscles ... and then dropped back in the chair, silently blessing Stephen Neville.

It was all there; everything he'd hoped for and more. Detailed evidence of the most damning kind, complete with names, dates and locations and signed at the bottom of the coded sheet in Neville's own hand.

It began with the firm assertion that Edmund Wakefield was his own son by Arabella, Lady Northcote. Then came shocking details of the depths of depravity to be found in the brothel known as the Painted Angel, located on the corner of Seething Lane and Crutched Friars. This was not owned, as was apparently the case, by the man who ran it but by Edmund Wakefield himself – whose property it had been since April, 1648. After this, Stephen listed the names of four gentlemen he believed might be persuaded to admit having submitted to extortion by Edmund Wakefield, now Lord Northcote; and finally, a high-ranking Naval official who had been blackmailed, not for money, but for information about the Fleet which Stephen believed had played a part in Admiral Blake's defeat at Dungeness in November of '52.

There was sufficient here, Eden realised, to put Northcote in prison. If a charge of selling information to the Dutch during the recent war could be made to stick, it might even send him to the scaffold. But that meant handing everything over to the proper authorities ... and he didn't want to do that. Northcote had been hounding Lydia for months. He'd hurt her and those belonging to her; he'd frightened her, caused her endless anxiety and made it impossible for her to live her life as she chose. So although Eden knew what he *ought* to do, he also knew that leaving Northcote's fate up to magistrates and judges was never going to be enough. He wanted the satisfaction of looking the bastard in the eye and meting out his own justice.

And Quinn, he thought grimly. *Once I've dealt with Northcote, I'll find a way of getting my hands on Quinn as well. And won't* that *be enjoyable.*

NINE

Lydia awoke slowly to the unfamiliar sensation of a warm body pressed against her back and an arm around her waist.

Eden.

She smiled, luxuriating in the feel of his skin against hers ... and then smiled a bit more as she remembered the piercing sweetness and overwhelming pleasure of the night before. He'd told her he loved her over and over again, both in whispered words and with the skilled worship of his hands and mouth. It had been so perfect that, had he not still been here, holding her to him even in sleep, she might have wondered if it had really happened.

She found herself recalling the moment he had emerged from his self-imposed seclusion and walked in holding his translation of Stephen's coded notes. Just for a second, his expression had remained one of sustained concentration. Then his eyes had found her and filled with warm appreciation as they travelled over the *décolletage* of the watered-taffeta gown ... and his smile had made her blush.

After that, the evening had been one of mingled celebration and argument. Eden had read out his transcription over supper and, once the natural euphoria had passed, this had naturally led to a debate on how to proceed. Gilbert favoured handing the matter over to the appropriate authorities; Eden, seconded by Nicholas, had flatly refused to do so. Then, when Gilbert had reluctantly agreed to leave the matter in Colonel Maxwell's capable hands, he admitted that he had no idea where his brother might be found. There were obvious places where he might be, of course; Northcote Park in Sussex or the family house on the Strand ... or as Nicholas distastefully remarked, the brothel. But if he wasn't currently in any of those places, Gilbert's opinion was that he might be anywhere.

Beside her, Eden stirred slightly, one of his legs tangling with her own and sending an unexpected flare of heat into the pit of her belly. Her breath caught and she forced herself to lie still. He wasn't awake yet and he'd been so tired last night she wondered now how he'd had the energy to ... well, to do what they'd been doing. It was a little disconcerting, however, to discover that if he woke wanting to do it again, she'd be more than willing.

'Why are you pretending to be asleep?' asked a voice in her ear.

Startled into a tiny gurgle of laughter, she said, 'Because I thought you still were.'

'I think, if you were to take a brief inventory, you'd swiftly realise that I'm not.'

Just for a second, his meaning escaped her. And when it didn't ... when she felt the evidence of it pressing against her, she was incapable of saying more than, 'Oh. Yes.'

Laughing, he turned her to face him, his thigh still distractingly between hers.

'Good morning.' He kissed her and then, glimpsing her expression, said gently, 'Don't be embarrassed, Lydia and don't ever feel you have to hide it. I'm happy that you want me as I want you. Marriage wouldn't be much fun if you didn't.'

'No.' A tremor ran through her when his hand slid down the curve of her spine to her buttock; and when that same hand travelled up and around to caress her breast, the tremor became a gasp. 'I suppose not. It – it's just that I didn't know it could be like this.'

'No, darling. Neither did I.'

* * *

After joy and the lassitude that followed it, came practicalities.

'Much though I regret the necessity,' said Eden, 'I think you should go home today. Mr Wakefield doesn't know where you spent the night and, as far as Nick is concerned, it may be possible to maintain the fiction that you slept in the next room. But until we can marry, I want to safeguard your good name.'

'Since we *will* marry, does that matter so very much?' she asked, whilst tracing lazy patterns on his chest. 'Who will care?'

'*I* will,' came the firm reply. Then, softening the blow with a kiss, 'I'd like to delay announcing our betrothal until Toby gets back. If Tabitha's safely delivered of her infant, it should only be a couple of days now –

and then we can give the glad tidings to both of our brothers at once.' He grinned. 'I suspect Toby will be happier about it than Aubrey.'

'You had him arrested and then interrogated him.' Her hand explored his rib-cage and started to drift lower. 'Is it any wonder you make him nervous?'

Eden trapped her wandering hand beneath his own.

'Since it's high time we got up, may I regretfully suggest that you save where that was going until later? We have to plan.'

'Yes, Colonel.'

'Hussy. Now ... with regard to the wedding, I'd like to do it as quickly as possible which, with things as they are and no bishops to grant licences, means I need a vicar who'll waive the reading of banns if I pay him enough. We can have a proper and more elaborate ceremony later when I take you to Thorne Ash to meet my mother – and please don't worry about that. Aside from the fact that she'll probably fall on your neck with gratitude, she'll love you. But that, since dealing with Northcote has to come first, may have to wait a while – hence my desire to tie the knot sooner rather than later. Will that be all right with you?'

'Yes. I'll marry you tomorrow, if you like.'

'I *would* like. And but for Toby and a cooperative vicar, we could. Damn.'

* * *

Dealing with Viscount Northcote was dependant on finding him and it came as no surprise to any of them that this proved next to impossible.

Mr Wakefield visited the house on the Strand only to be told that his lordship was not presently in residence. He sent his servant hot-foot to Sussex and got the same result. In a note informing Eden of this, he added, *I believe he once mentioned having business premises in the City but have no idea where these might be. If I learn anything further, I will send word.*

Nicholas, who happened to be with Eden when the note arrived, said, 'Business premises? That probably means the brothel. Are we going to have to try there?'

'No. Aside from the fact that I don't want to, the chances of any of us getting past Quinn's bravos are more or less non-existent – though if we can't get hold of Northcote, we're going to have to try hooking Quinn instead. And to be honest, I doubt Northcote spends any time at the brothel anyway. If he did, his nice cloak of anonymity wouldn't have lasted long.'

'So how do we find him?'

'We can't. The only solution I can think of is to somehow lure him to us – but so far I haven't figured out a way of doing it. And in the meantime,' he sighed, brandishing a second note, 'I'm ordered to report to Lambert's office; something, just at the moment, that I could well do without.'

The day wasn't destined to get any better.

'There is an uprising in Hampshire – one of several but the only one with teeth,' said the Major-General tersely. 'The latest intelligence says that some four hundred Royalists under Colonel Penruddock assembled at Winchester two days ago, planning to capture the assize judges. However, the Winchester garrison was reinforced a week ago and this seems to have caused Penruddock to change his plans. The next assize court is at Salisbury so that is probably where he's currently headed. Major-General Desborough is preparing to take command in the West but won't be ready to move for another three days so I've mustered two hundred Horse to assist the local Militia temporarily – and I want you to lead them.'

'No.' Eden heard the word come out of his mouth before it had gone through his brain.

'*What*?' Lambert both looked and sounded stunned.

It occurred to Eden that, in the thirteen years since he'd enlisted under the Earl of Essex, this was the first time he'd refused an order. True, he'd adjusted a few from time to time – but never actually *refused* one. Then a dozen other thoughts replaced it. First and foremost were Lydia's safety, their wedding and the search for Northcote. After them came, *If Desborough's been given command, why the hell can't he go and get on with it?* And finally something completely radical that he hadn't previously considered at all but suddenly knew to be right.

He said, 'My sincerest apologies, sir – but I can't leave London now. In fact, I believe it's time I gave you my resignation.'

If possible, the Major-General looked even more disbelieving.

'Your *resignation*, Colonel? Isn't that a trifle extreme?'

'No, sir. And this isn't a matter of some temporary inconvenience. Indeed, I think it's been inevitable for some months now – although I hadn't recognised it until today.'

'This sounds like a spur of the moment decision you may come to regret.' Since he did not want to lose one of his best officers, Lambert chose to be conciliatory. 'If the problem is that personal circumstances require your presence here at the moment, so be it. I can send another officer to Salisbury. In return, however, I would ask you to reconsider resigning.'

Eden stood up, smiling faintly.

'Thank you, sir. But my life is about to change in ways incompatible with my military duties – such as they are. I'll remain in my post at the Tower until the current situation is resolved and if you still need a go-between with the Cavaliers, I'll do that, too. But I must ask you to regard my decision as final.'

Lambert also rose, his dark gaze inscrutable as ever. Then, to Eden's surprise, he held out his hand and said, 'I don't pretend I'm not disappointed. But you've given exemplary service over the years and are entitled to know your own mind. I wish you the best of good fortune, Colonel. But should circumstances change, I hope you will come to me.'

'You may rely on it,' said Eden, gripping the Major-General's fingers. 'And thank you.'

* * *

On leaving Lambert's office, Eden paid a flying visit to his former clerk and informed him that he could tell the agent in Cologne to cease wasting his time on Ellis Brandon.

'I no longer need him. What I need *now* is to find Viscount Northcote. To the best of my knowledge, he's somewhere in England but I have no idea where. Any help you can give would be greatly appreciated.'

'Certainly, Colonel,' said Mr Hollins calmly. 'I will do my best. Is there anything else I can do for you?'

'Not unless you know a man of the cloth who'll perform a marriage ceremony without banns,' said Eden, not holding out much hope.

'The Reverend Dawson at Saint Michael's in Cornhill,' came the calm reply. 'Since the episcopacy was abolished, he has been making a very comfortable living supplying that particular service. We have known about his activities for some time, of course ... but have chosen to turn a blind eye. Am I to understand that felicitations are in order?'

Eden grinned and grasped the man's hand.

'They are indeed, Mr Hollins. And thank you.'

* * *

The Reverend Dawson promptly agreed to unite Colonel Maxwell and Mistress Neville in holy matrimony as soon as the Colonel's brother returned from the country and for the trifling sum of ten pounds. Eden didn't think the price trifling at all but would have happily paid it twice over for the privilege of being able to call Lydia his wife.

He set off for Bishopsgate with a spring in his step to give his love the glad tidings. Henry greeted him imperturbably as ever and informed him that Mistress Neville would be very happy to see him since she was currently engaged in repairing the household linen. Eden surrendered his hat, refrained from remarking that he hoped she'd be pleased to see him regardless of her occupation and strolled into the parlour.

Lydia promptly stabbed herself with the needle, tossed her sewing aside and got up saying, 'Eden! Between the hunt for Lord Northcote and your duties at the Tower, I didn't think you'd have time to come here today.'

'I missed you,' he said, catching her around the waist and licking the spot of blood from her injured finger before plunging headlong into a deep, lingering kiss. Then, 'I particularly missed that. And I have at least one bit of good news.'

Lydia let him pull her down on to the settle and nestled into the curve of his arm.

'Oh?'

'I've given Major-General Lambert my resignation.'

'What?' She turned to stare at him. '*Why?*'

'He wanted me to go racing off to Salisbury to put down an insurrection that the local Militia have probably already dealt with by now. For obvious reasons, I refused. Also, I'm tired of being a glorified errand boy and thought you might be able to find better uses for me. Can you?'

'I daresay I'll think of something, if I put my mind to it. But are you *sure* you want to quit the Army?'

'Perfectly sure. Peacetime soldiering doesn't suit me. Neither does it belong in the future you and I are going to build together. And speaking of that ... we can get married the instant Toby drags himself back here.'

A flush of pleasure touched her skin. 'You've found a vicar?'

'Yes. I'd like to pretend it was an arduous task but it was actually very simple.' And, having explained, added, 'In the hope of word not reaching Northcote or Quinn, I'd have liked to keep it very private; just you and I with Toby, Aubrey and Nick. But I have the strangest presentiment that isn't going to happen.'

'Not unless we continue living in separate houses,' objected Lydia. And then, with a touch of consternation, 'We won't, will we?'

'Absolutely not.' He toyed with an errant lock of her hair, waiting with some amusement for her to realise what he'd already foreseen. 'I recognise that Henry and the rest of your household will have to know. But it's not going to end there, is it?'

'I don't ... oh.' She stared at him helplessly. 'Even if I swear Nancy to secrecy, she won't be able to resist telling her sister and in a matter of hours all the women will know and they'll tell the men. And they'll all want to come.'

'I know.'

'They're – they're like family, Eden. How can I tell them I don't want them?'

'You can't, darling.' He smiled and dropped a fleeting kiss on her brow. 'You can't. And I wouldn't ask it of you. But because, at present, I can only think of one ruse that might tempt Northcote out of the woodwork, I *will* be demanding another oath of silence.'

* * *

On the following afternoon, Tobias walked in, windswept and lightly mud-spattered.

Eden said, 'Finally. I was beginning to think you'd decided to stay until Easter. How's Tabitha?'

'Well and blissfully happy. It's a boy. Richard Tobias.' He tossed his bags in a corner and threw his hat after them. 'As for what took me so long, we had word that Kate and Luciano were on their way so I waited to see them.'

'Kate's at Thorne Ash? *Now*?'

'Yes. Tab wants her to be godmother.'

'How long do they intend to stay?'

'Until after the christening, obviously. And since, for some peculiar reason Ralph wants you to be the boy's *other* godfather, you'll see her then.' Tobias poured a tankard of ale and downed half of it in one gulp. 'God – that's better. My throat was full of dust.' He dropped into a chair and took a long look at his brother. 'All right. Clearly something's happened. What?'

Eden debated the various ways in which he might answer this. Finally, he settled for, 'How long will it take you to make Lydia a wedding ring?'

With a perfectly straight face, Tobias shrugged and said negligently, 'Bring me the appropriate finger and I can have it done by tomorrow evening.'

'You don't,' grumbled Eden, hiding a smile of his own, 'seem very surprised.'

'I'm surprised it took you so long and I'm surprised she said yes. Isn't that enough for you?' Then, abandoning his pose and grinning broadly, he surged to his feet and crushed Eden's hand in his own. 'Congratulations. I couldn't be happier for you. She's a lovely woman and you're damned lucky. So when's the wedding? You'll do it in the chapel at home, of course – ah. *That's* why you wondered how long Kate will be here. Well, the timing couldn't be better, could it? Have you already written to Mother?'

'Stop,' said Eden laughing a little but recognising he might be facing a hurdle. 'It's complicated, Toby. While you were away, we found out who's been hounding Lydia all this time but I've yet to bring him to book – or that bastard, Quinn, either – and I can't leave London until I have. But neither can I risk him getting his hands on Lydia again, so ...' He stopped and said, 'I'd better explain properly.'

'Yes. Perhaps you should.'

Twenty minutes and half a jug of ale later, Eden said, 'So that's it. Now we have Stephen Neville's evidence, the situation becomes even more volatile. I imagine Northcote's getting ever more impatient with Quinn's failure to deliver – which means something else is likely to happen very soon. I want Lydia safe under this roof before --'

'I know *precisely* where you want Lydia,' interposed Tobias with a leer, 'and I don't blame you. But I don't see why you can't wait and be married properly at Thorne Ash – unless you're just frightened she'll change her mind.'

'She won't. But aside from her brother, the only family she has are the men and women she gives work to and she'd like them at her wedding. Consequently, since I can't transport all of them to Thorne Ash, we'll have an *im*proper wedding now and something better later. I'll even write to Mother telling her to have the banns read. But I'm marrying Lydia the day after tomorrow whether you like it or not.'

Tobias sighed and heaved himself to his feet.

'In that case, you'd better fetch the bride-to-be and *I'd* better search out the piece of Welsh gold I've been saving for just this occasion. No peace for the wicked. Isn't that what they say?'

* * *

By the end of the day, Eden had taken care of numerous details. He spent an hour at the Tower, called in at the lorinery, informed the Reverend Dawson that the wedding could now take place, sent a message to Aubrey Durand summoning him to sup in Cheapside that evening and collected Lydia from Bishopsgate. And throughout all of it, he found he had only one thing on his mind; how to lure Northcote from the heather and bring the whole matter to a head without further delay – preferably before his nephew's christening. The trouble was that he could only see one way of doing it; a way he didn't like at all and couldn't be sure would succeed.

Sir Aubrey Durand arrived in Cheapside an hour before supper and wearing an expression that was half disgruntled and half wary. Finding his sister sitting cosily beside Colonel Maxwell, his brows rose a little and he said, 'What's going on? Has Quinn done something else?'

'No.' Eden rose and went to pour wine. 'This is about something rather more pleasant ... though we will have to discuss the business with Quinn later. Lydia says she's told you everything we've recently discovered. What do you make of it?'

'A viscount dabbling in brothels and blackmail? To be honest, I'm having trouble believing it. But if it's true and Stephen knew about it – why didn't he get the fellow arrested years ago?'

'I imagine because doing so would reveal the fellow's mother to be not just as an adulteress, but as an adulteress who'd given her unsuspecting husband a son and heir sired by another man,' replied Eden, handing him a glass. 'If Arabella had died before him, I think Stephen would have used the information ... but she didn't.'

'I suppose that may be true. But I still don't see why he didn't just tell Lyd what he knew and where to find the proof of it. Or if not her, his own son. It would have saved a hell of a lot of trouble.'

'I think he intended to tell me,' said Lydia. 'But in the last weeks, his illness became so acute that he rarely had enough breath to talk.'

Aubrey nodded and was about to speak when the door opened to admit Nicholas and Tobias.

'Good.' Eden poured more wine and handed it to the newcomers. 'Now we're all here, Lydia and I ...' He paused to reach out and draw her to his side. 'Lydia and I would like you to congratulate us. We are to be married at St Michael's on Cornhill the day after tomorrow.'

Aubrey's incredulous '*What?*' was lost in Nicholas's delighted, 'At last! That's wonderful news!' And while Nicholas immediately shook Eden's hand and gave Lydia a swift, hard hug, Aubrey remained rooted to the spot.

To cover the awkwardness, Tobias sauntered over to kiss Lydia's cheek and murmur, 'Welcome to the family, my dear – and thank you. We thought we'd never find a lady willing to take him off our hands.'

She laughed up at him, shook her head and then said, 'Aubrey? Aren't you happy for me?'

He didn't look at her but continued to stare unsmilingly at Eden. Finally he said coldly, 'This is very sudden. And why so soon, Colonel? Have you got her pr--?'

'No,' returned Eden, equally coldly. 'And I suggest you accord your sister more respect.'

The blue eyes finally encompassed Lydia.

'Perhaps I'm missing something. Have the banns been read?'

'No. We wanted to --'

'Then it won't be legal,' he snapped. 'I don't know what the hell you're thinking, Lyd – but I absolutely forbid it.'

'You've no right to forbid anything,' replied Lydia flatly. 'And for the last time, will you stop calling me *Lyd*!'

'I'm your brother, damn it – your only living relative. Of course I --'

'Shut up,' said Tobias pleasantly, taking Aubrey's arm in a crushing grip and marching him to the far side of the room. 'You're behaving like an ass. Sit down and get a grip on your temper. Or failing that, go home.'

'Thank you, Toby. You said you had something in the workshop to show Lydia … so perhaps now might be a good time?' Eden slid an arm about Lydia's waist and dropped a kiss on her brow. 'Go and tell my brother what a clever boy he is while I put *your* brother straight on a few things. And don't worry. If I'm tempted to hit him, Nick will remind me not to.'

She hesitated, glancing across at Aubrey, leaning sulkily against the wall and then decided that he and Eden would be best left to sort out their differences without her. Nodding, she smiled at Tobias and let him lead her from the room.

'If,' said Eden crisply to his future brother-in-law, 'you had kept your mouth shut for a moment before putting both feet in it, you would have learned that I love Lydia and am doing my damnedest to protect both her person and her reputation. No, the wedding won't be entirely legal – though I personally see little difference between paying a bishop for a licence and paying a vicar to do without one. However, there will be a second wedding in Oxfordshire with virtually my whole family present. There is also the matter of Lydia's people in Duck Lane and Strand Alley – all of whom, unlike yourself, will want to wish her well and --'

'I *do* wish her well,' said Aubrey angrily. 'How dare --?'

'Be quiet. I haven't finished yet. Lydia wants those men and women there on her wedding day. That won't be possible at Thorne Ash – hence the ceremony at Saint Michael's. Also, despite its slight irregularity, it will mean that she can come and live here, where it will be easier to keep her safe while I attempt to take down Northcote and Quinn.' Eden stopped and fixed the younger man with a hard gaze. 'I trust that covers everything?'

Aubrey scowled into his wine and hunched one shoulder.

'It would seem to.'

'Good. So when Lydia comes back, perhaps you could manage a shred or two of civility. Dislike me, if you wish – I really don't care – but you'll keep it to yourself for your sister's sake.'

'I don't dislike you particularly,' muttered Aubrey. 'I was just taken by surprise. And you have to admit it didn't sound good. *Anybody* would have thought what I did.'

'Possibly. But if anybody but you had been stupid enough to *say* it, they'd be picking their teeth off the floor by now,' replied Eden. Then swivelled to face the door as Lydia came half-dancing back through it, glowing with pleasure.

'Look!' she said. 'See what Toby has given me as a bridal gift. Isn't it lovely?'

Eden shot a surprised glance at his brother and then looked at the dainty necklace of sapphires and moonstones set in gold that encircled Lydia's throat. He said, 'Yes. It's almost as beautiful as you are.' And to Tobias, 'That's extremely generous of you. Or are you merely wooing my lady away from me with expensive trinkets?'

'I thought it was worth a try,' grinned Tobias. Then, more seriously, 'I made it a couple of months ago but never put it in the shop. As soon as it was finished, I realised I'd already seen the one perfect neck for it.'

Lydia beamed at him. 'That's a very nice thing to say.'

'My charm is legendary,' said Tobias modestly. 'Ask anyone.'

'Lydia?' Aubrey eyed her uncertainly. 'I'm sorry. I shouldn't have said what I did.'

'No,' she agreed, 'you shouldn't.' She was careful not to look at Eden who, she supposed must have given the truth a wide berth. 'Eden and I will marry on Wednesday. I would like it if you felt able to – to take Father's place.'

'Of course.' He put his arms around her. 'And I'm glad for you. Truly.'

With Aubrey's capitulation, supper became a more pleasant meal than it might otherwise have been. But when it was over, Eden kept everyone gathered around the table and said, 'I need to bring Northcote out into the open. Has anyone any ideas on how to do it?'

Aubrey said nothing and Nicholas shook his head.

'Send a troop of Militia into this brothel of his. That should bring him out fast enough.'

'It might bring Quinn out,' agreed Eden, 'but if I take *him* down, I'll never get his employer. So it has to be Northcote first.'

'Offer him what he wants,' said Lydia simply. 'He wouldn't be able to resist that, surely.'

'No. Probably not and it's the way my own thoughts have been running. But our problem would be managing the how and the where – and I haven't found a satisfactory solution to that yet.'

'I could do it.'

Four pairs of male eyes were suddenly riveted on her face.

'No,' said Eden curtly. 'I don't want you anywhere near this.'

'Why not? He visited me once before – so why shouldn't he do it again? And if I pretended I didn't know what it was all about ... that I just wanted to be quit of the whole problem ... surely he'd have no reason not to believe me.'

'No,' said Eden again.

There was a brief silence and then Nicholas said slowly, 'I don't think you should dismiss it out of hand. Obviously, we wouldn't leave her alone ... and it's the only idea we have, let alone the only one that might work.'

'It wouldn't,' snapped Eden. 'If she pretends she hasn't read or doesn't understand Stephen's dossier – how come she knows that Northcote wants it? The man may be evil but nothing we know suggests he's also stupid. He'll see through her in an instant and we'll be worse off than we are now because he'll know for certain that we have the damned papers.'

Everyone stared gloomily into their wine.

After a while, Lydia said musingly, 'His name is on it somewhere I couldn't help noticing it. Wakefield? Northcote? Both, perhaps. I'm sure we can manage that. And I write him a letter. I'll say I couldn't understand any of that nonsense about mythology ... but seeing his name and recalling Gilbert's incessant talk about Stephen having letters from their mother, made me realise it had to be a family matter. Of course, I *could* give the letters to Gilbert ... but since I rejected his proposal of marriage, relations between us are not what they were. And really it matters little to me *which* of them has the letters so long as one of them does and I'm free of the whole, nasty business.'

She paused and Nicholas said, 'The bit about Gilbert is a stroke of genius. Go on.'

Lydia's eyes narrowed in concentration and she said slowly, 'I've experienced a lot of unpleasantness on account of these letters which – which only came to light recently thanks to severe damage inflicted on my Duck Lane premises. A blackguard named Quinn was behind that – I can only assume for nefarious purposes of his own such as the intention to blackmail his lordship. I am hoping that handing the letters to their rightful owner will spare both myself and the Wakefield family further pain. But if Lord Northcote has no interest in the matter ... I'll just send the wretched letters to Gilbert. *Anything* to be rid of them.' She stopped and looked hopefully at Eden. 'Well? Will it do, do you think?'

He said nothing, every instinct rebelling against involving her.

But Tobias said, 'It might. Admit it, Eden – it sounds pretty plausible. And as Nick said, Lydia doesn't have to see him on her own – or even at all, come to that. She sets up an appointment and we keep it.'

Eden finally unlocked his jaws to say, 'Aubrey? Do you have an opinion?'

'I'd rather she didn't have anything to do with it,' came the reluctant reply, 'but things can't go on as they are. Unless you have an alternative … I'd have to agree with Toby.'

'You see?' Lydia slid her hand into Eden's. 'It's a chance – and I'd be perfectly safe.'

His fingers closed hard over hers and he drew a long, painful breath.

'All right. But not until after the wedding. And then I want it locked up so tight that nothing can go wrong. If I've any doubts at all, we find another way.'

TEN

On the following morning, his stomach still queasy with anxiety, Eden went to the Tower in search of Major Moulton for the purpose of asking him to the wedding.

'I think I'm entitled to reinforcements of my own,' he explained, 'since Lydia is busy inviting her sewing women and everybody from Duck Lane.'

'All of them?' asked Ned feebly, thinking of Troopers Buxton and Hayes.

'*All* of them. So you'll come?'

'I wouldn't miss it.'

'Good – and once that's over I'll need your help with the Northcote situation.' Having already told the Major everything they knew, Eden proceeded to explain the current plan and then added bluntly, 'It's giving me nightmares, Ned.'

'That's understandable. And of course you can count on me – probably a few others, as well.'

'Thank you.'

'I'm beginning to see,' remarked Ned, 'why you found it necessary to resign your commission. Busy as a body-louse these days, aren't you?'

'It certainly feels like it.' Eden paused. 'Is there any news from the West?'

'You mean you haven't heard? Colonel Penruddock led his fellows into Salisbury at dawn a couple of days ago and caught the High Sheriff and the assize judges napping. Literally, in fact. Rumour has it they were still in their nightshirts. At any rate, Penruddock took the Sheriff hostage and rode on through Sherborne and Yeovil, trying – unsuccessfully, by all accounts – to rouse the country as he went. He got as far as South Molton in Devon before a troop of Horse out of Exeter stopped him.'

'And then?'

'A skirmish through the streets till the Cavaliers broke and fled,' shrugged Ned. 'A few escaped – but Penruddock and some of the other ringleaders are in gaol awaiting trial.'

'Which, in the case of Colonel Penruddock, will doubtless have the usual result.'

'I'd say so. But hopefully he'll be the last for a while.'

Eden shook his head.

'We think that every time,' he said.

* * *

Shadowed by Peter, Lydia went home with a smile on her face. The women had greeted the news that she was to marry the Colonel with sighs of envy; the men had made no bones about the fact that she was getting a good man – the very best, said some. All of them were stunned and delighted to be bidden attend the wedding; and all of them overwhelmed her with their good wishes.

Back in her bedchamber with Nancy, she pushed all thoughts of Lord Northcote to the back of her mind. There would be time enough for that later. Today was for a long and leisurely preparation for her bridal; for bathing, for washing her hair in scented water, for laying out the pale pink, pearl-trimmed gown ... and for dreaming about Eden.

A part of her still found it almost impossible to believe that tomorrow she would become his wife ... that this strong, clever, beautiful man would be hers to love and cherish all the days of her life. And that maybe ... just maybe, God would grant her one more miracle. Eden's child.

By the following morning Lydia felt a great deal less relaxed. She stared at the pink dress and said edgily, 'Do you think the blue would be better?'

'A gown you haven't worn before would be *better*,' replied Nancy tartly, 'but the Colonel's given us no time for that, has he? So stick with the pink one. At least you've only worn that once.'

At Yule, remembered Lydia. And then flushed as she also remembered what had happened on that day.

She smiled. 'Oh yes. *Definitely* the pink one.'

* * *

At much the same time, Eden was tying the laces of his coat and putting up with his brother.

'For God's sake, Eden – is that the best coat you've got?'

Eden glanced down at his forest-green broadcloth sleeve and said, 'Yes. Why?'

Tobias groaned. 'It – it's ordinary.'

'I like ordinary. But what, in your opinion, should I be wearing?'

'The fact that you need to ask that question says it all.'

'Does it?'

'Yes. You're not merely trotting over to the Tower or down to Whitehall. It's your *wedding* day!'

'Yes. I had remembered that.' He took in his brother's burgundy velvet and extravagant lace collar. 'But cheer up. You look splendid enough for both of us.'

'Don't be so bloody aggravating. When was the last time you visited a tailor?'

Eden smiled to himself and calmly continued fastening his coat.

'Not much more than a year ago, I think.'

'*A year*? Well I hope you're going to change that before we go to Thorne Ash.'

'I'll think about it. In the meantime, in case you haven't noticed, I've been rather busy.'

'I appreciate that. But --'

'Toby. Will you please stop nagging? You're worse than Mother. Just tell me you've got the ring, there's a good fellow. That's the only thing I'm interested in right now.'

* * *

At intervals and as unobtrusively as possible, just over forty men and women dressed in their Sunday best made their way into St Michael's, Cornhill – much to the surprise of the Reverend Dawson. In his experience, weddings which were required faster than the reading of banns permitted were usually clandestine affairs, attended by no more than the two necessary witnesses. Perhaps, he thought, Colonel Maxwell was about to go into battle and wanted the knot tied and his lady secure in case he didn't come back. Reverend Dawson, who was possessed of a romantic streak, liked that idea.

Arriving with his magnificently-clad brother, the Colonel took his place without ceremony while Nicholas, Major Moulton and Mistress Wilkes all slid into to place amongst the rest.

'She's late,' muttered Toby after a few minutes.

'She's entitled to be late,' replied Eden patiently. And then, with a grin, 'God, Toby ... if you're this twitchy when it's *me* getting married, what are you going to be like when it's *your* turn?'

Surrounded by her brother and her entire household staff, Lydia paused in the porch to hand her cloak to Nancy and shake out her skirts. Then, waiting while Henry and the rest of them took their seats, she looked at Aubrey and said just a little unsteadily, 'Do you think Eden's as nervous as I am?'

'No. From what I've seen of him, he hasn't got a nervous bone in his body,' came the candid but not very tactful reply. And then, 'Come on. It's time.'

There were neither music nor flowers and the Reverend even appeared to have skimped on the candles. Nevertheless, forty-odd smiling faces warmed Lydia on her way down the aisle to the place where Eden waited, his eyes alight with that special look he kept only for her.

That look turned slowly into a smile when she laid her hand on his sleeve. And covering it with his own, he murmured, 'You came. Toby thought you wouldn't.'

'But you knew better.'

'I certainly hoped I did.'

Since he had a surprisingly full house, Reverend Dawson decided to deliver the complete wedding service rather than the truncated version he usually performed on these occasions. He'd wondered what connection this undoubtedly motley congregation had with the bridal pair. Then he became aware that the bride and groom looked only at each other and that the female half of the motley congregation were all shedding tears. It was, he thought, almost enough to quell his worry that any one of the persons here present might inform the authorities that he performed weddings without either licences or banns.

The voice in which Eden spoke his vows resonated deep through Lydia's being. Her own voice was husky with emotion and her fingers trembled a little in his. She wondered if he understood the all-encompassing strength of her love for him and how, if he didn't, she could ever show him. Then she realised that they had the rest of their lives … that this day was just the beginning.

Eden hadn't ever had a woman look at him the way Lydia did; as if he was God, Hercules and Galahad all rolled into one. It filled him with awe, pride and a fierce determination to always be worthy of it. It was that thought which – when the Reverend finally pronounced them man and wife – that caused him to sweep her virtually off her feet and, much to the delight of their friends, kiss her long and hard.

Once outside the church and after a great deal of hand-shaking and back-slapping, Eden invited everyone to join himself and his wife at the Black Dog on Gracious Street where food and drink awaited them. This time no one bothered about being unobtrusive and the procession to the nearby tavern was a merry one.

Holding her close to his side, Eden smiled down at Lydia and said, 'Happy?'

Her answering smile dazzled him.

'Yes. Oh yes. But the word is inadequate. I feel as if – as if I'm floating.'

'Then I'd better make sure you don't fly away completely, hadn't I?'

'I won't,' she promised, suddenly serious. 'Not ever. But I won't mind you keeping hold of me. In fact, I wish you would.'

'Minx,' he whispered, snatching the chance to kiss her ear. 'We've a whole afternoon of celebrating to get through before I can hold you the way I'd like.'

Heat flared through her but she said, 'I'm told anticipation is half the fun.'

Eden grinned. 'Whoever told you that must have been very unlucky.'

The Black Dog had opened up both first floor parlours for the accommodation of Colonel Maxwell's extremely large wedding-party, serving enormous quantities of food in one and equal amounts of ale and wine in the other. At first, everyone tried to maintain their best behaviour – the men from Duck Lane seeming somewhat overawed as much by Mr Tobias Maxwell's size as by his lace-trimmed elegance. But by the time he'd made them laugh with the kind of disrespectful speech that only a brother could get away with, they all came to the conclusion that looks might be deceptive; and when the Colonel, having said all the right things on behalf of himself and his bride, added a brief but frankly hilarious codicil at Mr Tobias's expense, the room rang with laughter and all awkwardness fled.

At first, Eden kept Lydia within the circle of his arm while they accepted a flood of good wishes. All the women bashfully demanded a kiss. Smiling, Lydia watched him melt even the most sensible of her women with a salutation to the hand and another to the cheek. The men, of course, insisted on wringing his hand and, as often as not, clouting him merrily on the back for good measure. Buffets from Tobias and Peter almost threatened to overset him. Lydia caught his eye and failed to suppress a giggle.

A little later, when everyone had eaten their fill and with the wine and ale still flowing, Eden left Lydia surrounded by a laughing, chattering group of women who, having learned that there was to be a second wedding in Oxfordshire, were anxious to discuss what Mistress Neville – beg pardon! Mistress *Maxwell* – thought to wear on that occasion. Moving away from her, Eden discussed the recent Cavalier activity in the West with Nicholas, Ned and a couple of the lorinery fellows; and Major Moulton said the latest news spoke of five thousand Militia to be mustered in the City – possibly linked to a rumour that the Earl of Rochester had been captured but immediately escaped.

Good, thought Eden. *Let's hope his lordship takes himself back to France.*

Later still, Eden noticed with some amusement that, after his first startled glance, Henry Padgett was eyeing Alice Wilkes' abundant attributes with evident appreciation. He also watched Tobias making most of the younger women flutter and blush, prior to settling in a corner with Troopers Buxton and Hayes and saying, 'And now, gentlemen ... tell me *exactly* what my brother did in the war. He's very close-mouthed about it — which naturally leads me to suppose that he sat about with his feet up and left the dirty work to you fellows.'

Eden laughed and left them to it. The afternoon was wearing on and he was conscious of an increasing desire to have his wife to himself. The trouble was that the party was still in full swing and no one showed any sign of leaving. Repressing a sigh, he looked around for Lydia. If he couldn't steal her away just yet, a glimpse of her bright face would have to suffice. Most of the women seemed to have congregated in the other room so he sauntered in to look for her. As soon as he appeared, Lily Carter approached him and said, 'Colonel, we're all grateful to you for giving us this day with Miss Lydia. We know you didn't have to. You could've waited to be married with your own family without taking account of us. So we wanted to thank you.'

'It's unnecessary,' he replied easily. 'The bond of affection between Lydia and all of you runs both ways. Today means as much to her as it does to you ... so how could I not want her to have it?'

Rachel Walker and Mary Dawson sighed. Seeing possible embarrassment looming, Eden said quickly, 'Now ... can anyone tell me where I might find my wife?'

They all giggled and Mary said, 'She went off a bit ago with our Nancy. Said her hair needed fixing and one of the maids told her there was an empty bedchamber along the passage they could use.'

'Thank you.' He bowed slightly and moved away in the direction the girl had indicated.

In case Lydia had wanted privacy for more than replacing a few hairpins, he tapped at the door and waited. Then, when there was no reply, he opened it and went in. It was empty.

Frowning a little, Eden walked back to the top of the stairs and narrowly avoided colliding with the inn-keeper.

'Colonel!' He ran a distracted hand over his face. 'You'd better come down. There's been a — well, I reckon you need to see, sir.'

A sudden chill slid down Eden's back. Without hesitation, he pushed past the landlord and ran down the stairs. In the shadows at the foot of them and attended by a worried chambermaid, Nancy Dawson sat on the floor clutching her head.

Eden dropped on one knee beside her.

'Nancy? What happened? Where's Lydia?'

She drew a shuddering breath and tears began streaming silently down her face.

'I d-don't know. We came down because somebody asked for her – only then I was hit over the head and --'

Eden didn't wait for the rest. Cold with dread, he shot out into the street, his eyes searching in vain for a glimpse of Lydia's pale pink gown. Then, realising how useless this was, he swung back inside and asked again what had happened.

'A woman was at the door,' volunteered the chambermaid. 'Said she didn't want to barge in to the party but'd like to give the bride her good wishes – so I went and told your lady. I reckon she must've come down but I didn't see 'cos I was --'

'How long ago?' snapped Eden.

'Dunno. Ten minutes? Maybe a bit more.'

'You saw this woman?' And when the girl nodded, 'Was she alone?'

She shrugged. 'Far as I know, she was.'

'Describe her.'

'There ain't much to --'

'Her height, the colour of her hair, the kind of clothes she was wearing. Everything you remember – and quickly!'

'About as tall as me, I reckon ... and blonde. Pretty.' Her brows drew together in concentration. 'Didn't see her clothes but for a dark cloak. But I *did* notice as she painted her face 'cos I remember thinking --'

Eden nodded, tossed a curt word of thanks over his shoulder and went up the stairs two at a time. He knew fear. He'd met it head on, time and time again in battle. He'd feared for himself and for his men. But he'd never known fear like this; a helpless, frozen terror that drove the air from his lungs and paralysed his brain so that the only thought he had was, *I have to find her. I have to find her quickly. But I don't know where to go.*

Cutting across several conversations from the parlour door and trying to keep his voice steady, he said, 'Toby, Nick, Ned. I need – I need ...' He took a second to swallow the bile rising in his throat, 'Lydia's been taken.'

The silence these words produced was immediate and total. But after what felt like an age, Nicholas said, 'Quinn?'

'I don't know. Yes. Probably.'

Behind him, the women were crowding the doorway and he could hear mutters of shock.

'How long ago?' demanded Aubrey.

'Not long. A quarter of an hour --'

'So why are we still standing here?' Aubrey started pushing his way towards the door. 'Let's go!'

'Go *where*?' asked Tobias impatiently, striding across the room to lay a firm hand on his brother's shoulder. 'It won't help Lydia to go rushing off at half-cock.'

'Very true.' In an attempt to drag Eden out of what was plainly the bloodiest kind of nightmare, Major Moulton said sharply, 'Colonel? Your orders, sir.'

Eden shoved his hands through his hair and tried to get command of himself. He felt as if some wild thing was trying to claw its way out of his chest ... but knew he had to ignore it. Every second he hesitated was a second wasted.

'We don't know where they've taken her,' he said flatly. 'My first guess would be the brothel. But they used the lorinery before and, since it's been empty all day, they might have gone there again. Then there's the Steelyard.'

'No,' said the Major. 'There isn't. That's been deserted since we took back the women.'

Eden nodded. 'Cheapside, then. If Lydia offers them what they want – and I hope to God she does – they'll have to go there to get it.' Another brief pause. 'Also, though least likely, there's Northcote's own house on the Strand.'

'And so?' This time it was Nicholas who asked.

'So we hedge our bets. Ned, Toby and I will go directly to the brothel. Nick … you and Aubrey check on Duck Lane, then follow us. We can --'

'Just a minute, Colonel,' said Trooper Hayes. 'You wasn't thinking the rest of us was going to sit on our arses and leave you to get on with it on your own, was you sir?'

A chorus of approving grunts greeted these words.

'Aye,' said Trooper Buxton. 'Maybe there ain't one whole man amongst us – but we ain't *completely* useless.'

'Nor us neither,' called out Jenny Sutton. 'There's a good few of us ain't afraid to fight.'

'Count on me as well.' Alice Wilkes started rolling up her sleeves.

'Peter and I,' remarked Henry Padgett decorously, 'will also be happy to help.'

Eden looked around at the grim determination on every face. Then, his voice a little more ragged than usual, he said, 'I don't have the right to involve any of you because I can't guarantee your safety. But just now I need all the help I can get … so I'll accept your offer and be glad of it. Thank you.'

'That's settled then,' said Dan Hayes. 'Give us our marching orders and we're with you.'

Tobias gave a choke of unsteady laughter.

'Well done, Colonel. You've got a bloody army.'

ELEVEN

Lydia sat huddled on a strategically-placed chair in the centre of the large, brilliantly-lit room and faced a man, richly-clad in gold-laced blue satin; the man who had ordered her abduction and who now perched silently on the edge of a Turkey-covered table.

Aside from that table, what little furniture there was stood against the walls; two massive dressers laden with silver-gilt plate; a black lacquered cabinet displaying china and jade; and a set of intricately-carved high-back chairs. And the walls themselves were hung with dozens of paintings; portraits in some master hand ... religious scenes ... huge canvases in vibrant colours depicting naked nymphs and semi-clad gods and goddesses. Slowly, Lydia realised that everything she could see represented vast sums of money.

Still the man did not speak but merely sat, contemplating her thoughtfully. They hadn't restrained her this time but then they didn't need to. The woman who'd acted as decoy had gone but Lydia knew that the fellows who'd brought her here, and probably others as well, were just beyond the closed door – which meant that running wasn't an option even if she could out-distance the man in front of her. Even if she wasn't still shaking so badly she didn't think her legs would support her.

They'd swaddled her in a cloak and bundled her into a carriage almost before she knew what was happening. The woman and one of the men had sat beside her while the other man drove. Neither of them spoke. Neither answered her breathless questions about what they'd done to Nancy or where they were taking her. And with the leather flaps covering the windows, she had no idea of their direction ... only that it had been some distance across the City.

She kept her hands tightly clenched in her lap and tried to decide what best to do.

Eden will come. He will. But he won't know where I am. How long will it take him to find me? The chilling notion that he might *not* find her lay in wait at the edges of her mind. She did her best not to let it in. *It's up to me, then. I need to give Eden as much time as I can. So I'll sit here and say nothing. Not one word until I have to. And then I'll talk myself silly,*

The trouble was that the long silence was gradually shredding her already screaming nerves. She didn't know how much longer she could stand it. She tried comforting herself with the thought that at least she knew what to say. *I'll tell him the story I concocted for the letter and make it as long-winded as possible. It might work. But I wish I'd written the letter. If I had, I might not be here now.*

Finally, after another excoriating minute or two, her captor said dispassionately, 'If you're waiting for rescue, Mistress, I fear you may be waiting for a long time.'

Lydia swallowed and concentrated on keeping her voice steady.

'You think you can abduct me and no one will come looking, Lord Northcote?'

'Meaning that troublesome Colonel you married this morning?'

Even though he'd had her snatched from her own wedding party, it still gave her a jolt that he knew. 'Yes. He got me out of the cellar, after all.'

'The fellows being paid to keep the two of you under lock and key on that occasion were lax. Colonel Maxwell should not count on it happening again – or indeed, on finding you at *all*.'

'He'll come,' said Lydia stubbornly. 'He will.'

His mouth curled slightly in a chilly smile that didn't reach his eyes.

'Perhaps. But perhaps you should neither wish nor wait for his arrival. I'm sure you'd sooner not be a widow before you've been a wife.'

Ice slid through her veins but she said, 'Actually, I was waiting for something quite different.'

'Really?'

'Yes. I was waiting for you to explain your extraordinary behaviour.'

'I wouldn't have thought that, by now, it would need explaining.'

'I have no idea what you mean.'

'Of course you do. You have something of mine ... and I want it back without further prevarication or delay.'

Lydia stared at him for a moment and then said doubtfully, 'Are you ... can you be talking about the letters?'

His expression – or rather the lack of it – didn't change but somehow she had the feeling she'd surprised him. He said, 'What else might I mean? The letters my lamentably indiscreet mother wrote to your late husband and the conclusions, if any, he drew from them. I know you have them. You must always have had them – despite the inability of my employees to wrest them from you.'

'*Your* employees? But I thought --' She stopped abruptly and then added bitterly. 'Of course I should have guessed.'

'Guessed what, Madam?'

She took her time about answering. So long, in fact, that Northcote was eventually prompted to say, 'Well?'

'When I finally found the letters, my first thought was that they were the ones your brother asked me about.'

'They were. Did he tell you why he wanted them?'

'No – and I didn't ask. I just assumed his reasons were sentimental.' She managed an acid-edged smile. 'Yours, I take it, are not.'

'Neither, as it happens, are his.' He continued to regard her with a complete absence of expression. 'Have you shown them to him?'

'No. I – I might have done. But since I rejected his proposal of marriage – *not*, I should add because of anything you said – relations between us have become less cordial.'

'Naturally. However ... you were saying?'

'What?' For a moment, she couldn't remember what she *had* been saying. 'Oh – yes. Well later, when I realised the letters were responsible for the attacks on myself and my people, I assumed the man Quinn had been acting on his own initiative and for his own purposes. I thought he intended to use them against your family in some way – probably to extort money.' Lydia paused again, hoping she wasn't making a complete mess of this. 'If you hadn't abducted me today, I'd *still* think that.'

'Ah.' His lordship folded his arms. 'But now you know better.'

'Clearly, he's your lackey,' she shrugged. 'But had you waited a day or two more, this could have been avoided. I'd planned to write to you offering to *give* you the thrice-blasted letters.'

'Had you indeed?' The cold eyes narrowed. 'And what would your heroic Colonel have had to say about that, I wonder?'

Lydia bent her head and fiddled with her new and very beautiful wedding band.

'I know *exactly* what he'd say – which is why I'd no intention of telling him. I just wanted to be rid of the wretched things and it didn't matter *who* had them so long as I didn't. The few that I read are either completely uninteresting or make no sense whatsoever. And they've been nothing but trouble.'

'If that is so, why hold on to them until now?'

'Because – and purely thanks to the damage Mr Quinn and his bullies did to my lorinery – I've only recently *found* them.'

'Explain.'

'They virtually dismantled the upper floor. It was while putting everything to rights that a concealed space was found behind an old cupboard which Quinn's men had all but destroyed. Your precious letters were in it. Until then, I had no idea that they even existed.'

Lord Northcote regarded her silently for a long, unnerving minute. Eventually he said softly, 'Where are the letters now?'

She almost told him and then, with a sickening lurch, realised that she couldn't. He would immediately send a search party to Cheapside and if Alice or anyone else had gone back there ... she shuddered at the thought of what might happen. She said, 'It would be very stupid of me to tell you that, wouldn't it?'

'It will be extraordinarily stupid of you not to,' he replied in the same cool, level tone he'd conducted the entire conversation. 'Do you seriously believe I will hesitate to have my men hurt you?'

'No.' She licked her dry lips and tried not to sound as frightened as she felt. 'I've encountered your Mr Quinn before and I know how dangerous he is. But if I tell you what you want to know, you'll have no further use for me, will you? And I'd quite like to have some chance of surviving the night.'

* * *

As soon as Eden realised how much help was on hand, the fog that had been clouding his brain lifted and he wasted no time changing his orders. Up to this point, he'd withheld the information contained in Stephen Neville's boxes from Lydia's work-force; partly because he didn't want to share his discoveries with more people than was necessary but also because he'd thought it was safer. But the latter was no longer true. Safety now lay in spreading that information far and wide. Quinn might murder two or three people but even he couldn't kill fifty and expect to get away with it.

And so, deciding it was time to lay his cards upon the table, he said crisply, 'The situation is this. We are hunting two men. One is a criminal named Quinn and the other, Lord Northcote, is the man who is paying him. Amongst other things, Quinn is a murderer ... and Northcote has an arsenal of dirty secrets which I now share. One of those secrets is ownership of a house catering to every known perversion on the corner of Seething Lane and Crutched Friars – and that, I believe, is where Quinn will be holding Lydia.' He glanced round at nearly two score attentive faces. 'Since Ned, Aubrey and I are already armed, we'll take half a dozen of the fittest men from the lorinery, armed with whatever knives and cudgels this inn can supply and head directly for the brothel.'

Tobias scowled. 'I'm coming as well.'

'Not immediately, Toby. First you'll go to Cheapside. Take Trooper Collis, Mr Potter, Henry, Peter and Alice with you. Gather up every blade, pistol and all the powder and shot – along with my translation of Stephen's coded page – then follow me to the brothel. One of the men should stay at home with Alice and make the house secure. It will be our command-centre through which messages can be passed at need.'

'Allow me,' volunteered Henry promptly.

Too preoccupied to smile, Eden merely nodded.

'Nicholas. Take Trooper Hayes, half a dozen of his colleagues and some of the women and see what the situation is in Duck Lane. If you think Quinn or any of his men are there, do *not* go in. Surround the place as best you can and send word. But if there's no sign of activity, gather up anything that might be used as a weapon and join the rest of us in Seething Lane.' He looked round at his assembled troops. 'Those who have doubts about involving themselves should either return to their homes or join Alice and Henry in Cheapside. Now ... does anyone have any questions?'

No one did.

'Good. One last thing. I'd ask you all to be careful. Lydia won't thank me for rescuing her at the cost of one of you – and I'd sooner not begin my married life by having my ears boxed.' He won a scattering of laughter which he hoped put some heart into them but which did nothing for the lump of ice in his own chest. 'It's boot and saddle, then. Let's go.'

Out in the street with everyone going their separate ways, Eden grasped Ned Moulton's arm and said quietly, 'Get four or five of our own fellows from the Tower.'

The Major's brows rose. 'Officially?'

'Preferably not – but however you can do it. This time Quinn won't take any risks, so I can't either. If Lydia doesn't give him what he wants right away, he'll hurt her. And if he hurts her, I'll kill him. Slowly.'

Ned quickened his pace to cover the short distance past Seething Lane to the Tower. Eden delivered a few low-voiced orders to Trooper Buxton and the others, then turned to Aubrey and said bluntly, 'Are you capable of guarding my back?'

'Yes. Do you really think they've brought Lyd to a damned brothel?'

'It's the most logical place – so I hope so. At any rate, we'll soon know.'

Eden was glad he'd previously made a point of strolling past the Painted Angel. Now he was able to gather his little troop on the opposite corner and say, 'There it is. As you can see, it's a big, sprawling building. The door leading off Seething Lane leads to what appears to be an ordinary tavern. I think the door on Crutched Friars with no lights showing leads to the brothel. Somewhere inside, however, there will be a way of getting from one side to the other. Buxton ... leave one of your fellows out here to point the way to our friends when they arrive and take the rest of them into the tavern. Find the connecting door and get through it without attracting attention.'

Buxton could see difficulties with this. He said, 'And if we can't?'

'Find a way. Create a diversion. I'm sure you'll think of something. Aubrey ... you and I are going to bribe our way in upstairs. Let's go.'

Crossing the road into Crutched Friars, Eden walked straight up to the brothel door and hammered on it with his fist. After a minute, a grille slid back and a pair of eyes peered out at them.

'Open up, man!' demanded Colonel Maxwell peremptorily, simultaneously flashing a gold coin in his fingers. 'You think this is a place we want to be seen?'

There was a second of hesitation, then the bolts slid back and the door opened just wide enough for Eden and Aubrey to slip into the darkened passage-way.

Tossing the coin to the door-keeper, Eden said casually, 'Is Quinn in tonight?'

'Might be,' came the unhelpful reply, 'or might not. You gentlemen been 'ere before?'

'Might have – might not,' retorted Eden, heading up the stairs. 'And you shouldn't be asking.'

Aubrey clattered up in Eden's wake, pausing on the turn to check that the man below wasn't following them. He hissed, 'Shouldn't we knock that fellow out?'

'No. Nothing to tie him up with and if he came round and raised the alarm, we'd be finished. Now stop talking and leave the thinking to me.' Lanterns were lit on the first landing, from which the stairs carried on upwards. Light and voices came from rooms to their right but Eden focussed his attention on a bolted door at the far end of the passage-way. Pointing to it, he said softly, 'Unbar that. With luck it links to the tavern.' And when it was done, 'Good. Now let's find out what we're dealing with.'

'What do you intend to do?'

'No idea. Yet.'

Eden pushed open the nearest door and sauntered in, rapidly assessing the scene before him. Comfortably furnished, the large room was occupied by seven or eight semi-clad courtesans, none of whom were currently occupied. Plainly, the main trade of the evening had yet to begin. Three of the girls were playing cards, two were dressing each other's hair and the rest merely reclined in comfortable indolence. As soon as he and Aubrey appeared, a well-endowed red-head rather more respectably dressed than her fellows, undulated towards them, smiling.

'Welcome, gentlemen. I'm Mistress Clarinda and it's my pleasure to see to yours. We cater to all tastes here ... so what would be your preference this evening?'

'We are both open to suggestion,' returned Eden smoothly. 'But first we have business with Quinn. Where might we find him?'

The practiced smile faded.

'Quinn doesn't receive visitors without an appointment, sir.'

'He'll receive me. Where is he?'

Clarinda's eyes strayed to the far side of the room. Instantly one of the whores opened the door to an adjoining room and summoned its occupants with a jerk of her head. Two burly servants stepped into view. One of them was the fellow Eden had last seen in Duck Lane, standing behind Lydia with a knife in his hand.

His hand gripping his sword-hilt, Eden said, 'Ah. Chaff, isn't it?'

'What you doing 'ere?'

'I want to see Quinn. Preferably without hurting people and ruining the furniture – though I will if I have to.'

Chaff growled and rushed Eden, his knife appearing as if by magic. Eden half-drew his sword, side-stepped and felled his would-be attacker with a blow to the underside of the jaw using his sword-hilt. Chaff went down as if pole-axed, taking the card-table with him and making the courtesans sitting around it dive out of the way, squealing.

'Damn it, Stoner!' yelled Mistress Clarinda to the other servant. 'What're you waiting for?'

With a roar, Stoner stormed towards Eden, fists raised like a man who knew what to do with them. Eden twisted, extended one foot and, as his assailant stumbled, delivered two rapid punches that sent him down on one knee. An unkind but well-placed kick ended Stoner's resistance and left him curled up on the floor, howling.

Unfortunately, at this precise moment, a third servant appeared in the doorway.

Eden swore and at the same time heard footsteps in the corridor and what sounded like Buxton's voice. He snapped, 'Step to it, Aubrey! I didn't bring you just to watch!' And whirled out of the room to collide with the loriners head-on.

'That was quick. Well done.'

'Thank Cooper. He's running the Three Card Trick. Penny a go to win a half-crown.'

'Christ. Remind me to pay him back. Meanwhile, some of you go and help sodding useless Aubrey and the rest follow me.'

Buxton snorted and set off in Eden's wake.

'Cooper won't lose, Colonel. Where d'you think he got the half-crown?'

Eden barely heard him. There were eight closed doors spread to either side of the passage-way. He said, 'Check all these. If they're locked, kick them in.'

The first room was empty. The second was occupied by a naked fellow with a pot-belly and three whores – all of whom were completely oblivious thanks to the clouds of opium fumes filling the air. And in the third, two men – one of whom Eden recognised – lay entwined on the bed. Stepping back, he slammed the door shut behind him and moved on. On the other side of the corridor, Buxton and his team had disturbed other, more conventional couples and backed out with a bawdy remark or two. Meanwhile, Eden reached the last door on his side and found it locked.

It took two violent kicks to send the door flying inwards with enough force to bring it bouncing back off the wall. Eden stilled it with one hand, time seeming to freeze as he took in the tableau in front of him.

Naked but for the torn chemise lying tangled about her hips, a girl was curled up on the bed, half-hidden amidst a torrent of black hair. Her back was criss-crossed with savage wheals and her whole body was shaking with sobs, the sounds of which she was trying to stifle with her hands. And beside her stood a muscular man wearing only his breeches, his arm poised to deliver another blow with the whip in his hand.

Eden bit out a curse and was across the floor without conscious thought. He'd wanted to hit someone ever since he'd learned of Lydia's abduction; an urge the two servants in the antechamber had failed to satisfy – but that battering this bastard might.

He wrenched the whip from the momentarily slackened grip and hurled it aside. Then he smashed one fist into fellow's jaw and the other into his stomach. His opponent staggered but kept his balance and fought back, landing a blow on Eden's shoulder and a second on his ribs. Eden was scarcely aware of either. Fuelled by white-hot anger and his bottled-up fear for Lydia, he fought on furiously, wanting nothing but to pummel this pervert into a pulp.

Somewhere behind him, a voice said sharply, 'Colonel – stop!' But he didn't heed it and would have gone on grappling had not his opponent suddenly dropped like a stone.

Breathing heavily, Eden frowned up at the half-naked girl now standing on the bed clutching the handle of a heavy stone-ware pitcher ... the rest of which lay in pieces on the floor about her defunct torturer.

Ned Moulton strode across to grasp his shoulder.

'Come away. Rob Trotter and four others are outside. Toby has arrived with the arms and Nicholas says all's quiet in Duck Lane. Have you found Quinn?'

Eden shook his head to clear it. 'No. Not yet.'

'He's got rooms above,' said a woman's voice from the door.

Eden looked across at one of the courtesans from the antechamber. 'Is he there?'

'Don't reckon so – or he'd be down here by now.' She walked over to put her arms about the shaking, sobbing girl who Eden thought looked about fifteen. 'Dunno what you want with 'im. But if you want to *really* 'elp ... the worst of it's in the attics.'

'The worst of what?'

'What goes on 'ere.'

'Jesus, Eden,' muttered Major Moulton. 'It's a mad-house below here and chaos in the bloody street. If Quinn's not here --'

'Take a couple of men and check the next floor. I'm for the attic,' said Eden grimly. Then, yelling for Trooper Buxton, he charged up the stairs.

The attic was locked from the outside. Eden rammed the bolt aside and opened the door.

The gloom was such that it was several moments before he could distinguish the shapes within. But gradually his eyes made out the forms of three little girls, wraith-thin and none older than ten, huddled together against the far wall.

'Bloody buggering 'ell,' swore Buxton softly.

Eden's throat closed and he merely nodded. Then, swallowing, he said quietly, 'They're terrified and we'll just frighten them more. Get some of our women ... Jenny or --'

He stopped abruptly and looked down as something he hadn't previously seen stirred near his foot. It was another child. A little boy, probably about six years old, with matted blond curls and huge eyes. But what froze Eden to the marrow was the fact that, despite those eyes being awash with terror, the child's mouth was curled in a desperate smile as a pair of small arms wrapped themselves around his boot.

Eden suddenly wanted to vomit. If he permitted himself to contemplate the role of these children in a cess-pit like this, he *would* vomit. It took all his self-control to remain perfectly still whilst repeating his order to Buxton. Then, when the trooper's presence behind him had been replaced with that of his Major, he said with soft implacability, 'I'll have this place closed down and see Northcote and Quinn in hell. Go and hurry those women up here.'

Equally sick, Ned nodded and disappeared.

Very slowly, as he would to a frightened animal, Eden bent and extended one hand to where the child could reach it if he chose. He said, 'It's all right. I won't hurt you.'

The little fingers clutched his boot even more tightly and that terrible, caricature of a smile wavered.

His eyes stinging and pure agony excoriating his throat, Eden tried again.

'Don't be frightened. I'm here to help. I promise.'

Across in the corner, one of the girls came uncertainly to her feet. Her voice frail and far older than her years, she said dully, 'Help? Nobody helps. Nobody ever has.'

'They will now,' replied Eden unevenly. 'By *God*, they will now.'

TWELVE

Leaving four of the women and one of Sergeant Trotter's troopers to coax the terrified children out of the attic and take them to safety, Eden gained the street where the rest of his little army were anxiously waiting. He forced what he'd seen inside to the furthest corner of his mind. There would be time enough to clean out that particular rat's nest later. Right now, his priority was Lydia ... and he knew of only one other place where he might find her.

The possibility that he might *not* find her – or not find her in time – was beginning to impair his ability to think clearly. He tried to work out how long it had been since she'd been taken. A little over two hours, he thought, though it felt longer. But everything that had happened since then had happened very quickly so ... two hours; at worst, two and a half.

Competently handing him a loaded pistol along with a small bag of additional powder and shot, Tobias said succinctly, 'Anything?'

Eden shook his head and met his brother's unusually austere gaze.

'No. No sign of either Quinn or Lydia. It just ... wasted time.'

'You don't believe that. Ned told me what you found inside. But for now, we're all awaiting your orders.'

'Northcote's house.' Eden hesitated and then added tonelessly, 'If she's not there ... Toby, I don't know where else to look.'

'There *isn't* anywhere else,' came the bracing reply. 'She'll be there and this time I'm coming with you. So let's get moving. You can hand out your instructions along the way.'

By the time Colonel Maxwell and his troop reached Temple Bar, he had formulated and outlined a plan. In order to create a diversion that would draw the attention of both neighbours and occupants to the front of Northcote's house, Eden simply asked them to start a riot.

'You've all seen a mob at work. Be angry and threatening. Throw stones at the windows, hurl insults at Northcote himself ... and one of you women can scream that he's snatched your sister or your daughter for his evil brothel. Make it as noisy as you can and don't hold back with the accusations and curses. If someone opens the door, push forward as far as the steps and set up a shout for Northcote to come out and show himself. Trooper Hayes ... regard yourself as acting-sergeant for the evening and take charge out here.'

'Gawd! Thank you, Colonel. Honoured, sir.' Dan saluted. 'Come on, folks – better start gathering missiles. Don't want to turn up empty-handed, do we?'

Leaving them to it, Eden turned to Sergeant Trotter.

'Rob ... you and your men stay on the fringes as if you're waiting for reinforcements – which is what you'll say if anyone asks why you're not doing anything.'

'You mean we can't join in?' asked the Sergeant regretfully.

'And while all this is going on?' asked Tobias, as they continued their way down the Strand, 'what will you be doing?'

'We,' corrected Eden. 'You and I, along with Ned, Nick, Peter and Trooper Buxton – will be breaking into the house from the back.'

'And me,' snapped Aubrey. 'I'm coming as well.'

'No. You're going to stay here and back up Sergeant Trotter if any Militia turn up with questions. If they do, insist on them entering the house. No one in their right mind is going to shoot a Militiaman.'

'But --'

'No!' said Eden, long past being tactful. 'There won't be any time to stand about dithering – so I'm taking the five men I can best rely on.' Slowing his pace, he called softly, 'We're nearly there. Those coming with me turn off towards the river now. The rest of you ... start surging and grumbling. And be careful.'

* * *

Inside Northcote's house, Lydia had talked, persuaded and cajoled herself to a standstill. None of it had done any good. His lordship not only wanted to know the location of Stephen's papers ... he also refused to believe that she didn't know what was in them. In between long enervating silences under that empty dark gaze, his questions veered back and forth between the two and, between fatigue and fright, Lydia knew that sooner or later she was going to make a bad mistake. The only thing that surprised her was that so far he hadn't laid a hand on her – or, more likely, summoned one of his minions to do so.

For what seemed like the hundredth time, he asked her what – aside from his mother's letters – was contained in her late husband's papers; and for the hundredth time she replied wearily, 'Nothing that I saw. There were pages and pages and I'd neither the time nor the inclination to read it all – nor even to see what else might be there apart from the letters. Why won't you believe me?'

'Because I am not a credulous man – and you, Madam, are not a stupid woman. When you found something that you had repeatedly been asked to produce, you knew it contained information that someone wanted very badly. You would have been determined to find out what that information was. And even if, by some stretch of the imagination, *you* were not – your new husband undoubtedly *would* have been.' He allowed a glacial silence to touch the edges of the room and then said, 'I will ask one last time. What have you learned about me?'

I know you're a misbegotten cur who makes his money out of prostitution and blackmail. But if I admit to knowing anything at all, you'll guess that Eden and I both know everything. And after you've killed me, you'll go after him. I can't let that happen.

'Nothing! Truly – I swear it. Nothing.'

Without a word he stood up and rang the small bell that stood beside him on the table.

Instantly, the door opened to admit one of the men who had hauled her out of the Black Dog.

'Yes, milord?'

'The lady proves uncooperative, Herbert. I believe I will permit you to exercise your talents.'

Herbert grinned and his fingers strayed to the knife at his belt. 'Thank you, milord.'

All the air promptly evaporated from Lydia's lungs and she was suddenly very cold.

'No blades,' said Northcote negligently. 'Not just yet. Something a little more ... inventive, I think.'

'Hot irons, sir?' suggested Herbert hopefully.

'Mm. Perhaps. But she is so stubborn, I believe it might be entertaining to try something a little more lingering.'

'Lingering, milord?'

'Yes. Put your imagination to work, Herbert. Surprise me.' He looked Lydia over in a considering manner and then resumed his seat. 'I'm curious to discover how deep her obstinacy goes. See to it.'

The man bobbed a bow and went out.

Lydia stared at Northcote, trying not to show her panic. She'd known that eventually they'd resort to violence but she'd expected a few blows; something she'd been fairly confident she could withstand. But *this*? Mention of knives, hot irons and *something lingering* had sent her heart ricocheting around her chest like a wild thing.

She said raggedly, 'You d-don't need to hurt me. I've promised to give you what you want. You can have it first thing in the morning if --'

'Enough. You have exceeded my patience. The next time you speak, it had better be to say something I want to hear.'

Lydia pressed her lips together so she wouldn't say anything stupid. So that she wouldn't shame herself by pleading with a man who hadn't a scrap of humanity in him.

The door opened again and Herbert plodded in. He wasn't bearing any of the implements of torture that Lydia's imagination had conjured up in unpleasant detail. He was carrying ... a bucket.

A bucket? she thought incredulously. And still uncomprehendingly as what appeared to be water sloshed over the side, *What can he do with that - unless it isn't just water. Or – or there's something else in it.*

'Think you might like this one, sir,' Herbert said cheerfully, setting down the bucket. 'Beauty of it is, we can make it last as long as you want. There's two ways of doing it, of course – and if it was a man, I'd go for t'other. But her being such a slip of a thing, I reckon this'n should do.' He hesitated. 'Maybe I should just roll the rug back? Don't want it getting wet, do we, sir?'

'Since it is a century-old Bokhara, we most assuredly do not.'

Lydia felt a bubble of hysterical rising in her throat.

Oh yes. By all means, protect the damned rug. It would be dreadful if I threw up over it. And with an involuntary shudder of apprehension, *Eden ... where are you? If you're coming, now would be a good time. I don't know what they're going to do. If I did, it might be easier. But right now I'm really quite ... afraid.*

The carpet was rolled away to the side of the room and the bucket ceremoniously placed in the space mid-way between the Viscount and the chair on which Lydia sat.

'Shall I begin, milord?' asked Herbert.

Northcote yawned. 'I am all anticipation.'

'Milord?'

'Just get on with it. Today, if possible.'

Herbert nodded, walked over to Lydia and hauled her to her feet, pinning her arms behind her in the same move. He shoved her towards the innocent-looking bucket and forced her down on her knees.

She looked into the contents of the bucket. Water. It was just ... water.

Then, before she had time to grasp his intent, Herbert grabbed the base of her skull and bore her head down into the cold depths.

Shock caused an indrawn breath. Water invaded her nose, her mouth, her lungs; she choked, making everything very much worse. Unable to breathe or see or rid herself of the incoming tide, she struggled wildly but unavailingly against the iron grip that held her down. More choking ... pain in her chest and in her head ... a feeling of fading. Darkness.

Herbert hauled her up, brought her round with a hard thump between her shoulder-blades and released her hands. Lydia bent double, coughing, wheezing and regurgitating water from her nose and mouth. Desperate for air, she tried to breathe – but too soon and only brought on another fit of coughing to expel yet more water. Her head felt too large and her throat and chest hurt. People said drowning was peaceful. It wasn't. It was terrifying and it hurt. More cautiously this time, she drew in gasps of blessed air; and was just beginning to breathe again when Herbert resumed his grasp and plunged her back into the bucket.

* * *

Northcote's house was one of handful of narrow dwellings situated between Arundel House and the Savoy Palace which backed on to the river. Eden and his companions were therefore able to gain the rear of the property without undue difficulty – only to immediately find themselves facing four hulking brutes armed with what Eden was coming to recognise as the usual assortment of knives and cudgels.

Dodging a blow to his head, Eden snapped, 'No firing – just put them down fast.' After which everything happened at once.

One of the bruisers laughed. He stopped laughing when Tobias kicked him in the knee, wrenched the billet from his grasp and brought it down on the back of his skull. Ned dealt with his opponent with almost lazy precision, dropping him with a sword-thrust to the thigh before knocking him out. Nicholas struggled with a fellow nearly twice his size until Jem Buxton tripped him with a length of pipe and he went down with the two of them on top of him. Eden, meanwhile – having taken a hefty buffet to his shoulder and no longer caring for anything except getting to Lydia as fast as possible – didn't trouble to disarm the man trying to dash his brains out. He simply ran him through the throat. Ned cast him a sharp glance and Tobias muttered a startled curse under his breath.

Peter, meanwhile, had slithered past the fight in favour of seeking a way into the house. When Eden arrived beside him, he said, 'Window unlatched here, Colonel. If one of us got through, they could open what looks like the scullery door. I'd do it myself except I think I'd get stuck.'

With the exception of Trooper Buxton, everyone clustered about Eden to eye the window in question. It was a little above even Peter's reach and far too small, they all agreed, to admit any of them with the possible exception of Nicholas – for whom pulling himself through with only one arm was going to be difficult.

'What do you think, Nick?' asked Eden dubiously. 'It's tricky but --'
'Colonel?' came a whisper from a few feet away.
'-- if Toby and Peter boost you up, you might be able --'
'*Colonel!*'

Eden spun round with an impatient, *'What?'* on his tongue and then stopped dead.

Standing in front of the open door, picklocks dangling from one hand, Buxton said modestly, 'Thought this might be easier, sir.'

Tobias gave a snort of laughter.

'Christ, Jem,' muttered Eden, dropping a hand on the man's shoulder. 'You brought a set of picklocks to my wedding?'

'Habit, sir.' Buxton gave a bashful shrug. 'Never know when they'll come in handy.'

'So it seems. Right, gentlemen – here we go.'

They were all only too aware of their limited knowledge. They might be facing two men or twenty, armed either as those in the garden had been or with loaded pistols. And they didn't know the lay-out of the house or the particular room they needed to find. All they could be grateful for as yet was that they'd got inside apparently undetected and that the only occupant of the kitchen was a sleepy scullery-maid.

She gave a squeal but fell silent when an extremely large young man gave her a beautiful smile and said, 'Now, darling. If I lock you in the larder, there's no saying how long it would be before someone came to let you out. So why don't you stay quietly by the fire and forget you ever saw us?'

Bemused and faintly dazzled, the maid nodded and was rewarded with a kiss on the cheek.

'For God's sake, Toby,' muttered Eden, as he led the way out of the room. 'What *is* it with you?'

Tobias grinned and shrugged. 'Why use rope when a bit of charm can serve just as well?'

They gained the main floor of the house without incident but as they reached the hall they could hear the tell-tale sounds of an angry crowd outside. Something heavy thudded against the front door, followed by the sound of breaking glass. A thick-set fellow rushed out from an adjoining room and stopped dead when he clapped eyes on the invaders. He opened his mouth to shout but changed his mind when both Eden and Ned levelled their pistols at him.

'How many bruisers in the house?' demanded Eden softly. 'Quickly, now. Including yourself, how many?'

'Four. And four others out the back.'

'Not any more,' came the silky reply. 'Those inside ... where are they?'

'Two on the second-floor landing and another in with the boss.'

'And that's all?'

The man kept his attention fixed warily on the pistols.

'Far as I know. He – Sir sent all the servants off for the night.'

'No prizes for guessing why,' remarked Eden grimly. Then, 'Peter, Buxton ... tie him up, gag him and get him out of sight. Knock him out, if you have to – then open the front door and let Dan and a few of the others in to keep watch down here, so you can follow the rest of us upstairs.'

They reached the first floor and were about to continue up when Tobias dropped a hand on his brother's arm and said, 'Wait. Listen.'

From above them, they heard booted feet clattering along the landing. Someone hammered on a closed door, presumably burst through it and shouted, 'Sir – look outside! There's a bloody riot, right up to the steps. They're throwing mud and bricks and God knows what besides. One of the windows has been broke already and – and they're shouting things, sir. Th-things about you. What d'you want done about it?'

There was a moment of silence, before a low-pitched voice said something they couldn't hear. Then the guard said unhappily, 'Well, we can try. But there's an awful lot of 'em, sir. I'll fetch the men from the garden but I still don't rightly see as how wiv just them and Barker downstairs we're going to --'

His words were cut off by that maddeningly indistinct low-pitched voice. Then came the sound of a door closing and feet heading back towards the stairs.

'They're coming down. How very helpful of them,' murmured Eden; and signalled Tobias and Ned to one side of the staircase while he and Nicholas took the other.

The guards came down muttering to each other, then froze when each of them felt something cold and deadly pressed against the back of his skull.

'Don't do anything rash,' advised Eden to the one he held at pistol-point. 'None of your friends are in any position to help you ... and it sounds as if *my* friends are coming inside just about now. Am I making myself quite clear?'

The fellow swallowed and nodded.

'Good. Where is my wife?'

A quiver of shock ran down the man's spine. 'That woman's your w-wife?'

'Yes. Where is she?' And jamming the pistol hard under the man's jaw, '*Where?*'

'Next floor, third door on the right,' said the other guard quickly. 'Look – we never touched her. None of it's our d--'

'Be quiet. Ned – Nick – take these two down for Buxton and the others to deal with, then come back up. Toby – with me.'

Upstairs, Lydia was still on her hands and knees, gasping for air following a fourth ducking. Although scarcely able to think, she was distantly aware that she couldn't endure much more of this; that next time or the one after that, she was going to break and tell Northcote what he wanted to know. His voice seeming to come from a long way off, she heard him say, 'Again, Herbert.'

With a moan of misery, she snatched a ragged breath as the rough hands took hold of her again and plunged her head down into the bucket. Struggling made everything worse but she couldn't stop herself doing it. Once again, she started to choke and feel consciousness fading. And then, miraculously and sooner than before, she found herself free.

From the doorway, it took Eden less than a second to assimilate the scene before him. He shot across the room and, using the sole of his boot with every ounce of his strength, he sent Herbert scudding away over the polished floorboards.

'Toby – kill the first one that moves,' he snapped coldly. And was on his knees beside Lydia almost before the words were out of his mouth.

'Easy now, darling. Just breathe.' He slid a supporting arm under her ribs and massaged her back as the water came up. Silently, he damned these men for what they had been doing to her ... and himself for not getting here sooner. Then he damned the circumstances that meant he couldn't simply pick her up and carry her away; couldn't, in fact, even stay with her when she so clearly needed him. 'Slowly. Yes. That's right.'

'Eden?' she croaked, finding his wrist and clinging to it, not yet quite able to believe that the ordeal was over. 'Oh. You c-came.'

The words brought on a coughing fit and a red mist of fury filled Eden's brain.

'Yes. I'm here, love. Hush now.' With his free hand, he stroked back the dripping hair about her face and simultaneously realised that she was greenish-pale and shaking with cold and shock. Briefly releasing her, he dragged his coat off and wrapped it round her, before very slowly raising her to her feet so that he could hold her properly and warm her with his body.

'How very touching,' remarked a chilly, expressionless voice.

For the first time since he'd entered the room, Eden allowed himself to look into the face of a man he fully intended to destroy, the murderous rage he could barely contain showing unmistakeably in his eyes. In a tone that could have scored glass, he said, 'Nice coat, Quinn. Torturing women pays well, does it?'

The other man showed no reaction but, against his chest, Eden felt Lydia draw a harsh, painful breath.

'No,' she managed to say. 'Eden – no. Not Quinn. *Northcote.*'

Shock and momentary incomprehension froze every nerve and sinew. '*What?*'

'He – he's Northcote.'

For the space of a heartbeat, it didn't seem possible. He heard Tobias mutter, 'He's *both* of them? Holy hell!'

For a long, airless moment Eden frowned at the satin-clad man perched negligently on the edge of the table. And then the tumblers clicked into place and he saw that, of *course* it was possible. Lydia had met Northcote but never seen Quinn; *he* knew Quinn but had never laid eyes on Northcote. It was not only possible; it was the single fact that explained everything.

Eden let loose a long, slow breath. It was one of those things that, once you knew, became suddenly blindingly obvious. The bastard was successfully leading a double-life ... and enjoying the best of both worlds. The only thing Eden couldn't understand was why the possibility had never occurred to him before.

Behind him, he heard sounds betokening the arrival of Nicholas, Ned and some others but he didn't turn to look. Instead, holding Northcote's remote gaze with a very different one of his own, he said, 'Well, well ... two birds with one stone, then. This is going to save me a great deal of trouble. But I hope you've found the game entertaining enough to be worth the candle.'

Finally, the Viscount stirred. 'You think it's over? It isn't.'

'Almost. Your men are down and the house is full of mine. Unless you can conjure reinforcements out of thin air?'

'I don't need to,' came the dismissive reply. 'I have money, influential men who will do my bidding the moment I snap my fingers and a dozen or more fellows with skills you wouldn't imagine. You won't hold me for more than a day.'

Very slowly and in a way that Lydia would never have recognised, Eden smiled.

'I know that. So I've no intention of holding you at all.'

For the first time, something flickered in the empty eyes but Eden didn't give Northcote the chance to speak. Turning to find Peter standing beside Rob Trotter, he gently detached Lydia's fingers from his shirt and said, 'You're going home, love.'

'No!' She snatched her hands back, clenched her fingers on his shirt and, through chattering teeth, said, 'He d-doesn't matter. Too many people know about him now. All that c-counts, is that *you're* alive and *I'm* alive. And I'm not going *anywhere* without you.'

'Yes. You are.' The fact that – dripping wet, shivering and after being half-drowned God only knew how many times – she could still stand her ground and argue, made something twist painfully in his chest. But he shook his head and said, 'This is no place for you now, Lydia. So you'll do as I ask and leave me to follow you presently. No.' This, firmly, as she embarked on another impassioned denial. 'Stop. Nothing is going to happen to me. But I have to finish this because – as this piece of filth has just said – if I don't, he might find a way of squirming out of it. So you'll go and leave me to do what must be done.' He dropped a fleeting kiss on her brow. 'Peter – take her away, please. Over your shoulder, if necessary. Rob – organise an escort, will you? And tell any of those downstairs who wish to leave that they may now safely do so.'

'No!' said Lydia again, as Peter advanced towards her. 'You mustn't --' Her words ended in an outraged grunt when the young man tossed her up in his arms like a wisp of straw. Spitting out a mouthful of hair and belatedly recognising that she wasn't going to win, she sought Tobias's eyes across the room and said, 'Toby? You – you'll be here?'

'I'll be here,' he agreed grimly. 'You may count on it. And for the rest, you have no need to ask.'

THIRTEEN

Without removing his eyes from Northcote, Eden waited until Lydia – still furiously complaining – had been borne away. Then, his tone chillingly conversational, he said, 'You really *are* a sick bastard, aren't you?' And, over his shoulder, 'Would anybody like to shove Lord Northcote-Quinn's head in the bucket?'

'All of us,' replied Nicholas, disgustedly. 'He's not a man. He's a piece of shit.'

'Your insults grow tedious,' remarked Northcote, rising to his feet and brushing an imaginary speck from his cuff. And then, as if the matter were of little interest, 'What did she mean? Too many people know?'

'She meant that, as of this evening, roughly fifty people are aware that you are – quite literally – a bastard. They know of your criminal activities in the guise of Quinn ... and they know you own a brothel where the most despicable of all perversions are permitted.' Eden paused before saying in a tone of flat contempt, 'We have the children.'

There was a long silence during which Northcote's face remained completely expressionless. Then, 'I see,' was all he said.

Eden began to wonder what it would take to shatter that rigid composure and whether there was even a shred of decency behind it. He said, 'By tomorrow, those fifty people will become five hundred. And by noon, everything I know and everything Stephen Neville knew will be on both the Secretary of State's desk and also that of Major-General Lambert. Since this includes the implication that you sold information to the Dutch and arms to the Royalists, your personal outlook would be bleak even if I permitted you to walk out of this room right now. Not,' he finished, 'that there is the remotest chance of me doing so.'

'What, then? You said you intend to end this matter. How? With murder?' There was an infinitesimal and vaguely pitying pause. 'I don't somehow think so. Aside from your position within the Army, you have too many scruples.'

'Wrong on both counts. I've resigned my commission. And whatever scruples I may have had fled in the face of what I and some of my friends have seen tonight. I could blow your brains out right now and there's not a man behind me who would call it anything but justice.'

A decade-old image entered Eden's head; an image of bursting into the Marquis of Winchester's private study to find Cyrus Winter's head splattered all over the room while Luciano del Santi stood over him holding a still smoking pistol. Then he banished it. He hadn't been able, once in possession of all the facts to blame Luciano for what he'd done and had even found a measure of respect for the strength of will that had allowed him to do it. But it was not what he wanted now, in this not entirely dissimilar situation, for himself.

So he said, 'But I won't shoot you in cold blood. Not because I lack the stomach ... but because it would be too quick.' And with another unpleasant smile, 'You may have chosen to spend half of your life in the gutter, Northcote, but you were reared as a gentleman and must, I assume, have retained at least some of a gentleman's skills. Ned ... give him your sword.'

Without hesitation, Major Moulton stepped forward already unsheathing his blade. But Tobias said, 'Eden – what the hell are you doing? You don't owe him any kind of chance.'

'I'm not giving him one.' Eden drew his own sword, discarded his baldric and, catching sight of Herbert, still crouched mouse-still against the wall, 'Buxton – get that vermin out of my sight.'

Smiling grimly and hoisting a hefty cudgel, Trooper Buxton sauntered over to Herbert. 'Mind if I hurt him a bit, Colonel?'

'As much as you like, Jem. Toby, Nick – move that bloody bucket and find something to mop up the spillage.'

Tobias unrolled the Bokhara with a kick and sent it into the puddle. Then, noting the twitch of Northcote's brows, he stamped about on it, dragging the roughened heels of his boots as he went and said cheerfully, 'Oh dear. Valuable, is it? Pity.'

Northcote turned his eyes back to Eden. He still had not taken Ned's proffered sword.

He said, 'You can't make me fight.'

'No? You're going to simply stand there and let me kill you by inches, are you ... without seizing the opportunity to inflict some damage of your own?' Eden shook his head and strolled towards the other man. 'I don't think so. Unless,' he added deliberately, 'on top of everything else, you're a damned coward – which would, of course, come as no surprise to any of us.'

'And if I kill you?' Northcote finally closed his hand on the sword-hilt.

'You won't. But I'll make it worth your while to try.' Eden cast a swift glance at Tobias and the others. 'If I die, let him go. Give --'

'Bugger that!' snapped Tobias. 'And don't tell me it's an order. *I'm* not one of your damned troopers.'

Eden sighed. 'Have a little faith, will you? *If* he kills me, give him an hour before you hunt him down; and take what we know to Thurloe and Lambert.' He turned back to Northcote and lifted his own blade. The red haze that had filled his brain when he'd first entered the room had evaporated, leaving behind it a purposeful, ice-cold rage that he now intended to satisfy. 'Fight or don't fight, Northcote. Your choice.'

And without further warning, his sword made a lightning sweep that delicately sliced through one of the bows on the Viscount's sleeve. Northcote hopped back, then retaliated with a fierce lunge. Eden sidestepped and continued to circle, tempting the other man away from the table and out into the centre of the floor. Then, when he had Northcote where he wanted him, he embarked on an apparently lazy exchange of attack and riposte designed to tempt his opponent into believing he actually had some chance of coming out of this alive.

Looking on with little real knowledge of swordplay, Tobias wondered what his brother was doing. After seeing Eden spit the fellow in the garden, he'd expected some species of blood-frenzy – not this seemingly idle, almost teasing display of finesse. As for Northcote-bastard-Quinn ... he probably fought as well as most gentlemen who'd learned to handle a sword as a matter of form rather than as a life-saving necessity. At times, he even appeared to have the advantage – though he never quite got through Eden's guard. Tobias kept his eyes on the fight and a firm grip on his pistol. Then he became aware that Ned Moulton was leaning against the wall with folded arms and a half-smile bracketing his mouth – suggesting that the Major knew something he didn't. Tobias relaxed a fraction.

And suddenly Eden stopped playing. In a series of rapid, complex moves, he drove Northcote back and back across the room until he collided with the wall, his breath coming in uneven gasps and the tip of Eden's sword resting lightly against the base of his throat.

Eyes and voice cold and razor-sharp, Eden said, 'How many times did you drown my wife?'

Northcote swallowed but said nothing. The blade didn't move but a bead of blood blossomed around it.

'How many?'

'I ... wasn't counting.' The bead became a tiny trickle. 'Ask her.'

'I will. Not that it makes any difference now.' Without warning, the sword skimmed down from throat to navel, slitting the laces of Northcote's coat, slicing through his shirt and scoring a trail down the flesh beneath. 'Once was one time too many.'

For the space of perhaps three heartbeats, implacable hazel eyes held dark ones that were no longer empty. Eden read the hate there and his mouth curled slightly. 'Good,' he said and took a few paces back, beckoning with his left hand. 'You want to kill me? Try.'

Another moment of stillness. Then Northcote erupted from the wall to slash savagely but unsuccessfully at Eden's wrist before making an equally clumsy attempt to disarm him. Eden parried both moves with minimal effort and said derisively, 'No wonder you need hired cut-throats. Ever killed anyone with your own hands, have you?' A perfectly-judged flick drew a bloody line diagonally across the Viscount's cheek. 'Ah. I forgot. You suffocated your mother, didn't you? Quite the hero, in fact.'

Furious colour darkened Northcote's complexion. He took another vicious swipe at Eden's sword-hand but managed only to graze his knuckles as their blades tangled before slithering to a disengage. Then, without a second's hesitation, he pulled a pistol from his pocket and fired it at Eden's chest.

It was a left-handed shot but, even so, there was no warning and, had Eden not chosen that exact moment to make a sudden cross-wise sweep, he'd have been a dead man. As it was, the shot tore through his left sleeve and buried itself in the wall inches away from where Nicholas was standing. Ned and Peter started forward, swearing. From his position on the other side of the room, Tobias simply levelled his own weapon and prepared to fire it.

'Toby – no!' snapped Eden, ducking smartly as Northcote hurled the empty pistol at him. Then, with a disquieting smile and once more circling with predatory intent, he said gently, 'Dirty tricks, my lord? Splendid. I know a few of those myself.'

'Oh – for Christ's sake, Eden!' growled Tobias. 'Just kill him and have done.'

Eden ignored him. Instead, with a swift, hard kick, he sent the sword flying from Northcote's hand. Then, dropping his own point and still smiling, he said, 'Pick it up. I'm not done with you yet.'

'No.'

'Pick it up.' Blood was staining his shirt-sleeve scarlet and beginning to drip down his hand. 'I'm giving you another chance. Your last.'

Northcote's glance flicked over the cold, contemptuous faces gathered near the door and returned to the Colonel, moving slowly towards him with flint-hard eyes. Then, lithe as a cat, he swooped on the fallen blade and, in the same movement, swung it at Eden's chest – only to find it once more blocked and twisted from his grasp. It dropped at his feet and a boot hit him hard in the thigh, sending him down on his knees.

Seeing his brother wiping the blood from his hand on his breeches, Tobias held out a handkerchief, saying tersely, 'Here. Take this.'

In the second Eden turned slightly to stretch out his hand, Northcote lurched to his feet and Nicholas roared out a warning – but just an instant too late. The tip of Northcote's sword sliced across Eden's ribs in a long ribbon of red. Tobias swore and Ned stepped away from the wall. Eden, however, merely shook his head slightly ... and finally exerted the full sum of his skill.

Finding himself engaged in a fast and furious assault which earned him a number of pricks and cuts whilst driving him back again across the room, Northcote had no time for anything except defence. His breath coming in ragged gasps and knowing he couldn't stand this pace for long, he sought an opening and suddenly thought he saw one. It was a mistake. His last one.

Lunging precisely as Eden had intended he should, his sword was once more deflected ... and Eden's own blade travelled unerringly on to bite deep into his heart.

He dropped slowly, blood bursting over his coat and a look of surprise on his face.

Somewhere, into the abrupt moment of total silence, a clock chimed the hour.

Eden stood over him, watching him die; watching those dark empty eyes go sightless and even emptier with death. Then, turning away, he said unevenly, 'Ned ... get Sergeant Trotter's men to deal with this carrion. I'm going home.'

* * *

Back in Cheapside, with a borrowed coat over his ruined shirt, Eden found the parlour full of people all of whom wanted to know what had happened. None of them was Lydia.

For a minute or two, he responded mechanically, as best he could. Then he said, 'I'm sorry. I'm more grateful than I can say for everyone's concern and help – but just now, you'll have to excuse me. Toby and Nick will explain everything. I need to ...' He stopped and, managing to locate Henry Padgett's face, asked bluntly, 'Where?'

'Mistress Lydia is in your chamber, Colonel. Worried, of course – but warm, dry and with a little something to combat the shock.'

'Thank you.' He turned to go and then, looking back, 'Toby. Can you ...?'

'Yes,' said Tobias simply. 'Go.'

On his way upstairs, Eden realised that he'd have liked to wash off the sweat and get rid of his bloodstained shirt before Lydia saw him but that this wasn't going to be an option since the things he needed were in the same room she was. Then he told himself not to be stupid. He couldn't hide his injuries forever, so she might as well see them now.

When he entered his room, Lydia – having recognised the sound of his footsteps – was already uncoiling from the chair by the hearth, her face white with strain. This time, instead of Alice's hideous green wrapper, she was wearing something that looked like a mass of pale blue ruffles, interestingly fastened with darker blue ribbons. Eden swallowed. It was their wedding night; and he was coming to her filthy, aching and bleeding, his every bone and muscle protesting, less from the actual fight, than from the sheer weight of worry and fear that had preceded it.

Once on her feet, Lydia remained quite still for a moment, staring at him. Then, hurling herself at him amidst a torrent of words, she said, 'You're hurt, aren't you? Don't trouble to deny it! Why are you so *stubborn*? You didn't have to fight him. He's finished anyway. What has he d-done to you? How bad is it?'

'It's nothing,' said Eden. 'A couple of scratches --'

'Yes. You *would* say that. Of all the stupid, obstinate m-men in the world, you're probably the worst. You have to d-do everything yourself, don't you? Always so sure that you know best and that no-one else could p-possibly do it half as well as you can!'

Eden put his arms round her and let her continue to rant, uninterrupted.

He understood this phenomenon. He'd seen it before after their escape from the cellar. His Lydia didn't crumble when things were at their worst. It was relief that destroyed her defences; and even then there were no sobs to betray the silent cataract of tears he could feel drenching his throat.

So when the torrent of words finally stopped, he said mildly, 'I'm not arguing. But I'd think you might want to come up for air. I can only imagine how rank I smell right now.'

And was rewarded with a tiny tremor of unsteady laughter.

'That's better.' Quite gently, he lifted her chin to look into her face. Then, brushing away some of the tears with his thumb, he said, 'I'm sorry you were worried. But I fight my own battles, Lydia. And this wasn't something I could ask anyone else to do.'

The drenched silvery-blue eyes looked back at him gravely.

'Is ... is he dead?'

'Yes. It couldn't have ended any other way. But what about you? Are you all right?'

She nodded. 'Just a bit ... shaky.'

Despite everything he pulled her back into his arms and, against her hair, mumbled, 'I'm so sorry. If I could only have got there sooner --'

'Don't! Don't think like that. What matters is that you came – just as I knew you would.' She pulled back from him. 'Alice brought up a can of water a little while ago, so it should still be hot. Take off your shirt and wash. Then I can see what the damage is.'

'You're very free with your orders,' he grumbled, shedding the coat.

'Yes. You're on my territory now, Colonel – and will do as you're told.'

He winced involuntarily as he pulled the shirt over his head and heard the hiss of Lydia's breath. She said, 'What happened to your arm?'

'Bullet. It went straight through.'

'Oh. That's all right then,' she said sarcastically so she wouldn't start crying again. 'And that? One of those scratches you mentioned, I suppose.' She stopped, hauled in a steadying breath and said, 'I'm sorry. I sound like a shrew. Be still and let me see to you.'

While Eden washed his face, arms and chest, Lydia sponged his back and tended to the long shallow cut which mercifully seemed to have stopped bleeding. Conversation was kept equally superficial due to an unspoken understanding that as yet, some things were too painful to be discussed in any depth.

So they agreed that neither of them had ever suspected that Quinn and Northcote might be one and the same, but that the discovery had been less surprising than might have been supposed. Her voice under rigid control, Lydia admitted to having been told about the children in the brothel and Eden replied that he intended to see the place shut down if he had to demolish it brick by brick with his own hands. Neither of them speculated openly on what those children might have suffered; both of them knew that would come tomorrow.

And finally, when – having applied salve to the less serious cuts and bruises – Lydia finished binding the torn, angry flesh of his arm, she said expressionlessly, 'Will they charge you with murder?'

'No. It was a fair fight before witnesses.' He peered at her sideways. 'Will you please stop finding things to worry about?'

'With pleasure – when you stop giving me cause.'

She stood up, intending to tidy things away but was swept back down as, laughing a little, he said, 'You are amazing. Do you know that? But sometimes ... just sometimes, you understand ... I'd appreciate being allowed the last word.'

'You get it far too often, in my opinion,' she retorted, leaning into his shoulder and sliding one palm over the muscles of his chest. Then, 'Is everyone still in the parlour?'

'Most of them, probably.'

'Do you need to go back down?'

'No. You and I can do the rounds together tomorrow but, for now, Toby and Nick are giving chapter and verse. They don't need me.'

'Good.' She glanced up into his face. 'Then you can come to bed.'

Eden toyed idly with one of the pretty dark blue ribbons under her chin. He said carefully, 'This is a very inviting robe. I imagine it covers an even more inviting night-rail.'

Lydia's colour rose but she said prosaically, 'It does. But it isn't an invitation you'll be accepting tonight.'

'Oh. I won't?'

'No. You look exhausted. And if you're not, *I* am. All I want ... all I *need* right now is to sleep with my arms about you and yours about me.' And with a seductive sideways glance, as she disengaged herself and rose, holding out her hand, 'As for the invitation ... assuming you feel you need one ... it will still be there tomorrow.'

Tangling the fingers of one hand with hers and sliding the other into her hair, he took her mouth in a long, leisurely kiss – during which he wondered if perhaps he wasn't quite as tired as he'd thought. Then, because the idea of wrapping her close while they slept suddenly seemed incredibly nice, he said wickedly, 'By tomorrow, my darling, I'm likely to be taking unfair advantage. But for now, I'll settle for a glimpse of that night-rail.'

* * *

Cradled in Eden's arms, Lydia fell asleep very quickly. For him, given the evening's events, it took rather longer. But eventually oblivion overtook him ... and the next thing he knew, light was creeping in through the casement and Lydia's hair was tickling his face.

Eden lay very still for a moment, enjoying the faint scent of lavender. Even more enjoyable was the fact that the length of her body was pressed close against his side and a bent leg lay – rather suggestively, he thought – across his thigh. Unfortunately, she was still asleep.

He told himself not to wake her. He even tried convincing himself to make his way carefully out of the bed and leave her to sleep. It took less than two minutes for him to do neither. Unable to resist, he slid one hand lightly along that smooth, shapely leg ... tracing from the upper curve of her calf, past her knee and on to her thigh. Instantly, his body tightened rather more than he'd anticipated.

He withdrew his hand and waited for his blood to make a similar retreat from inconvenient places. It didn't. It didn't because Lydia sighed and stretched ... and that tempting leg shifted a little higher up his own. Eden gritted his teeth and, for roughly thirty seconds, lay very still. Then, consoling himself with the knowledge that he'd warned her, he gave up being considerate in favour of taking unfair advantage.

Lydia awoke slowly to the lazy drift of his hands and his mouth feathering light kisses against her cheek and jaw. Her eyes drifted open and she blinked at him.

Eden propped himself on one elbow and grinned. 'Good morning.'

She smiled back but he saw her eyes searching his. Finally, she said huskily, 'You look better.'

'Yes.' He paused. 'I'd say I didn't mean to wake you ... except that it wouldn't be true.'

'No. I – oh.' Her breath hitched as his hand strayed a little further along her thigh. 'I gathered that.'

'Subtlety is beyond me this morning.' He pushed the bed-covers back a little way and tugged at the ribbons of her night-rail. 'This is very pretty. One might even say ... seductive.'

'You *did* say it. Last night.'

'That doesn't count.' He had the first bow undone and was tugging gently at the second. 'Last night I wasn't allowed to appreciate it properly. And I always like to be thorough.'

'Yes.' The second bow surrendered and then the third. Laughter and dawning anticipation, making her voice less than steady, Lydia said, 'I've always admired that about you.'

'Thank you.' The last bow gave way and he brushed the flimsy garment away to better enjoy the view. He wanted to trace it with his tongue. Instead, electing to tease her a little longer, he murmured, 'What else?'

The look in his eyes was as potent as a touch. 'What?'

'What else do you admire about me? Hopefully, there's something.'

'Yes.' Lydia put an arm about his neck and tugged. He didn't move. 'Yes. Everything.'

His gaze rose to meet hers, hot with desire but also brimming with wicked amusement.

'Be specific.'

'*Now?*'

'Why not?' *Darling ... if I can wait a little while, so can you.* 'Unless you can't --'

'All right – yes,' she said rapidly. 'Your honour and courage and intelligence and – and even your sense of humour.'

The words, *Though I could do without it right now* remained unspoken but he heard them anyway. Managing not to laugh, he said plaintively, 'Is that all? It sounds rather ... dull.'

'You asked what I *admire*.' Deciding two could play at this game, Lydia slid her palm temptingly over his chest and then began a slow descent. 'Your face and hair ... your devastating smile ... and utterly beautiful body ... those are things I *love*.' She smiled when he trapped her fingers mere inches from their goal. 'Better?'

'Marginally.' His voice was suddenly ragged and he released her hand to pull her hard against him. 'It will do. For now.'

He kissed her and there was no longer anything teasing about it; only naked hunger and a great wave of emotion. Lydia sighed against his mouth and pulled him even closer. And suddenly all the hurts and fears of the previous day ... everything that happened since the moment when they'd bound themselves to each other before God was simply wiped away.

Passion flared and spread.

Eden slid the night-rail from her shoulders so that his mouth could follow the trail forged by his hands and Lydia tugged her arms free in order to take her own voyage of discovery. Skin met skin, fingers tangled with fingers, tongue with tongue. Inch by glorious, tantalising inch, he kissed his way down her throat, while Lydia worshipped the taut muscles of his shoulders and back. And when he finally allowed himself the long-awaited pleasure of tasting the sweet, delicate swell of her breasts, he was rewarded with a shuddering moan of unconcealed wanting.

Flames became wildfire and mutual hunger raged like a hurricane.

Eden treasured each tremor, each ragged gasp of pleasure, each incoherent endearment. As he had done before ... as he suspected he might always do ... he found the way she responded to him something akin to a miracle. She offered herself completely, holding nothing back and it intoxicated him. So when self-restraint finally melted before the force of her desire for him as well as his for her, he moved slowly into the molten silk of her body ... and saw in her eyes that he felt as exquisite to her as she did to him. And suddenly, helplessly, the world turned on its axis.

Later ... very much later, when he lay at peace with her head on his shoulder, he murmured vaguely, 'Did I happen to mention that I love you?'

A smile invested Lydia's mouth and she continued tracing lazy patterns on his chest.

'You may have done. I was a bit ... preoccupied.'

'A bit?' he echoed. 'You were *a bit* preoccupied?'

'Well ... maybe more than a bit.'

'Thank God for that. If I need to try harder, it may well kill me.'

Lydia heard the lazy contentment in his voice and lifted her head in order to kiss his jaw.

Silence fell for a time but eventually Eden said reluctantly, 'I suppose we should get up. Aside from visiting all your people, I ought to thank Ned and Rob Trotter. I also need to lay information against Northcote with both Lambert and Thurloe – which is likely to take a lot longer than one would think necessary. But I want that bloody hell-hole in Crutched Friars closed down without delay and that means putting it in official hands.'

'And all this has to be done today?' asked Lydia, sitting up and shaking back her hair.

'Today and tomorrow.' He folded his arms behind his head in order to fully appreciate the view of his wife clothed only by a yard of glossy brown hair. 'If it's all right with you, I'd like to leave for Thorne Ash by the end of the week.'

She stared at him, torn between admitting she'd go anywhere with him whenever he liked and another, decidedly feminine thought. The latter won and she said, 'You want me to marry you for the *second* time in a gown I've worn before?'

The hazel eyes drifted seductively over her and, in a voice that slid through her like warm honey, Eden said, 'Darling, I'd happily marry you wearing nothing more than you are right now. But Mother might not like it.'

EPILOGUE
Thorne Ash, Oxfordshire

'What,' asked Eden, 'are we waiting for *now*? We've been here a week. The christening is over and the banns have been called; Toby has finally arrived and the alterations to the gown Kate's giving you *must* be finished by now. So why, in the name of God, can we not simply walk into the chapel and get married?'

Lydia smiled vaguely over the letter she was writing and shrugged.

'I think your mother is still hoping your other sister will come or that Aubrey may change his mind.'

'Amy won't come. As for Aubrey – you know what I think of that.'

'Yes. But if I don't mind, you need not either.'

He eyed her bent head narrowly.

'Why do I think there's something you're not telling me?'

Because there is, she thought. But said lightly, 'Working for Mr Thurloe has left you overly suspicious.' And then, before he could cross-question her further, she stood up and looping her arms about his waist, murmured, 'You're very impatient.'

'Yes.' Eden pulled her closer. 'Aren't you?'

She eventually managed to escape with an excuse about joining Kate to choose flowers for the chapel and he let her go because he had a secret of his own.

Outside in the garden, Eden's sister shot Lydia an amused, sideways look and said, 'Is he still bemoaning the delay?'

'Yes. Sooner or later, he's going to guess. I'm only surprised he hasn't done so already.'

'Then it's a good thing we only have to hold our nerve until tomorrow, isn't it?'

'We do?'

'Yes. Mother had a note giving us advance warning. You can distract him until then, can't you?' And with a sudden grin, 'Silly question. Of course you can.'

Exactly as Eden had predicted, Lydia and Kate had formed an immediate friendship. Indeed, reflected Lydia later, his entire family had welcomed her warmly.

At their first and only completely private meeting, Dorothy had held her hands and talked to her for an emotionally charged hour, often with tears in her eyes; Tabitha had thanked her for caring for Tobias after he'd been shot – completely brushing aside Lydia's confession that, but for her, he *wouldn't* have been shot; and Ralph swept her off her feet in a bear-hug, then teased her until she blushed. Jude, having introduced his sister, bubbled over with questions about everything from the Yule baskets to the lorinery; and after a period of careful overtures on Lydia's part, Mary began shyly seeking her out whenever Eden wasn't there.

This, Lydia decided, needed to be put right. She waited for two days and then, drawing the girl to one side, said, 'Mary, we don't know each other very well yet but I thought ... I was *hoping* you might be my attendant at the wedding. What do you think?'

The cornflower blue eyes lit with delight, then clouded again. In a flat little voice, the girl said politely, 'Thank you, Mistress Lydia. But I don't think Father would like that.'

Oh Eden. You really have *made a mess of it, haven't you?*

'I think you're mistaken.' She leaned closer. 'Just between you and me, your father knows he has made mistakes and he's sorry. He wants to put things right ... but he's a man, so he doesn't quite know how to do it - which means you and I have to help him.'

A faint glow appeared and Mary said, 'You and I? Together?'

'Absolutely together,' said Lydia firmly.

And knew by the girl's smile that she'd won the first battle. Or would have done by the time she'd had an even firmer word with Eden and sent him off to repeat her request as if it was quite his own idea.

* * *

The one member of the family Lydia found both unfathomable and disconcerting was Kate's diabolically good-looking Italian husband; but that changed when she met him sneaking in through a side door with three exceedingly muddy children – the smallest and muddiest of which was perched on his shoulders, holding on to handfuls of blue-black hair.

Signor del Santi stopped, fixed her with a night-dark gaze and said, 'Ah. This is awkward.' And to the eldest child, 'Caught red-handed, Sandro. What shall we do?'

Seven-year-old Alessandro stared soulfully at Lydia and said, 'Can you *please* not tell?'

'Anyone?' asked Lydia, trying not to laugh. 'Or just your mama?'

'Anyone,' replied Alessandro positively.

'But most *definitely* not their mother,' added Luciano, setting little Vittorio on his feet and laying a hand on his daughter's coppery curls. 'Sandro and Mariella were supposed to be practicing their letters and Torio should have been having his nap. But ... well, the sun was shining, you see.'

'Of course.'

'And we wanted to go fishing,' offered Mariella. 'It was fun – but a bit dirty.'

'So I see.' Lydia looked at the coatless, dishevelled man and noticed, for the first time, the slight imperfection of his left shoulder. 'Can I help you clean them up before Kate sees?'

'That,' said Luciano, with a sudden blinding smile, 'would be extraordinarily kind. But I fear for the state of your gown.'

'It's of no consequence,' she said tranquilly. 'A little dirt never hurt anyone.'

Later, when three marginally cleaner children had been despatched to Meg in the nursery, the signor's gaze rested on the sapphire and moonstone necklace and, lifting one hand, said, 'May I?'

She nodded and he scrutinised it carefully, running a light finger over the setting. Then, 'Not bad. Rather good, in fact. Tobias's work?'

'Yes. You taught him, didn't you?'

'Everything he knows,' said Luciano. And then, with a slightly wicked laugh, 'Or at least, everything he knows about gold. The *rest* of what Tobias knows is entirely his own affair.'

* * *

On the following morning, Eden detected a sense of suppressed excitement running through the house and concluded that whatever everyone had been waiting for was now imminent but still had no idea what this was. All was revealed, however, when he returned from an errand in Banbury to find a travelling carriage in the middle of the stable-yard; and on the steps of the house, wearing a familiar sardonic smile, was Colonel Brandon.

'Venetia and I,' remarked Gabriel, 'were sorry to have missed your first wedding and somewhat piqued that an invitation to your second came, not from you, but from Toby via Nick. However, as you can see, we decided to overlook the insult and come anyway.'

* * *

Inevitably, the evening took on an air of celebration. Supper was noisy and cheerful and, after it, Venetia, Kate and Tabitha whisked Lydia off for vital pre-nuptial preparations while the gentlemen plied Eden with ale, over which he finally told Ralph and Luciano the full story of what had happened in London.

Having already heard the tale from Nicholas who, as soon as the crisis was over had made his way hot-foot to Yorkshire, Gabriel said thoughtfully, 'That must have been a shock – discovering that Quinn and Northcote were the same man.'

'Yes and no,' said Eden. 'Once I knew, it made a bizarre sort of sense.'

'The bastard nearly killed you,' growled Tobias. 'And you damned nearly let him.'

'No. I didn't. Aside from everything else we'd found out about him, he'd been repeatedly drowning Lydia in a bucket. Do you honestly think I was going to let him live after that?'

Tobias grunted and reached for the ale jug.

'I never understood why you didn't just blow his head off.'

'So you've said.' Eden's eyes met Luciano's in a moment of shared recollection; then he looked across at Gabriel and deliberately changed the subject. 'How is Nick?'

'Happier than his future mother-in-law. They've put the wedding off until July in the hope that Lady Clifford will get used to the idea. Personally, I wouldn't be holding my breath. She doesn't like *me* any better now than she did eight years ago.'

'I,' offered Ralph complacently, 'am the apple of my mother-in-law's eye.'

'Only because Luciano lives on the far side of Europe, you smug idiot,' objected Tobias. And pushing the ale jug in the Italian's direction. 'Speaking of which ... are you still consorting with the Medici and the Vatican?'

Luciano declined the jug and passed it to Ralph.

'From time to time.' He paused, a glimmer of amusement in his eyes. 'The necklace you made for Lydia is an interesting piece. Quite original.'

Tobias looked inordinately pleased. 'Thank you.'

'Not at all. It's so well-suited to the lady that it might have been made for her. Was it?'

'No. It was done before I'd met her. Only when I *did* meet her, it suddenly felt ...' He stopped, shrugging.

'It felt as though it ought to belong to her,' finished Luciano with a smile. 'Yes. It's rare. But it happens sometimes. My congratulations.'

Tobias grinned and Ralph muttered, '*Now* who's smug?'

The door opened and Kate's head appeared around it. She said, 'Eden ... no nocturnal wanderings tonight, if you please.'

Ralph gave a crack of laughter

Eden stood up, feeling his colour rise. 'What are you talking about?'

'You know perfectly well,' sighed Kate. 'Mother insisted on you and Lydia occupying separate chambers – so you've been slipping into her room as soon as the house is quiet.'

'Eden, you sly dog!' said Tobias. 'I'm shocked.'

'Shut up,' muttered Eden. And defensively to Kate, 'We are married, you know.'

'Not legally and not in Mother's opinion. So tonight you'll sleep in your own bed.'

Upon which note, Kate closed the door and listened, smiling, as her brother fell victim to a deluge of laughter and good-humour ribaldry.

* * *

The morning of this wedding dawned without a cloud in the sky. Surrounded by Kate, Venetia, Tabitha and Mary, Lydia had no time to dwell on that other day or even to wonder what Eden might be doing.

Then, a little while before it was time to dress, Dorothy laid a small box in front of her, saying, 'Something old, my dear – and also a bridal gift. Open it.'

Lydia looked down on a gold heart-shaped pin set with small diamonds. Eyes misting with sudden tears, she said, 'It's lovely. Thank you. Everyone is ... you've all been so kind.'

Dorothy smiled and shook her head.

'Nonsense. You've given Eden back to us. And that is a gift beyond price.'

After Dorothy had gone, Venetia finished arranging Lydia's hair while Kate laced Mary into a new and very grown-up gown ... and Tabitha slipped away on the excuse of having forgotten something.

'I'm having second thoughts,' remarked Kate presently from the doorway where she appeared to be having a whispered conversation with someone on the other side of it. 'I'm not sure my gown is quite right for you.' She paused and stood back to allow her sister to come in. '*This* one, however, will do splendidly.'

Lydia turned and then came uncertainly to her feet, her vision dazzled by yards of silvery-blue shot-silk, edged with exquisite sapphire and silver-thread trimming that could only have been made by one pair of hands. Drawing an unsteady breath and stretching out equally unsteady fingers, she said, 'How ... where ...I don't understand.'

'Eden wanted it to be a surprise,' explained Tabitha. 'He arranged everything with your sewing women and they made the gown but didn't quite have time to finish it before Toby left London. So they sent the trimming and instructions on how it was to be used ... and Mother and I have been kept very busy. Do you like it?'

'*Like* it? How could I not?' Tears threatened again. 'Eden did this?'

'Yes.'

'But he was so *busy* before we left. I can't believe he found the time.'

'Yet apparently he did,' said Kate matter-of-factly. 'So stop worrying and put it on. We've all been worried silly that it might not fit.'

It did, of course ... and the mirror told Lydia how well it suited her.

'That,' remarked Venetia critically, 'is a triumph. The Strand Alley ladies have outdone themselves. And if Eden chose that silk himself, he's a man of rare discrimination.'

'Let's just say that his taste has improved over the years and leave it at that,' said Kate astringently. 'Upon which note, ladies ... it's time to go.'

* * *

Partly due to Aubrey's defection and partly, he claimed, because he'd stood up for his brother before, Tobias waited at the chapel door to escort the bride. Offering his arm, he said, 'I thought you might turn tail and flee before doing this a second time.'

Lydia lifted disbelieving brows. 'Did you? Really?'

'Not for a minute,' he admitted cheerfully. 'And my brother is a lucky man.'

Lydia's silk gown hadn't been Eden's only extravagance. Mindful of Tobias's strictures, he'd paid a tailor an exorbitant sum for speedy delivery of a new suit and now stood before the altar resplendent in grey brocade and Flanders lace. And beside him as groomsman and looking ready to burst with pride, was Jude.

The small, beautiful chapel was ablaze with candles and heavy with the scent of flowers. From the ornately-painted ceiling, the Fall of Lucifer – bearing, as Kate was wont to remark, an uncanny resemblance to Luciano – looked down on the congregation; and a pair of viols played in gentle counterpoint from the recess near the altar where a lamp burned beneath Richard Maxwell's memorial plaque and where Dorothy would go privately later. But now, as she watched Lydia's progress down the aisle, she thought, *I wish you were here, Richard. But I know that, somehow, you're with our son now. This is the marriage we always wanted him to have. The one he deserves.*

On her journey to the altar, Lydia recognised the trouble his family had taken to make this day perfect in every respect. Then she was at Eden's side and aware only of that slow, bewitching smile.

This ceremony was as emotionally-charged as the other had been and even Kate was seen to be surreptitiously dabbing away tears. Jude performed his role with dignity which quickly dissolved into a huge grin;

Mary, by contrast, was solemn and careful ... but just a little less wary of her father than she'd been a week ago.

Back in the house, while the bridal pair accepted everyone's congratulations and good wishes, Goodwife Flossing and the maids served wine and then bustled in and out with platters of food.

Eden hugged his wife and murmured, 'Thank God we are now incontrovertibly legal. I've had enough of creeping back to a cold bed at the crack of dawn.'

'Is that the *only* thing this day means to you?' asked Lydia, refusing to smile.

'By no means.' He tightened his hold on her waist and kissed her, taking his time about it. 'But right now, it's the thing I'm most looking forward to.'

'There'll be time enough for that later.' Ralph clouted him on the back and prised Lydia from his arm. 'And if you don't come and eat, you won't have the strength for it.'

'Stop,' said Eden. 'I had enough of that last night ... and plan to strangle my bloody sister.'

'Go to it,' remarked Tobias cheerfully. 'My money's on Kate.'

Laughter became the key to the evening and later there was dancing. Breathless from an energetic reel with Tobias and dizzy after being whirled about the floor by Ralph, Lydia collapsed against Eden and whispered, 'It isn't that I'm not enjoying myself or ungrateful for everything that's been done for us ... but how long before we can slip away?'

'Now, if you like.'

'Won't anyone mind?'

'No. I doubt they'll even be surprised,' responded Eden, towing her unhurriedly towards the door. 'You and I have hardly had a private moment in which to talk since we got here.'

She sent him a slanting smile. 'You've been in my bed every night save one.'

'Yes. And if you expected sensible conversation under those circumstances, you must have a very mistaken view of my ability to resist temptation.' He continued sweeping her up the stairs. 'I don't recall telling you how beautiful you look.'

'It's the gown. I still don't know how you managed it but --'

'Lily Carter took charge the instant I said what I wanted. And it isn't the gown. It's you. No – don't argue. And don't thank me, either. It's the only gift I've ever given you and it was my pleasure.' Eschewing Lydia's bedchamber which Venetia and his sisters had been in and out of all morning and would probably presently re-visit to reclaim things they'd left behind, he drew her into his own and shot the bolt. Then, stopping her mouth with his own, he handed her to a chair by the hearth, discarded his coat and sat down on the rug at her feet saying, 'How much thought have you given to the future?'

'Not very much as yet. Have you?'

'Yes.' He paused for a moment, as if wondering where to start and then said, 'You'll have gathered that, though Thorne Ash belongs to me, I've spent scarcely any time here since the summer of '42 ... and nowadays, Ralph does a splendid job of looking after it. We could live here, if you chose ... but I'm not needed. And since I'm also unemployed and not used to being idle, I doubt if it would suit me.'

'No. I suppose not. And though I hadn't really considered it, I'd assumed we would continue living in London. Only I *would* like Jude and Mary to be a part of our lives there; to know they have a home with us whenever they want it.'

'I think you've made me tolerably aware of that fact.'

'And so?'

He grinned up at her. 'Do you hear me arguing?'

'No. Not yet.'

'And you won't. But we can talk about the children later. For now there are other things I want to explain and ideas I'd like you to consider.' He paused and then said, 'When I resigned my commission, I told Lambert I'd continue assisting him in certain areas if necessary. He's been indulging in discreet talks with the Cavaliers. My own view is that nothing will ever come of these but I don't mind pursuing them if Lambert asks. I suspect that two of the men I've spoken with are a good deal more important than either he or Thurloe have yet guessed.' *And a third knows something about me that I'd much rather he didn't.* 'This means I may be called on from time to time – but not often enough to stop me getting under your feet. So I had an idea for something that might.'

'I won't mind you getting under my feet,' she murmured.

'Any time you like, sweetheart.' His voice dropped to a seductive purr and one hand slid beneath her skirts to caress her ankle with lazy intent. 'I'm all for innovation.'

Lydia flushed a little but withdrew her foot and said severely, 'Very likely. But not until you've told me your idea.'

'Spoilsport,' sighed Eden. Then, 'The lorinery is doing well so I thought we might perhaps expand it. Thus far you've concentrated on saddlery items and not explored the market of carriage and cart harnesses. I could help with that. Indeed, I ... I wondered if you'd consider letting me take over management in Duck Lane.'

'Of course – if that's what you want.'

Stunned that she'd agreed without a blink, he said, 'Shouldn't you think about it?'

'No. I'm *glad* you want to be involved and I don't know why you're surprised.'

'Knowing you, neither do I – and I thank you. But there's more. That gown you're wearing proves that the Strand Alley ladies have untapped talents ... so would a seamstress service available only to a small and very exclusive clientele work?' He grinned. 'Unless I'm mistaken, the word *exclusive* translates in female terms as *desirable* and *expensive*.'

'That's very true,' nodded Lydia admiringly. '*What* a devious mind you have.'

'Thank you again. So?'

'It would need additional premses – but I like the idea. The women will, too.' She smiled. 'You've obviously been doing a lot of thinking. Is that everything?'

'Not quite.' Eden stopped and his expression turned rather grim. 'You know about the children we found in that hell-hole ... but you didn't see them, Lydia. And I thank God for that because I can't get them out of my head. Worse, I can't help thinking that there may be others like them. I have the connections that can help me find and rescue any such cases – but the problem will be what to do with them afterwards. And I hoped that we might work on that together. What do you think?'

For a moment, Lydia remained where she was staring at him. Then, sliding down from the chair and into his lap in a billow of silk, she placed a soft, sweet kiss on his jaw and said, 'I think that every single day you give me new reasons to love you. And for the rest, you must know that you didn't need to ask.'

'Yes.' His mouth trailed down her throat. 'But I don't take what you are for granted.'

He turned her in his arms so he could embrace her more fully. It was as well, he reflected distantly, that she hadn't been this close before for the scent and the feel of her was already clouding his mind. The silk gown was smooth and supple but he knew the skin beneath was silkier still. Hot and intent, his eyes lingered on her mouth until he saw her breath catch and a tiny tremor rippled through her. Then he kissed her, enjoying the way one of her hands tangled in his hair while the other found its way inside his shirt.

Anticipation stirred … but he continued to let it build. He knew her now; knew how to summon up a storm or how, as now, to create a long, shining ribbon of pleasure. So he pulled enough pins from her hair to allow it to tumble about her shoulders and he allowed himself to contemplate erotic images of undressing her very, very slowly; of gradually peeling away gown, corset, petticoats and chemise to discover the lovely lines and curves of the exquisitely responsive body they covered. He got as far as mentally removing her stockings before it became impossible to wait any longer and his fingers finally sought the laces of her gown.

Lydia whispered something he didn't catch but didn't need to because she had become liquid fire in his arms, wanting him as he wanted her.

Hovering nearby but as yet unrecognised, were a myriad of dazzling possibilities that they might fulfil together.

The future beckoned. And it was bright.

Author's Note

The period between Cromwell's forcible expulsion of the Rump in April 1653 and the Rule of the Major Generals in the summer of 1655, is not one of either shining success or landmark moments.

The Nominated Assembly was a failure as was the first parliament of the Protectorate; the Dutch War and the Western Design both cost a fortune but achieved nothing; and the mood in the country as a whole was one of surly discontent.

Nor were the Cavaliers doing any better. Endless failed plots to murder Cromwell; idiotic notions of fermenting risings that would topple the government; a lengthy but hopeless campaign to conquer Scotland; and a new executive body to coordinate Royalist conspiracies and control radical elements which never actually did anything.

The Sealed Knot was formed in late 1653 and Secretary Thurloe first got wind of it in February '54 during the course of the Ship Tavern investigations. It comprised just six members. Eden met three of them; Edward Villiers, William Compton and Richard Wyllis. But despite Thurloe's best endeavours, it wasn't until 1658 when Wyllis began supplying information that he would have learned these names. Eden may have had his suspicions ... but history dictates that he had to keep them to himself.

With the exception of Aubrey Durand and Ellis Brandon, all the conspirators named as participants in both the Ship Tavern and Gerard's Plots were real people and Roger Cotes was Thurloe's informer throughout. Cromwell did indeed keep a loaded pistol in his pocket and the incident in Hyde Park happened as I have described – though I'll admit to having used my imagination about the widespread sniggering that followed it.

All these things explain why I have called this book *Lords of Misrule*. I hope, however, they have not spoiled your enjoyment of it.

Stella Riley
April 2016

Printed in Great Britain
by Amazon